Have you met Barbara Holloway?

"A dynamic attorney."
—*Atlanta Journal & Constitution*

"Complex, maddeningly flawed, brilliant,
and altogether believable."
—*Salem Statesman Journal*

"A passionate lover of truth."
—*Portland Oregonian*

"The sort of level-headed heroine
you learn to like and trust."
—*Orlando Sentinel*

"Something of a slob."

DATE DUE

KATE WILHELM

DEFENSE
FOR THE
DEVIL

ISBN 1-55166-628-6

DEFENSE FOR THE DEVIL

Copyright © 1999 by Kate Wilhelm.
First published by St. Martin's Press Incorporated.

MIRA and the Star Colophon are trademarks used under license and registered in Australia, New Zealand, Philippines, United States Patent and Trademark Office and in other countries.

Visit us at www.mirabooks.com

Printed in U.S.A.

For Jon, Kitte, Mo, and Roxanne—
sharers of hearth and home.
And special thanks to Julie A. Stevens
for her continuing support and advice
in legal matters. Any mistakes
(of course, and alas) remain mine alone.

Every man before he dies shall see the Devil.
—Old English Proverb

Mitch

1

Eddie carries, you handle the paperwork. Have a shower, eat something, relax, just be sure to call this number exactly at one.

Using the name on the credit card and driver's license—R. M. Palmer—Mitch signed for two steaks, fries, beer. He ate his steak with a towel wrapped around him, his hair dripping. At one he made the call. "Mitch," he said. "We're here." *Here* was Miami, not even the beach, just Miami.

"Let me speak to Eddie for a second."

He handed over the phone. Eddie's end of the conversation was a series of grunts. Eddie was six feet three, and nearly that broad, with a brain that would have left empty space in a peanut shell. Eddie handed the phone back to him.

"Her plane gets in at four, Swissair from Zurich. Let her make the first move. If she doesn't, return to the motel and call this number at seven. You remember the rest of it?"

"Sure," Mitch said.

"Good. I'll be waiting to hear from you."

After he hung up, Mitch pulled the spread off one of the beds and lay down. "We'll head out at two-thirty," he said. "I'm going to snooze." Eddie grunted, watching a ball game on TV. When he got up to go to the john, he took the suitcase with him; when he sprawled again, he kept it at his side. It looked like an ordinary twenty-six-inch suitcase, except for the keypad lock. The first time Mitch and Eddie had done this, Palmer had said, "Pick a number, Mitch, see if you're lucky." When he touched the keypad, a little red light had come on. "Message is, don't touch," Palmer had said. His was the scariest voice Mitch had ever heard.

The problem with Eddie was that he slept like a cat, dead out one minute, wide awake the next. He had gotten plenty of sleep while Mitch drove from New York. Mitch had slept little when they switched places, and he felt sore now, but the adrenaline was pumping; he was primed.

At two he got up and took his duffel bag into the bathroom. He brushed his teeth and then took out a length of weighted pipe and a six-inch-long leather holder that slid over the end. He swung it, nodded, and kept it in his hand under the towel when he went back to the bedroom. He moved around a lot; he went to the window, checking out the sun, grabbed his slacks from a chair and shook them. Eddie scowled and hunched lower, closer to the television. When Mitch began to whistle, Eddie reached over to turn up the volume. Mitch swung the pipe hard, catching him in the temple.

Eddie went down to his hands and knees, and Mitch hit him again, harder, and then again. Eddie slumped to the floor.

When Mitch left at two-thirty, he hung the DO NOT DIS-TURB card on the door, and he carried his duffel bag and the black suitcase.

Park the car and go in together. Buy a red rose and slip it under the strap on the suitcase, then go to the customs section and wait. Don't stay too close together, just keep each other in sight. Give it time, there might be a delay in customs; but if no one approaches by five-thirty, go back to the motel.

He arrived at Miami International at three-twenty, and

by a quarter to four he was near customs, waiting, with what seemed to be a million other people. All he knew was that it was a woman this time.

She was short and plump, forty maybe, expensively dressed in a beige silk jacket and skirt, carrying a big shoulder bag and a briefcase. She looked around anxiously-amateur—then spotted the suitcase with the rose and walked toward him.

"Eddie?"

He nodded.

"I thought there would be two of you." Scared.

"He's over there," Mitch said, nodding toward a man leaning against a post.

She reached for the suitcase tentatively; he moved it back. "We have to make a phone call first," he said.

"Oh, of course."

He led the way to a bank of telephones. She looked alarmed when the man leaning against the post left it and walked away in the opposite direction and was lost among the hordes in people. "Don't worry about him," Mitch said. "He'll keep us in sight." He used the phone card and punched in numbers. The telephone rang once at the other end. He made a grunting noise. No one expected Eddie to talk much on the phone.

"No problems?"

"No."

"Let me speak to her."

He handed the phone to the woman. She listened a second, then after a quick glance at the suitcase, she said, "No problems. They're here. Everything is well." After another pause, she said, lowering her voice, "Of course. Penelope. Wait a second." She fumbled in her shoulder bag, found a notebook and a slim gold pen, and jotted down something. Then she handed the phone back to Mitch.

He listened to the instructions he already had memorized,

and the line went dead. He continued to hold the phone to his ear. "Yes," he said. "Sure. Right." He nodded, listening to a dead line, then hung up.

"Change of plans," he said. "I've got to drive you to a hotel. He's afraid for you to drive back alone. You've read the stories about carjacks along that route?" He looked around, as if searching for his partner. "Wait here. Don't move a step. Be right back." He strode off, carrying the suitcase. The area was packed with arrivals, piles of luggage, people milling about. He mingled a minute or two, then returned to her. "All set," he said. "Let's go."

Her anxiety had returned. She eyed the suitcase, gave him an appraising look, then glanced around for the other man.

"Look," he said irritably, "I don't like this any more than you do. You don't have to register at the hotel. Once we get there, I hand over the suitcase and the car title and keys, you give me the briefcase, and you're on your own." He looked past her into the crowd, nodded, as if to his partner, then said, "Let's move. I've got to be back here in time to catch another plane. My partner will keep us in sight until we get to the car. And we'll both hope and pray I get back in time to make the flight. Let's move."

"He should have told me," she said.

"Yeah, but he didn't. Now, are you coming or not? Lady, I don't give a fuck one way or the other." She looked at the suitcase. When he started to walk, she did, too.

As soon as Eddie makes the transfer, he'll take her to the car, give her the title and keys, and you're done with her. While he's doing that, you pick up your tickets at the Delta counter. Someone will meet your plane at La Guardia. Right.

The car was a black two-door Lexus. The sight of it seemed to cheer her up a little. He tossed the suitcase into the back, but she kept her bag and the briefcase with her.

The lead pipe was under the driver's seat. Traffic was fierce. It was five-fifteen, rush hour.

When he exited the freeway, she seemed unaware that they were nowhere near downtown yet; her alarm didn't go off until he turned onto a mean little side street. She clutched the briefcase harder. After another minute or two, she asked hoarsely, "Where are we going?"

"Not far," he said, making another turn. There was little traffic in this section of the city; a hurricane had hit hard a year before, few repairs had been made and a lot of the buildings were uninhabitable, but he knew people were watching the expensive car. This part had to go fast. He pulled into an abandoned convenience-store parking lot and stopped. She was trying futilely to open her door when he hit her with the lead pipe. It was a backhanded blow without much room for the swing, even with his seat all the way back, but it was a heavy pipe, and his arm was strong. Carefully he pulled the briefcase from her limp hands, then he grabbed her bag and riffled through it swiftly, searching for every scrap of paper, her airline ticket folder, receipts.... He took out the notebook and her wallet. He pulled out a couple hundred-dollar bills and the smaller ones and dropped them back into the bag loose, kept the wallet. Then he undid her seat belt, released the lock, opened the door and pushed her out, tossed her bag out after her. Let the local greaseballs have a few bucks to play with; by the time someone got around to calling the cops, there'd be nothing to find but another unidentified stiff, and nobody would have seen anything.

Hours later when he gassed up, he jotted down the name she had said on the telephone: Penelopy. He searched through the notebook for the message she had written and found it near the end, the code for the suitcase lock.

"Message is, don't touch," he said.

Maggie

2

It was four in the afternoon, muggy outside, and Barbara Holloway had been rushing for an hour and a half by the time she rang the bell at Martin's restaurant. He was closed at this time of day, she knew, and probably he was busy doing prep in the kitchen, but he opened the door almost instantly. He was so big that seeing him in an open doorway was always something of a jolt; he seemed to fill the entire space. And he was so black that the glare of his white beret was blinding and appeared to her sun-dazed eyes to be floating. He couldn't wear a chef's high hat, he had explained a long time ago, because ducking all the time killed his back.

"Is she here yet?"

He shook his head. "Look at you, dripping wet. You been running races or something?"

"Or something. I got two luscious salmon steaks, and lettuce and spinach for a salad. I washed it and have it in the fridge. And little red potatoes. Is that enough? Oh, and green beans."

"Sounds like plenty. You want some lemonade or iced tea? We're having iced tea."

"That would be wonderful." She sat at her usual table and pulled a cookbook from her briefcase. "Salmon is easy, isn't it? And quick?" She glanced up at him as he was entering the kitchen; she could see that his shoulders were shaking with laughter. The problem was, she thought glumly, that people who knew how to do things had no sympathy for people who didn't. And she didn't know how to cook.

She should have been out of here by three with the whole afternoon ahead of her, plenty of time to think, to plan, to try things and toss them if they didn't work out. But at two or a little later a frantic woman had called and begged for an appointment, now, today, as soon as she could drive over from the coast. And she, Barbara, had agreed.

She and John had explained to her father at dinner on Saturday night the arrangement they had come up with. "What we'll do is take alternate days, John one day, me the next. Then over here on Saturday, as long as your invitation is still good, and a restaurant one night a week."

Frank had turned to John, who nodded and said, "I have six dishes that are incomparable. Two weeks before I have to repeat."

Barbara had not missed the amusement in her father's eyes. He knew as well as she did that she had three dishes in her repertoire: steak and baked potatoes, canned soup, and frozen entres.

Anyone can cook, she told herself frequently, anyone who can read a recipe and understand the directions and follow them without fail. Of the three necessary skills, she was very good at one. She was reading more than she wanted to know about salmon when Martin brought out iced tea. A fat fish? Rolls of fat around the waist? What waist?

"Salmon's easy," Martin said without a smile. "You going to put a sauce on it? It's good without sauce," he added quickly, "just a squeeze of lemon juice, a little butter."

It needed a sauce, she understood, with a feeling of desperation, remembering the one time she had tried white sauce and it had come out with little gooey lumps like hard library paste.

The doorbell rang and he turned to go answer it.

She shoved the cookbook back inside her briefcase and watched as he admitted a man and woman, both dressed in jeans and T-shirts and running shoes, exactly the way Barbara was dressed. The woman was carrying an oversized tote bag with a picture of a whale. She was thirty-something, he a little younger. Both good-looking, fit.

"Thank you for seeing me on such short notice," the woman said. "I'm Maggie Folsum." She held out her hand. "And this is Laurence Thielman."

"Barbara Holloway," Barbara said, shaking hands with her first, then with him.

"Laurence will wait out in the car," Maggie Folsum said. "He just wanted to make sure everything was okay first."

"Too hot out there," Barbara said. "You could hang out in a booth."

Laurence Thielman looked at Maggie. She glanced back at the booths, then nodded.

"You folks want some iced tea? Coffee? Coke or something?" Martin asked.

They both said iced tea and he went back to the kitchen. Laurence settled himself in the most distant booth, not very far away in this small restaurant, but out of hearing.

Not hysterical, Barbara decided, studying Maggie Folsum, but either exhausted or ill. She had deep shadows under her eyes, and the drawn appearance that came with sleeplessness. About as tall as Barbara, slender and muscular, with long dark hair pulled back on her neck loosely with a ribbon. No makeup. Her eyes were lovely, brown with thick lashes, very steady as she submitted to the scrutiny without embarrassment or shyness.

"While we're waiting for your tea," Barbara said, "tell me how did you know about me? Why me?"

"My daughter is your devoted fan," Maggie said. "She wants to do what you do, work with poor people in a ghetto somewhere. As a doctor, not a lawyer, though. She's seventeen," she added.

"You have a seventeen-year-old daughter?"

"And an eighteen-year-old daughter," Maggie said. "I'm thirty-five."

Martin came out with a tray and put her glass down, glanced at Barbara's, went back to Laurence Thielman with another glass, and returned to the kitchen, all without a word.

Maggie said apologetically, "There's really no way I can get into it without going back to day one. I'm sorry. I'll try to make it brief."

"Day one it is," Barbara said. She sipped her tea and waited.

"I live at Folsum, over on the coast," Maggie said. "I grew up there, and the Arnos lived there until recently. I've known them all my life. I was sixteen when Mitch Arno swept me off my feet. He was twenty-two. His nickname, which I didn't understand until much later, was Mitch the Cherry Picker. Anyway, same old same old. I got pregnant, and his family and my parents got together and made him marry me. My mother was mortified, my father furious, Mama and Papa Arno outraged, like that. Mitch took off as soon as I started to show a lot, by May. Then, in February, six months after Gwen was born, he showed up again. I was living with my parents, they were both gone when he came, and he roughed me up and raped me. I was seventeen."

Her voice was steady, but she had to pause to sip tea often.

"My folks came home and found me bruised and crying,

and him in the kitchen. There was a lot of yelling.'' Her voice faltered and she drank again, then continued almost in a monotone. ''My mother called Ray, Mitch's brother. He came with Papa Arno, and they dragged Mitch out to the yard and Ray beat him up. Really beat him up. They took him to town and put him on a bus to Portland. I never knew what all was said, but probably everyone else in Folsum knows. Papa disowned him publicly.''

Very faintly then she said, ''Karen was born nine months later. I was eighteen, with two daughters. I divorced Mitch. I took my maiden name back and changed the girls' names to Folsum. End of day one.

''Day two,'' Maggie said, in a near whisper. ''Last Thursday.'' Her hands were on the table, shaking. She looked at them, then put them in her lap, drew in a deep breath, and let it out slowly. ''Okay. I own and manage Folsum House, a bed-and-breakfast inn, and I decided months ago to throw a big family reunion, a birthday/graduation party for Gwen, and make it something she'd never forget. She'll be going to the university in the fall, here in Eugene. I wanted it to be very, very special for her. And Mitch came back.'' She closed her eyes hard.

When Maggie opened her eyes and started speaking again, her voice was even lower. ''It was late, after eleven. We'd all been busy, there had been guests in the inn, and one couple was still there, planning to check out the next morning. I was expecting sixty or seventy people. Anyway, I had just put some pies in the oven when he walked in through the kitchen door as if he'd never left. He smelled bad, was road dirty, unshaven, rumpled, as if he had been driving for days without sleep. He came in carrying all his stuff—suitcase, briefcase, a duffel bag, a sport coat over his arm—and just let it all drop inside the door. I told him to get out or I'd call the police. He...'' She shrugged. ''He came at me and said he'd break my arm if I gave him any lip, and he grabbed my wrist. I hit him with the first thing I could grab, the rolling pin from the worktable.'' She shook her head, and a very faint smile appeared and vanished. ''What a cliché, hit him with a rolling pin. Anyway, he went down and didn't make a sound or move, and I thought I had killed him.''

She drank thirstily then and wiped her mouth with the back of her hand. ''I had to get him out of the kitchen. One of the girls might not be asleep yet, come out for water or something. I kept thinking he had come back to spoil Gwen's party. Crazy. Anyway, I ran out to the shed and got a wagon we use to haul firewood, and got an old beach blanket from the garage. I rolled him up in the blanket and dragged him to the wagon outside the back door, and I took him to the garage and got him inside the house van, wrapped up like a mummy. I locked the van so no one would get inside. I really was crazy, but it was all I could think of. I couldn't call the sheriff. They'd arrest me... Gwen's big day ruined, my mother could have a heart attack, more scandal, all those people on the way. They'd come for a party and attend a wake. And my daughters...I was crazy.'' She stopped again, longer this time.

''I hid his gear. I cleaned up the kitchen and took the pies out of the oven, and I remembered he must have left a car somewhere. It was in the drive near the garage. I had to get rid of it before people started to arrive the next day. That day. It was after one by then. All I could think of was to drive the car to a day-use park about two miles away and leave it there. Just before dawn that's what I did, and I waited in the park until there was enough light to walk home on the beach, where no one would see me.''

She drank more tea, gazing past Barbara. ''I made breakfast for the two customers, we cleaned their room, my housekeeper was there by then.... My parents arrived in time for lunch, and Mama and Papa Arno got there in the afternoon. I had a reservation for an early dinner for all the grandparents, the girls, and myself; by eight or nine, others would be pulling in, and we had to be back by then. There wasn't any time to do anything about Mitch. Then the Arnos decided to let me have a couple of hours with my folks—they said they would visit friends in Folsum—and we left them and went to dinner at about four. Mother wanted a little walk on the beach before dinner, and there's easy access down in Folsum, so we left early. When we got home Dad wanted to put his car in the garage, so I had to back my car out first, not the van, a little Nissan. I looked in the van to make sure nothing showed, and it was empty. I nearly fell down in relief; I felt as if I had been living a nightmare all day and finally woke up. He had come to and left, that's all I could think.

"On Sunday," Maggie went on, "most of the guests left, but a few stayed over until Monday. We had arranged for me to ride up to Portland with my brother and his wife Monday morning, and we'd leave right after my mother and father did. They took the girls down to California with them to spend a month. They adore their granddaughters. Irene and her crew came early to clean up the place; high-school kids would be around to collect chairs and tables I'd borrowed from the school, and everything would be ready for customers on Tuesday. So I went to Portland and spent the day with Laurence. He had a show in a gallery that I wanted to see; he's an artist. Anyway, we took all day, had dinner on the way back, and got home about eleven. Irene and her husband met us at the door. Tom's a deputy sheriff. My house had been torn apart.

"He had ripped open mattresses, chairs, couches, dumped things out of drawers, torn clothes out of closets, broken things. Every room was a disaster." Her hands were clenched hard and her voice was vehement now. "That bastard destroyed everything he could get his hands on."

"Easy," Barbara murmured. "Back up a second. How? When? I thought the place was crawling with people?"

Maggie shook her head. "Irene said she got through at two-thirty, and the kids were done loading stuff in their trucks before that. She left a lot of windows open to air the place out; she said people had been smoking, and I guess they had been. Anyway, she left it airing out at two-thirty, went back at eight-thirty to close up, and found the mess. She called her husband, and he brought in the sheriff. By the time we got home, no one was there except Irene and Tom, who was going to spend the night and make sure no one did any further damage. Tom said I couldn't stay, and Laurence couldn't. Even his apartment was a wreck! We would have to go to the hotel in Folsum. I couldn't move anything or touch anything until the insurance adjustor inspected it all and the sheriff's office investigated. They said it was malicious vandalism, and I didn't tell them about Mitch. I was too…I couldn't say anything," she said. "I actually couldn't speak. We all went to my room, and suddenly Irene shoved me into the bathroom and I threw up. I could hear her telling Tom to leave me alone a minute. I looked in the hiding place where I put Mitch's stuff, a little space you can get to from the bathroom. Everything was still there." She started to pick up her glass but pushed it away instead. "That was yesterday."

"Intermission," Barbara said quietly. "You want a glass of wine?"

Maggie nodded. Barbara stood up and went back to ask Laurence if he wanted wine, beer, anything else. He didn't. He was drawing in a small sketchbook. Taking her time, she went to the kitchen, where Martin and Binnie were hard at work preparing entres. "Sorry," she said. "Martin, could we have a couple glasses of chardonnay?"

"You got it," he said.

She returned to the table. Maggie was standing at a window, gazing out over dazzling white café curtains. Barbara watched her for a moment, then made a noise moving her chair, and Maggie jerked and returned from wherever she had been.

"All right," Maggie said as she came back to the table and sat down again. "Today. I was up really early making phone calls to head off customers; Tom let me take the reservation book. And I had to find rooms for my guests. The insurance adjustor couldn't get there until ten or eleven, and I couldn't touch a thing at the house, so I was still in the hotel, in the coffee shop, when a man approached me and said he wanted to talk to me. I told him some other time. I really didn't have time."

Martin brought out their wine, and she said thank you and sipped hers gratefully. "The man said his name was Trassi, and he wanted to talk about Mitch. I hadn't told a single person that I had seen Mitch. No one. I still haven't, until now," she added.

"He said Mitch worked for a company in Southern California, and he had been sent to their Seattle branch with important papers. He said Mitch had mentioned that he might stop off and see his ex, that he had a debt to pay, but everyone assumed he meant on the return trip and had thought little of it. He was due to arrive in Seattle on Friday and never showed up. Instead, he called and at first claimed that his car had broken down, but when his supervisor told him to rent a car and get to Seattle, he said his ex had thrown him out and he couldn't get back in to collect the stuff until Monday because there were a hundred or more people around. When he didn't show on Monday, the company sent Trassi, the company lawyer, to get the papers and find out what was happening."

Maggie stopped there and sipped her wine again. Her eyes were narrowed and a slight frown creased her forehead. "He told me they would give a thousand-dollar reward for the suitcase and briefcase, and the company would cover the damage Mitch had done to the inn. He described the briefcase and suitcase.''

Barbara drank her wine and waited the few seconds it took for Maggie to resume. There was no point in prodding her; she knew what she wanted to tell, what she had to tell, and her report was as clear and precise as Barbara's would have been.

''I was tempted,'' Maggie said. ''Really tempted. My insurance is pretty limited, the minimum that I have to carry. So there's a big deductible, and partial coverage. Anyway, before I could even ask a question, Mama and Papa Arno and Ray came rushing in, over from Eugene. I told Trassi I had to leave. He tried to keep me another minute or two, but the Arnos were all over us, and he saw it was useless. I left with the Arnos. We drove up to the inn, and Mama was crying, Papa cursing, like that.'' She flashed her fleeting smile again. ''It begins to sound like a farce here,'' she said, almost apologetically.

''They were all talking at once,'' she said. ''But what happened on Friday was that Papa Arno saw Mitch getting a drink from a hose near a shed, and he thought it was a bum who had stumbled out from the woods. Then he saw it was Mitch. He ran over to him and told him to turn around and beat it, but Mitch was muttering that he was going to kill me, and Papa Arno knocked him down. He thought he had to hide Mitch or someone would be killed that weekend. He shoved him inside the shed and told him to stay or he'd have him arrested. Mama and Papa Arno got together to decide what to do, and they called Ray and told him to wait at his house for them. When the rest of us went to dinner, they took Mitch to Ray's house, here in Eugene. Ray told him to clean himself up and they'd talk on Monday, that if he showed up at the inn, he'd beat him to a pulp. Then he came over. But on Monday when Ray got home, Mitch had left. He broke some lamps, spilled beer, left a mess; we think he might have broken into Papa's house, too, but he didn't do any damage there. Then he hit my house," she said furiously. "What if I'd been there with the girls?"

Her hands were shaking again. Barbara patted one and said, "Easy. You weren't, they weren't. So he tore up the place, no one got hurt."

"Right," Maggie said after taking another of her calming, deep breaths. "Anyway, Monday when I got home from Portland, there was a message on my phone machine from Ray, for me to call him back that night. And I called him from the hotel later. He told me Mitch had been there and was gone, and I began to cry, I guess, and I told him about the inn. He wanted to come over then and hang out, just be there if Mitch came back, but I told him that Tom Lasker was on guard, and he wouldn't be allowed in. That's why Mama and Papa came over the next morning with him. We got to the inn and Mama went to pieces again, but Irene kept saying it was her fault, for leaving the place open to air out, and Tom was there telling everyone it was simple vandalism. I really wanted to tell them, at least to tell Ray that Mitch had been there, get his advice about what I should do, but Mama was crying, and everyone talking at once, and Mama and Papa so upset.... I didn't mention that I had seen Mitch. No one mentioned Mitch. I got Ray to take Mama and Papa back home. No one could do anything until the insurance man finished. Then, the first chance I got, I really looked at Mitch's stuff. The suitcase looks very expensive, leather, with a keypad lock. And the briefcase is leather, with a keypad lock. It's really heavy. His sport coat is silk, with a New York tailor's label." Her voice dropped to a whisper. "He had seven hundred dollars in his wallet and eighty-two hundred dollars in a money clip. And I remembered something I hadn't thought of again.

When I went to back my car out of the garage on Friday, I saw something shining on the floor and picked it up. A watch. I just put it in my pocket, and when I went inside the house again, I put it in my bag and forgot it.'' Now she rummaged in the big tote bag and drew out a Rolex and laid it on the table.

Martin stepped from the kitchen and stood in the doorway. ''Barbara, you and your friends are welcome to sit as long as you need, but I have to warn you that in a few minutes I got to unlock the door and let customers in. It just won't be as private.''

Startled, Barbara looked at her own watch. It was ten minutes before six. ''We'll be done by six,'' she said. ''Thanks. Maggie, tell me something about Ray. He keeps figuring in what's happened. Do you suppose he knew Mitch was coming back?''

Maggie shook her head hard. ''No way. It's just that we all rely on him for so many things, he's the one we all call if the car won't start or the furnace makes weird noises. He was the first one I told when I got pregnant; he and Lorinne were engaged, and they offered to take me in, take care of me. For a while I was afraid my parents would kick me out. He's just always been there for me, for my daughters.'' She shrugged. ''He's my pal and my big brother.''

Barbara nodded, and Maggie leaned forward and asked, ''Will you handle this for me? Have I told you enough?''

''Exactly what do you want me to do?''

''I want to track down Mitch and make him pay for all the damage, make him help send the girls to college, collect back child support. I don't know! But he must have gotten rich somehow. And my daughters have gone without a lot of things over the years. I don't want him to get away with this again. I want you to take all Mitch's stuff out of my house and put it away in a safe place, and keep that, too.'' She pushed the expensive watch toward Barbara. ''I don't want to touch anything of his. And will you deal with Trassi?"

"You're on," Barbara said. "As of right now we have a verbal agreement that will have to be put into writing, but later. A few quick questions. Is his car still in the day-use park? And what kind of car is it?" She slipped the Rolex into her bag.

"It's gone. It was gone on Monday when I went up to Portland with my brother. We drove past the park and I looked. I don't know what kind it was. Black, with leather seats, is all I know. Expensive."

In the next few minutes they agreed that Barbara would go to the inn and collect Mitch's stuff and put it in a safe-deposit box. Maggie gave her a brochure about the inn, where it was, how to get there. Barbara said she would bring out an agreement to be signed, and Maggie wrote a check for five hundred dollars, a retainer.

"I'll bring a detective with me," Barbara told her. "I'll want pictures of the damage. And you're not to say a word about any of this to anyone, and don't talk to Trassi at all. Not a word." She gave Maggie two cards, one to be handed over to Trassi, and they both stood up just as Martin walked out to unlock the door.

"By the way," Barbara said, beckoning Laurence to join them, "if you and your friend need a recommendation for dinner, you can't do better than right here."

Then she muttered, "Oh, God! Dinner! So long, Maggie, Laurence. I just remembered something I have to do. See you tomorrow." To Martin she said, "I'll settle up tomorrow or the next day. Okay?"

"Hold it just a second," he said. He went into the kitchen and returned with a paper bag. "Sauce for the salmon. Seven minutes an inch, under the broiler. Got that? Let it rest a minute, then sauce it. And a nice vinaigrette for the salad. Don't use that bottled stuff. I think Binnie tossed in something, don't know just what.''

She hugged him and took the bag, feeling guilt and relief in equal measure. The last glance she had of Maggie and Laurence was of rather bewildered expressions cast her way, before they reseated themselves. They at least would eat very well.

3

Where had May, June, and July gone? It was not amnesia, because if she put her mind to it, she could fill in the weeks and months, most of them anyway. Although the first few weeks were a blur of lovemaking, eating, swimming, and more lovemaking. Then Aztec ruins. After she and John Mureau had spent weeks in Mexico, an earthquake had struck and John had been drawn to it irresistibly, and they had climbed rocky places so he could examine the wreckage, lecturing her on the physics of earth movements all the while. They had flown to New York and spent a few days, then on to Wheeling, West Virginia, so she could meet his two children. Barbara understood very well that part of her confusion about time was due to the fact that there were periods she had put away out of mind, to be thought about later.

She imagined that in her mind was an infinite file cabinet where she could store things that needed considering someday, but not right now. The meeting in Pikeville, Kentucky, with his mother and other family members was tucked away there, too.

Eventually they had flown to Denver, where he had stripped out a large four-wheel-drive camper van. As a geologist working as a mine-safety consultant, he spent a lot of time out in the field in the camper. She had been dismayed at the amount of stuff he had to move from his apartment, and more dismayed when she first saw his office. The desk alone would have filled her living room back in Eugene. He needed it to spread maps on, he had said. It had taken many days for him to pack up the things he would take in the camper, and then to arrange for movers to come for the rest.

Days and days in Denver had been followed by a slow drive to Eugene in the overloaded camper that struggled on hills in a way that made him clench his jaw hard enough for his scar to flare.

For more than a week they had stayed at Frank's house after they finally arrived in Eugene. A frantic search had started, a race to beat his belongings that were then in transit, a race that had ended here. And here was too small by half. A three-bedroom apartment that had looked good when it was empty. Now it was jammed with boxes, with *things*. Rolls of maps, file cabinets, big mover's boxes, some opened, some still taped, the camping gear he had taken out of the camper...

They ate on a card table that had to be folded up again when they were done. Two of the bedrooms were big enough for offices, they had thought at first, when the rooms were empty; the biggest bedroom would be theirs. And the little ones, after they were organized, were big enough for cots when the kids came to visit, he had said. Very carefully, wordlessly, she had stored that item away in her secret mental file cabinet.

That morning she was drinking a cup of coffee, standing by the sink with it, since the table was already folded up against the wall. Bailey was due any minute. She watched John finish cutting the tape on another box; he groaned.

"Only thing to do is open a window and start heaving stuff out," he said.

"Promises, promises."

Grinning, he crossed the few feet of space between them and took the cup from her hand. "Be back early?"

"As early as I can."

He nuzzled her neck.

"I'm sorry I said no," she said softly. "It turns out there was time."

"You'll pay, and pay, and pay," he murmured.

She laughed and pulled free, aware that if he kept it up, by the time Bailey arrived she'd look as sappy as little Mary Sunshine. The doorbell rang.

"And pay," John said ominously, and went to admit Bailey.

Bailey Novell came in, carrying an old denim daypack that he claimed held his junior detective kit. He said hi, and gazed about noncommittally. If Queen Elizabeth sashayed in with a rose between her teeth, he would look noncommittal, Barbara thought, picking up her briefcase and shoulder bag. Bailey was the best detective on the West Coast, her father sometimes said, and she had no reason to disagree, but he looked like a tramp in old hand-me-down clothes that never fitted right. John blew her a kiss and they left.

"Your car or mine?" Bailey asked outside the apartment building.

"Mine," she said, thinking of his expense account. Not only the best detective but one of the most expensive, that was Bailey.

"Okay, but you know your driving puts me in heart-attack territory."

She gave him a look. The apartment was at Fifteenth and Patterson, a nice walk to downtown and the office and courthouse, but too far to walk to Martin's, another annoyance. They got in her car and she headed for Eleventh, and westward.

"You might give a guy a little more warning next time," Bailey commented, slouched down in his seat.

She had not gotten around to calling him until almost ten-thirty last night. "Sorry," she said.

"You going to tell me why we're going to the coast, and why you wanted me to bring a gun?"

"Okay, just the highlights first. A woman's ex is on the rampage, he tore up her bed-and-breakfast place, and he may be crazy. I want a lot of pictures of everything. We're going to pick up some stuff and put it away in a safe-deposit box, so we have to get back before the bank closes. That's why the early start." It was then nine-thirty.

"Where's the place?"

Barbara bit her lip. She had not gotten around to looking at the brochure. "Somewhere between Florence and Newport. There's a brochure in my purse, with directions. You want to root around and find it and guide me in when we get to the coast?"

She pretended not to notice his swift glance at her; she was afraid the deadpan Bailey might be smiling.

He found the brochure and began to read, then he whistled. "It's only seven rooms to rent out, but pretty fancy. The lady loaded?"

"With seven rooms? Not likely. I think she must work pretty hard at it."

"Says her breakfasts are four-star events."

She sighed. She might have known Maggie would be a great cook.

"About ten miles south of Newport," Bailey said. "You should have gone up and out through Corvallis. Quicker that way." He put the brochure on the dashboard. "You going to give me any more than that?"

Traffic picked up; it was always heavy in the summer, and it would be worse coming back. The road was still straight, here on the outskirts of Eugene, but it would start snaking around hills, then mountains in the Coast Range, up and over and around for thirty miles, posted anywhere

from ten miles an hour all the way up to thirty. She began
to fill Bailey in on the details. When he began asking questions, she had few answers.

"Bailey, I just took her on as a client yesterday. Late
yesterday."

"Be nice to know," hc said gloomily. "See, the car
could have been stolen. But if the ex got the car, and there
was a gun locked up in the glove box, that's something
else."

Her hands tightened on the steering wheel.

It was twelve o'clock when she pulled into the drive to
Folsum House. Another time, she wanted to come back and
explore the little town of Folsum, but not today. A white
three-story building came into view, gleaming in the sun-
light. There were several cars in front of the building, and
as she got closer, she could see mattresses stacked at the
top of several stairs that led to the open front door.

Maggie came out to meet them. She was hot and sweaty,
her hair was tied up in a high ponytail to keep it off her
neck; she looked years younger than the thirty-five she had
admitted to. The deep shadowed hollows under her eyes
were less noticeable, as if she had gotten some sleep the
night before.

"Let's start at the top and work down," Barbara said
after introducing Bailey. Two young men emerged from the
house with another mattress. Bailey was already taking
photographs.

A woman came toward them from a long hallway when
they entered the building. She was muscular and lean, forty
or forty-five, dressed in chino pants and a plaid shirt. "Irene
Lasker," Maggie said. "This is the lawyer I told you would
be coming. Ms. Holloway and her associate."

Irene Lasker nodded. "I told her not to trust that insurance man," she said. She stalked away again, muttering,

"I hope they catch them and nail their hides to the wall, that's what I hope."

"Well, upward?" Barbara said, eyeing the stairs. Two men were starting down, carrying an upholstered chair; the seat, arms, and back had all been slashed, the stuffing pulled partway out.

"We'd better use the back stairs," Maggie said faintly, watching the men wrestle the chair down the staircase.

It was carnage from attic apartment all the way through. Paneling in the halls had been broken, storage spaces under eaves and stairs had been emptied, closets ransacked, drawers dumped, overturned. Worse than Maggie had described. Finally Maggie took them to her room, and closed and locked the door. Part of the room had been outfitted as an office; there was a twin-size bedframe, and clothing scattered everywhere. Papers were on the floor, drawers overturned on them.

Maggie went on to the bathroom, a large, oddly shaped room with hyacinth-blue and white tiles, a blue oversized tub, with a blue tile ledge in a sharply angled corner, blue cabinets.... Evidently a large flowerpot had been on the ledge; dirt, greenery, shards, were in the bottom of the tub. The cabinets had been emptied, hair dryer, towels, cosmetics, bowl cleaner.... A second door led to the girls' room, Maggie said. On the wall opposite the window were floor-to-ceiling open shelves that had been swept clean, and a lighted mirror over a vanity table and small chair. Maggie went to that wall.

She moved an upturned clothes hamper out of the way, moved the chair and then the vanity. Then she opened a panel in the wall. "Dad added the bedroom and bath when my mother got pregnant the first time. She didn't want an upstairs room and she wanted an adjoining room for a nursery. They angled it out for the view," she added. "And that made the bathroom this shape. They squared off some of the corners, but still there was space left where the pipes come in, and it was unusable, I guess, so they walled it off but left access to the plumbing.''

She stood aside to let Barbara and Bailey get to the opening. It was too dark to see much. ''Let's get pictures first,'' Barbara said, moving out of Bailey's way.

While he was getting the photographs, she glanced inside the girls' room. More carnage, more clothes strewn about. This room was lavender, and now she saw a painting of lavender flowers on the wall, a graceful spray of lilacs, and she recalled that every room had a flower painting. Lilacs, roses, sunflowers... She examined the painting; it was Laurence's, and it was very fine. Each room was decorated with colors that matched the colors he had used. The lavender bedroom, blue tinged with lavender in the bath, rose in Maggie's room. It must have been a very elegant bed-and-breakfast.

As soon as Bailey was done, he dragged the stuff into Maggie's bedroom and took more pictures of everything.

''Tape and seal the suitcase and briefcase, will you,'' Barbara said to Bailey. ''I'll get the paperwork out of the way. Not over the keypad locks,'' she added. He scowled; he knew that, she understood. Maggie cleared enough space on her desk for the laptop, and very quickly Barbara filled in the information on the fee agreement, and then quickly keyed in another agreement, her obligations and Maggie's. She finished almost as soon as Bailey was done.

''I want a look in the duffel bag,'' Barbara said.

Very quickly Bailey said, ''We should find something to dump it out in, something smooth.''

Maggie rummaged in the tangle of clothes and brought out a white blouse, which she spread on the floor.

After Bailey dumped the bag, they all gazed at a lead pipe and leather holder. ''What...?'' Maggie said, reaching for it. Bailey caught her hand.

"Don't touch," he said. He found a plastic bag in his gear, and latex gloves that he pulled on; then he carefully picked up the pipe and holder and put them inside the bag. He held it by the top and let them look. "Hair, fibers, blood, all that expert detective stuff." He put the plastic bag back inside the duffel. No one commented as he picked up the other items and replaced them in the duffel bag. Dirty shirts, underwear, socks, shaving kit... After that, he made a note of the tailor's name in the silk coat, then he counted the money in the clip. "Eighty-two hundred." Maggie nodded. In the wallet they found $728 and identification in the name of Gary Belmont. Driver's license, insurance card, Social Security card, all in Belmont's name.

Barbara picked up a little notebook. "Okay if I keep this with me? Could help track him down."

Maggie shrugged, and Barbara slipped the notebook into her bag and brought out the Rolex, which she added to the duffel bag.

"Is that Mitch?" she asked then, handing the driver's license to Maggie.

"Superficially it resembles him. Dark hair, at least. The statistics are almost right: six feet two, a hundred ninety-five pounds. Mitch is six one, and not that heavy."

"Okay. I'll write up an inventory of the stuff you're turning over to me, explain the various agreements, then a quick look outside, and we have to beat it."

It didn't take long. She explained the various papers to Maggie and was pleased to see that Maggie was actually reading them. She feared for clients who didn't read what they signed. A few minutes later they were ready.

"This end of the house can be closed off from the paying guests," Maggie said at an outside door near her room. "We have a little privacy that way, and use this as a private entrance."

"How close can we get my car?" Barbara asked.

"The driveway is over there, past my room," Maggie said, opening the door to a terrace. "You can't see it from here."

Barbara could see why the room had been angled as it had been. One wall with many windows faced northwest, one faced southwest; the view in either direction was magnificent—ocean, beach, cliffs.

"Be right back," Bailey said; he started around the house toward the garage.

"I want to walk out there a bit," Barbara said. She left Maggie in the doorway. The house was two hundred feet in from the edge of the rocky cliff, which was like a peninsula jutting out from the mainland. At the edge she stopped to gaze down. It was almost a straight drop from here to the beach, about seventy-five feet down, although on both sides the cliff sloped in a scalable fashion. A rustic split-log fence outlined the edge in both directions. She followed it to a break, where a trail zigzagged downward.

When she returned to Maggie, she said, "Wow! It's great!"

"Yes," Maggie said. "It is. When there's a storm, a real gale, spray comes up over the fence."

Bailey came around the corner of the house. "Both cars torn apart," he said morosely. "Walk over and look around. I'll bring the car back to pick you up, and while you're looking, I'll load the stuff. What did you do with his car keys?" he asked Maggie.

For a moment she looked blank, then she paled. "Oh, God, I forgot all about the keys. They're in my jeans. The jeans are—they were in the bathroom hamper."

They all went back to the bathroom. Maggie pulled the jeans out from under other things and felt in the pockets. "They're gone," she whispered.

When they left the bed-and-breakfast, Barbara headed north and drove slowly past the day-use park. It was jammed full, and the cars were visible from the road, which was no more than a narrow access road to the park and the inn. A mile farther up, it joined the coast road, 101. At Newport, Bailey told her to pull in at a drive-through fast-food place. Then, eating hamburgers, they headed out of Newport, back toward Eugene. It was ten minutes to three. She waited until Bailey had finished his second hamburger to ask, "Well? Comments? Observations? Anything?"

"Two guys. They were searching and being fast and careless about it. One's a lefty," he added.

"How do you know one's a lefty?" she asked, passing a truck. He groaned.

"Close your eyes and imagine—God help me, I didn't say that! Just imagine, open-eyed, how you'd go about yanking stuff out of a closet. Which hand you open it with, which one you grab stuff with, how you toss it."

She had no trouble visualizing it, but she had not seen it herself. "Gotcha," she said.

"And he's got the car keys," he said gloomily.

A little later she said, "See what you can dig up about Belmont. Could be Arno's alias. And if Mitch has a record. You know the drill."

"Barbara, Belmont's from New Orleans."

"So? I don't expect you to go there and pound on doors. Just dig a little." She drove for a minute or two, thinking, then said, "Maggie will stay at the hotel for a while, and no doubt Trassi will get to her. He'll probably give me a call tomorrow. It would be helpful if I had a little information before I talk to him."

"Wish for the moon. Tomorrow?"

"It's a thought."

They got to her bank in Eugene ten minutes before it closed at five-thirty. There had been a log truck on the

Corvallis road with traffic lined up behind it for miles. She parked illegally out front long enough to carry the stuff from the trunk inside the bank, then handed the keys to Bailey, who would move the car. When she was finished with the safe-deposit rental business, she made a Xerox copy of Maggie's check and deposited it and two other much smaller ones, and she was done.

Bailey was waiting for her. "Now the notebook," she said, but hesitated. He had to look through it, but where? Her office at the apartment was impossible; she couldn't even close the door. Not her father's office; the firm was closed by then, and she didn't want to use her key to get in. "How about a drink?" she said finally.

"How about that," he said with more enthusiasm than he had shown all day.

"Where's the car?"

"Two-hour parking slot. It's okay. Let's walk over to the Park Bar and Grill."

They crossed the street and walked through the small urban park with its big fountain, walked one more block and entered the cool, dim bar.

There, in a booth with a gin and tonic before her, a double bourbon on the rocks before him, they sat side by side and looked over the notebook.

"What the hell?" he said. "Foreign telephone numbers?" He flipped the page to find more foreign numbers. Not written by a European, Barbara thought; the sevens were all American, not slashed. Bailey flipped to the next page. "These I know. Seattle area codes. San Francisco." He copied all the numbers in his own notebook.

There was a long string of numbers without any notation to indicate what they were for. Under them was a flight number. The letters *f* and *l* and the number.

A woman's handwriting, Barbara thought, studying the

two letters. At the bottom of the page, printed in capitals with a different pen, a felt tip, was the word PENELOPY.

Bailey closed his notebook and stowed it away in a pocket, and she slipped the other one back into her bag. They finished their drinks and walked to her car, and she drove to her apartment.

"I'd offer to give you a call," he said at the car door when they got out, "but damned if I know where to call."

"Shit! Look, I'll see Trassi in Dad's office. When he makes the appointment, I'll leave a message on your machine. If you can get there half an hour or so before him, that should give us time enough."

Bailey saluted and slouched away toward his own car, and she thought, Goddamn it! She would have to use the office, after all. There wasn't any other place where she and Trassi could have a private talk.

When she opened the apartment door, the fragrance of spicy enchiladas hit her. The card table was set, with an unlit candle, a bottle of wine, and a rose in a glass, and John was hurrying from his office.

"You said you'd be home early," he whispered into her ear, drawing her in close.

"I said as early as I could," she murmured, setting her briefcase down, letting her shoulder bag slide to the floor.

4

When she closed the bedroom door without a sound the next morning, she saw the clutter that she had overlooked the night before. It was worse than ever. At her office door she stopped, rigid with rage. He had moved her desktop computer to the side and put two of his file drawers on her desk. She went to shower and took a long time, willing her anger to ebb and flow out with the water.

He had to work, he had said days ago. It had been months since he had done any serious work. He would get to the stuff as soon as he could; every day he would get more of it stowed away, but he had to work.

Every day he unearthed more junk, and nothing vanished.

The shower had helped some, she thought, wrestling the card table out from behind a box. She set up the table in the kitchen space, started a pot of coffee, and retrieved her laptop from the floor where she had placed it the day before. In spite of herself, she had to smile at the briefcase and purse just inside the door. *All right,* she told herself, *just go with it for now.*

She had finished her notes and was working on a plan of action when John came from the bedroom, naked.

"How can it be? You look as good at eight in the morning as at midnight." He kissed the top of her head and was in the process of turning her chair toward him when she pushed him back.

"Working," she said as lightly as she could.

"Can't it wait?"

"No. Go take a shower."

"In a minute. You know that Staley mine I told you about? The assholes are challenging my findings! I spent hours trying to find my original notes and pictures."

She looked at her monitor. Her hand had been on the keyboard; nearly a whole page of *F*'s filled the screen. "Shit!"

"My thought exactly," he said, pouring coffee. He carried it out with him through the little hallway to the bathroom. She heard the shower.

After cleaning up the *F*'s, she sat staring at the last word she had keyed in, *Trassi*, then had to backtrack in an attempt to recover her train of thought. Where was his office? Who were his clients?

John returned with a towel around him. Water dripped on her arm as he passed her. Very carefully, she saved her work and closed the laptop.

"Don't go," he said. "You're not in the way. Want some scrambled eggs?"

Standing up, keeping her voice calm with great effort, she said, "What's all that stuff on my desk?"

"What stuff?" He went to look, then said, "Oh, God, I'm sorry. I was looking for that Staley file. I'll get it off today."

"But you thought it was perfectly all right to put it there. I can't go in my own office and use my own desk, close my own door. And you say I'm not in the way."

"Hey," he said softly. "I'm sorry. I shouldn't have done it. Can't you use the downtown office today? Or your father's place?"

Still unnaturally quiet, she said, "I've tried hard to keep my private business out of the office. Today I *have* to go there because I don't have anywhere else." Her voice rose and she stood up. "And I hardly think it's my father's responsibility to provide me with working space."

"Barbara, Christ, what else can I say except I'm sorry. Can't you put off working until we get things better organized?"

"My office *was* organized, but I can't use it." She picked up her briefcase and purse. "I have to go."

She started for the door, then stopped and spun around to face him. "Oh, my God," she said. "We're fighting."

He nodded miserably, and this time when he tried to hold her, she did not resist. "I'm sorry," she said. "Frustration, I guess."

"My fault. I just kept thinking of that damn Staley file. I'm really sorry."

"Okay." His arms tightened around her. "I really do have to go." Drawing back from him, she touched his lips with her fingertip. "Not much of a fight, slugger. We'll do better next time."

He shook his head. "No next time. Back early?"

"As early as I can."

She sat in her car for a minute or two. Go, but where? Eventually she had to go to the courthouse and do a little research, and she had to get to a phone and call Ruthie at Frank's downtown firm, and she had to call her father, and... *Oh, cut it out,* she told herself then. She headed for her father's house.

When he met her at the door, a huge smile crossed his face instantly. "Bobby! Just in time for some breakfast."

Not *How are you? Is anything wrong?* Just *Come on in and eat.* She smiled back gratefully.

In the kitchen a few minutes later, she eyed him suspiciously. "Is that oatmeal?"

"You betcha. Good, too. Maple syrup on it. Cyrus tells

me I eat too much high-cholesterol food.'' Cyrus was his doctor.

She felt a pang at the reminder that her father was considered elderly, was elderly, and a possible candidate for a heart attack or plaque-clogged arteries or something else. Frank was seventy-four, seventy-five? Somewhere around there.

''Where are the monsters?'' she asked, watching him spoon oatmeal into a bowl for her.

''Backyard. They can't come in. Fleas. Later on I intend to walk over to the garden shop and see if they have any of those nematodes you can use on the lawn. Just spray it on and the little buggers knock off all kinds of pests. Then I'll give the cats a bath. And hope for the best.'' He didn't sound hopeful.

The oatmeal was good. They ate in silence. Then she asked if she could use his downtown office sometime during the day for about an hour or two.

''Honey,'' he said reproachfully, ''that's your office, too. You know you can, anytime you want. What's up?''

''Another lawyer, maybe from California, maybe not. I want to make him believe I'm for real.''

Frank laughed. ''You going to look him up in the ABA reference? Quote his own lies to him?'' He felt about Los Angeles attorneys the way most people felt about all lawyers.

''Something like that. And would you mind if I park in the upstairs office for a time? Our place is still uninhabitable.''

She was well aware of his shrewd appraisal, but he made no comment, asked nothing, just said sure.

One of the golden coon cats started to scratch on the screen door. She no longer could tell them apart, just Thing One and Thing Two. The other one pounced on the first one and they both rolled across the porch and tumbled down the few steps to the ground.

She told Frank in vague terms about a "he said, she said" case she had taken on; he told her about Mrs. Gillespie's new will. She called Ruthie at the office and told her to set up an appointment with Trassi anytime after two, and to call back here. When she hung up, she caught Frank's gaze on her. He was smiling.

"It's good to have you here like this, shooting the breeze," he said.

"Yeah, it is. I'll wash up. You can go about your business," she said.

"Just don't let those fool cats in." He went to his den to collect his own briefcase and notes.

Barbara worked awhile, paced, worked some more. Ruthie called, and Barbara called Bailey's number and left the message on his machine: "He's coming at two. I'll get there at one. See you."

By the time she entered the offices of Bixby, Holloway, and a couple dozen others, she had done all her chores: laptop work, courthouse records, notes, a game plan for "he said, she said"…

One o'clock was slack time at the office; nearly everyone was off to lunch. One of the stenographers was filling in at the reception desk; Barbara asked her to send Bailey on back when he got there, and went down the corridor to Frank's office.

It was spacious with high and wide windows, a lot of fine paneling, glass-fronted bookcases, forest-green leather-covered chairs and couch, a very nice coffee table—the kind of room where you could tell your lawyer your deepest, darkest secret without fear.

Bailey arrived ten minutes later. "Hi," he said. He glanced toward the bookshelves that concealed a bar.

"Help yourself," she said, and watched him go straight to the shelf with the *T*'s, open it, and stand considering the choices. "You could start talking," she suggested sarcastically.

"Oh, yeah. Forget Gary Belmont. Dead. Mugged, killed with the good old blunt instrument down in New Orleans during the night of July twenty-three. Found on the twenty-fourth by a biologist pursuing the mating habits of alligators." He poured bourbon, then seated himself in one of the client's chairs. "That one was easy, New Orleans newspaper, on the Web. Nothing on Arno. Clean, or he uses some other alias. The telephone numbers. Two restaurants and a pharmacy in Zurich, Switzerland. A restaurant and a hotel in Paris. A deli and a bookstore in Seattle. A hotel in San Francisco." He shrugged. "There are a couple of others, but you get the drift. All places like that—bookstores, restaurants, nothing personal, no individual." He sipped the bourbon straight and eyed her over the glass.

"I'm afraid your guy might be wanted for murder."

"Tell me about it," she said, frowning. "Anything else about Belmont?"

"Born and raised in the area, live-in girlfriend. Worked the docks, hit the bars and nightspots, gambled. Last seen in a bar in the Quarter. Arno might have cruised looking for a good-enough resemblance, then hit. Or maybe he knew the guy. However that goes, he ended up with the ID."

And added a whole other dimension to the case, she thought glumly. She couldn't conceal evidence of a felony crime. She remembered a saying a friend of hers had quoted once: "Heaven is high and the emperor is far away." She said, "Back burner. At least for now."

Bailey shrugged and finished the drink. He rummaged in his bag and brought out some folded papers, his reports.

"The flight number is United out of Miami, a daily nonstop to San Francisco."

She watched absently as he regarded the glass for a moment, as if considering. He set the glass down and waited.

"Look," she said, "Trassi's due in a few minutes. Can you hang around to get a peek at him? And I might have something after he's gone. Can do?"

"Barbara," he said reasonably, "it's my job, what I get paid for. I'll mosey back in when he's gone. See ya."

"Take that with you," she said, pointing to the glass.

By the time Ruthie called her to say Trassi was there, she had put Bailey's report in her briefcase and spread some yellow pads on the desk, one of them opened with her notes. She left them and walked out to meet Trassi.

"Barbara Holloway," she said at the reception desk. "Mr. Trassi?"

"Yes." He was slightly built, fiftyish, with sparse hair carefully combed over a bald spot, and he was very pale and gray—hair, eyes, expensive suit, all gray. His handshake was perfunctory, hardly more than a touching of her hand.

"The office is this way," Barbara said. He was looking around at everything; people had returned from lunch, some were still trickling in; there was a murmur of voices, a laugh from the stenographer's room.

In the office, with him in the chair Bailey had used, and her behind the desk, she asked pleasantly, "Would you like a cup of coffee? Tea, perhaps?"

"No."

He had examined the office with the same careful scrutiny he had shown in the corridor. Now he sat primly with his feet together, his hands on the arms of the chair in what looked like a very uncomfortable position.

"I don't know why your client thought it necessary to

employ legal counsel for what is a very simple request," he said.

Barbara glanced down at the open legal pad and closed it. "As you see, however, she did seek counsel," she said.

"Mitch Arno is basically a messenger," he said, "a courier, no more than that, but a highly trusted courier until this incident." He told the same story she had heard from Maggie. When Barbara did not comment, he said coldly, "Arno left our material at his ex-wife's inn. We need to recover it."

Barbara nodded. "So they sent you. Why you?"

"Because I can identify the bags, and I can open them. I can identify the contents. We assumed I could reason with Ms. Folsum, explain the situation to her, and compensate her for any trouble this has caused."

"Have you requested police help in locating Mitch Arno?"

"No! Absolutely not! We are constrained by the nature of the papers he was carrying. It must not be known that such sensitive material was out of our hands for even a second. This must be kept confidential."

He leaned forward. "What we propose, Ms. Holloway, is a meeting with Ms. Folsum, long enough for me to demonstrate that I have the combination to both of those locks. I shall show her enough of the papers to prove my point. In your presence, of course. We are willing to pay her five thousand dollars, and to cover any uninsured losses to her inn."

Barbara shook her head kindly. "I'm afraid that won't work," she said. "Ms. Folsum doesn't have anything of Mitch Arno's lying about, nothing less than eighteen years old, from the time he abandoned her. Of course, you could get a court order to force anyone who might have happened across your material to release it. With the proper identification, verification of employment of Arno, a statement from him, certified authorization from your company, you know, all those petty details, you might gain possession. No doubt everything would have to be opened in a judge's chambers to verify the contents of the bags, in such an event.''

"What do you want?''

He had not shown any anger and showed none now. Ah, she thought, he had been kissed by the Snow Queen. He could neither laugh nor cry.

"I was working on that earlier,'' she said, and opened her legal pad. "At five hundred a month for child support for the older child, for eighteen years, I arrived at one hundred and eight thousand dollars. For the younger daughter, the figure is one hundred and two thousand. Seventeen years,'' she said, looking up pleasantly. "The damage to the inn has yet to be determined, as has the cost of the loss of business.''

His eyes narrowed, his only reaction.

"We want to talk to Mitch Arno and arrange a settlement with him,'' she said, closing the pad again. "If we can't reach an agreement with him, we are prepared to institute garnishment proceedings, in which case a third party who happens to hold property or money belonging to the defendant would be ordered by the court to retain such property awaiting due process. An investigation, of course, would follow—full disclosure, proof of ownership, and so forth.'' She stood up. "Is that all?''

"For now,'' he said, rising.

She went to open the door for him, then watched him walk down the corridor and out of the reception area.

She was deep in thought when she heard Bailey's characteristic tap on the door. "It's open,'' she called.

He shambled in and took his chair.

"Get a look at him?''

"More. I tagged along after him. He headed for the pay

phone in the lobby downstairs, changed his mind, and used one half a block up the street. Called two numbers, one probably long-distance. At least he used a card on that one. One local. I had to keep back because he's got smarts. He was watching his tail. Then he went to the Hilton."

She nodded. "Can you get those two bags open? The suitcase and briefcase?"

"Sure. I'll bring a hacksaw."

"I want a look," she said. "Now, today, tonight."

He nodded, then said, "But I'd like a little reassurance that my hand isn't going to be blown off."

She told him about her meeting with Trassi, and finished saying, "He doesn't want cops, and he never batted an eye when I said two hundred ten thousand. I want to see what's in them. I think he believes we've already opened them. He'll consult with his client and come back with a better offer."

"Where?" Bailey asked then. "Not at the bank."

"No. Here. We'll have to get the stuff over here, preferably without his knowing, just in case he's keeping an eye on us. And Maggie will have to be present."

He reached down and pulled a glass from his bag, then held it up inquiringly. It was her father's glass, the one Bailey had taken out with him. When she motioned toward the bookshelves, he went over, opened the bar, and poured himself a drink. Bailey was polite; he never helped himself without permission.

She waited. At last he said, "Can you get Maggie over here by seven-thirty?"

Barbara said yes, and hoped it was true. She was aware that everything she was doing was involving her father deeper and deeper in whatever it was she was mixed up in. She had to involve him. She couldn't put that stuff in his office safe without his knowledge and permission.

"Use your phone?" Bailey asked. She nodded and went

to sit on the couch; he pulled the phone around to him and dialed. She heard his greeting: "Sylvia, how's things?" His voice dropped then and he talked, listened, even laughed once, but finally he hung up and came to sit in an over-stuffed chair across the coffee table from her.

"Okay, all set," he said.

5

At ten minutes past three Barbara decided that Frank was not home, and she stood undecided what to do next.

Finally she unlocked the door, then entered his house, and heard him cursing. She followed the sound through the wide hallway, past the living room and the dining room, and found him in the downstairs bathroom on his knees at the bathtub.

"Goddamn it, you do that again and I'll wring your neck."

There was a tremendous splash, and water sprayed from the tub all over him. "You little fucker, you misbegotten son of a bitch!"

Grinning, she backed away and went to the kitchen, then called out, "Dad, you around somewhere?"

Now she heard a cat's furious yowling. Frank yelled, "Be right with you." The bathroom door slammed.

She stood at the back door, laughing. He came out in a few minutes, and one of the Things streaked past the kitchen and up the stairs, yelling. It was soaked to the skin.

"Turn on the sprinkler and those fool cats play in it like kids. Roll around in the birdbath. A real bath and they turn into maniacs," Frank said. "But I did them, both of them, blast their eyes."

He went to the sink and washed his hands, then got a glass of water and drank most of it before he turned back to look at her.

"Are you going to go get dry?" she asked.

"No. Feels good this way."

"Can we talk a little?"

"Sure. Coffee? Something else?"

"No, thanks. It's about private business, a case I've taken on at Martin's, but I've already used your office, and I have another favor to ask. I need to use the safe."

"Okay. So use it. You going to fill in more than that?"

She told him about it. He whistled when she said $210,000.

"And he didn't bat an eye," she said. "I'm convinced he thinks we've already gotten inside that suitcase, that we know what we're talking about. But we don't."

"Drug money? Drugs? Secret plans to take over the world? New and better Pentagon Papers? Maps to militia caches? Could be anything. Industrial spying, national security stuff... Corporate plans to conquer the stock market. It could be FBI or CIA business." He shrugged. "Could even be what he claims it is, legitimate company business. You on contingency?"

"Of course not."

"Okay. Wishful thinking. So you and Bailey will get the stuff to the office around five. I'll drop in, check my mail, cheer up Patsy. She thinks I spend too much time somewhere else." Patsy was his secretary.

"Thanks," she said. "I've got to run. Bank at four-thirty. Bailey said he and Sylvia would be there waiting."

"Sylvia? He's bringing in Sylvia?" Frank laughed. "You'll love her."

"You know her?"

"Oh, Lord, yes. Sometime when you have an hour, I'll tell you about Sylvia. Beat it now, or you'll be late."

Get there at four-thirty, Bailey had said, *and go to the safe-deposit boxes.* She did that, and her bank escort used her key to open the box, then watched as Barbara inserted hers and turned it. The door swung open; the escort withdrew and pulled the vault door closed behind her. Barbara brought out the suitcase, the briefcase, and duffel bag, shut the drawer, and rang the bell for her escort. She had forgotten how heavy the briefcase was.

"I'm ready," she said.

Her escort was careful not to glance at the things Barbara had, but they both turned to look toward an open door outside the safe-deposit area, where a woman was saying in a quarrelsome way, "I told you I wanted to put the earrings in there. Why didn't you watch?" Another escort was standing at the door, gazing fixedly at her shoes, as if this has been going on for a while. "Now I have to get back in." The door swung open all the way, and a man pushed a wheelchair out of a small private room. Barbara blinked. Bailey, in a black suit and tie. The woman was grotesque, orange hair frizzy about her face, big dangling earrings that looked like emeralds, a long multicolored skirt, and a garish red filmy top; one leg was in a cast. She looked to be seventy or older.

"Barbara! Barbara Holloway! You remember me! Sylvia Fenton, we met at some silly luncheon. My dear, you look wonderful."

Bailey gazed at the ceiling with a wooden expression; both escorts looked at the floor.

"How are you?" Barbara said, feeling inordinately stupid. The old woman had a broken leg, that's how she was.

"Not too bad, considering. My dear child, you surely don't intend to carry all that by yourself, do you? Ridiculous! Ralph, help her."

"Oh, I couldn't impose," Barbara said hurriedly.

"We'll deliver it wherever you say," the old woman said. "Ralph, put it in the office here, while I go get rid of those earrings. Miss," she said to her escort, "I'm afraid we have to open the door again. If it's not too much bother. Ralph, where's my key? Put this bag somewhere and help me with my crutches. If you'd been paying attention, we wouldn't be having all this fuss.''

Bailey took a large paisley print bag from her, carried it back inside the office, and came out with crutches. They all watched anxiously as she got up and supported herself on the crutches. "Put that damn chair back in the office and stay with my bag,'' she told Bailey. Then she said to Barbara, "Just tell him where you want the stuff delivered, dear. I won't be a minute, then we'll drop it off on our way home.''

"Centennial Bank,'' Barbara said. "I was going there from here.'' She looked at Bailey, who appeared bored unto death. "If it's really no bother—''

"No, ma'am. No bother. I'll just put your things in here with her bag. And stand guard,'' he added.

"Thank you,'' Barbara said, and shrugged at her escort. "I guess that's all.''

She left the bank and walked the two blocks to the other bank, where she rented a box exactly like the one she had just emptied, and ten minutes later Bailey entered, carrying all three bags. "She said I should carry them down for you,'' he said in a patient voice. They were escorted to the vaults by a male this time.

Bailey put the bags down, and she handed him a ten-dollar bill. "You've been so kind,'' she said.

"Thanks. Appreciate that.'' He left, and she put the bags in a drawer. Ringers, she realized; they looked all right, but were subtly different, and also empty, and lightweight.

Afterward, back in her father's office, she paced. Frank sat on the couch, grinning. "Now what?'' she demanded.

"I wouldn't spoil this for anything. Relax, he'll be along in a minute or two.''

In a few minutes Ruthie buzzed them; Bailey had arrived. Barbara ran to open the door and saw Bailey pushing the wheelchair down the corridor toward her. Mrs. Fenton's big paisley bag was on the seat, and Bailey was smiling.

"Nothing to it," he said.

Barbara watched as he opened the paisley bag and drew out the duffel, then opened the back of the wheelchair and took out the briefcase, and finally removed the seat and brought out the suitcase. "See? Slick as a whistle. Sylvia was great." He reassembled the chair.

"Where is she?" Barbara asked, imagining the woman hobbling down on the street, giving orders right and left.

"Talking to her broker on the first floor, making a scene, I bet. I came up the service elevator. Gotta run. Take her home, get a bite to eat, back here at seven-thirty. See ya."

Oh, God, Barbara thought in dismay. Eat. Again. She waited impatiently as Frank took his time opening the wall safe tucked way behind the bookshelves. As soon as everything was put away, the safe locked up, she said, "Dad, I have to go. Seven-thirty."

He watched with a faint smile as she snatched up her bag and ran out. Under his breath, he said, "Ah, Bobby."

Maggie was late; she had borrowed Irene's car, she said, and it was cranky and slow. After Barbara introduced her to Frank, they gathered around the coffee table and the suitcase and briefcase. Bailey touched a key. A tiny red light came on in the upper corner, blinked once and went out. He scowled.

"You understand that there are people who can get into them without destroying them," he said darkly. "I'm not one of those people." He looked at Barbara, who shrugged. Then he turned to Maggie.

"Break them open," Maggie said. "I don't care."

"Right. Over at the desk." He carried both cases to the

desk and picked up his denim bag. When Barbara started to move around the desk to watch, he said, "Beat it."

She went back to the couch with Maggie and Frank.

When everyone was settled, Frank asked, "Has Folsum House been an inn a long time?"

"Ten years," Maggie said. "That was another reason for the party, to celebrate my tenth year there."

"You started it?" Barbara asked, surprised again by this young woman. "At twenty-five?"

"I had some help," Maggie said. "Laurence's father made it happen. After Mitch left for good, Papa Arno got me a job at Cliff Top Hotel. Mama Arno baby-sat the girls while I worked, and gradually I was learning something about how a hotel is run. Then Mr. Thielman bought Cliff Top. He does that, finds a hotel with potential and buys it, renovates it and trains local people, then sells it to a chain. He trained me."

"All this leads up to how you became an innkeeper at twenty-five?" Frank asked. Barbara pretended she was not watching Bailey.

Maggie nodded. "About then, my mother began to talk about moving to California to be closer to my brother Richard, and then one day they told me they were putting our house up for sale. I was still living with them with the girls; it was all I could afford. Everyone just assumed I would go, too. Then Mr. and Mrs. Thielman asked me to come into his office for a talk, and he asked me if I wanted to move to Los Angeles, and I said no. He made a proposition. Why didn't I buy the house and turn it into a bed-and-breakfast? He had trained me well; I knew everything there was to know about how to run it, and it would provide a living for me and my children as long as I wanted it to. I nearly laughed in his face. I didn't have a penny to my name."

Across the room Bailey muttered something unintelligible. Of course, Barbara thought, it was a metal case and the lock was probably an integral part of the frame. She wanted to call out for him to use a blowtorch.

Maggie was still talking. "Mrs. Thielman said Laurence was unhappy about their coming sale of Cliff Top and moving on, this time to Singapore. He refused to go. He was in art school in Chicago and wanted to finish, and then live on the coast and paint. She said they both understood his need to prove himself, but on the other hand he was so young, only nineteen then, that if he did manage to find a suitable apartment, he would never keep it. It would be robbed in his absence or he would spend rent money on art supplies or a trip somewhere or something else." She smiled faintly. "Their offer was incredible. If I would let Laurence have the attic apartment, they would pay his rent in advance every year for ten years. They had already sent someone out to look over the house and see if it could be converted, and Mr. Thielman had an estimate of what it would cost. Mrs. Thielman said they would be relieved, knowing that Laurence had a home to return to, where his belongings would be safe, where he could paint, and after ten years he would be on his own.

"They made it happen. I had no credit and I couldn't borrow the kind of money it would have taken, but they bought our house, and the next day they sold it to me. They carry the mortgage. I've never missed a payment, and next month Laurence has to start paying rent or get kicked out."

"Hats off," Frank said quietly. "You did it and you did it alone."

"Not altogether," she said. "The second year I was about to go under, and Papa Arno came to my rescue and loaned me money. If it hadn't been for his and Mama Arno's trust and faith, and Mr. and Mrs. Thielman's belief that I could do it, it wouldn't have worked."

There was a loud snapping from the other side of the

room. They all watched as Bailey pushed the suitcase aside and pulled the briefcase around.

A little later Frank and Maggie were discussing whether commercial art, illustrations, could be considered real art. Laurence hated doing commercial art, she said, although he was very good at it, but he refused to do more than enough to scrape by. Evidently that was a sore point in their relationship.

Just then there was another snapping noise and Bailey said, "Done."

They hurried across the room to the desk.

"They're unlocked," Bailey said. "Tape's still in place. Whose move?"

"I'll do it," Barbara said. No one stirred or spoke as she peeled the tape off the suitcase, then lifted the lid. Maggie gasped. Barbara let out a long low whistle. Money, stacks of money bundled in neat rows.

"Don't touch," Bailey said. He got a pair of latex gloves from his kit and pulled them on, then he lifted out a bundle of hundred-dollar bills and riffled through it, replaced it, and pulled out a second one. "Ten thousand in the bundles." He counted. "Two hundred fifty thousand, looks like, except one's been tapped." He counted that one. "Ten grand missing. Two hundred forty thousand bucks. Used bills. Not in sequence. If they're marked, it's going to take a real examination to see how."

Silently, leaving the suitcase open, Barbara peeled off the tape on the briefcase and opened it. Papers. A thick stack of papers. Bailey, still wearing the gloves, lifted the stack out and set it on the table. Computer printouts, hundreds, perhaps thousands of sheets of flimsy fanfold printouts in computerese, totally meaningless to Barbara. The print was so small, it appeared almost illegible.

Bailey examined the briefcase; nothing else was in it. After a quick look at Barbara, then Frank, who both nodded, he returned the stack of printouts to the briefcase; Barbara closed it. Then, more slowly, she closed the suitcase.

Bailey left soon after that, saying he'd be in touch.

Maggie sat on the couch with a dazed expression. "Where did that money come from?"

Barbara shrugged. She was thinking it was no wonder that Trassi had shown no surprise at the figure she had arrived at for child-support arrears.

"What we should do," she said, thinking out loud, "is keep all that in the office safe until we know where it came from, whose money it was, and why Mitch had it. And he's the one who can tell us those things." She looked steadily at Maggie. "He'll have to get in touch with you. He doesn't know about me. Don't stay at the inn at night for the time being; stay down at the hotel, with a lot of people around you. If he calls, give him my name and number, and if he shows up, the same. Tell him you'll meet him here, but don't talk to him alone anywhere." Maggie was wide-eyed and pale. She moistened her lips.

"If he tries to get rough," Barbara said matter-of-factly, "scream, yell, make noise to get others to gather around. Just don't go off alone with him for even a minute." She waited for Maggie's nod. "Okay, then. We'll put everything back in the safe. Bailey's running down what he can, and until we get some answers, or see Mitch himself, there's nothing else we can do except sit tight and wait. And don't talk to anyone, not a word. Agreed?"

"Yes," Maggie said.

Then Frank said, "Maggie, you can't drive home alone, not at this hour. I have three upstairs rooms going to waste, without a living soul in them, unless it's a cat. Cats in my house are bootable. Stay over and drive back in daylight."

"He's right," Barbara said. "You shouldn't be out alone at night, not until we know more than we do now. I left gowns and things in the closet and drawers. Please help yourself.''

Maggie hesitated only briefly, then said thanks, she would be glad not to drive out now. After putting everything back in the safe, they left; Maggie followed Frank home, and Barbara hurried to her own apartment.

In his house, after showing Maggie the upstairs rooms, turning on lights for her, Frank went to his own bedroom and eyed the coon cats at the foot of his bed, well aware that they had not forgiven him.

He admired Maggie quite a lot, he reflected. Courage, good sense, determination, all admirable qualities that she had in abundance. He understood her need to throw a big party, to demonstrate to everyone that she had done it. He had great sympathy for young women like her, working so hard to prove their worth to a world that was either disbelieving or indifferent, or both. Even when they succeeded, the world tended to say, So what, can you cook?

He realized he had switched tracks and was considering his own daughter, who was also struggling to prove something. Of the two, Maggie and Barbara, Barbara's self-appointed task was the harder. She had a tougher critic: herself.

"Okay, you monsters," he growled then. "Move over." Usually when he turned down the bed, the cats moved, took up their positions like two warm guardians, one on each side. Tonight they looked at him with golden eyes and did not move. When he took them in to have them neutered, they had not forgiven him for a week. He wondered which they considered worse, having a bath or having their balls cut off. He squirmed into bed and pushed one with his foot until he had room enough, and although usually he promptly fell asleep, that night he lay thinking about the suitcase and briefcase, thinking about Mitch Arno. Why hadn't Mitch Arno called or come back?

He didn't like the answer he was getting.

6

"Hot," Barbara murmured when she and John returned home from a hike up Spencer's Butte on Saturday. John fiddled with the air conditioner, and she hit the MESSAGE button on the phone, then began to unlace her boots. She stopped moving when Maggie's voice came on.

"Barbara, it's Maggie. Are you there? Please pick up!" she sounded panic-stricken. "Please. Okay. I'm coming to town and I'll go straight to Martin's. Please, if you get this, be there. I need help!" The machine voice said, "Saturday, August tenth, eleven forty-five a.m."

"I've got to go out," Barbara said, retying her boot. It was ten minutes past one. She looked up to see John regarding her with a hurt expression. All the way home they had been talking about a shower, a little nap....

"John, I'm sorry." She sounded desperate. "I have to go."

"Sure."

"When I get back, I'll tell you what this is all about." She picked up her bag and hurried from the apartment. So much for weekends together.

If Martin was surprised to see her at the restaurant, it didn't show.

"I'm sorry to barge in," Barbara started at the door. Past him she saw Binnie at one of the tables, the remains of a salad, a pitcher of something still in place. "A client said she was coming here. I'll take her to Dad's office when she shows up."

"What for? We were just waiting for the kitchen to cool down before we get to work. It has by now."

Just then a car pulled up with a squeal; Maggie jumped out and ran toward Barbara.

"Have a seat," Martin said, stepping aside to let Maggie enter. "We're out of here." Binnie was clearing their table.

"Mitch is dead," Maggie whispered. "The police had Ray identify the body, and they asked him questions and sent someone to Papa Arno's to question him. What am I going to do?"

"Three deep breaths, first thing," Barbara said calmly, feeling anything but calm. Dead! Police! Good God!

The long breaths were not working as well as they had before when Maggie first talked to her, but she was more coherent when she said, "Ray called me, just before I called you. He said the police asked him to go downtown to try to identify a body. It's Mitch. Someone killed him. Ray said he was beaten up and killed." She drew in another futile breath, let it out too fast. "They kept Ray and questioned him; he told them the truth, that he left Mitch in his house on Friday and he was gone on Monday. That's all he could tell them. He doesn't have anything to lie about! But what will I tell them?"

"The truth," Barbara said sharply. "After Ray told you Mitch was back, you retained me to deal with him."

"I told Ray I'd come right over, as soon as I could get a ride. He'll be expecting me."

"Let me think a minute," Barbara said. She got up and walked the length of the restaurant and back again. Martin came from the kitchen with a tray of iced tea, silently put the glasses on the table, and returned to the kitchen. Barbara sat down again.

"Maggie, you have to stay calm and not go to pieces. I

need some information. Did the police question Ray downtown or at his place?''

"Both. He said they kept him in the living room and two men went all over the house. They scraped something from the floor.''

"Is his wife back from her parents' place yet with the children?''

"No. They'll come home tomorrow.''

"Did the police fingerprint the house?''

"I don't know. He didn't say.''

"That probably means no. You told me that someone had knocked things around there; you assumed it was Mitch. And you said someone had broken into Papa Arno's house but hadn't done any damage there or stolen anything. Remember?''

"Yes,'' Maggie said in a faint voice. She was calmer now, paying close attention.

"Has it occurred to you that there's more than one possible scenario to account for the breaking and entering at Papa Arno's house, then for things being knocked over at Ray's, and Mitch being gone?''

Maggie's eyes widened, then narrowed as she thought. After a moment she said, "Someone could have been looking for Mitch; they could have taken him away.''

Barbara nodded. "Remember, you said that, not me. It could become important. Another thing to consider, Maggie. The police did a scraping, but they didn't fingerprint the house.''

"They didn't believe Ray,'' Maggie said. "They won't bother to look beyond him.''

"Good,'' Barbara murmured. "Anything else?''

"No.'' When Barbara remained silent, Maggie closed her eyes hard. Finally she opened them.

"Someone should fingerprint the house before Lorinne gets home tomorrow. She'll clean things.''

Barbara wanted to hug her, but she remained silent, waiting.

"I don't know what else you want," Maggie cried. She studied Barbara for a moment, then closed her eyes again, and this time when she opened them, she asked, "Would the detective you use do it for me?"

"You could ask him," Barbara said. She wrote down Bailey's name and number on the back of one of her cards and handed it to Maggie, then pointed to a phone on the cashier's desk. Maggie hurried to it.

In a moment Maggie said, "He isn't home. A woman said he'll be back any minute." She was holding her hand over her mouthpiece.

"Leave your name and this number, and ask her to tell him to call, that it's important."

Maggie spoke into the phone again, then came back to the table.

"We need a couple of minutes to talk," Barbara reassured her. "Maggie, you absolutely must not say a word about seeing Mitch, about the stuff he left at your house. Not a word. If you even breathe that you saw him, you could be compelled to tell it all. At this moment, we don't know anything about this murder, or even if it was a murder. Not how, when, where—nothing. If he was killed when all of you were at your place, there's nothing to worry about, and the police will look further. But if it turns out that Ray was back home when Mitch was murdered, and if the police seriously suspect Ray, then if a large amount of money surfaced, it could be seen as a motive. You can't tell Ray or anyone else anything. If they ask Ray to take a lie-detector test, he has to be free to tell the exact truth, or he'll be in serious danger." She paused. "Do you understand?"

"Yes." She was very pale.

"All right. If the police ask you if you saw Mitch that

weekend, tell them the truth, you didn't. It isn't a lie. You didn't see him after Thursday night.''

Maggie started to say something, but stiffened as the phone rang. Martin picked up in the kitchen, then, after a moment, opened the door and said from the doorway, ''It's for Ms. Folsum.'' His voice was very gentle. She ran to the telephone.

''He'll do it,'' Maggie said when she returned to the table. ''I told him I'd meet him at Papa Arno's, that's where Ray was going, and I'll take him over myself. I'll tell them all what I think happened, that some men got in the house and took him out.''

''Will you have a reason for saying it?'' Barbara asked.

''Sure. Ray told the truth, and Mitch didn't have a car and wouldn't have left on foot.''

It would do, Barbara decided. She jotted down phone numbers on one of her cards and handed it to Maggie. ''Whatever happens, keep in touch with me. Try my place first, then my father's, then the office, and if all else fails, call here. Someone will know where I am. I'll find out what's going on, and we'll talk again soon.''

Maggie started to walk to the door, but she wheeled about and rushed back to the table, where she grasped the tabletop with both hands and leaned forward, her face close to Barbara's. Her voice was low and harsh when she spoke. ''I told you Ray was the first to know when I got pregnant. It was more than that. I was down on the beach, in a little cove that gets cut off at high tide, no exit if there's a heavy surf. I was waiting for the ocean to come get me. I wanted to die, an accident in the ocean, something that would be regrettable but not scandalous, for my mother's sake. It was all I could think of, to die, be done with Mitch, with my life, with the baby. All right, teenage angst, but it's real, Barbara. It's real enough to kill yourself. And Ray spotted me from the cliff, and he came down and got me. I fought him, but he carried me out, climbed up the cliff with me over his shoulder and waves crashing over both of us. We could have been killed, both of us. He took me home with him and gave me a hot bath; I couldn't stop shaking I was so cold. He poured hot cocoa down me and talked to me. Really talked to me. He promised that my baby would not be a bastard, an illegitimate baby that people would scorn and hate and mock, but a respected member of the Arno family, complete with grandparents who would be silly about it, and three big Arno uncles who would protect it, and I would inherit three brothers and in-laws who would welcome me like a daughter. He made me believe it all. And it was all true," she said, her voice dropping to a whisper. "It all came true." She straightened up then, drew back from the table, and said very precisely, "We know other people were looking for Mitch, and why, but the police don't know that. If I have to tell them, I will. Ray, all of the Arnos, they're my real family. I can't let anything happen to them."

"I can't stop you," Barbara said. "Promise me this, though. If you make such a decision, you'll tell me first."

"I'll tell you first," Maggie said, and hurried out.

As soon as she was gone, Barbara went to the phone and hit the redial button. Bailey answered. "It's me," she said, and he said he thought it might be.

"Right. Maggie hired you to do some work for her, and you bill her directly, not through me. Got that?" He said sure. She told him what little she knew, and then said, "Find out what you can about it. And while you're with the Arno clan, keep your eyes and ears open. Okay?" He asked if she wanted to teach him how to tie his shoes. Ignoring that, she said, "I'll be at Dad's tonight, and you're welcome to drop in for dessert and coffee, if you'd like. And if you have anything for me."

He laughed. "You're hitting a new low. In my books that's bribery. See you around."

She drove home deep in thought, and only when she entered the apartment and John emerged from his office, still with a distant, hurt expression, did she remember that she had promised to tell him what was happening.

"I made some tuna fish," he said. "I'll fix you a sandwich while you get the boots off and wash up. You look hot."

He wasn't going to ask anything, demand anything, she understood, yet this would be between them, her silence, her abrupt departures, staying out past office hours with no explanation, and it would fester and grow.

The card table was in the kitchen with the two folding chairs in place. She sat down and started to unlace her boot. Not looking at him, she said, "If I talk with my clients about legal matters, no power on earth can make them or me reveal what was said, but that doesn't apply to you. If you know anything about a case and you're put under oath, you would have to testify, or possibly be held in contempt of court, possibly even go to jail. There's no protection, not even spousal protection in our case."

She finished with the boots and wriggled her toes; her feet were hot and sweaty, she thought with disgust.

He had stopped moving at the tiny counter by the sink. "You think I'd reveal a confidence," he said flatly.

"No, I don't. It's just that you could be at risk." She pulled off her socks. "I want to spare you any possible problem."

"Is a problem going to come up? Spousal protection. You mean one spouse can't be forced to give evidence that might be incriminating to the other, don't you? Are you involved in something that's going to cause you trouble?"

"There could be trouble down the road. Sometimes

things that start very simply turn complicated. A pretty simple case just went postal.''

He finished making the sandwich and put it down in front of her. ''Wash your hands at the sink here and then tell me about it. And eat something first.''

She ate first and then told him about it.

He was silent a moment when she was done, then he asked, ''Can I comment?''

''Sure.''

''She can't collect from a dead man, and the bum's dead apparently. Why not hand the stuff over to the cops and let them deal with Trassi, get to the bottom of it?''

''She has a child who wants to go to medical school,'' Barbara said. ''She'll come out with a hundred-thousand-dollar-plus debt to pay back. That's for openers. But worse, suppose the police come up with a different story. Mitch arrived and told her about the money, maybe showed it to her. She killed him and hid his body and called Ray for help. Or Ray killed him for a share of the money. I have to stall for now, until we know more about Mitch Arno's death.''

''Barbara,'' John said thoughtfully, ''granted that you like Maggie Folsum, but has it occurred to you that maybe she hasn't told the entire truth?''

''It's always a possibility that a client's been lying. They often do. But let's drop it now. I'm so sticky and stinky, I can't stand myself a minute longer. I have to have a shower.''

It did not surprise her at all when he joined her beneath the spray a few minutes later.

Frank's dinner was mainly garden vegetables, all crisp and tender and brightly colored, done to perfection in a way that Barbara decided could only be magic. His halibut was moist and flaky, with a luscious lemon-and-garlic sauce.

Her salmon had been tough and dry; she had forgotten to set a timer. She had told him when he admitted her and John that Bailey might join them for dessert. He had raised his eyebrows. "Always plenty."

Then, at the dining room table, he began to talk about Sylvia Fenton. "You know who Joe Fenton is, don't you? The jewelry-store owner?" Barbara nodded. "Yes, well this started back, oh, thirty or thirty-five years ago, when this rich bachelor was on a jewelry-buying trip to New York. Can't say he was handsome, he never would have won a beauty contest, but he was rich and eligible. Every gal in the county was after him. Anyway, he was in New York and someone took him to an off-Broadway show, and he saw Sylvia. She was a bit player, did character roles— the Irish waif, the saucy French maid, tough honky-tonk dancer. You know what I mean. But something hit Joe hard that night. He came home with a bride."

He was grinning. He helped Barbara to another serving of spinach salad with feta cheese, talking all the while.

"Well, Joe's mother tried to have a heart attack, and his father threatened to disinherit him. But a funny thing happened. In just a couple of months the mother-in-law was Sylvia's champion; she took her everywhere and introduced her as 'my daughter.' And the father-in-law began talking about doing it right, a real wedding with no expense spared. Joe was the happiest man in the county. She has a way, that Sylvia." Frank looked at John then. "Now, I know a few things about folks around here. Barbara knows more, I'm sure. Bailey knows just about everything. And Sylvia knows more than Bailey.

"She fitted in, kept busy, volunteer work, stuff like that, but it wasn't quite enough. Then one day she came to see me and brought a maid in with her, and the maid's story was that a nursing home had killed her mother through neglect, wrong medication or something. Sylvia believed her, but there wasn't a shred of evidence. Inspectors never found a thing out of line. Bailey said he might be able to get a ringer, someone to send in undercover, and Sylvia said she'd do it herself. Right before my eyes she changed from queen of high society to a barely literate, ignorant drudge. So she went in and got a job emptying bedpans and scrubbing; she took a camera with her, and she nailed them. The usual thing, sugar pills instead of prescription drugs, and pocket the money, a lot of things like that."

He laughed. "Thing is, Sylvia loved doing it, and Joe was so proud, you'd have thought she just invented heaven. Sylvia told Bailey she'd be available if something else came along. And, by God, every now and then something does come along." Very softly he added, "Everybody loves Sylvia, and no one more than Joe. He's still the happiest man in the county."

They all cleared the table, and Frank brought out a raspberry torte and a carafe of coffee. As if on cue, Bailey arrived at that moment.

Finally even the dessert was gone, and Bailey put sugar in his third cup of coffee and said, "You tell him anything yet?"

"I told John about it, but not Dad." She told Frank then about Maggie's visit, Mitch's death. "What did you find out?" she asked Bailey afterward.

Frank's face had been jovial, a look of fond reminiscence had softened his features; now he was grim-looking.

With a reproachful look Bailey said, "You sent me straight into bedlam. Three sons—Ray, James, and David—two wives, a thousand kids, Maggie, the old man and old lady all talking at once. Nobody listens, everyone talks."

She shook her head impatiently, and he continued.

"Okay, okay. Problem is, you ask Ray a question and while he answers it, so does everyone else, a chorus of answers, and no one seems to notice. I fingerprinted the whole crew, even little kids wanted their fingerprints made, so I did them, too.''

John looked bewildered. "Why?"

"Elimination. Match up what I can, and anything left over goes to the FBI lab for identification," Bailey said. "So, no point in doing that house, not with people swarming everywhere like they were. Maggie, Ray, James, and the old man, we all went to Ray's house and I did that one. Got a nice footprint in the bathroom, and another one on a hassock in the living room. Looked like someone had put his foot against it and shoved it across the room.''

No one moved as he talked. "Okay, out at his house, I asked Ray to show me around the property, alone. And I got to ask him some questions without the Greek chorus helping out. Ray says that the old man showed up at seven or a little later on Friday, hauling Mitch in with him. The old man took off in his truck, and Ray told Mitch about the party at Maggie's place and warned him if he showed up, they'd make the last beating look like practice. Then he took off, collected his brother James, and they went to the coast.

"On Monday when Ray got home, the living room looked like Mitch had gone wild. Two broken lamps, a can of beer spilled on the floor. Mitch had shaved with Lorinne's razor, and he had eaten and left dishes on the table. He had showered in the big bathroom and left a footprint. He had put on a pair of Ray's jeans and a shirt with the shop logo on the pocket. Mitch was gone and so were his own clothes. That's all Ray knows about that.

"This morning at seven two cops come to the house and seem a little surprised to find Ray. They might have thought he was the dead man. Anyway, they split up—one goes in with him to identify the body, and the other one tags along behind. They're being helpful, they'll help him with parking, show him the right place to go, and generally be of assistance. He's grateful, and after he identifies Mitch, he tells them everything he knows.''

Barbara groaned and he nodded. ''Right. I doubt it would have occurred to him to clam up, get some advice, not his style. They ask questions, he answers, and they send a couple of detectives back to the house with him. They send someone out to talk to the old man, and the questions are getting tougher with Ray. The way he sees it, they're doing their job and he'll help any way he can. Simple.''

''What do the police have?''

''Last night they got a tip about a body up at a cabin around Blue River. The caller said it was behind a place that's for sale. He was hiking with friends and they spotted a foot sticking out of the ground and did their duty and called. And hung up. The cops went out last night and found him, buried, except for one foot. The cabin had been broken into, and he had been beaten and probably killed inside. And they found the name *Arno* in blood on the floor, so tracking Ray down was easy enough, that and the shirt.''

''Jesus Christ!'' Frank muttered in a low, savage voice.

Barbara asked, ''Anything else?''

''They've been up there today poking and prying. No time of death yet, no direct cause of death. Hell, the autopsy hasn't been done yet, more than likely. But the police will be all over Folsum asking questions, and if they don't already consider Ray their prime suspect, they will soon. Who else?''

John was watching her so closely, she felt almost as if rays were being emitted from his eyes, burning her. ''Are you going to take him on if he asks? Get involved in another murder case this soon?''

''Even if I wanted to, and I don't, I couldn't,'' she said. ''Conflict of interest.'' She stood up. ''Excuse me. Right back.'' Outside the dining room door she paused, listening to her father's voice.

"See, John, she already has a client, and it's her duty to protect that client, to fulfill her obligation to her, and not bring harm to her."

"Wouldn't that be a criminal offense, to withhold information in a murder investigation?"

"Now you see the problem."

She hurried to the bathroom, where she gazed at herself in the mirror. "Oh my, yes," she whispered. "Certainly a criminal offense."

7

Sunday was going to be another hot, bright day; at ten in the morning it was already too hot to be carrying the camping gear from their apartment down a flight of stairs that collected heat and stored it. By the time all the equipment was beside the van, sweat was running down her back, down her legs. John was unbearably cheerful; she suspected he had been more oppressed by the cluttered apartment than he had admitted, and now they were doing something about it. He regarded with satisfaction the piles of bedding, the stove, refrigerator.... There was so much, it seemed impossible that it would all fit into the van.

"Go on and cool off," he said. "This will take a couple of hours."

Thank God for air-conditioning, she thought as she returned to the apartment. And thank God for silence, she added. She felt desperate for time without distraction.

She took her briefcase to her newly cleared office and sat down to think. Already dates and times were slipping away; she had not made sufficient notes to set them in her mind.

John came back; she heard him moving boxes in the living room, and she put down her pen. In a moment there was a very soft tap on her door, as if a low noise would be less intrusive than a real knock. John pushed the door open and asked, "Have you seen a box about like so? Tools in it.'' He held out his hands to indicate size; she shook her head, and he withdrew.

It took a long time for her to remember something she had started to jot down. She finally got it back and wrote: *What if Mitch had not recovered his car, and instead some kids had hot-wired it and taken it joyriding? Had it turned up wrecked anywhere? If so, what was found in it?* Bailey work.

If there was any way she could keep Maggie out of the murder investigation, she would do it, she had decided; something in the car might drag her in anyway.

The phone rang and she went to the kitchen to listen. ''Ms. Holloway, I have to talk to you. It's imperative that I talk to you today.''

She picked up the phone. ''Barbara Holloway,'' she said.

The caller let out an audible sigh. ''Thank God,'' he said. ''My name is Brad Waters, in San Francisco. I'm catching the first flight I can get, and I'll go to the Valley River Inn. Can you talk to me this afternoon? At four? It's about Mitch Arno and what he was carrying?''

''Hold on, Mr. Waters—'' She hit the CALLER ID button and quickly jotted down the number that came on the display.

''I can't. I have to run to make that flight. In the lounge at Valley River Inn, at four. Please be there.'' He hung up.

''Shit,'' she said under her breath. The number she had written down had a Seattle area code. She tore the page off the pad and took it to her office, where she compared it with the numbers they had found in the notebook from Mitch's bag. It didn't match any of them. More Bailey work.

Barbara walked into the lounge at exactly four. ''I believe Mr. Waters has a table already,'' she said to the woman at the reservation stand.

The woman checked her list and smiled. "Oh, yes. He's here." She beckoned a waiter. "Mr. Waters's table."

The waiter led Barbara to one of the dimly lighted tables on the upper tier, not down by the wide windows overlooking the Willamette River. The lounge was very busy, every table filled on both tiers. Waters was sitting facing the wall. He rose instantly when she drew near.

"Ms. Holloway? Brad Waters."

There was not enough room for the waiter to get behind her chair to adjust it, but he hovered. "Can I bring you anything?"

"Iced coffee," she said. She shook hands with Waters, then seated herself.

The light was dim, especially after the brilliant sunshine outside, but as her eyes adjusted, she could see that Brad Waters had dark hair and was smooth-shaven, and from what little she had seen, he was athletic, with broad shoulders. She couldn't tell the color of his eyes, just dark. A tall glass of beer was in front of him; it looked untouched.

"No trouble getting on a flight?" she asked. "Sometimes, this time of year, it's difficult."

"No problem. I checked in here at two. Then I did a Web search on Barbara Holloway. I'm glad I had time to do that."

"How did you come across my name in the first place?"

"I called Ms. Folsum's inn early this morning, and someone there gave me another number to try. Then Ms. Folsum referred me to you and gave me your number."

She understood that they would kill time waiting for her coffee, and he seemed to have the same understanding, but it was irksome.

He was saying, "—afraid you might be tied up with a client at the diner—" when the waiter reappeared and placed the coffee before her.

As soon as the waiter was gone, Waters leaned forward.

"Ms. Holloway, I'm the head of security for a large computer company. What I'd like to do is give you a little background and then make a serious request, so please, be patient for just a few minutes. And please be understanding if I don't mention real names just yet, including my own." He was watching her closely. She nodded. "All right. My company is big, not as big as Microsoft, but big, and the principals, a man and a woman, are, or were, the company. The two of them started it as partners, and they produced some very important programs over the years, working as a team. A few years ago, we had a major theft of a program in development; a rival company introduced it weeks before we were ready. We were able to track down the guy who sold us out and promised him immunity if he would tell us how the theft had been worked." He leaned back and began to move his glass of beer in circles.

"It was a simple scheme," he said flatly. "How they worked it was to have a lawyer draw up papers to have a car brokered and delivered to the guy. The driver was to deliver a large sum of money along with the car, and he was to receive the program. Simple. The transfer of an automobile was aboveboard, not suspicious in any way. How much the broker knew, anyone's guess, but the lawyer was in on it, and so was the driver. That driver was Mitch Arno. We pieced it together bit by bit, and tried to track down Arno, with no luck. And there was no way to prove a theft had taken place, that it hadn't been parallel research. We tightened security, did what we could to prevent it happening again."

He finally tasted the beer and set the glass down again, as if the taste had not registered. "Okay," he said then. "That's the history, the background you need in order to understand what comes next. My two bosses had a big falling-out; they had been lovers for more than fifteen years, but they fought and split in a very public and very ugly way. It was bad. He started to date pretty young things. She was not a pretty young thing, and it hit her hard. She got back by stealing the new program that was in development and selling out. She had access to everything I had found out about the first incident, including the lawyer's name.''

He drew in a long breath and shook his head. "They were both my friends. I saw how hurt she had been, but I never imagined this. Anyway, the last day she showed up at work, she left with a new fancy briefcase with a keypad lock and she got on a plane for the States. The next day she was found dead, murdered. The police said she had ordered a car, a Lexus, and the broker furnished the names of two delivery men; one of them was found dead in a motel room, the other one vanished. He was using a different name, but the description fits Mitch Arno. The briefcase did not turn up, and neither did the suitcase. The police think the missing man killed them both for the car, and for the cashier's check for the balance due—forty-two thousand dollars. What we think happened is that Arno grabbed our programs and the check, as well as the suitcase of money, and took off, probably planning to get bids on what he had. Other research groups have bits and pieces of the program; she had it all.''

As he spoke, Barbara felt as if the chill from her iced coffee had entered her hand and traveled throughout her body, until she was chilled all over. He continued to push his glass back and forth in a distracted way.

"Why are you here now?" she asked. "How did you track Mitch Arno here?"

He rubbed his eyes. "As soon as we learned she was dead, and a Lexus was involved, we started a continuous-search program for him. His name came up when he was reported murdered. His name, his former wife's name, the trashing of her inn.''

"Why do you think the other company doesn't already have the program?"

"Because Trassi's hanging around. I've been having him followed. I knew when he flew into Portland, rented a car, and came here to Eugene. I just didn't know why, until we got Arno's name. The stuff hasn't come to light, or Trassi wouldn't be here. Folsum still has it, or turned it over to a third party. If there's a suitcase like the one they used before, it has a fancy keypad lock on it. The briefcase has another one. I hope and pray the program is still intact, hidden away where it's safe." He added, "But whoever has it isn't safe, Ms. Holloway. If Maggie Folsum and her kids had been home when her place was torn up, they'd all be dead."

Carefully Barbara asked, "If what you believe is actually true, would these people be less dangerous if they learned the program was in your company's hands once more? Wouldn't they go after the suitcase?"

He shook his head. "Such men will kill if they have to; they killed Mitch Arno, but they don't kill out of revenge. Once they know we have the program back, they'll vanish into the slime and move on to a different project. The last thing any of us wants is an official investigation and publicity. As soon as they know we have the program, this matter will wind down, finis. You know the saying 'All's well that ends.'"

"Maybe," Barbara said. "I understand why they wouldn't want an investigation, but what about you, your company? Why haven't you gone to the police?"

He began sliding his glass around again. "I can't. My boss is shattered. He takes complete responsibility for what she did, blames himself for everything up to and including her death. He said if her reputation is damaged, he'll give away everything he has, kill me and then himself.

"Ms. Holloway, I said that I had a request. Two, actually. All we want from you is the program. We're not interested in the suitcase, or anything else Arno might have had, just the briefcase, our program. That program is the biggest and most important thing they ever produced together, and that's the only complete program in existence; she destroyed the tapes, the backups, everything else. If our competitor brings it out as his, that will be the last straw for my boss."

"The other request?"

"Your silence. An agreement of confidentiality. If a single question arises, my boss will deny everything—the original theft, any knowledge of a new program, everything."

"I see. Are you going to be staying here at the hotel?"

"Yes. I doubt anyone would recognize me; I keep a very low profile. But they might. I'll hang out around here. You have to understand that they are very clever. They'll get to you through Folsum, threaten her children, force her to back out of whatever arrangement you have with her. And you have to understand that it's not just Folsum who might be in danger. Anyone with that program is at risk, and if they learn that I'm around, the risk would become uninsurable. I know you have to discuss this with your client, but don't take too long to reach a decision, Ms. Holloway."

Abruptly she stood up. "I have a lot to think about, as you are aware. I'll be in touch, Mr. Waters." She left him signing the tab for the drinks neither of them had wanted.

She walked out into the blinding sunshine. Maggie's children at risk? She had thought of them safely tucked away in Southern California, but how safe were they?

8

The next morning she sipped coffee in Frank's kitchen, watching him eat a bran muffin that looked terribly healthful. "Wait for Bailey and tell us together," he had said when she told him there was a new wrinkle.

One of the coon cats approached, rose to its hind feet, and put its paws on the table to look over breakfast. "My God, how big do they intend to get?"

"I've been reading up on them," Frank said complacently, ignoring the cat. "Don't reach full growth, fill in bulk and such, until the second year. He's still a kitten." The kitten weighed in at eighteen pounds now.

The Thing rubbed his cheek against Frank's arm, dropped lightly to the floor, and strolled away to his own food.

When Bailey arrived, Frank motioned toward the coffee. Bailey helped himself and joined them at the table. "Got the prints separated out," he said. "I'll send them in when I leave here. You know it's going to take two, three weeks to get a report back?"

She knew. "What about the murder? What do you have?"

"Thought I'd wait until your dad finishes eating," he said.

Frank pushed his plate away with a half-eaten muffin still on it. "Done," he said.

"Someone really worked him over," Bailey said gloomily. "Good old blunt instrument. They're saying maybe a baseball bat, something like that. One arm broken, some fingers broken. Back of his head caved in, that's what killed him. And someone doused both his hands with lighter fluid or gas or something and set him on fire."

"Christ," Frank muttered. He stood up and went to gaze out the sliding glass door.

"Time of death?" Barbara asked after a moment.

"No word yet. Maybe Sunday, no later than Tuesday. They're working on it."

She was silent, thinking, when Bailey added, "Thing is, he should have stayed buried. The hole was deep enough to cover him, but one foot was poking out of the ground. They're saying an animal started to dig him up and got spooked or something."

"Shoes?" she asked, remembering the barefoot print he had recovered at Ray's house.

"No shoes. They roughed him up in the cabin and burned him inside. Maybe they meant to burn down the cabin itself, but he kept going out."

Barbara glared at him. He shrugged. "Sorry. He managed to scrape the letters *A-R-N-O* in blood on the floor."

Frank sat down again. "Was he burned before or after death?"

"Don't know. Maybe they don't know yet."

"They'll go for aggravated murder," Frank said. "Maybe torture and murder."

Bailey said he might be getting information about Trassi later on, then Barbara told them about her meeting with Brad Waters. "It shouldn't be too hard to find names," she said. "How many female partners in a computer company got killed recently?"

"Barbara," Bailey said, "you realize that if Mitch Arno killed his partner and the woman, they probably have his prints on file. And if I send in my batch of unknowns, they're going to find his among them.''

"Shit." She thought a moment. "I'll see if Maggie has anything with Mitch's prints on it. About the car, we know a little something about it now. A forty-two-thousand-dollar black Lexus. The other day you said maybe it was stolen. If some kids took it joyriding, what next?"

"They finally wreck it, or take it to a chop shop," he said promptly.

"If they wrecked it, someone must have found it. See what you can dig up. Especially what was in it. And the broker who arranged the deal. Who is he, where?"

He was eyeing her with a detached expression. He never questioned strategy or asked why about anything; they had their jobs, he had his. But he always asked if the client was prepared to pay his expenses. He asked now.

"I'll find out," Barbara said. "But for now, the answer is yes."

"Okeydokey." A few minutes later he left her and Frank at the table.

Frank began to clear the few dishes, and she went to stand at the door. The two cats were engaged in what looked like a battle to the finish; they were distracted by a hummingbird and started a new game of catch-me-if-you-can. "Do they stray off?" she asked.

"Some. But they come back when I whistle. Bobby, what are you planning? What's on your mind?"

She turned around. Almost helplessly she said, "I don't know. I feel as if I've been sucked into a whirlpool and more and more junk gets pulled in with me until I can't tell flotsam from jetsam. I haven't had time to think."

"You're just reacting. Things are happening too fast, and all you can do is react. Find yourself a quiet spot and sit there and think a long time."

"Okay. I can take the money and the program in to the

police right now. Today. Then what? Even if we knew the names of the companies fighting over the program, they'd both deny everything. Trassi would be horrified that Mitch had a sideline that no one else knew about. Waters would disappear back into his high-security cubbyhole, which he can prove he never left. Nope, he was never in Eugene, never met me or discussed anything with me. All I would give the police is a whole lot of money and a program that no one seems to know anything about.'' She drew in a breath, then added, ''And a powerful motive for either Ray or Maggie or both working together to have murdered Mitch. A motive everyone understands.''

''Maybe some significant fingerprints,'' Frank said.

''Maybe. We don't even know that yet.'' She shook her head. ''No matter how much bait I toss out for Trassi, he comes back for more. How far will they go? And the other guy, just keep all the money. Hah! I have to keep stalling until I have more information.''

''If a single damn one of them is telling anything near the truth, I don't think you're going to have much stalling time. I'm going to mosey down to the office for an hour or two.''

All right, she thought then, someone who had information and would give her straight answers: Lou Sunderman, the firm's tax expert. She called him and made an appointment for eleven. In succession she called Maggie and arranged for a six or seven o'clock meeting, then John.

''Hi,'' she said. ''It's me.''

''On your way home?''

''Nope. Up to here. Want to drive over to the coast this evening, fourish?''

''You just don't want to make dinner.''

She laughed. ''I know a great seafood restaurant over there.''

"Cheap?"

"On me."

"You just talked me into it. Be home early?"

"As early as I can."

She was smiling when she hung up. One last call, she told herself after a moment. She gritted her teeth and called Wes Margollin, king of the nerds. He was a computer consultant who had set up the systems at the office, and talked.

"Jeez, Barbara," Wes said aggrievedly, "you guys got another problem? I'm really busy."

"No, no. I just want to open your brain case and take a quick peek inside. Information. Can you spare a little time today?"

"No way. Like I said, I'm really busy. Lunch? We gotta eat, right?"

Not only was he a talker, he was a moocher. They agreed on lunch and she hung up. Then it was time to go talk with Lou Sunderman.

He was only five feet six, possibly weighed 120, and no doubt was the most valued member of the law firm.

"A hypothetical problem," Barbara said when she took a chair across his desk from him. "If a woman collected back child-support payments for eighteen years for two children, and the sum came to a very big number, would it be taxable?"

"No. The amount is unimportant."

She restrained herself from uttering, "Hah!" then she asked, "Could she collect from his estate in the event he died before he paid up?"

"Much would depend on circumstances. Did he have a will? Are there other children from a different marriage? Did he leave large medical bills? And so forth. If he died intestate, probably the best she could hope for would be for her children to inherit whatever would be left after all accounts are settled. That money would be taxable."

"What if he paid her and soon afterward died, before she had a chance to do anything with the money?"

Lou looked as if his patience was nearing an end. "If it can be proved that the sum due her was transferred to her before his death, that money is no longer part of his estate. It is hers and it is not subject to seizure by his creditors, if she can prove delinquency in his support payments. The Internal Revenue Service would conduct its own investigation and issue a closing agreement before she could claim the money legally."

Pushing her welcome, she asked how long it would take. He said, "Months," and looked pointedly at his watch. She thanked him nicely and walked out to meet Wes Margollin.

She groaned when she saw how packed the Greek restaurant was that Wes had chosen. He was standing at a table across the dining room, waving a menu at her.

"Hey, Barbara, how you doing?" he called before she reached him. "You know what I'm up to my nose in? See, everyone's got a modem, everyone's surfing the Net, everyone's got to have a Web page. Shoeshine boy, bank president, janitor, they all got to have a Web page, and not a one of them knows diddly about HTML. You want a Web page?"

She shook her head. A harried waitress came and took their order and rushed away. The noise level was decibels above comfort, but it didn't slow Wes down a second.

"See, you tell me what you want, how fancy you want it, music, bells, dancing bears—"

"Tell me about a company started fifteen or twenty years ago by a man and woman partnership. She died recently."

He didn't even change gears. "You mean Major Works. You want to buy stock, go for it. Imagine Einstein with two heads, that was Major and Wygood, and she got herself mugged and killed. Everyone's watching to see if he can hack it alone, but it won't matter to the company. With what they already have, they'll coast a long time. You never thought of just Major, or just Wygood; it was like one word, you know. Major/Wygood. He began showing up places with babes on his arm, and she took off.''

Barbara listened, confirming item by item what Waters had told her. Their lunch came and she ate her Greek salad and he his kebabs, and he never stopped talking. It was awesome, his talking, eating, drinking wine all at once, and just a bit disgusting, too, she thought, looking away from him.

Finally she interrupted. ''What will the next big breakthrough be?''

''Lots of stuff,'' he said promptly. ''First, AI—that's artificial intelligence-but not this century. Next, TV, computer, telecommunications combo, big bucks, big brains, big-power machine chugging in the background. Big, really big fights. Then, a voice-recognition system. You know, like Dick Tracy talking to his watch and his watch answering. Right now it's like speech-class training, you know. Ev. Er. Y. Syl. La. Ble. has to be enunciated clearly. We gotta train people how to talk all over again. And people don't train too good. Not just that, either. It's how we talk. 'That guy's a beanpole.' What's a computer supposed to do with something like that? Or 'He's sawing logs.' Or 'She's pickled,' or 'He's a real lady killer.' But that's not even the worst of it. What about the homonyms, the synonyms, dialects, accents, not even touching yet on irony or symbolism? Nobody understands symbolism. People from Boston don't understand Mississippi. No one understands Texans. What about Brooklyn? It's a headache. See, there's another one. But, Barbara, baby, you get that and you connect it with telecommunications, you just bought yourself a key to heaven. For a while people thought Major/Wygood was working on it, but nothing came out, so if they were, they got mired down just like everyone else. I saw Wygood on a panel once talking about the problems, and suddenly she got real quiet, but she flashed a funny look at Major first. I was there, I saw it."

The waitress came back and Wes ordered baklava. They both had coffee. Barbara let him ramble on about Major/ Wygood until he had his dessert, then she asked, "What would a workable program like that be worth, do you suppose?"

He snorted. "Can't even put a price on it. Millions? Lotsa millions." He wagged a finger at her. "But it's got to work on the platforms out there. And that's the rub. You need more memory, more RAM, more speed, more everything than we've got."

He finished his coffee and stood up. "More Web sites, more home pages, more, more, more. You decide you want a page, give me a buzz. Of course, you'll have to get in line...."

"Thanks, Wes," she said to his back as he hurried away. She had forgotten the noise in the restaurant, she realized then when it hit her as a cacophony. She put her credit card on the table; the waitress was there almost instantly, and soon Barbara was back outside. It had grown many degrees hotter; she crossed the street to keep in the shade, and walked slowly, thinking of what Wes had told her.

A block from the office, as she crossed the open, downtown plaza where food vendors were doing a brisk business—tacos, Scandinavian pastries, ice cream, espressos— she saw Trassi, the gray man, who looked out of place here in his gray suit and sour expression. He rose from a bench and watched her approach.

"I want to talk to you," he said curtly.

"All right."

"Not here. There's a little park up there." He pointed toward Park Street, a block away.

"Fine."

Neither spoke again as they walked to the little park. An ice-cream vendor was set up and busy; people were sitting on several of the benches, others strolling aimlessly, a few with quick purpose. Shade from the tall fir and pine trees cooled the air magically. Barbara slowed her pace and let Trassi select a bench. There were only two choices.

He nodded toward the one closer to the fountain, and they went to it and sat down.

The fountain had a twenty-five-foot catch basin with a broad outer lip. Water flowed into it from a center pipe, then over the lip to a second, wide return basin, almost soundlessly. The sheen of water as it overflowed made it look like satin at times; when the lighting was just so, it looked like mercury; other times when the wind was blowing a certain way, the overflow was disturbed in such a manner that it looked bunched up, uneven. Barbara had spent many hours on this bench, gazing at the fountain, considering her next move, her next witness, the last witness.... Now she gazed at the water and waited.

"My client is prepared to pay a fifty-thousand-dollar finder's fee for the return of our material," Trassi said without preamble. "Plus whatever damage costs the insurance doesn't cover."

She shook her head. "I told you what we want," she said. "Did you forget? Two hundred ten thousand, for the past-due child support, and so far the damage is up to forty-five thousand, and counting." She paused, then said musingly, "I haven't even considered yet the intangibles—fear, worry, loss of goodwill." Her voice became very brisk again. "We want it aboveboard, without the IRS or other creditors seizing any of it. Child support isn't taxed, I understand."

"That's impossible! The man's dead! You can't collect from a dead man who didn't have anything. He never saw the kind of money you're talking about."

"Oh, I don't know," Barbara said thoughtfully. "What if he was a private contractor who earned a lot of money and didn't trust banks? In addition to working for your company, of course. There could be a number of safe-deposit boxes with hundred-dollar bills tucked away inside. Could be that he worked under several different names, lived frugally, saved his money."

Contempt was thick in his voice when he said, "You'll end up with nothing. A dream of riches, that's all, a fairy tale. Go back to your law books, Ms. Holloway. You can't start garnishment proceedings against a dead man; all you can do is present your claim to the probate court and get in line with his other creditors. We are prepared to prove that the material he was carrying belongs to our company, that he was on a legitimate business trip acting as a courier. What he was carrying will be returned to its owners; it will not be included in his estate, believe me. And no matter how many creditors line up, they'll all get exactly the same thing: nothing. He didn't have anything. Nothing divided among three or three hundred is still nothing."

"The way I see it," Barbara said, "Mitch Arno got religion and decided to pay his ex-wife for the many years of neglecting to support his children. You know; he told you he had a debt to pay. He decided to make a grand gesture, pay her in cash, and came here on a side trip to do so. You arrived to make certain it was all legal, with authorization to deliver the suitcase to Ms. Folsum or her attorney. She told you to talk to me, which you did, and after you delivered the suitcase, your mission was accomplished. I, of course, immediately put the suitcase in a safe-deposit box until I had time to determine the legality of the procedure." She paused, then continued in a thoughtful way, "Of course, if that scenario were true, there would be records, payment records, a document to show that he intended to pay his ex-wife what he owed her, an attorney agreement. You know, papers and records, the bane of civilization. That's what I want, Mr. Trassi, all the paperwork that proves it was his money and he retained you to deliver it, and, further, a statement that you carried out his instructions faithfully before he died. When it's ready, call the office and set up a meeting with our tax attorney, Mr. Sunderman, and he will contact the IRS to arrange for a closing agreement with them.''

"You are proposing an illegal action that could get you disbarred. We would never agree to such a scheme.'' He stood up.

"Okay. So we could auction off what we have and call it quits.''

"What you have is valueless to anyone except my company.''

"So we won't make much with it. Scan a page or two and put it on the Internet, with a plea for help, might work. Something like 'Found, pages from someone's manual. What does it mean?' Maybe someone would make an offer.''

He did not move.

"One more thing,'' Barbara said, keeping her gaze on the water. "I moved things from my own bank to the safe-deposit box the firm rents, one that requires two senior members to open. I've given instructions that in the event I am incapacitated, those senior members will turn over everything they find in the box to the police. And if I hear that Maggie Folsum has been pressured in any way, I'll turn them over myself. You see, when you start out with nothing, there's little to lose. Is there?'' She looked up at him. "And, Mr. Trassi, I see no advantage in further dickering. When you're ready, call Mr. Sunderman and set up a time.''

"I'll be in touch," he said. He walked away like a marionette with an inept handler.

She turned her gaze back to the fountain. A thin cirrus cloud had dimmed the sun slightly, turning the smooth water into molten gold that was just out of reach.

9

"When I was a little girl," Maggie said, "I named all these rocks."

They were walking on the beach, where fog was gathering and the surf was gentle for the moment. The rocks were basalt, John had said, old volcanoes sailing out to sea on a raft of tectonic plates. Now John and Laurence were walking ahead, out of hearing.

"This one's the Black Knight," Maggie said, patting a smooth columnar monolith that rose ten feet high. "He saved my life when I was about eight or nine. An erratic wave caught me. He held me, or I held him. Never turn your back on the ocean," she added. Laurence turned to look at them and waved, and she waved back. Her voice became strained. "I remember how my mother used to handle my brothers when we were kids. If they got on her nerves too much, she'd send them to town for a loaf of bread or something."

"Send him on an errand," Barbara said. "Let him go buy the chairs and love seats and things."

Maggie looked surprised, then she nodded. "All I could think of was that it took me two years to find the furniture I wanted; you saw, oak in one room, wicker in another, cherry…. He could do that." Suddenly she grinned. "He could do that."

"Okay," Barbara said brusquely. "Do you know when

the funeral will be, and will you bring your daughters home for it?''

''We don't know yet when they'll release Mitch's body. I talked to Mama and Papa Arno, and we agreed not to drag the kids home now. I'm not even sure where they are, Mom and Dad had a lot of things planned. The Arnos will have a very small private service, and later on I'll take the girls to the cemetery.''

''Good. I'll need a copy of the divorce decree, and do you have anything with Mitch's fingerprints? Bailey needs to eliminate him, the way he did with the rest of the family.''

''Mama Arno gave me his birth certificate and the prints they made in the hospital when he was born.''

''Next, about that money. You could just keep it and burn the contents of the briefcase. You'd have to destroy the papers in the briefcase if you decided to go that route. Keeping them would be dangerous. They are very valuable, and there are powerful people who want them.'' Maggie started to say something, but Barbara said, ''Let me lay it all out first. The next option is to turn everything over to the police and tell them what happened. The downside is that you'll give yourself a motive for killing Mitch, and you'd never see a penny of the money again. You would put not only Ray in danger but yourself as well. Or you could deal with either Trassi or another man who may have a legitimate claim; Trassi's upped the offer, and he will again, and the other one has no interest in the cash. You'd end up with a lot of money, perhaps all of it.'' Maggie gasped. Barbara continued. ''The downside is how you would then handle the cash. If you put it in your bank, the bank would inform the IRS; it's the law. And then you'd have to account for it, and there would be an investigation. Word would leak, and there's a motive for murder again. You could stash the money in a safe-deposit box and spend it little by little without ever saying a word about it. It's risky, and the chance that your sudden affluence would be noticed is very high.''

"What you're telling me is heads I lose, tails I lose," Maggie said. "Where did that money come from? How did Mitch get it? What are the valuable papers? Who are those powerful people? I can't make choices in the dark."

Barbara was always grateful when her client was intelligent, but sometimes, she would also admit, it complicated her life. Slowly, picking her words with care, she said, "I can't tell you a lot because we are still checking out various stories, and I'm stalling everyone until we have hard facts. It could be a case of industrial espionage. Two competing companies, one stole a product from the other one, using Mitch as the delivery man who was to have paid off the thief and receive the product. He double-crossed them all and ended up with everything."

"Then *they* killed him," Maggie exclaimed. "The police would understand that much."

"Neither company would admit a thing," Barbara said patiently. "We don't have a shred of proof. We don't even know for sure the names of either company. I'm afraid the police might decide that Mitch had acted on his own and was involved in something yet to be determined; meanwhile, a quarter of a million dollars in cash would be irresistible as cause for murder."

They became silent, walking slowly in the packed sand. The fog had thickened; it was like a misty rain defying gravity. Laurence and John had turned, were coming their way.

"Barbara," Maggie said tiredly, "you've told me the things I can't do, but what's left? What can I do?"

"Let's wait until they get past and let them lead the way back," Barbara said. She looked at the sea; only a hundred feet away the fog eclipsed it wholly and hushed the sound of invisible waves breaking over invisible stacks out in the water.

"Hey," Laurence said, still dozens of feet from them, "can we stop being pariahs yet?"

Barbara shook her head. "Nope. Girl-talk time." She could see water droplets sparkling in John's hair.

The men walked past them, and after giving them a good lead, they followed. Then Barbara said, still speaking carefully, "You remember our agreement, what I agreed to do?" Maggie nodded. "That's what I want to do, Maggie. I want to get you all the back child-support payments that are owed you. I want to do it in a way that won't compromise the money or you, and won't jeopardize either Ray or you. But to do that, I need your confidence, your trust. I need to know that you won't decide that you have to go to the police until I say so, and then we'll go together. I promise, we will go. Further, I have to know that you won't talk to Trassi or anyone else, including the family. I need to have the same kind of trust in you that I'm asking from you. Also, to do that, the expenses might run up more than you anticipated."

Maggie put her hand on Barbara's arm and stopped her. "What kind of money are you talking about? And expenses? I have to know before I can agree."

"I'm talking about two hundred and ten thousand dollars, and expenses will go to several thousand, at a minimum."

Incredulity swept over Maggie's features. She laughed, a bitter, choked sound. "I don't believe you."

"That's what I'm going after, if I have your permission and cooperation."

"Did you tell me all the things I can't do so I'd jump at this?" Maggie asked, her voice subtly different now; she spoke as a businesswoman who had learned some things along the way.

''I told you why you shouldn't do the various things you've been contemplating, and the one thing you didn't contemplate.''

''That's for sure,'' Maggie said. They started to walk again. After a moment Maggie said, ''I won't talk to anyone and I'll do what you advise me to do.'' She looked at Barbara. ''Shake?'' They shook hands solemnly. Then Maggie said, ''The police came here to ask questions. They already knew about the party and the vandalism. It was like you said, they just asked about Friday and afterward. They've been all over town asking questions. They know all our past history by now.'' She paused, then asked, ''If they arrest Ray, will you defend him?''

''I can't. It would be a conflict of interest.''

Maggie kicked a clump of seaweed. Then she said, ''If they arrest him, his trial won't be for months. Could you take him later?''

''Maggie, you'll be my client for months. Ray needs an attorney now, before he talks to the police again. I have several names for you to give him, if you choose. All people my father and I would recommend.''

''What if I decide I don't want you to represent me anymore, then could you take Ray?''

''No.''

''Why not?'' Maggie demanded.

''Because if I were defending him, you'd be at risk.''

''You'd use what you know about me?'' Maggie stopped again.

''Yes,'' Barbara said. ''Nothing that was confided when we had an attorney-client relationship, but anything that developed afterward. If I had to use it, I would.''

Maggie stared silently at her, then abruptly started to walk. Neither spoke again until they were back at the inn.

They dried themselves while Maggie went to get Mitch's birth certificate, the fingerprints, and the divorce decree.

She handed Barbara an envelope, without comment, and Barbara gave her the paper with attorneys' names. She said she would keep in touch, and she and John left and drove to Newport.

At Mo's Seafood Restaurant, eating clam chowder, she asked John what he had made of Laurence.

"He's thirty, going on twenty," John said judiciously. "He complained that Maggie treats him like a kid much of the time." They both laughed. Then John said, "He thinks he wants to get married; she doesn't. He wishes there were dragons around so he could kill one for her. I know the feeling," he added.

For a time they sat holding hands, not eating, not talking, but when the waiter came to remove the soup bowls, Barbara said, "Not yet." She pulled loose from John and picked up her spoon. "Not another word about me or my client's problem child. What's happening with the Staley mine?" He had not brought it up for many days, she realized with a twinge of guilt.

"The usual bullshit," he said. "The miners lodged a complaint, unsafe working conditions. The commission hired me. The company hired its own experts, and now we snap and snarl at each other."

He was being too flippant; the little twinge of conscience was replaced with a stab of fear. "You'll go back, won't you?"

"Finish your chowder," he said. "I'm ready for halibut and the works." He looked around the restaurant. "I like this place."

The tables were picnic tables, with plastic tablecloths, and benches that were to be shared with whoever wanted to sit down and eat. The food was delicious, perfectly cooked seafood; the house specialty was clam chowder for which people traveled many miles. Outside the windows was a dock on Newport Bay, where people were fishing, children playing, seagulls swooping. Fishing boats were returning, riding the incoming tide, racing the fog.

By the time they left the restaurant, fog had shrouded all of Newport, turned lights into multicolored glowing clouds, made distances unpredictable, and played optical-illusion tricks with moving vehicles. "We could check into a motel," Barbara said doubtfully; she knew they would not find a room so late in the evening during the season.

"Let's go home," John said. They went to the car and he drove.

She could feel John's relief when the fog cleared and he picked up speed. She well knew that for many miles this road wound its way up and down, around and around, and each time it went down, it would be smothered by fog again, probably all the way through the Coast Range, possibly all the way home. They started down the hill they had just climbed, and before them lay a white lake of fog. John eased up on the gas and crept ahead cautiously.

And so it went, up into clear air, down into fog, mile after mile after mile. Neither spoke. Other cars were on the road; approaching they appeared to be formless glowing clouds that became defined slowly, then vanished. Now and then someone passed them in a suicidal rush, and their taillights were clouds on fire.

She should have driven, Barbara thought; she knew this road, not in a way that was communicable, but her hands, her reflexes knew it. Soon they would reach Mary's Mountain; when they curved around it, descended again, they would enter the broad Willamette Valley. Usually summer fog didn't get beyond that point, although winter fogs recognized no boundaries. If she were driving, she would know without question whether she should drive on east to I-5 or turn south onto Highway 99, a crooked narrow black road. It was her preferred route because it was twenty miles closer to home that way, and it didn't have the din and roar of an interstate with its countless trucks. But not in fog. She breathed a sigh of relief when they left the mountains and the valley lights shone clearly ahead.

"Good job," she said when John turned south on 99.

"Hairy," he said. "Thanks."

They were quiet until they reached their apartment, pulled off their sweatshirts, and had drinks in their hands. John had cleared out enough stuff so that they could sit in the living room, she in the good chair she had moved from her previous house, he in a new chair that they both suspected was not quite right but had bought anyway.

"Something's got to give," he said tiredly. "I didn't want to tell you about the Staley mine like that, in a public place. I wanted to talk it over, explain."

"No explanation is called for. You said the mine is unsafe, and you'll go back in it to prove your point. What's to explain? Besides, did I say a word? Did I scream or faint or throw a tizzy fit?"

"You screamed, all right," he said. "Inside you were screaming your head off, and it showed all over you."

"Well, shee-it," she said. "I'll just have to learn to hide my feelings, won't I?"

"Goddamn it! Don't do that! I told you up front what I do. And you said you weren't going to get involved in anything yet, not until we've had some time to sort things out about us."

"What do you want? A pledge that I'll sit home and not worry when you're in the field? Make dinner and do the laundry and be the sweet little housewife with nothing on her mind? If that's what you want, you should have stuck with Betty! You knew up front what I do, too."

His face twisted in anger at the mention of his ex-wife. "I know, all right. I know you hate what I do as much as I hate what you do. That's a given. But you don't have to get involved the way you do, that's what's different, everything on the line—professional life, personal life—all hanging out. Obsessed. You get obsessed with what you do, and it goes on and on until it's your whole life."

Shocked, she drank deeply of her gin and tonic. Then she said, "Surgeons get obsessed with the cut-open patient; I guess firemen get obsessed with a raging blaze; I know you get obsessed looking for a crack in a rock wall that might bring a mine down on your head. But I can't get obsessed with my work. I see. Now I understand. Of course I hate what you do. It's the test-pilot's-wife syndrome. But I didn't understand before that you hate what I do." She glanced at her glass but didn't pick it up again. She stood up. "I'm going to bed."

"Wait a minute, we're not through."

"I don't know. Maybe we are."

"Well, ask yourself why you have to identify with every client who comes along. Why you have to make them all personal crusades. What are you trying to prove?"

She walked from the room to the bathroom and brushed her teeth, and then went to bed. She was still awake much later when he got into bed beside her. They were careful not to touch.

In the morning she was ready to leave when John came from the bedroom. Before he could speak, she said, "I have to go. I think from now on, for the time being, neither of us should talk about our work. If you have to go somewhere and I'm not around, just leave a note. I'm not sure where I'll be all day."

"Fine," he said.

He didn't ask if she would be home early.

10

Barbara realized, driving to Frank's house, that the secret file cabinet in her mind had sprung open overnight, and all the things she had tucked away to be considered later had surfaced.

John's mother hadn't liked her; his children had been silent and watchful, resentful of her presence. His ex had become a burden, worrying about him; Barbara had filled in details silently. His ex had become the test pilot's wife, unable to still or conceal her fear. Now Barbara was playing that role.

Well, she demanded savagely, *what did you expect? That those problems would evaporate, vanish?* Maybe, she thought, and maybe she could have dealt with them a little at a time. Maybe there wasn't enough time in the space-time continuum to deal with the fact that he hated her work, what she did, probably who she was when she did it.

When she pulled into Frank's driveway, Bailey's car was close behind her. Frank opened the door.

She and Frank exchanged good mornings. "Two with one blow," he commented. "Coffee's on the table."

She went past him to the dinette and sat with her back to the glass doors. He had cleared away his breakfast; there were cups and the coffee carafe on the table, and the newspaper folded open to the editorial page.

"Hiya," Bailey said cheerfully, coming in with Frank.

They took chairs, and Bailey began to go through his denim bag. "You get some prints for me?"

"Yes. His hospital birth record, hands and feet." She pulled the document out of her briefcase and passed it over.

"Good. I'll start with Wygood. You hit the jackpot with those names, Barbara. Thelma Wygood ordered a car from a broker in New York, to be delivered in Miami. Two guys drove it down, Eddie Grinwald and a guy called Steve Wilford. They were supposed to deliver the car and collect a cashier's check for forty-two grand and take it back home. They never got back. The police found Grinwald's body in the motel they used, and the next day they found Wygood's body. Car, cashier's check, and Wilford were all missing."

Bailey pushed a folder toward Barbara. "It's all in there. Wilford's clean. Grinwald has a record from twenty years ago, manslaughter. Did four years. Funny coincidence, though. Wilford's description fits Mitch Arno to a T."

He pulled out a second folder. "Another coincidence. Happened that a second customer ordered another Lexus coupe, just about like the one headed for Miami. And this time Mitch Arno was supposed to deliver it, drive out from New York to somewhere up in Washington. On Saturday, August third, three a.m., Corvallis police found the Lexus in a ditch. All the goodies were gone—stereo, CD player, like that—but in the glove compartment they found a title transfer with the customer's name not filled in; the transfer was by the delivery company, R. M. Palmer Company. They get in touch with Palmer, and lo and behold, happens his attorney is on the West Coast, and he'll handle it. Enter Trassi on Saturday, August third."

"Story number three," Barbara commented.

Bailey grinned. "Cops are figuring Mitch picked up hitchhikers, kids who never even saw the title, didn't realize the car was up for grabs. They drove him around on the coast, he got away within walking distance of Maggie's place on Friday, and old man Arno found him. They have it all figured out.''

"Let them figure," she said. "Anything else?"

"Major Works," he said. "Seems to be common knowledge that Russ Major's had a nervous breakdown, or is having it. Wygood left just about everything to Major, except for a few bequests for family, friends, like that, and she was buried on his island hideaway with only the family members present. He hasn't left the island since. Jolin, his security guy, has been everywhere. No one knows where he goes, when he goes, when he gets back. He reports only to Major. Not there now, though.''

She gave him a dark look. Jolin, calling himself Waters, was at Valley River Inn, which he well knew. "She was buried on his island?''

"Seems it was in her will, written years ago, and she never got around to changing it. When you're her age, you're not too worried about kicking.''

"Anything new about Mitch's murder?''

"Not much. They're digging through history, and they think they have the answers. It's not a big deal for them. Just another family feud.''

Barbara stood up and went to the door to gaze out at Frank's immaculate garden and the two golden cats stalking shadows. That summed it up, she thought, shadow dancing, what she was doing.

She returned to her chair and gathered together the various reports Bailey had produced. "Okay," she said. "Go with the prints. I may want something later, but I can't think of anything right now.''

And that summed it up, too, she thought bleakly; she couldn't think, period.

After Frank took Bailey to the door and returned, he asked bluntly, "What are you planning to do?''

"Don't know. Something's bugging the bejesus out of

me, though. I feel like I'm stuck in the briar patch, and everywhere I look, the thorns are big and sharp.''

"And poisonous. Keep that in mind, too. I've got stuff to plant in the garden." He watched her shove papers inside her briefcase, refill her cup, and walk out slowly to go upstairs.

When they came home from their prenuptial honeymoon, he had seen her walking around so lightly that she wouldn't have left footprints in snow. And now her feet were shod in lead. "Old man," he told himself sharply, "butt out. You knew it was going to happen."

He picked up the seed packets and went outside.

Upstairs, Barbara read through Bailey's reports, as meticulous as ever, and not helpful.

She picked up a magazine article Bailey had dug up about Major and Wygood. She didn't read the article, but studied their pictures. In one they had been posed waist deep in computer printouts arranged like waves and hills around them. They were both grinning like idiots and were as stylish as turnips. His hair was longer than hers, and he wore oversized glasses that had slid down his nose. Her hair had been cut with little regard to her plump face. She wore no discernible makeup, no jewelry except a watch. They both had on company T-shirts. The other picture had been taken at a trade show; he had on a business suit and tie, and running shoes; she had on a suit also, the skirt too short for her figure, and flat shoes, and her hair had been pouffed unbecomingly. They were holding hands in that picture. Barbara wondered if either of them had known the other was not pretty, not handsome. When he started dating models, Thelma would have come to know it, she thought sadly.

She began a Web search for Major and Wygood, and found thousands of entries. It was a familiar story, their rise from poverty, developing a program in a bed-sitting-room, the new programs, the company. Einstein with two heads, always Major/Wygood, or Wygood/Major, always paired, one as good as the other in their field, until he had become distracted by pretty young things.

So Thelma went to Europe to plot her revenge. Not for the money, but to hit hard where Major was vulnerable, probably the only place he was vulnerable. If she'd been after money, it would have been to her benefit to finish the program, put it on the market, and watch the cash flow in. She had been a full partner, after all. Not for money. In fact, she had spent money—

"Where's the damn cashier's check?" Barbara said under her breath.

She found the inventory of things from Mitch's belongings, then reread Bailey's account of the police report about the wrecked Lexus. No cashier's check for forty-two thousand dollars. Mitch might have cashed it; she rejected the idea. Not with all that money in the suitcase.

She started to pace again.

When Frank finished his garden chores, he looked at the two cats, both with muddy feet and bedraggled muddy tails, and shook his head. "You guys can't come in," he said. "Clean yourself up." He went inside the house, fastened the latch on the cat door, and cleaned himself up. He started up the stairs then to see what Barbara wanted for lunch, but halfway up, he stopped. He could hear her pacing, the way she did when she was engrossed in a puzzle. He hoped it was the Folsum dilemma that was making her move, not her own personal dilemma. That problem, he was certain, would not yield to logic and reason, no matter how many gray cells she put into action. Quietly he returned to the kitchen. She would eat whatever he fixed.

She ate salad, but he knew she was not tasting it. "Are you due over at Martin's at one?"

She blinked, then said, "Oh, God. I forgot." She looked

at her watch. "It won't take me long. It's that 'he said, she said' business. Wrap that up, and then hand over a check to a couple of kids who got robbed by a car dealership...."

He recognized the signs; he had done exactly this many times, thinking out loud, juggling people, happenings, things.

"Oh," she said then, still thinking, "are you going out? I'll pick up stuff upstairs if you are."

"I'm not going anywhere. Leave it."

"Thanks. I've got to run. I won't be long."

She had finished her business at Martin's and was preparing to leave when a couple walked in hesitantly.

They were both in their forties, she guessed; the woman looked it, but he didn't at first glance. She was about five feet five and a little overweight, with a round face and pale blue eyes. Her hair was light brown, almost frizzy, it was so curly, and she looked terrified. He was over six feet and lean, with black hair and eyes.

"Ms. Holloway?" he said, still hesitant. "Ray Arno, and this is my wife, Lorinne. Can we talk to you?"

"Of course," she said, trying to hide her dismay. "Please, sit down."

Ray was anxious, but he looked more puzzled than frightened. He cleared his throat. "We know you're helping Maggie," he said, "and we've read about you before, the cases you've worked on, I mean. And my family keeps telling me to talk to a lawyer." He glanced at Lorinne. "She said we should at least talk to someone."

Lorinne nodded vigorously. "They might arrest him! They keep asking questions. You know about his brother Mitch, how he was murdered? They think Ray did it!"

"We had a fight nearly twenty years ago," Ray said patiently. "They're just doing their job, asking everyone questions. No one holds a grudge for nearly twenty years.

Kids fight, but it doesn't mean anything when they're older. They know that's—"

"They do think it! All those questions! Maggie thinks they'll arrest him, too! Everyone thinks it except Ray. They think they had another fight and Ray killed him. That's what they think! You can tell by the way—"

"Honey, take it easy," Ray said. Almost apologetically he said to Barbara, "If you could just reassure her a little that it's just a routine investigation, something like that?"

"It isn't! Tell him it's more than that!"

There had not been a gap wide enough for Barbara to get in a word yet; now she did. "Mrs. Arno, please, I know how afraid you are, and you have cause, but it's very important that you keep control. And, Mr. Arno, you have to understand the situation, or you could do yourself damage. Please, both of you, just listen a minute," she said swiftly when it appeared that both of them were going to start talking again. "Mr. Arno, I can't act as your attorney, but I can give you some advice—"

"Why can't you?" Lorinne cried. "We don't have much money, but the whole family will pitch in." She was near tears.

"It would represent a grave conflict of interest," Barbara told her, "because I already agreed to be Maggie's attorney in another matter. If the two cases came into conflict, I would have to withdraw from both of them. And no one knows when such a conflict might arise, especially when both cases involve a single family."

"But—"

"It's the law, Mrs. Arno. There's nothing I can do about that." She looked at Ray then and said soberly, "And you, I'm afraid, have not accepted the seriousness of the situation. They might arrest you and charge you with murder. Statistically, they know that murders are frequently committed by family members. And the fact seems to be that you were the last person who saw your brother alive, other than his killer or killers. You should have your own attorney. I gave some names to Maggie to pass on to you. Has she done that yet?''

He had gone pale with her words. "No."

Lorinne took his hand and held it, wide-eyed, panic-stricken.

"Call her and get them. My advice is for you to retain an attorney immediately and to refuse to answer any more questions except in your attorney's presence. Everything you say will be noted, and if there is a contradiction, they will seize upon it and use it in a way that could be damaging to you. People contradict themselves; they misremember; they leave out details. That's human, but it can look incriminating months later.''

He looked more puzzled than before. "Ms. Holloway, there's nothing for me to leave out, or misremember. I've told them the truth. I don't have anything to lie about. There's nothing—"

"He can't lie! He's never told a lie in his life! He can't even fib a little. He's a good man, Ms. Holloway. A really decent man. He never learned how to lie because he's never needed to hide anything.''

Studying Ray Arno's face, Barbara believed every word Lorinne was uttering. She said, "Mr. Arno, I'm on your side, I believe you, but that's beside the point now. Get a lawyer and take his advice. And please, accept that very good people, innocent people, sometimes get charged, put in jail; sometimes they get convicted of crimes they didn't commit. It happens, Mr. Arno.''

"We've taught our kids that if they tell the truth, no harm will come to them," he said slowly. "It always seemed a good lesson to pass on.''

"It is a good lesson," Barbara said. "The best. And you must keep telling the truth, no matter what.''

He stood up and held out his hand to Barbara when she and Lorinne also got to their feet. "Thanks," he said. "I was deluding myself, wasn't I?" He grinned and looked boyish for a moment. He put his arm around Lorinne's shoulders and gave her a squeeze. "Time to march. I'll get a lawyer, Ms. Holloway. I'm grateful to you. I needed a swift kick, I guess. Thanks."

They walked out with his arm around his wife's shoulders.

When she returned to Frank's house, she told him about the Arnos' visit. "They're good people, fine people. You'd like them. Oh, shit!" She went upstairs.

Dinner for three, he thought, watching her out of sight. She was too troubled to give food a thought. He'd go round up John himself, if that's what it would take. Barbara's efforts toward domesticity had both amused and alarmed him. His alarm button had gone off only when he saw how important Barbara considered it, how she equated failure in the kitchen with something a hell of a lot more meaningful than that.

A little later he lifted the phone to call a fish market and was startled to hear Barbara saying, "That's right, Sally Bronson. My Visa number..." She rattled off a string of numbers and gave the expiration date, then said, "May I have a confirmation number?" The other person gave her a different string of numbers, and Frank hung up. What the hell...?

When he tried the phone half an hour later, she was on it, again reciting a Visa card number. He started up the stairs to see what the hell, but he resisted the impulse; she would tell him when she had something to tell. Then he called up to her, "I'm going dinner shopping." He had to say it once more before she came to the top of the stairs.

"I'm sorry? What did you say?"

He said it a third time. "Won't be long. Everything's locked up down here."

"Oh," she said vaguely. "All right."

After shopping, he dropped in at the Patterson Street apartment. John opened the door, looked past him, then at him, not hiding his anxiety at all.

"Is something wrong?"

"Nope. I was in the neighborhood, came by to invite you to dinner. Bobby's at the house, working, not a thought in the world about the next meal."

John's face tightened. "Thanks, but not tonight."

"Well, it will be there, a plate out for you. Six-thirty, if you change your mind."

"Thanks again," John said stiffly. "You should have called, saved yourself the trip."

"Couldn't," Frank said. "I think she's into telemarketing or something. Kept the phone tied up all afternoon. Sometimes, watching her when she's hot after something, I wonder how the hell my wife put up with me for more than thirty years. Never thought to ask her, never guessed she had anything to put up with."

John grinned slightly. "She's like you were?"

"Yep. Not saying it's admirable, just that it's how she is. I recognize myself over and over. It's a little uncanny. Well, I've got to hustle some nice fat tiger prawns home and do interesting things to them."

Barbara came down the stairs as he was washing snap beans. "Wine for a dying-of-thirst voyager," she said piteously. He pointed toward the refrigerator, and she helped herself. He then pointed to a small glass dome covering an assortment of cheeses, and she helped herself to a bit of cheese, too.

"I've run up a terrible phone bill," she said then. "When it comes in, let me know how much. See, I got to thinking about the cashier's check, but of course Wygood never had one, not for forty-two thousand. The car was part of the payoff. But why would she want to be paid off? She was filthy rich already. Then I got to worrying about all those telephone numbers, the other numbers." She was wandering in and out of the kitchen. When she paused, she sipped wine or nibbled cheese.

"Okay," she said. "What if that long string was a hotel confirmation number? So I began calling every hotel number in her notebook—Zurich, Paris, San Francisco—and I made reservations each time and got a confirmation number each time. They'll check the credit card and know it's a fake, but meanwhile, I have what I was going after. It's a confirmation number, all right, for the Hilton at Miami International. Then I called United and said I was trying to clear up a credit card misunderstanding, and an obliging man told me that Thelma Wygood had had a reservation for the flight to San Francisco on July twenty-third, that she was a no-show, but unfortunately they had not received a cancellation, and the charge would have to be paid. I said I understood."

Frank studied her; she showed not a trace of embarrassment or guilt. She caught his searching gaze and grinned, lifted her wine glass and drained it.

"Then I started to wonder about the other phone numbers—bookstores, and a deli in Seattle. Why? A long way to order a pastrami on rye, don't you think?" She poured more wine. "I called the Seattle numbers to find out where they're located, a bookstore and a deli, within half a block from the Major Works headquarters. Useful, if you happen to be working in Seattle, but from Zurich?"

She was pacing again, her voice rising and falling as she moved close to the sink, then farther away. Frank turned off the water and dried his hands.

"I began to do some heavy thinking about Thelma Wygood," she said. "Looked up things about her on the Internet, and found out a lot. She and Major were equals in every way; her name came first as often as his did when they released a new program. She wasn't shy about taking credit for her work, either. She knew damn well what she had done and what it meant. I'm getting ahead of myself," she said apologetically, returning to the kitchen.

"I tried to put myself in her place. I'm in Zurich, and leave carrying nothing but the briefcase with the program and my purse, maybe with a toothbrush and a nightgown in it. I have a reservation for the Miami airport motel, and a flight out early the following morning. What do I plan to do with the car and the money? I can't get through airport security with a metal suitcase full of money, and I sure as hell wouldn't check it through. So what? Why the stopover in Miami? Why not a connecting flight on to San Francisco if that's where I wanted to be?"

She paused. "Putting myself in her head made me realize that in many ways Maggie Folsum is like her. She had her party to show her family, her parents and brothers, that, by God, she had done it and done it alone. Rub their noses in it a little. Women like that are fed up with achieving a lot and having the credit go somewhere else."

Her voice had become a bit hard-edged.

"If I argued a case and won it before the Supreme Court, do you imagine for a second that I'd go all demure and shy and say, 'Daddy told me what to say'?"

Frank burst out laughing, and she grinned again, broader. "Anyway, you can see where my thoughts were taking me. I just don't believe Thelma Wygood would have let someone take her program and claim it as his own. And if that wasn't the case, then she and Major might have done something extremely foolish. And, as it turned out, fatally dangerous."

Frank's eyes narrowed, and now he poured wine for himself. "Let's have a seat," he said, motioning toward the dinette. He carried the bottle in with him.

"Okay," Barbara said. "I can imagine how bookstores would be useful if you're conspiring. A simple message left with a secretary: The book Mr. Major ordered will arrive on the third, something like that. But it would be limited, don't you think? But a deli that's open until two in the morning, all day, that offers more possibilities, especially if you own the building, the deli, all of it. I haven't checked it out, but I'd put down money that Major owns that whole block."

"You're suggesting that she might have planned to turn over the car and the money in Miami to private investigators, FBI, something like that?" Frank said. "Then fly to the West Coast. Another trip to the island next? Maybe." He drank his wine, deep in thought, then said, "It's a stretch, Bobby. You're speculating a lot, and assuming a lot, too."

"Yes," she admitted. "It just makes sense this way. Nothing else does. Would they have had a fight in public that everyone seems to know about? Then the elaborate separation, all the way to Europe for her. And for him to have sported Barbie dolls in public? I bet they scared him to death. None of that's in character with anything I've been able to find out about them."

"But what's that program she was selling, then?" Frank asked after a moment.

"I don't know. I want to ask Major."

"If Major's in seclusion, occupied with having a nervous breakdown, that step might be in the range of hard to impossible."

"I know. I'm going to try something. First I wanted to air it all, and have a bit of wine." She drew the notebook from her pocket. "Dave's Deli, my next move."

She went to the kitchen phone; Frank followed, then

stood nearby as she dialed. When a man said, "Dave's Deli," she said, "I have an urgent message for Mr. Major."

The man on the other end said, "Hold on." Then he yelled, "Dave, you want to take this?" There was a lot of background noise; apparently the deli was busy.

"This is Dave," a different man said after a moment.

"I have a message for Mr. Major. It's urgent. Tell him it's about Thelma and Penelope." She gave Frank's number, and Dave hung up without another word.

"Now we wait," she said, then let out a long breath.

11

When Frank mentioned that he had invited John to dinner, Barbara momentarily looked startled, then she shrugged. "I'm not telling him any of the new developments," she said. "I think it's best not to involve him further."

"Okay," he said, but he had mixed feelings. One day he would be the one kept in the dark, and he knew very well how that would sit; on the other hand, John was curiously innocent about a lot of things. Also, the fewer people who knew about this matter, the better. Still, there would be injured pride. None of your business, he reminded himself, and turned the shrimp in the marinade of garlic and oil.

Barbara went to the door when the bell rang at six-thirty. John was holding a bottle of wine. She had a flashing memory of the first time he had come here to dinner, and had brought flowers and a bottle of Grand Marnier. The flowers were for her father, he had said gravely when she reached for them.

"Hi," he said, his gaze sweeping over her—up, down, then fixing on her face. "No flowers, no coals to Newcastle."

Her voice was husky when she said, "Come on in."

Inside, he set the bottle down on the side table in the hall and took her in his arms. "I missed you."

She nodded. "Me, too."

Frank stopped at the other end of the hall when he saw

them, and backed up again, returned to his food preparation. It might just be a temporary truce, but truces were good. They led to negotiations, which sometimes led to compromises and even agreements.

The truce lasted through dinner, although neither Barbara nor John had much to say. They listened to Frank's stories and laughed at the right places. Twice the phone rang and Barbara jumped up from the table with a hasty "Excuse me." Each time she returned and did not say a word about the caller.

After dinner, John washed the pots and pans the way he always did at Frank's house; Barbara dried them and put them away. Then there was an awkward moment.

"You're waiting for a phone call?" John asked.

She nodded.

"Any idea when to expect it? How long you'll wait?"

"No. It might not even happen."

He regarded her without any expression for a time, then said, "I better get on my way. It's a long walk."

"You walked over?" She realized that he had expected them to drive back in her car.

"Give you a lift," Frank said.

John thanked him and said no. "I need the exercise."

Barbara walked to the door with him. "You could hang out for a while. The call might come any minute, and we'd both leave."

"And it might not. See you later."

He didn't ask if she'd be home early.

She paced while Frank read, then she played with the cats, then she paced again. She sat down and stood up many times. She should see a counselor, she thought; no, John should see one. They should both see one. But he wouldn't. She realized she was chasing her own tail and stopped, then went over her reasoning about Thelma Wygood again.

At eleven she said, "Dad, go on to bed. I'll just read for a little while. He isn't going to call this late."

Wordlessly Frank left the living room; he returned with a sheet, which he draped over the back of the couch. He knew she would go nowhere until that call came, or morning came, but maybe she would stretch out and get some rest.

At fifteen minutes before twelve the phone rang. She ran to pick it up before the machine took it. "Hello."

A hoarse voice demanded, "Who are you? Did you leave a message for me? I'm Russ Major."

"I called," she said, and sank down into a chair. "My name is Barbara Holloway. I'm an attorney in Eugene, Oregon. I think I have something that belongs to you."

"How much do you want?"

"Just to talk."

"How do you know anything about Penelope? What do you know about Thelma?"

"Not on the phone, Mr. Major. I have to talk to you in person."

"Get up here to Seattle. I'll have you met." To someone else he said, even more hoarsely, "Shut up. I'm handling this."

"I can't do that," Barbara said. "Mr. Major, there's an attorney in town who works for the Palmer Company. I don't want them to know I'm in touch with you, and if I leave, they might follow me. You'll have to come here."

At the mention of Palmer, there was a strangled sound, then a different voice said coldly, "I don't know who you are, or what game you're playing. We'll get back to you. In the morning. Nine o'clock. Be at this number." He hung up.

When Barbara got home half an hour later, John was asleep in the living room, sprawled out in a chair. He would be stiff and sore, she thought in dismay. He roused, rubbed his eyes, and peered at her.

"Can we go to bed now?"

She held out her hands to pull him upright.

12

Frank was in his robe and slippers when he let her in the next morning. He picked up the newspaper, led the way to the dinette, where he tossed the paper on the table, and walked out.

"We have to come up with a good place to put Major where we can talk to him," she said to his back. He vanished into the hall to his bedroom and closed the door hard.

The doorbell rang and she went to admit Bailey, who looked as out of sorts as her father. "Eight o'clock!" he grumbled. "Jeez, Barbara."

"I've been up for hours," she said. "Where can we hide a guy, maybe more than one?"

He shook his head. "It's eight o'clock," he explained.

"Oh, right." After pouring coffee for them both, she filled him in. "So, they'll call back at nine. And I want to be able to tell them where to hole up."

"And maybe they won't call," he pointed out. "And if they call, maybe they won't come down here."

"Let's pretend they will."

Frank came in then, with wet hair but dressed. "I've found that what helps digestion is silence until after breakfast," he said coldly. "You guys want to eat? Just a simple yes or no."

"Yes," they said simultaneously.

Frank busied himself at the refrigerator, pulling out things, setting them down on the counter.

"Well?" Barbara said. She began to drum her fingers on the table.

Bailey scowled and said, just as coldly as Frank had done, "That's no help."

Frank was folding an omelette when Bailey said, "Sylvia's place."

For a moment Frank stared at him, then he nodded.

Bailey made the call from the wall phone. He had to get past two people before Sylvia was on the line. "Hiya, Sylvia. Want to play cops and robbers?" He grinned broadly. "Yeah, right. A guy or maybe two—hell, I don't know, maybe more—need a place for a private conversation."

He listened, nodded to Barbara, and said, "I'll tell them. And I'll call back with some details."

After he hung up, he said, "Okay. They're houseguests, but they'll never know anyone new has arrived, way that place is set up. And they should come in a limo if possible, so they won't be conspicuous," he finished, absolutely deadpan.

Major called at five minutes past nine. Barbara snatched up the wall phone. "Holloway."

"We're coming. Tell me where to meet you."

She gave him the Fentons' names and telephone number, then said, "I'll turn this over to my associate, who can give you driving instructions. Can you come in a limousine, with darkened windows, perhaps?"

"Yes." He said something to someone else, then said, "Here, you do this part."

Barbara handed her phone to Bailey.

Later, in his downtown office, Frank opened the wall safe and brought out the briefcase. Barbara removed a few sheets of printout and put them in her own briefcase; he returned the other one to the safe and locked it.

At twenty-five minutes after twelve Barbara went out to Bailey's car, and they left. At twelve-thirty, Ruthie buzzed

Frank to tell him Mr. Fenton's driver had arrived to pick him up.

"Anyone tailing us?" Barbara asked Bailey as he headed out Franklin Boulevard.

"Nope. But they're watching the office, two of them. Local guys."

They drove out Franklin, past the university buildings, past the I-5 cloverleaf, over the river, and then turned south. The road became narrow and winding. An overloaded hay truck crawled along in front of them. Strawberry fields, farms, a miniranch or two, more subdivisions... Bailey turned again, onto a county road that began to snake up into the hills. He turned once more, and they were driving along a high stone wall. When they came to a gate, he stopped and rolled down his window. "Ms. Holloway to see Mrs. Fenton," he said into a speaker. The gate opened soundlessly; he drove through, and the gate closed again. There was a wide meadow all around them now, with horses and cattle grazing, and no fence in sight. Barbara knew she was gaping, and couldn't help it. A real, by-God ranch twenty-five minutes out of Eugene! Dense forest was in the distance, on this side of the stone wall; a bridge over a creek; gardens, fenced off from the cattle.

"How big is this place?" she asked.

"Eight hundred acres. A thousand. Somewhere about that. Jeez! Can you imagine what the property tax is?"

When the house came into view, at first glance it seemed small, then wings began to appear, and the wings had their own wings. Part of the building was two-story, most of it was one. The closer they got, the bigger it grew. They passed a swimming pool with half a dozen people lounging about, no one in the water. Bailey followed a curve around the house and stopped at a side door, at least two wings removed from the front entrance.

"We are here," he said cheerfully. "And there's Sylvia herself. What a doll!"

The limousine with Frank inside pulled up behind them as they got out of the car.

Sylvia was more garish than she had been before; she was wearing lime-green silk pants and a pink overshirt with a blue sash. She glittered with jewelry. Her hair was more yellow than orange today, and her earrings were dangling rubies.

Her broken leg had made a miraculous recovery. She rushed to the limousine door and opened it herself. "Frank, you beautiful hunk! Come on out." As Frank climbed out, she said to Barbara, "I've warned him fair and square, the day Joe kicks, I'm coming after him. Haven't I warned you, Frank?" She threw her arms around Frank and kissed him on the mouth. To Barbara's amazement, he hugged and kissed back. "Of course," Sylvia said, disentangling herself, "Joe enjoys perfect health, so it won't be tomorrow, but I want Frank to take good care of himself, so when I'm ready, he'll still be full of piss and vinegar. This way, this way."

The door was only steps from the car; they entered a spacious hallway filled with art: paintings on the walls, sculptures on the floor and on stands, tables adorned with gilt and inlays of mother-of-pearl, red-velvet-covered chairs.... The result was one of clutter, expensive clutter, but too much, too mixed, too crowded, the worst taste Barbara had ever seen west of Versailles.

"There are a couple of bedrooms," Sylvia said, gesturing, "and a sitting room, and a little dining room. As soon as Mr. Smith and company arrive, lunch will be brought in to the dining room. If you need anything, there's the telephone." She looked around for it, then said, "Maybe it's in the sitting room. It's somewhere. You'll find it. The

Smith party will be met at the gate and driven around by one of my boys. Well, enjoy."

She started to walk down the hall; Barbara walked with her. "Mrs. Fenton, this is so very generous—"

"Dear, if I'm going to be your stepmother someday, I insist that you call me Sylvia. I wish I could work more with Bailey. But he holds back. Well, this is better than nothing...." She continued to talk until she reached the door, and left.

When Barbara turned around, both Frank and Bailey were laughing. She grinned, then said, "Well, you beautiful hunk, let's look over the sitting room." Bailey went out to move his car and wait for Major and company.

Frank and Barbara were in the sitting room, exclaiming over the excessive art, when Bailey knocked on the door, then entered with three other men.

Barbara stepped forward. "How do you do, Mr. Major. I'm Barbara Holloway, and this is my father and colleague, Frank Holloway." Major's handshake was limp. Barbara turned to the next man.

"Garrick Jolin," he said. His handshake was almost too hard. "This is our driver, he'll wait outside."

"As will our driver," Barbara said, nodding to Bailey. He left with the other man. Her thoughts were swirling; if this was head of security for Major Works, who was that man at Valley River Inn?

Major was exactly what she had expected, bespectacled, unruly long hair, nervous. Jolin was stoop-shouldered, with a receding hairline, and a hardness that was very much like the hardness Bailey showed sometimes. He had a perceptive gaze that was direct and wholly skeptical.

"There's a washroom, second door down the hall," Barbara said. "Mrs. Fenton said she would have lunch brought in."

"Ms. Holloway, we didn't come here to party," Jolin

said rudely. "What do you have? What do you know? And how do you know anything?"

"Let's sit down and I'll tell you."

Major was moving around the room as if examining the various objects—a Ming vase next to a crude pottery vase with some cattails in it, a Miró surrounded by what looked like calendar art.... He didn't stop at any one thing long enough to take it in, though, just kept moving. Now he perched on the edge of a chair. He looked ill, haggard.

"I have your program, and a suitcase with over two hundred thousand dollars in it," Barbara said. "I know who killed Thelma Wygood and why. I think I know what she was doing and why."

Major jumped to his feet and started his aimless walk-around again. Jolin said in a hard voice, "Don't play games. What do you want? How did you get anything? Can you prove what you say?"

She opened her briefcase and withdrew the sheets of printout, handed them to Jolin. Major made a soft moaning sound and sat down again, his gaze fixed on the printouts. Jolin handed them to him, and after no more than a cursory glance, he nodded.

"Just tell us what you know," Major said thickly. "How did you get them?"

"I can't tell you everything," she said. "I have a client involved in this, but I'll tell you as much as possible. Afterward, will you fill in some blanks for me? Quid pro quo?"

Major nodded. Jolin was impassive.

"Some time ago an employee stole a new program from you, and you staged a charade to catch the people responsible. Ms. Wygood played her role brilliantly and the trap was set, but the delivery man got greedy, killed his partner and Ms. Wygood, and then he came here to Oregon, no doubt to hide and contact a high bidder. However, he himself has been murdered. And the money and the program ended up in my hands. An attorney named Trassi has been in touch with me to negotiate a sale, and I've stalled him.''

Major was on his feet again, with both hands clenched hard. ''Wilford's dead? Who killed him?''

''His name wasn't Wilford, and he's dead. I believe Palmer's men tried to force him to reveal where the money and program were hidden, and then they killed him.''

''How did you get your hands on anything?'' Jolin asked then. His eyes were narrowed to slits, and he looked as tense as Major.

''For now, it's enough that I have the items, and Trassi knows I have them. There's another man in the picture, and he has made a generous offer also. I don't know where he fits in, but he knows all about this.''

Jolin looked surprised, then his face became expressionless again.

''It's your turn,'' Barbara said then. ''Was the scenario I gave pretty accurate? You were deliberately baiting a trap?''

Major nodded. ''God help us all, we did.'' He went to stand by a window, facing out. ''For nothing,'' he said in a choked voice. ''Nothing.''

There was a light tap on the door. Frank went to open it. A pretty young woman in a maid's uniform said lunch was in the dining room.

Briskly, Barbara said, ''Why don't you both go wash up, and then we can pick at lunch. We all have things to think about.''

After they left together, Barbara said, ''I might as well tell them more; Jolin's going to start digging and find out anyway.''

Frank agreed. ''But who the hell is Waters? Let's go see what kind of a spread Sylvia sent our way.''

There was gazpacho in a crystal bowl set in a second

bowl of crushed ice, surrounded by crystal cups. There were several pâtés, and baguettes and crusty brown bread, little sandwiches, flutes of paper-thin pink ham....

Jolin and Major joined them in the dining room a few minutes later. Major didn't even glance at the table but started roaming. Jolin spread pâté on brown bread, ladled out gazpacho, took them both to Major, and practically forced them into his hands. Major looked as if he didn't understand.

"Try it," Jolin said, and returned to the table. No one sat down; they moved around the table and picked at lunch.

"You guessed it almost exactly," Jolin said. "It was a trap. We had men in Miami at the motel, waiting for Thelma to get there with the car and the money. We had an FBI number to call when it happened. There wasn't any reason to suspect violence would occur. There hadn't been any violence in the Palmer deals we were able to learn about; simple business transactions, that's all they were." He sounded very bitter. "The plan was to turn over the cash and the car to the FBI, put a tail on the delivery men with the program, and go after Palmer and his client. We know who he is, but there's no proof. Thelma would have been our star witness; she kept a meticulous diary from day one." He drank some gazpacho and set the cup down hard. "It was all worked out. For nothing. We've spent all this time chasing after Wilford."

Across the room Major had put his food down, untasted.

Jolin ignored him. "How did you come into it? Who told you about the theft?"

She gave a bare-bones synopsis of her talk with Waters. Jolin didn't move while she spoke, but Major prowled aimlessly about the room.

"It's almost right," Jolin said when she concluded. "A few details are off, but it's close enough. Our version of what took place," he said harshly, then told about the theft

three years earlier. "So we knew the guy had bought a car
from the Palmer Company; it was delivered by Steve Wilford and Eddie Grinwald, who flew back to New York afterward, and our guy headed for California and within a
few months started his own company. No proof, parallel
research, back luck, bad timing—there wasn't a damn thing
we could do. The other company brought out the program,
and that was that." He glanced at Russ Major, who was
standing at a window, possibly even gazing out. "Russ and
Thelma knew in a second it was theirs; they told me, and
none of us ever mentioned it to anyone else. Our research
teams suspected, of course, but since no one talked about
it, the matter died. We tightened security, and tried to ferret
out the spy."

"Do you know yet who the in-house spy is?" Barbara
asked.

"Yes. The day after Thelma was reported dead, a woman
left without warning, terrified." He scowled. "A little late
to find out, though. Anyway, about eighteen months ago
Thelma came up with the scheme to trap the thieves. It
looked good on paper," he added, bitter again. "She reasoned that if it had happened once, it would happen again
with the ncxt big program, and she was determined to stop
it. She didn't call Trassi or make any movement in that
direction. Instead, she and Russ both let out a leak about
an exciting new program that was coming along, and, of
course, our spy informed our competitor. We tightened security again, as if we intended to guard our work to the
hilt. Then they staged the first of their fights. The fights
became nastier and more public; they separated, and she
finally took her research team to Zurich and waited for
someone to make the first move. The last time she flew
home, she and Russ went to the island, then came back to
Seattle and threw a big party, a celebration party, not to
announce anything, but to suggest the last bugs had been

worked out. Russ showed up with a model draped on his arm, and Thelma took off that night for Zurich. Our spy was probably on the phone before she got to SeaTac. Two weeks later a man approached her and the opening gambit was played out.''

He studied Barbara, then said, ''I don't quite understand how Waters knows as much as he does, what his game is. Can you describe him?''

''Smooth and personable, six feet tall, broad-shouldered, a good voice, dark hair and eyes. He claimed he was head of security for the company involved and he was persuasive and believable.''

''Gilmore!'' Major said suddenly. ''That son of a bitch!''

''Maybe,'' Jolin said. ''Stuart Gilmore is the man who approached Thelma in Zurich. He's an ex-actor turned con man who's worked for the Palmer Company for a dozen or more years. He makes the first move. It could be him. But why tell you as much as he did? Too much maybe.''

''Probably several reasons,'' Barbara said. ''They had no idea how much I already knew, what all Mitch might have had with him. He could have kept Thelma Wygood's ID, her wallet or something that would have led us to her murder and eventually sent us to the police. He made a special plea that I not go to the police, that the affair be kept confidential. But also, I think, to give me an alternative choice, one that appeared honorable and just. And lucrative. His offer was all the money, no questions, and justice served. To cover the possibility that we had her name, he had to make it authentic and detailed enough for me to accept. He was good,'' she added.

''Why didn't you take his offer?''

''I didn't trust him. And after I read about Thelma Wygood, I came to disbelieve she would sell out her company. Also, I really do have a client to protect.'' She looked at

Major again and said very sharply, "Mr. Major, I need your attention. What do you want me to do with your program?"

"Give it to Palmer's lawyer," he said in a low voice.

"It's a setup, isn't it? How long before they'll know it's a phony?"

He looked helplessly at Jolin. "We worked for more than two years on it, Thelma and I, before we knew it was all wrong. It will take them longer. Our teams never found out, and no one else ever had access to the entire program. Everyone was excited. It would have revolutionized the telecommunications industry, but it was wrong."

"After you knew Thelma was dead, why didn't you go to the police?"

Major looked agonized.

Jolin answered. "What was the point? We didn't go to them beforehand, too afraid of a leak. And afterward? We had no proof, the diary of a dead woman, unsigned, coded, no names in it. Not even a real diary, just pages that she sent on as she wrote them. It would have been pointless, but the rumor would have spread that she had sold out. We weren't willing to do that. We didn't have anything," he said bitterly. "No car, no money, no witness—nothing!"

Barbara could no longer contain her impatience with Major and his ceaseless movements. "Mr. Major, please sit down so I can talk to you."

He stopped walking and looked at her with a bewildered expression.

"Please, just sit down a minute." She waited until he did so. "Do you have any interest in that money? It's two hundred forty thousand dollars."

He shook his head and looked as if he was ready to move again, but Frank spoke now. "Would anyone pay out that kind of money for a program sight unseen, without a demonstration or something?"

Jolin and Major exchanged glances. Jolin said, "You know what vaporware is?"

"Not a clue," Frank admitted.

"Okay. A company announces a new program that's to be released at some future date. The day comes and goes, and the product doesn't appear. It's so common in our field that there's more vaporware than software out there. Major Works has never in twenty years announced a vaporware product. Never. And people know that. Thelma let out a hint early on that they were working on a voice-recognition system; not a blatant hint, but enough, and then she and Russ clammed up. They both let their research teams in on the fact that they were interested in the telecommunications problems and were tackling them. Then they had the big party to celebrate; and another, final, hint was dropped: they would have an announcement for the fall trade show. That was last spring, just before their last big battle. The other company had to bite."

Frank shook his head. Rumors and rumors of rumors. A crazy business.

"All right," Barbara said. "However that went, they did pay out a large amount of money and they don't yet have what they paid for. Mr. Major, your people can't go after Palmer now or the person who hired him. Neither can you get involved with Trassi or Gilmore. The minute they detect your presence, they'll know you're onto them, and they'll cover their tracks thoroughly. There's no way you should know about any of them, is there?"

He looked at Jolin, as if for help, then said, "No. They think we don't know anything."

"Right," she said. "The man who killed Thelma was Mitch Arno. His ex-wife is owed just about the amount in the suitcase for past child support. I intend to get it for her, in a way that will satisfy the legal requirements. But I'm talking about justice more than law, Mr. Major. Ray Arno very likely will be arrested for the murder of his brother Mitch, and he is innocent. I don't intend to stand by and see him get the death penalty for that murder.''

"You'll throw Thelma out for them to gnaw on," Jolin said heavily.

"No, I won't. You can't punish her killer, and you can't go after Trassi and Palmer; I can. But I'll need your cooperation, and Mr. Major's cooperation.''

"Why would you?" Jolin asked.

"My client is due that money, but she'll turn it over to the police along with the program before she'll let Ray Arno hang for Mitch's death. They wrecked her bed-and-breakfast inn and would have killed her, no doubt, if she had been home. They threatened her children, and me. They tortured and murdered Mitch Arno. An innocent man is at deadly risk. I think they've gone far enough.'' She knew that was only the surface of her reasons, but she would not have been able to explain herself to these two men, since she could not explain it even to herself.

Jolin continued to study her, his face as expressionless as stone.

Major was up again, on his feet, on the move. "We'll do whatever you say," he said, going to the window. "If you can keep Thelma out of it." He swung around to face her. "I intend to destroy Dan Frisch; getting the program into his hands will do it. It will take time, but he'll be ruined, he won't steal another program. Can you keep your client in line? Will she cooperate, not hand anything over to the police? Ms. Holloway, I want Frisch and I want Palmer, even more than the tools they used.''

"I can't defend Ray Arno until my client and I conclude our business, but at that time I want to step in. I want the men who killed Mitch and tore up Maggie Folsum's inn, and I want Trassi, who was more than likely directing the killers. To get them, I'll have to involve Palmer. I can't work out in the open yet, but there's a lot I can start with in the background.''

Jolin shook his head. "You can't get them. They've been too careful too long.''

"Maybe not,'' she admitted. "But I have a chance, and you don't. It's that simple. And for openers, I'll want everything you've learned, and then for your people to back off, or work under the direction of my own detective.''

He pursed his lips and looked at Major, who nodded. "She's right. She has a chance. Tell us what you need.''

"Can I hold out some pages of printout until Trassi makes good on promises? Would that satisfy the person behind all this?''

Major's expression changed, became almost demonic. "Yes! Keep out the first hundred pages, and the last fifty or so. Frisch's team will go crazy trying to fill in the missing pieces. They'll have enough to do to keep them busy for six months, longer, but Dan Frisch will be driven to finish it himself.'' Abruptly he swung around to face out the window, where he stood rigidly with his hands thrust into his pockets.

Watching him, Barbara realized he wanted to destroy Frisch, his rival, competitor, thief, and he knew how to do it, because whatever it was that drove Frisch drove him as well, just as it had driven Thelma Wygood.

"Let's iron out some details,'' Jolin said then, and for the next two hours Barbara and Jolin worked on their plans.

Suddenly Major participated again. "Ms. Holloway,'' he said bleakly, "you know the expression 'Money is no object'? Usually no one really means that. I do. Just get them, any way you can, legal or not. Just get them. If you can't, I'll get them myself. I wanted to. He stopped me.'' He gave Jolin a bitter look. "But he won't stop me again if I have to do it.''

13

Major and Jolin left as soon as they finished; Frank left with the Fenton driver, Ralph, and Barbara with Bailey.

"So you got real backing," he said after she told him about the meeting. "Good work."

"They have an airstrip they use out of Vancouver, Washington. They'll drive there, then fly back to the island, and by eight or so, Jolin will start faxing me all the stuff they've gathered so far."

"Tonight? Barbara, remember Hannah, my wife? You know, I've got a whole other life?"

"You don't need to be there. But I've been thinking. If Waters really is Gilmore, he's going to fly away free as a bird. He romanced a lonely woman in Switzerland, so what?"

She was well aware that Bailey had gone into his hard-listening attitude. He said sourly, "But you've got an idea."

"I may have an idea," she said. "What if a failed actor turned con man met a foolish, rich old woman who longed for the roar of greasepaint and the smell of the crowd, and above all else her own theater, a return of glory? How much do you suppose he'd try to take her for?"

There was a strange sound from Bailey; she glanced at him and realized he was chuckling.

"You want Sylvia to work a sting," he said. "Jeez, she'd love it!"

"Could she pull it off?"

"Barbara, she looks and acts like a nut, but she's as shrewd as they come. And Joe indulges her. She'd love it, and Joe will play along and be happy as a clam. And when the time comes, they know every judge in the state. If she goes for a sting, consider him stung."

"Would she be willing to testify, go the whole distance?"

Bailey laughed out loud. "Are you kidding? Jeez, I wonder what getup she'll wear."

Very softly, Barbara said, "They'll send Gilmore's picture. I'll let you know if he's calling himself Waters."

She had Bailey drop her off a few blocks from her apartment at a Safeway, where she studied the gourmet section of frozen entres, picked two, and lettuce and tomatoes, and thought with relief that dinner was under control. She walked home.

The truce was still holding. John laughed when she unloaded her bag of groceries. "Look in the freezer," he said. She found half a dozen more frozen entres there.

He didn't ask what she had been up to all day, and she didn't ask about the Staley mine. After they finished eating and washed the few dishes, she said, "I left my car in the office lot. I'll go over, pick up some faxes, and drive home."

"I'll walk over with you."

Neither had been truly relaxed, but a new tightness appeared on his face, sounded in his voice.

"There's no point in that," she said.

"I'll come," he said.

She shook her head, and suddenly he grinned. "See, you're still doing it. You get impatient and shake your head like a dog with a bone. But, impatient or not, I don't think it's a good idea for you to be out alone at night when you're dealing with the kind of people you seem to gravitate to.''

She sighed in exasperation. ''I've been a big girl for a long time—''

''I'll tag along a few paces behind you,'' he said.

''Jesus!'' she muttered.

''You have any idea how much like your father you just sounded? When do you have to be there?''

They walked to the office together. Half a block from the apartment, he reached for her hand.

The next morning she started to read the faxes. At eight-thirty a special-delivery parcel arrived: Gilmore's picture from his acting days, and two snapshots that Thelma Wygood had taken. Gilmore was calling himself Brad Waters these days. He had been blond in Zurich. There was also a photocopy of Thelma's diary, starting with June fourth. ''A blond man introduced himself as Brian, and bought me a drink at the Hilton Bar. His first words were 'God, you look like an American. Please be American. A Kansas drawl would sound like heaven.' It was a very good way to start. We talked a few minutes, nothing of consequence.''

Barbara flipped through the pages; some of the entries were quite long, and there were a lot of them.

Bailey arrived a few minutes before nine, and Frank a few minutes later. They both started on the faxes. Bailey concentrated on Gilmore's dossier.

''A snap,'' he said after a few minutes. ''Sylvia will chew him up and spit him out.''

''If Trassi actually calls Sunderman to set up a time for a meeting, I'll call Waters and make a date. It won't take me long to shake him, and he might be in a rush to get out of town afterward, once his role is played out here. I'll let you know when.''

Frank looked up sharply. "What the devil are you conniving?"

When Barbara told him, he looked troubled, then grudgingly he nodded. "It probably will work. But you're cutting it pretty close, Bobby."

"I know." She motioned toward the faxes. "I'll go through all this stuff and wait for Trassi's call." She was relieved that no one asked what her backup plan was if Trassi didn't call.

"Word is, they're going to arrest Ray Arno today," Bailey said.

"I know," Barbara said morosely.

She made copies of all the Gilmore material, and Bailey left to talk to Sylvia. Barbara and Frank settled in to read. At eleven Frank wandered down the corridor to Lou Sunderman's office to tell the tax attorney that he had an interesting problem for him. He was humming under his breath; he and Lou regarded each other as members of alien species. Frank thought anyone who liked spending all his time studying new tax laws and trying to find ways to get around them was straitjacket material. And he well knew that Lou thought anyone who chose to hobnob with criminals, possibly murderers, was a seriously deranged pervert.

When Frank returned an hour later, he handed Barbara a sheet of paper nearly covered with his heavy scrawl. "Lou says that's what he'll need from Maggie. Marriage license, divorce decree, kids' birth certificates… He's probably being fussy, but he says the more he can produce at the first meeting with the IRS, the better."

She called Maggie, who sounded terrible, frantic with worry. She would get the documents together and bring them over the following day.

"They'll arrest Ray, won't they? He has a lawyer, a man named Bishop Stover, someone who comes in to the sports shop now and then. I told him to try one you recommended, but he said a lawyer he knew would be better.... Barbara, I'm so scared for him."

"Take it easy," Barbara said. "Don't go to pieces. We'll talk tomorrow. When will you get here? You might as well come to the office."

When she hung up, she cursed. "Stover! For God's sake!"

"Maybe he'll shake himself for a friend," Frank said. Stover was not a bad man, not evil; he was lazy, and too many of his clients ended up going for a plea bargain. No doubt, most of them were guilty of something or other, everyone was, but a plea bargain should be used as a last resort, not the first.

At three-thirty Trassi called. "I told Mr. Sunderman to arrange a meeting with IRS as soon as possible," he said curtly.

"Good. I shall remove a couple hundred sheets of print-out and hold them until the Internal Revenue Service signs a closing agreement. That will take several weeks, no doubt. Meanwhile, you will have enough of the material to satisfy your clients."

"You don't know the people you're trying to outsmart," he said in a low voice. "You don't know what kind of danger you're inviting."

"Maybe not, but I have a very good idea of what my bargaining chips are."

When she hung up the phone, she had to wipe her hand, suddenly sweaty on the phone. Good God! she thought in wonder, Trassi was going to do it! He was going all the way.

At four-thirty she arrived at Valley River Inn, asked for Mr. Waters's table, and was led to the same table they had sat at before.

Waters/Gilmore jumped up. "I thought you might not make it," he said. "I've been trying and trying to reach you." The waiter was hovering. Barbara waved him away. "Russ is really losing it," Gilmore said. "It's really bad. He's threatening to throw himself off a cliff. Ms. Holloway, Barbara, please…" He reached across the table and took her hand. "For God's sake, please. I'm begging you. Let me tell him I have his program."

She pulled free and shook her head. "Sorry, Mr. Waters. I'm going with Trassi."

He leaned back in his chair, as if stunned. "Why? I thought you were an honorable woman, a decent human being. Why?"

"Because he can give me what I need, and you can't. Not just the money, but legal justification for it."

"We'll find a way," he said. "If that's all, we'll fix it. Russ will make it legal as hell."

"I don't think so," she said. "Trassi can do it easily in a way the tax people will understand and accept. So, sorry. I have to run."

"You're like the rest, after all," he said harshly. "A lawyer through and through. Don't let decency get in the way of a buck. You'll be directly responsible if Russ does something desperate, if he kills himself. It will be on your head."

"I don't believe your employer's emotional or psychological distress is any of my business. And if two giants nibble each other to death, let them." She walked away.

In the lobby a small group of women were standing under a banner: GRANDPARENTS' RIGHTS ADVOCACY ASSOCI-ATION. Most of them were silver-haired with a touch of blue here and there, and most of them were extremely well dressed with discreet jewelry. Sylvia stood out like an orange in a snowbank. Her hair was bright orange, frizzed in an Afro; she was wearing leopard-spotted silk pants, and a gold lam top, and every finger was dazzling with diamonds; diamond pendants dangled from her ears.

Barbara walked past her. In a moment she heard Sylvia's carrying voice: "Excuse me, Lucy. I'll be damned if that isn't Stu Gilmore!"

14

Frank strolled into the office at nine in the morning. Barbara would drop in around eleven, she had said, and Maggie was due by eleven-thirty. There were a few things for him to attend to, nothing of great importance, no matter how Patsy regarded them.

She scurried from her office as he drew near his own. Patsy had coal-black hair she tended so carefully that no white root had ever shown itself. He was very fond of her.

"Mr. Bixby asked you to give him a buzz as soon as you arrived," Patsy said.

He grinned amiably at her. "All right." He entered his office and gave Sam Bixby a buzz. "What's up, Sam?"

"I'd like a few moments, if you have time," Sam said. "I can come over if you're not tied up."

"Come on over."

Moments later Sam arrived. He knocked and waited to be invited in, the way he always did. They exchanged pleasantries and seated themselves in the comfortable chairs by the coffee table.

"What's on your mind?" Frank asked.

"I heard that the Fentons sent a car for you," Sam said, not quite nonchalantly. "I thought it was agreed that if we took on a new client, we would discuss it."

"I didn't take them on," Frank said. "A little advice, no more than that."

Sam looked disappointed. "Oh," he said. "But there's

something else. I hear that Barbara's been in and out a lot this past week, even working late. Has she taken on someone we should talk about?''

"Sam, knock it off," Frank said. "You know as well as I do that we're consulting with Lou Sunderman, and yes, it's going to involve him and the office. A tax matter, Sam."

Sam looked uncomfortable. At one time he had worn a hairpiece, but he had given it up and, in fact, had been ridiculous in it; but his head did gleam, and it was very pink. Frank suspected that Sam was a little jealous of his, Frank's, abundant hair, gray as it was.

"What's really bugging you?" he asked bluntly.

Sam took in a deep breath, then said, "I don't believe you're unaware of how this whole office has changed over the years. Drastically. The day you retire, we no longer will be concerned with criminal cases, for example."

"Ah," Frank said. "You haven't forgotten that my cases kept us in chow for a good many of those years, I hope."

"Of course not. But things change. Our image has changed. And criminal cases do not enhance it."

"So when I walk out, you assign this office to whom? Got that far yet?"

Sam turned a shade redder. "No, no. Frank, I'm not suggesting you leave, for God's sake. I haven't forgotten anything. But things change. That's all I'm saying. Things change. High-profile cases alienate people. They take sides. People associate the firm with unsavory publicity, with a lack of discretion. It isn't good for us as a firm. That's all I'm saying."

"I give you discretion. You handle more crooks in a month than I see all year, but discreetly. Now I get it."

"No, you don't! I know you aren't pulling in those cases yourself anymore. But you let Barbara drag you into the middle of them. She uses this firm when and how it suits her. She's a maverick like you. There was a time when we needed that, but we don't any longer. Let her open her own stable of criminal attorneys if that's what she wants. I don't want us to get involved in another murder trial, Frank. Now, do you get it?''

Frank laughed. "Sam, if I decided to take on Manson, there's not a damn thing you could do about it.''

Sam jumped to his feet. "Don't do this, Frank. This isn't just my opinion. I told you, things change. This firm, without exception, does not want to get involved in another high-profile criminal case.''

Very silkily Frank said, "Oh, you've had meetings? Is that it? Anything else on your mind?''

Wordlessly, Sam Bixby left the office. His scalp was cherry red. Frank knew very well that when he retired, this office would go to one of the associates, and from then on the firm would handle trusts, corporate business, wills, matters guaranteed not to alienate important clients. And the only criminals who would be free to come and go within these august walls would have clean hands, manicured nails, white collars. And their crimes would only affect hundreds, thousands, possibly millions of other people, not the simple one-on-one that he preferred. But, he told himself, things change.

Maggie arrived soon after Barbara, and they all went down to Lou Sunderman's office, where the gnomelike man looked over the documents Maggie had brought and pronounced them satisfactory.

"Very well," he said. "Our next step is to transfer the money to an escrow account and obtain a court order to keep it there until we finalize a closing agreement with Internal Revenue. If Mr. Trassi produces the appropriate documents, we should have no trouble arriving at a closing agreement; however, it will take several months, more than likely. There is no need for you to be present at our initial conference, Ms. Folsum, although your presence will be required at the closing-agreement formality. Also, I think it is in everyone's interest to have this matter kept confidential, and I shall so stipulate in the court order and at the conference. Otherwise, you may find yourself inundated with requests of various kinds, and, of course, there would be unwanted publicity which might make much of the fact that Mr. Arno has been murdered, arousing unnecessary speculation."

He stood up. They would need a separate agreement, he said, since the one Barbara had drawn up was for her, not the firm. Frank said they'd be in his office and to send it around when it was ready for Maggie to sign, and they left the little man.

Maggie stopped just inside Frank's office, staring in disbelief at Barbara. "You're getting it for us? Is it going to work?"

"Looks like it," Barbara said.

"But what if they ask me questions?" Maggie said.

"You answer." She was watching Maggie closely. "The only thing you have to conceal is that you saw Mitch or even knew he was back before Ray told you."

"You make it sound so simple," Maggie said.

"Just listen carefully to any question put to you, and answer it as briefly as you can. Don't volunteer anything and don't stray from the question. You'll be fine."

Maggie looked at Frank, who nodded.

"When we get the fingerprint report, do I give it to his lawyer, or to the police, or just to Ray himself?"

"What's your instinct about that?"

"Both the police and his lawyer," Maggie said after a moment.

"I think you should pay attention to your own instincts,"

Barbara said. "Have you accepted that if Ray's arrested, there's nothing you can do or should do immediately?"

"Yes," Maggie said. "I'd just make it worse for him if they knew so much money might be involved. I understand that." She looked miserable.

"That's exactly right," Barbara said. "As soon as we have a formal statement from Trassi that the money is legally yours, we'll go to the D.A. and I'll try to get them to drop the charges against Ray. He's in for a bad time, so is his family, and so are you. It can't be helped now. He'll be frightened. They'll tell him the penalties for various degrees of murder, for manslaughter. They'll tell him his cooperation and a statement of remorse can lighten his sentence, and they'll pretend to assume he'll be convicted."

There was a tap on the door; Lou Sunderman's secretary was there with the agreement for Maggie to sign, and she didn't stay long after that. She would reopen the inn on Sunday, she said; she had to.

Barbara let herself into the apartment quietly, then stopped with her hand on the doorknob, the door not closed all the way yet. John was talking to someone. She hadn't realized how sound traveled in their small apartment; his words were quite audible.

"Yes, vaguely familiar with it. When would you need a report?" After a moment he said, "When do you expect it to start snowing?" Then, "That's cutting it pretty fine. Look, fax me what you already have, and I'll get back to you later today."

She finished closing the door, and called out, "I'm home."

John stepped out of his office, holding the telephone. He waved. He said into the telephone, "Right. I'll call back as soon as I have a chance to look it over. Might be late this evening."

She went in to wash her hands, and when she came out of the bathroom, he was in the kitchen, peering into the refrigerator.

"Time to go out for a hamburger?" she asked.

He shook his head. "Waiting for some faxes. We have some tuna fish, or soup. Flip a coin."

They had soup, and Barbara found herself biting her tongue when she started to ask what was up. He went back into his office, and she went to hers and closed the door. But she could hear his fax machine, and a few minutes after it stopped, she heard papers rustling, a noise she couldn't identify, more rustling.

Finally she stood up and began to gather her things to return to the downtown office. John's door was open; he was bending over a map spread out on his mammoth desk.

"Leaving again," she said.

He looked up, then came around the desk and kissed her. "Short visit."

"Way it goes. I think I'll be out from under all this mess soon. Then back to routine stuff."

He nuzzled her earlobe. "I'll be waiting."

She left and as she drove to the office she thought how different they were. He could leave something he was doing in the middle of a word, then get back to it as if he had an on/off switch. If she became distracted, it took a long time to recapture whatever she had been thinking. Not his problem, she told herself, hers. When his kids were around, it would be just like that, too. He would do things with them, and return to work. On/off/on. Simple. It was as if he could turn his focus into such a narrow beam that what was immediately at hand was all that he was aware of, but her focus wanted to take in everything. Again she told herself, sharply this time: not his problem, hers.

She was in the office, reading more of the Jolin material, when Frank entered. He went to his desk and sat down.

"They arrested Ray Arno, charged him with aggravated murder."

There was nothing to say.

"Lou met me in the hall outside," Frank said after a moment. "He's getting a court order for Monday to transfer the money to an escrow account. I'll be glad to get it out of here."

There was still nothing to say. She returned to the report she had been reading about the Palmer Company and finished the last page. "Palmer probably delivers for the Mafia," she said. "Never arrested, never seriously questioned about anything, but there are rumors."

Barbara picked up the copy of Thelma Wygood's diary. She had found it hard to read, and not because of the handwriting, which was small and precise. They were still in the getting-acquainted period—early seduction period, she corrected. She read: "I told him I can't dance and he was delighted. He will teach me, he said, not in a public place where I might feel shy, but somewhere without an audience. 'But you can dance. Anyone who walks like you do, with the natural grace of a princess, was born to dance. Let me teach you....'

"June 15. I met him at the Hilton Bar, as usual, and he said he had a car waiting. There is a restaurant he wants to share with me. I said no.... He said, 'You won't heal until you have struck back, stop feeling beaten, fight back'...I had my drink and walked out. He did not follow, as I thought he might. He is clever in a reptilian way. I won't make another move until he does.

"June 17. Tonight I took a walk, then sat at a little café and had coffee. He found me there. He said he had a present for me. He left the present on the table. It's the book *Don't Get Mad, Get Even.* I think things will pick up speed soon."

The phone rang, and Barbara turned over the last page she had read and stood up as Frank answered. "Right, Ruthie, she's here." He held out the phone.

"Mr. Trassi is on the line," Ruthie said.

"Put him on."

"Ms. Holloway?"

"Yes, I'm here."

"Next Thursday afternoon at three, same place as before. I'll have the material you require."

"And I'll bring the material you need," she said. He hung up.

She let out a long breath. If anyone had told her just a couple of weeks ago how close she would be to the edge today, she would have laughed. If anyone had told her the bomb would explode and in the fallout there would be obstruction of justice, withholding evidence, trying to pull a fast one on the IRS, the real conflict of interest represented by Maggie and Ray, possible charges leveled at her, Barbara... She shook her head in bewilderment; at no time had she planned any of it to work out the way it was moving. But Thursday would see her take a step back from the abyss, not in the clear yet by any means, but not hanging by her fingernails, with any luck. She knew very well she would be at risk until after the IRS signed an agreement with Maggie, and Ray was set free by a trial of his peers or his case was thrown out of court or the cops took off their blinkers and found the killers.... But Thursday was a step in the right direction, away from disaster. She turned from the phone to see Frank regarding her; he averted his gaze swiftly.

"Thursday, three o'clock," she said. "Federal Building."

Going home, she considered the coming days and weeks. They would have Saturday and Sunday free, and next week, on Friday, maybe they could drive out to the coast together in the camper and spend the weekend after she talked to Maggie. She began to hurry.

This time when she entered the apartment, she called out instantly, "I'm home."

He came from his office. "All wrapped up?"

"Pretty much. A little tidying remains, that's all."

"Great! Want to take a trip?"

"You've been reading my mind," she said. "When, where?"

"Up to the Canadian Cascades first. It's an all-day drive, get there Sunday night, do a little work for a few days, hike, camp, then swing down through Idaho for a couple of days."

"I have a meeting I have to attend on Thursday," she said, deflated. "Could I get to an airport from where we'd be?"

"No. It was just an idea." He started to turn away, then stopped and faced her again. "Is it okay with you if I leave? You're sure that other problem is settled?"

"Of course," she said. "Just another afternoon meeting or two, and it's over for now."

"I have to make a phone call," he said, and reentered his office. She could hear every word when he told someone he'd drive up on Sunday, arrive before ten at night, and hope the weather didn't change.

One day to drive up, three or four days in Canada, a day to drive to Idaho, three more days, then a day to drive home, ten days at least. And the Staley mine was in Idaho.

15

Frank grilled dinner on the back porch that night, and he had set up a table and chairs out there. The weather was turning hot again; it was pleasant in the shade scented by a blooming jasmine vine that spiraled up a wire mesh. Thing One and Thing Two apparently considered it an adventure, having the big people eat outside. They took turns trying to climb up on the table.

"Grilled veggies are the best," Frank said contentedly. He had prepared eggplant, zucchini, brilliant orange peppers, new potatoes, tomatoes…all touched with a hint of garlic, olive oil, oregano, basil, a faint tang of lemon. There was a whole salmon with a spicy sauce.

She could do this, Barbara thought, then admitted to herself that, no, she couldn't. There were secrets about cooking food to perfection. The secrets were jealously guarded by a cabal, a guild of cooks who had sworn never to tell all.

"How did you fix on geology?" Frank asked John. He poured more wine and leaned back in his chair, in no hurry to start clearing things away and get on to dessert.

"When I was a kid," John said, as relaxed as Frank now, "one day it hit me that we were burning rocks. We had a coal stove. Most people around us did—coal was cheap, free for the taking if you knew where to go dig. Filthy fires, with clouds of sulfurous fumes, creosote in the flues, sooty dust in the house, but we burned it. What was available was low-grade bituminous coal, more junk than coal actually, but it was cheap. Anyway, I was putting coal in the stove, and it hit me, we were burning rocks. I tried to burn other kinds of rocks, until my dad made me stop, and when the fire was out, he made me clean up the mess I'd made. So I got to see the rocks that didn't burn— some had exploded—and the ashes and clinkers. I thought it was a miracle that some rocks would burn and others would explode. Magic." He laughed a low amused rumble of a chuckle. "It never occurred to me until years later that you could go out and study rocks. I just liked them and began picking them up everywhere I went."

"When I was about nine I knew I'd be an Arctic explorer," Frank said. "All that snow, the wilderness, Jack London, Byrd... That's what I wanted to do."

"When did you get sidetracked?" John asked.

Frank didn't answer immediately. He drank his wine, and put his glass down first. "I was about thirteen. Back in the thirties, a bad time, a very bad time. My father was lucky, landed a job with the Corps of Engineers, building dams in the West, and we were living in a small town in Oklahoma. Well, there was a killing and a black man was arrested, followed by a speedy trial. They hanged him. A few weeks after the execution there was another killing, same method, same everything. Same killer. I'd followed that first trial, just like everyone else, and it hadn't occurred to me that the guy might not have done it. There was a big town party the night he was hanged. Soon after the second killing, we moved on and I never found out if they got the real killer, but after that I went around picking up trials the way you picked up rocks. I didn't have any idea what I'd do with them, but I couldn't leave them alone, either."

Frank changed the subject then by asking John what he would be doing up in the Canadian Cacades. Barbara had not asked a question, refused to ask a question, but she listened intently to the answer.

"A mining company is trying to pull a fast one, get an approval during the winter months when no one can get near the mine they want to open. An environmental group got wind of it, and they've been lining up experts to investigate—a hydrologist, a forester, a biologist, geologist. I'll tramp around the hills and pick up rocks, take some pictures, look at the hole in the ground, and by January, when they hold the hearing, we'll have our reports ready to present. With any luck," he added. "If it starts snowing, and it could, we'll be limited in what we can find."

Barbara and John didn't stay long that night; he still had things to get ready, and he wanted an early start in the morning, by dawn. It was going to be a long drive.

After she saw John off on Sunday, she went back to bed, on his side, and dozed, fantasizing about being a photographer, taking the vital pictures for him, developing and printing them in her own darkroom. She drifted into sleep again.

Later she read the for-rent ads in the newspaper. All they needed was more space, she had come awake thinking, more separation while they worked, a place where words didn't carry from room to room. Four bedrooms. Not too far from the university library and the public library. Not too far from Frank's house and the courthouse, and Martin's.

Frank called Monday morning to say he would wander over to the courthouse, see what was going on; she understood he would hang out, gossiping with old pals, and learn all there was to know about the arraignment of Ray Arno. "Also," he said, "Lou tells me his escrow officer and the judge's clerk will be here around three to take charge of that loot."

She had a few things to attend to that morning. A visit

to a Realtor, another to a rental agency, and last, a book-store to buy a cookbook for beginners. There was no point in trying to start anywhere else, she had admitted to herself; she had no idea of the basics, how to make white sauce without lumps, for instance. Or what a roux was.

By the time she arrived at Frank's house, she was grumpy. The sales clerk had asked how old the child was who was showing an interest in cooking. Young teens, Barbara had said, feeling stupid. Although the cookbook was insultingly simple, it was exactly what she needed. How to make a stuffed baked potato. How to roast a chicken. How to steam vegetables. Four simple pasta sauces. Easy stuffed peppers. Just what she needed.

When Frank arrived, he was as grumpy as she was.

"Goddamn that man," he said. "They had a meeting in chambers—assistant D.A., Stover, Jane Waldman—and among them they decided there wasn't any reason not to set the trial date for December second. It was that or late February. December!"

Barbara groaned. December second! Not enough time to prepare a decent case. "Who's prosecuting?"

"One of the new guys, Craig Roxbury. It's a low-priority case: do it fast, send the guy up, or to his death, and be done with it. Speedy justice."

"Bail?"

"No."

"Shit! Stover must think there's no defense; he'll let Arno sweat it out in jail for a couple of months and then press for a plea bargain. He doesn't think it will ever get to trial."

Lou Sunderman and the escrow officer and clerk arrived; they counted money, examined bills closely, then made out receipts, which everyone signed. There were two rent-a-cop uniformed men waiting to escort the escrow officer back to his building.

"That's a relief," Frank commented when it was done. "Bailey called. If we're free around four-thirty or so, he'll drop by the house and tell us a funny story."

She drove him home. He changed clothes, back into his slouch shorts and shirt, and they sat on the back porch watching the cats try to catch butterflies.

"May be the best present I ever had," Frank said.

She had gotten him the cats for Christmas the previous year.

When Bailey arrived, Frank brought him to the back porch, and they sat in the shade, sipping wine.

"Full report from superspy Sylvia," Bailey said. He was grinning broadly. "She snagged Gilmore at Valley River Inn and practically dragged him back into the lounge, and demanded a window table, which they managed to provide, no doubt canceling someone else's reservation. I wish I had seen her, how she was dressed."

Barbara told him, and his grin broadened even more. "Isn't she something else! I'd love to know what he thought. Anyway, they reminisced about the good old days, off-Broadway theater, directors, other actors, God knows what all. Then she suddenly remembered Joe, and dinner at seven-thirty, and things like that. So she dragged Gilmore home with her. Gave him an eyeful."

He helped himself to more wine. "Gilmore didn't say anything about why he's in the area on the first day. She had Ralph drive him back to the hotel at about eleven or so. He must have done some homework then, and found out a lot about Sylvia and her past career as an actress, because he called her on Saturday and suggested lunch, and on Saturday, he talked about her acting, how great she had been, plays he had seen her in. And he confided that he's here on a mission. A famous director is looking for a good location to launch a small intimate theater, like the good old off-Broadway theaters used to be. He's had no luck finding the right place. Boulder, Austin, Taos, Ashland… now Eugene. The place has to be just right, you see, not too big, not too small, with a good sophisticated audience, a nearby university. Eugene looks good to him, so far." He laughed. "Sylvia gets all fluttery just thinking about it."

"What's the scam?" Barbara asked.

"Matching money, probably. He's being cagey. He hinted that his director, who might be Woody Allen, or maybe not, has to be kept out of preliminary searches. No names. But he'll go for whatever Gilmore recommends, if the conditions are right. What he'll probably come up with is that if Sylvia can put dough into a special account, to demonstrate strong local support, his director will more than match it, and they're in business. He was talking about *Arsenic and Old Lace* as a possible production."

"But that's so blatant! Surely no one would really go for it," Barbara said, somewhat awed.

"Honey, you've seen Sylvia," Frank said. "Doesn't she look ripe for the picking? And to dangle a part in a grand old play under her nose. If Sylvia was what he thinks she is, she'd be in his pocket by now." He looked at Bailey. "Any idea when he'll take the next step?"

"Soon, a day or two. Work it fast and get out of town, that's the way to do it. Tomorrow, next day."

"Then what?" Barbara asked.

"See, she'll put the money in the special account, which he will have access to, of course, so he can deposit the director's money. Sylvia will bring it up with her lawyer, one of her other lawyers, and if he doesn't smell a rat, she'll guide him to the rathole very gently. He'll get in touch with the bunco squad, and they'll watch Gilmore clean out the account and hightail it to the airport. They'll wait until he's ready to board the plane and grab him. He's got a record; he's done time. They'll get him and throw the book at him, a smart New York con man trying to take our own Sylvia Fenton. Meanwhile, Sylvia's having a ball! I might not be able to hold her back after this."

Sitting alone on the porch later, Frank was wishing that Barbara had accepted his invitation for dinner. He would be in there now cooking happily, knowing he had an appreciative guest, but he had no inclination to start anything for himself just yet. He was troubled more than he had realized at the time by the talk he had had with Sam Bixby. Again and again he had found himself going over Sam's words: things change. They do, he conceded.

He suspected that a good part of the problem Barbara and John were having arose from her working habits, maybe the work itself. Many people despised criminal lawyers even more than other lawyers.

Because he was methodical, Frank separated the Barbara problem into parts now. That was one. Not his business, he reminded himself. The other part was his business. Sam wanted her out.

Frank had no illusions about what would happen the day he retired, or fell over dead, whichever came first. If he was kicked out, would she leave the law again? She had left once and he had dragged her back in, but if he couldn't play that role, then what? She would still have Martin's restaurant, but that was child's play, something she would never give up, but not what she was meant to do full-time.

Then he thought, Sam was right after all: she should have her own office, her own people, her own stable of lawyers. Sam would have a fit if she brought in another murder case, especially a Cain and Abel case, which Frank knew she would do, if she could get out from under the Maggie Folsum business in time. And if she wasn't clear of that, she would do something very foolish, he felt certain. What she wouldn't do was let a lazy son of a bitch like Stover allow Ray Arno to be found guilty either by a plea or by a jury.

So there was a double-barreled shotgun getting primed for her, he thought with deepening gloom. Sam would not hesitate to fire. And the other barrel was one she might prime herself, and end up being kicked off the Folsum matter as well as out of Arno's case. And possibly face charges before the bar. She was withholding information, obstructing justice in a murder case, a serious charge. She had made it all but necessary for another attorney to commit perjury, and there was the question of how that money got into her hands. If she was asked directly, would she lie? He thought not, but, he admitted, he didn't know. If she had deliberately set out to cause herself serious trouble, maybe serious enough for disbarment, she couldn't have done a better job of it.

Or, he thought bleakly, had she done it not altogether consciously to achieve exactly that? The idea filled him with such disquiet that abruptly he stood up, too abruptly; for a moment the porch floor tilted. He didn't move until it was stable again, then shakily he reentered his house.

At that moment Barbara was scrubbing out a skillet for the third time. "Goddamn it," she muttered. "You can make a goddamn pancake, for Christ's sake!" But she couldn't. No matter what she did, they stuck to the skillet. She went back to the recipe: *If the batter is too thin, thicken it with a little flour.* She had done that and ended up with what looked like German pancakes, thick ugly things that she couldn't roll, no matter how carefully she tried. If she followed the recipe to the letter, the batter looked like cream and stuck to the skillet. The illustration was of crepes filled with a spinach-ricotta mixture. She washed out the bowl and started over. The batter looked like cream. "Butter the fucking skillet.'' She buttered it, then added just a little more, then poured in some batter. ''Don't stick, damn you!'' It stuck to the skillet.

She flooded the bowl with water to dilute the rest of the batter in order to pour it down the drain, scrubbed the skillet one more time, and opened a can of soup.

16

Over the next two days Barbara looked at rental properties, then in desperation at houses and townhouses and condos for sale. Wrong place, wrong room arrangement, especially wrong price.

On Thursday she and Frank prepared to go to the Federal Building for the meeting with the IRS representative. Barbara tore off the top hundred or so pages of printouts, and the last fifty, which she returned to the safe.

At the Federal Building they were kept waiting in a desolate room with wooden chairs occupied by dejected-looking people awaiting their turn with auditors, no doubt. Mr. Chenowith would be with them in a minute, the woman behind the information counter said, but he would be with them only when the entire party had gathered, they understood. Trassi was late. Lou Sunderman looked quite happy.

At ten minutes past two, Trassi hurried in, carrying a suitcase, and he looked as if someone had been tramping on his corns. He nodded curtly to Barbara and did not offer to shake hands with Sunderman or Frank when she introduced them. A door opened and a tall thin man appeared.

"Good afternoon, Lou," he said. "Thomas Chenowith." He shook hands all around as they introduced themselves.

"Please come in." The room he showed them to was marginally less desolate than the anteroom. In here was a round, much-scarred wooden table and too many chairs and nothing else.

After they were seated under a harsh white light, Chenowith said genially, "Now, what can I do for you?"

"Well, Thomas," Lou Sunderman said, "we have a pretty little tax situation that needs clarification." He outlined the situation as he drew papers from his briefcase. "So the money is in the escrow company's keeping, under court order. But all we really need is a closing agreement, and we'll be out of your hair." He smiled, but Chenowith's geniality had vanished; he appeared to be battling with a pain. "Here I have Ms. Folsum's agreement with Ms. Holloway...." He described the documents as he pushed them across the table to Chenowith, who did not touch them. "I believe Mr. Trassi has a statement to add to my account," Lou said.

"My statement, as you insist on calling it, is quite simple," Trassi said coldly. He took a paper from his coat pocket and read from it. "On July nineteenth I happened to meet Mitch Arno in the outer office of the Palmer Company in New York City. I was there on business, as he was. He overheard Mr. Palmer bidding me a safe trip to Oregon, and approached me and drew me aside. He asked if he could retain me for a private matter he was concerned about. I found that I could accommodate him, and I did. I asked one of the girls in Mr. Palmer's office to type out a simple agreement between Mitch Arno and myself to the effect that he would deliver into my hands on July twenty-fifth a suitcase containing valuables, which was the property of his ex-wife, Margaret Folsum.

"I met him as planned in Portland, and he gave me the suitcase and told me again that it belonged to his ex-wife and that I should give it to her and inform her that he would be there in time for his daughter's birthday. As soon as I delivered the suitcase, my duties to him would be concluded, and he would open the suitcase himself at the proper time."

"Why didn't he just deliver it himself?"

"He said he had to deliver an automobile to an out-of-the-way place and would then take a bus back to Portland, where he would rent a car. Evidently he was uncomfortable carrying anything of value on a public bus."

"Did he at any time say what the valuables were?"

"Yes. He said it was a large sum of money, long overdue."

"No more than that, it was overdue?"

Trassi said impatiently, "He said a great deal, but what pertains is that he had not paid his ex-wife for child support over the years, his children were now of college age, and the money was theirs. Also he wanted to regain the favor of his father."

Chenowith remained impassive, but now and again his face twitched in a way that suggested an ulcer was paining him and he was being brave about it. "When did you deliver the money?"

"Not as quickly as I desired," Trassi said. "My other business in Portland took longer than I had anticipated, and I was still in the city on Friday, August second. I called Ms. Folsum to make an appointment for Saturday or Sunday, but the person who answered the phone said she would not be available until Monday or Tuesday. So I postponed going to Ms. Folsum's inn. On Monday, August fifth, I finally drove to the coast, but no one answered my phone calls all evening. On Tuesday, I was horrified to learn that hoodlums had vandalized her inn severely, and when I finally saw her and tried to deliver the suitcase, she was too harried and distraught to talk to me. The following day she referred me to her legal counsel, Ms. Holloway. A day or so later I contacted Ms. Holloway and concluded my legal obligation to Mitch Arno." He hesitated a moment, then passed the statement over to Chenowith.

If she had an Oscar, Barbara thought, she'd hand it over

on the spot. Instead, she said, "I put it in a safe-deposit box immediately and left it there until I could talk to my client and decide what the legality of the situation was. We decided to do nothing until Mitch turned up to explain it all. After we learned of his death, I consulted with our tax attorney, Mr. Sunderman, and subsequently turned the matter over to him."

His ulcer was hitting him again, Barbara thought sympathetically, when Chenowith looked at Lou Sunderman.

"I, of course," Sunderman said, "realized that Ms. Holloway couldn't simply release the money to her client, not without a closing agreement from the Internal Revenue Service, even though the money was legally hers from the time Mitch Arno handed it to Mr. Trassi, who was acting as his agent. Mr. Trassi kindly agreed to cooperate, to furnish Mitch Arno's address and other information that would be pertinent to settling this matter. Hence this meeting."

"You have that information regarding Mitch Arno?" Chenowith asked Trassi.

"It's all in here," Trassi said, sliding a file folder across the table.

"Gentlemen," Barbara said then, "since Mr. Sunderman is Ms. Folsum's counsel of record in this matter, if you have no further need for my presence, I do have other business to attend to."

"We'll be in touch with you," Chenowith said.

"Before you leave," Lou Sunderman said. "One more little item. I request that this meeting be held in confidence, by court order, if necessary, until the matter is settled conclusively."

Trassi nodded, and after a moment Chenowith did also. "I'll get an order," Chenowith said, then looked at Barbara and Frank in turn. "You both agree to hold this meeting in confidence pending such an order?"

They said they did. "With one exception," Barbara said.

"As an officer of the court, it's my duty to report this matter to the district attorney, since it could be of material interest as that office investigates the death of Mitch Arno. The district attorney will, of course, be under the same court order regarding confidentiality as the rest of us."

For a moment it appeared that Trassi might turn into a leaper before their eyes. His body tensed and his expression was disbelieving and furious. She met his gaze coolly. "If I don't, Mr. Chenowith will. Not to disclose a matter of this significance could be construed as obstruction of justice."

"The district attorney's name will be added to the restraining order," Chenowith said.

Barbara and Frank stood up and walked out.

She had to fight an impulse to hop, skip, and jump her way through the anteroom toward the outside door.

At the door, they stopped when Trassi called out her name. "Outside," he snapped. He was carrying the suitcase.

They stepped out, away from the door, and she handed him the briefcase, which he put inside his suitcase, and without a word turned and reentered the building.

"Round one," she said in a low voice.

Back at the office they found Bailey waiting for them. "Sylvia opened the account at ten," he said. "They went out for a cup of coffee. At twelve Gilmore cleaned out the account. The vice president was in on it, and he called bunco. They nabbed him at the airport, and he's in the county jail. He called his lawyer. Another funny coincidence, happens his lawyer is named Trassi, who gave him holy hell and hung up on him."

Frank nodded. "They won't let him stay in jail long, too risky. Someone will show up and bail him out."

"Trassi is scurrying," Bailey said. "Canceled a flight out of town, making a lot of phone calls. Mad as hell."

"Guess Gilmore knows how Adam felt," Frank said. "Just couldn't resist that one little bite, and here comes the sky down on his head."

He would jump bail, Barbara thought, and there would be an arrest warrant issued. He was of no further use to Palmer, Trassi, any of them. He would go to jail or be a fugitive. "I wonder how long it will be before he realizes his life isn't worth very much," she said.

Frank shrugged. "You want some dinner tonight?"

"Love it, but I might be a little late, after John calls at seven or seven-thirty. And I have to set up a meeting with the D.A. Maybe for Monday."

"You going out to Maggie's place tomorrow?" Frank asked.

She nodded. "I might stay over a night or two, walk out some kinks."

She and Maggie talked in Maggie's bed-sitting-room. Maggie gazed out the windows at the ocean as Barbara recounted the meeting with the IRS. "Do you think they'll accept that story?" she asked when Barbara finished.

"Hope so. No real reason for them not to."

Maggie turned to Barbara then. "Is it extortion or black-mail? You're selling them the printouts, aren't you?" She looked pinched and cold, and years older than she had before. "I've been thinking a lot about this and I've decided I can't go along. I can't start my kids out in life with dirty money. I've been tempted before; there are opportunities for a single woman, as you probably know, but never quite so much money." She laughed, a bitter, harsh sound. "I dreamed about what all we could do with so much money, what it would mean, then I'd wake up and wonder how I could explain it if they ever ask hard questions. Give the printouts to their owner, get rid of the money. I don't care what you do with it.'' She stood up and crossed her arms over her breasts. ''Just don't keep tempting me with it.''

Startled, Barbara shook her head. ''I want you to believe me when I say this. I'm not doing anything I'm ashamed of or that would shame you.'' Maggie was like a statue, remote and unreachable. ''Sit down, Maggie. It's an ugly story, and you have to promise me that you won't reveal it to anyone now, possibly never.''

''I can't make such a promise in the dark,'' Maggie said.

''If you trust me, you can.''

For a long time Maggie didn't move; her gaze on Barbara's face was intent, searching. Finally she sat down. ''All right.''

''I can't tell you names,'' Barbara said then. ''I'm sworn to secrecy. But I'll give you the rest of the story. Mitch was working for a company that acted as a go-between in serious industrial espionage....'' She told it briefly, leaving out only the names. Maggie turned very pale when Barbara said that Mitch had killed at least three people. ''Company A authorized me to turn the bogus program over to Company B and to keep the money. That's what I'm doing. What I've done. The money is yours, or will be in a few months.''

''And everyone's letting it go at that?'' Maggie asked incredulously.

''No,'' Barbara said. ''One day I will tell you the rest. When Ray Arno is free, exonerated, and this is really all over, then I'll tell you everything.''

''Is he going to be free?'' Maggie asked. ''His lawyer doesn't believe that.''

''He's going to be free,'' Barbara said.

Maggie continued to study her face, and finally nodded. Barbara told her about the meeting being arranged for

Monday with the district attorney, and they started going over the questions that might come up.

When they were done, Maggie said, "Would you like to see the rest of the inn, restored more or less to normal?"

It was beautifully furnished, beautifully decorated, with Laurence's flower pictures serving as palettes for each room.

"He did a good job," Barbara said in the Sunflower Room, where a small couch and two chairs were covered in a rich umber fabric, the curtains were pale yellow, and drapes a deeper golden yellow. Red-brown cushions on the couch, and one on each twin bed finished the scheme. Perfect.

"He's good at many things," Maggie said. "There's an art walk in Portland this weekend, or he'd be at my elbow. He keeps hovering," she said with a sigh.

Barbara gave her a swift glance.

"You might as well ask," Maggie said. "Everyone else does. Why don't I marry him?"

"Do you answer?"

"Sometimes. See, the problem is, I can't afford him. I have my daughters to consider first. Maybe when they're both done with school, if he's still around, if he's grown up yet, maybe then. He doesn't really want to be married. We have an…arrangement, but if he had a free ride, he'd take it. He really thinks the world owes him that much." She gave the lovely room a last glance and turned toward the door. "I told him I'm serious, that he has to start paying rent or get out, and he took off in a temper. He might stay away for days, weeks, even months, and all the time he's gone, I doubt he'll give me a thought. When he's here, he's like my shadow. That's how it is."

After leaving Maggie, Barbara drove north on 101, through Newport, nearly to Yachats, where she had managed to book a room, on the wrong side of the highway and in a simple motel, but sufficient. She checked in and found no surprises. Then she went down to the beach.

Later, sitting on a massive driftwood log, she watched the play of light on the ocean as the sun set. No flamboyant sunsets here, not like in Hawaii or Florida, or even out on the desert; the sun just rode its path down to the horizon, turning redder as it sank, until it was an orange globe that quietly dipped into the sea and the afterglow turned violet and very gradually darkened.

She was thinking of the women in this affair: Maggie, who was so clear-eyed about what she had to do, and strong enough to do it. And Sylvia, who knew the kind of world she wanted to live in and had arranged it to suit herself. Even Thelma Wygood had done what she had to do from her earliest years.

If she were as clear-eyed as Maggie or Sylvia or even poor Thelma Wygood, she would know what she had to do, but she wanted two mutually antagonistic things: she wanted to live with John and be his love, and she wanted freedom to work her own hours in her own space.

Abruptly, she stood up to climb the trail back to the highway, then return to the motel, and in a little while drive out somewhere for dinner. Tomorrow, she promised herself, tomorrow she would think more clearly.

Tomorrow she would think of the implications of what John had said, that he hated her work. She had tried to think through that many times and had always been distracted by something or other. Tomorrow, she promised again, and started up the trail.

17

When Barbara went home on Sunday, she listened to the phone messages, one from Frank, one from Bailey. She called Frank.

"Want some dinner?" he asked.

She said sure, and then sat gazing at the apartment. It looked like a bachelor's pad. Her good chair and a lamp were the only possessions of hers in sight. Everything else she owned was put away in her little office or in the bedroom; she felt like an intruder here. "A room of one's own," she said under her breath. Then, *an apartment of one's own.* She jumped up and hurried to her office to find some photocopies of apartments and houses one of the real estate people had given her. She stared at the one she had been looking for.

"Rose Garden Apartments, lovely two-bedroom apartments in three groups of twelve units, each group with its own swimming pool. Easy access to the bike trail by the river. Walking distance to town. Ready for occupancy October first..."

That evening, while Frank prepared dinner, she explained. "See, this way we'll have four bedrooms, and two baths. Plenty of space to spread out our stuff, for both of us to work at home. And when his kids come, they'll fit, too."

"You signed up for two apartments?"

"One definitely, one conditionally." She added, "I can't breathe in our apartment. Even if we could divvy up the space equally, it's too small. I can't move in it. You know as well as I do that in December I'm going to need breathing room."

He knew. "I say it's a grand idea." He didn't ask the next question, the one she had been asking herself ever since signing the rental agreement: What if John hated the idea?

As Frank sliced tomatoes, he thought that maybe she had found a fine solution to a problem that would only have grown worse. Two adjoining apartments, not the usual mode for live-together lovers, but it would do. And he decided to postpone mentioning his reason in asking her over tonight. He had planned to bring up the idea of her forming her own group, getting her own office space, a secretary, the whole works, now, before she found herself tangled in a mare's nest in December. He didn't believe any more than she did that the D.A. would drop the charges against Ray, and he was more than a little worried about how she planned to work it later.

"I've got a long list for Bailey to start on," Barbara said, "but I wasn't sure where to tell him to meet me. Here?"

"You know here," Frank said.

It was a bad night; she alternated from imagining John in a mine he had declared unsafe, to stewing about how to tell him she wanted separate apartments, to refusing to look down as she balanced on a tightrope across a bottomless chasm....

By nine in the morning, she was at Frank's house ready for Bailey, aware that her father had noted the effects of not enough sleep.

"Okay," she said briskly as Bailey stirred sugar into coffee. "Let's go over some of the things I want us to follow up on.'' Bailey nodded and took out his notebook; she opened her legal pad, and Frank leaned back in his chair to listen.

Later, she put down her pen. ''That's for openers,'' she said. Bailey was still writing; she waited for him to finish, then said soberly, ''I've been stewing about the lead pipe and holder. I want to get them to the New Orleans police, along with the Gary Belmont stuff.''

Bailey scowled. Ignoring that, she continued, ''The stuff should be packaged up and mailed to the cops with a New Orleans postmark. And you should call the cops with an anonymous tip—you saw Belmont get in a Lexus coupe with this guy who could have been his brother, they were so alike.''

Bailey's scowl was ferocious. ''You want me to fly down to New Orleans with a lead pipe in my hip pocket!''

''I didn't think it would be that easy,'' she said. ''But you're the expert. If you think that would work...''

He turned his glare toward Frank, who simply shrugged.

''We handled the license and other items,'' Barbara murmured. ''I suppose it would be a good idea to clean off our prints.''

He didn't even bother to respond, just gave her a murderous look.

She glanced at Frank. ''Anything else?''

''Maybe,'' he said. ''I've been thinking about something you said the other day, that Gilmore's life might not be worth much these days. They'll set bail this morning, more than likely, and he'll be out and gone. But he's had time to consider his ways, I suspect. It might be that if someone like my old friend Carter Heilbronner got a tip that Gilmore knows something about big-time espionage, carrying illegal stuff around the country, or anything like that, the FBI might get in touch with him. They could make a deal.

Course, we wouldn't know anything about it; they play it too close. But it could be a way to get to Palmer.''

Barbara nodded thoughtfully. Then she said, ''But we would know. They would want Sylvia to drop the charges against Gilmore. They'd have to guarantee him that much up front, wouldn't they?''

Bailey snorted. ''Sylvia working with the FBI! Jeez, where will it all end?''

''Is Gilmore smart enough not to bring in the Major-Wygood deal and her murder?'' Frank asked. ''Would he have anything else to give them? That's the question.''

They all thought about it. Finally Barbara said, ''I doubt that he would say anything that would implicate him in a murder, not Wygood's, or Mitch's, either. He's worked for Palmer a long time, twelve years or longer. There must be a lot of things he could talk about.'' She frowned; then, thinking out loud, she said, ''Gilmore could become a threat to Palmer; he's faced with a prison term and he might cut a deal with the state or the feds. He'll be a fugitive, a convict, or hidden away in a witness-protection safe house; in any event, no longer an asset. I wonder if Palmer would be worried enough to want him removed? If so, when? My guess is, sooner rather than later. Later he might be whisked away out of sight. Heilbronner isn't likely to put a lot of effort into a tip without any foundation, but if Gilmore got knocked off and he has the tip in mind, he might then stir a finger and poke around.''

She looked up at Frank, who was frowning also; he nodded. ''Or Gilmore could go to ground and hide out for the next few years,'' he said, ''which also might make Heilbronner curious about Palmer.''

Abruptly she stood up. ''Mind if I put on some more coffee?'' she asked. It had occurred to her that John would consider this conversation evil, that this was what he hated about what she did. She, Frank, and Bailey were looking at the situation dispassionately, knowing a man's life might be at risk but also knowing that if it was, the machinery was already in place, the lever already pulled. No one's past could be undone. Gilmore's past had made it impossible for him to walk away from a soft touch like Sylvia; he had not resisted the apple. Although he couldn't have known he was leading Thelma Wygood to her death, he had done nothing about it after the fact, except take on yet another role, well aware that his boss had had Mitch Arno killed. But, Barbara thought bleakly, none of this would be understandable for John, for others like him. And perhaps, she thought then, those others were right, after all. How guilty would she feel if Gilmore got killed because she baited a trap he found irresistible?

"Does he have enough sense to know that maybe his only chance is to cooperate with the FBI?" she said, returning to the table.

"A con man gets pretty good at figuring the odds," Frank commented.

She recalled Gilmore's implicit threat to Maggie's children; he had known the threat was real, or could be made real. "Can you tip off Heilbronner in such a way that he won't come sniffing around us?"

Frank said to leave that part to him.

They discussed some of the points Barbara had raised earlier, and afterward Bailey and Frank agreed on a time for him to pick up the lead pipe and the Belmont material.

"Just give me the fucking stuff. I'll think of something," Bailey said.

Barbara and Frank both raised their eyebrows; Bailey never used such language.

18

Craig Roxbury was not intimidating in any way, she decided when they met on Monday. Not the district attorney, just an underling, the one who would prosecute Ray Arno, he was clearly uncomfortable here in Frank's office, and clearly suspicious. She knew a good bit about him already: thirty-one, divorced, no children, in town less than a year, after three years in the Indianapolis district attorney's office. Methodical and unimaginative, a good worker, conscientious and thoroughly unremarkable, the kind of man who would pass through life leaving little trace. He had dark brown hair cut short and neat, and a clean, freshly shaven appearance. His hands were large and rough-looking, the hands of a man who had worked at hard labor for many years, which fitted the biography she had read. He had worked his way through school as a carpenter's helper. He seemed very earnest.

After the introductions, they all sat down in the visitors' end of Frank's office, Maggie on the couch by Frank, Barbara and Roxbury in the facing chairs. Barbara leaned back and said, ''Thanks for agreeing to come, Mr. Roxbury. We really wanted to keep this as informal as possible, but we feel that we have information that may prove vital to your investigation of the murder of Mitch Arno. As you are aware, Ms. Folsum and Arno were married many years ago....''

His suspicious glance toward Maggie said that indeed he

was aware. Barbara continued, starting with the Monday after Maggie's big party, repeating the same story Trassi had told.

She smiled pleasantly at him when she concluded; his face had turned a dull red, and for a time he seemed speechless.

"I have copies of all the documents—"

"Just hold it!" Roxbury finally blurted. "Back up! You've known about this for weeks! Why haven't you mentioned it before?"

"Mr. Roxbury," she said gently, "please. If I had called your office and said I happened to have a suitcase of money that came from Mitch Arno, where would it be now?" She shook her head. "I had no idea you'd jump the gun and arrest the first suspect you got your sights on, and meanwhile, we handled this matter in a timely and orderly manner. I am prepared to deliver copies of all the documents to you at this time. Mr. Chenowith at Internal Revenue handled it for the government; Mr. Trassi acted on Mitch Arno's behalf. I'm sure that both of them will be happy to answer any questions you may have."

"I have questions, all right," he snapped, and began barking them at Maggie, the same questions Barbara had predicted he would ask. Maggie answered them all without hesitation.

Then Barbara handed the file folder to him. "Of course, we'll be available to answer any questions; however, I have advised my client to talk to you only in my presence."

"Why?" he muttered. "If it's all as aboveboard as you say, what's she got to hide?"

Barbara laughed. "Goes with the turf, Mr. Roxbury." She sobered again. "After you've discussed this at the office, and talked with the other principals, I expect you'll agree that you arrested the wrong man. Obviously, others learned that Mitch Arno was delivering a large sum of money in cash to his ex-wife. No one here knew it, but Arno's colleagues, his friends, or even his enemies could well have found out.''

Roxbury's eyes narrowed, and abruptly he stood up. ''We never suggested he did it for money,'' he snapped. ''If what you're telling me checks out, it doesn't make a damn bit of difference in our case. We'll be in touch.''

Frank escorted him from the office. As soon as the door closed behind them, Maggie said in a low voice, ''You did it! They'll have to investigate those people now! They'll see that they're the ones with a reason to kill Mitch!''

''Maybe,'' Barbara said.

''Can't I tell the family anything?'' Maggie asked. ''Just a hint that things will work out?''

''They know I'm trying to get back support payments. Don't breathe a word more than that,'' Barbara said sharply. ''For one thing, it's a court order and you could be held in contempt. But more important, we might need it later. If word leaks, I want to know who leaked it. If it leaks from the D.A.'s office, it will say a lot about how seriously they're taking this.'' She stopped; it was too complex to explain. If a little came out now, a little in a week or two, then a full disclosure, it might mean they intended to release Ray and go after persons unknown. If a rumor of unspecified wealth started to float around, it could mean they wanted to defuse it now, not have a surprise later. If they sat tight and nothing leaked, it could mean they really didn't consider it important to their case and would be prepared to deal with it later. Or...

She grinned at Maggie and spread her hands. ''Anyway, from what I hear about the Arno family, it's a real talk machine set full speed ahead all the time. How long would it be a family secret?''

Reluctantly Maggie accepted that.

After Maggie left, and Frank was behind his desk again,

his expression turned grim. "They won't buy it," he said flatly.

"I know. Roxbury thinks it's chalk dust."

"Well, he thinks you're trying to pull a fast one."

Alone later, he brooded about Roxbury. He had sounded very sure of himself when he declared the new development wouldn't make a damn bit of difference in his case. Frank had never met Ray, or any of the Arnos, and for the first time he wondered if Barbara had come to a conclusion prematurely.

By forcing Trassi's statement, Barbara had effectively given Mitch Arno an alibi for the murders of Thelma Wygood and the other Palmer courier in Florida, as well as for Gary Belmont's murder in New Orleans. Defending Cain, he mused, but what about the brother? They knew Mitch was a killer. How did they know his brother was not?

You never know for sure, he told himself sharply. So you risk a lot, take chances; that had been his life, too. But then he thought, this was different. He wasn't risking anything these days. He no longer had a damn thing to lose, he thought, surveying his office bleakly, but, Christ, she was way out there and the limb was fragile.

He became very still, remembering the laughter and happiness in her voice when she reported in from Mexico, from New York, from Denver; the sparkle in her eyes when they came home, the lightness of her step. And he wondered, had he acted for her sake when he asked her to come back years ago, or for his own? She had left once, packed her few things, cleaned out her bank account, and had taken off for parts unknown. And he had brought her back. For good or evil? It was one thing to walk because you decided to go that route, but quite a different matter to be forced out, to leave in disgrace. Or would that hidden engine that drove her think it was a pretty good trade-off? He leaned back in his chair with his eyes closed and cursed his helplessness, aware that she had to fight this battle alone.

19

All Monday evening Barbara pretended she was not listening for the phone to ring, and she learned how to make chicken breasts with green chilies. The sauce looked strange, but it tasted good.

Tuesday she didn't leave the apartment and pretended she was not listening for the phone. When it did ring, it was Bailey. He and Hannah were going to take a trip, he practically snarled; he would bill her for it. She didn't press him for details, but she thought, New Orleans in August, yuck.

She browsed through the children's cookbook for a few minutes, then began to walk.

He should be out of the mine by now. He should be back somewhere with a telephone handy. He should have called by now.

His call came at eight. "Hi," he said softly. "God, I've missed you."

She sank down into a chair. "Me, too. Where are you?"

"Boise. We just pulled in half an hour ago. I'll be out of here at dawn, home at eight or nine. Unless there's heavy traffic or something. If there is, I'll fly over it."

"Don't drive too fast. No, scratch that. Drive like hell."

He laughed.

After they hung up, she continued to sit with her hand on the phone, her eyes closed hard. Finally she roused. "And that's how it is, kiddo," she said softly.

* * *

He got home at eight-thirty Wednesday night. They didn't bother to eat, just tumbled into bed, and got up at midnight to scrounge for food, then back to bed.

On Thursday he told her the Staley mine was closed for good. "I dragged a couple of commissioners down with me and scared the shit out of them."

Then he said, "Up in the Canadian Cascades, I had plenty of time to think. It's beautiful country up there; we'll go back one day. I'd like to show you. Anyway, I got to thinking, what if you asked me to give up little jaunts like that, take up teaching or something instead. In time, a long time probably, but in time, after the honeymoon wore off and every day I had to face another classroom of kids who'd rather be out playing, or fucking their heads off, or something else, I'd come to resent my decision and blame the one I decided was responsible."

She looked at him in dismay. "I wouldn't ask you to give it up. You can't believe I'd ask that."

"No, I can't. But isn't that what I've been asking you to do? Give up the biggest part of your life? I don't know. If I have been, by implication or outright, I can't tell. If I have been, I'm sorry."

"But you said you hate what I do."

"What you get involved in, the people who might be dangerous, the risks you take. I'm afraid for you, and jealous of that part of your life because it takes you away from me. Out there in the wild I realized I'm a lousy test pilot's spouse."

She put her finger on his lips. "I have to show you something," she said. "We'll drive part of the way, then walk a little. Okay?"

She drove to the riverfront park, where they left the car and walked across the grass to the trail that followed the river for many miles. It was not crowded at one in the afternoon. Blackberry brambles were lush and weighted down with fruit on one side of the trail; the ground sloped to the flashing, sparkling river on the other.

"No hint about where we're going?" he asked.

"Not even a hint. Remember the great blue heron we saw that first day?"

He nodded; his hand tightened on hers.

After a walk of several minutes, she pointed to a trail through the brambles. "Up there," she said. It was not a very steep ascent; when they emerged, the Rose Garden was in front of them. She led him through it, and out the far side, past hundreds of blooming rose bushes; the air was heavy with perfume.

They crossed a street and went up several stairs, and before them was the Rose Garden Apartments complex. John looked at her curiously, but she didn't explain yet.

The apartments were laid out in three groups; a landscaping crew was at work putting down sod, planting bushes, some balled and burlapped trees. She headed for the apartments nearest the river. Four units of two apartments each faced one another across a courtyard with a swimming pool. Two more double units one floor up spanned the distance between them at the ends, enclosing the whole. She went to two doors, one leading to stairs, the other to the interior space between the apartments on the lower level. She unlocked the door to the stairs and they went up to a small landing with two facing doors, both locked. She opened the apartment to their right and led him inside to a short hallway with a closet on one side and an open door to the first bedroom on the other. Another short hallway led to the bathroom. Straight through was a hallway to the living room on the right and the kitchen on the left, open space now, with folding doors pushed all the way back. Beyond the kitchen was the door to the second bedroom. It was bright and airy throughout.

"What do you think?" she asked. He had been absolutely silent.

"I don't know what I'm supposed to think," he said in a curiously flat voice. "Small?"

"Yes, it is. But watch." Now she led him back out the way they had entered, and unlocked the second apartment, a mirror image of the first one.

She watched him walk through the rooms; in the kitchen he turned to face her. "Two of them! My God, you're a genius! Two apartments side by side. Four bedrooms!" He was coming toward her as he spoke; he took her in his arms and held her, kissed her. "I had decided to rent an office and clear out my stuff, so there'd be room to move. This is a hell of a lot better. Two apartments!" He began to laugh, and she felt weak with relief.

Ray

20

Barbara smiled as she watched Shelley McGinnis walk toward her table in the Ambrosia Restaurant. Shelley had to be aware that eyes turned to follow her progress, but she gave no indication of it. She had grown prettier than ever in the months since she had moved to California in pursuit of a job; maturity, sadness, distress, were all becoming to her, although her outfit suggested anything but maturity. She was dressed in a pink raincoat and pink high-heeled boots. Her smile was radiant, belying her unhappiness at not finding a job here in Eugene.

"Hi," Barbara said when the younger woman drew near. "You look terrific, as usual."

"Hi. Bill keeps complaining about how gray the weather is, how miserable everything is, so I just brought bright and cheerful clothes this time. I have a yellow jacket that looks like sunshine. How are you?"

"Not bad." Barbara had talked to Bill Spassero quite a few times during the past months, just in passing usually, and she knew how miserable he was; he had made no secret of it. She wondered how many miles the two had traveled going back and forth, taking turns visiting, and how many triple-digit phone bills each had paid. "Let's order and then talk," she said. "Okay?"

"Sure." Shelley took off her raincoat to reveal a bright pink knit dress. "See?" she said complacently. Her cheeks matched the color almost exactly. Frank called her the golden-haired pink fairy princess, and that was just about right.

They ordered soup and salad, and then, waiting for it, Barbara asked what work she was doing now.

"I'm researching rights-of-way," Shelley said mournfully. "A lot of them. Hundreds and hundreds."

"Sam Bixby was an idiot not to take you on permanently."

"Well, you know. He interviewed me and asked me point-blank if I had any interest in trusts and corporate law, and I had to tell him no. He said the firm won't be handling any criminal cases in the future, and that was that."

"He said that?" Barbara asked, surprised. Shelley had not told her anything about the interview, which had taken place while Barbara and John were in Mexico. Shelley had worked as an intern for the firm for a year; most of the work had been done for Barbara.

"I thought you knew. He said the day Mr. Holloway retires, that's the last day they'll be associated with a criminal lawyer."

Barbara nodded. "I knew, but I didn't realize he was telling people that." The waitress brought crusty bread and herb butter. Barbara let Shelley carry the conversation until they finished eating and were ready for coffee.

Finally, with espressos before them, Barbara said, "I have an ulterior motive, as you probably guessed." Shelley leaned forward. "I'm mixed up in something that's going to be pretty messy in a few weeks, and I need help. But it wouldn't be permanent."

"I'll take it," Shelley said.

"Not so fast." Barbara laughed. "Can you get a leave of absence? Would it jeopardize your job?"

"I don't give a damn about my job! Rights-of-way! Good heavens! I'll take whatever you have."

"You have to know a little bit more before you make a

decision. Just a few highlights for now, and then let's talk again before you fly back to Sacramento. Okay?''

Shelley's expression said she had decided already, but she nodded.

"Okay. I'm in a conflict-of-interest dilemma...." Barbara gave her no more than a hint of the two overlapping cases, watching Shelley's face as she talked. Shelley was extremely intelligent, as she had proved during her internship, but she had little real experience yet; Barbara was uncertain how much of what she was relating needed more explanation. "So if you were on the scene, applying for jobs again, and sitting in on a couple of trials, then getting interested in this one, you would be in a perfect position to be my second counsel and fill me in on what you saw and heard. You would be doing it on your own, not in my employ, although there's no law that says you can't chat about things."

"I'll take it," Shelley said firmly.

They made a date for Shelley to visit Barbara's new apartment on Monday. "It has to be kept completely confidential," Barbara said; they both knew she was talking about Bill Spassero, who was in the public defender's office.

When they left the restaurant, the rain was pelting down; Barbara felt shabby next to the sparkling pink of Shelley's outfit. She laughed when Shelley opened an umbrella, transparent, with golden sunflowers hanging in space, aglow in the rain.

At home, she hung up her raincoat on the coat tree they had installed on the upper landing, then looked in on John, who grinned and waved, blew her a kiss. He liked for her to look in on him, and he never came to her office to do the same. His living room held his massive desk, a dining table and chairs, the television, and two easy chairs. They cooked in his kitchen, and she used hers to continue her lessons.

She went through the other door, past their bedroom, past her living room with reading chairs and lamps and bookcases, past her kitchen, and into her office, where no sound he made ever penetrated. She closed her door and stood at the window, gazing out through the trees, which looked ghostly in the rain, at the river, thinking about what Sam Bixby had told Shelley.

The next night at Frank's table, she brought it up when they were lingering over coffee. "Dad," she said hesitantly, "would you consider it abandonment if I struck out on my own?"

He blinked. "What do you mean?"

"I talked it over with John last night, and we both think I should have my own offices and stop using yours. It would be a stretch financially at first, but I think in time it would work out. You know how happy that would make Sam."

"Has he been at you again?"

"No. But to be truthful, I'm not very comfortable using your office space all the time. I can't stand the accusing look Patsy gives me."

Frank laughed. "I think it's a grand idea." Thoughtfully he said, "Patsy's problem is boredom. I've been thinking how good she'd be at organizing some of my book, retyping parts of it, proofreading it for me. It's just about ready to send off, and I keep finding reasons not to do the grunge work that needs doing. She'd love it." He eyed John diffidently. "You read it. What would you think about a title like *The Zen of Cross-examination?*"

They talked about the book he had been writing for the past five years, and Barbara kept giving him suspicious looks, unable to shake the feeling that somehow she had done what he had planned for her to do all along.

On Monday when Shelley arrived at the apartment, they went into Barbara's office and closed the door, and Shelley said she most definitely wanted the job.

"The situation has changed," Barbara said. Shelley's bright expression dimmed, and she looked near tears. "You see," Barbara said, "I'm going to start my own firm. Do you want a permanent job? As permanent as mine will be, anyway."

Shelley did not jump up and down, but it was obvious that she was pulling in unsuspected reserves of self-control. "Do I want it! Does an angel want wings! You don't have to pay me anything!"

"Well, let's start." Barbara had not told her anything in detail; now she did, starting with Maggie's seduction and abandonment, bringing it all up to date. "So Gilmore's dropped out of sight. Sylvia was approached by the FBI to drop charges, which she did, of course. Bailey got the lead pipe and the Belmont material down to the New Orleans police; nothing I have to do there. The D.A. decided the money is a side issue, and Ray's trial will start on December second. Between now and the trial date, you'll have to read every scrap I have—there's a ton of stuff—and become familiar with every detail so you'll know what to watch and listen for at the trial. But you won't be hired officially until the day of the closing agreement, when I discharge my obligation to Maggie. I can't cut her loose until I know that business is over and done with, and I don't dare show my face at the trial. I don't want even a suspicion of conflict of interest to arise, so it's going to be on your shoulders."

She scowled and added, "Meanwhile, Stover's been

frightening the Arnos with talk of the death penalty, as opposed to copping a plea for a lesser offense.''

Shelley had been making notes as Barbara talked. She looked up. ''What about the fingerprints Bailey lifted? Isn't anyone chasing down those two men?''

''Nope. It's the one-armed-man syndrome. Except there are two of them, Stael and Ulrich, ex-cons. Stover's willing to bring them in, but only to muddy the water. He hasn't done a thing with them. He warned Ray that they aren't worth a damn, since no one can prove when they got in. That's the line the D.A.'s office will take if they're brought up.''

Shelley looked shocked, and again Barbara thought how young she was, how inexperienced.

''Okay,'' Shelley said then. ''I'll give two weeks' notice, and be done at the end of next week. I'll need an apartment here. Are there still any vacancies in this complex?''

There were three. She said she would take one today. ''I'll need to be in touch with you every evening,'' she said. ''That will be perfect.''

''Perfect,'' Barbara agreed. ''And I'll start looking for office space.''

Almost shyly, keeping her gaze on her notebook, Shelley asked, ''Would it offend you if I asked to decorate the offices? You know, pick out the drapes and desks and things like that?''

Barbara hesitated. Shelley was a very rich young woman with expensive taste who had never had to skimp or save a dime in her life.

''I won't go overboard,'' Shelley said hurriedly. ''And no pink or anything like that. We could work out something about paying for it, if you'd just let me take care of that part.''

''Done,'' Barbara said, mentally kissing her meager budget good-bye. They talked about what kind of space they would need, what they would need to start with, and then Shelley left to talk to management about her own apartment. When she walked out, her feet skimmed over the floor as she reverted to the fairy princess, who had no need for earthly contact.

21

From two until four, people had drifted in, oohed and aa-hed, had drunk champagne, and congratulated Barbara on the appearance of her offices, misplaced praise, since Shelley had been the interior decorator, but no one knew that yet. Shelley and Bill Spassero had been guests among many other guests. No one mentioned Bailey's invisible contribution—a state-of-the-art security system and a safe built into the wall behind bookcases.

The carpeting was a deep burgundy plush wool. Shelley had explained it with a helpless shrug. "Daddy wanted me to have it," she said. "It's his gift to both of us." The furnishings were Danish modern, pale gleaming wood with wonderfully simple lines. A couch covered with dark green leather and matching chairs were in Barbara's office; her desk was big, her swivel chair was high-backed, with a golden-tan leather seat cushion and armrests, and the clients' chairs were comfortable, with pale green cushions. A coffee table before the couch had an inlaid border of jade and ruby-colored stones. Three brilliant Chinese urns held plants, which Shelley swore she would take care of, and vertical blinds admitted soft light from windows on three walls.

"Shelley, how could you?" Barbara had cried after the furniture was delivered.

Shelley had already explained about the carpeting. She

looked a little confused at Barbara's shock and dismay. "Don't you like it?"

"That's not the point. I love it, but I can't afford it!"

"Oh, that. Mr. Holloway said it was on him. Daddy gave me the carpet; your father gave you the rest."

"I can't let him do this," Barbara had said to John.

"I don't think you realize how much pleasure it gives him to be able to do it," John said.

That day Frank had come early and stayed until the last visitor left, and his pleasure had not been at all concealed. Now Barbara and John were alone in her office, sitting side by side on the couch, their feet on the coffee table.

"Good party," he said lazily. "Everyone's mighty impressed."

"Me, too," she said. "Other girls dream of dancing with Prince Charming. I dreamed of my own offices."

"Lucky girl," he said, taking her hand.

"I know." Then hastily she leaned forward and knocked on wood. John laughed.

After a moment she said, "You know I'm gearing up for Ray Arno's trial, don't you?"

"Just for the past three months."

"Well, it actually starts on Monday, and we'll have our closing agreement for Maggie the following Monday. That's cutting it terribly fine if the prosecution starts to steamroll and Stover doesn't slow it down. In any event, I'm going to be pretty busy from the start of the trial until it's over. Just a warning."

"Okay. Will it be over by Christmas?"

"I hope so. That's all I can say. I'm afraid there will be a lot of objections to the various lines I'll open; there may be a continuance."

John stood up and walked to the window, moved the blind aside, and gazed out. His children were due the day after Christmas for a week's visit. "I understand." He sounded distant.

"I'll gather up glasses and then we'll go eat." They picked up glasses and empty bottles together and she groaned melodramatically about having to wash everything, but he stayed remote.

Then the trial began. It was as bad as Barbara had feared; Shelley was outraged by Stover's performance. Her own performance was exemplary. Every day she reported in full, how people had appeared, how they had dressed; she commented on the jurors, on the judge's demeanor—everything.

Every night Barbara listened to the tapes. And that had to be done in real time, hours and hours of real time. On Thursday, four days into the trial, she asked Maggie to come to the office after court recessed for the day.

Maggie looked at her accusingly. She was staying in town all week, but she was not sleeping well, and she was more nervous than Barbara had ever seen her. "They're going to nail him," she said. "They keep adding more and more details to prove that no one else could have done it, and they showed the autopsy pictures and kept going on about how sadistic the attack was. They'll convict him!"

"They won't," Barbara said. "I told you, and I meant it. What do you want me to do?"

"What can you do at this point? Tell the truth? We should have done that at the beginning!"

"What did you say you wanted me to do months ago?"

"I wanted you to take Ray's case. But it's too late! Can't you understand that?"

"All right, today you asked me to take his case. But I can't simply agree and take over. Has Ray indicated that he would like to change his attorney?"

Maggie was on the couch, twisting her hands in a helpless gesture again and again. She became very still. "What do you mean?"

"Has he indicated dissatisfaction with his attorney?"

"Yes! He can see that Stover's not doing anything. He isn't blind."

"Now listen carefully, Maggie. Have you noticed a pretty young woman with a whole lot of beautiful blond hair in the courtroom every day?" Maggie nodded. "All right. Her name is Shelley McGinnis, and she has applied for a job with me. If I had a big case on hand that required a second attorney, I would hire her in a second. Tomorrow, during the first recess, Shelley will approach you and chat, and she will say how badly this case is being handled. You confide in her that there are fingerprints that no one is doing anything about, and she will advise you to tell Ray to get someone who will do something about them. She'll tell you to have Ray ask to see me, and to tell his attorney how unhappy he is. Got that?"

Maggie was stone still. She nodded.

"Okay. During visiting hour at the lunch recess, visit Ray and repeat what Shelley said, and tell him that she worked with me in the past. Tell him you asked me to take over, and I can't unless he requests it. Just tell him what Shelley says and urge him, if he needs urging, to ask to see me. Be very careful what you say. Your conversation will be taped. I'm counting on you to be very careful."

Maggie leaned back and closed her eyes for a moment. She drew in a deep breath, then another. "What else?"

"If Ray says he wants to see me, then you'll have to come and tell me that. Come straight over here after you talk with him. Maggie, you may be questioned about all this; probably it won't happen, but it might. It's important that you act on what Shelley says, that she solidified your doubts and worries. Can you do that?"

"God, yes!"

"Okay. Let's go over it all again. Then when you come to see me tomorrow, we'll take the next steps."

"It's really bad, isn't it? Is it too late?"

"They're rushing this through so fast, they could wrap up the state's side tomorrow, and that would be bad for Ray. They're on a downhill slope racing toward the bottom without any resistance at all, and probably feeling pretty cocky about the whole thing. I have to slow them down. I want the state to bring up the possibility of outsiders."

When they walked out through the hall to the reception room, Barbara was surprised to see Frank at the desk.

He greeted Maggie and held her hands a moment; after she left, he said, "Did you start wheels rolling?"

"Afraid so."

He was concerned, but he had expressed his worries already and did not push her again. "What I've been wondering," he said too innocently, "is if you'd let Patsy use your outer office over the next week or so. See, I hate to have her working on my private stuff downtown, and I couldn't bear to have her at the house. She'd want to straighten out my socks and sew buttons on my shirts. But she sure could sit at that desk and try to make an index for me." In a very offhanded manner, he added, "Of course, I'd have to hang around to consult with her now and then."

Barbara hugged him. He knew that getting a secretary who could be privy to what was going on right now was impossible.

Then he said thoughtfully, "You realize that if I have to do anything real, anything legal, I'd have to be an associate. Not just someone off the street."

"I don't think I could afford you," she said, also thoughtfully.

"We'll work something out. Am I in?"

"You are."

"Okay, about those subpoenas, someone will have to

talk a judge into agreeing to an enjoinder for the witness not to leave the state until he testifies. I think I might be better at that than Shelley. It's hard to take a cream puff seriously.''

"That little cream puff is doing one hell of a job," Barbara said fervently. "Did you get to yesterday's tapes yet?"

He nodded. "You're right. They want to wrap it up this week, and there's not a damn thing to stop them at this point. They're making a strong circumstantial case.''

"Maybe after lunch tomorrow they'll tread water for a while," she said.

Although she had given up any pretense at cooking, she nevertheless insisted that they stick to their alternate days, and her meals were microwavable. That night it was chicken Kiev, which was actually pretty good.

"Another late night?" John asked as they finished eating.

"Afraid so.''

"You look tired, and you don't even have the case yet.''

"I know. This is not—repeat, not—the proper way to do it. First and last time for me." She got up to pour coffee. "Tomorrow all hell just might break loose. And from then on, I'll be involved," she said in a low voice. "You should be warned.''

He nodded. "It's all right. Remember, I saw you at work before. I know pretty much what to expect. An absentee lover. But then, afterward, another honeymoon? The payoff's worth the wait.''

The doorbell rang, and she started out. "That's Shelley. Time to go to work." She left, feeling him watching her out of sight.

"It's really bad," Shelley said in the office. "Today Roxbury brought in the Corvallis police and made the case that Mitch was in the area on legitimate business. And that no one but the Arnos knew he was here. He read a statement from Palmer, claiming that Mitch had worked for him for the past fifteen years, had been trustworthy and all that. Stover didn't challenge a thing. It wasn't even a deposition, just a statement. Roxbury brought in the first witness to testify about the fight eighteen years ago. He was rough with him. Treated him like a hostile witness with no cause. Then Stover tried to make him admit he couldn't really remember what happened so long ago. It was pathetic to watch him. He was rough, too.''

"Was that the last witness? Was he dismissed yet?"

"Yes. It's all like that: they testify, Stover asks the wrong questions, and on redirect, they repeat what Roxbury wants the jury to hear, and they're out of there."

"Okay," Barbara said. "I talked to Maggie earlier. She'll be expecting you to approach her at the first recess."

The next day Maggie arrived at fifteen minutes before two; she was nearly breathless, from excitement or from running up the stairs to the office, or both.

"I did it. Stover tried to keep me away, he said he had to have a conference with his client, and I'd be interfering. Ray insisted on seeing me, and he wants to see you as soon as possible. He said he'd tell Stover to beat it, and he'd write a note to the judge to request a change of attorney." She said this without pause, the words tumbling almost incoherently.

"Good. Can you hang around for a while?"

"Yes."

"As soon as I can get in to see Ray, that's your cue, you go tell the Arnos that I'll want to talk to them. Ray's parents and James, that is."

Her phone rang and she picked it up. "Holloway."

A man said, "This is Clyde Dawkins, Judge Waldman's

clerk. The judge would like a word with you. Can you hold a second?''

"Yes, of course.''

Judge Waldman came on the line. "Ms. Holloway, a situation has arisen in court. Have you agreed to represent Mr. Raymond Arno?''

"His sister-in-law has asked me to represent him. I was going to talk to him later today.''

"I would appreciate it if you could go there now and talk with Mr. Arno and make your decision. Is that convenient?''

"Yes.''

"Very well. Then I want to have a meeting in chambers with you. Three-thirty. Is that convenient?''

"Fine. I'll be there.

"Well," Barbara said when she hung up. "It's starting. I'll go see Ray now, and you arrange with the Arnos to come over here at ten in the morning. Okay? And I'll want you at nine. Time to go to work.''

Maggie was walking out when Barbara called Frank to tell him they were on, and to get Bailey over there that evening after dinner. "Marching time," she said. Frank laughed.

22

Ray Arno was handsome, even with deep shadows under his eyes and a tic in his cheek that seemed new enough to be bothering him. His hand kept edging up to it, as if feeling his cheek for something unfamiliar. He no longer looked younger than forty-seven. They shook hands and sat on opposite sides of the small conference table and studied each other.

Barbara knew he had been in Vietnam; although the war had been winding down by the time he served, he no doubt had seen horrors. He was a businessman, married with two children, the first of four sons in the Arno family, and none of his past experiences had changed him the way the past few months had done. When she had met him before, he had been open, unguarded, just puzzled. He had been trusting, had faith in the system—the criminal law system, the police—had believed in their mission to find the killer of his brother. Today he was withdrawn and watchful, wary and suspicious of her, of the conference room, this meeting. He had lost weight, and the shadows under his eyes were not as worrisome as the shadows that had appeared in his eyes, as if he had pulled himself back into a very dark place with a curtain between him and the world. His complexion, naturally a little saturnine, had paled to an unhealthy, lusterless grayed tone.

"Mr. Arno," Barbara said, "since I am not your attorney, we will assume that our every word is being recorded.

Maggie tells me that you're not satisfied with the way your defense is being conducted and that you would like me to represent you. Is that right?''

His mouth tightened when she said they were being recorded, and his gaze flicked around the tiny room, searching for a hidden microphone or some other device. "That's right," he said. "Stover's an ass."

"Have you notified Judge Waldman of your wish to drop him, retain someone else?"

"Yes. I sent her a letter telling her that."

"You understand that she has to approve of the change at this late date?"

"Yes. Stover said I can't switch now, it's too late."

"We'll see," she said. "I'm on my way to a meeting with the judge. If she approves, I'll be back, and we'll be able to talk freely then."

He stood up; the look of total despair he had had earlier, while not erased, seemed a little less overwhelming.

Outside the jail, she drew in a deep breath before she got into her car; it was a cold day with the smell of wood smoke in the air. Eugene was the only city Barbara knew where wood smoke overcame the smell of automobile exhaust. She got behind the wheel and started to drive. Christmas lights shone from windows, twinkled, blazed; a line of cars inched along Willamette Street in a futile effort to find parking spaces close to the post office, which had its own line of customers on the sidewalk. She drove past them all to the courthouse.

There, after parking in the lot across Seventh, she went through the tunnel under the street and emerged in the lower level of the building, where she saw Bishop Stover watching the people entering as if on guard duty.

He strode forward to meet her, his face a dull red, his expression one of outrage and fury. He was in his fifties, a stocky man who would go to fat if he let up on the exercise and didn't keep a sharp eye on his diet. His hair was brown with a tinge of red, streaked with a little gray. "What the hell do you think you're trying to pull?" he demanded, stopping directly in front of her.

"Mr. Stover? How do you do?" She sidestepped him and continued to walk.

"You know damn well I'm Stover. You can't jump into my case and grab my client. You've been on the sidelines, coaching everyone all the time, haven't you? What for, Holloway? Arno's broke. Don't look to make a cent off him. You want to start a new office with a few headlines? Grab a little free publicity? Is that it?"

She looked him up and down contemptuously. "I'm sorry I can't stop and chat," she said. "I'm on my way to a command performance with Judge Waldman."

"So am I. I don't intend to get pushed aside and let you play your little game. You've had Folsum acting as your spy, and now McGinnis. You're too clever for your own good, Holloway. Go get your headlines somewhere else."

Very pleasantly, Barbara said, "I don't believe you look well, Mr. Stover. Perhaps you should check into the hospital, have a few tests."

"You're threatening me! My God, you're threatening me!"

"Don't be silly. Just passing the time of day. Now, if you'll excuse me, I should comb my hair, wash my hands before I meet the judge. See you in chambers, Mr. Stover."

Frank had said that Jane Waldman was a lady, and meeting her, Barbara understood exactly what he meant. She was fifty, but she could have been any age between thirty and sixty or even seventy. She was tall and slender, dressed in a mid-calf-length black silk dress with long sleeves; she wore a strand of pearls and pearl earrings. Her ash-blond hair was in a loose chignon. And her slender hands with long tapered fingers would have made an artist reach for his brush. She shook hands with Barbara and motioned toward the others in the room.

"I understand you've all met," she said. "Craig Roxbury, assistant district attorney, and Bishop Stover, defense attorney. Gentlemen, Ms. Holloway."

They were all very polite, shaking hands, taking chairs around a low coffee table set with silver coffee service and lovely bone china cups and saucers.

The judge did not waste time. She asked, "Ms. Holloway, have you consulted with Mr. Arno? And have you made your decision?"

"Yes, I have. If it please the court, I'll take his case."

"Before we continue, I must advise you that serious charges have been leveled in this office. Mr. Roxbury, please repeat your concern for Ms. Holloway's benefit."

He cleared his throat. "Yes, your honor. At this stage of the trial, I believe Mr. Arno is grasping at straws in an attempt to delay the outcome, to delay the trial until it is very close to Christmas, when he hopes the jurors will be more likely to be charitable. He has had ample opportunity to make a change such as this in the months past; to put it off until the state is nearly ready to rest is intolerable."

Judge Waldman nodded, then turned to Stover. "And your concerns?"

"She's been pulling strings behind the scenes for months," he said angrily. "I've done all the work, and she wants to step in and grab headlines. I agree with Roxbury that Arno's desperate, but the defense hasn't had its chance to tell the rest of the story yet. And she's using his desperation for her own purposes. She and Maggie Folsum cooked up this plot months ago, and she planted McGinnis in court to act as her spy, so she would know exactly when to step forward and make the power play." More belligerently, he said to Barbara, "If you have information concerning my client, it's your duty to let me in on it. You could even come aboard as part of my team. You don't have to grab him."

"You have the same information I have," she said coolly. "I just intend to use it, since you don't seem to grasp its importance."

Judge Waldman gazed at Barbara without expression. "Did you discuss this case with Ms. Folsum months ago?"

"Yes, I did. Maggie Folsum was already my client when she asked if I would defend him. I had to tell her no, that it might result in a conflict of interest. I didn't know at that time how either case would develop. She asked me again today, and since I will fulfill my obligation to her on Monday and I now see that no conflict could arise, I told her that if Ray Arno wanted me, I would talk to him about it."

Without pausing she continued, "Ms. Folsum has two major concerns. In August she and I met with Mr. Roxbury to inform him that Mitch Arno had brought a large sum of money in cash to the state, but his office apparently has chosen not to follow up that line of inquiry, and this alarmed her. She also said that since certain fingerprints she had given to the district attorney's office as well as to Mr. Stover appeared to have been overlooked or even deliberately put aside, she was even more alarmed. Today Ray Arno asked me personally to take his case, and I said I would if the change was approved by the court."

"Is Ms. McGinnis your employee?"

"No, your honor. She is a friend and she was a colleague in the past. She has applied to a number of firms for a position; she asked me for a job. I started my own firm only recently, and I had nothing on hand that required a second attorney as yet. I suggested she might fill in her time by observing as many trials as she could."

Careful, she told herself, aware of the judge's close scrutiny. "I shall hire Ms. McGinnis the minute I leave here. I know how intelligent and what an excellent observer she is. I think she will be invaluable to me in defending Ray Arno.''

''You mentioned fingerprints,'' Judge Waldman said. ''What fingerprints are you talking about?''

''Ms. Folsum told me she asked a detective to fingerprint Ray Arno's house last summer and that when the report came back, she gave it to the district attorney and to Mr. Stover. She said the detective had recovered prints of two ex-convicts in Ray Arno's house, but no one has brought them up at the trial.''

''They're a red herring!'' Roxbury said angrily. ''They go nowhere! We investigated them, and they mean nothing!''

''Mr. Stover, did you intend to use the evidence of the fingerprints?''

''Yes, of course. Next week, when we have our turn.''

''And which witness would have introduced them?'' she asked politely.

''The detective,'' he said. His face had turned a darker shade of red.

''Have you subpoenaed him?''

''Not yet. I was waiting for the state to rest.''

''Is his name on your witness list?''

''Not yet.''

''I see.'' She leaned in toward the table. ''Perhaps we should have coffee. I have a few more questions.'' No one moved or spoke as she played hostess, and although no one wanted coffee, they all accepted and murmured their thanks.

She asked about the money then, and Barbara gave her a very abbreviated account, aware of Roxbury's increasing fury as she spoke.

''Your honor,'' he said harshly, ''that's a simple red herring. We looked into it. Mitch Arno didn't even have it, his lawyer did. It has nothing to do with the murder.''

Judge Waldman regarded him thoughtfully for a moment, then turned to Stover and directed her remarks to him. "Since Mr. Arno has requested a change of attorney, I shall grant his wish. That is his constitutional right, of course, even if it delays the trial somewhat. And, Ms. Holloway, I shall not allow this trial to be delayed unduly. The jurors have every expectation of being through here before Christmas.''

"What am I supposed to do, just bow out and let her take the stage?'' Stover demanded.

"I expect you to cooperate fully with Ms. Holloway, to furnish her with all the information provided by the state, and to be of any other assistance possible. Ms. Holloway, I charge you with the duty to inform me if there has not been complete cooperation. Mr. Roxbury, your office will also cooperate with Ms. Holloway and provide any materials to which she is entitled without delay.''

She asked Roxbury how much longer he intended to take. He said bitterly that he had planned to rest the following day, but the delay meant he would need at least two more days. She consulted a calendar, then said with a sigh, "Very well. Mr. Roxbury will finish on Tuesday or Wednesday. On Monday, December sixteenth, I expect you to present the case for the defense, Ms. Holloway. That does not give you a great deal of time, but as I said, I want this jury to be finished with its work before Christmas. And as you said, Ms. McGinnis is an excellent observer. I shall instruct Mr. Dawkins to provide you with a complete transcript of the trial to date as soon as he can.''

"Your honor,'' Barbara said, "if I find it necessary to ask additional questions of witnesses who have already testified, may I have them recalled, or must I subpoena them as defense witnesses?''

Judge Waldman considered for a moment, then said, "After you have gone over the transcript, show me the list of witnesses you want to recall on Monday morning. At what time on Monday will you be prepared to start your defense?"

"I can prepare my list for you by eight that morning and I can be in court by eleven."

"Very well. Monday morning at eight in here," Judge Waldman said. "I'll talk to the jurors and explain the new development, and we shall delay the start of Monday's proceedings until eleven o'clock." She looked at them severely and added, "This meeting is to be kept confidential. If any of you gives out a hint, I shall hold you in contempt and put you in jail."

By five Barbara was back at the county jail, back in one of the conference rooms, this time with her notebook and pen.

"I should have gone with one of the people you suggested at the start," Ray said unhappily when they were both seated. "You saw the condition I was in, still disbelieving, going along. I thought since I knew Stover—he's gone fishing with me, for God's sake! I thought he would work for me."

"It's done, Mr. Arno," she said. "No point in fretting about it now."

He seemed oblivious of her attempt to derail him, to start working. "At first you think it can't happen, not really," he said, looking over her head, at the wall, at the past, at nothing. "Then you think, well, it happens, but to other people, not you. Then, in the middle of the night one night, you think, why me? Why, God, what did I do to deserve this? You know? You warned me, and I simply didn't understand what you meant, as if you had been speaking a foreign language or something—"

"Mr. Arno—Ray! Please, there's no point in this. We have a little more than a week to prepare your defense. You have to help me; I can't do it alone."

"Just one more thing," he said; he gazed at her for a moment, then rubbed his eyes. "I'm sorry, but you see, my family...I can't say things like this to them. They're still in the opening phase—it can't happen, not here, not to us— and I can't seem to talk to them. They come in and say things like, It's just a big mistake, they'll see it's a mistake and turn you loose. But I've had my nights of asking God why it's happening, and that puts me in a different place from the family. It's as if I've finally seen into the pit, but they keep closing their eyes or turning away their heads. Today, when you showed up earlier, I knew you understood what I'm facing, you and the judge, a few others in court, but not my family. And, Barbara, I have to say this before you take over, today for the first time I felt like maybe I won't be tossed overboard into that pit. I'm grateful to you for coming, for taking me on. I just had to tell you that."

"Save your thanks for after the case is over with," she said; her effort to sound kidding and lighthearted fell a bit flat, but it was the best she could do at the moment. She patted his hands, folded on the table. "For now, please bear with me if I seem demanding and abrupt; tell me if you want a break. I really don't want this to become a new torment for you. It's just that the pressure of time is very much a factor."

"Shoot," he said.

At eight, going up the apartment stairs, she was overwhelmed by the fragrance of chicken and green chilies, one of John's specialties. He met her at the top landing and for a time he held her, his face pressed into her hair. Then he drew back slightly and said, "Dinner is being served at this very moment, madam."

She held on another second, until he took her by the shoulders and turned her toward the living room, where the table was ready. "Dinner," he said. "Did you have any lunch today?"

She had to think, then she shook her head.

"Dinner," he repeated. She thought the yearning look on his face must have matched her own, but they went in to eat.

When the first ravenous hunger pangs had been satisfied, she said, "On Monday we'll have the closing agreement and I'll be done with the Maggie Folsum business."

"Then what?"

"Tonight I have to collect Shelley and go to Dad's to consult. We'll all be dashing around for the next ten days. All the stuff I couldn't do in the past few months will have to be crammed into a little more than a week. It will take all of us, full-time, and then some."

"I meant what about the Palmer affair? You're not letting it go, I can tell."

A week after moving into the apartments, relaxed, with breathing space, she had decided that if they were to live together, there could be no secrets between them, and she had told him everything she knew and suspected about the case. She shook her head. "I'm not letting it go. I intend to force Trassi and Palmer to hand over Mitch Arno's killers."

He stared at her. "You'll need a bodyguard."

"Bailey's taking care of that."

"I'll go to Frank's with you tonight. I don't want you out at night alone, or just with Shelley. Don't even bother to try to talk me out of it."

"All right," she said. "But it's not a threat for now. Please believe me. I still have papers they need, and Trassi doesn't know the trap he's in. Monday afternoon he will, but not now, not yet."

* * *

Frank was relieved to see John arrive with Barbara and Shelley. "Go on in," he said. "There's Bailey driving up. I'll just wait for him."

They went into the living room, where Frank had a fire going, and both cats were on the couch, sprawled across most of it. "Beat it," Frank growled at them when he entered with Bailey. Neither cat stirred until he moved them.

"First," Barbara said as they were getting settled, "Judge Waldman gagged us all until the trial resumes on Monday. She doesn't want the jury speculating over the weekend about news stories of the change. I don't think the D.A. will find it to their advantage to leak anything yet. So we just might have the weekend without interference."

Barbara began to outline the following week. She had been planning the defense for months; now they could openly implement the plans.

"Starting next week," Frank said later, "no more restaurants. We'll eat here and I'll cook or we'll order carryout food. You, too, Shelley. No running around alone, no late hours driving by yourself." She was wide-eyed, and nodded emphatically. "Now, how about a snack and something to drink?"

Bailey was on his feet almost instantly. "How about that."

Barbara's gaze came to rest on John, who might have been carved from cold, hard stone.

23

Barbara accepted that she could never compete with the other professional women she met day after day, as far as clothes or hair or general appearance were concerned. She especially could never compete with Judge Jane Waldman, who that Monday morning was dressed in a mauve-colored sheer-wool knit dress with matching shoes. A simple gold chain and small gold hoop earrings finished her outfit; she looked more elegant than ever. Grumpily Barbara thought that she had tried; she had had her hair cut sometime in the fall. She couldn't remember when, only that for a while her own hair had looked wonderful, until she shampooed, and magically it had turned into her usual style, which was to say no style at all.

Craig Roxbury and Barbara had been admitted into Judge Waldman's chambers together, and this time the judge was sitting at her desk and motioned them to chairs across from her.

"You have your list?" she asked Barbara.

"Yes. It's only four names." She handed over the list.

"I have to warn you that I won't allow you to recross-examine these witnesses. If there is anything new to bring up from their various reports, you may do that, but you have the transcript, and we will not reopen the cross-examination. Is that understood?"

"Yes, your honor. However, there are two missing reports, one concerning what was found in Ray Arno's car when it was impounded, and the last page from the medical examiner's report.''

''We turned over everything we have,'' Roxbury said. ''If Stover lost the stuff, we can't help that.''

''You will make copies of those two reports and see that Ms. Holloway receives them both this morning before court resumes,'' Judge Waldman said. She put on gold-framed glasses and looked over the list Barbara had handed her. ''For the sake of continuity, I suggest that these four witnesses all be recalled on Monday, December sixteen. After that, of course, you will conduct your defense without further suggestions from the court. Is that agreeable?''

''Yes, your honor.''

Judge Waldman took off her glasses and laid them down. ''I have been informed that Mr. Stover was admitted to Sacred Heart Hospital late Saturday with chest pains,'' she said. ''That is what I shall tell the jury. I don't want to sequester them at this season; they have shopping to do, other things to attend to. For that reason I am imposing a no-comment order from now until the case goes to the jury. I don't want stories in the newspapers, or television news concerning this trial. No press conferences, no news releases. The court will contact these four witnesses and recall them all for Monday, the sixteenth. I trust you will finish with them all on that day. And I trust you will finish the defense case by the end of next week.''

The discussion continued until nine-thirty, when Barbara finally left the judge's chambers and walked across the street to the Federal Building, where Maggie met her at the entrance. Maggie was very nervous.

''Relax,'' Barbara said. ''Now, as soon as I know beyond any doubt that there's no last-minute snag, you're no longer my client. You understand? I'll turn you over to Sunderman, who will handle the paperwork and arrange for a transfer of the money to your account.''

She spotted Trassi standing at a table covered with handouts, facing away. ''Excuse me a minute,'' she said, and walked to the table by Trassi. ''They won't want you in there today, will they?'' she asked him, picking up a pamphlet.

''No, of course not. Where are the printouts?''

She patted her briefcase. ''I'll go in with Sunderman, but I won't have to stay long, I'm sure. The minute I'm done, I'll leave and hand them over.''

''This is a farce. I have a plane to catch. Do you think I'll burst in there and cry foul? Give me the printouts.''

''As soon as the signatures are on paper,'' she said. ''There's Mr. Sunderman now.''

At that moment a woman came to tell them that Mr. Chenowith was waiting for the group.

They were taken to the same room they had occupied before, under the same harsh white light. Both men began to pull papers from briefcases.

''Mr. Chenowith,'' Barbara said as he shuffled his stack of papers, ''I have to be in court by eleven. I don't believe my presence is required here. Mr. Sunderman is representing Ms. Folsum in the matter.''

He looked pained, but she had to assume that was his normal expression, unless he was conducting an audit with an unfortunate tax dodger caught red-handed.

''There is the matter of the amount of the arrears,'' Chenowith said. ''Your original claim was for two hundred ten thousand dollars, and the money has since accrued interest; and there is the additional sum of thirty thousand dollars, which will be returned to Mr. Arno's estate. I have drawn up papers to the effect that Ms. Folsum will receive the original sum, plus the interest on that part of the money only. Is that satisfactory?''

"Yes. Absolutely. Mr. Sunderman, I no longer am Ms. Folsum's attorney of record. Now, if you gentlemen will excuse me...."

Trassi was in the lobby near the entrance door. He walked outside and she followed. "It's done," she said. "Here's your package."

She took a manila envelope from her briefcase and handed it to him; he opened it and examined the contents as well as he could without removing anything. She waited until he closed it again. "Now, we're all finished," she said. "Good day, Mr. Trassi." She turned away at the same moment a young man in a windbreaker approached from behind him.

"Mr. Trassi?" he asked. The lawyer jerked around, startled, and the young man handed him a paper.

Trassi looked as if he had received a snake. He stared at the paper, then finally looked up at Barbara. "What is this? What are you trying to pull?"

"It's a subpoena," she said. "See you in court, Mr. Trassi."

She met Shelley in the courthouse at fifteen minutes before eleven. All the Arnos were milling about—James and his wife, David and his, Lorinne Arno, several of their various children, Mama and Papa; Maggie's daughters were with them, and it appeared that everyone in that cluster was talking at once. Gwen and Karen Folsum hurried to Barbara. They were both very handsome, tall like the Arnos, and with Maggie's lovely eyes and hair.

"Is Mother going to be here?" Karen asked.

"She may be delayed a few minutes, not for long, I'm sure," Barbara said. Mama Arno was approaching her. "Excuse me, I have to speak with Shelley a moment before we begin," Barbara said hurriedly. Talking with the Arnos was hard, she had learned on Saturday, when in desperation she had separated them and had talked to them one by one.

All the Arno sons were tall with dark hair and dark eyes, athletic, all like their father, who at seventy was still upright, strong, and vigorous. His face was deeply lined, weathered by salt spray, sun, wind; he had been a fisherman off the coast all his adult life until recently. His hands were very large and heavily veined. Mama Arno was five feet two and stout, not fat, but husky-looking; her hair was a soft golden blond with white roots. And her skin was unlined and as pink and creamy-white as a baby's. She liked to touch the people she was talking to, and since she seemed to talk to everyone within earshot at the same time, she was busy touching someone here, patting there, caressing another, smoothing down the hair, or straightening a collar.... Barbara had found it so disconcerting, she had kept her desk between them Saturday when they talked. The Arno clan all had the ability to listen to multiple conversations simultaneously, without any sign of confusion. And the wives had been trained over the years to participate in exactly the same way. Barbara could imagine what bedlam a big holiday must be in their households; sitting day after day silenced in court must have been a strain nearly beyond endurance for them.

Now, escaping Mama Arno, she drew Shelley aside and said in a low voice, "Trassi was served with the subpoena, and he's hopping mad. You might get in touch with Dad and let him know."

"Right. Roxbury handed over the two reports and snarled at me." She grinned. "He acted as if I had been Delilah to his Samson."

They talked a few more minutes, then people started to file into Courtroom B. Barbara entered and took her place at the defense table. Shelley left to call Frank.

* * *

Judge Waldman very politely introduced Barbara to the jury, and then she introduced the jurors to Barbara. Shelley entered and was introduced, and they started.

"Mr. Roxbury, your next witness, if you will."

He called Cory Sussman, a stooped man with a weathered face and thick gray hair, clearly nervous and unhappy about testifying. He kept glancing at Ray Arno, then at the rest of the family, as if apologizing.

After establishing that Sussman lived in Folsum, where he managed the Exxon service station and a small store, Roxbury steered him to the day of the fight between Mitch and Ray Arno.

"Just tell us in your own words about what you saw that day."

"Well, Papa Arno, he come into—"

"You mean Mr. Anthony Arno? Mitchell's father?"

"Yeah, Papa Arno. He come in to the store and bought a one-way ticket to Portland...." It was the same story Barbara had heard many times, one the jury had heard twice already. He didn't add anything new to it.

"Mr. Sussman," Barbara said kindly when Roxbury was done, "you've known the Arno family a long time?"

"All my life," he said.

"Were the Arno boys fighting, brawling kids?"

He looked shocked. "Never were. Quietest bunch of kids on the coast."

"That day you've described, was Papa Arno bloody or dirty?"

He shook his head hard. "No way. Not at all."

"Was Ray Arno messed up, bloody and dirty?"

"Yeah, just like Mitch. Looked like they was both rolling in the mud and hitting each other hard."

"You said that Papa Arno got the bus ticket, and he was the one who put Mitch on the bus. Did you see Ray walking around that day?"

"He got out of the car and watched, maybe took a step or two toward the bus with them, but Papa didn't need no help."

"Was Ray wobbly and unsteady on his feet?"

"Yeah, maybe not as bad as Mitch, but he'd took a beating, too."

"Was Ray much bigger than Mitch in those days?"

He looked surprised. "Not bigger at all. They was all big boys, six feet or over, and strong. Fishermen, you see, strong."

"So you think they were pretty evenly matched if they had a fight?"

"Yeah, real even."

"And you think they looked about the same afterward?"

Now he shook his head. "No, ma'am. Not the same. Mitch looked whupped, and Ray looked like the whupper."

The next witness was Eric Rubens, a neighbor of Ray's. He had known Ray Arno for fourteen years, ever since Ray moved across River Loop One from him.

"Last summer, did Ray Arno ask you to keep an eye on his property while he was away for a few days?" Roxbury asked.

"Yes."

"Did you see him leave his house on the evening of Friday, August second?"

"Yes."

"At what time was that?"

"A few minutes after seven."

Barbara suppressed a smile. This witness was going to stick to the questions with the shortest possible answers. Let Roxbury pull teeth for a while.

Slowly, painfully, Roxbury dragged it out that Rubens had seen Papa Arno drive past at about seven and leave again almost immediately, and a few minutes later Ray drove out past him. In the same slow way he testified that he had been in his yard all day Sunday and had not seen any strangers around, had not seen any strange cars drive into Ray's driveway, had not seen anything out of the ordinary.

"Did you see lights come on in the Arno house each night of that weekend?" He said yes. "Friday night?" Yes. "Saturday night?" Yes. "Sunday night?" Yes. "Did you hear any sounds of distress, calls for help, yelling?"

"No."

"In other words, all weekend it was quiet over there, and you saw no one strange and heard nothing out of the ordinary. Is that correct?"

"Yes."

"And on Monday, did you see Ray Arno return home and enter his driveway?"

"Yes."

Pulling teeth, Roxbury got him to say that Ray had returned home around one in the afternoon and had left again about an hour later, then returned at about seven or seven-thirty. He had not seen him again that day or evening. When Roxbury nodded to Barbara, he was clearly glad to be rid of Eric Rubens.

"Mr. Rubens," she started, "your house is across the road from the Arno house, is that right?"

He said yes, then added, "Not straight across, down a piece."

"I have a map here of that area. Would you please show us where your house is, and where the Arno house is located?" Shelley was setting up a large map on an easel as Barbara spoke, and she turned toward it. "Maybe you could step down and point out the two properties." She looked at Judge Waldman, who nodded.

"You may step down, Mr. Rubens," the judge said.

He stood up and moved very deliberately to the map, studied it a moment, then pointed. "That's my place, twelve acres, and that's Ray's, six acres, down the road a piece.''

"Before you take your seat again, could you explain how it happened that you were outside during those few days in early August?''

"I was selling apples,'' he said. "Gravensteins were in.''

"And where was your stand?''

He pointed. "Had a stand right there, by the driveway.''

"There are two more properties on River Loop One, before the name changes to Stratton Lane. Is that right?''

He said yes, and she asked him to take his seat again. Then, tracing the route on the map, she said, "So River Loop One turns off River Road, curves around past orchards, and finally ends here at the intersection with Stratton Lane and Knowles Road. Are those the routes most residents use to get to their places on River Loop One?''

"Mostly Stratton,'' he said.

"Is there anything on River Road to indicate that either Stratton Lane or Knowles Road joins River Loop One?''

He said no. "Stratton goes through the development, and Knowles goes past the school and has sharp turns. Not too many folks know about them, unless they live along there.''

"Did you advertise apples in the newspaper when the crop came in?'' Barbara asked.

"Yes.''

"Were you at the stand most of the time when you had them for sale?''

He said yes.

"Did most of the customers come in by way of Stratton or by way of River Loop One?''

"River Loop One,'' he said.

"How far was your stand from the Arno driveway?''

"Four, five hundred feet.''

"So, if a car came by way of River Loop One and turned in there, you wouldn't have seen it, would you?''

"Not likely."

"All right. You said lights came on every night that weekend. Did they come on Monday night, as well?" He said yes. "And Tuesday, Wednesday, all that week?"

He said yes. Every night.

"Can you explain that, Mr. Rubens? Do you know why they come on every night?"

He said yes, and she thought for a moment she would have to ask him to explain, but he continued. "There aren't any streetlights out there until you get in the subdivision. Most of us have lights on timers, or else on automatic, so they come on at dusk and go off in the morning. Every night."

"On Monday, did you talk to Ray Arno?"

"Yes. I picked up his mail on Saturday and took it over to him on Monday. We talked a little."

"How did he appear?"

"Same as always."

"Was he bruised, or cut? Did you notice any swelling on his hands? Anything of that sort?"

He said no.

"What time did you talk to him on Monday?"

"Seven-thirty, a little after. When he came home the second time and was putting his car in the garage."

"What kind of car was he driving?"

"Honda. Hatchback. Lorinne had the van."

"He was putting the car in the garage then? Did you see inside the car?"

He said yes. "He was taking stuff out to put it away— an overnight bag, cooler chest, things like that. We stood at the garage door and talked a minute or two."

She thanked him and listened to Roxbury make his same few points: Rubens had not seen any strangers, no strange cars, had heard nothing out of the ordinary.

Judge Waldman called for the recess then, and told the

jurors that they must not talk about the case and they would resume at two.

Barbara and Shelley went to the office, where Patsy was at the receptionist desk, working on Frank's book. Frank, she said, was explaining to the magistrate that no one had singled out Mr. Trassi for special treatment, that all Barbara's witnesses were being subpoenaed and told not to leave the state. Patsy reported this perfectly straight-faced, knowing well that Trassi was the reason for all the subpoenas.

That afternoon Stan Truckee was the next witness. He worked in Ray's sports shop, had worked there for twelve years, mostly part-time. He was a gangly man in his fifties, with a crippled hand, the fingers drawn inward in a clawlike position. All Roxbury wanted from Truckee was the fact that Ray often took customers home with him to see his collection of flies.

"So, since you work only part-time, you have no way of knowing who he takes home with him, or when? Is that right?"

"Well, he's not real close-mouthed—"

"Just a yes or no, please. You have no way of knowing, do you?"

"He tells me—"

"Your honor, will you please instruct the witness to answer the question."

"Just answer the question, Mr. Truckee," she said kindly.

"No," he said. "Except—"

"The answer is no," Roxbury snapped. "Your witness," he said to Barbara.

Shelley had said Roxbury looked like an accountant, and at the moment he did, an accountant who had found a plus instead of a minus in the books. She smiled at him and stood up.

"Mr. Truckee, what exactly does your shop handle, what kind of merchandise do you sell there?"

"Fishing gear, hooks, lines, tackle, flies, lures, waders. Anything to do with fishing, freshwater or saltwater fishing."

"No baseball bats or golf clubs? Just fishing gear?"

"That's all. And we have customers from all over the world."

"Objection," Roxbury said. "The witness is advertising."

"Sustained."

"All right," Barbara said easily. "You just sell fishing gear. Let's talk a minute about the collection of flies Mr. Arno shows to some customers. Can you describe the collection?"

"Yes, ma'am. See, there are some people who have a real gift for tying flies, so real they would fool the insects' mamas. One of our suppliers is famous for his flies, he wins competitions, has private showings. And another one is a lady down in Medford, who gets her material from around the world—alpaca from South America, phalarope feathers from South Africa—"

"Objection!" Roxbury cried. "This is irrelevant."

"Overruled," Judge Waldman said. "You may continue," she said to Stan Truckee.

"Well," he said, "it's like that. Where common flies might use a copper bead, some of our suppliers use gold, real gold. Or instead of muskrat, they get wild boar, or instead of dying some pale fur orange, they get orange from an orangutan from Borneo. I mean, these are special, real works of art. And over the years Ray's built up a real collection of those flies. He mounted them in glass boxes, and he shows them at conventions, and sometimes he sets up a display at the shop.''

"Does his collection have value for anyone besides other fishing enthusiasts?''

"Yes, ma'am. They're insured for a lot of money. They're all one of a kind, the best.''

"All right. So he has customers who know about the displays and ask to see them? Is that right?''

"Yes, ma'am. Some regulars bring in new people and they can't wait to see them, they get real excited about them.''

"If strangers come to the shop and ask to see the special collection, then what happens?''

"Well, he tells them when the next show's going to be, and where. Or when he intends to bring them in to the shop.''

"To your knowledge, has he ever taken a stranger to his house to show off his collection?''

He shook his head emphatically. "No way. No, ma'am.''

"Would he be secretive about such a thing?''

Roxbury objected and Barbara said, "You brought it up, that he might do it without telling anyone.''

"I didn't say anyone. I said this witness has no way of knowing that.''

"Sustained. Move on, Ms. Holloway.''

She nodded. "Mr. Truckee, do you know how much Mr. Arno pays for the special flies?''

Roxbury objected, and this time was overruled.

"Yes, ma'am. I'm in on everything.''

"You know all his suppliers?''

"Yes, ma'am.''

"And most of his regular customers?''

"All of them.''

"Do you set aside special lures and flies for special customers?''

"Yes, we do."

"And discuss in advance that a customer might like the new ones? Something like that?"

"Yes, ma'am. We talk about it."

"You talk about most of the business?"

"I'd say all of it."

"If you got a new customer who proved to be an avid fisherman who wanted only the best you had, you would talk it over with Mr. Arno?"

"Every time. We keep an eye out for the real fishermen."

"And he would do the same, mention to you that an avid fisherman had come in?"

"Yes, he would. We talk about the business all the time."

"And it would take an avid fisherman, a real enthusiast who was knowledgeable about flies, who would gain admittance to his private collection?"

"Unless he knows the difference between an English Gold Bead Headstone and a Glass Bead Caddis Pupa, there wouldn't be any point in it, would there?"

She smiled and shook her head. "I don't think so, Mr. Truckee. If such a customer came along, a new customer, would you learn about him?"

"Sure, I would."

"Mr. Truckee, without giving any names, can you tell the jury the last time that you know Ray Arno took a customer to his house to look at the collection?"

"Yes, ma'am. It was in May, early May. A customer, a regular, came in with two friends from Michigan, and they asked if they could see them. Ray said sure, and they all went out to the house."

She thanked him and sat down. "No more questions."

Roxbury snapped at him, "The days you don't work in

the shop, you don't know who comes in for certain, do you?''

''I find out.''

''You can't know unless Ray Arno tells you, and you have no way of knowing if he tells you everything, do you?''

Truckee looked puzzled, then shook his head. ''No, not if you put it that way. But he tells—''

''That's all. The answer is no.''

When Truckee left the stand, Roxbury called his next witness, Alexandra Wharton.

24

Alexandra Wharton was a large woman in her forties, five feet ten, one hundred eighty pounds, with dark brown hair, little makeup, dressed in a no-nonsense navy blue suit and white blouse. She walked to the stand, took her oath, and seated herself with a minimum of fuss, hardly a glance at the jury, and none at all toward Ray Arno.

Roxbury led her into her testimony quickly, and her story was simple. She went to the *Register-Guard* dock every night at two-thirty to collect bundles of newspapers, which she then distributed to route carriers.

"The corner of Stratton and River Road is the next-to-last stop I make," she said. "I always get there between five-thirty and a quarter to six, and usually the Dyson kids are there waiting and we transfer their bundle to their truck and I take off. That's Derek and Lina Dyson. She drives and he delivers the papers to the porches or the boxes out front."

"Do you recall what happened on the morning of Tuesday, August sixth?"

"Yes. I pulled in to the church parking lot, and the truck hadn't come yet, so I opened the back of my van and was getting the bundle ready for them when I saw headlights coming up Stratton. I thought it was the Dyson truck, but it wasn't. A gray Honda Civic came speeding to the corner and hardly slowed down at all, took the turn, and raced up River Road toward town."

"How far were you from the Honda?"

"No more than fifty feet."

"And you saw it clearly?"

"Yes."

"Did you see the driver?"

"Just that it was a man with dark hair; then it was gone."

"Could you see how he was dressed?"

"Not really. A dark sweatshirt or sweater is all I could see."

"What time did you see the Honda?"

"It had to have been about five-thirty. I got to my next stop at ten to six, and it's usually about fifteen minutes after I leave Stratton that I get up to it."

Roxbury was being silky smooth with this witness, showing not a sign of brusqueness or impatience. He drew her out slowly and carefully, covering every point with precision. She knew it was Tuesday, August sixth, because she had a dental appointment that day at nine, and the speeder had upset her and was still on her mind when she went to the dentist's office; she had mentioned it there, how kids who delivered newspapers in the dark were at risk from speeders.

Barbara did not interrupt, not even when he showed Alexandra Wharton a photograph of a car and asked if that was the one she saw speeding that morning. She said yes. He identified the photograph as Ray Arno's automobile and had it entered as a state exhibit. Soon after that he finished with her.

Barbara stood up and asked, "Ms. Wharton, was it still dark that morning when you got to Stratton?"

"Not real dark, but the sun wasn't up yet. Twilight."

"You said the speeding car had its headlights on, so it was dark enough to be using headlights?"

"Yes."

"Are there traffic lights at that intersection?"

"No, just a stop sign."

"Are there streetlights on the corners there?"

"No."

"Are there any lights at all?"

"Yes. The church has a lightpole; that's why I pull in there, so we can see what we're doing with the newspapers. And there's a light on in the grocery store across Stratton."

"A night-light in the grocery store? A dim light?"

"Yes."

"All right. When you pull in, do you turn off your headlights? Stop your engine?"

"Yes. Sometimes I have to wait for them, and the church light is enough. They can see me fine."

"Do you always pull in close to the church light?"

"Yes, so we can see what we're doing."

"Yes, of course. So the light was about fifty feet from the intersection, as you were. Is that correct?"

She nodded, then said, "About that far."

"And the automobile you saw was a gray Honda Civic? Do you know what year it was?"

Wharton hesitated, then said, "I wasn't thinking of what year it was or anything like that. I recognized it when I saw it, though."

Barbara nodded, then went to her table, where Shelley handed her a photograph; it was a montage of fifteen gray hatchback automobiles—a Honda, Toyota, Nissan…. The years ranged from 1987 to 1994. The individual cars were numbered, and there were no other identifying marks. She showed the picture to Judge Waldman, then to Roxbury, who leaped up and objected.

"On what grounds, Mr. Roxbury?" the judge asked.

"May I approach?"

Roxbury and Barbara approached the bench, where Roxbury said furiously, "This witness made a positive identification. That picture is just to confuse her, make her doubt her own eyes. All those cars look—''

Both the judge and Barbara waited for him to finish. When he didn't, Barbara said, "Alike. Is that the word you want? You had the witness pick out one from one. Let's see if she is that positive when there's a real choice."

"Are the cars identified somewhere?" Judge Waldman asked.

"Yes, on the back. Ray Arno's car is one of them, in fact."

The judge glanced at the back of the montage, then nodded. "Very well. Overruled, Mr. Roxbury."

Barbara took the sheet of photographs to the witness then and handed it to her. "Ms. Wharton, can you identify the car you saw in this collection?"

Alexandra Wharton looked confused at the number of cars on the montage, then she began to study them; she pursed her lips and a frown creased her forehead after a moment. It took her a long time, but finally she looked at Barbara and shook her head.

"I can't say for sure which one it was."

"Can you be sure it was a Honda?"

"No, not for sure, I guess."

"Can you say for sure it was a 1991 model?"

"No."

"How would you describe the car you saw that morning?"

"A little gray car, a hatchback."

"Thank you," Barbara said. "No more questions." She had the sheet of photographs entered, and watched the bailiff pass it to the jury foreman. And some of them would know in a second which was the '91 Honda Civic, she thought, satisfied.

Roxbury tried to undo the damage. Her memory when she identified the car in August had been clearer than it was

now, after so many months. She had been certain at the
time. Looking at so many gray cars was confusing.... He
didn't help the situation and might have hurt it. Some of
the jurors knew a Honda from a Toyota.

Roxbury called Anthony Arno next.

When Papa Arno's name was called, to Barbara's surprise and consternation, Ray stood up; she heard a com-
motion behind her and twisted around to see James and
David Arno also on their feet. Roxbury was shouting, and
the bailiff was bawling for all to be seated. Judge Waldman
raised her gavel, then gently put it down again; the jurors
appeared as amazed as everyone else by this spontaneous
display. They stared at Papa Arno, at the three tall sons,
back to Papa Arno.

Then Judge Waldman said in her firm no-nonsense way,
"Gentlemen, be seated. Please, there must be no further
demonstrations of any sort in this courtroom."

Papa Arno had seemed unaware of his sons' actions; now
he glanced behind him and nodded; it was as if his signal
to sit down again was the one they needed. A guard had
rushed to Ray Arno's side when he rose; he withdrew as
Ray took his chair again. James and David Arno sat down,
and only then was Papa sworn in.

Craig Roxbury turned a bitter, icy glare toward Barbara;
she shrugged. If he believed she had had anything to do
with that, she was certain he was the only person in the
courtroom who did. The jurors regarded Papa with height-
ened interest.

On Saturday Papa Arno had said to Barbara, "A father
should not have to testify against his son. Can they make
me?"

"I'm sorry," she had said. "If you appear reluctant, not
cooperative, they will call you a hostile witness and it
would be worse for Ray. I don't think your testimony will
be damaging."

"I am talking about the son I had, Mitch. I don't know anything about Ray that could hurt him."

After going over his testimony, Barbara had said, "Just tell the truth, Mr. Arno. The jury will know you're telling the truth."

And now Roxbury was leading him into the fight between Ray and Mitch nearly eighteen years ago.

"Mitchell Arno was married to Maggie Folsum. He claimed his marital rights with her and she was in tears. So you and the defendant forced him outside and beat him up. Didn't you?"

Barbara objected to his leading question; Judge Waldman sustained the objection, and Roxbury backed out of it and asked the same questions, one at a time.

"Did you and the defendant force him outside and beat him up?" he concluded.

"No, sir. Ray took him outside and they fought."

"Wasn't the defendant so enraged that he was uncontrollable?"

"He was outraged."

"Did you publicly disown your son Mitchell that day?"

"Yes, sir."

"Did the defendant tell Mitchell Arno that if he came back again, he would not be able to walk away next time?"

"Yes, sir."

"All right. Last summer on Friday, August second, did your son Mitchell return?"

"Yes, sir."

"Did you see him yourself that day?"

"Yes, sir."

"And what did you do?"

"I pushed him into the shed and told him he had to leave because there was a big party at the house. I told Mama to call Ray and tell him to wait for us. And we took Mitch to Ray's house in Eugene."

"So, aware of the threat the defendant had made, you delivered your son into his hands. Aware of his uncontrollable temper, his violence toward Mitchell—"

"Objection!" Barbara cried. "Improper questions, as the prosecutor knows very well."

"Sustained. Ask your question, Mr. Roxbury."

"You delivered Mitchell into the keeping of the defendant, who had threatened him in public at their last meeting. Is that correct?"

"I took him to Ray's house."

"Did you give him an opportunity to explain the reason for his return?"

"No, we didn't talk."

"Was the occasion of the party his older daughter's birthday?"

"It was her birthday."

"Did it occur to you that Mitchell had come to celebrate his daughter's birthday?"

"No, sir."

"Did you give him an opportunity to explain his presence?"

"No, sir."

"Did you talk to him on the drive to Eugene?"

"No, sir."

"How did you transport him to the defendant's house?"

"In the back of my truck."

"You shoved him into the shed, then you bundled him into the back of a truck, the way you might transport an animal. Is that correct?"

Barbara objected, and it was sustained. Roxbury had made the point, though. He hammered away at Papa Arno. No one had permitted Mitch to explain himself. No one had talked to him, except to tell him to keep away from the inn. Papa Arno didn't know what took place between Ray and Mitch after he left them. Finally Roxbury looked at the old man with open disgust and said no more questions.

"Mr. Arno," Barbara started, "what happened in February of nineteen seventy-nine?"

"Doris Folsum called Mama and said—"

"Objection. Hearsay."

"Your honor," Barbara said quickly, "this goes directly to the state of mind of Mr. Arno at that period. It explains his subsequent actions."

Judge Waldman looked thoughtful for a moment, then nodded. "Overruled," she said. "You may continue, Mr. Arno."

"Mama told me that Mitch was back at the Folsum house and had hurt Maggie." Papa Arno's face was set in rigid lines, but his voice was steady. He kept his gaze on Barbara and spoke in a low tone, pausing now and then, as if in pain. "We went up there and saw she was crying and had a big bruise on her face and on her arms. She said he raped her in front of the baby, that he hurt her down there. She said she told him to leave her alone and he knocked her down and raped her, and then hit her in the face." He looked down at his big hands clasped together on the witness stand.

"You said that he was back. Had he been gone?"

"Yes, ma'am. He left in the spring and came back in February."

"Did you know where he was during that time?"

"No. He just left one day."

"How old was Maggie when he left?"

"Sixteen."

"And how old was she in February when he came back?"

"Seventeen."

She led him through the rest of it.

"Why did you disown Mitch, Mr. Arno?"

"Because he brought dishonor to his wife, our daughter Maggie, and to our family. He no longer could be my son."

"You think of Maggie Folsum as your daughter?"

"She became the daughter we never had."

"In all the years since that day in February until last summer did you ever hear from Mitch?" He said no. "Did he send Christmas presents or birthday cards, or call, or get in touch in any way?"

"No. Not once."

"Why did you feel you had to get him away from Maggie Folsum's inn?"

"There was a big party, a family reunion. It was Gwen's eighteenth birthday, her graduation party, and all the family would be there—all the Folsums, all the Arnos, other relatives. There was a lot of bad feeling about Mitch, how he abandoned Maggie with two babies. I was afraid there would be terrible trouble if he stayed."

"When you took him to Ray's house, you said he was in the back of the truck. Why was that?"

"The truck was what I was driving. With a canopy on it. We hauled a lot of stuff out to the party in it. I put a blanket back there for him to use if it got drafty. Only two of us could ride in the front."

"When you arrived at Ray's house, did he talk then?"

"We didn't stay long enough to talk. I just told Ray to let him stay until after the party, and we'd talk on Monday when we all got back. Ray said he would do that."

"Was Ray enraged?"

"No, ma'am. He was surprised, same as me. And disgusted by the way Mitch looked. Not mad or anything."

Slowly she then asked, "Mr. Arno, if you asked Ray to do something, would it occur to you that he might not do it if it was within his power?"

He looked surprised and shook his head. "No. Anything I asked, he'd do if it killed him."

"And you asked him to let Mitch stay in his house until you all returned home on Monday, when you planned to talk. Is that right?"

"Yes. He said he would."

"At what time did you get home on Monday?"

"About one-thirty or a little after."

"Did you call Ray?"

Roxbury objected. "Beyond the scope of direct," he snapped.

Quickly Barbara said, "This whole line of inquiry was opened by the state. I want to complete it."

"Overruled."

Barbara repeated the question.

"He called me. He said Mitch had left, that he had torn up the place first and then took off. I told him someone had broken in at my house, and he said he would come to our place right away."

"Objection!" Roxbury cried. "Irrelevant."

"Your honor," Barbara said, "this goes to the core of the defense. It is highly relevant."

Judge Waldman beckoned them both to the bench, and there, out of hearing of the jury, she asked Barbara to explain.

"Someone was looking for Mitch Arno, first at Papa Arno's house, then at Ray's, where they found him."

Judge Waldman frowned, tapping one finger lightly on an open notebook before her. After a moment she nodded. "I'll permit the question and answer, but if it turns out to be a red herring, or irrelevant, I'll so advise the jurors and have it stricken."

Barbara thanked her and continued to question Papa Arno. "Did you tell anyone else about the break-in at your house, or that Mitch had come back?"

"Yes. I called both James and David and told them, and

we decided that Ray would call Maggie so she wouldn't be taken by surprise if he showed up at her place.''

Barbara finished with him soon after that, and Roxbury stood up and walked around his table to approach the witness chair. In a soft voice he asked, ''Mr. Arno, on the occasion that your two sons fought, and you then put your injured son on a bus and sent him away, did you at any time consider filing charges against him, or even reporting the incident to the police?''

''No, sir.''

''Did you consider it a family matter, something to be taken care of within the family circle?''

''Yes, sir.''

''Your testimony is that you consider Maggie Folsum to be your daughter. Is that right?''

''Yes, she's our daughter.''

''And as your daughter, she is to be protected, shielded from harm, and avenged if she is mistreated—''

''Objection!'' Barbara said. ''That's a leading question if there ever was one.''

''Sustained. Rephrase your question, Mr. Roxbury.''

He bowed slightly to the judge, then asked, ''Is it your belief that a daughter is to be guarded and protected by her father and her adult brothers?''

''Yes, sir.''

''And do you believe that it is proper for a father and adult brothers to seek to punish anyone who brings harm or dishonor to that daughter?''

Barbara cried out an objection. ''May I approach?'' she asked.

''Your honor,'' Roxbury said smoothly, ''I am merely trying to clarify the position Ms. Folsum holds within the Arno family. We all know that different cultures regard the honor of the family in vastly different ways—''

''Your honor—'' Barbara called out, but before she

could say more, the judge beckoned her and Roxbury to approach the bench.

"Your honor," Barbara said furiously in a low, intense voice, "he's deliberately introducing a cultural distinction where none exists. The Arno family is an American family from generations back, not part of some big Mafia family. This is an outrageous attempt to prejudice the jury against Ray Arno."

Judge Waldman nodded. "Mr. Roxbury, I am sustaining the objection, and I want you to back away from that line of questioning. We will not have a jury racially or culturally prejudiced in this case."

But the damage had been done, Barbara knew. The jury had been prejudiced even if only infinitesimally. When Roxbury resumed his redirect, she watched him closely, aware that he was far more dangerous than she had originally assumed. His move to characterize Ray Arno as a stereotypical Italian-honor-crazed brother was as smart as it was reprehensible. She had no doubt he would allude to it again before this trial was over.

25

Today the media were on hand, newspaper and television reporters as well as cameras; there had been little interest in the case before Barbara's entrance. Frank bantered with the reporters good-naturedly, the way he always did, and Barbara said simply, "Of course, Ray Arno didn't do it. And no comment beyond that."

Then Frank drew her aside in a huddle with John and Shelley. "They'll go on to the house," he said. "We have a date with Trassi."

Bailey was waiting at the curb in Frank's Buick. "Hilton," Frank said.

"What's up?" she asked. "How did it go today? Will Trassi be held?"

"You kidding? He was given a choice: stay put or answer to an arrest warrant and face thirty days in the pokey for every hour he's out of state. He's not happy. Might say he's boiling over, but it's hard to tell with him." Frank clearly was quite amused. "No New York lawyer should come to the boonies and try to outtalk a judge. Gets their back up for some reason."

She grinned. "So what's up now? This meeting?"

"Not sure. I told him no private talks except in your office, or in a public place. He opted for the Hilton bar. We'll see. I made a reservation."

Bailey drove them to the hotel and even got out to walk to the door with them, looking over everyone on the way.

They took the elevator to the second floor, where Frank motioned toward a bar. "He didn't want the top floor, too open," he said.

The bar was dim, noisy, and crowded; after they were shown to a table at the back of the room, Frank excused himself to give Trassi a call. When he returned, they both ordered wine; Trassi appeared before it was served. He was stiffer than ever, and in the faint light, his complexion suggested that he had probably died since the last time Barbara had seen him.

"Mr. Palmer wants to talk to you," he said curtly.

The waiter brought the wine, and Trassi snapped at him, "A telephone."

No one spoke while they waited for the telephone. A pretty young woman was playing very good jazz on a piano; there were loud voices, an undercurrent of lower-pitched voices as counterpoint, now and then bursts of laughter.... Barbara sipped her wine.

The waiter returned with the telephone and plugged it in, retreated again. Trassi dialed a number; apparently an operator came on, and he gave his room number and name, then he waited.

Finally he said, "Trassi," then handed the phone to Barbara.

"Hello," she said. "Barbara Holloway."

"Ms. Holloway, in the company I keep, when you make a deal, you honor it. What are you after now?"

She was very surprised at his voice; it was deep and almost lilting, with just a touch of a brogue, enough to sound charming. "I kept my end of the deal," she said. "I delivered everything I said I would."

"Let's not play games," he said. "Let Trassi go, release him from the subpoena, and let's be done with all this business."

"I can't do that," she said. "I'm afraid he has to testify,

and the only way we can be assured of his presence is by subpoena.''

"What do you want?''

"I want the two men who killed Mitch Arno, and the one who handled them.''

She was watching Trassi as she said this; his expression did not change by even a flicker. Dead man, she thought again.

Palmer paused only a second, then said easily, "I'm afraid I don't have any idea what you're talking about.''

"If you don't, then you have some very dangerous loose cannons in your organization,'' she said. "You should be warned about them and take measures before they do you grave harm.''

"I understand that you have a great number of admirers, Ms. Holloway. I confess that against my will and my determination not to be drawn into their circle, I have found myself joining them. I found myself helpless to resist admiring and, yes, appreciating your cleverness and dedication in pursuing the interests of your former client. I trust you wouldn't now nullify all the very fine work you've done or jeopardize her future enjoyment of her new wealth through any indiscretion, however minor it might appear.'' He sounded pleasant, musing aloud as he went on. "I didn't order the world we find ourselves in. I never would have made it such a dangerous world for the indiscreet.''

"I can assure you, I am very discreet,'' she said coolly. "Now, if there's nothing else on your mind, I have to go. I have work to do. Good-bye, Mr. Palmer.''

"Oh, I don't think we're through yet, Ms. Holloway,'' he said, sounding almost lazy. "Let me talk to Trassi.''

She handed over the phone and picked up her wine. Trassi said, "Yes.'' After a moment he said it again, then hung up. Without another word he rose and left the table, walked out through the lounge.

"Good wine," Barbara said. "Good music, too." She was glad Frank couldn't see how clammy her palms were; she hoped he didn't notice that her hands were trembling.

"Let's get the hell out of here," Frank said.

It was very late when Barbara went to bed that night. The last thing she did was look in on Alan Macagno, who was reading a book in the other apartment, John's apartment. When Bailey said Alan would be staying over for the next few nights, John had said dubiously that he supposed someone could sleep in the extra bedroom on his side. "He isn't being paid to sleep," Bailey had said. And Alan hadn't looked a bit sleepy at two-thirty; he had looked like a college kid cramming for an exam. He would prowl around a little now and then, he had warned Barbara, but he'd try to be quiet about it.

For the duration of the trial Shelley was staying at Bill Spassero's townhouse, where security was okay, Bailey had said after looking it over. And every morning a driver would pick up Frank and Shelley, then come to collect Barbara and take them all to court together.

She was unable to account for the way she barely had time to close her eyes before the alarm went off, and how she dragged through the morning routine of shower and breakfast, only to come wide awake instantly when court convened. Another one of Pavlov's dogs, she thought, disgusted; bell rings, saliva flows, except in her case it was adrenaline.

Roxbury called his witness, and they began.

Winnie York was a young woman, handsome without being pretty, sensibly dressed in a navy wool skirt with a pale blue cardigan, low heels, her only jewelry a single strand of cloisonn beads.

Roxbury led her through the preliminaries quickly: she

was thirty-four, had been born in Newport, and had lived there until she was about sixteen, and she had known all the Arnos and the Folsums. Now she was employed as a sales representative for a publishing company; her territory was the Northwest. She had been transferred to Portland in the spring this year, after working in California for a number of years.

"Please tell the jury what happened last May," Roxbury said. He was being very pleasant to this witness, not rushing her, not pressing.

"Yes," she said. "During a regional book fair here in Eugene, one of the girls I had known as a child suggested we get together for dinner with a couple more old friends. We did that, and went to a microbrewery pub. I hadn't been back to the coast or heard from any of them for nearly twenty years, and they talked about who married whom, children, divorces, gossipy things like that. One of them mentioned Maggie Folsum, and I asked if she had had the baby and if it had been a girl. Maggie had been pregnant when I left. They told me about Maggie and Mitch, and how Ray had beaten him up, and that whole story. I hadn't known any of it. I said that it was a wonder Ray hadn't killed Mitch then, that if he had known about Mitch and Lorinne, he probably would have killed him." She gave her testimony in a steady, uninflected way, as if she had rehearsed it until all the emotion had been wrung out of the words. She kept her gaze on Roxbury throughout.

"What happened next?"

"Sue grabbed my arm and shook her head. A man and a woman had come out of the next booth and walked past us. When they were gone, Sue said that was Ray and Lorinne. I hadn't recognized either of them."

"Did they hear your conversation?"

Barbara objected, and it was sustained. He rephrased the question.

"At the time did you believe they had heard your conversation?"

"Yes. We were not speaking in whispers; we might have been a little loud at times, recounting the past."

"Ms. York," Roxbury said then, his voice dropping to an almost confidential level, "exactly what did you mean by what you said, that if he had known about Mitch and Lorinne, he might have killed Mitch?"

For the first time she hesitated, and her voice was less steady when she answered, "I meant that Mitch had slept with Lorinne several times."

"How did you know that?" Roxbury asked softly.

"Mitch told me."

Roxbury nodded to Barbara with a smug expression. "Your witness."

At first Ray Arno had gone very still when Winnie York was testifying, then he had started scribbling notes. Barbara glanced at them and nodded.

"Ms. York," she said, "let's back up a little to the summer of 1978, the summer that you moved away from the Oregon coast. You said you were almost sixteen? When is your birthday, Ms. York?"

"October twenty-ninth."

"So you were fifteen that summer. Were you a friend of Maggie Folsum, in classes together?"

"No. Not really. She was older, a year ahead of me in school."

"Were you a friend of Lorinne Talbot, now married to Ray Arno?"

She shook her head. "No. She was a lot older. I knew who she was, that's all."

"Eighteen years ago Newport was a much smaller community than it is today, wasn't it?"

"Much smaller," Winnie York said, nodding.

"And Folsum is quite a bit smaller than Newport, isn't it?"

"Yes."

"In those days, before you left, did the local residents pretty much know what was going on in one another's lives?"

"It was a tight community," Winnie said after a brief pause. "I doubt there were many secrets."

One of the women on the jury nodded slightly.

"Were there places where the young people, kids in their teens, hung out together? Danced, played music, things of that sort?"

"Yes, a couple. In Newport, not in Folsum."

"Did Mitch Arno hang out with the young crowd?"

"Sometimes." She had grown cautious now and was watching Barbara intently.

"Did he hang out after he married Maggie?"

Winnie hesitated, then said, "Sometimes."

"Can you tell us exactly when and where Mitch made his comments about Lorinne?"

She shook her head. "I don't remember."

"Well, we know from testimony that he left the area early in May that year, so it must have been before that. Is that right?"

"I guess so."

"All right. Were other people present who heard him?"

"I... No. Just me."

"Were you a good friend of his?"

"He just liked to talk to me."

"Do you know how old Mitch Arno was that spring?"

Roxbury objected on the grounds of irrelevance.

"But it's relevant," Barbara said. "If Mitch Arno was making claims of conquest, we have a right to know something about the circumstances."

"Overruled," Judge Waldman said.

"Do you know how old he was?" Barbara asked again.

"Twenty-two," Winnie said in a low voice.

"And you had become his confidante when you were fifteen? Is that what you're telling us?"

"I... He said there weren't many people he could really talk to, and he liked to talk with me."

Barbara nodded and went to stand by her table. "Did the two of you leave the group and go off to talk alone?"

"Sometimes," Winnie said in a very low voice.

"Do you recall now what led up to his comment about Lorinne?"

"Yes. I said I wouldn't see him alone because he was a married man with a pregnant wife. He said the marriage was a big joke; as soon as the baby was born, it would end. He said Ray told him he'd beat the crap out of him if he didn't do right by Maggie, and he laughed and said if Ray knew about him and Lorinne, the times they had gone to bed together, he might try to make him marry her, too, and turn him into a bigamist."

"Did Mitch say he loved you?"

She looked startled, then ducked her head and gazed at the table before her. "Yes, he did."

"Did you believe him?"

"Yes."

"Did he tell you he was going away?"

"Yes."

"Did he say he wanted to take you with him?" It was a long shot into a very dark place, but she asked it and didn't hold her breath for fear someone would notice.

"Yes," Winnie said in a near whisper.

"Did Mitch Arno seduce you when you were a fifteen-year-old girl and he was twenty-two?"

Winnie hesitated and Roxbury yelled an objection. Before Judge Waldman could respond, Barbara said quietly, "I withdraw the question."

Instead, she asked, "Did he borrow money from you?"

"Yes."

"And did he pay you back?"

She shook her head. "No."

"After Mitch left in early May, did he get in touch with you at any time?"

"No."

"Did he tell you good-bye?"

"No."

"Did he lie to you?"

"He lied."

"All right. Last May, when you met your friends at the brew pub, did the conversation continue after Ray and Lorinne left the restaurant?"

"Yes, for a long time."

"Did anyone refute what you had said about Mitch and Lorinne?"

She nodded. "They all did. They said people would have known, but besides that, she was too old for him. He couldn't have been more than thirteen when she left to go to college, and she never was back much after that." She stopped, but looked as if there had been more, and Barbara waited for her to continue. "They said he just liked young girls, very young girls."

"Was his nickname brought up?" Barbara asked when Winnie stopped again.

"Yes," she said faintly. "They used to call him Mitch the Cherry Picker."

"Thank you," Barbara said. "No further questions."

After a brief recess, Roxbury called the next witness: Judith Ludlum. She was seventy, bent with osteoporosis and she had sharp features, a long bony nose, sharply pointed chin, frail-looking wrists and fingers. Her hair was gray, in a frizzy perm; she wore bifocals.

She stated that she lived in Corvallis, where she owned and managed an apartment building, two quads for college girls. Her voice was high-pitched and wavery.

"Do you recall a time when Lorinne Talbot lived in one of the quads?" Roxbury asked.

"Yes, back in the seventies, seventy-seven and seventy-eight. Two years."

"Is there a particular reason for you to recall her?"

"Yes, there is. I thought she would be a steadying influence on the younger girls. She already had some degrees and she was going to Monmouth to get her teaching certification. She must have been about twenty-eight then. The others were all real young, hardly old enough to be away from home."

"Was she a steadying influence?"

"For a while I thought so, but then I changed my mind."

"Why was that?"

"Well, she got engaged, you know, and they were out all hours, her and Ray Arno. Then she took off with his brother Mitch for a weekend or two. I changed my mind, all right."

"Tell us about when she took off with his brother Mitch," Roxbury said softly, glancing at the jury as if to make certain they were listening.

"Well, I live downstairs in the building, and the quads are on the second and third floors. All women, no men allowed except in the front room. This was on a Friday, in early April; I was out front weeding in the daffodils when a man drove up, and he began to blow the horn. I don't allow that. If they come for a girl, they can go in the front room like civilized people. I was just starting to go over and tell him to stop. I thought at first it was Ray, but it wasn't. I heard Lorinne yell out the window at him. Mitch, she called him, and she told him she was coming. Then I heard her tell one of the other girls she'd be back Sunday night, and she came out with her suitcase and got in the car. He leaned over and kissed her, and they took off."

"That was on a Friday afternoon?"

"Yes, before dark; I was still out weeding."

"Did you see her come home on Sunday?"

"Yes. I heard the car stop out front, and I looked out just to see if someone was about to come in. It was late, after ten, and they were in the car kissing and hugging. Half an hour or longer. Then she came in all smiling. And he took off."

Roxbury nodded gravely. "I see. You said she went with him more than once. Can you recall another time?"

"Yes. A few weeks after that. She put a lot of camping stuff in her own car that afternoon, and he called her on the telephone. One of the girls told her it was Mitch on the phone, and she came down to talk to him. She said she would meet him as soon as she got off work. She didn't come home that time until Sunday late."

"You didn't see them together that time?"

"No. I just heard her ask him where he was, and she said she knew where it was, and would be by as soon as she got off work at nine. I thought at the time that was a pretty late hour to be meeting someone, but I didn't say anything to her."

"Did you overhear anything else she said to him?"

"Yes." Her lips tightened until they nearly disappeared. "She said, 'Don't tell Ray anything.' I thought maybe she was fixing to break off with Mitch and was afraid he might tell his brother about them and their meetings."

Roxbury finished with her soon after that, and Barbara stood up. "Ms. Ludlum, you said at first you thought it was Ray Arno blowing his horn that afternoon, then you saw that it wasn't. What made you change your mind?"

"Well, I got a good look at him," she said. "I got up

and walked to the end of the hedges, where I had a good look at him.''

"Could you see him or the car he was driving before you walked to the end of the hedges?''

"Not much. Just a glimpse of the car, dark, like the one Ray usually drove, that's what made me think it was him.''

"When she got in the car, did he put his arms around her?''

"No. Just leaned over and kissed her.''

"Did he kiss her on the lips?''

"I don't know.''

"Well, did she turn toward him?''

"Not much. She knew I was watching.''

"Was she facing the windshield, the front of the car?''

"Yes, like I said, she knew I was watching.''

"Yes, you said that. All right, when she came back on Sunday night, what were you doing at the time?''

"Watching television in the front room.''

"But you were able to hear the car drive up and stop? Is that right?''

"Yes, I heard it.''

"Then what did you do?''

"Like I said, I got up to have a look, to see if anyone was coming in.''

"Where did you look from? The windows in the front room?''

"No. I went to the hall and the front door; there are two windows by the door, one on each side.''

"Was it very dark outside?''

"It was after ten, yes, dark.''

"Did they have the dome light on in the car?''

"No. They wouldn't do that, not with all the hugging and kissing and such.''

"Were they parked under a streetlight?''

"No. There isn't any light out there.''

"I see. How far back is your front door from the curb?"

"I don't know. I never measured it."

"Let's reconstruct your property," Barbara said pleasantly. "Is there a porch?"

"Yes."

Step by step Barbara drew from her a description of the house and the landscaping in the front. Finally she said, "So there are bushes, a hedge, several trees. Forty feet? Is that about right?"

"I don't know. Maybe that's about right."

"Was there a porch light on?"

"Yes."

"All right. Was there a light in the hall where you were standing?"

"No."

"So you left watching television to stand in the dark hallway, where you looked out past the porch light, past shrubs and trees, to a dark car at the curb. Ms. Ludlum, what could you actually see in the car under those conditions?"

"Enough," she said indignantly. "I could see them just fine."

Barbara shook her head. "Were you watching television again when she entered the house?"

"Yes. I could see her fine. I turned on the hall light by then."

"Do you usually stay in the front room with the door open to the hall?"

"Yes, of course. I have to know who's coming and going."

"Oh, I see. The other time you mentioned, you said Lorinne had put camping gear inside her car earlier. Is that right?"

"Yes, a sleeping bag, a pack of some sort."

"Did you answer the phone when the call came for her?"

"No. I was in the front room. One of the girls picked up the phone."

"But you could hear what was said?"

She hesitated, then said yes.

"Were you watching television that afternoon?"

"Yes, but the sound was turned real low. I could hear her."

"You testified that she asked him where he was, and said she knew where that was. Do you know where she met him?"

"Yes, at the Black Angus Motel."

"Before, you said she knew where it was. Is it now your testimony that she mentioned the motel by name?"

Ludlum's lips tightened even more and she nodded, then said almost defiantly, "Yes. The Black Angus."

"Is there an extension phone in the front room?" Barbara asked coolly.

"Yes, of course."

"Ms. Ludlum, in fact, didn't you listen to part of her conversation on the extension phone, up to the point where she asked you to hang it up?"

"I can explain that," Ludlum said swiftly. "Sometimes the girls upstairs don't hear if someone yells for them to come to the phone, and it stays off the hook for hours. I wanted to make certain she took her call and then hung up, that's all."

"Did you hear what Mitch told her when she said she would meet him after work?"

"No, that's when she came to the door and said to hang up the phone."

"Did you hear her say for him not to tell Ray something in particular?"

"Just not to tell him, not to call him."

"So, after you hung up the telephone, you continued to listen to her half of the conversation?"

"I could hear every word."

"Do you know where she went camping that weekend?"

"No."

"Did you see her with Mitch that weekend?"

"No, of course not."

"Did it make you angry for her to tell you to stop eaves-dropping on her private call?"

"I was doing my duty, trying to keep my house respectable, that's all."

Barbara gave her a scathing look, then took her seat. "I have no further questions for this witness."

26

Lunch that day was a hurried business in Barbara's office. Bailey was waiting for her with a report on the neighbors of Victor Radiman, the next witness; she read his report as she ate a sandwich.

"Good job," she said. "All right, Roxbury will wrap it up today, and we'll have the rest of the week to get our act together. Anything yet on Palmer?"

"Nope. Hasn't budged," Bailey said. "And Trassi hasn't had a visitor yet, but he's burning up the telephone lines."

Frank walked in and looked over the remaining sandwiches. "Got it," he said, giving Barbara a Xerox copy of an inventory. "Took a court order, but I got it." He had a police report of the possessions that had been taken from Radiman the night he was arrested, which had been the first night that Ray Arno had spent in jail. Frank helped himself to a sandwich while Barbara scanned the list he had handed her.

Then they were back in court and Victor Radiman was called. Roxbury was brusque with him, as if he wanted the jury to know he had little sympathy for this witness, but it was necessary to hear him out.

Radiman was a florid-faced man in his late forties, with the telltale broken veins in his cheeks and the bulbous nose of a heavy drinker who suffered from rosacea. He was a scaler for a lumber mill, he said. He kept his gaze fixed on

Roxbury, listening intently to the questions, then turned to address the jury when he answered in a too-loud voice. His story was that he had been arrested on the night of August sixteenth for disorderly conduct and had spent the night in the Lane County jail.

"Tell the jury what happened that night," Roxbury said.

"I was trying to sleep and I kept hearing this guy sort of moaning and making noise. He woke me up and I couldn't get back to sleep. I could hear him crying and saying he was sorry, that he didn't mean to do it, and praying for God to forgive him, things like that."

"Can you repeat his exact words?" Roxbury asked harshly.

"Some of them. He said, 'I didn't mean to hit him that hard. I didn't mean to kill him. I couldn't help it. I'm sorry. God, I'm sorry. Dear God, forgive me, I'm sorry.' Then he said, 'God, have mercy on his soul. Have mercy on my soul.'" His voice was not only too loud, the words were curiously uninflected, almost flat, turning the prayer into a recitation that could as easily have been a laundry list.

"Then what happened?"

"I yelled at him to shut up, and after that he was quieter, but he kept praying for a long time."

"Do you know who that man was?"

"It was the defendant over there. Ray Arno."

"Was he in the same cell with you?"

"No. I saw him in a cell when they took me to lockup. I noticed because he looked wild and like he'd been crying. His eyes were red, like they get when you've been crying. And one of the other guys in my cell said he was in for murder."

"You got a good look at him, at Ray Arno?"

"Yes. And I heard him like I said."

Roxbury sat down.

"Mr. Radiman," Barbara said, standing at her table, "what were you arrested for that night?"

"Like I said, disorderly conduct."

"That's the charge you pleaded guilty to, but what were you charged with by the arresting officer?"

Roxbury objected. "Prejudicial," he snapped.

"No, it isn't," Barbara said quickly. "There is no one clear definition of disorderly conduct; what constitutes disorderly conduct is in the eye of the beholder, and since Mr. Roxbury brought it up, the jury has a right to know precisely what is meant in this situation."

She was allowed to continue, but Radiman shook his head. "All's I know is that my lawyer said if they asked me if I was disorderly, I should say yes, and I did."

"I have here the arresting officer's report from that night," Barbara said, picking it up. "Let me refresh your memory." She showed the report to the judge and to Roxbury, then read from it: "Suspect was in a drunken state; the television was on loud enough to hear from the street; his neighbors—" She stopped and said, "I'll leave out the names of the neighbors who brought the complaint." Judge Waldman nodded, and Barbara read the rest of the report: "His neighbors complained that other times when they asked him to turn down the volume, he threatened to set his dog on them. When they knocked on his door on the morning of August seventeenth, he shoved one of them off the porch and used loud and abusive threatening language. Plaintiffs then called the police...." She looked up at Radiman and said clearly and slowly, "The arresting officer charged you with drunkenness, with maintaining a public nuisance, with assault and battery, and with resisting arrest. Do you recall those charges, Mr. Radiman?"

He shook his head. "I said I was probably disorderly and that's what I was guilty of."

"Did you pay your neighbor's doctor bill as a result of that incident?"

"Yeah, I agreed to pay it."

"What time of night did all this take place?"

"I don't remember."

"The arresting officer has the time on his report, Mr. Radiman. It's given as twelve-forty a.m. Do you recall that now?"

"It wasn't that late."

"And it says here that you were booked into the Lane County jail at one-ten in the morning. Do you recall that?"

"No. It wasn't that late."

"I see. So everyone else has the time wrong. Do you recall what time was right?"

"No. I don't remember."

"After a person is taken to jail, there is a certain routine that they follow, isn't there? Fingerprints are recorded, an inventory of possessions is made, things of that sort. Do you recall being searched and fingerprinted?"

"Sure."

"Do you recall being taken to a cell where there were others already locked up?"

"Yes. I was drinking earlier, but by then I was pretty sober."

"Were lights on all through the jail?"

He hesitated, as if trying to remember, then nodded. "Not real bright lights, but there were lights."

"Lights in the various cells? Really? At two in the morning? Are you sure, Mr. Radiman?"

Roxbury objected. "Witness has already answered the question."

"But perhaps he misspoke," Barbara said.

"Overruled," Judge Waldman said.

Radiman was watching Barbara as closely as he had

watched Roxbury. When she repeated the question, he nodded. "I could see in the cells just fine."

She smiled slightly, although his loud, flat voice was starting to grate on her nerves; then she turned her back to pick up a second report. "I have here the inventory of your possessions from that morning. Do you recall signing it?"

When he didn't reply, she faced him again. "Did you hear the question?"

"No, I didn't. Your back was turned and you were mumbling."

"Sorry," she said. "Do you recall signing the inventory of your possessions on that occasion?"

"Yes," he said.

Still facing him, but holding the sheet of paper in front of her mouth, she asked clearly, "Why do you play the television so loud that it can be heard from the street?"

He fidgeted a little, glanced at Roxbury, then at the jury, and finally said, "Can you ask the question again? I didn't catch it all." His face, florid to start with, was a darker red.

She repeated the question, and he said angrily, "I don't play it that loud. They're just troublemakers, looking to make trouble for me."

She covered her mouth again and read from the list of belongings the police had taken from him the night he was arrested: "A wallet, and the amount of money in it, credit card, driver's license, change, pocket knife, keys, hearing-aid battery pack and hearing aid…" She put the list down and asked him, "Did you sign the inventory for those items?"

He hesitated again, then nodded. "I signed something. I don't remember what it was."

"When did you tell the police that you had heard Mr. Arno talking in the next cell?"

"I don't know, after a day or two."

"Was it after you retained an attorney? As a result, were the charges reduced to disorderly conduct?"

Roxbury was shouting his objection before she finished the question.

This time, with a look of sharp rebuke, Judge Waldman sustained the objection.

Barbara nodded and turned to her table again; then facing away from Radiman, she asked, "How long have you used a hearing aid?"

She had to repeat the question, and he flushed even darker and said, "I hardly ever use one. Just for movies."

"In fact," she said coldly, "you are an expert lip reader, aren't you?"

"I can hear you."

"But not if I cover my mouth, can you?" she said, covering her mouth.

"I can hear you," he said angrily.

Keeping her hand in front of her mouth, she asked, "What time is lights-out in the jail?"

"I can hear you, I said," he snapped.

"Then answer the question," she snapped back, even sharper.

When he made no response, Barbara said to the judge, "Please direct the witness to answer the question, or else admit he couldn't hear it." When she turned to look at the judge, Radiman did, also.

"Did you hear the question, Mr. Radiman?" Judge Waldman asked clearly.

"No. She's playing tricks with me, trying to trap me."

Before Barbara could say anything, Judge Waldman asked, "Mr. Radiman, did you at any time indicate to the police or the district attorney's office that you suffer a hearing loss?"

"I don't," he said. "Not really. Just a little bit at movies."

Judge Waldman leaned back and nodded to Barbara. "You may continue."

She studied Radiman for a second, then said, "No further questions for this witness." She hoped the jury read her meaning: what was the point, since he had impeached himself already?

Roxbury tried to salvage something. "Do you have more trouble with some voices than with others?" he asked.

"Yeah. Soft women's voices are harder than men's. High voices, like hers, are the hardest to hear." He inclined his head toward Barbara, who grinned.

"Are you certain you saw Ray Arno in his cell the night you were booked?" He said yes emphatically. "And are you certain you could hear his voice clearly, hear his words plainly?" He said yes, in an even louder, more assertive voice.

Roxbury read from his notes: "I didn't mean to hit him that hard. I didn't mean to kill him. I couldn't help it. I'm sorry. God, I'm sorry. Dear God, forgive me, I'm sorry." He looked up at Radiman. "Were those the words you heard that night?"

"Yes, they were. Plain as I heard you right now."

"Try a question facing away from him," Barbara suggested. Roxbury yelled an objection, and the judge used her gavel to make them both behave.

"The jury is instructed to disregard counsel's remark," she said sharply.

When Roxbury finished with Radiman, Judge Waldman summoned Barbara and Roxbury to the bench.

"We will have a recess at this time, and I want you both in chambers in ten minutes," she said.

Returning to her table, Barbara saw Matthew Gramm at the rear of the courtroom, standing near the door with his arms crossed over his chest. Gramm was the district attorney. Roxbury rushed to him, and they left together.

"What's up?" Frank growled when she cursed in an undertone.

"Don't know. But Gramm's in on it, and we're due in chambers in ten minutes. I want you to go with me. If they're trying to pull a fast one at this late date—"

"Don't panic until you see the fire," Frank said.

Today Judge Waldman did not serve coffee; she had not taken off her judicial robe, and was seated at her desk with the visitors' chairs arranged in a semicircle across from it. Gramm and Roxbury nodded at Frank and Barbara, and that ended the civilities. If Roxbury could have been described as an accountant with fair accuracy, Gramm would have fitted anyone's description of a wrestler, which he had been in his youth. He was fifty-five, sandy-haired and tanned, and large in every dimension, with thick shoulders and a deep chest, over six feet tall, well over two hundred pounds, and most of it muscle. He worked out, he liked to tell people; athletes got flabby if they didn't continue to work out all their lives. He was not flabby.

"Mr. Gramm has filed a motion requesting a short continuance of the trial," Judge Waldman said crisply. "Mr. Gramm, will you explain please."

"Although this is highly irregular, which we admit," Gramm said easily, "under the circumstances, we are compelled to ask for a delay. A witness has come forward today—this morning, in fact—with a statement of such gravity, it cannot be ignored. We are forced to investigate, and our investigation will cause a brief delay in the proceedings."

"A surprise witness!" Barbara exclaimed in disbelief. "You've got to be kidding! With no discovery? Please!"

Ignoring her, Gramm addressed the judge. "This witness called my office earlier today, and came in person three hours ago. She has made a formal statement in which she swears she saw Ray Arno throwing a large bundle into the McKenzie River at eight o'clock on the morning of August sixth. At this moment we have divers in the water, searching for the bundle.''

Barbara made a rude snorting sound. "Is your witness certifiably blind? A partner for Radiman?"

"Our witness," he said smoothly, "is Marta Delancey, the wife of California senator Rolfe Delancey."

For a moment no one moved, then Gramm reached into his briefcase and withdrew a folder, which he handed to Barbara. "Her statement," he said, not quite smiling, but close enough for her to want to kick him. "I already handed a copy to Judge Waldman." He turned back to the judge then. "Of course, we will call her even if we don't find the bundle, but it would be a dereliction of our duty not to search for it."

"How long a delay are you requesting?" Judge Waldman asked. She had been cool at the start of the meeting; now she was icy.

"Two days only," he said. "Mrs. Delancey said the bundle appeared quite heavy. It could have been weighted with something, and it is quite possible that it has not moved very far."

Frank and Barbara both began to make objections, and the judge heard them without interruption; then she said, "I will grant the continuance for two days only. Presumably, Mr. Roxbury, in the event that a bundle is found, you will then want to call a witness to identify the contents. I warn you to have any discovery in the hands of the defense by Friday morning when we resume. You will not be permitted to rest the state's case until the defense has had an opportunity to examine all the evidence you uncover, and statements from all the witnesses you intend to call to testify."

"Your honor," Barbara said very quietly then, "this de-

velopment means that the defense very likely won't be able
to conclude during the period we agreed upon earlier.''

''I'm afraid that's correct,'' Judge Waldman said with
some bitterness. Evidently she was already considering
what the news of a delay would mean to the jury panel.

''They can use this hiatus exactly as if we had rested,'
Gramm said. ''It shouldn't make a bit of difference to
them.''

Judge Waldman regarded him silently for a moment.
''Don't push too hard, Mr. Gramm,'' she said. ''I'll inform
the jury that we will be in recess until Friday morning.'
She stood up. The meeting was over.

27

They had read Marta Delancey's statement in Barbara's office. A glum silence had followed. "She was a local girl," Frank said thoughtfully. "Can't recall her maiden name, but she married Joel Chisolm, and after he died, she latched on to the senator. She's on committees, boards of directors, things of that sort. Respected."

The silence had settled again, until Barbara broke it the next time. "Shit!"

Now she was waiting for Ray to be delivered to the conference room at the jail. Her father was having a tête-à-tête with Sylvia Fenton, and Bailey and Shelley had been dispatched to dig up what they could about Marta Delancey.

Ray was almost bouncy when he entered the small room and sat down. "Wow! You did a real job on that creep today."

She shrugged. "He was easy. Ray, do you know Marta Delancey?"

He looked blank, then shook his head. "Why? Who's she?"

"Of course, we knew Marta after she married Joel Chisolm," Sylvia said to Frank.

They were in a small sitting room, Sylvia, Joe, and Frank, having a glass of wine and some very fine spiced shrimp and lobster tidbits. The room was overcrowded with furniture, as were all the rooms in the mansion, but it was an intimate setting, and the artwork had been held to a minimum here. Only one wall had paintings, Picassos, and the tables had space for the Waterford wineglasses, after some of the knickknacks had been rearranged. Lovely crystal fish and Dresden bowls of candies, a hand-beaten copper bowl of agate marbles...

Joe Fenton had a little bit of fuzzy white hair, hardly enough to cover his scalp, and fuzzy white eyebrows; his eyes were bright blue, and his cheeks as pink as any Santa's. He was wearing a gorgeous Chinese brocade jacket and old worn house slippers. Sylvia had on a silk sari in a wild red print. On the table at her elbow was a silver bowl with a lot of rings in it; the gemstones flashed and glittered as if with an inner life.

"Joel Chisolm was an idiot," Sylvia said complacently. "He got an MBA, and God alone knows how he managed to get through the courses—we always thought Marta did the work for him—and they went off to New York for him to make a million or two, but he was mugged and killed. What else do you want to know?"

"What about her, Marta? Tell me about her."

"Marta Perkins, gold digger," Sylvia said promptly. "Greta, Joel's mother, wanted to kill her when she snatched little Joel. She told me all about it. I reminded her that people had talked about me that way, and she pooh-poohed that, said this was different. And maybe it was." She looked at her husband, who was beaming at her.

"The Chisolms made a fortune in wood products," Joe Fenton said then. "They had three kids, none of them able to tie their own shoes, so there was a lot of disappointment in that house. But they had hopes, always had hopes, you see. Marta's father was a working logger, worked for the Chisolms, in fact. She was a pretty girl, I remember."

"She tried to snag you," Sylvia said with good humor.

"When was that?" Frank asked.

"Oh, we were married by then. And she was married to Joel. Fat chance she had, but she gave him the eye plenty. He would have been a better catch than Joel, you understand. Anyway, they got married and after five or six years moved to New York, and a few months later, his father died from a massive heart attack. No warning symptoms or anything, just keeled over one day. Poor Greta was devastated. Her kids were a mess and she was a widow. She hit the bottle, and that and prescription drugs did her in within a few months. Found dead one morning. So the kids suddenly inherited a lot of money. There's Harry, he's up in Portland, I think, with his third or fourth wife, and broke. And Connie, who's off in Italy, last I heard. And Joel was mugged and shot soon after his mother died; after he and Marta came home and cleaned out the old house; they took everything worth a cent and moved it all back to New York, and probably had a big yard sale. Harry and Connie fought like devils to prevent it, but Greta had left the house and everything in it to Joel. She told me that Joel needed money, that things just seemed to go wrong for him. The rest of the estate, stocks and such, was split three ways. I don't believe any of them ever spoke to one another after that." She speared a piece of lobster and ate it, then went on. "So there was Marta, a very pretty widow with a fortune of her own. She's smart, got herself a college degree in history, I believe, and she learned how to eat with a fork and everything. She married the senator within the year. And he has an even bigger fortune. She's done well, little Marta Perkins."

By the time Frank left, he felt he knew more about Marta Perkins Delancey than any tabloid reporter could ever uncover. At the same time, he felt that all this information was as useful as a tabloid story that proved the aliens had landed.

* * *

Rain moved in before dawn on Wednesday, not a hard, driving rain, just insistent and continuous, and it was still like that when Barbara and Bailey left her apartment before nine. She drove to I-5, onto Highway 126, through Springfield, past Weyerhauser with its loathsome smoke curling up to merge with the clouds and turn them a dirty yellow, then the straight shot toward the McKenzie River bridge. She didn't exceed the speed limit; when the bridge came into sight through the relentless rain, Bailey said. ''Twenty-two minutes.''

She slowed down. Ahead, on the other side of the bridge, a turnoff access road wound down to a parking area near a small beach where the river was shallow and not too fast for swimming, although the McKenzie was always so cold, summer and winter, that warnings about hypothermia had to be repeated year after year in the hottest weather. Now the beach was crowded with official cars; a dozen men in waterproof ponchos, under umbrellas, were standing around, a camera crew huddled by their own van…. There were two drift boats in the water.

Barbara didn't stop; she felt sorry for the divers in the swirling frigid water. Today the river looked black; the sky at treetop level and the steady rain dimmed what little light there was at this time of year. She hoped that Gramm and Roxbury were freezing their asses off down there in the rain.

''Tell me where to turn for the cabin,'' she said. She had been there once, but on a sunny fall day, and the road had been easy to spot.

''There it is,'' Bailey said a minute later.

She made the turn off the highway onto a county road and the forest closed in on both sides immediately. They had been in farmland until now—fields, pastures, filbert orchards, farmhouses—but here the forest took over with massive fir trees that blotted out the sky.

"Third turn on the right," Bailey said, watching closely. The next turn put them on an even narrower road that twisted and climbed through the forest. There were driveways, but the cabins themselves were invisible. "There," Bailey said. She turned onto a gravel driveway, and ahead was the Marshall cabin.

"Okay," she said, and started backing and filling until she was heading out again. It would be faster going out, she knew; it took ten minutes to get back to the bridge, then another twenty minutes to return to Eugene.

Neither commented again until she parked at the office on Sixth. "It's a fuckup," he said then.

"You got that right," she agreed unhappily.

Late in the afternoon she visited Ray. "How are you holding up?" she asked.

He looked very tired and worried. "Okay, I guess. I've tried and tried to come up with a time I might have run across Marta Delancey, and there's just nothing. I never saw her in my life."

"Did you know her first husband? Joel Chisolm. They were still married eighteen years ago, just about when you were opening your shop. Could he have been a customer?"

He shook his head. "Good God, eighteen years ago! Chisolm. You mean the lumber-company people?"

"He was one of the sons."

He shook his head more emphatically. "I don't believe the Chisolms mingled much with the Arnos. I never met him, never even saw him that I'm aware of."

"Were you keeping records back then? Would his name be in your books if he bought anything from your shop?"

"No. Probably not. I learned about good records later, the first time I was audited, five or six years into the business." He leaned forward then and asked harshly, "Why is she doing this? What's in it for her?"

"I wish I knew," Barbara said.

"I didn't throw anything in the river," he said with great intensity. "She didn't see me. I didn't kill Mitch. But right now I feel like I'm losing my mind. A strange woman can come forward and convict me with a lie. Why is she doing it?"

Barbara reached across the table and took his hand. "I know all that, Ray, and you're not convicted yet. Try to relax, get a little rest while you can."

Some of the tension left him; she knew, because she could almost feel it flowing into her through their joined hands.

That night Frank ordered food from Martin's. Too busy to cook, he said, they'd have to make do with second best. Martin had prepared roast duckling in a sweet and hot mustard sauce, asparagus tips with herbed butter, a potato-leek casserole.... Binnie had added one of her specialties: raspberry cream tarts in hazelnut crust.

John didn't stay long after they had dessert and coffee; he was working hard to wrap up his report on the Canadian mine, which he had to finish before Christmas.

She walked to the door with him. "This is a bitch," she said. "But it won't be much longer. Promise."

"Better not be. If I'm sleeping when you get in, wake me up." Then, in a whisper, he added, "If Alan's sleeping leave him alone."

Frank was just bringing in a carafe of fresh coffee when she returned to the dining room. "Let's talk about Marta Perkins Delancey," he said. "After I talked with Sylvia, I spent some time with Bud Yates, up at his place in Pleasant Hill. He suspected I wanted to pump him, and when I said it was about Marta, he said pump away." Bud Yates was one of his old friends, older than Frank, and retired now.

"Bud was the Chisolm attorney for a good many years,"

Frank said. "And he gave me an earful. Between him and Sylvia, I reckon I got the whole story. After Marta hooked Joel, they stayed in Eugene for a few years and went through his money, took it down to zilch. Then Marta got an itch to move to New York. So off they went. Greta, the mother, was heartbroken, and the money problem got worse. She hated Marta with all her soul, and probably with cause. Anyway, after the father died, Joel began talking about his marriage being a mistake after all, and Greta bought it. Joel and Marta came home to discuss things. He said he was going to leave Marta and live in the family house with his mother. That's when she added the clause to her will, leaving it to him, and everything in it. It had priceless antiques the Chisolms had collected and she had added to, things like that. She told Bud that she knew Joel was irresponsible about finances, but at least he would have the house and its contents, and maybe after the divorce he would find a nice local girl and really settle down. She also said that Joel was in desperate trouble and that she had made him a big loan. Something to do with brokering phony stocks. Two weeks after they left again, with a big check, Greta died. Harry, the other son, accused Marta of poisoning her, but nothing came of it. Alcohol, sleeping medications, and tranquilizers, that was all, and his accusation was treated as sour grapes.

"After the estate was settled, they had this fancy mover come in, crate up everything, and haul it off to New York, and they put the house in the hands of a real estate company and left town. Two weeks later, Joel was shot in the street and killed. They had gone to a play and were on their way to a supper club when it happened. Marta was not injured."

He stopped and regarded Barbara with a knowing look. "Sylvia said they used a mover who specialized in handling expensive goods, one based in New York."

"Oh, my God! Palmer?"

"Possibly. She didn't know the company name."

Barbara remembered Ray's question and repeated it: "What's in it for Marta? Why would the wife of a United States senator come forward to commit perjury?" She shook her head. "We have to try to find the link between her and Palmer. Your job, Bailey, whatever it takes. And I need some ammunition by Friday."

Bailey groaned. "You know we can't dig deep that fast."

"Whatever you can find. And, Bailey, a three-way link maybe: Marta, the senator, and Palmer. See what you can find about Joel's death." She frowned, thinking, then said slowly, "She knew about Palmer's moving business eighteen years ago. Was it operating then the way it is now, a little business deal of moving something to cover up the real transaction? In that case, maybe a murder?"

Frank made a throat-clearing noise, which she ignored. She knew he hated it when she went leaping over obstacles blindly. She turned to Shelley. "Your work is in Portland. Find Harry Chisolm and talk to him. Did Joel ever go fishing? Buy stuff from a local shop? That line. We may want him to testify, but you'll have to judge that. Remember, a bad witness is worse than no witness, and if he hates Marta enough, he might be a very bad witness. But we need to know. I'll want dates, when Marta and Joel left town here for New York, when and where Ray opened his shop...."

When she got home, John was sleeping. She stood inside the bedroom door for a moment, then quietly left again and went to her office, where she sat at her desk and thought about time. All this business about Marta was cutting into the hours she had budgeted for other things. She swiveled in her chair to examine the calendar on her wall. Christmas was on a Wednesday. Would Judge Waldman take the entire week off, or just Tuesday and Wednesday? What she wouldn't do, she had made clear, was sequester the jury at this point, nor would she work them on Christmas Eve or Christmas Day. Barbara did not believe the judge would send the jury into deliberation on Monday, two days before Christmas.

And John's children were due the day after Christmas. He had motel reservations at the coast, for them to see Keiko the whale. And a day planned in the mountains, sledding and snowboarding. A day in Portland to visit the science museum... Plans for shopping for their presents.

She closed her eyes hard; then, very roughly, she cursed Palmer and Marta, and finally she opened her briefcase, pulled out papers, and started to work.

28

At four-thirty on Thursday Barbara and Frank joined a group of people in the forensics lab. There were detectives, forensic personnel, Matthew Gramm and assistant D.A. Craig Roxbury, and now Frank and Barbara gathered around a long table that held a shallow black plastic pan, such as a photographer might use for developing large negatives. A stark white light glared on a black plastic bag in the pan. The table was covered with a white plastic-coated sheet of paper, and there was a second shallow pan, empty.

Two cameras were recording everything, one on a fixed tripod, the other handheld by a photographer who moved in and out among the assembled witnesses.

The black plastic bag was heavy-duty, industrial strength, fastened by a wire that had rusted and fused together but was so brittle that when the forensics technician cut it, it broke in several places. There were a few small slits in the plastic bag, and it was still partly filled with water; when it was opened, the water ran out into the pan.

The technician was wearing elbow-length rubber gloves and a rubber apron. Carefully he opened the bag and held it open for the photographer, then he reached inside and drew out the contents, moving slowly, stopping frequently for the pictures. A sodden stained shirt, black slacks, black shoes, filthy white socks, very brief briefs, a pair of leather work gloves, a second pair of canvas gloves, a lead pipe like the one Mitch had carried in his duffel bag, six big rocks. The technician identified each item as he pulled it out and laid it in the pan. After the plastic bag was empty, he examined the pockets of the slacks and the shirt, all empty.

"Ms. Holloway, Mr. Holloway," the district attorney said then, "may we have a word? Outside, in the corridor."

They followed him and Roxbury to the hall.

"Obviously, they can't do anything with that stuff until it dries out," Gramm said. "We can't tell if those stains are just muddy water or blood at this point. What I propose is that we ask Judge Waldman for another postponement, until Monday morning. By then we'll know something about this evidence. Is that agreeable to you?"

Barbara nodded. "You understand that you're asking for this delay, not I."

"I know that," he said curtly. "I informed Judge Waldman as soon as I received word that the bag had been found. She wants to see us in chambers. She said as soon as we had opened it, to come over directly; she'll be waiting."

She was at her desk, toying with gold-framed glasses, with a calendar before her. Her nod was frosty and her words were clipped and sharp when she said, "Please be seated." As soon as they had taken chairs opposite her, she turned toward Roxbury. "What do you propose to do?"

"Well—" he started, but Gramm interrupted him and answered.

"Your honor, we regret very much this unforeseen development, but we all are experienced enough to know that sometimes the unexpected does occur."

Judge Waldman shook her head at him. "Mr. Gramm, no speeches. We are all experienced enough to know that an enraged jury panel is a bad jury panel. How they will vent their displeasure is an unknown factor. Will you introduce this new evidence, and how long will it take?''

"We need until Monday,'' Gramm said bluntly. "We can't examine the items until they dry out, and that will take a day or two.''

Judge Waldman was tapping her fingers on the calendar.

"Your honor,'' Gramm said then, "we have an alternative to propose. It would be highly irregular at this point, but we would consider a plea bargain with Mr. Arno, let him admit to manslaughter, and be done with the whole thing. Those clothes, the incontrovertible testimony of the next witness, Mrs. Delancey, is overwhelmingly convincing. To drag out these proceedings further serves no purpose whatever.''

Judge Waldman looked at Barbara.

"Impossible,'' Barbara said. "Ray Arno didn't kill his brother.''

"Can you speak for him?'' Judge Waldman asked.

"I'll talk with him, but he won't accept a plea bargain.''

"In the event that we continue with the trial,'' Judge Waldman said, addressing Roxbury, tapping the calendar, "how long do you expect to take with Mrs. Delancey, and then with any follow-up witnesses you require?''

"Half a day with Mrs. Delancey, half a day with follow-up,'' he said. "Providing defense counsel doesn't drag things out the way she's been doing.''

"I already have a lot of questions for Mrs. Delancey,'' Barbara said. "I don't think the state will rest until the middle of next week.'' She added thoughtfully, "It would not be fair to the defense or to the jury for us to start and then be interrupted by the holidays. Such a break in the continuity of the defense case would be grievously damaging.''

Judge Waldman put on her glasses and looked at the calendar, frowning. "What I propose,'' she said after a moment, "is to let you recall the state's four witnesses next week, then recess until the day after Christmas. I'll advise the jurors of this schedule and warn them that we could continue into the New Year, and that if we do, they should be prepared to work half a day on New Year's Eve, then off for New Year's Day, and back the following day. And I warn both sides now that the jurors are not going to be happy about this."

Gramm and Roxbury both raised objections, politely, but with some force, and she heard them out. If Arno would not accept a plea bargain, and he needed time to think about it, they wanted the trial postponed until after the first of the year. She rejected their arguments. Then Barbara said, "Your honor, would it be possible to let them know that this delay is not a sinister machination of the defense?"

"I object to such a statement being made to the jurors," Roxbury said. "That would be grossly prejudicial."

"I shall consider carefully what I tell them," Judge Waldman said dryly.

Ray Arno leaned back in his chair and studied Barbara with a disbelieving gaze, then he turned the same incredulous gaze on Frank. He shook his head. "I told Bishop Stover on day one that I didn't do anything and wouldn't plead to a lesser charge, because it would be a lie. Nothing's changed. Why are you bringing it up again?" His handsome face had become ravaged-looking, and strangely more attractive than before.

"Because Gramm made the offer before the judge," Barbara said. "That makes it more or less binding. You would get twenty years, or we could go for a lower number and argue about it; in any event you'd be out on parole in seven or eight years at the most. On the other hand, under the sentencing guidelines, you could get life without parole if you're found guilty, or you could even get the death sentence.''

''So those who are guilty get the breaks, and the innocent get life, or the final shot in the arm,'' he said bitterly after a moment. He was very pale. ''I didn't do anything, Barbara. I won't say I did.''

Gil Wilkerson, one of Bailey's hired guns, was waiting to drive them home when they left the jail. It was raining very hard.

''My place,'' she told Frank. ''I'll give Bailey and Shelley a call, meet back at your place around eight. We'll scrounge up something to eat first.''

She heard John's printer at work when she let herself into the apartment; he came to the small landing to meet her and help her off with her coat.

''You're shivering,'' he said. ''Let's have a hot drink. Irish coffee?''

''God, yes! But first I have to get out of these clothes.'' Then, a few minutes later, in her jeans, sweatshirt, and sneakers, she called Bailey and Shelley, and finally she sat at the table, sipping Irish coffee, and told John about the new developments.

His forehead furrowed, the way it did when he was troubled, and the scar on his face drew up his mouth in a crooked grimace. ''You won't even start your case until the day after Christmas?''

''No.'' Then she said, ''I told Dad we'd eat here. I have to go to his place at eight. I'll see what we have.''

''I'll do it,'' John said. He quickly went into the kitchen, and she understood that he needed time to think.

She felt almost numb as she gazed at the living room, at his massive desk spread with maps, opened books on end tables, pages of printout on the couch.... She looked down at the steaming coffee and took another sip. Not too much, she thought, and realized she had eaten nothing all day, not since a hasty breakfast. Her system was miswired, that was the problem; she never got the signals for hunger or fatigue or...John had stopped rummaging about in the kitchen.

"Barbara," he said, his back to her, his posture stiff and even hostile-looking, "you can't really believe a man like Palmer has a woman like Marta Delancey in his pocket. Aren't you taking a gamble a little too far?"

"I do believe it," she said. "And it's a gamble, but not mine. It's Ray's gamble. He's innocent!"

"She saw him, recognized him, fingered the place where he dumped the bag, and they found it there, or nearby." Now he turned to look at her. His face was expressionless, the way it became when he was unwilling to reveal his thoughts, his feelings, a way that revealed everything by concealing too much.

"She's lying," Barbara said.

"Someone's lying. This whole case started with a big lie, and it's gone on from there. You got it into your head from the beginning that it's a single case, the Palmer affair and Mitch's murder, but maybe they're really not connected. Can't you even consider the possibility that there's no connection? The murder might be a family affair; most murders are."

"And sometimes they aren't that simple."

"Have you considered that if you're right, if Palmer can send in a senator's wife to do his dirty work, no one here is safe, no matter if you have armed guards? Have you considered what it would mean to bring two kids into an armed camp where they could become targets?" The scar on his face flared, then turned livid. His mouth drew up, and abruptly he spun around and stalked from the kitchen. "I don't think I'm hungry. I'm going for a walk."

She didn't move as she heard him at the coat tree, then

going down the stairs fast and hard; she heard the outside
door close with a bang.

He had not returned when Bailey rang the bell with his
characteristic signal; she had made herself a sandwich but
after a few bites had put it down. She tossed it into the
garbage. When she went down, swathed in her heavy pon-
cho, it was still raining hard. He would get soaked, she
thought distantly, and hoped he would come home and take
a hot bath, hoped he had ducked inside somewhere to brood
over a beer or two, that he was not out tramping around in
the weather.

In Frank's living room, Barbara reported on the day's
events and the new schedule. Both Shelley and Bailey
groaned. Batting a thousand, Barbara thought.

"Forget Harry Chisolm as a possible witness," Shelley
said glumly. "He thinks Marta's guilty of whatever sin has
been reported, starting with the Fall of Rome. But he said
that Joel Chisolm never went fishing in his life and he,
Harry, never did, either. He was able to give me some
dates—when Joel and Marta got married, when they moved
to New York, when they came home for the father's
funeral, and then again a couple of weeks before their
mother's death, and so on. He said all the antiques went
straight to an auction house." She pushed her report across
the table to Barbara.

"Also," she said, "I talked to Lorinne and went over
old photograph albums with her. We found pictures of the
various places where Ray's had his business, starting with
day one. She let me have copies made of the snapshots.
They're in here, too. Then," she said, "I did a little research on the various sites, what they were like when Ray
was there, things like that, and what they are now. There
have been a lot of changes since he started in 1978."

"Why?" Barbara asked.

"I thought that if Marta Delancey is lying, she might not know where Ray's shop was back then, what it looked like. I was surprised by it; that's what sent me searching."

She opened her file folder and drew out the pictures. "See, a corner in a warehouse in an area that was zoned industrial. It was temporary, but still, there it is."

"Good work," Barbara said, studying the photograph. "You've had yourself a real day, earned your keep plenty."

Shelley beamed at her and blushed.

The corner in the warehouse looked like a dismal, poorly lighted space with a picnic table that kids might have used to sell lemonade.

Bailey had been less successful. "Okay," he said, "the cops were suspicious of Joel Chisolm's death, but they didn't have a thing to go on except a gut feeling. Joel and Marta left the show at ten after eleven and decided to walk three or four blocks to the supper club, where Joel had made reservations earlier that day. After a block, a car drove past them and stopped, and two guys got out. One of them grabbed Joel's arm and snatched the wallet from his coat pocket; the other one shot him in the head. No one could describe the guys, happened too fast, they said." He spread his hands. "Gut feeling says it was a setup. Hard facts, zilch."

"Any link between Marta and Palmer? Did he move the family heirlooms?"

"Don't know. They're trying to find out, but it might take days, weeks. That was a long time ago, remember."

Barbara frowned. "So, unless and until it's proved one way or the other, we go on the assumption that he did, that he and Marta were acquainted, and she used his services."

Bailey nodded noncommittally. "She and the senator were married nine months after Joel bit the dust. According to interviews, they had met years earlier. Two kids: a son by Joel, a daughter by the senator. One of the successful marriages, not a word of scandal, Caesar's wife, all that.'' He shrugged. ''We need a little time, Barbara. You know how it goes. They'll make her out to be Mother Teresa.''

She did know, and ignored his complaint. ''So Palmer's got something on her that makes her jump when he gives the word. Why would he get involved? Why now? He doesn't want Trassi and his two goons implicated, for openers. Is that enough to bring out a big gun like Marta?'' She stopped, considering, then said, ''Trassi could be making demands. Maybe he's hanging on to the printouts until Palmer gets him out of this mess. He must think that Ray will take the plea bargain. They must believe they have an unimpeachable witness.'' She looked at Frank and asked, ''Is that how most lawyers would think at this point?''

''A plea bargain is a powerful inducement to deal,'' Frank said after a moment. ''Trassi knows that.'' Slowly he went on. ''Most attorneys who aren't trial lawyers would say, 'Take the deal.' Many trial lawyers would say the same simply because there isn't enough time to refute Marta's statement, to discredit her. Stover was ready to deal even without her testimony. They could be counting on you to dig as much as you can in the time allotted, and then conclude that you can't impeach her. And, Bobby, maybe you can't. We know things from the old boys' network, but they aren't worth a tinker's damn in court. If you can't impeach her, can't convince the jury that she's lying, will she carry the burden of a conviction with her testimony? That's the question. They must think the answer is yes, and that you will arrive at the same conclusion.''

At twelve Bailey and Barbara drove Shelley to the townhouse and he saw her safely inside; then he drove Barbara to her apartment and went up with her, ostensibly to have a word with Alan Macagno, but she knew it was to see her all the way in, not leave her at the outside door. Armed camps, she thought; Pete McClure had arrived at Frank's house at eleven to spend the night in his living room.

John and Alan were watching a movie, which seemed to involve a lot of men on horses, a lot of dust, and a lot of shooting. A pizza tray was on the table.

John left Alan and Bailey and followed her into the other apartment. He didn't get closer than arm's length. "I put pizza in the fridge," he said. "It needs a minute in the microwave."

"Thanks. Maybe later."

"Coffee's in the carafe. Are your feet wet?"

She looked down, then nodded. "I'll change. How about yours?"

"Okay. Well, back to justice, frontier-style. Don't work too late."

She watched him walk stiffly through her hall, through the landing, into his own hall, then vanish into the other living room, where the gunfire sounded like corn popping.

29

If Barbara had kept a diary, what she would have written for Friday was: *Notified Judge and Roxbury, no deal. Rain.* For Saturday it would have been: *Reports, work. Rain. Sunday: Work. Rain.*

What she would not have written was an account of the strange new behavior that had developed between her and John. Either they clung to each other like desperate teens or they were as distant as polite, well-mannered acquaintances. No middle ground. Ominously, neither of them had referred even once to his outburst of Thursday, or to the new schedule she had to observe, or to the trial in any way.

On Monday, Marta Delancey was sworn in and seated herself gracefully. She was tall with broad shoulders, very handsome in a salon-finish gloss from head to foot. Her hair was an indeterminate color between blond and brown, cut stylishly short, with a few wisps down on her forehead. Her jewelry was discreet—small pearl earrings, a pearl necklace against a pale blue silk blouse that was exactly the right color to go with her dark blue silk suit. Her blouse matched the blue of her eyes.

Roxbury led her through her past history, her marriage to Joel Chisolm, his untimely death, and her later marriage to the senator from California. He had her list the various committees on which she had served, those on which she was presently active. It was all very impressive. Her voice was pleasant, carrying without being strident or overly forceful as she answered his questions concisely.

Barbara could tell nothing about what the jury was thinking. The members were as unreadable as petroglyphs on granite walls.

"Mrs. Delancey," Roxbury said, finally getting to the point, "are you acquainted with the defendant, Ray Arno?"

"Not really. I have seen him two times in my life."

"Will you please tell the court the circumstances of the first occasion on which you saw him."

"Yes. It was in the fall of 1978. My late husband and I were in Eugene visiting his mother. We were strolling, looking in windows, and noticed a new shop, The Sporting Chance. Joel, my late husband, said he would try to find a gift for his brother there. It was a fishing supply shop, and Joel knew nothing about fishing; therefore, he engaged the young man at the counter in a rather lengthy conversation. I knew even less about fishing than Joel did, and I was not interested in the conversation, but I found the proprietor very interesting. He said he had recently opened the shop and business was not very good, but he had great hopes for the future. He was very handsome and, frankly, I studied him quite a bit, enough to make him uncomfortable, I'm afraid. I realized I had embarrassed him, and stopped, of course. When we left the shop, I turned and wished him luck, and he said thank you. He was the defendant, Ray Arno."

"Was he very different from the man you see today? Has he changed very much since then?"

"He's hardly different at all. He might be a few pounds heavier, but he looks almost exactly the same as he did then."

"Would you have been able to pick him out of a crowd?"

"Objection. Speculation," Barbara said.

It was sustained, and Roxbury moved on. "Mrs. Delancey, please tell the court the circumstances of the second time you saw the defendant, Ray Arno."

"That was last August. I had come to Eugene to visit my mother, who is quite ill and resides here in a nursing home. On the morning of August sixth, I decided to take a drive up in the mountains. I left early that morning, and I was on the McKenzie Highway, heading east, when I saw a car stopped on the bridge ahead. I slowed down, thinking the driver might need assistance. Then, just as I had driven onto the bridge, a man came from around the back of the car, carrying a large plastic bag that appeared to be heavy. He lifted it over the bridge railing and let it drop into the water, and then he looked in my direction, as if he had not previously heard my approach. He seemed startled, and for a second or two he didn't move, just looked at me. I had drawn up almost even with him by then. Suddenly he hurried to the driver's side of his car and got in and drove away fast, toward Eugene. I recognized him, although I didn't know his name then. I don't believe I had ever heard his name, but it was the same man I saw in the fishing shop, the defendant, Ray Arno."

"Are you positive it was Ray Arno you saw on the morning of August sixth?"

"Yes."

"Do you recall what time that was?"

"About eight."

"Do you recall what kind of car he was driving?"

"I don't know makes and models, but it was a small gray car with a hatchback. I watched it out my rearview mirror as he drove away."

She was a very good witness, Barbara had to admit silently; her answers were fluent and to all appearances unrehearsed. Roxbury asked what she had done after seeing Ray Arno, and she answered readily.

"I was troubled by what seemed to be illegal dumping, but I was here because my mother was having a crisis, and by the time I returned to visit her later that morning, I'm afraid I let the matter of Mr. Arno slip my mind. I was trying to decide if I should take my mother to California, where I could visit with her more often, weighing the pros and cons of moving her away from doctors and nurses she had grown fond of, a comfortable setting with other residents she had become friends with. It was a difficult decision, one that occupied my thoughts for the remainder of my visit. I forgot about Mr. Arno."

"Did you read about the murder of Mitchell Arno?"

"Not at that time. I was gone before it was reported in the local newspapers, and I didn't know anything about it."

"And what made you come forward now?"

"I was visiting again last week. I try to get up here as often as possible. I came across an account of the murder; it was summarized when Ms. Holloway joined the defense case, and there was a picture of Ray Arno. I remembered seeing him on the bridge that day, and I knew I had to tell what I had seen."

Roxbury finished with her soon after that, and Judge Waldman called for a short recess. That morning the courtroom was filled to capacity; Marta Delancey's appearance had made the news both locally and nationally.

"Mrs. Delancey," Barbara said after the recess, "your testimony is that you first saw Ray Arno in the fall of 1978. Can you be more precise about the date?"

"I'm sorry. I don't think I can. We were back and forth between Eugene and New York several times that fall. On one of those trips, but the date...?" She shook her head. "It was a long time ago."

"I understand. Nineteen seventy-eight was a momentous year in your life, wasn't it? Was your son born that year?"

"Yes, January twenty-eighth."

"And your father-in-law died unexpectedly in March. Is that right?"

"Yes."

"Then, in October, your mother-in-law died, also unexpectedly. Is that correct?"

"Yes."

"Was there an investigation regarding her death?"

"There was. It was determined that she died from an accidental overdose of a prescription sleeping medication."

Barbara picked up a paper from her table. "This is the official report following the conclusion of that investigation." She showed it first to the judge and then to Roxbury, who looked bored and resigned. It was admitted. "According to the report here, Mrs. Delancey, the autopsy report attributed her death to a high level of alcohol in her system, in combination with the sleeping medication, antidepressants, and tranquilizers. Do you recall that?"

"Yes," Marta Delancey said in a low voice. "She had become very depressed that year. I believe her children, and I, all made a statement to that effect."

"Yes, your statements are included. Your statement also says that you and your late husband visited Mrs. Chisolm two weeks before her death, that you arrived on October fourth and left on October seventh. Is that correct?"

"Yes."

"Did you accompany your late husband and your mother-in-law when they went to her bank and arranged a loan?"

Roxbury was on his feet with an objection instantly. Judge Waldman was frowning at Barbara, who said, "Your honor, I am trying to pinpoint exactly when Mrs. Delancey might first have seen Ray Arno."

"Please rephrase your question," the judge said crisply.

"Mrs. Delancey, did your late husband have business to attend to with his mother on that visit in early October?"

"Yes. It was a business trip."

"Did they spend time on both days of your visit conducting their business?"

"Yes."

"And did you visit your own mother while they were doing that?"

"I did."

"In fact, did you spend the nights of October fifth and sixth in your mother's house?"

"Yes. Her health was failing, and I wanted some time with her."

"You flew all the way from New York City to Eugene in order to spend two days with your mother? Is that what you're telling us?"

"Yes. I didn't know at the time how ill she was, and I had a nine-month-old baby back in New York. I was torn between them. After I reassured myself that she was in no immediate danger, I was eager to return home."

"Was your mother employed at the time?" Barbara walked to her table and picked up a sheet of paper. She looked at Marta Delancey, who was watching her closely.

"I really don't remember when she retired."

"Wasn't she given a luncheon in 1982 and presented with an award for thirty years of service with the Lane County government?"

"I don't remember when that happened."

Barbara nodded and said, "I have a photocopy of a newspaper account of her award and her retirement, dated December third, 1982. Would that refresh your memory?"

Marta Delancey shook her head sadly. "What happened was that my mother began to suffer from a debilitating illness that was intermittent for several years before it progressed so much that she could no longer hold her position."

Her point, Barbara thought almost in admiration. "I

see," she said, putting down the photocopy of the newspaper account. "So on that first occasion in October of 1978 you arrived in Eugene at seven or later in the evening on the fourth, your late husband and his mother were occupied with business the following two days, during which time you stayed with your mother; then you left Eugene at ten in the morning on the seventh. Was there an opportunity for you to stroll and shop during that brief visit?"

Marta Delancey glanced at the police report Barbara was still holding, then said, "I don't think so. It must have been when we came back later that month."

She continued to be very calm and poised, to all appearances unruffled and quite willing to be as cooperative as possible. A good witness for the prosecution. Painstakingly, keeping her own voice as pleasant and conversational as Marta Delancey's, Barbara led her through the next visit, following the death of Greta Chisolm.

That afternoon Barbara summarized: "So you flew back to Eugene on October twentieth, and the funeral was not until the twenty-fifth. In the intervening days, there was the reading of the will, and many discussions about the new codicil that Mrs. Chisolm had added on October fifth. Did Harry Chisolm retain his own attorney to represent his interests?"

"Yes. It was a very emotional time for everyone. We all felt it was best to let attorneys handle all the details."

"Was Harry Chisolm not only shocked and stunned by his mother's sudden death but also furious that she had left the house and furnishings to your late husband?"

Roxbury objected fiercely, and this time asked permission to approach the bench. Judge Waldman motioned him and Barbara to step forward.

"Your honor, this is harassment, pure and simple. Innuendos that are certain to be prejudicial. This witness is not on trial here, and what happened nearly twenty years ago is irrelevant.''

''But she said she first saw Ray Arno nearly twenty years ago,'' Barbara said reasonably. ''I just don't quite see when that was possible.''

Judge Waldman considered for a second or two, then she said, ''I'll permit you to continue, but I don't want you to rake up old scandals and gossip. And I direct you to rephrase your question with that in mind.''

After Roxbury and Barbara returned to their tables, Judge Waldman said, ''Sustained. Counsel will rephrase the question.''

''Mrs. Delancey,'' Barbara said then, ''did Mrs. Greta Chisolm leave her house and furnishings to your late husband?''

''Yes.''

''Was the codicil added to her will on your previous visit in early October?''

''I believe so,'' she said. ''That was Joel's business and hers. I didn't know she had done that until after she died.''

''All right. So the funeral was on the twenty-fifth. Did you have an inventory made of the furnishings before you returned to New York?''

''Yes, of course.''

''Was that done by a local person?''

''I don't know. Joel handled it.''

''Did all three of the Chisolm children oversee the inventory?''

''Yes. Harry and his sister had some personal belongings they wanted to recover, and naturally there was no question about that. Those items were not included in the inventory.''

''How long did it take to inventory the furnishings?'

''I don't remember precisely. A day, perhaps two days.''

''Were you all staying in the house during this period?''

"No. Harry had his own residence and was staying at home, and his sister chose to stay with him."

"So the inventory might have taken two days, and you remained in the house during that time, and that brings us up to the twenty-seventh of October. Is that right?"

"I really don't remember how long it took. Possibly not two whole days."

It was slow, and there was always a risk that the jury would get too bored to keep listening, but for the moment they were following closely, maybe intrigued by the witness or by the timetable Barbara was constructing. She could tell little about them; it made a difference not being there from day one, not being there for jury selection. They were an unknown quantity to her now.

"When did you return to New York?" Barbara asked.

"A few days after the inventory was made."

"I see. There was a third catastrophic event in your life that year, wasn't there? Was your late husband shot and killed on a sidewalk in New York City on December thirteenth?"

Marta Delancey looked down and said yes in a low voice.

"During the ensuing investigation did the police ask you to retrace your steps for several weeks prior to that incident? And didn't you tell them that you had returned to New York on October twenty-ninth?"

Marta looked startled momentarily, then nodded. "Yes, that was my statement. At the time, of course, I remembered it very well."

"Of course. And did you make one more visit to Eugene between the twenty-ninth of October and the time of your late husband's death?"

"Yes. When the movers crated up the furnishings, we supervised them. In November. We didn't go shopping then, we went the day after the inventory was made in

October. Joel said he needed a distraction, and we left the house for several hours.''

That was good, Barbara thought. Marta had seen the timetable narrowing to nothing and had taken steps to fix it. A good move.

Barbara nodded, as if satisfied. ''So on the twenty-eighth of October you and your late husband took some time off and went shopping. Is that right?''

''Yes. Not to shop, actually, just to get out of the house.''

''When did Harry Chisolm and his sister remove their personal possessions from the house?''

''Immediately following the inventory. I believe it was early the next morning. We went out soon after they left.''

''Were there servants in the house?''

''No, they had left several days earlier.''

''Did you just lock up the house and go out for a stroll?''

''No. My husband made arrangements for a security firm to maintain a watch in the house until we had the furnishings moved. An empty house is too tempting to leave unwatched.''

''I see. Do you recall what company was used for security?''

''No. My husband took care of it. I know a guard arrived before we went out.''

''Was he instructed not to let Harry Chisolm or his sister enter the house?''

''I don't know.''

''You said earlier that your late husband was interested in buying a gift for his brother. Was that not the case?''

''Not really. He was being ironic, I think. He just wanted to get out, to get his mind off the past week, I think.''

''In fact, had there not been a number of very emotional scenes that week, a lot of tension and turmoil?''

Barbara waited for Roxbury to object, but he remained silent, and Marta answered almost sadly, ''There was a lot of tension. It was an emotional week. Losing the second parent in such a short time had everyone's nerves frayed. Joel was in a highly emotional state and he said he had to get out and get some air. We drove, then we left the car and walked past some shops in south Eugene. I don't recall exactly where. I don't even know what kind of shops they were, and that's when we spotted the new shop and went in, just to be doing something.''

"While he was being shown fishing gear, what did you do?''

"Just wandered around the shop a little. I was not interested in fishing equipment.''

"Did you pick up items, examine them at all? Just to keep yourself occupied, perhaps?''

"I might have done so. Probably I did.''

"Were there other customers in the shop?''

"Not that I recall.''

"Are you certain it was The Sporting Chance shop that you entered that day?''

"Yes. My husband commented on the name. He liked it. That's really why we entered, the name sounded interesting.''

"Were you standing near your husband and Mr. Arno when you began to study Mr. Arno?''

"No. I might have been near the door, or across the shop. I don't remember where I was standing, only that I was bored and that I found his face interesting and very handsome.''

"How far from Mr. Arno were you when you observed his face?''

"Not far. Fifteen feet or so. It was a small shop.''

"And how was the lighting?''

"It was quite good. I could see him clearly.''

"Did you ever see him again between then and this year?''

"No. I have a very good memory for faces, and names as well. I would remember if I had seen him again. Besides, following the death of my husband, my trips to Eugene were solely to visit my mother."

"Are you certain you entered his shop that day in October, and not the next month when you and your late husband returned for your last trip together to Eugene?"

"Yes. You reminded me by mentioning the police report concerning Joel's death. In November we were very busy supervising the crating of the furniture. There was no time for shopping."

"You said 'crating' again. Did each piece have to be crated up?"

"Most of them. They were very valuable antiques. And we had to check each piece against the inventory list. We didn't go out shopping on that trip."

"Who moved the furnishings, Mrs. Delancey? Was it the Palmer Company from New York?"

Roxbury objected that it was irrelevant, and his objection was sustained, but she had seen a flicker of startlement in Marta Delancey's eyes. If Barbara hadn't been watching closely, she would have missed it. But finally she had shaken the witness just a little.

"Mrs. Delancey, when you came to Eugene last August, did you fly in?"

"No. I drove."

"Up from California? That's a long drive."

"I often do if the weather is pleasant."

"Where did you stay while you were in town?"

"One of the motels off I-5."

"Can you be a little more precise?" Barbara asked, just a touch sharper than she had been before.

"I'm afraid not," Marta said, still at ease, still trying to help. "Usually when I come to visit my mother, I simply stop at a motel and sign in, often with a fictitious name

because I don't want any publicity about my visits, and
don't want to become involved in any social obligations o
interviews, anything like that. When I visit my mother
that's all that's on my mind."

"I see," Barbara said. "What name did you use in Au
gust?"

"I don't remember," Marta said regretfully. "Once
said I was Mary Pickford. Another time I registered as Jane
Austen. I just pick a name at random because I want to
remain anonymous. And I pay in cash. I've been doing that
for many years."

Barbara let her disbelief show, then asked coolly, "When
you visit your mother at the nursing home, do you sign ir
with a fictitious name?"

"I seldom sign in," Marta said. She made a little gesture
with her hand, as if waving away gnats. "One time, re
porters got wind of my visit and they pestered my mothe:
afterward, and it was traumatic for her. Many of us with
long-term residents in the home don't bother to sign in; we
just visit and leave again."

"So there's no record of your visit to Eugene in August'
No motel record, or nursing home record, or credit car
record?"

"I'm afraid that's right," Marta said. "There's just my
word that I was here and why." She said this with absolute
self-confidence mildly tinged with regret.

"Have you used the same method for your present vis
it?"

"No. I don't drive up when the weather might turn bad
I flew into Eugene last Wednesday and rented a car. I didn'
have a hotel reservation yet. I had a slight headache and
went to the lounge for a cup of coffee and an aspirin, and
there I picked up a newspaper someone had left and I read
about the murder and I realized that I couldn't keep this
visit private and anonymous. I called my secretary and

asked her to make a reservation for me. I'm registered in a local hotel under my own name.''

Once, many years earlier, before Barbara had passed the bar exam, she had watched Frank question a witness, then abruptly stop, and she had asked him why he hadn't nailed the guy. "Being a trial lawyer is nine-tenths facts and evidence and knowing it by heart backward and forward, and one-tenth intuition," he had said. "But when that one-tenth clamors for attention, you listen hard before you utter another word. That's the part that wins or loses your case."

Her intuition was telling her to stop. She wasn't going to crack Marta Delancey open, and she had become aware that the jury was developing a great deal of sympathy for Marta. Barbara wouldn't have been able to say how she knew that, just that it was so. It would not benefit her to play the heavy now, to pound away.

Very politely she said, "Thank you, no further questions."

It appeared that everyone in court was astounded by her stopping without even trying to refute Marta's positive identification of Ray Arno on the bridge, and maybe that was a point, she thought. Ray had scribbled a big *Why?* on his notepad. She whispered, "I'll explain after we adjourn." She didn't know if she could explain to his satisfaction, but she had been reassured by an almost imperceptible nod of approval from Frank.

30

That night Barbara dreamed: She was standing in a sleety rain, watching divers at work in water so clear, she could see their every movement. The water kept freezing over with a thin layer of ice that acted as a magnifier and did not obscure her view; then a wave would come and the skim of ice would crack and break and float away, only to re-form after a second or two. She could have told the divers to come out, to look from the surface, that they didn't need to enter the water, since it was clear enough to see every rock on the bottom, every bit of floating seaweed, tiny fish darting, but her dream self did not move, did not speak. Eddies formed and vanished. She leaned forward in an effort to see them more clearly. Then fear and wonder seized her as she realized they were faces. She struggled to turn away, to close her dream eyes, but her dream self was frozen in place, leaning over, then falling toward the water, toward the watery faces.

She snapped awake, still caught in the deep-dream paralysis, until a shudder passed through her; she was freezing, soaked with sweat. Carefully she slipped out of bed, groped for her robe, and padded barefoot to the bathroom. Her face was streaked with tears, her hair clung to her sweaty forehead and cheeks, and she was shaking with a chill. Even as she tried to recapture the dream, it vanished from her mind, leaving only a dull headache.

* * *

That morning the courtroom was as packed as it had been the day before, but without the air of expectancy that Marta Delancey's appearance had roused. Last night's television news had shown Marta getting into a limousine, being whisked away after her testimony; she had returned to California. An item in the morning paper, more commentary than news, had suggested that she had been the state's star witness, that her testimony had been devastating to the defense, which was not expected to recover.

As the jury was being brought in, Shelley whispered that Bailey said there was an FBI agent present. Then Roxbury brought in his next witness.

Harrell Trainer was twenty-eight and looked years younger, a little ill at ease at his role in the trial but extremely confident when he began to talk about the underwater search. In excruciating detail Roxbury had him describe the procedure, the strategy of a water search in a fast-moving river, and finding the plastic bag.

His fifteen minutes of fame stretched out to over an hour, but that was incidental; he looked very proud when he left the witness stand. Barbara did not ask him a single question.

A laboratory technician was next. Gus Moxon was a stout man with a pale complexion and a very grave demeanor, with deep worry lines in his forehead. He had been in charge of cataloging the items recovered. It had been his responsibility to see that the items were air-dried and that all the water was collected to be analyzed.

Roxbury had him identify the various items: a pair of shoes, socks, underwear, shirt.... The articles of clothing were all in separate, tagged plastic bags.

Roxbury finally got to the gloves and had them identified: two pairs of gloves, one leather, one canvas. Then he held up the plastic bag with the lead pipe. There was a profound hush in the courtroom as he described it—hollow, lead, two feet long—and asked Moxon if he had identified it and cataloged it. Moxon said yes after thinking about it for a second.

"And can you tell the court what is in this bag?" Roxbury asked, holding up one more plastic bag.

"Yes, sir," Moxon said. "Detective Ross Whitaker removed those items from the pipe. There's nine pounds of metal washers, two steel key rings, and a piece of nylon line."

Roxbury had a few more questions, and he got the same kind of slow, thoughtful answers.

When Barbara had her turn with Moxon, she asked, "When did Detective Whitaker dismantle the pipe?"

He thought about it, then said ponderously, "We put it in the drying room with everything else until everything was good and dry on Sunday, and then they tried to recover prints, and did other tests, and then he took it apart and I cataloged the washers and key rings and the nylon cord at that point in time."

"Thank you," she said. "No further questions."

The glance Roxbury gave her was deeply suspicious, as if he sensed a trap and could not quite fathom how it would be sprung.

They ate lunch at Frank's house that day. He had made a pot of chicken soup over the weekend, and he brought out a loaf of good French bread.

"Bailey, are you sure the printouts are still in the hotel safe?" Barbara asked.

"Never sure about anything," Bailey said. "What I know is that Trassi put the stuff in the safe, and the guy who stands to earn a buck hasn't alerted us that he's taken it out again."

Bailey's beeper went off. He cleaned his bowl before he ambled away to the study to return the call.

"Palmer's on a plane heading toward Seattle," Bailey said in the doorway a minute later. He grinned at Barbara. "A herd of guys will pick him up at SeaTac and hang on him like burrs."

"If they lose him, I personally will go on a vendetta," she said. His grin broadened. After a moment, almost absently, she stood up and headed for the stairs, not because she had anything in particular to do up there but because she had to move.

"When she gets restless like that," Shelley said in a near whisper to Frank, "I feel like I should start pacing, too. But I'm too hungry."

The forensics investigator, Detective Ross Whitaker, was a slightly built man in his forties; his hair was black and straight, and he wore eyeglasses with black frames. Neatly dressed in a charcoal gray suit, a blue tie, black socks and shoes, he looked studious and sincere, rather like a Mormon missionary.

For the benefit of the jury Roxbury had Whitaker describe his education, his police training, his specialized forensics training, his duties.... Barbara would have been willing to stipulate all this; she knew Whitaker's credentials were flawless. But Roxbury went on and on with him, with numbing exactitude.

They had recovered no usable fingerprints, he said when Roxbury finally got around to the evidence. The water in the bag had trace amounts of blood, and the bloody water had soaked all the items, so that they all had the same traces of blood; the blood was in Mitchell Arno's blood group. There had not been time for DNA tests. They had recovered hair samples, which were not incompatible with Mitchell Arno's hair.

Roxbury tried to get him to state that the hair samples

matched Mitch Arno's hair, but he would only say they were not incompatible.

"Did you find hair samples that were not incompatible with Ray Arno's hair?" Roxbury asked.

"Yes, sir."

"Detective Whitaker, why did you take the lead pipe apart?"

"After we examined it for fingerprints and trace evidence, we saw that both key rings had bits of additional trace material wedged in them. We took it apart to examine the key rings more thoroughly."

"Your honor, at this time, I ask permission to show a video we made of the procedure," Roxbury said then.

Barbara objected; she had not seen the video yet. Judge Waldman called for a recess, and she and the attorneys met in her chambers to view it.

On the television screen in the judge's chambers, they watched the scanning of the entire pipe when it was still intact. At both ends large key rings had been used to hold the nylon line in place. At one end the line was unbroken and had been slipped between the coils of the key ring wire; on the other end the cord had been knotted, then the ends burned and fused together to hold the second key ring securely. Whitaker, wearing latex gloves, cut the line to free the key ring at one end. He picked it up with tweezers and put it on a dish, with a short piece of the line still attached. He tilted the pipe, and the washers slid out in a neat row. He pulled the line through the pipe, slid the second key ring off and placed it on another dish.

"There's more," Roxbury said then. "We wanted to reconstruct a pipe to inform the jury of the process, and to show the weapon complete." He looked at Barbara as if expecting an argument. She merely shrugged.

The scene shifted to a desktop that held packages of washers, a length of pipe, a roll of nylon line, and two key rings. Whitaker's hands were ungloved now. He moved swiftly and surely. First he stretched out the line and cut it, then slid a washer on it and centered it, then he doubled the line and slipped it through the holes in one package of washers after another until the line was filled, like a string of beads. The first washer acted as a stopper for the rest. He inserted the string of washers into the pipe far enough that several of them were visible at the other end, and he worked the loop at that end between the coils of the key ring. He pulled the string tight, placed the second key ring on the other end of the line, and tied a knot to hold it in place. He fused the knot with a cigarette lighter and then cut off the excess line. The entire process had taken only a few minutes. The four-pound lead pipe had become a more lethal weapon that weighed thirteen pounds.

"Satisfied?" Roxbury asked smugly.

Barbara nodded. "Nasty," she said. "Very nasty."

When court resumed, it was nearly four o'clock. He would take half a day with follow-up, she thought derisively, and listened to Roxbury inform the jury about the video they were about to see.

Barbara watched the jurors as they watched the video. One of the women began to look ill when the implication of what she was seeing struck her. One of the men, who had appeared sleepy and even bored that morning, had come wide-awake, his eyes narrowed in concentration.

Roxbury resumed questioning Whitaker after the video ended. He showed him various bags, the washers, the key rings, the cord, and finally the pipe itself. "Is this pipe we just saw being assembled like the one you took apart?" He held up a pipe and handed it to Whitaker, who said yes.

"Did you assemble this pipe?"

"Yes, sir."

"Where did you get the materials you used? The washers, pipe, all of the items?"

"At a local home builder's supply house."

"You just walked in and bought all those items, no questions asked?"

"Yes, sir."

"Detective Whitaker, when you examined the key ring on the end of the pipe more thoroughly, what did you find?"

"There were bone fragments wedged in between the coils of the ring. And there were traces of skin tissue and head hair also wedged in the loops."

"Can you determine if the skin tissue is from the scalp?"

"Yes, sir. The hair follicles of the skin tissue indicate that it was from the scalp, and there were three hair fragments, also from the scalp."

"If that pipe had been wielded with enough force to crush the skull of a man, would you expect to see bone and tissue fragments lodged in the loops of the key ring?"

"Yes, sir, I would."

"And that's what you found, bone and skin. Is that correct?"

"Yes, sir."

When Roxbury said he was finished with this witness for now, Judge Waldman excused the jury for the day with her usual strict admonition about talking about the case or watching any news broadcast or reading about it.

Barbara reassured Ray Arno that she would be by later to discuss the day, and the days to come; he looked very gloomy. Then his guard collected him, the spectators began to disperse, and Frank said in a low voice close to her ear, "Your office. We have a visitor coming by around six. Carter Heilbronner."

Carter Heilbronner was with the FBI, maybe the head of the Eugene office, maybe chief of operations of the entire

Northwest; she never had found out exactly what his place in the hierarchy was. And he, no doubt, would want to know how she had managed to reel in R. M. Palmer, she thought with satisfaction.

31

Barbara and Frank talked to Ray briefly in the conference room and then had Bailey take them to her office, where she regarded Carter Heilbronner. He was tall and well built, about fifty, with brown hair and brown eyes, and a crisp no-nonsense air about him. He sat on the couch, crossed his legs, and looked relaxed and reflective. He had said no, thank you, to coffee or wine, to anything she had to offer.

"Ms. Holloway," he said, "your questioning of Mrs. Delancey has stirred up quite a bit of interest. I believe you've never worked in Washington, have you? It's like a big spiderweb. I watched a documentary about spiderwebs once, very interesting and complex structures. If you touch a strand anywhere on it, the vibrations are carried to every strand, and the spider hiding in her corner knows exactly where the original touch occurred, and even if it's something she has to do something about. If it's prey or predator, or too big and threatening, or too insignificant to bother with, even if it's a suitor come calling. Her response to the touch is instant, or so nearly instant as to make no difference. Amazing creatures."

Barbara waited.

"If you get Palmer out here, what are your plans?" Heilbronner asked.

"I'll subpoena him."

"I thought that was the case. Others thought not. So I said, what the hell, I'd come around and ask." Obviously he had not said that; it was not his style, and he even smiled faintly, but he was serious when he said, "You've got the web in motion, Ms. Holloway, a lot of telephone lines are vibrating. You're an unknown factor to most people, of course, but since we did work well to the same ends previously, it was decided that I should ask you a few questions and make a request."

Not quite mockingly she said, "You realize that at this point in the defense case, I may not be at liberty to answer your questions. Do I get to ask questions, also? Or is it to be one-way?"

"Ask," he said. "Of course, I may not be at liberty to answer."

She grinned and settled back. "So ask already."

"Do you have a basis in fact for asking Mrs. Delancey if the Palmer Company moved the furniture? Or was it a wild shot?"

"It wasn't a wild shot," she said.

"I thought not, but others... If you get him on the stand, do you intend to bring up her name again?"

She shrugged. "Do you know where Stael and Ulrich are?"

"Yes."

"Are you keeping them under surveillance?"

This time he shrugged. "I would be very careful if I were you." He regarded her soberly. "I must tell you, Ms. Holloway, that if a federal agent advises an individual that certain actions would result in obstruction of an official investigation, that individual would be held responsible if he or she persisted in those actions and did indeed cause an official investigation to go awry."

"I saw that same documentary about the spiders," she said. "Every night the spider rebuilds the web, whether it was torn apart by a stick or any natural event, or hardly touched at all; overnight it gets rebuilt in a virtually identical structure. Isn't that interesting? If you're really determined to be rid of the web, you should step on the spider.''

He recrossed his legs and tented his fingers in a contemplative way. ''You can't step on this particular spider. All you can do is stir it up and get in the way. Perhaps even suffer a dangerous bite.''

''A murder charge or two is a serious effort toward eradication, Mr. Heilbronner.''

''You can't make it stick. We're not interested in local murders, as you well know. Go after Stael and Ulrich, and Trassi, if you have the ammunition. I hope you get them. Our request is that you do not subpoena Palmer. And I advise you that we will consider it obstruction if you do.'' He spread his hands apart, palms up. ''Don't start something you can't finish, Ms. Holloway. Any more questions?''

''Am I likely to get any more answers?''

''Probably not.''

She spread her hands in a gesture that mimicked his. ''No more questions.''

''I have one,'' Frank said suddenly. He had been watchful and very still until now. ''Off the subject, I'm afraid. An old friend of mine, Sylvia Fenton, told me an interesting story recently. Seems a con man tried to take her for a big pile and she called bunco. Then, strangely, the FBI asked her to drop the charges. Seems she got to worrying about the con man out there bilking other old ladies, and it's really preying on her mind that she went along with the FBI. She got it in her head that he might be FBI, too, and since he's a crook, someone should know about him. I told her to let it be and I'd see if I could find out anything about it.'' He looked as guileless as a child. ''Carter, she's afraid she made a mistake, and she thinks that guy belongs in the pokey. And Sylvia can be a handful when she sets her mind to it.''

Heilbronner's thoughtful expression became as innocent as Frank's. "I'll tell you an interesting story. Confidential, of course. Seems one of the offices back East thought a man had information for them, and they were planning to interview him as soon as he returned home from a trip, but an unfortunate drive-by shooting occurred; he was hit and killed instantly on his doorstep. End of story. Tell your old friend not to worry about him, Frank."

Very gravely Frank said, "I'll tell her his conning days are over. Thanks."

Heilbronner stood up. "I've kept you from your dinners long enough. I'll be on my way. Maybe, with luck, the rain has let up. You know, they expect flooding." He pulled on his raincoat, and they all walked through the hall to the reception room. "Every winter I think I'll ask for a transfer to someplace where the sun shines once in a while, then every summer I think this is the only place to be." They shook hands all around, and he left.

Bailey emerged from Shelley's office.

"You've got to get in touch with Jolin," Barbara said. "Tell him they're investigating Palmer, big-time."

"What we have to do is collect John and beat it to my place and eat," Frank said.

Bailey left to get the car, and she said accusingly, "You know Heilbronner came to find out how much we know, and you practically told him everything."

"But we had to find out how much Gilmore talked," he pointed out. "Not much, apparently, but it set them in motion. Besides, he already knew we were on to Palmer and Delancey. Come on. Bailey must be around front by now."

Frank called Martin and ordered whatever Martin recommended. "Half an hour," he said, hanging up the phone in the kitchen.

They sat at the dinette table, and Barbara filled in Bailey

about Heilbronner's visit. "So call Jolin and tell him Gilmore's dead, and they're going after Palmer on the QT. And that Stael and Ulrich are probably in the area somewhere."

"You still want to serve the subpoena?" Bailey asked.

"I have to think about it," she said.

"Well, you've got a little time. His plane was an hour and fifteen minutes late, fog. And Seattle's fogged in tight. Nothing's moving. Palmer headed for an airport motel. He'll be stuck there until sometime tomorrow, more than likely."

Suddenly John spoke. He had been listening silently, not moving, not touching the wine Frank had put before him. "He told you Stael and Ulrich are around?"

"Not in so many words," Barbara said. "But that was the message."

John's face was almost totally without expression; his scar was a pale line, his mouth straight. She knew what kind of effort it took for him to do that, and she reached across the table for his hand. It was unresponsive to her touch. "We expected them," she said. "We thought they'd turn up, remember?"

"Gilmore's dead; two killers are loose out there; Palmer's on his way. When do the fireworks start?" he said tonelessly. "How many more bodies do we get to count? What's the score to date?"

Bailey stood up. "Use the study phone?" he asked Frank, carefully not looking at Barbara or John.

"Help yourself," Frank said, also standing. "I aim to set the dining room table."

They both left the dinette, and Barbara pulled her hand back from John's. "You know we're taking precautions," she said. "Do you have any suggestions to add to what we're already doing?"

"You can't guard against a drive-by shooting or a bomb

or a guy on a roof with a rifle. I had a suggestion months
ago; you chose not to listen.''

''I told you then why that wouldn't work; nothing's
changed. If I'd told them, they wouldn't have Major Works
or Jolin, or Gilmore, or the other company back East, or
the Palmer Company connection. They'd have Maggie and
Ray, period.'' She shook her head. ''I can't change anything now, it's done, and I'm on the roller coaster until it
stops.''

''I know you are,'' he said softly.

The doorbell rang, and he stood up. ''That's probably
Martin. I'll catch a ride home with him. You have work to
do here; I have work to do there.''

Frank admitted Martin, and they took the food to the
dining room. Barbara walked to the front door with John.
Neither spoke now. Martin came back and said sure, he'd
be glad to give John a ride, and they left together.

When she got home to the apartment that night, it was
after eleven; Alan Macagno was reading a book in the living room; John was in his office, with his door closed. She
went into her own office and closed the door behind her.

''Detective Whitaker,'' Barbara asked the next morning
in court, ''would you say that some of the tests you ran
were inconclusive?''

''Not really,'' he said. ''We put in a lot of overtime on
that material.''

''I'm sure you did,'' she said. ''But you said earlier that
you could not do DNA tests because of time limitations. Is
that correct?''

''Yes.''

''And all you could say about the hair samples you found
was that they were not incompatible with Mitchell Arno's
hair, and neither were they incompatible with Ray Arno's
hair. Is that correct?''

"Yes."

"How does a person pick up hair samples from someone else, Detective Whitaker? Do you have to use their comb, for example?"

"No. If you brush against someone, or sit in their chair or their car, you might pick up hair fragments. They're all around, even floating in the air."

"I see. From testimony, we know that Mitchell Arno was in Ray Arno's house for a period of time. Would you find it surprising that he had picked up some of Ray Arno's hair on his clothes?"

"No."

"Did you find other hair samples that were not similar to either Ray or Mitchell Arno's hair?"

"Yes."

"Did you try to match them with anyone else's hair?" He said no, and she asked why not.

"Because there's no way of knowing when or where they were deposited on any of the material."

"How many different types of hair did you find?"

"Five."

"And they are all unidentified? Is that correct?"

"Yes."

"You also said that you found no usable fingerprints. Does that mean you found some that you could not identify?"

"Yes. Not complete prints, just smears, and some partial prints."

"Did you try to identify the partial prints?"

"I tried."

"Where did you find those partial prints?"

"On the washers."

"How many fingerprints did you recover altogether from the washers?"

"Seventeen partial prints."

"And you examined each washer individually?"

"Yes."

"Did you try to match those partial prints to Ray Arno's fingerprints?"

"Yes, I did."

"And could you make a match with any of them?"

"No, there wasn't enough to work with."

"Did you try to match them to anyone else's fingerprints?"

"No."

"When you tried to match them to Ray Arno's prints, did you think you had enough to work with?"

"It was a long shot, just a faint possibility, so I tried."

"Did you try to make a composite print? Put two or more of the partials together to try to obtain a complete fingerprint?"

"Yes, I tried that."

"And it still didn't match Ray Arno's prints, is that right?"

"I didn't even know if I had partials of the same finger," he said.

"My question was: Did the composite print you assembled match Ray Arno's fingerprints?"

"No, I couldn't match it."

"And did you try to match it with anyone else?"

"No."

"So all you were interested in was matching your partial prints to Ray Arno's fingerprints, wasn't it?"

Roxbury objected; it was overruled.

"That isn't the case. I would have sent it to the FBI lab if I had recovered enough for a positive identification," Whitaker said.

"You stated that you had forensic training with the FBI. Is that correct?"

"Yes, I did."

"Isn't it a fact, Detective Whitaker, that the FBI labs can take partial fingerprints and make a composite print that then can be used for identification purposes?"

"If they have enough material to work with."

"Is that a yes answer?" she asked coolly.

"Yes."

"Did you send your partials to the FBI to see if they could do that in this instance?"

"No."

"Why not?"

"I didn't have enough for them to use."

"But you thought you had enough to try it yourself at one time, didn't you?"

"I tried."

"Did you think you had enough that you might get an identifiable composite fingerprint?"

"It was a faint possibility, that's all."

"Is that answer yes, Detective Whitaker?"

"Yes, I thought I might have enough."

He hadn't lost his detached, neutral demeanor, but she knew she had pricked him. "How long would it take for the FBI laboratory to report back on such a task, making a composite print from partials?"

"I don't know," he said.

She had him describe the procedure: photographers would take pictures and enlarge them, then fingerprint experts would try to match whorls and ridges in a complex jigsaw puzzle.

"You wouldn't expect a report overnight, would you?" she asked then. He said no. "In a week?" He said no.

"When did you recover the partials?" she asked then.

"A few days ago," he said.

"Please, let's be precise," she said coldly. "You had to let everything dry before you began your examinations. You had to go out and buy the materials to assemble a facsimile of the pipe. You had to have a photographer and a video cameraman come in. Is all that correct?''

"Yes."

It took time, but she got him to admit that he had recovered the partial prints Sunday evening at about seven or eight o'clock. He had gone out to eat while the photographer made the enlargements, and had worked with them from about nine until after midnight.

"So you spent a few hours at a job that FBI technicians might spend weeks on, and you decided you couldn't make a match with Ray Arno's fingerprints. Whose decision was it not to send the material to the FBI lab to see if their technicians might have more success?"

"It was my decision," he said flatly.

Slowly she walked to her table and stood by it, then asked, "Detective Whitaker, if you had recovered those partial prints back in September, or even October, would you as a matter of routine have forwarded them to the FBI laboratory for possible identification?"

Roxbury objected, and this time his objection was sustained.

"Is it a matter of routine forensic investigation to forward partial fingerprints to the FBI for possible identification?" she asked deliberately.

"Sometimes we do, yes."

"What determines the instances when you do?"

"If the identification is crucial to a case, we would send them in usually."

"And you decided without consultation that those partial prints were not crucial to this case? Is that what you're telling this court?"

"I decided there was no point in sending them in, yes."

She regarded him for a second; then she went to the evidence table and picked up the pipe he had assembled.

"You described in great detail what you found in the

key ring at one end of the pipe. Was there any material, any trace material at all, in the other ring?''

While he didn't really refuse to answer any of her questions, it took a long time before she got him to say the material at the other end of the pipe had been leather, pigskin, and that it was discolored not so much by the stains from bloody water as from age and wear.

Before the lunch break, Judge Waldman summoned Barbara and Roxbury to the bench, and asked somewhat wearily how much longer Barbara planned to take with this witness.

"Your honor, I'm sorry, but you can see how it's going with him. I need a shoehorn to pry out basic information.'' She glanced at Roxbury. "You could speed things up by telling him to stop dodging, no one's after his scalp.''

"You're just picking apart every word of his testimony,'' Roxbury snapped.

"I'll keep picking away,'' she snapped back, "until we hear the full report of his findings, all the things he conveniently left out in direct.''

Judge Waldman shook her head at them both. "Mr. Roxbury, it would be helpful if your witness would simply answer the questions more directly.'' Then she said to Barbara, "And I hope you will finish with him before we adjourn today.''

As if to emphasize her point about time, she allowed only an hour for lunch, an hour Barbara spent pacing back and forth from her office to the reception room.

Whether it was because Roxbury spoke sharply to him, or he simply foresaw many more hours of cross-examination looming, Detective Whitaker stopped dodging that afternoon and answered her questions directly.

He stated that the canvas gloves and the leather gloves were new, both size large. As work gloves they were readily available. The leather gloves were cowhide, and he had found traces of pigskin in two seams of the leather gloves.

"Detective Whitaker," she asked, "would it be fair to say that the person who wore those leather gloves handled the same object that left pigskin traces in the key ring?" He said yes.

"Can you speculate, based on your experience, what that object might have been?"

"Yes," he said to her surprise. "I believe it was a hand-grip for the pipe."

"Are you familiar with such an object?" He said yes, and she asked, "Did you find such an object in the plastic bag?"

"No."

She held up the pipe he had put together. "Would it fit over the end of the pipe and be tight against the edges?" He said yes. "Would you expect the sharp edges of the pipe to fray the pigskin?"

"It might get worn down that way," he said cautiously.

"You testified that the pigskin fragments indicated that the pigskin was old, discolored by age, not merely stained by water and traces of blood. Would you say the pigskin handgrip had been used more than once on a pipe such as this one?"

Roxbury objected finally, and it was sustained.

She worked around the objection, and Whitaker admitted that the fragments of pigskin had been frayed and worn thin, and the discoloration was due to both age and staining by lead.

It was nearly four-thirty when Barbara thanked the witness and sat down. Roxbury went directly to the problem of the handgrip.

"Is it not possible that such a grip would be useful for other purposes? Such as at the end of a sickle for cutting brush and weeds?"

"Yes, it would work for that."

"Or even as a grip for a fishing rod?"

"Yes."

After Roxbury was finished with his redirect examination and Whitaker was dismissed, Judge Waldman asked Roxbury if he had another witness.

"May I approach?" he asked. Wearily she beckoned him and Barbara to the bench. "I have another witness," he said in a low voice.

"You've got to be kidding!" Barbara exclaimed.

"Who?" the judge demanded.

"An FBI agent, to explain more fully about partial prints and composites," he said.

Judge Waldman said, "No. If you have concluded your case, the state may rest at this time. We have heard quite enough about composites and partial prints to understand the matter."

"Your honor," he said, "she's left the jury thinking Whitaker shirked his duty, that his investigation was less than thorough. I don't believe that's a fair assessment, and it's misleading and prejudicial—"

"Rest your case," Judge Waldman said.

32

When Barbara, Frank, and Shelley left the courthouse, Barbara could not suppress a groan. Fog eclipsed Skinner Butte; it hid the upper floors of the Hilton Hotel, it pressed down on the bank under construction across the street and wrapped the world more distant than a block away in ghostly shrouds. Lights were haloed everywhere, sounds muted. The fog was insidious; no clothing could keep it out. It was cold and penetrating, chilling to the bone. Bailey was at the curb, with the Buick door open, a scowl on his face.

"John said for us all to come up to the apartment," Bailey said at the car door. "He's got a surprise." He sounded only marginally less gloomy than Barbara felt.

As soon as they were inside the car, and Bailey was waiting for a chance to enter traffic, Barbara asked, "Where's Palmer?"

Bailey took his time answering. The traffic was creeping as if following invisible tentacles that had to test each inch of road ahead. "Vancouver, Washington," he said after making his turn off Seventh. "Nothing's moving from the North Pole down to the middle of California. Fog all the way."

John's surprise was dinner: his specialties of green chili and cheese enchiladas; do-it-yourself tacos, with many bowls of various fillings; a beautiful salad with green and red peppers and slivers of red onions, white mushrooms, and black olives; black beans and rice…. He was as anxious and nervous as a newlywed serving in-laws their first meal in his house.

Cornering him in the kitchen, Barbara whispered "Thanks."

"Can't compete with your old man," he said, "but I hated the idea of your being in and out of the fog all night."

She kissed him. "It's wonderful."

The first witness to be recalled the next morning was the medical examiner. At first glance it appeared that Dr. Tillich was a frail old man, but that was deceptive. He was going on seventy, but he was sinewy and muscular without a trace of fat, a runner who ran a mile every day. As he regarded Barbara through thick lenses, his attitude suggested that he had not been surprised in fifty years, and didn't expect to be surprised now.

"Dr. Tillich," she said, "good morning." He nodded. "I won't keep you long today," she said. "There are just a few points I'd like to clarify. Have you had the opportunity to review your report, refresh your memory?"

"I have."

"In your report you wrote that Mitchell Arno's death could have occurred anytime between Sunday night, August fourth, and before noon on Tuesday, August sixth. Is there any scientific or medical reason for choosing one of those periods over another for the time of his death?"

"There's no reason to pick one over another."

"Dr. Tillich, is it usually possible to tell how long before death the victim has eaten a meal? And even what that meal had consisted of?"

"Often that is the case. However, where serious trauma is inflicted, the digestive process slows or even comes to a stop in some cases."

"Based on your autopsy findings, can you tell us what

Mitchell Arno's last meal was and how long before his death he ate it?''

"Not precisely. The stomach contents indicated a meal based largely on meat protein, partially digested, as it would have been during a two-to three-hour period following consumption. There was little further digestion following that, indicating severe trauma had occurred. Also, he had been drinking beer, within minutes of the severe trauma. It had not been assimilated to any extent.''

"Later, in your report, you wrote that based on the amount of swelling present and internal hemorrhage present, you estimated that his right arm was broken and that he suffered the injury to his testicles two to three hours before death. Is that correct?''

"It is.''

"So, he had his meal, then two or three hours later he was drinking beer when he was attacked, and two to three hours later he died. Does that sum up the times correctly?''

"Yes, it does.''

"Would the initial attack, the breaking of his arm and the trauma to his testicles, have caused unconsciousness?''

"More than likely. He would have been in shock and incapacitated, at the very least.''

"In your original report you provided drawings of the wounds on Mitchell Arno's feet. Do you recall that?''

"Yes, of course.''

"I'd like to go into more detail about those lacerations and other wounds at this time,'' she said. He had included the injuries in his report; no one had referred to them when he first testified. Now she picked up his drawing from her table and showed it to him. "Is this the drawing you made of Mitchell Arno's feet?'' He said yes, and she turned to the judge and said, "Your honor, I had an enlargement made of this drawing, and would like Dr. Tillich to use it in order for the jury to see more clearly what he is talking about.''

Shelley set up an easel and placed the enlarged drawing on it, several views of both feet. Dr. Tillich left the stand to position himself before the drawing, then used a pencil as a pointer as he explained his marks.

"I'll start with the heels," he said. "Here, there are two cuts on the left heel in the upper region." He had found slivers of glass from a lightbulb in both heels, but only two had cut through the skin.

Barbara stopped him to ask if those cuts had bled, and he said yes, a little.

Then he said concrete dust and particles were embedded in both heels.

The soles were both embedded with slivers of fir bark, the sort that comes from bark mulch; there were several bruises where the deceased had stepped on sharp gravel, and there were bits of cedar splinters in both soles. The upper parts of the toes and the tops of the feet had splinters of cedar, and several deeper lacerations from gravel cuts, and they had fir splinters and embedded dirt.

"Did those wounds on the toes and upper fleet bleed?" Barbara asked.

"No. They occurred after death."

"From the nature of the lacerations and the glass cuts, can you surmise how the deceased received those wounds?"

"Yes. He was dragged through the glass and then over concrete. The cuts and the embedded concrete are in parallel lines, and concrete dust was on top of the glass fragments. Then he was dragged after his death, facedown this time, across rough cedar, flooring maybe, and over fir bark mulch and peaty dirt. Again, all the lacerations and cuts are in parallel lines. He walked through the bark mulch and gravel, and his weight caused the gravel to bruise his soles."

She thanked him and asked him to resume his seat. After he had done so, she asked, "When you perform an autopsy, do you also examine the deceased's clothing?"

He said yes, and explained that he would look for holes, entrance or exit holes for bullets or sharp weapons, for possible tears that would help explain and identify various wounds.

"What did you find on the deceased's clothes?"

"The lower legs, the bottom three inches in the back of the jeans, had slivers of lightbulb glass, and some concrete dust. The front of the jeans legs, the lower three inches, had embedded cedar, fir bark mulch, and dirt. There were slivers of cedar on the front and the back of the jeans and the shirt."

"Dr. Tillich, if the deceased had been conscious and struggling, would you expect the cuts on his heels to be parallel?"

"No," he said promptly.

"How high would you need to lift an inert man in order for the lower three inches of his jeans to scrape the floor, and only his heels to show signs of being dragged?"

Roxbury objected that this was beyond the scope of the doctor's expertise. No one knew the condition of the deceased at that time. His objection was sustained.

"Dr. Tillich," Barbara said slowly, "in your previous statement, you said that the deceased's hands were burned after his death, and that the flames had reached as high as his wrists. Is that correct?"

He said yes.

"Was flesh and skin sloughed off his wrists or hands?"

"Where they were in contact with the floor when they burned, some tissue sloughed off," he said. "And there was a small track of tissue two inches long trailing from one hand area.''

"What about the rest of the cabin? Any burned tissue anywhere else?''

"No.''

"As a medical examiner, do you sometimes try to reconstruct the events at a homicide to clarify in your mind the sequence of actions, how it might have happened?''

"Yes, I usually do that.''

"Can you do it for the jury in this instance? There is a dead man lying facedown, with his hands outstretched over his head. How could you lift him in such a way that only the tops of his feet drag on the floor, in such a way that you don't slough off the burned tissue from his wrists or hands, in such a way that his hands, necessarily dangling down from his body, avoid contacting the floor? Can you reconstruct that scenario, Dr. Tillich?''

Roxbury had started objecting halfway through this, but she persisted to the end. For the first time, Judge Waldman used her gavel, not a heavy-handed banging, a tap only.

"Object!'' Roxbury said furiously, red-faced. "Same grounds as before. Beyond the scope, not his expertise.''

"But it is within his scope,'' Barbara said coldly. "This is what he often does, as he stated, and this time we do know the condition of the man being moved. He was dead.''

During this exchange Dr. Tillich leaned back in his witness chair, frowning thoughtfully. Waldman overruled the objection.

Before Barbara could repeat the question, Dr. Tillich said, "I don't know how one person could have moved him without leaving a trail of tissue and blood.''

"Could two people have done it, one grasping each arm, lifting him under the armpits?''

Roxbury objected on the grounds that it was sheer speculation. The objection was sustained.

"Back in your autopsy room, having only the evidence of the dead man and his clothes, during your attempt to reconstruct what had happened at the crime scene, did you surmise that more than one man had moved the deceased?" Barbara asked.

Roxbury objected, but this time Judge Waldman allowed the question.

"Yes," Dr. Tillich said. "That was my first assumption."

Barbara nodded. "In your original testimony you stated that you could tell approximately how long before death the deceased had suffered various injuries. His broken arm, for example, had time for a great deal of swelling to take place, and the fingers were swollen to a much lesser extent. Is that correct?"

"Yes."

"Did he have blood under his fingernails? Could you tell?"

"I examined them; there was no blood."

"Would the deceased have been able to use his hands in a meaningful way at the time he received the final, fatal blow?"

"The right hand, absolutely not; the left hand, I doubt it."

"Would he have been able to grasp a stick or any other object and write his name with his left hand?"

"It would be most unlikely."

"Just one more detail, Doctor," she said then. "When you examined the deceased, did you find any teeth marks or claw marks on his leg or on the jeans?"

He said no, and she thanked him and sat down.

Roxbury came on hard then. The doctor was not at the scene when the deceased was injured and moved, was he?

He couldn't know how the defendant handled the body, could he? Hadn't he seen domestic pets, cats and dogs, carry objects, move them, play with them, leaving no teeth marks?

Barbara kept thinking she had laid the first stone in the structure she had to build.

After a brief recess, the next witness was Detective Gil Crenshaw. He had been one of the detectives sent to search Ray's house and car. He was a heavyset man in his thirties, with blond hair so pale that it looked white. It was cut short, in almost a skinhead effect, and he squinted as if he needed glasses.

Barbara had the schematic of Ray's house placed on the easel and now pointed to it. "Detective Crenshaw, you testified in some detail about your search for additional bloodstains, out here on the back patio, along the stepping-stones to the garage, and in the garage itself. Did you examine the front walk?"

"We looked it over," he said.

"But did you give it the same kind of painstaking examination you gave the other areas?"

"I looked it over and didn't see anything."

"Did you test it with chemicals the same way you tested the garage and stepping-stones, and the patio?"

"No, I didn't."

"Why not?"

"The defendant said they always used the back entrance, and that's a long walk around the front to the driveway. It didn't seem likely that he would have dragged the victim all that way when it was so much closer to a car from the back door."

The house was laid out in such a fashion that the front walk from the driveway passed two bedrooms, then the living room, to the main entrance. The garage was detached and set back even with the edge of the patio, and reached by slate stepping-stones from a redwood deck and patio. Barbara pointed to the drawing of the house and garage, then asked, "Would a stranger to the premises be able to tell how much closer the car would be to the back entrance? It isn't evident from the road, is it?"

Roxbury objected, and his objection was overruled.

"You'd have to walk around it to tell," the detective said.

"Is that front walkway concrete?" He said yes. Then she asked if there was concrete anywhere else on the premises.

"The garage floor is concrete," he said.

She picked up his report and asked politely if he could summarize his findings regarding the garage floor.

"There wasn't any blood," he said.

"In your report did you state that the floor was dusty and dirty, with old oil stains, and no evidence of having been disturbed for a long time?"

"Yes, I wrote that."

"All right. Did you fingerprint the house?"

"No, we didn't."

"Why not?"

"It wasn't the crime scene. And the defendant admitted his brother had been in the house. There wasn't any point in it."

"Did Ray Arno tell you he found evidence of a scuffle when he returned home from the coast that weekend?"

"Yes, he said that."

"But you determined that no crime had been committed here. Is that correct?"

"We knew the cabin was the crime scene," he said doggedly.

"Did he tell you his father's house had been broken into over the same weekend?"

"Yes, he told us that."

"Did you investigate the break-in?"

"I asked his father some questions."

"Did you fingerprint his house?"

"No."

"Why not?"

"They had changed the locks, there wasn't anything t find there. Too many people had been in and out."

"Did you remove the vacuum cleaner bag from Ra Arno's house?"

"We did."

"What did you find in it?"

"Just the usual dust and stuff, and a little bit of glass.'

"Glass from a lightbulb?"

He said yes.

"Did you remove a shovel and a garden spade?"

He said yes.

"Did you find any forest duff, forest dirt, or fir needle on either of them?"

He said no, and she quickly went down the list of thing they had not found: no lighter fluid, no charcoal starter, n bloody clothes, no shoes with forest dirt embedded in then no pigskin handgrip, no plastic sheeting....

"Did you remove a gasoline can with approximately gallon of gasoline in it?"

"Yes, we did."

"Why?"

"We knew an accelerator had been used on the victim we didn't know yet if it was gasoline or something else.'

"Did you notice a lawn mower in the garage, or a tracto in the barn?"

"Yes."

"Yet you thought a can of gasoline might be incrimi nating? Is that what you're telling us?"

"I thought it might be evidence," he said. He wa

squinting at her, ignoring the jury, and he looked a little flushed. He was so fair that any flush at all on his cheeks was apparent.

"Did you search Ray Arno's car?"

He said yes, and she asked him to tell what he had found. A gum wrapper, a boy's sock, a soda can, some comic books, a library book, the usual tire tools and spare tire.

"After you removed those items, did you proceed to vacuum the car?" He said yes, and she asked him if he found bits of glass from a broken lightbulb, forest dirt, fir needles, bark mulch, forest duff, trace evidence of plastic sheeting, or blankets. He said no to each item.

She asked if he found bloodstains, and he said no.

"Detective Crenshaw, in your entire search did you find any incriminating evidence?"

"Yes, the bloodstains in the family room."

"When you questioned Ray Arno, did you consider him to be not only the prime suspect but the only suspect in this case?"

His flushed deepened perceptibly. "No. We never make an assumption like that."

She shook her head at him, then said to Roxbury, "Your witness."

"Detective Crenshaw," he said briskly, "on what day did you question the defendant and search his house and car?"

"Saturday, August tenth."

"And on what day was the deceased killed?"

"Early morning, on Tuesday, August sixth."

"Was the defendant alone in his house during those intervening days, to your knowledge?"

"Yes, he was."

"With plenty of time to get rid of incriminating evidence?"

"Objection," Barbara said. "Speculation."

It was sustained.

"Were there any visible signs of a struggle in the house—broken furniture, forced entry, anything of that sort?"

"No, sir."

"If the deceased had been wrapped in a plastic sheet, something of that sort, would you expect to find traces of blood in the car? Or anywhere else?"

She objected; there had been no evidence of the use of a plastic sheet or anything of that sort.

"You brought it up," Roxbury snapped.

"Only to indicate that there was no evidence of such a thing," she said calmly. "If I had brought up a teleportation device, would you now suggest he might have been moved with it?"

Roxbury wanted to argue about it, but evidently the judge didn't want any more argument; she sustained the objection and almost brusquely asked the prosecutor to get on with it.

He was surly when he asked the detective, "Do you know how the victim was transported from the defendant's house to the cabin?"

"No, sir, I don't."

As soon as he was finished with the detective, Barbara said no further questions, and Judge Waldman recessed for lunch.

The fog had not lifted: it was even denser than it had been earlier, and everyone was edgy. Palmer was still holed up, Bailey said, no planes were flying, little traffic was moving. There was a mammoth pileup on I-5 down around Medford. A bright spot was provided by Patsy Meares, who had ordered duck soup, along with potstickers and spring rolls with shrimp filling. She ate with them that day, as reluctant to go out into the fog as Barbara was.

* * *

Lieutenant Stacey Washburn had been the lead detective in the case, heading the joint special homicide investigation team made up of county and city detectives.

Washburn looked hungry; he always looked hungry. He was lean with sharp features, and black hair and eyes. His teeth were bad, which might have accounted for his hungry look; they were crooked, and his bite probably was terrible. Frank said rumor had it that because his temper was fierce, the only way he could testify in court was by taking a tranquilizer first. In the witness chair he appeared relaxed and at ease now.

"Lieutenant Washburn, during your investigation of the murder of Mitchell Arno, did you become aware that he had carried a large sum of money into the state?" She could hear a ripple like a collective sigh pass through the spectators; this was the first mention of money in the case.

"Yes."

"When did you learn about the money?"

"Back in August. I don't remember the exact date."

"In your testimony you stated that Mitchell Arno had been driving a Lexus automobile that had been wrecked and recovered by the police in Corvallis. Do you recall that?"

He snapped his answer, yes.

"Did you go to Corvallis at any time to inspect the automobile?"

"No. I talked to the officers by phone."

"Did you interview Mr. Stanley Trassi, the attorney representing Mitchell Arno regarding the large sum of money?"

"Yes."

"In person?"

"Yes."

"Did you talk with R. M. Palmer, the man Mitchell Arno was working for?"

"Yes, by telephone."

"Not in person?"

"No. He's in New York."

"Did you request a sworn deposition from Mr. Palmer?"

"No. I took his statement over the phone."

"Do you know when the Lexus was repaired and released to Mr. Palmer's representatives?"

"No."

"Were you aware that fingerprints from Ray Arno's house had been collected and delivered to the district attorney's office?"

"I learned about them."

"Did you do an independent check on those fingerprints?"

"No."

"Did you do a follow-up investigation of the men identified through those fingerprints?"

He said no, more sharply.

"When did you become aware that such fingerprints existed?"

"Back in September sometime."

"Perhaps we can refresh your memory for exact dates. In your report you state that you talked to the Corvallis police officer on August tenth. And it says that you talked to Mr. Trassi about the Lexus on August twelfth. And on September second you learned about the fingerprints. Are those dates in your report correct?"

"If they're in the report, they're correct."

"All right. So you knew a very expensive automobile had been wrecked, possibly stolen, and that Mitchell Arno had been wandering around on the coast. Did you at any time consider a different reason for the murder of Mitchell Arno than the one you proceeded to pursue?"

"No. His business had nothing to do with his death, that was our conclusion."

"On August twenty-sixth you learned that a large sum of money might be involved in the case. Did that make you consider a possible different motive for the murder?"

"No."

"Then, on September second, you learned that two unknown men had left fingerprints in Ray Arno's house. Did that make you reconsider his story about possible intruders, and about his father's statement that his house had been broken into as well?"

"No."

"At any time from the moment you entered the case until the present did you consider an alternative suspect?"

"We considered all those other things and decided they were not relevant."

She nodded. "So your attention was focused on Ray Arno from the start, and you did not allow yourself to become distracted by anything that might conflict with your first assessment. Is that correct?"

He said no, it was not. He was angry now, but still controlling it. "There are always false trails that have to be looked into, false leads, and we investigated them all."

"But not to the extent of obtaining a sworn deposition from Mr. Palmer, or examining the Lexus in person. Did you ask the Corvallis police to make a thorough search of the automobile?"

"No. They reported that they had looked it over. I didn't see any need to do anything else about it."

"Do you know who collected the Lexus after it was repaired?"

"No. The car wasn't part of my case."

"I see." She went to her table and picked up a photograph of the shallow grave near the cabin. It was one of the first pictures that had been taken, and showed the grave and one foot exposed quite clearly. She asked him if he recalled it. He said yes.

"Did you find any evidence of an animal? Any footprints or droppings, anything of that sort?"

"No, we didn't."

"Yet in your report you stated that it was obviously the work of an animal. Why did you conclude that, Lieutenant?"

"In my experience," he said coldly, "I've found that that's what an animal would do. It smells blood and digs for it."

"Then why didn't it dig in the area where there was a great deal of blood? That's the right foot exposed, isn't it? Wasn't the only blood from the head wound, and a trace amount on the left heel?"

Roxbury objected that she was piling on questions and not giving the witness a chance to respond. Judge Waldman sustained the objection.

Barbara didn't belabor the point, but moved on to the name scrawled in blood inside the cabin. She produced the photograph and showed it to the lieutenant. "Did you have an enlargement made of this picture in order to study it more thoroughly?"

He had not done that.

"I did," Barbara said. She found the enlargement on her table and showed it to him, then to the judge and Roxbury, and had it admitted. "Lieutenant Washburn, those letters were scratched into dried blood, weren't they?"

"I don't know how dry it was," he said. "We know it was not flowing any longer."

She pointed out the flaking and cracking, and the fact that the blood had not flowed back into any of the markings, and he admitted that it had been dry when the letters were written.

"Yes," she said. "Further, whatever was used to write those letters made scratches in the wood floor, didn't it?"

He said yes, the floor had been marked.

"Would that have been a metal object? A nail or a key, possibly the point of a knife, something like that?"

"I don't know what was used."

"Did you find a nail or key, or even a sharp stick, with blood on it?"

"No."

"Would it have taken a bit of strength to scratch through the dry blood hard enough to mark the flooring?"

"Not much," he said. "The cedar's old and soft."

"Would a man with a broken arm and broken fingers on his other hand have been able to do it, in your opinion?"

"Yes, certainly."

"Would a dead man with a broken arm and broken fingers have been able to do it?" she asked scathingly.

He tightened his lips and Roxbury objected stridently. Judge Waldman frowned at Barbara and told her to rephrase her question.

"You heard the testimony that the head wound was the only wound to produce blood, and that the head wound was instantly fatal, that the brain stem had been broken, his skull crushed. He had no awareness, no cognitive function; he was dead. Are you telling us it is your opinion that he survived long enough for the blood to dry first, and then he scrawled his name in it with a sharp object that then disappeared?"

"That's how it must have happened," he said darkly.

She shook her head. "You mean that's how it had to have happened for your scenario to work, don't you?"

"Objection! She's arguing with the witness."

Very coldly Barbara said to Washburn, "You gave three possible reasons for burning the deceased's hands after he was dead. You said, first, to mutilate the body. Was the deceased's face marked, his nose broken, teeth knocked out, anything like that?"

"No. His face was untouched, except where it came in contact with the floor."

"Were there any other signs of mutilation on his body, not connected with the beating he received?"

"No."

"All right. Then you said possibly it was to torture him. Are you still of that opinion? That you can torture a dead man?"

"The killer might not have known he was dead at that point," he said.

"With his head crushed in as it was?" she said incredulously. "All right. Then you suggested that the killer might have wanted to burn down the cabin, hide the evidence of the crime through arson. With all the incendiary material around the cabin, would anyone have tried to burn it down in that grisly fashion?"

"Nobody sane would," he said harshly.

"I agree. Lieutenant Washburn, did you consider a fourth possible reason for burning his hands? That the killers might have wanted to obliterate his fingerprints?"

He shook his head. "No. That didn't seem reasonable."

"Did you consider a possible reason for sparing Mitchell Arno's face, his mouth and nose? That someone might have wanted information from him?"

"No."

When Barbara was finished, Roxbury had Washburn restate that they had investigated the business that had brought Mitchell Arno to Oregon, and they had concluded that there was no connection between that and his murder. Everything to the contrary was simple speculation.

Then Roxbury said, "Lieutenant Washburn, you've had many years of experience in police work. During those years do you recall instances when the perpetrators of crimes left incriminating evidence behind in a way that

ooked as if they did it on purpose in order to be appre-
nended?''

"They do it more often than people suspect," Washburn
said. "Either consciously or unconsciously."

Barbara objected. "This is really getting into the area of
abstract speculation," she said. "Philosophy 101."

"I agree," Waldman said. "Sustained. Move on, Mr.
Roxbury."

"Would you find it surprising if the perpetrator and not
the victim had scratched those letters, that name, in the
blood in the cabin?" Roxbury asked, with a sly glance at
Barbara, as if awaiting her objection, now that his point
had been made.

Since his point was exactly the one she intended to come
back to, she held her peace.

"I would not find that surprising at all," Washburn said.

After Washburn was dismissed, there was a brief recess,
and then the last state witness to be recalled came forward.
He was a police officer from Corvallis. His testimony
had been brief and not very informative earlier. Today he
looked a little nervous, as if he was afraid he had been
found negligent somehow.

She smiled reassuringly at him. "Officer Trent," she
said, "I have just a few questions for you. Do you recall
the incident of the wrecked Lexus and the subsequent
events?"

"Yes, ma'am."

"You testified that you went to the garage to inspect the
car, and you found the title transfer in the glove compartment. Was the glove compartment locked?"

"Yes, ma'am. The officers who found the car said it was
locked up, so I took a locksmith with me, and he got it
open."

"You testified that you then called Mr. Palmer in New York. Did you reach him?"

"I left a message on an answering machine, and he called me back in fifteen minutes, at seven-thirty our time. Ten-thirty his time. He told me the car was supposed to go up to Washington State somewhere, and he wanted to know about the driver, if he was okay. He said his lawyer, Mr. Trassi, would come around to take possession of the car.'

"When the car was in the possession of the police, did you make a thorough search of it?"

He looked puzzled, then shook his head. "No, ma'am. We looked in the trunk, just to make sure it wasn't carrying something illegal. After I talked to Mr. Palmer, it seemed like it was a legitimate delivery arrangement. No one had been hurt, and the guy who had driven it must have walked away after he ran into a tree. No one filed a complaint and it didn't seem like police business, more like insurance business."

"All right. When Mr. Trassi arrived, did you go with him to inspect the car?"

"Yes, I did. I had to make sure it was the right car, and he didn't know the town, so I went with him."

"Was the car locked when you went with Mr. Trassi to inspect it?"

"Yes, ma'am. We couldn't get inside, but he said it was the right car, and he had the license number and some papers that Mr. Palmer had faxed to him. I was satisfied that the Palmer Company was the owner, and he was their lawyer."

"But Mr. Trassi didn't have a key for it, is that right?"

"No, he didn't."

"Where was the car at that time, Officer Trent?"

"In a lot we use up in Corvallis, the back lot of a mechanic's shop. Mr. Trassi said he would have the car towed o a repair shop, and I told him it was in the best one in own, and he decided to let them fix it there.'' He added, 'Besides, nothing was open anyway, it being on a Satur-day. That's when he said he'd just leave it where it was. He didn't want to hang around and see to having it towed on Monday.''

"Could the car be driven at that point?''

"No, ma'am. Looked like the left front wheel was bent, and the radiator was leaking pretty bad, and the left head-light had to be replaced. They had to order parts.''

"But the damage was all to the exterior, is that right?''

It was clear that he was puzzled by her questions, but he answered readily. "As far as I could tell, the inside was in near perfect shape, except the radio and CD player were gone.''

"Thank you, Officer Trent,'' she said then. "No more questions.''

He was surprised and evidently relieved. Roxbury had no questions, and Officer Trent was dismissed.

Judge Waldman told the jurors again not to read about the case or watch television news concerning it, not to talk about it, and then she wished them all a Merry Christmas, and announced the court would recess until December twenty-sixth.

33

"What I thought we might do tomorrow," Frank said in the kitchen, preparing dinner, "is put up a tree and decorate it. Those damn-fool cats are old enough now to leave the ornaments alone, I hope." Last year, as kittens, they had undecorated the tree repeatedly and joyously.

"We should put our tree up," Barbara said. John had bought a tree, which was standing in a bucket of water in the storage space under their stairs.

"Is it really true that criminals, perps," Shelley asked, "often leave really incriminating evidence behind?"

"You bet," Frank said, slicing a beef filet into strips. "This guy goes into the bank and passes a note to the teller, the usual thing—I have a gun, give me money. She gives it to him and then gives the note to the police. It's on the back of one of his own deposit slips."

"Another guy goes into a jewelry store," Bailey said then, "and while he's waiting for another customer to get finished and skedaddle, he's playing with his car keys like there's nothing on his mind. So he takes a bag full of diamonds and stuff out and leaves the keys on the counter. Then the poor sucker goes back for them, and the clerk says he has to go to lost and found, and he walks to the back of the store and into the arms of the cops. True," he added.

They were all laughing by the time Frank told another story. "A guy bashed his wife in the head and put her behind the wheel of the family car and pushed it off a cliff, perfect accident. Except he took pictures of the whole thing and turned in the film to a local processing company to have it developed.''

No one drank much of the wine; Barbara had several hours of work ahead, and so did Shelley, and Bailey was antsy about Palmer in his motel in Vancouver. He hadn't asked again if she still planned to subpoena him if he entered the state, and she still hadn't made up her mind. That was something they had to discuss after dinner.

After they finished eating, John volunteered for kitchen duty. ''You all have to have your conference,'' he said. ''I'll clean up.''

Barbara suppressed a smile at the ''you all.'' Every once in a while his Southern roots poked through, not often, but when he addressed a group, there it was, not slurred as one word exactly, but close enough to betray his origins.

He began to busy himself in the working part of the kitchen, and Bailey asked bluntly, ''What do you want us to do about Palmer?''

''What do you think, Dad?'' Barbara asked.

''Heilbronner's a good man,'' he said. ''I don't think he'd steer you wrong. The real problem that I see is if you implicate Palmer without enough to make it stick, he will squirm free, and he might drag Trassi out with him. A confused jury is not a pretty sight when you've got a defendant depending on you.'' He paused, and she waited. ''As of today,'' he continued, ''you've probably got Ray off the hook, but the question is, if you try to go too far, will the jury decide you're throwing dust in their eyes? Palmer might be that kind of distraction for them.''

Barbara nodded slowly. She turned to Shelley, whose eyes had grown very round as she listened to Frank.

''Do you think Ray's really off the hook?'' Shelley asked.

Frank answered, "She laid the foundation today for se rious doubt in their minds, and she'll build on that foun dation day by day. Reasonable doubt, remember, is all i takes, and what she's giving them and will keep givin them is a tad more than just reasonable doubt. It would b a mistake to undo that doubt, maybe, by trying to do to much."

What she really wanted was to hang Palmer along wit his henchmen, Barbara thought, but she had to agree wit Frank.

She said, "If Trassi comes to think that Palmer is makin him a sacrificial lamb, what are the chances he'll do some thing drastic?"

"Turn state's evidence? Something like that?" Fran asked. "Hard to say. The way it looks to me is that he' so deep into Palmer's business, there's little chance he ca just walk away from it. But if the feds want to deal? I don' know. He's too much an unknown player, not like Gilmore He was pretty predictable."

Barbara was aware that John had stopped moving in the kitchen, that he had become as still as stone. And this con versation had taken a turn that was reminiscent of the tall they had had months earlier concerning Gilmore.

Decisively she said to Bailey, "Tell your people not to serve the subpoena. We may still want it later, but no now."

They continued to discuss the case, and Barbara was aware that John had become busy again in the kitchen, and she was aware later when he went to the living room, where he would read until they were through.

When she went to bed that night, John was waiting for her. They made love in silence, with an intense and terrible urgency.

The next morning she waited until she heard Alan leave before she wandered to the kitchen in her robe and slippers

John was reading the newspaper at the table. He put it down when she walked in.

"Still foggy?" she asked, helping herself to coffee.

"More than ever."

She shivered. "Yuck." She put bread in the toaster. "I wonder if *yuck* is just a euphemism for *fuck.*"

"Barbara, we have to talk," he said quietly.

She sat down opposite him, feeling as if the chill fog had entered the apartment, after all. "I know."

"From what I heard last night, you can get Ray off now with what you have. You don't need to drag in Trassi and Palmer."

"I can't go partway and then stop."

"You mean you won't."

She shook her head. "Put whatever slant you like on it. I can't do it."

His face twisted into a grimace; he was not hiding that morning. That was more frightening than if he had become stone-faced. He was letting her see a dangerous side, a dark and mean side. "Won't you try to see it the way I do?" she asked in a low voice. "I can't just say maybe two other guys did it and not give the jury more than that. Ray wouldn't be free of suspicion. It would follow him forever, even if we got an acquittal, and there's no guarantee that we would."

"I've been trying to see it your way from the beginning," he said angrily. "My eyesight's failing me, though. All I can see is you on a personal crusade of some kind." He rubbed his hand over his eyes, as if had meant that literally. "Your job is to get Ray off, but you're forcing Trassi and Palmer into a corner without a clue about how they'll react. They're killers, for God's sake! I can't bring my kids into this mess, put them in jeopardy. You know that."

"I do know," she whispered. "John, I'm sorry. God I'm sorry."

Abruptly he jerked up from his chair and crossed th room, then with his back to her he said, "I'm meeting ther in L.A. I'll take them to Disneyland or something, cam out, go to the desert. I don't want them in Oregon for eve: a second, not with those two killers on the loose. I calle Betty and arranged a different flight for them."

"Can't you just postpone their visit?" she asked after . moment. She felt stunned, shocked into mindlessness.

"To what end?" he demanded, facing her now. "I can' tell them to forget it and we'll make it up later. They're i school, remember? Spring break? God only knows wha you'll be mixed up in by then." He rubbed his eyes agai: "You don't need me hanging around. I'm just in the wa' here. But my kids need me, and I need them."

She wanted to protest, to cry out that she needed hir desperately, more than his kids did. They had their mothe and each other and a loving stepfather. She wanted to reacl for him and hold him, to explain that she had not planne this, had not wanted it to happen this way. She felt tha even language had deserted her; there were no words t: express what she wanted to tell him. When she found he: voice, she was surprised at her own question, not one tha she wanted to utter. "Will you come back?"

Now his face became expressionless, rigid with contro] "I need a little time to think," he said. "I may drive o: up to Canada after they leave."

"You're driving? When will you go?" It wasn't panic she thought bleakly; it was desolation, despair, misery tha made her voice sound strange.

"I couldn't get a flight on Christmas or Christmas Eve and I have to be there by four on the day after Christmas That's when they're due in. I can't risk a delayed fligh then. I have to drive down. I'll leave in the morning, give myself plenty of time to fight the fog most of the way.''

She stared at him. He had made plans, made preparations, called his ex-wife....

"Aren't you going to say anything?" he demanded. "No more explanations?"

She shook her head.

"Then hear me out," he said harshly. "I wondered at first if you were doing this on purpose, to test me, make me choose. You built your case on a big lie, and if you had played it straight from the beginning, we wouldn't be here like this now. But you had to play the avenger, you and your bloody sword. I don't really think you did it deliberately, cornered me to force a choice, but it happened. You crossed that line, and you're still on the wrong side, scheming, conniving, covering one lie with more lies.''

"Just hold it a minute," she said furiously. "I didn't put Mitch in Ray's house and I didn't send two murderers there after him. And I sure as hell didn't assume that one brother killed another, and then put on blinders to everything that pointed somewhere else. The day the law treats the Ray Arnos exactly the same way it treats the Trassis and the Palmers, then you can talk to me about morality, but until then, just shut the fuck up!''

"You keep saying things like that, but the way I see it—''

She was on her feet without being aware when she had risen; she was at the hall without being aware when she had moved. "Let me tell you something," she said icily, interrupting him. "At this moment I don't give a shit how you see things. If I had butted out, Ray would have been arrested anyway. Nothing I could have said or done would have prevented that. The state had an easy win, and they weren't going to mess around looking for complications. He would have been found guilty of murder preceded by torture. That's the reality. He probably would have gotten the death penalty. That's how the real world works when you're a nobody. But your cozy little Christmas with your children would not have been bombed out. Well, get your ass on the road, beat it down to La-la Land, and have yourself a dreamy vacation. Don't let reality get in the way.''

''Goddamn it, Barbara! Can't we even talk about it!''

''No!'' She was at the end of the hall. ''You don't have the authority to pass judgment on me or what I do. You don't know shit about how justice works in this country. Just fuck off!''

She stepped out onto the landing, and she saw Bailey at the bottom of the stairs. ''I'll be ready in half an hour,'' she snapped. She went to her bathroom and closed and locked the door. Then she started to shake.

It was a day just like the rest, she told herself that afternoon; she had more work than she could get through, more reports to read, more testimony to study, more pretrial statements to go over than she had time for. The days would be okay. And dinner with Frank, Shelley, and Bailey, that was okay, normal. Then more work to do; but after that, the long nights.

At four-thirty she had Bailey drive her home, planning to change clothes and then go to Frank's to help with his Christmas tree.

''I'll wait,'' Bailey said in the car, gazing straight ahead.

She didn't blame him. He had not referred to the scene he had overhead that morning, and she knew he never would, but he was uncomfortable now, and would be more uncomfortable if another scene started in his presence. Bailey was very proper in many ways; domestic problems alarmed him, and he would go to great lengths to be somewhere else when one occurred.

The apartment felt empty, deserted. On the table was a

large gift-wrapped box. The card had no name, simply the words in John's precise writing: *I love you*. Moving as if the box contained something very fragile, she picked it up, carried it to his office, and put it on his desk, then walked out and closed the door.

Palmer

34

"Of course," Frank muttered to the Things, "he couldn't bring his kids into this mess." He had known for days that John had a tough decision to make, but he had reasoned that he would simply put off his kids until after the holidays, after the trial was over, and then he and Barbara would take off for a delayed visit. He suspected Barbara had thought the same thing.

An awkward moment had come when she said that was enough work for the night, time to go home. Hesitantly Frank had suggested that she could move a few things over, use her old room upstairs, and she had looked distant and unapproachable. "Too much trouble," she had said. He knew from past experience that she would not talk about it, not now, maybe never.

They were all as jumpy as cats, although at the moment the two cats on the floor looked about as jumpy as bricks. Thing One had rolled over on his back, all four legs sprawled out in impossible angles, and Thing Two was draped partly across him, playing dead. But until the fog lifted, until they knew something about what Palmer was up to, where his stooges were, what plots were being concocted behind closed doors, the people involved would be on edge, and Barbara would be over there alone most of the time.

On Friday afternoon Barbara, Shelley, and Frank were discussing the batting order of the witnesses; Bailey was waiting for their final decision, not bothering to take notes yet. He would be in charge of getting witnesses to court. Some of them, he had warned, would rather go fishing. Barbara's phone buzzed and she crossed the office to get it; Patsy would not have put a call through unless she thought it important.

"Barbara," Patsy said, "there's a man on the line who said to tell you he's calling from Vancouver, and that you want to talk to him. Do you?"

"Yes indeed. Thanks, Patsy." She covered the mouthpiece and said, "Palmer."

He came on the line and said hello when she said, "Holloway." Frank came to her desk and she held the phone away from her ear for him to hear.

"Ms. Holloway, I understand the fog is lifting. I want to know if you intend to subpoena me if I set foot in your state. If you do, of course, I'll stay on this side of the river, but I really have some business to discuss with Mr. Trassi, and this is an awkward situation."

His voice, lilting, mellifluous, charming, sent a chill through her. He sounded almost amused.

"I won't subpoena you," she said.

"Mr. Trassi tells me I shouldn't trust your word, but, Ms. Holloway, I do. I have given a good deal of thought to the various aspects of our dealings and I have concluded that you don't actually tell falsehoods, although you may curl the truth around the edges a bit—but don't we all? To demonstrate my trust, I'll even tell you my travel plans. I shall drive down there with a companion, and register at the Hilton when we arrive. I have a reservation, of course. Then, after a bit of refreshment, may I call you again, to arrange for a brief face-to-face meeting? I find it helpful to talk in person whenever possible. Don't you?"

"We can arrange to meet," she said.

"Good, good. Has the fog lifted in your area? I understand driving can be difficult and slow in the present conditions. But never mind. We will drive slowly and with great care. Until later, Ms. Holloway. Tomorrow, possibly." He paused, then very smoothly he said, "It may be late when we arrive. Would you mind if I call you at this number?" He gave Frank's telephone number. "Yes, probably that would be best." He hung up.

Frank returned to his chair near the ornate coffee table, and Barbara leaned back in her desk chair. "Well," she said. "Well, well." She was icy. He knew Frank's number.

"I'll wire you," Bailey said.

"No way. He's not a dope. He'd never fall for that. Did you notice that he didn't say anything actually? Do you suppose he really trusts me to keep my word about the subpoena?"

"Maybe," Frank said. "In any event, I doubt a subpoena would hold him if he wanted to leave. Then, safely out of the state, maybe out of the country, he'd fight it with a pack of attorneys based in New York."

"Well," she thought, rising, "back to work." An hour later, after she had explained exactly what her game plan was, and which witnesses she wanted early and why, they were interrupted again. This time Patsy said Mr. Heilbronner was in the outer office.

Frank's eyes narrowed, and he said to Shelley, "You and Bailey better head for your office. Carter doesn't like an audience. I'll go fetch him."

Barbara felt the same anger that Frank had revealed. Those sons of bitches were bugging her telephone! When Frank left to bring Heilbronner back, she went to her desk and sat behind it.

Frank and Heilbronner came in, and she motioned toward the chairs. "Good afternoon, Mr. Heilbronner," she said coolly. "What can I do for you?"

He looked taken aback at her tone. He sat down and crossed his legs, regarding her. Then he said, "We're not tapping your phone, Ms. Holloway. His? That's different."

"In any event, it's still my private conversation that got put on a tape somewhere."

"Sorry," he murmured. "Would you consider a wire?"

"No. What else?" The last thing she wanted was for the FBI to tape a private conversation between her and Palmer, she thought savagely.

"Ms. Holloway, from his comments, I take it that you've had dealings with Palmer before."

"I've spoken to the man one other time in my life," she said coldly. "And you probably know about that conversation. He wanted me to release Trassi." She suspected that Palmer had used a secure phone for the first call; he had said too much not to have taken precautions.

"His remarks suggest there's more than just releasing Trassi on his mind," Heilbronner said. "What did he mean, you curl the truth around the edges?"

"Mr. Heilbronner, you have the records with our dealings concerning Maggie Folsum and Internal Revenue. You know very well that I had to request certain documents that ultimately came from Palmer, through Trassi. At present I am in the middle of a defense case, and I don't have time to involve myself in your investigations."

"I understand," he said. "I would like a formal interview with you following your conversation with Palmer, however."

"And I am at liberty to refuse your request."

"You are, but it could be to your advantage not to do so."

"Carter," Frank said then in a conciliatory tone, "when we find out when and where she'll meet him, we could let you know and you could drop in at the house for a glass of wine afterward. Christmas cheer, that sort of thing. Certainly not a formal interview, just a friendly chat.''

Heilbronner was watching Barbara; she shrugged. ''That would be pleasant,'' he said. ''Yes, I'd like that.'' He stood up. ''I know you're busy, sorry to interrupt. I'll expect a call.''

Frank walked out with him.

When he returned alone, she demanded, ''Why?''

''Because he knows where Ulrich and Stael are,'' Frank said. ''And God help us, we don't.''

Palmer's call came at eight that night. Barbara waited for the answering machine to take it, then picked up the receiver. ''Holloway,'' she said.

''It wasn't a bad drive at all,'' Palmer said. ''In fact, the hills were quite lovely wreathed in vapor, very picturesque. I'm afraid it has closed in again, however. Perhaps we could meet at the reception desk at the hotel here at eleven tomorrow morning? Quite public and open. We can decide then where we can share a cup of coffee and have a quiet conversation. Is that acceptable, Ms. Holloway?''

''I'll be there.''

''Very good. Don't worry about paging me or anything. I'll recognize you. Until eleven. Have a pleasant evening.''

''Eleven, Hilton front desk,'' she said after hanging up. Bailey nodded. He would have his own crew on hand, she understood, and he would be there himself, but she really didn't want to know the details.

Bailey had already reported on Palmer's arrival, at six-fifteen, with a Ms. Fredericks, who Palmer had said was his secretary. He had a suite; she had a single room on a different floor. Palmer had met Trassi in the bar, where they had a short talk and a drink, then both had gone back to their own rooms, where they remained. Trassi had ordered dinner in his room for one; Palmer had ordered for two. Trassi had not yet removed anything from the hotel safe.

That night she dreamed she was driving a very large truck with more gears than she knew what to do with; she was driving too fast when a deer appeared on the road ahead. She manipulated gears, but the truck simply sped faster and the deer did not move. She groped for the brake pedal and couldn't find it, then she got on the floor to search with her hands for the brake. She was speeding faster and faster, and ahead the deer gazed at her with luminous red eyes and did not move. She came wide awake, shivering, sweating. She was clutching her rock, the rock John had given her nearly a year ago.

She put it down on the bedside table and groped for the clock, turned it so she could see the hands. These nights she had been facing it away, not willing to register the time—two o'clock, three, four…. It was five after five. She got up to go to the bathroom, get a drink of water, wipe her sweaty face. Alan came to the hall almost instantly when she left the bedroom.

"It's only me," she said.

He withdrew, back to John's apartment, John's living room.

When she returned to bed, she again faced the clock away.

At eight Jory Walters relieved Alan. If Alan looked like one of the youths who always seemed to be hanging around at the mall, or riding a bike around town, Jory would be at home in a group of football linebackers. She had never heard him utter a sound that wasn't in direct response to a question; he simply nodded that morning and settled down on the couch with a newspaper. He had brought hers up as well, and she settled at the table with coffee and her own newspaper, and they read in silence.

At fifteen minutes before eleven they left the apartment and Jory drove her to the Hilton. He drove around the hotel to enter the underground parking level, where he could pull up within a few feet of the back entrance. Another escort opened her door and hustled her inside swiftly, then walked by her side up the stairs to the ground level, past the many convention rooms, a large lounge with a dozen or more groups of comfortable furnishings, couches and easy chairs with only a few people occupying them, although a lot of people seemed to be drifting aimlessly about.

As they approached the reception desk, a man in a dark suit turned her way, then walked toward her. "Ms. Holloway, good morning. I'm Palmer."

She knew he was fifty-two, but he looked younger, with curly auburn hair and blue eyes with a lot of crinkly smile lines, and very white teeth. He was trim, with a salon suntan. He didn't offer to shake hands, but his smile was broad, as if he really was glad to see her.

"Good morning, Mr. Palmer," she said, as pleasantly as he had spoken.

"Since the fog has come back so densely, and it is such a cold and dismal fog, I suggest we have our talk here in the hotel. Perhaps in the big lounge you passed on your way in. Or there's a coffee shop, a little noisy and crowded, but it would do."

"The lounge is fine."

"Good. You pick the chairs, since I more or less picked the setting. Fair enough?"

She nodded, and led the way to a couch and chairs with a coffee table, situated almost in the center of the big room.

"Don't you want to take off your coat?" Palmer said to Barbara. "I'm afraid this hotel, like so may of them, overheats the space terribly."

She took off her raincoat, and he was at her side helping her instantly. Holding the coat, without glancing around, he motioned to someone. A woman strolled to them. "Ms. Holloway, Ms. Fredericks," Palmer said. "She'll be happy to hold your coat for you, and your purse, if you don't mind. Not far away, and not for an instant out of sight, certainly. Just over there."

Barbara shrugged and handed the woman her purse. She was blond, in her forties, and had on too much makeup. She was dressed in a severe black skirt suit, with shiny black boots to her knees. Wordlessly she took the coat and purse across the lounge and sat down.

Barbara sat down, and Palmer sat across a table from her.

"Your maid travels with you?"

Palmer shook his head, smiling. "Not even my secretary, just a private investigator I hired for the occasion. She assured me that she could tell if you had a wire on your person, something about earrings, or a necklace, possibly a lapel pin, or buttons. I trust her to know her business, but I feel I must ask anyway: Are you wired?"

"Of course not. Are you?"

He laughed. "No, my dear Ms. Holloway."

"Mr. Palmer," she said, "another time, when I am not engaged in a trial, perhaps we can meet over tea and crumpets and have a nice cozy conversation, but at present I really am quite busy. What do you want?"

"Tea and crumpets," he said musingly. "My accent, of course. My mother would have tea and soda bread, and my father the crumpets. Irish and English, they fought constantly. I wanted to see you in person. Your photographs don't do you justice. I'm afraid Trassi is not a very good judge of women; he described you as a dragon lady. I like dealing with women, personally. Charm and business do mix quite pleasantly. I want to retain you, Ms. Holloway.

pay extremely well, and the work would be negligible, ut it would be comforting to know you're on hand if eeded. Perhaps for only a year, perhaps longer. We could lk later about renewing our relationship. One hundred ousand dollars for one year.''

She studied him thoughtfully. "You know I'll turn you own, and then what? Subtle threats?''

"Yes, I know," he agreed, smiling again. "I'm a bit fey, ou see. A legacy from my mother, I imagine; she was ever deceived in her life to my knowledge. What do you ant, Ms. Holloway? Everyone wants something; everyone as something he or she wishes to keep. What do you ant?''

"I want Trassi, Stael, and Ulrich.''

"I see. Suppose I hand you Stael and Ulrich.''

She shook her head.

"Do you have enough to get them on your own? I rather oubt it.''

"I have what I need.''

"But not enough to go after me? How unfortunate for ou, how lucky for me." He leaned back in his chair. "My ather was a simple man, Ms. Holloway. He had a truck nd he moved people, not far usually, from one address in Brooklyn to another, sometimes all the way to the Bronx, or even Staten Island. It was very hard work. And it was a ain. People complained that a waffle iron was missing or chair was scratched, petty details that were annoying, over nd over. Together we changed direction, thirty-one years go it was. We became specialists. Over the years the busi- ess has become very successful. I can move anything and lo, and I never ask questions about the origin of what I nove. I feel strongly that it's not my business to inquire; 'm not a detective agency. But over the years I have come o have a reputation for reliability, you see. I insure what move, and I deliver. Always." He sighed. "A reputation

is a precious commodity, Ms. Holloway, as I'm sure you';
aware. But something quite strange started happening in th
past few months. Quite strange, indeed. My staff has su
fered certain losses, not irreplaceable, but still, bothersom
And a customer is starting to get very anxious about a dela
in a certain shipment, and not only that, but the entire que
tion of confidentiality has arisen in an irksome manner.''

Briskly Barbara said, ''Mr. Palmer, I told Trassi what
wanted at our first meeting. He delivered, and so did
exactly as we both agreed. What has come up betwee
you and him since then does not concern me. I have n
breached the confidentiality of our transaction, and I don
intend to. When we first talked, you and I, I told you wh;
I want: Trassi, Stael, and Ulrich. That has not changed, an
I won't need to go into a matter that is concluded as far a
I'm concerned in order to get them.''

''You can't have Trassi,'' he said then, his voice flat an
very cold now.

''I already have him,'' she said. ''If he skips, an arre;
warrant will be issued and he will be brought back to fac
a contempt charge. Of course, he understands this quit
well. He'll never work as an attorney again, and whateve
problem you have with him you will have to solve withou
me. Now, I really do have things to do. Such a busy seaso
you know.''

''Ms. Holloway, I made you an offer. I'll deliver Stae
and Ulrich with whatever you need to convict them. I doul
you have enough to do it without help. But, understanc
turnabout's fair, now, isn't it? I can also offer you to them
don't you see?''

She laughed. ''Not very subtle, after all, Mr. Palmer. Yo
know very well that too many others are in possession o
my facts.'' She stood up.

''I cried like a baby when my mother died,'' Palmer sai
softly. ''I was eighteen. My father was very embarrasse

y such a display, of course, being English as he was.
Vhen he died, I was thirty, and I wept again. The Irish are
'ery sentimental, I fear. How Irish are you, Ms. Holloway?
can see the English in you, but Irish? I wonder if you
vould weep in public as I did.''

35

Half an hour later she, Frank, and Carter Heilbronner sa[t] in Frank's study with the drapes closed and few lights on, as if this really were a friendly get-together of old pals.

"He wants me to release Trassi. He offered to exchang[e] Stael and Ulrich, with whatever evidence I need to na[il] them, for his favorite attorney," she said. "He threatene[d] me, and he threatened my father. What more do yo[u] want?"

Heilbronner was watching her closely, and she appreciated now the reason Frank had arranged the lighting as h[e] had. Her face was in shadows. She had washed her hands, but she felt an almost irresistible urge to go wash the[m] again, harder.

Heilbronner was sitting comfortably, his legs crossed, hi[s] hands at ease on the arms of his chair. Frank was in hi[s] old brown chair that was gradually falling apart, and sh[e] was in a wing chair with a high enough back that she coul[d] rest her head against it. Heilbronner brought his hands together and steepled his fingers.

"Ms. Holloway, I need a little information. For instance, why did Palmer go along with your scenario and release that money to Ms. Folsum? That would be a good place to start, I believe. I've read all the statements and talked to Mr. Chenowith at Internal Revenue, and, frankly, it doesn'[t] really work. Does it?"

"I can't divulge confidential matters that concern my

lient," she said. "But I can tell you another story that you may find interesting. Then we can come back to that. Agreed?"

He nodded.

"Years ago," she said, "young Marta Chisolm and her husband, Joel, moved to New York City. His mother hated Marta and was very upset with the marriage. Following the death of her husband, she became depressed and relied for a time on sleeping pills, tranquilizers, and alcohol. Then Joel said that his marriage was over, that he was coming home to live with her, and she dropped the dope and booze overnight. She changed her will, leaving a fortune in antiques and an expensive house to him, with the expectation of having him with her once more. Marta and Joel came to town for him to obtain a loan from his mother, and oversee the change in the will, and to confirm that the marriage was ending. Sometime during the next two weeks something happened to Joel's mother, and she once more turned to drugs and alcohol, and this time she overdosed and died. Joel came into a very large inheritance, as well as the house and the antiques. Then he was shot and killed, and Marta was very rich."

When she paused, Heilbronner said coldly, "None of that is news. What are you getting at?"

"Marta was restless with her rather dull husband," Barbara said, as if he had not spoken. "She had met a man named Palmer, and no doubt at that time he was devastatingly charming and irresistible. What I'm suggesting is that she, with Palmer's help, planned to kill Joel's mother as soon as possible after she changed her will. Marta was in the house long enough to substitute something deadly, or maybe simply too potent to be taken with alcohol. Also, I'm suggesting that, back in New York again, she called her mother-in-law and said forget it, no separation was taking place, Joel would never return to Eugene, she would never even see her grandchild. Then she waited for the inevitable, which came about as planned. Soon after that Joel was shot and killed by unknown assailants.''

Heilbronner wanted to speak, but she held up her hand and said sharply, ''Wait a minute. What I'm suggesting is that someone could find the original inventory of those antiques, as well as the original insurance policies that covered them; both of the other children had copies, and so did their lawyer. That someone could find the appraisal and the auction records, and find out how much of what was inventoried was actually sold then. A real investigation might reveal that Palmer sold a lot of priceless antiques privately at some later date and pocketed the money. His payment. And from that time to this, Marta Chisolm Delancey has been his to use when the occasion arose.'' Very softly she said, ''It must be extremely important to get Trassi off the hook, for him to use such a big card in such a small case as the Arno murder.''

For a time Heilbronner didn't move. Then he tapped his fingertips together almost delicately, it seemed. ''Can you impeach her, beyond question?''

''Yes.''

The silence lasted longer then, until Frank said meditatively, ''I think the question now is, If you hook Calpurnia, do you also snag Caesar? Interesting little problem, isn't it? Carter, I suggested coffee a while back. Maybe now's a good time to reconsider.''

''Coffee would be good,'' Heilbronner said.

His face was turned toward Barbara, but she felt certain he was not seeing her. Frank left and they were both silent for a time, until Heilbronner said, ''You don't have an iota of proof, I take it.''

''Adding one plus one plus one; local gossip; a good dose of intuition and guesswork; end results,'' she said. ''And perjury.''

Frank returned with a tray. "Way I see it," he said, "a nap's worthless unless you know two things—where you tand, and which way is north. But if you know those hings, then it's dot-to-dot child's play. I don't keep up with politics the way I should, I'm afraid. I wonder how many committees Delancey's on, how much power he's gained n the past fifteen or twenty years. Cream?"

Heilbronner rose and walked to the window, pulled the drape aside, and stood gazing out.

Barbara accepted a cup of coffee from Frank, watching Heilbronner. After a moment she said, "You've read the statements and findings; you know I agreed to pursue Mitch Arno for his ex-wife and recover long-past-due child support. I did that, and as far as I'm concerned, that whole matter is history. At present, my only concerns are staying alive, keeping my father alive, and exonerating Ray Arno. He is a textbook example of an innocent bystander."

Heilbronner let the drape fall back into place and turned once more; he went to the table and added cream to a cup of coffee, then sat down. "I understand," he said almost absently. After another moment he focused on her again, sipped his coffee, then said, "One of the theories that has arisen, Ms. Holloway, is that you or Maggie Folsum found the money along with something else that had great importance to Palmer, and that you used the other item or items to force him to deal. This suggested that it was not his own money, of course; he would have been more reluctant to relinquish his own money. But, as you say, the past is done, history. He recovered his item or items, you accomplished your mission for your client, and it's over. Theories come and go, but we have the official record, statements, the IRS final agreement, and I see little profit in trying to ferret out each and every detail of historical incidents."

Then Frank said bluntly, "Carter, there are a couple of

little items that do need clarifying. Where are Stael and Ulrich? Palmer has made threats; they're his hired guns. Be nice to know where they are.''

''Yes,'' Heilbronner agreed. ''They were not very high-priority, I'm afraid. I don't know where they are. In Oregon, last seen in Portland, over a week ago. I'm afraid we've been more preoccupied with the senator's wife, and the reason for her appearance here, than with Palmer's hired hands.''

Frank nodded. ''Seems to me that there's been a lack of attention to several things. Losing a guy back East to a drive-by shooting; losing two ex-cons who are about to get accused of murder. One way or the other Trassi is dead in the water. I hope, Carter, that when all the bodies are laid to rest and the dust settles, Mr. Palmer isn't going to be the only one to walk away untouched. I trust there's no one with a vested interest behind the scenery manipulating priorities, making decisions about what is or isn't important enough to keep an eye on. You know, someone in an oversight position second-guessing fieldwork.''

Heilbronner's face was expressionless. He set his cup down and got to his feet. ''It's been informative and interesting talking to you both. Thanks. I'd better be on my way. I know you have work to do, and so do I. Fieldwork can be demanding—Saturdays, Sundays, holidays, no letup. Communications break down; people in the head office are out partying while you're in the field slogging away. I'll be in touch.''

He shook hands with Barbara, then left with Frank, talking about the fog, about Christmas shopping still to do, about nothing.

Later that day she moved into Frank's house. Whether she was trying to protect him or be protected in his house didn't matter.

"You think you can't possibly get through the days sometimes, but then the day's over and you did it," she whispered that night to Thing One, who was half on her lap and half on the couch. He grunted when she spoke. Both Things grunted a lot, the first cats she had ever heard make that particular noise deep in their throats, as if trying to speak. She stroked the cat and watched the fire, wishing for tomorrow, wishing for Christmas to be over.

Frank came in, trailed by Thing Two, and sat opposite her; the other cat tried to get into his lap. It was grunting, too.

"Rain's moving in," Frank said. "Maybe that will be the end of the fog for a time. Sylvia asked us over for eggnog and a cookie tomorrow. I said okay. I'll eat the cookie and drink the eggnog, and you can tramp around her hills in the rain. Deal?"

Tomorrow, Sunday. "Sure," she said. "Sounds good."

And so she got through Sunday; Sunday night, tired from climbing hills in the rain, she slept undisturbed by dreams. You do get through the days, she thought. You really do.

She worked Monday, and most of Tuesday, Christmas Eve. She visited Ray on both days, and, strangely, she felt almost envious of him; in jail over the holidays, his family pretending a cheer they couldn't be feeling, yet he was enduring the season in better shape than she was. She could envy him his faith, she thought, and envy his big family that was so supportive and comforting, even if they all talked at once.

Frank spent most of Christmas Eve in the kitchen, preparing dinner for Shelley and Bill Spassero, and Bailey and his wife, Hannah. A party, Barbara thought bleakly, putting on a long skirt and cashmere sweater, her party clothes.

Christmas night she stood in her upstairs room at the window, gazing at the city lights through the rain that continued to fall steadily. She had thought John might call, then had decided there was little point in it. What could either of them say, except "Merry Christmas"? And tomorrow, back to court, back to the real world. What a long holiday. Then, looking at the lights shimmering through the rain, she whispered, "Merry Christmas."

36

Court was not filled to overflowing that morning, the day after Christmas. No doubt, the usual hangers-on would wander in eventually, but the media had lost interest again since there were reports of flooding in the valley, and the immediacy of floods at the holiday season would make for more human-interest features than a humdrum murder case, at least for now. After the lunch recess, they would be back, Barbara knew. The jury was not happy to be in court again—that was evident from some dour expressions. Tough, she thought, and called her first witness.

Douglas Herschell was in his thirties, prematurely balding, a stocky man with a large open face and a good-natured grin. He was a machinist, he said, at a chicken-processing plant in Pleasant Hill, fifteen miles south of Eugene. He lived on Stratton Lane with his wife and a seven-year-old son.

Quickly Barbara led him to the first week of August. "Please tell the court what was different about that week," she said.

"Yes, ma'am. We were putting in new machines and we had to be on hand earlier than usual, by six in the morning, every day from the fifth of August until the middle of the month. It was hard because I had to get up at four-thirty and leave the house at a quarter after five. I was late the first two days," he said, then grinned sheepishly.

''What time did you leave the house on those two days?''

''Five-thirty.''

''On the morning of Tuesday, August sixth, you left your house at five-thirty in the morning, knowing you were going to be late for work. Did you speed a little?''

''Probably did,'' he admitted.

''What kind of car were you driving, Mr. Herschell?''

''An eighty-nine Toyota Tercel,'' he said promptly.

''And what color was that car?''

''Gray.''

She showed him the picture of fifteen gray hatchback cars, and he pointed to his. She had him initial it, had it passed on to the jury, then said no more questions.

Roxbury picked at him, but he didn't change a word.

Moving right along, Barbara thought, and called her next witness, Sally Arno. Sally was thirty-nine and married to James Arno, Ray's brother. Blond and dimply, a touch overweight, she had the contented expression of someone not obsessed with appearance. Her hair was showing touches of gray, and she was leaving that alone, obviously not concerned.

''When you and Lorinne Arno prepared a lot of food to take out to the family reunion at Folsum, why did you do the cooking at your house instead of hers?''

''Well, she had been painting and cleaning most of July, she does that in the summer when school's out—she's a teacher, you know—paints her cabinets, waxes the floors, cleans everything when school's out, and I said it would be a shame to leave a mess for Ray to deal with.'' She smiled at Ray, then at Lorinne, sitting among the spectators. ''And we knew we'd leave a mess. Someone would have to clean it all up, and I was going to be home, but she was taking her kids down to Gold Beach to visit her folks right after Maggie's party. So I said let's get together at my place and cook, and I'd have all the next week to straighten up again and she wouldn't have a mess to face when she got home again."

Two of the women on the jury were looking at Sally with understanding; they knew what it meant to leave a mess for a man to clean up.

"Did Ray Arno pick up your husband, James, and the two of them drive to the coast together that weekend?" She said yes, and that they had arrived before nine-thirty.

"Do you recall the spring of 1978?"

"Yes, very well."

"Will you please tell the court what was going on with the Arno family in April that year?"

"James and I were engaged, and Ray and Lorinne were, too, and none of us had any money. David and Donna were married by then, and they were really broke. And Mitch never had a cent in those days, and Maggie was pregnant. I mean, things were tough. Then Papa Arno said he knew about a fishing boat that was good and sound, and he could buy it at a really good price, but it needed a lot of work; it had been let go a long time, I guess, and it needed varnish, parts replaced, woodwork redone—just a lot of work. He said if the boys wanted to do the work, he'd buy the boat and they could fix it up and he'd sell it, and they could keep all the profit. We were all trying to save up a little, and the boys jumped at the chance. So starting on the last weekend in March and every weekend in April, we all headed out to the coast and worked on the boat."

Barbara let her ramble on and tell it her way without interruption. One weekend, she said, Lorinne had called to say her car was having a problem with the brakes and she wouldn't be able to drive over. Everyone else was there already, and Mama Arno said that since Mitch wasn't doing a lick of work on the boat, he could drive to Corvallis and pick up Lorinne and bring her over; then Ray would drive her home again on Sunday night. Mitch drove Ray's car and got her.

"Do you know when they arrived, what time it was?"

"Yes, before dinner, and we ate at six."

"What happened the last weekend of April, or the firs
weekend of May? Do you recall that time?"

"Yes. We were done with the boat, it was the first week
end in May that we didn't have that on our minds anymore
and we were all going camping, David, James, Ray, Lor
inne, another couple of friends, and me. Lorinne had t
work late, until nine, but she said for us to go on and ge
the camp set up and she'd drive over as soon as she go
off work. That same day, Mitch called me and asked if I'
lend him some money. He said he was in trouble, he'
borrowed money from a girl, and her father threatened t
throw him in jail if he didn't pay her back right away, bu
I didn't have any money to lend him and I said so. Anyway
Lorinne showed up at the campsite and she told me tha
Mitch had asked her for a loan, and said the same thing
he was in trouble, and he said he'd go to Ray for it if she
couldn't help out. She said she worried what it would d
to Mama Arno if he got in more trouble, and of course
Ray would have told her, so she gave Mitch fifty dollars."

"Did Mitch pay back the money, to your knowledge?"
Barbara asked.

"No. In fact, that was the weekend he took off altogether."

"Do you recall what time Lorinne arrived at the campsite
that night?"

"Yes. It was about an hour's drive, and it was pretty
dark, so we were watching for her, and she showed up by
ten. Then we ate and played cards and like that."

When Roxbury did his cross-examination, he tried to
back her down about dates and times, but she simply
wanted to explain things more fully.

Two down, Barbara thought when she did her redirect,
and then thanked Sally and excused her.

* * *

After a brief recess, she called Walter Hoven. He had not wanted to testify and resented being called, and had been furious about being served with a subpoena. He was sick, he had said angrily, and he had nothing to tell the jury anyway, and it was a fucking waste of his time.

He was sixty-one, heavyset, with a permanent frown that had been fixed so long, his face had become rearranged with deep scowl lines.

"Mr. Hoven, where were you employed in the fall of 1978?" she asked politely.

"Valley Warehouse," he snapped.

"What was your position there?"

"Manager."

"Where was the warehouse?"

"West Seventh Place."

Bit by bit she drew out of him a description of the area at that time, a warehouse district across the road from fields, with the train tracks not far away, railway sidings criss-crossing the roads and fields, no sidewalks, nothing for consumers, just warehouses.

"Did you have occasion to meet Ray Arno in the fall of that year?"

"Yes."

"Will you please tell the court how that came about, what your association with Mr. Arno was at that time."

"He wanted to rent space. I rented it to him."

She had known he would be difficult, but gradually she became aware of a growing sympathy toward her from the jury. A mean witness could do that, she thought, and asked her questions patiently, and he answered, begrudging every word.

Ray Arno had looked for space to rent because the shop he had counted on having was not yet available, and he had goods due to arrive through the fall. He had rented the corner of the warehouse from September tenth until December first. Barbara showed him the pictures Lorinne had provided, and he admitted that that was the warehouse, that was the space Ray had rented. It was a dim corner with a fold-away table, and rough board planks on concrete block, stacked with boxes. Fishing gear was spread out on the table.

"Did he show you his business license?" she asked.

"Yes. Wouldn't have rented the space to him other wise," he said.

"Did he have customers come to the warehouse?"

"No. Not allowed."

"Did he have a sign in his window?"

"There wasn't no window for a sign, and it wasn't al lowed anyway."

"When did he actually move out of the warehouse?"

"Last day of November. Didn't get through until the next day, and he paid for an extra day."

There were a few more details, but she had what she had wanted from him and turned him over to Roxbury soon after that.

Roxbury asked coldly, "Do you know where his shop was at the time?"

"No."

"Do you know that he didn't open his shop that fall?"

"No."

"Isn't it possible that he had his shop, and used the warehouse to store excess merchandise at the same time?"

Barbara objected, speculation. It was sustained.

"Do you know where he was when he wasn't in your warehouse?" Roxbury asked.

Hoven's face was a dull red; he looked ready to erupt in anger, but he simply snapped, "No."

"Was he there all day every day?"

"No."

"So he could have been in a retail shop, selling his wares," Roxbury said sharply.

Barbara objected; it was sustained. Roxbury was dogged,

...ough; he knew as well as Barbara that this witness was ...evastating to his case.

When Roxbury finally finished, Barbara said, "Mr. Ho-...en, you stated that Mr. Arno was not in the warehouse all ...ay every day, but isn't it true that your agreement with ...im was that he was to be there to receive his shipments ... person?"

"Yes. I told him I wouldn't do no unpacking or checking ...rders, wouldn't be responsible for signing for it, none of ...at. He had to do it."

"And isn't it true that his shipments were arriving ...rough the month of September and into October?"

"I don't know when they came," he said sullenly.

"But the agreement was that he would receive his own ...hipments in person. What did he use the table for?"

"He opened stuff and counted it, spread it out to check ...hings. Then he put everything back in boxes. Not allowed ... leave things out on the table."

She let it go at that. It was time for lunch.

It pleased her when they left the courthouse to see Hoven ...truggling furiously in the midst of several reporters and ...hotographers. He was not restraining his language any ...onger; obscenities were loud and coarse. Camcorders were ...etting every second of it, and that night on the news, there ...e would be for the world to see. Word had gone out ...hat he had contradicted Marta Delancey's testimony, im-...eached her.

Norman Donovan was Barbara's first witness that after-...oon. He was a bespectacled man in his fifties, now in ...nanagement at the big mall across the river. In 1978, he ...estified, he had been manager of a strip mall in south Eu-...gene. His testimony was precise and to the point.

Ray Arno had rented a store in the mall, but the then-...urrent tenant had not been able to vacate as planned during ...he first week of September. Ray had been upset; he had

his business license, and he had taken a Yellow Pages a
and had cards and invoices printed already, all with tha
address, so it was out of the question for him to look for
different location. The tenant had not moved out until th
middle of November; management had redecorated, th
sign painter had done the windows, and the last day o
November and the first of December Ray had moved h
goods in and taken possession.

"Was there any one particular cause for worry for M
Arno?" Barbara asked.

"Yes, there was. He had planned to be in the shop earl
in September and he had a lot of stock due to arrive startin
at that time and for the following few weeks, on into Oc
tober. He didn't know where to store it, until he located
warehouse that would rent him a small space temporarily.

When Roxbury did his cross-examination, he pressed th
same points he had with Hoven: Donovan didn't kno
where Ray was all that time, he didn't know if he wa
selling his merchandise out of a different shop, did he?

When Shelley stood up and called on Maggie, there wa
a ripple of interest in the court. They looked like Gi
Scouts, Barbara thought, watching. Shelley had tamed he
gorgeous abundant hair into a chignon and had dressed i
a very simple dark blue suit, with a dark red blouse, an
she wore simple gold hoop earrings. Maggie's hair wa
drawn back and held at the nape of her neck with a bon
clasp, and she was dressed in an equally simple suit, gray
with a gray blouse. Neither of them looked at all nervous

Shelley took her through her history with Mitch and th
Arno family quickly and briefly, then focused on the event
following the Monday after the party.

"Do you know what time Ray Arno called you tha
night?"

"Yes. The call was recorded at eight-thirty."

"At what time did you return his call?"

"A few minutes after twelve, from the hotel in Folsum."

Shelley produced both records of the phone calls and had them admitted. "When Mr. Trassi approached you in the hotel on Tuesday morning, why didn't you talk with him?"

"I was too upset. I believed that Mitch had done that to my inn. I didn't think I could discuss him with anyone at that time."

"Why did you stop believing that?"

"The deputy sheriffs said it was the work of at least two people, and the detective I hired confirmed that. He said two people had done it, and one of them was left-handed."

Point by point Shelley took her over the events concerning the money, hiring Bailey to fingerprint the house, the meetings with Sunderman, and then with the Internal Revenue representative. Maggie was a good witness. At no time did anyone mention how much money was involved, and Roxbury's objections were few and of little consequence.

"Following the initial meeting with the Internal Revenue Service, what did you do?"

"The next working day Ms. Holloway and I had a meeting with the district attorney and told him about it. That was August twenty-sixth."

"When you received the report about the fingerprints found in Mr. Arno's house, what did you do with it?"

"I gave a copy to the district attorney, and one to Mr. Arno's former attorney."

Shelley turned to Roxbury then and said, "Your witness."

"Ms. Folsum, when the defendant told you Mitchell Arno was at his house, did you express fear? Beg him to keep Mitchell Arno away from you?"

"Objection," Shelley said coldly. "Leading question based on a false premise."

"Sustained."

"Did the defendant tell you he would protect you from his brother, as he had done before?"

"No."

"If you had asked the defendant to defend you as before would you expect him to do so?"

"Objection. Speculation." It was sustained.

"When you informed the defendant that your bed-and-breakfast had been wrecked, did you tell him you suspected Mitchell Arno had done the damage?"

"Yes."

"Was he enraged?"

"No. He was very sad, and worried about my safety."

Roxbury hammered at her, making the point that the Arnos had their own code of justice; a daughter and sister had to be protected, that Ray as the eldest son had that obligation: to protect the cherished sister.

Without exception, Shelley's objections were sustained and Maggie remained calm and refused to be rattled.

Barbara had suspected that the state intended to play down the money Mitch had carried; the fact that there had been no leak concerning it had reassured her that they had accepted the IRS agreement, as well as the various statements, and that it was a closed issue. She was not surprised that at this time Roxbury never once referred to it. He was going to play his other card: the Arnos were not like the jury panel members, they pursued justice Mafioso-style.

"The Girl Scouts came through with flying colors," Barbara said to Frank when Maggie was finally excused and Judge Waldman called for a recess. Barbara walked to the women's room with Maggie and Shelley, and inside, they both started to shake. She laughed and put her arms around them, drawing them in close. "I do that, too," she said. "But never in court. You were both swell."

Then, back in court, still on schedule, moving exactly as planned, she called Bailey. He was not dapper, she thought as he was being sworn in, but he was presentable in a brown suit she estimated to be about fifteen years old and red-striped tie from some historical period. He had shined his shoes, she noted with approval. She would try to remember to compliment him on that bit of heroism.

She had him give an account of his training and experience: the police academy in California, work with the San Diego Police Department as a detective, special FBI training, then his move to Eugene and going into business as a private investigator.

She went straight to their visit to the bed-and-breakfast and the photographs he had taken. He identified the pictures and they were admitted as evidence. "What did you conclude about the damage done to the inn?"

He said two people had been searching, and explained how he had determined that one was left-handed. "It wasn't the pattern for malicious vandalism; they were looking for something."

"What is the difference between malicious vandalism and a hasty search?"

He explained: malicious vandalism involved scrawling obscenities here and there, spray-painting walls, breaking windows, defecating on beds, urinating on carpets, flooding the place, and it wouldn't involve the entire building, because that was too much work. The inn had been searched methodically from top to bottom; it had been fast and they hadn't cared how much damage they did, but there hadn't been any of the personal touches of malice.

"On Saturday, August tenth, did you receive a call from Ms. Folsum?"

He said yes, and recounted what he had done.

"Did you receive a report from the FBI?"

"Yes. On August twenty-ninth the report came back and I made a copy for my files and gave the original to Ms. Folsum on the following day, August thirtieth."

"Do you have that report?" she asked. He said yes, and she asked him to summarize it for the court.

"One set of prints," he said, referring to the report, "be-

longs to a man named Jacob Stael, who goes by the name
of Bud, address unknown, believed to reside in New York
City. He has a criminal record, served seven years in New
York State for assault and battery. Another set belongs to
Jeremy Ulrich, also of New York City, also with a criminal
record, for armed robbery. Both men are employed by the
R. M. Palmer Company of New York City.''

"Is either of them left-handed?" Barbara asked then.

"Bud Stael is left-handed.''

"Do you have photographs of those two men?" she
asked.

He did.

Roxbury objected strenuously when she asked that the
pictures be admitted. There was no foundation for introducing two new characters, he said meanly.

Barbara asked to approach, and at the bench she said
"Those two men will be identified by various people as
the defense case proceeds. We will demonstrate that they
were in the area throughout much of August, as well as in
the Palmer office when Mitchell Arno retained Mr. Trassi.''

"Picking out a man from a single picture isn't admissi-
ble," Roxbury snapped, "as she well knows."

"Not like picking out a single car from a single picture?" She turned to Judge Waldman. "We have witnesses
who will testify that they picked out these men from among
a group of mug shots.''

Judge Waldman looked thoughtful for a moment, then
said, "I'll sustain the objection at this time, but if your
witnesses testify as you state, then you may introduce the
photographs after the proper foundation has been laid.''

She thanked the judge and resumed questioning Bailey.

In his cross-examination, Roxbury wanted to make three
points, and he drove at them harshly. "Did you recover
other fingerprints that were not identified?" Bailey said yes.
"It is just an opinion, isn't it, that the inn was subjected to
a search?"

"It was a search," Bailey said.

"According to the official police report—"

"Objection," Barbara said. "Improper cross-examination. No one has introduced an official report on the damage. It was not part of discovery."

"I have it right here," Roxbury snapped, holding up a sheet of paper.

Barbara shook her head. "But you didn't supply the defense with a copy, did you, Mr. Roxbury?" She thought he was being very reasonable, and even sweet, but his flush of anger suggested that he didn't agree.

"Enough arguing," Judge Waldman said. "Overruled."

Barbara's exception was noted, and Roxbury continued.

He tried to give Bailey a hard time, but in Barbara's opinion, it would take a nuclear explosion to accomplish that.

When Bailey left the witness stand, Barbara called her final witness for the day.

Gene Atherton was a pale, nervous man who had confided to Barbara that he had never been in court before, and worried that it would be an ordeal. She had reassured him as much as possible, but now, today, it appeared that his worst fears had surfaced once more. For a moment he seemed to forget how to spell his name.

In a conversational tone, she invited him to tell the jury where he worked and what his position was. She kept her tone easy, almost soothing, as she drew him out about working in a motel; he began to relax a little.

He worked as desk clerk in one of the Gateway motels off I-5, and had been there for nine years.

"I suppose with so many people arriving and leaving constantly, you don't particularly remember any of them after a time has passed," she said. "Is that correct?"

"Usually," he said. "There's no reason to remember most of them."

"But if something unusual happens, then later on you might recall one or more of your guests. Is that right?"

"Yes, it is."

"Do you recall any of your guests from last August?" she asked, still easy.

"Yes, very well."

"And is that because something unusual happened to make you remember them?"

"Yes, it is."

"Please tell the jury about that, Mr. Atherton."

He hesitated, evidently not knowing just where to start. "You mean from when they checked in?"

"That would be fine," she said. "Just tell it in your own words."

"Well, two men checked in late on Saturday night, August third. They called first for a reservation and gave a credit card number and said they'd be late and to hold a room. So they checked in, and they said they were tired, ready for bed. New Yorkers, they sounded like, and I thought the time difference, jet lag, something like that, was bothering them. They said they'd be there three or four days, maybe longer, maybe not." He paused, watching Barbara for a sign of approval, a clue that this was okay. She nodded at him.

"The next morning they were up and out early, before I got off work, even. I work from ten at night until seven in the morning. I saw them take off."

Barbara interrupted him then. "Mr. Atherton, before you continue, just a few questions to clarify what you've already said. What is the procedure when a call for a reservation comes in, with a credit card number?"

"Whoever takes the call reserves the room and then puts the card through the machine for verification, he initials the charge information, and that's that."

"All right. So you had that information, a name and

redit card number. When they sign in, what is the proce-
ure?"

"They have to sign, or one of them does, in the regis-
ation book, and give the license number of their car and
home address, and sign the credit card charge slip. One
f them did that."

"Did you get a good look at them?"

"The one who signed them in, I did. The other one was
ooking over maps, the tourist information in the rack. I
idn't see him as well."

"You said they were New Yorkers. Did the one who
igned in give a New York address?"

"Yes, but it was the way he talked that made me think
lew York—you know, the accent."

"What were they driving?"

"A ninety-three Honda Accord, dark blue, with an
Oregon license plate."

"Do you know the number of the license?"

He produced a photocopy of the registration with the
icense number and read it.

"All right. Did they stay the few days they had said they
night?"

"No. They stayed until the morning of August four-
eenth."

"On Sunday morning, August fourth, you said they left
very early. Do you know when they returned Sunday
light?"

"Yes. I saw them drive in at two-thirty in the morning."

"Were both of them in the car?"

"Yes. The reason I noticed the time," he added, "was
hat I was thinking if they were still on New York time, it
vas like five-thirty in the morning for them, and it had been
a long day for them."

"Mr. Atherton," Barbara said, "so far this sounds like
very routine motel business. What was it that made it mem-
orable, made you remember them in such detail?"

"It wasn't then," he said hurriedly. "I mean, they didn' do anything to bring attention. It was a couple of week later, when a credit card investigator came around. The car was stolen, you see, and the company was looking into i They ran up a pretty big bill, eleven days, meals. And i turned out that the license plate on the car was stolen, toc and the car was stolen. They asked all of us questions, an it was still recent enough that we could remember, and afte we answered their questions, it's like we'll never forge now."

"Did you describe the men for the investigator?"

"Yes."

She asked him to describe the two men and he did, bu his description was not very detailed until he said, "Th one who signed in was left-handed."

"Did you identify them by looking at photographs?"

"Not then. He didn't have any. Later, another privat investigator came around with a book of pictures, and picked them out."

"Can you tell the jury about the book of pictures? Wha was it like?"

"Thirty pictures maybe, in a book, like a photograph album."

She went to her table and picked up the album and showed it to him. "Is that the book of photographs yo looked through?"

He leafed through it, then nodded. "That's it."

The pictures were all of ex-cons, dressed more or less the same in sports shirts open at the throat. Their age ranged from about thirty to about fifty and there was noth ing to make one stand out from another. A good mug book that Bailey had assembled over the years. "From those pic tures you were able to identify the two men who checked in on August fourth?"

"Yes. One of them was the guy who signed the regis tration, him I knew right off. I wasn't that sure about the

her one, like I said. But I picked out another picture and
told the investigator I thought that was the second man."

"Then what did you do?"

"Well, the investigator asked me to put my initials on
the back of the pictures, and I did."

Now Barbara picked up the photographs she had wanted
introduce earlier, and she asked Atherton to look at the
initials. "Are those the initials you wrote there?" He said
es, and she showed him the pictures. "Are those the two
en you identified?"

"Yes. That one for sure," he said, pointing. "That one
think is the other man, but I wouldn't swear to him, not
ke the other one."

Barbara asked to approach the bench then, and she and
oxbury stood before the judge and spoke in low voices.
There is peel-off tape on the back of those two photo-
raphs," Barbara said. "The pictures were provided by the
riminal justice department in New York City, and have a
ertification stamp and signature. May I identify the men,
r must I introduce yet another witness to do so?"

Judge Waldman took the pictures and peeled off the tape,
en showed them to Roxbury. "Will you stipulate the au-
enticity of the photographs?" she asked him.

It was clear that he wanted very much to say no, but
fter a moment of hesitation, he shrugged. "So stipulated."

Judge Waldman nodded to Barbara. "You may identify
em."

Back at her table, Barbara said, "Let the record show
at the witness identified Jacob 'Bud' Stael as the man
ho signed his registration book on the night of August
ourth, and tentatively identified the second man as Jeremy
Ulrich." She had the pictures admitted and passed them to
e jurors, and when they were done looking, she said,
"Your witness, Mr. Roxbury."

37

It was ten-thirty when Bailey and Shelley left that nigh. The rain was hard, relentless, although it was not very col.

"You planning to be up a bit longer?" Frank asked Bar bara in the living room. Alan was in the dinette with hi book.

"Awhile," she said. "I'm working on my closing ar gument. Maybe I'll even get a draft of it down. What abou you?"

"What I aim to do is take a very long bath, snuggle wit a book for half an hour, and then sleep. Sounds pretty goo don't you think?"

She grinned and nodded, then stood up and walked t the hall. "I'll tell Alan he might as well come share th fire with the monsters; I'll be up in the office." Both golde cats were stretched out full-length as close as they coul get to the fire without singeing their fur. In the corner th Christmas tree glowed and sparkled, untouched this yea every ornament in place. She almost regretted how fleetin childhood was for cats. Well, Alan could enjoy the fire an tree; she would leave the lights on it for him. She had take only a few steps when the doorbell rang, long and piercing as if someone was holding a finger on the bell. She turne toward the door; Bailey? Had he forgotten something Then, magically, Alan was passing her. He motioned he back to the living room, and Frank grabbed her arm. Ala

ent to the front door, looked out the peephole, then came
) them, just inside the living room doorway.

"Trassi," he said.

"Alone?" Frank asked.

"Didn't see anyone else, but there's shrubbery out
here."

"Let's turn on the floodlights," Frank said, walking into
he hallway. "Ask him what he wants; I'll do the lights."

Alan nodded and returned to the door. "Mr. Trassi, it's
retty late. Won't this keep until morning?"

Frank flipped the switch for the outdoor lights, and as if
n signal, gunfire erupted. Five, six shots, as loud as can-
ons. The cats streaked past Barbara, up the stairs. She was
mmobilized, and Frank stood with his hand on the light
witch, as motionless as she was. Alan now had a gun in
iis own hand, and he was opening the front door.

"Just back up," he snapped. "Palmer, put the gun on
he step, then back up, or I'll shoot you. Now!"

"Call nine-one-one," Frank said to Barbara, and he hur-
ied toward the door. She ran to the kitchen phone and
nade the call.

"Tell them two men are down, maybe three," Frank
elled as she spoke into the phone. "We need an ambu-
ance."

The dispatcher wanted her to stay on the line, to keep
alking, but she put the phone on the stand, and ran to the
loor. Trassi was leaning into the front of the house, with
Alan patting him down, holding his gun very steady as he
lid. He motioned Trassi away and told Palmer to walk very
lowly toward the house. Then Barbara saw two men lying
n the rain, with blood all around them both. Frank was
kneeling by one of them; he stood up, walked the few steps
o the other one and did the same thing, knelt down, felt
or a pulse.

"One of them might still be alive," he said. "Maybe a
couple of blankets."

She ran to get the blankets. Stael and Ulrich, she thought Palmer had killed Stael and Ulrich. He had delivered them to her doorstep, just as he said he would. Fighting hysteria she groped in the linen closet for blankets, then hurried back to the front porch. Frank covered the two men on the ground.

"Do you suppose we could get inside out of the rain? Palmer asked then. "I'm afraid Mr. Trassi is exhibiting signs of shock."

Trassi was shaking violently. His skin was blue-white even his lips.

"Are they clean?" Frank asked. Alan said yes. "Get inside," Frank snapped to Palmer. Already, the wail of siren was all around, the noise reverberating against the low clouds. Up and down the street, lights had come on; people had come to doorways, some all the way out to the street huddling under umbrellas. "We'll go in, too," Frank said "You okay out here?"

Alan said sure, and leaned against the house on the porch, out of the rain. Barbara thought irrelevantly how different he looked, no longer the friendly kid delivering a pizza, or one of the youths riding a bike aimlessly around He looked like a man Bailey would hire and trust to do his job. His gun had vanished again.

Inside, Frank said, "You want to put on some coffee" This might take a while." He ushered Trassi and Palmer into the living room, where they drew near the fire, both of them soaked. Frank was only slightly less wet. She hurried to the kitchen to make coffee, saw the phone again and hung it up. The siren sounded as if the ambulance or police car, or both, had turned the corner of their street.

After the initial confusion of uniformed officers asking questions, of medics whisking both men away to the hospital, Lieutenant Lester Cookson arrived with two plain-clothes detectives and asked what was going on. Without hesitation, Palmer said, "I shot them both."

Trassi was huddled in a chair with a blanket around him, still shaking, but less violently now. His color was better, more white than blue; he looked terrified. Palmer was seated comfortably in another chair close to the fire. His clothes were steaming; he had turned down Frank's offer of a blanket.

"We'd better go to the station and let you make a statement," Lieutenant Cookson said.

"I prefer to explain in front of Ms. Holloway and Mr. Holloway," Palmer said coolly. "They should know what happened on their doorstep, don't you think?"

Just then Bailey arrived, and after a little argument between Frank and Cookson, he was admitted.

"Why not?" Palmer said. "The more the merrier." He watched one of the detectives open a laptop computer, and he shrugged. "Tell me if I speak too fast. Earlier this evening Mr. Trassi and I had dinner together. Mr. Trassi is my attorney, and it was a business meeting and meal. Afterward, we met Ms. Fredericks, who is a private investigator in my employ. The three of us boarded an elevator together to return to our rooms, but we were stopped on the second floor. Two men boarded; they grabbed Mr. Trassi's arms and dragged him off the elevator, and were hustling him toward the stairs when the doors closed, and we began ascending again. They were Stael and Ulrich, both of whom I employ now and then, and, frankly, I was quite alarmed. I told Ms. Fredericks to lend me her gun, a forty-four I believe it is, and at the next floor I left the elevator and ran down the stairs, hoping to catch up with the kidnappers. I could hear them in the stairwell, and I followed them to the lower-level parking garage, where I glimpsed all three of them on the opposite side of the area. They got into a car, and I got into my own car, and was close enough to catch up with them at the street exit. I followed after them

out into the street, quite worried, and not knowing wha
other course to take, except to keep them in sight until the
stopped somewhere, and then confront them.''

He spread his hands in a gesture that suggested help
lessness. ''I had no idea of their intentions, of course, no
any idea where they might be going or what was being said
in their car, and the rain was very hard. It was difficult jus
keeping them in sight.''

He might have been describing a jaunt to the beach, he
was so self-assured and at ease. Watching him, Barbara
again felt the chill that his presence had brought on before
His voice was almost hypnotic in its rhythmic cadences.

''When they turned into this street, I didn't know where
we were,'' he continued. ''I saw a car pull out of the driveway at this house, and they pulled in. I stopped at the curb
down a way and came after them on foot. Stael and Ulrich
shoved poor Mr. Trassi to the door, and they both stepped
behind bushes; Stael had a gun in his hand, and that's when
it occurred to me that this could be the Holloway residence.''

He frowned and said with an air of apology, ''I'm afraid
it gets a little confusing now. I was close enough to hear
Stael say something like, As soon as the door opens, we
rush them. No one's going to walk away. I'm not repeating
his words verbatim; he was using very vulgar language and
I see no point in echoing his exact words; however, that
was what he meant. My worst fears were confirmed.'' He
looked at Trassi and shook his head. ''He was quite helpless. After all, Stael was holding a gun on him.

''My next move was to step forward and call out, 'Bud,
for the love of God, stop this. Put that gun away and get
out of here before someone gets killed.' Just as I spoke,
many lights came on, and the two events, my voice coming
from behind him, as well as sudden lights all around, made
him panic, I'm afraid. He spun around and started shooting.
I shot back. And Ulrich had drawn his gun from his pocket,

ıd I shot him also. Perhaps unnecessarily, but at the mo-
ıent it was quite a reflexive action," he added. A very
ight smile curved his lips for a moment, then he added,
Mr. Trassi did the only sensible thing. He threw himself
at on the ground when the shooting started."

He was going to get away with it, Barbara thought then.
rassi would back him up, and Palmer would come out a
ero who had saved the lives of her and her father, and
lan. He looked at her, and she could almost hear him say,
I delivered them right to your door."

Trassi added a few details: Stael and Ulrich had meant
ɔ rush the door as soon as it opened. They knew there was
security system, and it had to be opened from inside. They
oth had silencers on their guns, and they would have killed
im, too. They wouldn't have left a witness. In a high-
itched and tremulous voice he confirmed Palmer's story.
Ie didn't look at Palmer once.

It wasn't long after that when the lieutenant said, "Thank
ou, Mr. Palmer. I still have to ask you and Mr. Trassi to
ome downtown with us, but it shouldn't take long."

"I understand," Palmer said. "I shall be of any assis-
ınce possible, of course. I wonder if it would be permitted
ɔ go back to the hotel long enough to change clothes first?
did get rather wet, you know, and poor Mr. Trassi must
e even wetter, and neither of us in heavy coats. I am re-
ıctant to leave the warmth of the fire."

Cookson spoke with two officers and they left with Pal-
ıer and Trassi. At the doorway Palmer turned back toward
łarbara and ducked his head in a little bow. "I so regret
uch unpleasantness outside your door. I apologize." She
ıid not say a word.

After they were gone, Cookson said to Frank, "We have
crime-scene tape up, and a car will be parked out front
vernight. A television crew is out there now and it's going
ɔ get worse. I'd like to keep them off the property until
ve've had a chance to look around in daylight."

* * *

With everyone gone, the house secured again, Frank sa
bitterly, "Christ on a mountain! Rush the door, sho
everyone in the house! Lunatics!"

"They weren't going to get in," Alan said. "No wa
was I going to open that door. I meant to give Bailey a ca
and have him drive back over."

"That's how we set it up," Bailey said. "Once the se
curity system goes on, no outsider gets in unless he's e
corted by me or one of my guys."

"That wasn't the plan, anyway," Barbara said. "Th
plan worked exactly the way Palmer arranged it. He se
them up and then killed them. He delivered them to m
That's his business, special deliveries. Guaranteed." Sh
became aware of Frank's appraising gaze and stopped.

Alan nodded in agreement. "By the time I got the syste
off and the door open, Palmer was at Stael's side. I thin
he put his hand over Stael's on the gun and fired twice.
heard two more pops from the silenced gun after Palme
stopped shooting."

Bailey and Alan went to check out the house then, t
make certain nothing had been opened during the conft
sion, and Frank put his arm about Barbara's shoulders i
the living room.

"You going to be okay the rest of the night?"

"Sure," she said. "Safest night so far with a cop ca
parked out front."

Later, wide awake in bed, she was remembering John'
bitter words: *How many more bodies do we get to count*
Thelma Wygood, the other Palmer man in Miami, Belmo
in New Orleans, Mitch, Gilmore, now Stael and Ulrich. I
spite of the warmth of the room, the warmth of her blan
kets, she couldn't stop shivering.

She never had believed in evil as a thing in itself. Peopl
did evil things, usually for understandable reasons, mone
or power to gain possession of what they coveted, or kee
what they possessed, to exact revenge....

But evil infects some people, she thought, it gets in the ystem and stays like a virus that is never killed, that might ie undetected for years and then surface again, a virus that s so contagious that those who have even casual contact vith the carrier are endangered; no one is safe in its presnce, and it spreads like a plague.

Any accommodation strengthened evil, a wink, a nod, a urried glance away, a minor deal, a favor accepted or reurned, a denial of word or act, the slightest compromise— hey all added to its power, because such evil was very ware of its ability to ensnare, and finally enslave, those vho accepted it. Those it used might be unthinking, unware whose cause they served, but evil was never unware; it used its tools when it needed them, discarded them vhen their usefulness ended, and never without full awareiess.

She had met evil for the first time, she realized, and she vas afraid of it. She was afraid of Palmer, and he knew ier fear.

In her mind she heard his softly spoken words, almost)urring, *I don't think we're through yet, Ms. Holloway.*

He had offered her a deal, to deliver Stael and Ulrich, ind he had carried out his part even though she had said 10. But she had dealt with him before, over the money for Maggie and the return of the program. They were not hrough yet.

38

Frank looked terrible the next morning, drawn and old, a
if he had not slept, and she looked like death itself, but the
reassured each other that they were fine, just fine.

"Things are happening," he said at the table. "Story'
out, of course, but no names attached. Ulrich was DOA
Stael died an hour later in the operating room. The usual
names withheld pending notification of next of kin. Jan
wants us in chambers when we arrive in court. I expect th
good judge is a bit upset, and no doubt Gramm and Rox
bury are, too. The press is out there clamoring, as expected
Palmer's given a couple of interviews, modestly downplay
ing his part in saving our lives. Let's see, what else?"

"Eat," Barbara said, regarding her toast with disfavor.

"If you will, I will," he said.

Alan admitted Bailey, who said that Stael and Ulrich had
been driving a stolen car, and had phony ID. Stael's gur
had been fired twice.

"How do you find out stuff like that?" Barbara de
manded, watching Bailey eye her toast in a predatory way
She pushed it toward him, and he took it.

"Got connections," he said.

He said he had sent someone to pick up Shelley, and
Alan would stay in Frank's house until relief arrived, any
minute now. It was understood that he was planning to stick
close to Frank and Barbara all day.

Then, outside, she ignored the press being kept behind

he crime tape; two uniformed officers cleared a path
hrough the reporters to Bailey's car parked at the curb. It
wasn't raining, although the sky was gray and low. "Remember that old horror movie," Barbara said glumly, get-
ing into the car, "*The Day of the Triffids?* There was one
cene where the monsters were all pressed against a fence,
cornstalks gone wrong, something like that. There they are
n the flesh."

"Now, Bobby," Frank said, waving good-naturedly at
he reporters.

At the courthouse they went straight to Judge Waldman's
ecretary, who said the judge would be there in a minute
or two. Gramm and Roxbury were both waiting also. The
district attorney looked unhappy, and Roxbury was grim-
aced, chewing on his lip. Everyone nodded to everyone
lse; no one spoke.

Inside chambers, Judge Waldman was behind her desk,
not yet in her judicial robe. She was frowning and not in
a good mood. Her voice was crisp and cold when she invited them to be seated.

"Ms. Holloway, Mr. Gramm has requested a continuance in the trial, and his concerns must be addressed. Mr.
Gramm, please explain your reasons."

"Your honor, in light of the double shooting in front of
Mr. Holloway's house last night, and the fact that the two
men have been identified as Stael and Ulrich, both of them
named in court yesterday, the state is forced to ask for time
to investigate this incident, to ascertain if it has any bearing
on the case being tried. The jury must be aware of the
shooting, and could not help but be influenced by such
knowledge. We don't feel it would be fair to Mr. Arno to
continue with so many uncertainties."

Judge Waldman looked at Barbara.

"Absolutely no! Hold Mr. Arno in jail for another delay?
They had months to look into the Stael and Ulrich connection."

"Mr. Palmer and Mr. Trassi have been very coopera
tive," Gramm said quickly, "and will continue to cooper
ate, but it will take a few days to get information that coul
be vital. We're not planning for a lengthy delay."

Barbara shook her head. "I object to any delay what
ever."

"We would be willing to reconsider bail for Mr. Arno,'
Gramm went on, as if she had not spoken. "I agree that t
hold him in jail for the continuance probably isn't neces
sary."

Before Barbara could object again, Frank said musingly
"Bail? I don't think so. Of course, if the state is willing t
drop the charges and, further, to make a public statemen
of apology and exoneration for Mr. Arno, that would be
different matter."

Gramm flushed. "Based on the information we had, th
state acted with all due propriety. No apology is called for
and we can't consider dropping any charges until we com
plete our investigation."

"I'll fight it through every appellate court," Barbar
said.

"That won't be necessary," Judge Waldman said firmly
"Mr. Gramm, the court denies your request for a continu
ance. You have had sufficient time to investigate those tw
men. I spoke with the jury this morning, and since th
names of the men were not released, they don't know wh
they are, and they will not be influenced by the scant new
they might have seen or read. I shall speak to them again
at the end of the day, of course. Court will convene in ten
minutes."

Walking down the corridor toward the courtroom, Bar
bara said, "I want to be like her when I grow up."

"I think that's a possibility," Frank said. "Course,
you'll have to take up clothes shopping."

They met Shelley, and before she could ask a question,

arbara said, "Later." She told Ray the same thing; they
ould talk later.

Her first witness was Peter Stepanovitch. He was thirty-
ve, a salesman for an electronics company in Portland, a
b that required a lot of travel, he said importantly.

"Do you recall the first week of August?" Barbara
ked, and he said yes. "Tell the jury what made that week
emorable for you," she said.

"You see, on the third I had to fly to Chicago, so I drove
 the airport and put my car in long-term parking, like I
ways do. I flew back home on the eleventh, and the car
as gone. Stolen."

Barbara nodded. "I see. Did you recover your car?"

"Yes, on the fourteenth, the police called and said they
ad it. They found it outside Corvallis on the night of the
urteenth of August."

"What kind of a car is it, Mr. Stepanovitch?"

"A ninety-three Honda Accord, dark blue."

"And what condition was it in when you recovered it?"

"Well, it wasn't wrecked or anything like that, but it
as filthy, like they'd been using it for camping. The trunk
ad a lot of dirt, and fir needles and stuff like that, like you
et out camping. And there were a lot of beer cans in the
ack."

"Was there anything else unusual about the car when
ou recovered it?"

"Yes, there was. The license plates weren't mine. At first
ere was a little confusion about whose car it was, and the
olice called the wrong guy, because of the plates, but we
gured it out with the motor-identification number. The
rooks switched plates to make it harder to spot, I guess."

"Did you make a note of the wrong license plate num-
er?" she asked.

"Yes. When they called and said they had a car, they
ave me the number and I wrote it in my notebook."

She asked him to repeat the number for the jury, and he

recited it without looking in his notebook. It was the sam
number the motel manager had given.

Barbara turned then to Roxbury and said, ''Your wi
ness.'' He said, No questions. She thanked the witness, an
he left the stand.

She called Michael Murillo.

Murillo was twenty-seven, married, and lived in Corva
lis, where he worked for the repair shop that had receive
the wrecked Lexus. He described the shop and yard with
high security fence, topped with barbed wire, where th
police put impounded cars, and cars that had been involve
in wrecks. He remembered the Lexus very well, he saic
because it was the first one he had seen up close like tha
and then to see it brand-new and already smashed up, h
wouldn't forget it.

''What did they do with the Lexus?''

''They towed it to the back part of the yard and left
there. We all just looked it over.''

''Was it locked?''

''Yes.''

''Just tell the jury what happened with the Lexus afte
that, Mr. Murillo.''

''Okay, I mean, all right. First a policeman and a lock
smith came and opened it up and found papers. The
locked it again and left. Then, late in the day, the cop—
the policeman—came back with a lawyer, Mr. Trassi, an
said he was in charge of it. And he, the lawyer, wanted t
have it moved, but there wasn't any way to do it that lat
on a Saturday, so he said to just fix it enough to run, an
they'd take care of the stereo and CD player back in Nev
York. And we said that we didn't know what it needed
and in any case, we'd have to order parts and it might b
a week to get them. He said to do it as soon as possibl
and give him a call when it was ready. He said he'd cal
us back with a number where we could reach him. So w
ordered the parts and got it ready to run again.''

Barbara stopped him there. She smiled at him reassuringly. "Just a few details before you continue," she said. "When Mr. Trassi arrived, did he have a key for the car?" He said no.

"While the car was being repaired, did your mechanics do anything to the interior?"

He shook his head. "They just got it up and running."

"Where was the car being kept during the time it was at the shop?"

"Until we got the parts, it was out in the yard; then they moved it inside to work on it."

"Is the shop inside the security fence?"

"Yes, and there's a night watchman. We keep cars that are going to be used in trials, so we have to keep everything pretty much locked up."

"All right. So you got the car ready to run again, then what happened?"

"I called Mr. Trassi on the thirteenth, late—we were about to close—and he said someone would come for it the next day. On the fourteenth a guy came to get it."

"Were you present when someone collected the Lexus?"

"Yes. I work in the office mostly; I do the calling, ordering, all that kind of stuff. So I was the one that signed it out."

He went on to say the man had walked in, but he had seen a dark blue Accord pull away, and he thought the man had been driven there in it. He described Ulrich, then said he had picked him out of the album Bailey had shown him; he had initialed the picture, and now he identified it again.

"Did he have a key for the car?" Barbara asked. He said yes.

"Did he have any papers of authorization, or the title, anything like that?"

"He had the title transfer, and he had a letter signed by Mr. Trassi saying he could take it."

When Barbara finished with him, she turned to smile at Roxbury. He glowered at her.

Barbara's last witness before the lunch recess was Gloria Reynolds, who lived in the Blue River district. She said she and her husband had advertised a cabin for sale the first week of August, and two men had come by to look at it early on Sunday, August fourth, before ten in the morning.

"They took one look and said that wasn't what they were after," she said. "Didn't even bother to get out of the car or anything, just one look."

"Can you describe the men or the car they were driving?"

"A dark blue foreign car, that's all I can say about it. But they were from back East, real abrupt-speaking. One had a map and the classifieds, the other one was driving. They had on suits, I remember, dark suits. Not like fishermen, like we thought might be interested." She sniffed, then said, "They were rude, too. Said, 'Where's the Marshall place?' Just like that. So I told them how to find it and they left without a thank you or anything."

"Where was the cabin you had for sale?" Barbara asked.

"Just across the road from our place, a real nice little A-frame, walking distance to the river, easy to get to. A real nice little cabin. It's sold now."

Barbara produced the classified ads with the A-frame listed, and Gloria Reynolds said that was their ad. "The one immediately following it is for the Marshall cabin," Barbara pointed out. "Is that what they indicated they would look at next?"

"Yes. I told them to go back to the highway, down a mile or two, and turn right. The Marshall place is at the end of the gravel road down there."

In his cross-examination, Roxbury asked how many others had inquired about her cabin without bothering to go inside, and she said several. He demanded to know how many of the others she could recall with such detail, and

e said a few, but none of the others had been so rude, so
e remembered those two best. Her lips tightened when
e said that, as if she now would not forget him, either.
Did she know anything about those men, he demanded,
ether they had been agents for someone else, for ex-
ple? If they were real-estate agents? If they were bank-
s? She said no, all she knew was what she had said. He
ve it up with that.

Lunch was a seafood salad and crostini, ordered by
tsy. Between bites Frank and Barbara told Shelley and
tsy about the shooting at the house. Afterward, Barbara
ught how strange that they all had to keep reminding
e another to eat. Shelley was horrified and frightened,
dignant and furious, in a combination that kept changing,
she flushed, then turned pale, then flushed again.

"But that's so...so..." She swallowed hard. "He's the
vil," she whispered.

No one disputed her. Then Barbara said briskly, "Okay,
xt comes Trassi."

She watched as Trassi was sworn in. In her mind he had
come the little gray man, and today he was grayer than
er, and he looked shrunken, as if fear had drained some-
ing vital from him. At one time she had thought to keep
m on the stand for a whole day, or even more than one,
ringing denials from him; then, considering how restive
e jury had become, she had decided not to go that route,
it to drive directly to the points she wanted to make.

After Trassi had stated his background, she asked him to
count his association with Mitchell Arno, and he gave the
me statement he had made at the IRS office, in almost
xactly the same words as he had used then. She admired
s memory.

"All right," she said. "Because the various dates tend
become confusing, I have prepared a timetable to help

the jury keep them straight.'' She turned to see Shell
setting up the easel with a very large calendar printed
heavy cardboard. The dates began with the middle of Ju
and went through August into the first week of Septemb
There were strips of peel-off tape on many of the date
She went to the calendar and said, ''On the nineteenth
July you stated that Mitchell Arno approached you in t
anteroom of the Palmer Company in New York and ask
you to represent him. Is that correct?'' He said yes, and s
peeled off two strips on the nineteenth, revealing the nan
Trassi in green lettering and under it Mitch's name in r
letters.

''Were there others in the anteroom that day?'' He sa
yes, and she asked if Stael and Ulrich had been there.

He hesitated momentarily, then said, ''I didn't kno
them by name at that time, but they were there.''

She peeled off two more strips over their names, both
dark blue. She asked, ''Was mention made of the delive
of the Lexus in their presence?'' When he said yes, s
took off another strip and there was a cutout of a slee
black automobile, very small and elongated to fit. When I
admitted that the money had also been mentioned, she u
covered the final icon, a yellow suitcase with a dollar sig
on it. And that filled the space.

She backed away from the calendar in order to let th
jury see it more clearly, then she said, ''The next day yc
met with Mitchell Arno was on the twenty-sixth of July.
that correct?''

He answered her questions, and she peeled off more tar
on the twenty-sixth, to show Mitch's name, Trassi's, th
automobile, and the suitcase.

''During the following week were you in contact wit
Mitchell Arno?'' He said no. ''Were you in contact wit
either Mr. Ulrich or Mr. Stael?''

''No,'' he snapped.

''All right. From testimony, the next time we know any

ng about the Lexus was on August third, the day you
nt to Corvallis to claim the car for the Palmer Company.
that correct?''

He said yes; his answers were getting sharper, his eyes
rrower as he watched her peeling off the tape. His name,
: suitcase, and the car were revealed on Saturday, August
rd.

"Did you know who would actually pick up the Lexus
d drive it back to New York?"

"No."

"Did you know that Mr. Ulrich and Mr. Stael were in
: state? That they had checked into a motel in Eugene
at evening?"

"No!" He wasn't loud, but his voice was high-pitched
d strident.

She peeled the tape from their names on August third,
en regarded the calendar for a moment: Trassi in green,
: blues of Ulrich and Stael, the yellow suitcase, and the
:ek black Lexus.

"Did you take possession of the title transfer on August
ird?"

He hesitated, then said yes.

"Did you at any time have a key for the Lexus?"

"No!"

"You were on the coast at Folsum to see Ms. Folsum
1 Monday, August fifth, weren't you?" He said yes and
.e took off the strip of tape. "And Tuesday, August
xth?" Another strip came off. "And you had not yet de-
vered the suitcase and the money?" She revealed the suit-
.se.

"All right. Then you came over to Eugene and stayed
:re until the fifteenth." A row of green Trassis marched
:ross the dates, on to the next line. Under his name the
.ues of Stael and Ulrich were revealed as if in lockstep
ntil August fourteenth. "In your statement you said you
.d to delay your departure until the legalities of the trans-

fer of the funds for Ms. Folsum were settled. When w
you informed that Ms. Folsum and her attorney insisted
talking directly to Mr. Arno about the settlement?''

"I don't know when it was," he said. "I don't remem
the date."

"Mitchell Arno's body was discovered on Friday, A
gust ninth," she said. "Following that, did you agree
arrange for the necessary documentation to prove to
authorities the legality of the transfer of funds to Ms. F
sum?''

"Yes, I did."

"Then you left Eugene and returned to New York
the fifteenth." She regarded the calendar. "And on the p
vious day, the fourteenth, Mr. Ulrich picked up the Lex
presumably with Mr. Stael, but since that is less certa
we don't show his name here." Ulrich and the Lexus we
both revealed under Trassi's name on the fourteenth.

"Mr. Trassi, when did you give the title transfer to M
Ulrich?''

He blinked, then shook his head. "I didn't."

"Were you given the tittle transfer when you identifi
the Lexus."

"Yes."

"What did you do with it?''

He frowned, as if trying to remember. "I mailed it to t
Palmer Company in New York."

"Oh? Why? Were you not put in charge of the car a
its recovery?''

"I didn't know who they would send to get the car, b
whoever it was would need the title, so I mailed it to t
office."

"I see. When did you do that?''

"I don't remember just when it was."

"Well, did you use the post office at Folsum?''

He hesitated, then said no. "I mailed it in Eugene."

"So it must have been on or after Wednesday, Augu

venth. Weren't you afraid that was cutting it rather fine,
ice the car was due to be ready in just a few days?''

"I mailed it back to New York," he said. "I thought
ey could handle it any way they wanted to."

"What about the letter of authorization you signed for
r. Ulrich to pick up the car? When did you give that to
m?''

"I didn't sign it for any particular individual," he said.
I mailed it with the title."

She regarded him for a moment without comment, then
ood by her table. "Mr. Murillo's testimony is that he
illed you on the thirteenth, late in the afternoon, to inform
ou that the Lexus was ready to drive. Do you recall that?''

"Yes, he called me."

"Did you inform Mr. Ulrich that it was ready?''

"No. I didn't talk to him. I didn't even know he was in
e area.''

"Do you know how he found out the Lexus was ready?''

"No, I don't."

"Did you tell Mr. Murillo that someone would collect
e car the next day, the fourteenth?''

"I probably did. I don't remember."

"Did you tell the front desk at the hotel that you would
e leaving on the fifteenth?''

He was watching her like a snake; his eyes were almost
lazed over with his intense stare. "I might have told them.
don't remember when I checked out."

She nodded, then turned to shuffle through some papers
n her table. "I have a certified copy of your billing record
om that stay, Mr. Trassi." She showed it to him. "Is that
our signature?" He said yes. "According to this, you
ade no long-distance call to New York on the thirteenth.
ut there is one for five p.m. on the fourteenth. Is that right,
o your recollection?''

"I don't remember particular calls," he snapped.

"Did you meet with Mr. Stael and Mr. Ulrich on the

evening of the thirteenth, or the morning of the fourteen
of August?''

"No! I didn't even know they were in the state!"

Barbara regarded him for a moment, then turned aw
and said, "Your witness, Mr. Roxbury." In the last r
among the spectators, she saw Palmer; he smiled ve
slightly at her. The expression was so fleeting, it might n
have happened at all, but she knew he had smiled, that
knew where she had led Trassi, and it amused him. Shake
she sat down and listened to Roxbury try to undo some
the damage, to disconnect Trassi from Stael and Ulrich. S
couldn't stop the thought, looking at the little gray man
the witness stand: he was a dead man. He had outlived h
usefulness.

39

Although Roxbury was rather good with Trassi, the calendar spoke louder than he did. Trassi said, responding to his questions, that there were often half a dozen employees in the Palmer anteroom; they were a delivery service and had to keep people on hand most of the time. Some of them had familiar faces, most did not, and he knew none of them personally.

"Were you in a position to give any of those men direct orders at any time?" Roxbury asked.

"Never! I am Mr. Palmer's attorney for contracts, things of that sort. I have nothing to do with the day-by-day affairs of his actual business or the men who work for him."

"When you mailed the transfer title and the letter of authorization back to New York, who did you send it to?"

"The office manager, Mr. Henry McClaren. I told him that I didn't expect to be in the area when the car was finished, and it would be best to handle it from the main office."

"On the thirteenth of August, when you were informed that the Lexus was ready, did you notify anyone else?"

"Yes. I took a walk, and then realized that my number was the only one the garage had, so I placed a call to the main office and left a message that the car was now ready to be picked up."

It wasn't very good, Barbara thought, just the best he could do without more advance planning. When she started

her redirect, she came back to the evening of the thirteent
"The garage notified you late in the day, nearly five,
believe. Then you took a walk. At what time did you ca
New York?"

"Right away after I went out," he said. His color ha
improved under Roxbury's handling, but he was wary ar
gray again.

"So it had to be later than five, six possibly?"

"I don't know what time it was."

"All right. Of course, that would have been after eig
or nine in New York. Was the office open at that hour?"

"No."

"Do you know what office hours they keep in Ne
York?"

"No. I have nothing to do with any of that."

"Presumably your message was heard the followir
morning, if no one was there when you left it. Wouldn
you agree?"

Almost sullenly he said he didn't know anything abo
that.

"Do you know when the title transfer and authorizatio
as well as the key, were sent to Oregon, and then given t
Mr. Ulrich and Mr. Stael?"

"I said I don't know anything about that."

"Yes, you did. Do you believe that the company ser
someone else out here with those items in advance? Woul
that be a reasonable explanation?"

Roxbury objected that she was arguing with the wi
ness, and harassing him. "He said he doesn't know," h
snapped.

"Sustained," Judge Waldman said. "Please move or
Ms. Holloway."

She harassed him just a little longer, then said no mor
questions, and he was dismissed. Barbara watched hir
hurry out of the courtroom, past Palmer, without a glanc
in his direction.

* * *

The judge gave her usual warning to the jury and every-
ne else not to discuss the case, and she left, but she was
oing to talk to the jury, she had said. And Barbara had to
pend time with Ray. She had gone over all her questions
ith him already; it was time to warn him about the line
f questioning Roxbury would take.

"A couple of hours," she told Frank. "If someone can
ick me up around eight or eight-thirty, that should be time
nough."

They were standing outside the courtroom door; Barbara
lanced around, but Palmer was not in sight. Down the
orridor, held at bay, the press was waiting, and a crowd
f people were leaving work. Everything looked entirely
ormal, but, Barbara realized, she was as apprehensive as
Bailey. "Let's beat it," she said, steeling herself for the
eporters.

That night Barbara and Shelley talked about her char-
cter witnesses; they were an impressive lot. A church
member or two; a counselor from the juvenile rehab center;
a teacher from a local high school—Ray did a lot of volunteer work with troubled youngsters, took them fishing,
aught them to fly-fish, supplied the materials they needed.... He and Lorinne were active in church work, community affairs....

She and Shelly were talking in the study when the phone
ang, and she heard Clyde Dawkins on the machine. She
aised her eyebrows at Shelly and picked up the receiver.

"Ms. Holloway, I'm sorry to disturb you at this hour.
Judge Waldman asked me to call to see if it would be
possible for you to be in chambers at eight-thirty in the
morning."

"Yes, of course," she said. He said thank you and hung
up.

"Now what?" Barbara got up and went out to find
Frank; he was as mystified as she was. A few minutes later

she told Shelley she might as well go on home; Shelle
knew exactly what to do the following morning, and sh
was prepared.

"Something's happening," Bailey said. "Gramm and
detective talked to Palmer and Trassi around six, for abou
half an hour. Palmer and Trassi had dinner in the hotel afte
that, then they cleaned out Trassi's safe and took stuff u
to his room. He might have handed over the program fi
nally. While they were at the front desk, Palmer told th
desk clerk to get two first-class reservations on a flight to
morrow to New York. He went to the Hult Center to se
the show, and Trassi went out twice to use a pay phone
My guy said he looks like a chicken that can't find hi
head. Now he's in his room trying to get a call through t
a New York number; he stopped going out to do it, jus
using his own phone. No dice, so far. He gets a machin
and hangs up, then tries again in a few minutes."

No one spoke for a time, until Barbara shrugged an
said, "Palmer's up to something, but God knows what
Meanwhile, we stick with the scenario we've got. I don'
give a shit if they both fly to Bermuda at this point. Le
the cops haul Trassi back later."

A little later, alone with Frank, Barbara said, "Palme
must have told Trassi he'd back him up, but he won't. H
can't admit they knew Stael and Ulrich were here. If h
does, he drags the entire company into a mess."

Frank nodded. "That's the choice you gave them: throw
Trassi out for the wolves, or risk an investigation of th
whole outfit. Evidently the police aren't going to hol
Trassi right now, but they'll have to look into it, ask th
office manager questions about the title transfer and letter
What would you bet that's the call Trassi's been trying t
get through—to the office manager?"

"And he's suddenly unavailable. Think they'll questior
him by phone?"

"I doubt it. Not this time. They'll send someone. It's going to take a week or longer to get answers."

"By now Trassi understands he's being scuttled," Barbara said softly, "no matter what Palmer might have told him earlier. Now what?"

"God knows," Frank said. He watched her pace about the living room restlessly, and he was well aware that she knew, as he did, that if Trassi decided to deal with the police or the FBI, she was still at risk. And to save his skin, Trassi might have to deal.

The next morning, when he came around to drive them to the courthouse, Bailey said glumly, "Trassi skipped a while ago. He drove his rental car to the Eugene airport and got on a plane heading for New York, by way of Denver."

There was nothing to say. So Palmer would have two first-class tickets to use. Maybe he meant to take the Fredricks woman home with him. Barbara shrugged and pulled on her coat. "Showtime," she muttered.

At eight-thirty in the morning on a Saturday, the courthouse was a bleak, echoing shell. The coffee shop was closed, barred; the room for the jury pool was sealed off; the law library was closed; no bailiffs scurried about; no police officers milled about waiting to be called.

Judge Waldman's secretary was at her desk on the second floor, looking sleepy, and no one else was in sight. Barbara turned when she heard footsteps coming along behind her and Frank; Roxbury was hurrying toward them, his cheeks flushed by the cold morning air.

The secretary buzzed the judge, and Clyde Dawkins opened the door and motioned them to come in. Judge Waldman was at the coffee table, where the fragrance of coffee was welcome.

"Please," she said, "make yourselves comfortable."

She poured coffee for them all and handed out the cup
before she spoke again.

"As you know," she said then, "I spoke with the juror
yesterday after we recessed. The foreman, Mr. Tomlinson
speaking for them all, made an unusual request. He aske
if it would be possible to conclude the trial today and giv
them the case to deliberate by tomorrow afternoon. He sai
they quite definitely do not want to disrupt another holida
and have to return after the first of the year, and the other
agreed with him, without exception. I told them I woul
have to think about it, and discuss it with counsel."

Before anyone could speak, she held up her hand. "
questioned them in a group, and then individually, to try t
determine whether they have been discussing the testimony
and I don't believe they have. This is simply a unanimou
decision they have reached. They want to be done wit
this."

"They've made up their minds," Roxbury said in a grat
ing voice.

"It could become a mistrial," Barbara said slowly
"Have they been reading the newspapers, watching TV
news? Talking to people outside?"

"Perhaps," Judge Waldman said, "although they denie
it. If they've made up their minds, they gave me absolutel
no sense of how they intend to go with the evidence. I
believe Mr. Tomlinson. They want to be done with it. They
want to enjoy a remnant of the holiday without the tria
hanging over them."

Her turn, Barbara thought then, sipping her coffee. She
put the pretty little cup down and said, "I can be finished
by the end of the day today."

Barbara was aware that she would be cutting her defense
short, aware also that to do otherwise would risk alienating
the jury even more. A jury already in rebellion could jump
erratically. She looked at Roxbury, who was gnawing on
his lip, frowning. He appreciated the problem as much as

e did, she knew. If he was the one to drag it out beyond
e close of the day, would the jury retaliate? The jury
ight already blame the prosecution for the many delays,
r ruining their Christmas and now threatening their New
ear. He knew that Ray Arno would take the stand that
ternoon. How much tough questioning had he planned for
ay? How short would he have to cut that? No one spoke
 they waited for his response.

"I have to say that I never heard of a jury dictating
rms. Not like this." His tone suggested that the judge
uld shape them up, keep them in line if she chose. "I'll
 along. If she can close the defense today, the state will
 along as much as possible, but no guarantees that we
on't go overtime."

"I'll explain that to them," Judge Waldman said. "Now,
r the closing arguments. I propose one and a half hours
r each side; I'll need at least an hour for my instructions,
d they can have the case by the lunch recess." She
oked at Barbara and Roxbury in turn. "Is that accept-
le?"

Barbara thought of the pages and pages of closing ar-
ment she had already prepared; she suspected that Rox-
ury had at least as many pages ready. Cut it down to one
d a half hours. She glanced at Frank. He nodded and she
d, too. "I can handle that," she said. Then she thought,
oor Shelley; she had planned to take all day with her char-
ter witnesses.

"Half a day!" Shelley cried. "Just half a day! Good
eavens! Who can I leave out?"

"Look at it this way," Frank said, "you don't leave out
nyone so much as you leave out a few selected tidbits.
et's have a look at your list and your questions." He
ounded as comforting as a family doctor who knew panic
hen he saw it and could put an end to it before anyone
lse even recognized it as panic. He sat down with Shelley

at the defense table, and they looked over her list. Barbai
went to speak with Ray, who was already in the holdin
room at the courthouse.

Shelley's last witness before they recessed for lunch tha
day was Michael Conroy, a thirty-year-old high-scho·
teacher. He had testified that Ray Arno took four boys at
time out fishing, that he taught them how to fish, and som·
thing about responsibility, about life, loyalty.... "He chang
es their lives," he said.

"How do you know what he does with them out fisi
ing?" Shelley asked.

"Because I was one of four he took responsibility fo
fourteen years ago, and they tell me about it now. It's th
same thing that I experienced with him then. Of our fou
two of us became teachers, one's still in graduate schoo
a postdoctoral physicist, and one's a cook in a very goo
restaurant. But we were all headed for trouble when he too·
us in hand. So are the kids he takes in hand today. Hi
boys, those he guides, don't get into trouble."

Then, after lunch, Barbara had Ray tell about the pa·
summer, when Mitch showed up at his house, what hap
pened afterward. Ray was a good witness for himself, care
ful, just emotional enough, transparently truthful.

"Mr. Arno," Barbara asked, "did you consider it you
duty to protect Maggie Folsum last summer?"

"No," he said. "She's a very capable young woma·
who is quite able to take care of herself."

"But you felt it your duty eighteen years ago to protec
her? Is that right?"

"Yes. She was defenseless, with an infant of her own
and little more than a child herself, and my brother ha·
threatened her, had even hurt her. I felt responsible for m·
brother's actions and for ensuring that he didn't hurt he
again. I felt it my duty then to get between my brother an·
my sister."

"When you spoke to Maggie Folsum after you returned
me and found that Mitch had left your house, did she
ll you about the vandalism done to her bed-and-breakfast
n?"

"Yes."

"Did you assume that Mitch had done the damage
ere?"

"Yes."

"What was your reaction? Did you vow to get even with
m, to punish him yourself?"

"No. I talked to my father, and we agreed that if Mitch
rned up again, if he actually had wrecked her inn, we
ould have him arrested and charged. I told Maggie to stay
ith other people, not be alone at the inn, just in case he
turned."

Barbara led him through the past years, the spring he and
s brothers had worked on the boat at the coast, his en-
gement to Lorinne, when he went into business for him-
lf, the problem with the warehousing of merchandise be-
re his own space was available. She showed him the
ctures of Stael and Ulrich and asked if he had ever seen
ther of them; he said no. Quickly she went over the state's
ase with him, and he denied being on the bridge the morn-
g Marta Delancey claimed to have seen him; he denied
er being near or in the Marshall cabin....

She had allowed herself two hours with Ray, leaving the
me amount of time for Roxbury. At the end of her time,
e asked, "How long were you with your brother Mitch
ter your father left him at your house?"

"Ten minutes at the most. I showed him through the
ouse, told him to clean himself up, to help himself to food,
nd that I would be back on Monday, probably around
oon, and we would have plenty of time after that to talk."

"Did you see him alive again after that?"

He shook his head, and in a low voice said, "No. He
as gone when I returned home."

"Did you fight with him?"

"No."

"Did you kill your brother?"

"No!"

That night both Shelley and Barbara were glum, and n
amount of reassurance from Frank could lift their spirit
"Look," he said, "you both did a bang-up job today. She
ley, you had your witnesses so primed that if you'd c
them off in half the time you took, they still would hav
put the halo in place and lighted it. And, Bobby, the
crowned him with a halo, and you showed that it was
perfect fit. No more could have been asked of either of yo
if you'd taken a week."

"Well," Barbara said after Shelley left, "I'll go take a
ax to my closing argument. An hour and a half! God!"

But she found it hard to concentrate. Trassi had vanishe
in Denver. His plane had arrived there on time, apparentl
but Trassi had not arrived in New York. No one had fo
lowed him past the departure gate in Eugene; there ha
been little reason to do so, and the Major Works men wh
were keeping an eye out for him in New York said he ha
not been aboard the continuation of the flight. Denver wa
one of the big hubs; he could have taken off in any dire
tion from there. Later, the Fredericks woman had drive
Palmer to Portland, where he had caught his nonstop t
New York alone. Now, with the whole Palmer crew gone
Barbara should have been able to relax and concentrate
she kept telling herself. But, instead, she was as tense as
prima donna waiting for the curtain call.

She then stared at her computer screen filled with page
of closing argument. *Everyone goes away,* she thought. *Dis
appear without a trace, one and all.* She closed her eye
hard when she realized she was no longer thinking of Trass
or Palmer, either. Then, furiously, she began to red-line he
prepared text.

unday morning. Everyone looked sleepy and tired, and
cept for the Arno clan, the courtroom was nearly empty
nen Roxbury started his closing argument.

"Ladies and gentlemen, no oratory today, no flowery
eeches, or appealing to your sympathy; today the facts
ill be sufficient, and just the facts. You have been atten-
ve and patient throughout this ordeal of a trial, and now
ask only for your attention for a short while longer. The
cts will demonstrate that the defendant, Ray Arno, in cold
ood and with malicious intent to inflict the greatest pain
ossible, murdered his brother.

"It is a fact disputed by no one that Ray Arno attacked
s brother in a vicious fight eighteen years ago, and at that
ne threatened his life if he ever returned to the area...."
He laid out his argument with cool precision. "There is
o need to speculate about mysterious strangers with mys-
rious motives; the facts speak for themselves," he said.
Ray Arno was incensed that people were talking about
s wife and his brother. Did the defendant find his brother
his own bed, using his belongings as if he had a right
them? Did Mitchell Arno intend to move back into the
mily circle and give new cause for more gossip? We'll
ever know what transpired between the two brothers on
at fateful Monday when the defendant returned from the
ast and found his brother usurping his place.... He buried
s brother and put various items in the plastic bag to dis-

pose of them—the lead pipe murder weapon, his brother
clothing. But then fate stepped in and a witness saw hi
on the bridge. We know she saw him that morning; sl
identified him positively, and she pointed out where he ha
thrown the plastic bag. And we found it.

"We found the plastic bag exactly where it had to b
where it had been for months."

He took his full hour and a half, and finally summarize
"The defendant beat up his brother years ago, and threa
ened to kill him if he returned. He admits to feelin
responsible for the safety of Maggie Folsum, to feeling r
sponsibility for the actions of his brother. We all know th
in many families, protecting the honor of a sister, a niec
a mother is the prime responsibility of the males of th
family, especially the oldest son. I suggest that Ray Arr
feels this responsibility to an extreme. He alone had th
opportunity to commit the murder. He had a motive. H
was the last person known to have been with Mitchell Arn
and he killed him and tried to hide the crime."

After a ten-minute recess Barbara stood up. "Mr. Rox
bury is quite right in that there is no need for oratory th
morning," she said. "You have heard the testimony an
you have seen the evidence, but there is a difference in ou
approach to that testimony and evidence. Mr. Roxbur
would have you examine and consider only the evidenc
that supports his case, and I want you to examine and cor
sider all of it. It happens, ladies and gentlemen, that th
same evidence often yields more than one interpretatio
When it was generally believed that the earth was flat, th
only evidence most people saw supported that assumptio
Evidence to the contrary was there; it was simply not rec
ognized. And so it has been with this case; the evidence i
there and for a long time it went unrecognized, its meanin
lost. Today, I want you to consider all the evidence.

"First, let's examine the state's case."

She pointed out that one witness had not been able t

ck out Ray's car from others that were more or less sim-
ar. And she reminded them of the witness who had con-
ssed to speeding past the corner of Stratton and River
oad in another similar car. "When most of us look at a
ock of birds, unless we are avid bird-watchers, we might
y they were simply little gray birds," she said, smiling
intly. "To a real bird-watcher, they might be sparrows
nd finches, wrens and juncos, and so on. To most of us
he little gray bird is very much like another; to most of
s one little gray car is very like another. And we know
ho did drive past the corner that morning."

Another witness, she went on, could not have seen Ray
n his cell, not at two in the morning, and he could not
ave heard him praying and confessing, since he suffered
severe hearing loss that had been demonstrated in court.
third witness had misinterpreted what she had seen when
orinne got into a car with Mitchell Arno eighteen years
go, and misinterpreted what she had heard on the tele-
hone.

One by one she demolished the state's witnesses, and
hen she came to Marta Delancey. "It happens that we
ometimes misinterpret what we hear or see," she said
lowly. "We hear what we expect to hear and see what we
xpect to see, and there is no sinister intent; it is a simple
uman failure. However, there are times when misstate-
ents are harder to understand or explain. Mrs. Delancey
aid positively that she saw Ray Arno in his shop, that she
tudied his face to the point of embarrassing him, that her
usband commented on the name of the shop displayed on
he window, that she browsed through the merchandise and
icked up and put down items there. None of this could
ave happened. Ray Arno did not yet have his shop. By
he time his shop opened in December of 1978, Mrs. De-
ancey's first husband was dead. Her testimony was that
he returned to Eugene only to visit her mother, never to
o any shopping, and especially she would not have had

an occasion to visit a sports shop. This cannot be put dov
to a misinterpretation of what she saw or heard.'' Barba
read from her testimony, all positive statements about Ra
and his shop, and the visit there with Joel Chisolm.

''Ladies and gentlemen,'' she said, putting down tl
transcript, still speaking very slowly and carefully, ''if yc
find that a witness has spoken falsely, has distorted tl
facts, or has not recalled accurately what has been offere
as truthful testimony, you are entitled to disregard all ∙
that person's testimony. To do otherwise would be unjus
since you have no way of knowing where factual testimon
starts and stops.''

She was being cautious because she knew the jury ha
been sympathetic to Marta Delancey and might not tal
kindly to her calling the woman a liar. She continued. '
don't know what Mrs. Delancey saw on the bridge that da`
I don't know the state of her mind at that moment, cor
cerned as she was about her mother's health. I don't kno`
the state of her mind when she returned and read the ac
count of the murder in the newspaper and saw Ray Arno`
picture.

''I do know that she could not have recalled him fro⌐
the time she said he so impressed her in his sports sho┌
And if part of her testimony is demonstrably wrong, th
rest of it is suspect also.''

She moved to the calendar then, and pointed. ''Now, thi
is when we first hear of Mitchell Arno in the recent pas
talking to Mr. Trassi in the Palmer Company anteroom o
July nineteenth. Present were Mr. Ulrich and Mr. Stael. S∙
on that day, these four people and a stenographer all kne`
that Mitch Arno would be carrying a large amount ∘
money to Oregon.''

Using the calendar, she outlined the following days an∙
weeks and tracked down the known movements of Trass:
Stael and Ulrich, the Lexus, and Mitch. ''We don't kno`
where Mitchell Arno was or what he was doing in the pe

iod from the twenty-sixth of July until August second, when he was found on the coast...."

She moved away from the calendar and said, "Let's pause here and ask a few of the questions that all this raises. First, of course, what were Stael and Ulrich doing in Eugene? Why was Mitchell Arno taken to the cabin? If Ray had killed him, there was no need to go there. He knew he would be alone in his house for a week. He has five acres of ground, plenty of places where a body could be buried, with no questions asked. But if others had been looking for and then found Mitch Arno, they had no way of knowing when they would be interrupted. They needed a secluded place.

"Why was Mitchell Arno's face untouched? In the fight between the brothers, they had both been bloodied, faces and hands. But Mitchell's face was spared this time. I suggest that it was to make certain he could talk. A broken jaw would interfere with talking.

"Then, the actual physical act of moving him must be considered. Could one man have dragged him through broken glass in such a way that only his heels scraped the floor? Then he was dragged again, after he was dead, and this time he was dragged facedown with only his toes and the tops of his feet scraping the floor. Could one man, acting alone, have accomplished that? I suggest that you try acting it out when you start your deliberations, to see just how impossible that would be.

"Next, consider the weapon. This was not a crime of uncontrollable passion; this was premeditated, the isolated cabin was selected in advance, the weapon was assembled in advance with care. It was a weapon designed to inflict a great deal of damage; the parts had to be purchased, and this was done by someone who knew exactly what he was doing. You heard the testimony about the pigskin fibers, and the opinion that a leather holder, a handgrip, had been used on the pipe. In other words, this was a professiona weapon assembled by a professional in his own field.

"Why two pairs of gloves if there was only one killer?

"Why burn the hands of a dead man? Consider, he ha no identifying clothes; he was wearing his brother's clothes He had no papers, nothing to identify him, except his fin gerprints, and they were burned off.

"Now, as to the time of the attack and the murder. We know that Mr. Stael and Mr. Ulrich arrived in Eugene o the third of August, Saturday. When could they have lef their fingerprints in Ray Arno's house on surfaces that ha been washed, painted, waxed in July? Not before Saturday night, certainly. But isn't it likely that on Sunday, afte preparing the setting for the crime to come, they then wen looking for Mitchell Arno, and they found him Sunday eve ning, two hours after his last meal, in his brother's house?

"What did they want from him? He had already turned the child-support money over to Mr. Trassi; that was the arrangement from the start. When he was found, he had only the clothes on his back, and the Lexus was missing, presumably stolen by joyriders. Is that all he could tell them? Did they accept it?

"We know that on Monday Maggie Folsum's bed-and-breakfast inn was ransacked, ruthlessly searched. If they had found what they were looking for, would they not have left the area instantly? Why did they remain in the motel, risking discovery of a stolen car and stolen credit cards? I suggest they did not find what they were after, and that the only other place to search for it, whatever it was, was in the Lexus itself. But the Lexus was behind a security fence in Corvallis and could not be entered, could not be driven away."

She returned to the calendar and pointed to August eighth. "On Thursday Mr. Trassi was informed that Ms. Folsum demanded a meeting with Mitchell Arno, that she could not accept the past-due child support without ade-

ate proof that it was legitimate. And on the following
ght, as the result of an anonymous phone call, Mitchell
no's body was found. There were no tooth or claw
arks, no animals tracks, nothing to indicate that an animal
d dug up and raised one foot from the grave. And on
at night, in the blood that had dried and hardened, the
me Arno was scratched with a tool that dug into the floor
der the blood. Why?''

She walked back and forth before the jury as she spoke
w; they were rapt in attention. ''I suggest, ladies and
ntlemen, that Ms. Folsum's demand to see her former
sband in person made it imperative that his body now
ould be found. No one had paid much attention to the
xus; it was simply a business deal that had gone bad.
ut an investigation into the whereabouts of Mitchell Arno
ight bring about an impoundment of the car, might bring
out a real search of it. So, in spite of the care that had
en taken earlier to make identification of the body diffi-
lt or even impossible, it now became necessary to have
discovered and identified. And the Lexus remained in the
ckground, considered irrelevant, a minor crime that the
almer Company and their insurance company would han-
e. No one had inspected the interior with care, and no
ne did now. The investigation of murder was focused
lely on Ray Arno; the Lexus was ignored.

''Then, Mr. Trassi agreed to provide the necessary doc-
mentation to substantiate the legality of the transfer of
oney, but still he did not leave the area immediately. And,
fact, he didn't leave until the day after the Lexus was
tually released.''

She pointed again to the calendar. ''On the fourteenth,
Ir. Stael and Mr. Ulrich left the motel; Mr. Ulrich took
ossession of the Lexus, and the following day Mr. Trassi
ecked out of his hotel. And all three men and the Lexus
anished from the area.''

She shook her head and said slowly, ''But there are a

few questions to be answered about those last two days th
were still here. Who told Mr. Ulrich that the Lexus w
ready? How did he get possession of the title transfer a
letter of authorization? And most important of all, how c
he get a key?''

She stopped moving and said quietly, ''The last pers
who had the key was Mitchell Arno. I suggest that t
person who killed him took that key.'' She began to pa
again, moving very slowly back and forth before the juro
holding their attention.

''What happens when you buy a car? The dealer has tv
keys and gives them to the new owner. He doesn't ke
one for himself. So, no doubt, Mitchell Arno started o
with two keys. If joyriders, as the state suggests, stole t
car, they had one of the keys, but Mitchell Arno still h;
the other one, and then Mr. Ulrich had it.''

She turned to regard Ray then. ''You've observed R;
Arno day after day in this court; you've observed his far
ily. You saw and heard his friends and colleagues, t
teachers and church members; you've heard about the kir
of life he and his wife lead, the good work they do, the
involvement with their community. Everything you'
heard and seen about him reinforces the simple truth th
he is a good man who is not a killer....''

She spent the rest of her time talking about Ray and h
family, and finished by saying, ''He was caught up in
series of events that had nothing to do with him. He w;
carrying out his father's request, to provide a haven for h
brother for a weekend until they could gather and discu:
the situation, and he knew nothing of the other players wh
were in the field with their own sinister agenda. Ray Arr
was a truly innocent bystander in the deadly drama.''

Judge Waldman was as good with her instructions ;
Frank had predicted she would be, and then they were a

:nt away for the lunch recess, to return at two-thirty, at
·hich time the case would go to the jury.

Barbara and Frank had talked about the problem of lunch
)r the whole Arno crew, and agreed that a restaurant was
ut of the question. There wcre fourteen people to feed in
n hour, an impossible task for any restaurant. They ended
p going to Frank's house, where Patsy had arranged with
caterer to provide sandwiches and salad for an army. And
ιe Arnos talked, reassuring one another that it had gone
/ell, reassuring Barbara that she was the best lawyer they
ad ever seen, reassuring Patsy that the sandwiches and
alad were fine. But they were all nervous, and Lorinne
urst into tears when Mama Arno said she should eat some-
ιing.

Barbara felt as if she had to scream, go somewhere alone
nd scream. She kept thinking of the hurried explanations,
ιe scanty summation.... "I didn't even mention reasonable
ιoubt," she said to Frank.

"Not your job, and Jane told them all they need to know
bout it. Relax, honey. You did a great job. I didn't believe
ou could wrap it all up in such a short time, but, by God,
ou did. Relax."

Then it was time to return to court, time for the real
vaiting to begin. Judge Waldman gave the jury their final
nstructions and sent them out, then she said to Barbara,
'If the Arno family would like to wait in the lounge down
he hall, they are welcome. I believe we can have coffee
)rought in."

"She thinks it's going to be fast," Frank said as the
ιdge left the bench. "And I think she's right. That jury
vants to go home. The lounge?"

Barbara nodded. Ray was escorted out to a holding room,
ιnd the rest of his family made their way to the lounge,
vhere they began to talk again. There had been more spec-
ators that afternoon than earlier, but they were all barred
rom the lounge. Roxbury had vanished.

"Barbara," Maggie said hesitantly, "it did go we'
didn't it? Mama and Papa are so up about it. They're co
vinced that Ray will go home with them today. They'
planning a big party for tonight."

Barbara patted her arm. "I think it went well," she sai
and wished she felt the same confidence. If only she ha
not left out so much. She should have protested the tin
limit, she thought then. Would it be grounds for an appea
She wanted to ask Frank, but not now, not with the whol
family present, watching. How could they do that? Watc
everything, hear everything, and keep talking, too?

She heard snatches: "...one of those range turkeys,
bronze something or other. Best you ever tasted..."

"...a spiral, honey-baked ham..."

"And mashed rutabagas. You know how much he like
them."

"He says he has to go shopping for presents...."

"We should take him out fishing, first chance. Remem
ber how he needed to be out on the water after he cam
home from the army?"

"...so much new stuff to be sorted through. We're ju
leaving it for him. He'll need to do things like that."

"The kids will be fine with us, and you both need to ge
away for a while. He's so pale."

Barbara closed her eyes and thought about the coast,
rocky stretch of beach with no one in sight, no one in ear
shot, a place where she could scream and scream. Fran
touched her arm and she jumped, startled.

"Bobby, it's all right," he said. "It really is."

But what if it isn't? she wanted to cry. What if I los
him after all the promises I made? What if the jury believe
Marta Delancey in spite of everything? She looked acros
the room and met Maggie's gaze. What if I got the mone
for her, and lost Ray? She'll hate me. I'll hate mysel
What's the money worth if he's lost? This is what Joh
was afraid of, what he meant. He hates this—lying, cheat

g, conniving—and he's right. Nothing good can come out
a lie. My entire case was based on a lie....

Frank put his arm about her shoulders and squeezed, then
moved on to talk to Papa Arno.

At a quarter to five they were summoned back to the
courtroom; the jury had a decision.

She felt frozen as she watched the ritual; the sheet of
paper passed from Mr. Tomlinson to the bailiff, who took
to the judge. She put on her glasses to read it, then took
them off again and asked the foreman if the jury had
reached its decision.

"Yes, your honor. We find the defendant, Ray Arno, not
guilty."

Then it was bedlam. As if she knew the Arnos could no
longer be contained, Judge Waldman spoke over their cries
and laughter and shouts. She thanked the jury and dismissed them, and told Ray he was free, and she left the
bench as if unaware of the circus taking place in the courtroom.

Everyone was hugging everyone else, crying and laughing. Ray grabbed Barbara and hugged and kissed her. Roxbury wormed his way through the group and shook Barbara's hand, then walked out, and the jurors came to shake
Ray's hand, and talk and talk. They wanted to talk as much
as the Arnos. Again, Barbara could hear only snatches of
what was being said, as one after another of the Arnos
hugged her. Ray and Lorinne were both crying, surrounded
by brothers and wives and children, hardly giving him
breathing space; Maggie's daughters were holding Shelley;
all three were jumping up and down, laughing and crying.... Mama Arno was hugging the jurors, crying, thanking
them.... She invited them to dinner on New Year's Day,
all of them.

Then Frank was at Barbara's side; he touched her cheek
gently, and she realized her face was wet with tears.

"It's contagious," she said, and groped in her purse for a tissue.

"I reckon it is," he said, surveying the hordes of people who could no longer control themselves. He grinned. "Let's move this circus out before I start blubbering."

41

he Arno party was both raucous and reverent; food ap-
ared in an endless stream of casseroles and pastries, pasta
shes and salads, hams and smoked turkeys.... And they
l talked and laughed and joked and wept. The party was
James Arno's house; it was the biggest house available,
d it was crowded with family and friends in every room,
l of them eating and talking. No one ever finished a sen-
nce, and no one minded. They all touched one another a
t, hugged one another, patted, caressed, loved one another
ithout reservation.

At ten-thirty Barbara, Frank, and Shelley said good-bye
d escaped into the foggy night. Ray, Lorinne, and Maggie
ame out with them to the car, where Ray shook hands
ith Frank, kissed Shelley again, and then held Barbara's
oulders for a moment before he wrapped her in a bear
ug.

"I'll never forget you, what you did for us. Never," he
id huskily.

When he released Barbara, Maggie said, "I just want to
ay, you have a room at the inn anytime you want it, any-
me at all. You're family now. On the house, just like the
est of the family."

Then, finally, they were inside Frank's Buick, leaving.
one of them said a word as Frank drove Shelley to Bill's
ownhouse. Shelley got out but hesitated at the side of the
ar. Barbara rolled down her window and said, "I don't

want to see your face until the day after New Year's. G
some sleep. Rest.''

Shelley nodded. ''You, too.'' Suddenly she leaned ove
and put her head in and kissed Barbara's cheek. ''Thank
Barbara. Just…thanks. It's the best holiday of my life suc
denly.''

She turned and ran to the door, where Bill was standing
waiting for her. Frank started to drive. After a moment h
said, ''When we get home, let's have a bit of that goo
Courvoisier I've been saving for lo, these many years.''

Later, in front of a fire in the living room, with one o
the Things grunting on her lap, she tried to sort through th
days to come, the things she still had to do—write a repo
for Major and Jolin, start a search for a secretary, go ove
the accounting with Bailey, clean up her own files, mov
back to her own apartment. Change the lock on her door

She bit her lip. Change the lock. Move his things to hi
apartment, hers back into her place, although there was lit
tle of hers to move back. Suddenly she wondered, was th
price too high?

Frank got up to poke the fire, the other Thing complaine
at being moved. The Christmas tree glowed, the fire wa
comforting, the cognac was excellent, and, outside, the fo
pressed close to the house.

And she was thinking of the things she had intended t
accomplish. Palmer was spinning his new web; she ha
given him an out, defended him even. She shuddered: de
fending the devil. All his company had to do was deny
receiving the title transfer and letter of authorization in th
mail, and the suspicion would land on Trassi, who had van
ished, probably to Argentina or the Riviera, or who migh
even be dead now. Palmer had delivered the rest of th
program to his client, who no doubt was celebrating a
merrily as the Arno family.

This whole affair had started with a monstrous lie con

cted by Major/Wygood; a tissue of lies had followed, and
e trail from there to here was littered with bodies. Far
om feeling elated, jubilant over her victory in court, she
lt as if she was sinking into gloom and despair. She felt
certain about her own actions, uncertain how far she was
pable of going to save a client, win a case. She didn't
en know why she was doing this, what she was trying to
ove, if anything. Was the price too high?

"Bobby, let's talk a minute," Frank said quietly, back
the couch with the Thing settled in again, grunting.

She looked up, startled by the realization that he had
en watching her, maybe even tracking her thoughts.

"You saved a man's life this past week. You don't have
explain the ins and outs of it to Shelley or me or Bailey
Jane Waldman or Bill Spassero. We all know. And you
n't explain to a hell of lot of other people who will never
ow. That's how it is." He held up his hand to forestall
ything she might have said. "There was a time when I
as about your age, when I still believed the law was holy
rit, and I would have fought the devil himself to keep it
re. Then, one day, I came to understand that laws are
ritten by people like me, like us, fallible people, biased
ople, who are incapable of writing holy law. On that day,
came to realize that justice takes precedence over the im-
erfect laws we swear to uphold. And, Bobby, your sense
f justice is very fine. You're going to brood about cases
ow and again, try to replay them in different ways over
d over—that can't be helped, it's your lot in life. But
our instinct for justice won't be fettered by imperfect laws,
nd you have to live with it. You'll pay the price more than
nce, and you'll have black nights, but you'll go on doing
hat you have to do." He stood up. "And what I have to
o is get some sleep. Good night, honey."

She watched him walk from the room; both cats
retched, yawned, and followed him.

* * *

The main thing is to keep busy, she told herself, and sh
kept busy. She talked to Jolin, and then to Major, wh
begged her to come to the island, at her convenience,
discuss the whole case. She hesitated only a moment, the
said yes, she would like that. Jolin was especially intereste
in the fact that the FBI was looking into Palmer's conne
tion to Senator Delancey, who, he said, was chairman of
joint telecommunications committee.

She had her accounting session with Bailey, who said h
would send a guy to change her locks if she wanted hi
to. Next week, after the first of the year. She started to so
files and worked on her final report to Major Works.

Late in the afternoon she went to her own apartment t
see what needed doing there before she could move i
again. She came to a dead stop when she saw the desiccate
Christmas tree in a bucket.

Upstairs, she walked through both apartments, touchin
things lightly as she passed them—John's oversized desk
his chair, his robe over a chair in the bedroom. Next week
she told herself, and left again without moving anything.

New Year's Eve she went to a party at Martin's restau
rant, where many of her old clients greeted her like a long
lost kinswoman. Everyone danced at Martin's parties; ev
eryone sang. Hot and sweaty, she sat down to cool off, an
she spied Maria Velasquez dancing and realized that Mari
could be her perfect secretary. She had done a little wor
on Maria's behalf once, and knew the young woman wa
capable and smart, and with a little training, she could be
come for Barbara what Patsy was for Frank. She grinne
at the idea, and at the next break in the music she offere
Maria the job and hired a secretary. And, she chided her
self, this is the way you bow out, ease yourself out of th
filthy law business. Then she danced with Martin.

She didn't stay long after the midnight countdown
"Happy New Year," she whispered, pulling into Frank'
driveway. All over town fireworks were exploding, gun

re being fired. It was raining hard again, and Frank's car
s not in the garage yet. He was ringing in the New Year
h old friends and might be late, he had warned her.
retend you don't notice if I come staggering in in the
e hours.''

She didn't bother with an umbrella, but pulled her coat
er her head and dashed the few feet from the garage to
e front porch. Then, as she was unlocking the door, she
ard a soft voice, "Happy New Year, Ms. Holloway. No,
n't stop. Let's get inside and dry ourselves. I'm afraid
ur Oregon climate is rather wretched.'' Palmer had
pped out from behind the large azalea shrub at the porch;
grasped her arm and propelled her inside the house.

He was all in black, a long raincoat, black hat, gloves,
es. He was holding a gun with a silencer. "Ah, this is
tter,'' he said. "Living room.'' He drew her with him to
e living room and looked around approvingly. "Take off
ur coat, Ms. Holloway, and please sit on the couch, and
l see if a new log will rejuvenate the fire. I do appreciate
fire on a rainy night such as this. Does it ever not rain
re?''

She pulled off her coat and put it on a chair back, then
arted to sit down.

"Not at the end. Why don't you center yourself on the
uch? I think you'll find that more comfortable.''

"What do you want?'' She sat down in the center of the
uch, where nothing was in reach. Both cats wandered in;
e joined her, the other one went to sniff at Palmer's feet
d legs. He ignored it.

"You didn't really believe we were finished, did you? I
d that hard to accept.'' Slowly he took off his coat, hold-
g the gun steady as he pulled one arm free, then he shifted
e gun from one hand to the other to free his other arm.
e was wearing a black turtleneck sweater and black jeans;
didn't take off the black gloves. "Now, please, don't
ove while I tend the fire. I'm afraid I got a chill out there

in the rain, and I'm sure you must be feeling chilly
well.''

When he opened the fire screen, and then reached fo
log, she tensed, but he smiled at her and said, ''Nothi
foolish, Ms. Holloway. I really would rather not shoot yc
that's not part of the scenario, but if I have to change t
action, improvise, then, of course, I shall do so. I think
the leg. No lasting damage that way, but something mer
orable. You see, I don't intend to do you any real har
tonight, but I must have your cooperation.'' He poked tl
fire, and moved away from it as the log blazed up. ''A
how pleasant a fire is. Part of our heritage, I suspect,
satisfies the atavistic in our psyche.''

''What is your scenario?'' she demanded. There, in tl
middle of the couch, with a goddamn cat halfway in h
lap, she felt totally immobilized.

''I have come to think of you as my own personal dea
angel, Ms. Holloway. You know her, the mythic figure th
appears when a death is imminent? Those who move in
her sphere are doomed, and no one knows the breadth c
her sphere until too late. She appears with awesome beau
and awesome power, and often seems unaware of tl
deaths that follow her path. She herself is always unaffecte
by the deaths she foretells. A powerful figure indeed, or
to be feared and avoided if at all possible. I believe in h
with all my soul.'' His voice had taken on the lilt of
balladeer; he looked relaxed, at ease as he remained stan
ing near the fireplace with the golden cat at his feet. ''M
dear mother told me all the old legends, of course, and sl
told them as true stories, but she also said that the onl
way to win the struggle that is life was by confronting ou
fears and banishing them. I have found that a useful hon
ily.''

''We have no unfinished business,'' Barbara said coldl
''We both said at the start exactly what we wanted, and w
both delivered what we said we would. We are through.'

"No, not through, not quite. You see, there is also the
sky matter of reputation. I'm afraid mine has suffered
atly in the past few months. My organization has been
cimated. I have lost valued friends, allies, and employees,
d I fear that word will get around that an insignificant
man in a mudhole of a Western town was the agent for
e destruction of a powerful machine. That won't do, you
ist understand. I can't refute one by one the malicious
ssips who would relish such a revelation. And not many
them share my belief in the death angel, I'm afraid. We
ve lost our sense of wonder and awe; myth no longer
oves us or explains the world to us. No, people will say
et a small-town female lawyer wreak havoc and did noth-
g in return. In my business, as in yours, one's reputation
ist be jealously guarded at all times."

"But you don't intend to do me any real harm," she said
ingly.

"That's correct. Soon, I imagine, your father will return
om his revelries. I told you I wept when my father died;
did. Without shame, I wept."

Barbara felt a wave of ice crash over her. The Thing on
r lap stirred and complained. Then it raised its head, lis-
ning. The Thing at Palmer's feet was listening, too.

He raised his gun and said, "Shh."

Both cats relaxed again and Palmer said, "Even they
e appropriate. Early-warning systems. How very conve-
ent." He smiled at her. "And I see you already grasped
y intentions. You are a very intelligent young woman,
ry intuitive. I suspect there is a lot of the Irish in your
ood. I sensed it before, of course. Yes, the scenario. Your
ther will return and if you call out to him, he will come
to the living room here; if you don't call out, he will
me. So we don't have to concern ourselves with getting
m to walk through the doorway. And when he does, I'll
oot him. Will you weep for him, Ms. Holloway?"

"How many people can you shoot before you run ou
plausible-sounding explanations?"

"No explanation will be required. Mr. Palmer is ce
brating a joyous New Year's Eve party in California. M
important and influential people will attest to that. And
the time they get around to investigating the truth of
claim, I will be there, and express my shock and horror
an appropriate manner. You, of course, will relate this e
ning's events in great detail. But, Ms. Holloway, no c
will believe you. I'm afraid I shall have to inflict the sn
amount of damage to your person that I alluded to earli
No lasting damage, you understand. A blow to the he
enough to raise a bump; then I shall bind you and lea
you to watch your father bleed to death. I fear the blow
your head and shock will unbalance your mind. You s
the death angel herself cannot be killed; we shall see if I
mind can be destroyed. You, of course, will assume a n
role, that of avenging angel, and our little private game w
continue until the day comes that you will have to be
strained. I won't forget you, Ms. Holloway; I shall se
you flowers periodically, dark red roses. Which is wor
Ms. Holloway, death or the destruction of a super
mind?"

She didn't speak or move. He was leaning against t
mantel, alert and watchful, and she realized that he w
studying the room in swift appraising glances, taking I
eyes off her only for a second or two at a time, fully awa
each time she moved a finger.

"The lines I had imagined for you now," he said, "a
the platitudinous cries of desperation: you are mad, or, yo
can't get away with this. I underestimated you. Instea
you're trying desperately to think what you can do to thwa
my little playlet, not wasting time with foolishness. I a
mire that. I truly admire you, Ms. Holloway."

She visualized the space behind the couch, a long narro
table that held the cognac bottle on a tray with sever

asses, a lovely crystal candy bowl that had never been ed for anything but special Christmas mints, cut flowers a vase, a lamp.... All behind her, out of reach. At both ds of the couch were tables with lamps, a few books, out reach. Pillows on the end of the couch, out of reach. lmer was eight feet away, still at the mantel, and equally stant were three easy chairs and other end tables, out of ach. The Christmas tree in the corner had not been turned ; in the shadows it appeared strangely menacing, out of ace here.

The fire crackled, and outside there was the sound of ntinuing fireworks. She became aware that Thing One as no longer as relaxed as pudding but felt tense under r hand, as if she had communicated her own fear and nsion. Then both cats lifted their heads again, listening, d this time they both rose and trotted from the room. She alized that they, and she, had heard Frank's soft whistle. ore fireworks exploded closer.

Palmer raised the gun again, also listening.

"Firecrackers spook them," she said.

"It's time to reset the stage," Palmer said, his voice no nger easy. "I think you'll be more comfortable in the iddle chair, over there. Move."

She shook her head. "No."

"Don't start being tiresome now," he said in a hard, flat ice. He reached under his sweater and brought out a ackjack with a leather strap, which he slipped over his rist. He took a step away from the fireplace; the gun now inted at her legs.

She tensed, ready to spring up and away. He planned to e her to the heavy chair, she understood, one she couldn't rn over, couldn't move. She slid closer to the edge of the uch as he took another step toward her.

Then he stopped, listening again. There was the unmis-kable sound of a door being unlocked.

"Bobby, you still up? It's me," Frank said at the fr᷈
door. At that moment the lights went out.

She twisted and rolled even as Palmer closed the spa
between them. She grasped a pillow and flung it towa
him, continued to roll to the floor, and felt the sweep of
as the blackjack whirred past her head.

She scrambled to the end of the couch, around it; ɫ
fireworks had entered the house, not with great explosi
booms, but with pops and a compression of air. She rais
her head to see a man's shadow in the doorway; behind ʰ
she heard a gasp and then the sound of Palmer falli
heavily.

"Bobby! Are you all right? Bobby!"

Frank was on his knees at her side, examining her fa
by firelight, and she shuddered and grabbed him hard. "ↄ
right," she gasped. "I'm okay." She realized that som
one else had entered the room and she stiffened. "Whↄ
there?"

"Carter Heilbronner," Frank said, holding her. "It's ᷈
right." The lights came on again, and she could see t
FBI agent.

They sat in the study, where Frank put a glass of branↄ
in her hand; his hands were shaking more than hers. Sʰ
told him all of it, and they sat in silence afterward.

Burned into her retinas, into her mind was the last ima͛
of Palmer she had seen, black from head to foot, a shado
outlined by firelight, leaping toward her, rising from tʰ
flames.

Much later Carter joined them. He accepted brandↄ
gratefully and sank down into a chair, and Barbara told hi
what she had already told Frank. Her hands were no long
shaking, but her voice wavered now and then as she spok
and once it failed her altogether.

"I get the picture," Carter Heilbronner said. "We ha
him under surveillance, of course, and we knew when ʰ

de the switch in San Francisco. He flew in, went to the
n's room and changed clothes. Another man, dressed
e him, walked out and got into a limo and left. Our man
San Francisco called the office here to say Palmer had
arded a plane to Eugene. He got in at eleven-twenty;
re was a car waiting for him in the short-term lot, and
drove off in it, with a tail. He left the car near the train
tion and came the rest of the way on foot, and my guy
s trying to locate me for instructions. When I got here,
decided to wait until Frank showed up. We thought
lmer might be waiting for him to get home to do any-
ng, and we were afraid if we rushed the place, he'd shoot
u. It wasn't the easiest of calls.''

Carter said he had an agent wave down Frank when he
unded the corner coming home, and the agent told him
keep driving on past the house, not to pull into the drive-
ay, in case Palmer was watching. Then they huddled.
ey had to call off the security company, get in through
window, and let Carter get to the dark dining room. He
d that part because he was familiar with the house, he
id. Frank whistled for the cats, to alert Barbara that she
as not alone any longer, to prepare her to act, and so the
ts wouldn't give it away that someone had entered the
use. As soon as Frank opened the front door, called out,
agent pulled the main light switch, and Carter moved in
om the dining room.

"And so it ends," Carter said heavily. "Sometimes you
ve to step on them, after all." He drained his glass but
d not yet stand up. "Frank, Barbara, we've removed the
dy, and we'll clean up your place tomorrow—today. I'm
raid he shot up the couch a little. You deflected his aim
ith that pillow just fine, by the way. Anyway, nothing
appened here tonight. One day next week, or the week
ter that, the body of an unidentified man will wash ashore
mewhere on the coast; meanwhile Mr. Palmer is enjoying
holiday with friends in California. No doubt, in New York

there will be meetings and discussions about what to
with the business, the outstanding contracts. We would li
very much for those meetings to go forward. Without P
mer the web will disintegrate and blow away in the wi
but before it's gone, we'd like to pick up as many of t
pieces as we can. We believe some very important peo
are involved, some important projects are still in the worl
and we'd appreciate the opportunity to gather in the tatt
and remnants. We need your cooperation to do that. I
one knows that the FBI is interested in the activities of t
Palmer Company, so there's still the chance to go forwe
with our investigation. No one will know where Palmer
what happened to him, and our guess is that they will
to continue with business as usual while they wait for I
return.''

Barbara moistened her lips. ''Where's Trassi?''

''He had a fatal boating accident off the Virgin Islands

She closed her eyes. ''They're all dead,'' she whispere
''All of them.'' Death angel.

''Not all; the web spinner is dead, but those who are l
don't know that yet. Will you cooperate?''

She nodded, then said huskily, ''Yes.''

''Carter,'' Frank said, his voice almost as husky as Ba
bara's, ''when you take the couch and rug away, dor
bring them back.''

Carter Heilbronner nodded. ''We're all pretty exhauste
I'll be off.'' He stood up and walked to the door, where
paused to say to Barbara, ''It's really over. No one else
going to bother with you; they'll have too many oth
things on their mind.''

She stands at her window in the dark upstairs bedroo
and watches the city lights through the rain as they glitte
fade and brighten, then go out one by one.

Dawn comes very late in January in a process that is s
gradual, it is hardly distinguishable. Shades of gray, inte

angeable. She is thinking how it started with a monstrous
, and ended with an equally monstrous lie. Thinking:
ath angel, he was the angel of death, he, Palmer. All he
uched withered and died.

And now she believes in evil, believes in the devil; he
uched her and changed her. He knew her fear and cher-
hed it, played with it, nurtured it.

She remembers what John said: she got obsessed with
r cases, put everything on the line. A year ago it was
hn's life on the line, and together they won. Strange that
didn't mention that, that she gambled with his life, won.
nd she can never mention it, never refer to it in any way,
t it was strange that he didn't. Would he read about this
se, know that she gambled and won again? The dragon's
ead, she thinks, I killed the dragon. She presses her fore-
ead on the cool window.

"But the price is too high," she whispers to the gray
awn, the gray room. She feels as if she has crossed a
reshold that she never suspected was in her path, that on
is side of it she has become as ageless as the death angel,
at she can never grow older or more alone than she is at
is moment.

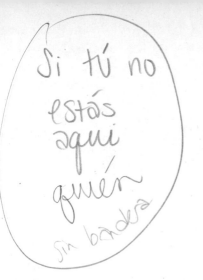

Si tú no estás aquí quién su bandera

Бриллиантовая ??
"Diamond arm"

Кавкаслая ПЛеННИЦа
(Prisoner of Kavkaz)
Kavkaskaya Plenитza

"not disapproving"
"not dangerous"
"i have no idea"
didn't know definition
send roots

Sophie 16?
p. 51 — 52
p. 53 — 54
p. 68 — 72 Sentence
completion
p. 98 — 100
p. 107 - 111 p. 74-86
Reading

CONTEMPORÁNEA

Gabriel García Márquez, nacido en Colombia, es una de las figuras más importantes e influyentes de la literatura universal. Ganador del Premio Nobel de Literatura en 1982, es además cuentista, ensayista, crítico cinematográfico, autor de guiones y, sobre todo, intelectual comprometido con los grandes problemas de nuestro tiempo, en primer término con los que afectan a su amada Colombia y a Hispanoamérica en general. Máxima figura del llamado «realismo mágico», en el que historia e imaginación tejen el tapiz de una literatura viva, que respira por todos sus poros, es en definitiva el hacedor de uno de los mundos narrativos más densos de significados que ha dado la lengua española en el siglo XX. Entre sus novelas más importantes figuran *Cien años de soledad, El coronel no tiene quien le escriba, Crónica de una muerte anunciada, La mala hora, El general en su laberinto,* el libro de relatos *Doce cuentos peregrinos, El amor en tiempos de cólera* y *Diatriba de amor contra un hombre sentado.* En el año 2002 publicó la primera parte de su autobiografía, *Vivir para contarla.*

GABRIEL GARCÍA MÁRQUEZ

Cien años de soledad

DeBOLSILLO

Diseño de la portada: Equipo de diseño editorial
Fotografía de la portada: © Jordi Sàbat

Primera edición en U.S.A.: diciembre, 2005

© 1967, Gabriel García Márquez
© de la presente edición para España y cono sur
  (Argentina, Chile, Paraguay y Uruguay):
  2003, Grupo Editorial Random House Mondadori, S. L.
  Travessera de Gràcia, 47-49. 08021 Barcelona

Printed in Spain – Impreso en España

ISBN: 0-307-35042-8

Distributed by Random House, Inc.

Para Jomí García Ascot
y María Luisa Elío

Muchos años después, frente al pelotón de fusilamiento, el coronel Aureliano Buendía había de recordar aquella tarde remota en que su padre lo llevó a conocer el hielo. Macondo era entonces una aldea de
veinte casas de barro y cañabrava construidas a la orilla de un río de aguas diáfanas que se precipitaban por
un lecho de piedras pulidas, blancas y enormes como
huevos prehistóricos. El mundo era tan reciente, que
muchas cosas carecían de nombre, y para mencionar-
las había que señalarlas con el dedo. Todos los años,
por el mes de marzo, una familia de gitanos desarra-
pados plantaba su carpa cerca de la aldea, y con un
grande alboroto de pitos y timbales daban a conocer
los nuevos inventos. Primero llevaron el imán. Un gitano corpulento, de barba montaraz y manos de gorrión, que se presentó con el nombre de Melquíades,
hizo una truculenta demostración pública de lo que él
mismo llamaba la octava maravilla de los sabios alqui-
mistas de Macedonia. Fue de casa en casa arrastrando
dos lingotes metálicos, y todo el mundo se espantó al
ver que los calderos, las pailas, las tenazas y los anafes
se caían de su sitio, y las maderas crujían por la desesperación de los clavos y los tornillos tratando de des-

enclavarse, y aun los objetos perdidos desde hacía mucho tiempo aparecían por donde más se les había buscado, y se arrastraban en desbandada turbulenta detrás de los fierros mágicos de Melquíades. «Las cosas tienen vida propia —pregonaba el gitano con áspero acento—, todo es cuestión de despertarles el ánima.» José Arcadio Buendía, cuya desaforada imaginación iba siempre más lejos que el ingenio de la naturaleza, y aun más allá del milagro y la magia, pensó que era posible servirse de aquella invención inútil para desentrañar el oro de la tierra. Melquíades, que era un hombre honrado, le previno: «Para eso no sirve.» Pero José Arcadio Buendía no creía en aquel tiempo en la honradez de los gitanos, así que cambió su mulo y una partida de chivos por los dos lingotes imantados. Úrsula Iguarán, su mujer, que contaba con aquellos animales para ensanchar el desmedrado patrimonio doméstico, no consiguió disuadirlo. «Muy pronto ha de sobrarnos oro para empedrar la casa», replicó su marido. Durante varios meses se empeñó en demostrar el acierto de sus conjeturas. Exploró palmo a palmo la región, inclusive el fondo del río, arrastrando los dos lingotes de hierro y recitando en voz alta el conjuro de Melquíades. Lo único que logró desenterrar fue una armadura del siglo XV con todas sus partes soldadas por un cascote de óxido, cuyo interior tenía la resonancia hueca de un enorme calabazo lleno de piedras. Cuando José Arcadio Buendía y los cuatro hombres de su expedición lograron desarticular la armadura, encontraron dentro un esqueleto calcificado que llevaba colgado en el cuello un relicario de cobre con un rizo de mujer.

En marzo volvieron los gitanos. Esta vez llevaban un catalejo y una lupa del tamaño de un tambor, que exhibieron como el último descubrimiento de los judíos de Amsterdam. Sentaron una gitana en un extremo de la aldea e instalaron el catalejo a la entrada de la carpa. Mediante el pago de cinco reales, la gente se asomaba al catalejo y veía a la gitana al alcance de su mano. «La ciencia ha eliminado las distancias», pregonaba Melquíades. «Dentro de poco, el hombre podrá ver lo que ocurre en cualquier lugar de la tierra, sin moverse de su casa.» Un mediodía ardiente hicieron una asombrosa demostración con la lupa gigantesca: pusieron un montón de hierba seca en mitad de la calle y le prendieron fuego mediante la concentración de los rayos solares. José Arcadio Buendía, que aún no acababa de consolarse por el fracaso de sus imanes, concibió la idea de utilizar aquel invento como un arma de guerra. Melquíades, otra vez, trató de disuadirlo. Pero terminó por aceptar los dos lingotes imantados y tres piezas de dinero colonial a cambio de la lupa. Úrsula lloró de consternación. Aquel dinero formaba parte de un cofre de monedas de oro que su padre había acumulado en toda una vida de privaciones, y que ella había enterrado debajo de la cama en espera de una buena ocasión para invertirlas. José Arcadio Buendía no trató siquiera de consolarla, entregado por entero a sus experimentos tácticos con la abnegación de un científico y aun a riesgo de su propia vida. Tratando de demostrar los efectos de la lupa en la tropa enemiga, se expuso él mismo a la concentración de los rayos solares y sufrió quemaduras que se convirtieron en úlceras y tardaron mucho tiempo en sanar. Ante las protestas de su mujer, alarmada por tan peligrosa inventiva, estuvo a punto de incendiar la casa. Pasaba largas horas en su cuarto, haciendo cálculos sobre las posibilidades estratégicas de su arma novedosa, hasta que logró componer un manual de una asombrosa claridad didáctica y un poder de convicción irresistible. Lo envió a las autoridades acompañado de numerosos testimonios sobre sus experiencias y de varios pliegos de dibujos explicativos, al cuidado de un mensajero que atravesó la sierra, se extravió en pantanos desmesurados, remontó ríos tormentosos y estuvo a punto de perecer bajo el azote de las fieras, la desesperación y la peste, antes de conseguir una ruta de enlace con las mulas del correo. A pesar de que el viaje a la capital era en aquel tiempo poco menos que imposible, José Arcadio Buendía prometía intentarlo tan pronto como se lo ordenara el gobierno, con el fin de hacer demostraciones prácticas de su invento ante los poderes militares, y adiestrarlos personalmente en las complicadas artes de la guerra solar. Durante varios años esperó la respuesta. Por último, cansado de esperar, se lamentó ante Melquíades del fracaso de su iniciativa, y el gitano dio entonces una prueba convincente de honradez: le devolvió los doblones a cambio de la lupa, y le dejó además unos mapas portugueses y varios instrumentos de navegación. De su puño y letra escribió una apretada síntesis de los estudios del monje Hermann, que dejó a su disposición para que pudiera servirse del astrolabio, la brújula y el sextante. José Arcadio Buendía pasó los largos meses de lluvia encerrado en un cuartito que construyó en el fondo de la casa para que nadie perturbara sus experimentos. Habiendo abandonado por completo las obligaciones domésticas, permaneció noches enteras en el patio vigilando el curso de los astros, y estuvo a punto de contraer una insolación por tratar de establecer un método exacto para encontrar el mediodía. Cuando se hizo experto en el uso y manejo de sus instrumentos, tuvo una noción del espacio que le permitió navegar por mares incógnitos, visitar territorios deshabitados y trabar relación con seres espléndidos, sin necesidad de abandonar su gabinete. Fue esa la época en que adquirió el hábito de hablar a solas, paseándose por la casa sin hacer caso de nadie, mientras Úrsula y los niños se partían el espinazo en la huerta cuidando el plátano y la malanga, la yuca y el ñame, la ahuyama y la berenjena. De pronto, sin ningún anuncio, su actividad febril se interrumpió y fue sustituida por una especie de fascinación. Estuvo varios días como hechizado, repitiéndose a sí mismo en voz baja un sartal de asombrosas conjeturas, sin dar crédito a su propio entendimiento. Por fin, un martes de diciembre, a la hora del almuerzo, soltó de un golpe toda la carga de su tormento. Los niños habían de recordar por el resto de su vida la augusta solemnidad con que su padre se sentó a la cabecera de la mesa, temblando de fiebre, devastado por la prolongada vigilia y por el encono de su imaginación, y les reveló su descubrimiento:

—La tierra es redonda como una naranja.

Úrsula perdió la paciencia. «Si has de volverte loco, vuélvete tú solo», gritó. «Pero no trates de inculcar a los niños tus ideas de gitano.»José Arcadio Buendía, impasible, no se dejó amedrentar por la desesperación de su mujer, que en un rapto de cólera le destrozó el astrolabio contra el suelo. Construyó otro, reunió en el cuartito a los hombres del pueblo y les demostró, con teorías que para todos resultaban incomprensibles, la posibilidad de regresar al punto de partida navegando siempre hacia el Oriente. Toda la aldea estaba convencida de que José Arcadio Buendía había perdido el juicio, cuando llegó Melquíades a poner las cosas en su punto. Exaltó en público la inteligencia de aquel hombre que por pura especulación astronómica había construido una teoría ya comprobada en la práctica, aunque desconocida hasta entonces en Macondo, y como una prueba de su admiración le hizo un regalo que había de ejercer una influencia terminante en el futuro de la aldea: un laboratorio de alquimia.

Para esa época, Melquíades había envejecido con una rapidez asombrosa. En sus primeros viajes parecía tener la misma edad de José Arcadio Buendía. Pero mientras éste conservaba su fuerza descomunal, que le permitía derribar un caballo agarrándolo por las orejas, el gitano parecía estragado por una dolencia tenaz. Era, en realidad, el resultado de múltiples y raras enfermedades contraídas en sus incontables viajes alrededor del mundo. Según él mismo le contó a José Arcadio Buendía mientras lo ayudaba a montar el laboratorio, la muerte lo seguía a todas partes, husmeándole los pantalones, pero sin decidirse a darle el zarpazo final. Era un fugitivo de cuantas plagas y catástrofes habían flagelado al género humano. Sobrevivió a la pelagra en Persia, al escorbuto en el archipiélago de Malasia, a la lepra en Alejandría, al beriberi en el Japón, a la peste bubónica en Madagascar, al terremoto de Sicilia y a un naufragio multitudinario en el estrecho de Magallanes. Aquel ser prodigioso que decía poseer las claves de Nostradamus, era un hombre lúgubre, envuelto en un aura triste, con una mirada asiática que parecía conocer el otro lado de las cosas. Usaba un sombrero grande y negro, como las alas extendidas de un cuervo, y un chaleco de terciopelo patinado por el verdín de los siglos. Pero a pesar de su inmensa sabiduría y de su ámbito misterioso tenía un peso humano, una condición terrestre que lo mantenía enredado en los minúsculos problemas de la vida cotidiana. Se quejaba de dolencias de viejo, sufría por los más insignificantes percances económicos y había dejado de reír desde hacía mucho tiempo, porque el escorbuto le había arrancado los dientes. El sofocante mediodía en que reveló sus secretos, José Arcadio Buendía tuvo la certidumbre de que aquel era el principio de una grande amistad. Los niños se asombraron con sus relatos fantásticos. Aureliano, que no tenía entonces más de cinco años, había de recordarlo por el resto de su vida como lo vio aquella tarde, sentado contra la claridad metálica y reverberante de la ventana, alumbrando con su profunda voz de órgano los territorios más oscuros de la imaginación, mientras chorreaba por sus sienes la grasa derretida por el calor. José Arcadio, su hermano mayor, había de transmitir aquélla imagen maravillosa, como un recuerdo hereditario, a toda su descendencia. Úrsula, en cambio, conservó un mal recuerdo de aquella visita, porque entró al cuarto en el momento en que Melquíades rompió por distracción un frasco de bicloruro de mercurio.

—Es el olor del demonio —dijo ella.

—En absoluto —corrigió Melquíades—. Está comprobado que el demonio tiene propiedades sulfúricas, y esto no es más que un poco de solimán.

Siempre didáctico, hizo una sabia exposición sobre las virtudes diabólicas del cinabrio, pero Úrsula no le hizo caso, sino que se llevó los niños a rezar. Aquel olor mordiente quedaría para siempre en su memoria, vinculado al recuerdo de Melquíades.

El rudimentario laboratorio —sin contar una profusión de cazuelas, embudos, retortas, filtros y coladores— estaba compuesto por un atanor primitivo; una probeta de cristal de cuello largo y angosto, imitación del *huevo filosófico*, y un destilador construido por los propios gitanos según las descripciones modernas del alambique de tres brazos de María la judía. Además de estas cosas, Melquíades dejó muestras de los siete metales correspondientes a los siete planetas, las fórmulas de Moisés y Zósimo para el doblado del oro, y una serie de apuntes y dibujos sobre los procesos del *Gran Magisterio*, que permitían a quien supiera interpretarlos intentar la fabricación de la piedra filosofál. Seducido por la simplicidad de las fórmulas para doblar el oro, José Arcadio Buendía cortejó a Úrsula durante varias semanas, para que le permitiera desenterrar sus monedas coloniales y aumentarlas tantas veces como era posible subdividir el azogue. Úrsula cedió, como ocurría siempre, ante la inquebrantable obstinación de su marido. Entonces José Arcadio Buendía echó treinta doblones en una cazuela, y los fundió con raspadura de cobre, oropimente, azufre y plomo. Puso a hervir todo a fuego vivo en un caldero de aceite de ricino hasta obtener un jarabe espeso y pestilente más parecido al caramelo vulgar que al oro magnífico. En azarosos y desesperados procesos de destilación, fundida con los siete metales planetarios, trabajada con el mercurio hermético y el vitriolo de Chipre, y vuelta a cocer en manteca de cerdo a falta de aceite de rábano, la preciosa herencia de Úrsula quedó reducida a un chicharrón carbonizado que no pudo ser desprendido del fondo del caldero.

Cuando volvieron los gitanos, Úrsula había predispuesto contra ellos a toda la población. Pero la curiosidad pudo más que el temor, porque aquella vez los gitanos recorrieron la aldea haciendo un ruido ensordecedor con toda clase de instrumentos músicos, mientras el pregonero anunciaba la exhibición del más fabuloso hallazgo de los nasciancenos. De modo que todo el mundo se fue a la carpa, y mediante el pago de un centavo vieron un Melquíades juvenil, repuesto, desarrugado, con una dentadura nueva y radiante. Quienes recordaban sus encías destruidas por el escorbuto, sus mejillas fláccidas y sus labios marchitos se estremecieron de pavor ante aquella prueba terminante de los poderes sobrenaturales del gitano. El pavor se convirtió en pánico cuando Melquíades se sacó los dientes, intactos, engastados en las encías, y se los mostró al público por un instante —un instante fugaz en que volvió a ser el mismo hombre decrépito de los años anteriores— y se los puso otra vez y sonrió de nuevo con un dominio pleno de su juventud restaurada. Hasta el propio José Arcadio Buendía consideró que los conocimientos de Melquíades habían llegado a extremos intolerables, pero experimentó un saludable alborozo cuando el gitano le explicó a solas el mecanismo de su dentadura postiza. Aquello le pareció a la vez tan sencillo y prodigioso, que de la noche a la mañana perdió todo interés en las investigaciones de alquimia; sufrió una nueva crisis de mal humor, no volvió a comer en forma regular y se pasaba el día dando vueltas por la casa. «En el mundo están ocurriendo cosas increíbles», le decía a Úrsula. «Ahí mismo, al otro lado del río, hay toda clase de aparatos mágicos, mientras nosotros seguimos viviendo como los burros.» Quienes lo conocían desde los tiempos de la fundación de Macondo se asombraban de cuánto había cambiado bajo la influencia de Melquíades.

Al principio, José Arcadio Buendía era una especie de patriarca juvenil, que daba instrucciones para la siembra y consejos para la crianza de niños y animales, y colaboraba con todos, aun en el trabajo físico, para la buena marcha de la comunidad. Puesto que su casa fue desde el primer momento la mejor de la aldea, las otras fueron arregladas a su imagen y semejanza. Tenía una salita amplia y bien iluminada, un comedor en forma de terraza con flores de colores alegres, dos dormitorios, un patio con un castaño gigantesco, un huerto bien plantado y un corral donde vivían en comunidad pacífica los chivos, los cerdos y las gallinas. Los únicos animales prohibidos no sólo en la casa, sino en todo el poblado, eran los gallos de pelea.

La laboriosidad de Úrsula andaba a la par con la de su marido. Activa, menuda, severa, aquella mujer de nervios inquebrantables, a quien en ningún momento de su vida se la oyó cantar, parecía estar en todas partes desde el amanecer hasta muy entrada la noche, siempre perseguida por el suave susurro de sus pollerines de olán. Gracias a ella, los pisos de tierra golpeada, los muros de barro sin encalar, los rústicos muebles de madera construidos por ellos mismos estaban siempre limpios, y los viejos arcones donde se guardaba la ropa exhalaban un tibio olor de albahaca.

José Arcadio Buendía, que era el hombre más emprendedor que se vería jamás en la aldea, había dispuesto de tal modo la posición de las casas, que desde todas podía llegarse al río y abastecerse de agua con igual esfuerzo, y trazó las calles con tan buen sentido que ninguna casa recibía más sol que otra a la hora del calor. En pocos años, Macondo fue una aldea más ordenada y laboriosa que cualquiera de las conocidas hasta entonces por sus 300 habitantes. Era en verdad una aldea feliz, donde nadie era mayor de treinta años y donde nadie había muerto.

Desde los tiempos de la fundación, José Arcadio Buendía construyó trampas y jaulas. En poco tiempo llenó de turpiales, canarios, azulejos y petirrojos no sólo la propia casa, sino todas las de la aldea. El concierto de tantos pájaros distintos llegó a ser tan aturdidor, que Úrsula se tapó los oídos con cera de abejas para no perder el sentido de la realidad. La primera vez que llegó la tribu de Melquíades vendiendo bolas de vidrio para el dolor de cabeza, todo el mundo se sorprendió de que hubieran podido encontrar aquella aldea perdida en el sopor de la ciénaga, y los gitanos confesaron que se habían orientado por el canto de los pájaros.

Aquel espíritu de iniciativa social desapareció en poco tiempo, arrastrado por la fiebre de los imanes, los cálculos astronómicos, los sueños de transmutación y las ansias de conocer las maravillas del mundo. De emprendedor y limpio, José Arcadio Buendía se convirtió en un hombre de aspecto holgazán, descuidado en el vestir, con una barba salvaje que Úrsula lograba cuadrar a duras penas con un cuchillo de cocina. No faltó quien lo considerara víctima de algún extraño sortilegio. Pero hasta los más convencidos de su locura abandonaron trabajo y familias para seguirlo, cuando se echó al hombro sus herramientas de desmontar, y pidió el concurso de todos para abrir una trocha que pusiera a Macondo en contacto con los grandes inventos.

José Arcadio Buendía ignoraba por completo la geografía de la región. Sabía que hacia el oriente estaba la sierra impenetrable, y al otro lado de la sierra la antigua ciudad de Riohacha, donde en épocas pasadas —según le había contado el primer Aureliano Buendía, su abuelo— Sir Francis Drake se daba al deporte de cazar caimanes a cañonazos, que luego hacía remendar y rellenar de paja para llevárselos a la reina Isabel. En su juventud, él y sus hombres, con mujeres y niños y animales y toda clase de enseres domésticos, atravesaron la sierra buscando una salida al mar, y al cabo de veintiséis meses desistieron de la empresa y fundaron a Macondo para no tener que emprender el camino de regreso. Era, pues, una ruta que no le interesaba, porque sólo podía conducirlo al pasado. Al sur estaban los pantanos, cubiertos de una eterna nata vegetal, y el vasto universo de la ciénaga grande, que según testimonio de los gitanos carecía de límites. La ciénaga grande se confundía al occidente con una extensión acuática sin horizontes, donde había cetáceos de piel delicada con cabeza y torso de mujer, que perdían a los navegantes con el hechizo de sus tetas descomunales. Los gitanos navegaban seis meses por esa ruta antes de alcanzar el cinturón de tierra firme por donde pasaban las mulas del correo. De acuerdo con los cálculos de José Arcadio Buendía, la única posibilidad de contacto con la civilización era la ruta del norte. De modo que dotó de herramientas de desmonte y armas de cacería a los mismos hombres que lo acompañaron en la fundación de Macondo; echó en una mochila sus instrumentos de orientación y sus mapas, y emprendió la temeraria aventura.

Los primeros días no encontraron un obstáculo

apreciable. Descendieron por la pedregosa ribera del río hasta el lugar en que años antes habían encontrado la armadura del guerrero, y allí penetraron al bosque por un sendero de naranjos silvestres. Al término de la primera semana, mataron y asaron un venado, pero se conformaron con comer la mitad y salar el resto para los próximos días. Trataban de aplazar con esa precaución la necesidad de seguir comiendo guacamayas, cuya carne azul tenía un áspero sabor de almizcle. Luego, durante más de diez días, no volvieron a ver el sol. El suelo se volvió blando y húmedo, como ceniza volcánica, y la vegetación fue cada vez más insidiosa y se hicieron cada vez más lejanos los gritos de los pájaros y la bullaranga de los monos, y el mundo se volvió triste para siempre. Los hombres de la expedición se sintieron abrumados por sus recuerdos más antiguos en aquel paraíso de humedad y silencio, anterior al pecado original, donde las botas se hundían en pozos de aceites humeantes y los machetes destrozaban lirios sangrientos y salamandras doradas. Durante una semana, casi sin hablar, avanzaron como sonámbulos por un universo de pesadumbre, alumbrados apenas por una tenue reverberación de insectos luminosos y con los pulmones agobiados por un sofocante olor de sangre. No podían regresar, porque la trocha que iban abriendo a su paso se volvía a cerrar en poco tiempo, con una vegetación nueva que casi veían crecer ante sus ojos. «No importa», decía José Arcadio Buendía. «Lo esencial es no perder la orientación.» Siempre pendiente de la brújula, siguió guiando a sus hombres hacia el norte invisible, hasta que lograron salir de la región encantada. Era una noche densa, sin estrellas, pero la oscuridad estaba impregnada por un aire nuevo y limpio. Agotados por la prolongada travesía, colgaron las hamacas y durmieron a fondo por primera vez en dos semanas. Cuando despertaron, ya con el sol alto, se quedaron pasmados de fascinación. Frente a ellos, rodeado de helechos y palmeras, blanco y polvoriento en la silenciosa luz de la mañana, estaba un enorme galeón español. Ligeramente volteado a estribor, de su arboladura intacta colgaban las piltrafas escuálidas del velamen, entre jarcias adornadas de orquídeas. El casco, cubierto con una tersa coraza de rémora petrificada y musgo tierno, estaba firmemente enclavado en un suelo de piedras. Toda la estructura parecía ocupar un ámbito propio, un espacio de soledad y de olvido, vedado a los vicios del tiempo y a las costumbres de los pájaros. En el interior, que los expedicionarios exploraron con un fervor sigiloso, no había nada más que un apretado bosque de flores.

El hallazgo del galeón, indicio de la proximidad del mar, quebrantó el ímpetu de José Arcadio Buendía. Consideraba como una burla de su travieso destino haber buscado el mar sin encontrarlo, al precio de sacrificios y penalidades sin cuento, y haberlo encontrado entonces sin buscarlo, atravesado en su camino como un obstáculo insalvable. Muchos años después, el coronel Aureliano Buendía volvió a atravesar la región, cuando era ya una ruta regular del correo, y lo único que encontró de la nave fue el costillar carbonizado en medio de un campo de amapolas. Sólo entonces, convencido de que aquella historia no había sido un engendro de la imaginación de su padre, se preguntó cómo había podido el galeón adentrarse hasta ese punto en tierra firme. Pero José Arcadio Buendía no se planteó esa inquietud cuando encontró el mar, al cabo de otros cuatro días de viaje, a doce kilómetros de distancia del galeón. Sus sueños terminaban frente a ese mar color de ceniza, espumoso y sucio, que no merecía los riesgos y sacrificios de su aventura.

—¡Carajo! —gritó—. Macondo está rodeado de agua por todas partes.

La idea de un Macondo peninsular prevaleció durante mucho tiempo, inspirada en el mapa arbitrario que dibujó José Arcadio Buendía al regreso de su expedición. Lo trazó con rabia, exagerando de mala fe las dificultades de comunicación, como para castigarse a sí mismo por la absoluta falta de sentido con que eligió el lugar. «Nunca llegaremos a ninguna parte», se lamentaba ante Úrsula. «Aquí nos hemos de pudrir en vida sin recibir los beneficios de la ciencia.» Esa certidumbre, rumiada varios meses en el cuartito del laboratorio, lo llevó a concebir el proyecto de trasladar a Macondo a un lugar más propicio. Pero esta vez, Úrsula se anticipó a sus designios febriles. En una secreta e implacable labor de hormiguita predispuso a las mujeres de la aldea contra la veleidad de sus hombres, que ya empezaban a prepararse para la mudanza. José Arcadio Buendía no supo en qué momento, ni en virtud de qué fuerzas adversas, sus planes se fueron enredando en una maraña de pretextos, contratiempos y evasivas, hasta convertirse en pura y simple ilusión. Úrsula lo observó con una atención inocente, y hasta sintió por él un poco de piedad, la mañana en que lo encontró en el cuartito del fondo comentando entre dientes sus sueños de mudanza, mientras colocaba en sus cajas originales las piezas del laboratorio. Lo dejó terminar. Lo dejó clavar las cajas y poner sus iniciales encima con un hisopo entintado, sin hacerle ningún reproche, pero sabiendo ya que él sabía (porque se lo oyó decir en sus sordos monólogos) que los hombres del pueblo no lo secundarían en su empresa. Sólo cuando empezó a desmontar la puerta del cuartito, Úrsula se atrevió a preguntarle por qué lo hacía, y él le contestó con una cierta amargura: «Puesto que nadie quiere irse, nos iremos solos.» Úrsula no se alteró.

—No nos iremos —dijo—. Aquí nos quedamos, porque aquí hemos tenido un hijo.

—Todavía no tenemos un muerto —dijo él—. Uno no es de ninguna parte mientras no tenga un muerto bajo la tierra.

Úrsula replicó, con una suave firmeza:

—Si es necesario que yo me muera para que se queden aquí, me muero.

José Arcadio Buendía no creyó que fuera tan rígida la voluntad de su mujer. Trató de seducirla con el hechizo de su fantasía, con la promesa de un mundo prodigioso donde bastaba con echar unos líquidos mágicos en la tierra para que las plantas dieran frutos a voluntad del hombre, y donde se vendían a precio de baratillo toda clase de aparatos para el dolor. Pero Úrsula fue insensible a su clarividencia.

—En vez de andar pensando en tus alocadas novelerías, debes ocuparte de tus hijos —replicó—. Míralos cómo están, abandonados a la buena de Dios, igual que los burros.

José Arcadio Buendía tomó al pie de la letra las palabras de su mujer. Miró a través de la ventana y vio a los dos niños descalzos en la huerta soleada, y tuvo la impresión de que sólo en aquel instante habían empezado a existir, concebidos por el conjuro de Úrsula. Algo ocurrió entonces en su interior; algo misterioso y definitivo que lo desarraigó de su tiempo actual y lo llevó a la deriva por una región inexplorada de los recuerdos. Mientras Úrsula seguía barriendo la casa que ahora estaba segura de no abandonar en el resto de su vida, él permaneció contemplando a los niños con mirada absorta, hasta que los ojos se le humedecieron y se los secó con el dorso de la mano, y exhaló un hondo suspiro de resignación.

—Bueno —dijo—. Diles que vengan a ayudarme a sacar las cosas de los cajones.

José Arcadio, el mayor de los niños, había cumplido catorce años. Tenía la cabeza cuadrada, el pelo hirsuto y el carácter voluntarioso de su padre. Aunque llevaba el mismo impulso de crecimiento y fortaleza física, ya desde entonces era evidente que carecía de imaginación. Fue concebido y dado a luz durante la penosa travesía de la sierra, antes de la fundación de Macondo, y sus padres dieron gracias al cielo al comprobar que no tenía ningún órgano de animal. Aureliano, el primer ser humano que nació en Macondo, iba a cumplir seis años en marzo. Era silencioso y retraído. Había llorado en el vientre de su madre y nació con los ojos abiertos. Mientras le cortaban el ombligo movía la cabeza de un lado a otro reconociendo las cosas del cuarto, y examinaba el rostro de la gente con una curiosidad sin asombro. Luego, indiferente a quienes se acercaban a conocerlo, mantuvo la atención concentrada en el techo de palma, que parecía a punto de derrumbarse bajo la tremenda presión de la lluvia. Úrsula no volvió a acordarse de la intensidad de esa mirada hasta un día en que el pequeño Aureliano, a la edad de tres años, entró a la cocina en el momento en que ella retiraba del fogón y ponía en la mesa una olla de caldo hirviendo. El niño, perplejo en la puerta, dijo: «Se va a caer.» La olla estaba bien puesta en el centro de la mesa, pero tan pronto como el niño hizo el anuncio, inició un movimiento irrevocable hacia el borde, como impulsada por un dinamismo interior, y se despedazó en el suelo. Úrsula, alarmada, le contó el episodio a su marido, pero éste lo interpretó como un fenómeno natural. Así fue siempre, ajeno a la existencia de sus hijos, en parte porque consideraba la infancia como un período de insuficiencia mental, y en parte porque siempre estaba demasiado absorto en sus propias especulaciones quiméricas.

Pero desde la tarde en que llamó a los niños para que lo ayudaran a desempacar las cosas del laboratorio, les dedicó sus horas mejores. En el cuartito apartado, cuyas paredes se fueron llenando poco a poco de mapas inverosímiles y gráficos fabulosos, les enseñó a leer y escribir y a sacar cuentas, y les habló de las maravillas del mundo no sólo hasta donde le alcanzaban sus conocimientos, sino forzando a extremos increíbles los límites de su imaginación. Fue así como los niños terminaron por aprender que en el extremo meridional del África había hombres tan inteligentes y pacíficos que su único entretenimiento era sentarse a pensar, y que era posible atravesar a pie el mar Egeo saltando de isla en isla hasta el puerto de Salónica. Aquellas alucinantes sesiones quedaron de tal modo impresas en la memoria de los niños, que muchos años más tarde, un segundo antes de que el oficial de los ejércitos regulares diera la orden de fuego al pelotón de fusilamiento, el coronel Aureliano Buendía volvió a vivir la tibia tarde de marzo en que su padre interrumpió la lección de física, y se quedó fascinado, con la mano en el aire y los ojos inmóviles, oyendo a la distancia los pífanos y tambores y sonajas de los gitanos que una vez más llegaban a la aldea, pregonando el último y asombroso descubrimiento de los sabios de Memphis.

Eran gitanos nuevos. Hombres y mujeres jóvenes que sólo conocían su propia lengua, ejemplares hermosos de piel aceitada y manos inteligentes, cuyos bailes y músicas sembraron en las calles un pánico de alborotada alegría, con sus loros pintados de todos los colores que recitaban romanzas italianas, y la gallina que ponía un centenar de huevos de oro al son de la pandereta, y el mono amaestrado que adivinaba el pensamiento, y la máquina múltiple que servía al mismo tiempo para pegar botones y bajar la fiebre, y el aparato para olvidar los malos recuerdos, y el emplasto para perder el tiempo, y un millar de invenciones más, tan ingeniosas e insólitas, que José Arcadio Buendía hubiera querido inventar la máquina de la memoria para poder acordarse de todas. En un instante transformaron la aldea. Los habitantes de Macondo se encontraron de pronto perdidos en sus propias calles, aturdidos por la feria multitudinaria.

Llevando un niño de cada mano para no perderlos en el tumulto, tropezando con saltimbanquis de dientes acorazados de oro y malabaristas de seis brazos, sofocado por el confuso aliento de estiércol y sándalo que exhalaba la muchedumbre, José Arcadio Buendía andaba como un loco buscando a Melquíades por todas partes, para que le revelara los infinitos secretos de aquella pesadilla fabulosa. Se dirigió a varios gitanos que no entendieron su lengua. Por último, llegó hasta el lugar donde Melquíades solía plantar su tienda, y encontró un armenio taciturno que anunciaba en castellano un jarabe para hacerse invisible. Se había tomado de un golpe una copa de la sustancia ambarina, cuando José Arcadio Buendía se abrió paso a empujones por entre el grupo absorto que presenciaba el espectáculo, y alcanzó a hacer la pregunta. El gitano lo envolvió en el clima atónito de su mirada, antes de convertirse en un charco de alquitrán pestilente y humeante sobre el cual quedó flotando la resonancia de su respuesta: «Melquíades murió.» Aturdido por la noticia, José Arcadio Buendía permaneció inmóvil, tratando de sobreponerse a la aflicción, hasta que el grupo se dispersó reclamado por otros artificios y el charco del armenio taciturno se evaporó por completo. Más tarde, otros gitanos le confirmaron que en efecto Melquíades había sucumbido a las fiebres en los médanos de Singapur, y su cuerpo había sido arrojado en el lugar más profundo del mar de Java. A los niños no les interesó la noticia. Estaban obstinados en que su padre los llevara a conocer la portentosa novedad de los sabios de Memphis, anunciada a la entrada de una tienda que, según decían, perteneció al rey Salomón. Tanto insistieron, que José Arcadio Buendía pagó los treinta reales y los condujo hasta el centro de la carpa, donde había un gigante de torso peludo y cabeza rapada, con un anillo de cobre en la nariz y una pesada cadena de hierro en el tobillo, custodiando un cofre de pirata. Al ser destapado por el gigante, el cofre dejó escapar un aliento glacial. Dentro sólo había un enorme bloque transparente, con infinitas agujas internas en las cuales se despedazaba en estrellas de colores la claridad del crepúsculo. Desconcertado, sabiendo que los niños esperaban una explicación inmediata, José Arcadio Buendía se atrevió a murmurar:

—Es el diamante más grande del mundo.

—No —corrigió el gitano—. Es hielo.

José Arcadio Buendía, sin entender, extendió la mano hacia el témpano, pero el gigante se la apartó. «Cinco reales más para tocarlo», dijo. José Arcadio Buendía los pagó, y entonces puso la mano sobre el hielo, y la mantuvo puesta por varios minutos, mientras el corazón se le hinchaba de temor y de júbilo al contacto del misterio. Sin saber qué decir, pagó otros diez reales para que sus hijos vivieran la prodigiosa experiencia. El pequeño José Arcadio se negó a tocarlo. Aureliano, en cambio, dio un paso hacia adelante, puso la mano y la retiró en el acto. «Está hirviendo», exclamó asustado. Pero su padre no le prestó atención. Embriagado por la evidencia del prodigio, en aquel momento se olvidó de la frustración de sus empresas delirantes y del cuerpo de Melquíades abandonado al apetito de los calamares. Pagó otros cinco reales, y con la mano puesta en el témpano, como expresando un testimonio sobre el texto sagrado, exclamó:

—Este es el gran invento de nuestro tiempo.

Cuando el pirata Francis Drake asaltó a Riohacha, en el siglo XVI, la bisabuela de Úrsula Iguarán se asustó tanto con el toque de rebato y el estampido de los cañones, que perdió el control de los nervios y se sentó en un fogón encendido. Las quemaduras la dejaron convertida en una esposa inútil para toda la vida. No podía sentarse sino de medio lado, acomodada en cojines, y algo extraño debió quedarle en el modo de andar, porque nunca volvió a caminar en público. Renunció a toda clase de hábitos sociales obsesionada por la idea de que su cuerpo despedía un olor a chamusquina. El alba la sorprendía en el patio sin atreverse a dormir, porque soñaba que los ingleses con sus feroces perros de asalto se metían por la ventana del dormitorio y la sometían a vergonzosos tormentos con hierros al rojo vivo. Su marido, un comerciante aragonés con quien tenía dos hijos, se gastó media tienda en medicinas y entretenimientos buscando la manera de aliviar sus terrores. Por último, liquidó el negocio y llevó a la familia a vivir lejos del mar, en una ranchería de indios pacíficos situada en las estribaciones de la sierra, donde le construyó a su mujer un dormitorio sin ventanas para que no tuvieran por donde entrar los piratas de sus pesadillas.

En la escondida ranchería vivía de mucho tiempo atrás un criollo cultivador de tabaco, don José Arcadio Buendía, con quien el bisabuelo de Úrsula estableció una sociedad tan productiva que en pocos años hicieron una fortuna. Varios siglos más tarde, el tataranieto del criollo se casó con la tataranieta del aragonés. Por eso, cada vez que Úrsula se salía de casillas con las locuras de su marido, saltaba por encima de trescientos años de casualidades, y maldecía la hora en que Francis Drake asaltó a Riohacha. Era un simple recurso de desahogo, porque en verdad estaban ligados hasta la muerte por un vínculo más sólido que el amor: un común remordimiento de conciencia. Eran primos entre sí. Habían crecido juntos en la antigua ranchería que los antepasados de ambos transformaron con su trabajo y sus buenas costumbres en uno de los mejores pueblos de la provincia. Aunque su matrimonio era previsible desde que vinieron al mundo, cuando ellos expresaron la voluntad de casarse sus propios parientes trataron de impedirlo. Tenían el temor de que aquellos saludables cabos de dos razas secularmente entrecruzadas pasaran por la vergüenza de engendrar iguanas. Ya existía un precedente tremendo. Una tía de Úrsula, casada con un tío de José Arcadio Buendía, tuvo un hijo que pasó toda la vida con unos pantalones englobados y flojos, y que murió desangrado después de haber vivido cuarenta y dos años en el más puro estado de virginidad, porque nació y creció con una cola cartilaginosa en forma de tirabuzón y con una escobilla de pelos en la punta. Una cola de cerdo que no se dejó ver nunca de ninguna mujer, y que le costó la vida cuando un carnicero amigo le hizo el favor de cortársela con una hachuela de destazar. José Arcadio Buendía, con la ligereza de sus diecinueve años, resolvió el problema con una sola frase: «No me importa tener cochinitos, siempre que puedan hablar.» Así que se casaron con una fiesta de banda y cohetes que duró tres días. Hubieran sido felices desde entonces si la madre de Úrsula no la hubiera aterrorizado con toda clase de pronósticos siniestros sobre su descendencia, hasta el extremo de conseguir que rehusara consumar el matrimonio. Temiendo que el corpulento y voluntarioso marido la violara dormida, Úrsula se ponía antes de acostarse un pantalón rudimentario que su madre le fabricó con lona de velero y reforzado con un sistema de correas entrecruzadas, que se cerraba por delante con una gruesa hebilla de hierro. Así estuvieron varios meses. Durante el día, él pastoreaba sus gallos de pelea y ella bordaba en bastidor con su madre. Durante la noche, forcejeaban varias horas con una ansiosa violencia que ya parecía un sustituto del acto de amor, hasta que la intuición popular olfateó que algo irregular estaba ocurriendo, y soltó el rumor de que Úrsula seguía virgen un año después de casada, porque su marido era impotente. José Arcadio Buendía fue el último que conoció el rumor.

—Ya ves, Úrsula, lo que anda diciendo la gente —le dijo a su mujer con mucha calma.

—Déjalos que hablen —dijo ella—. Nosotros sabemos que no es cierto.

De modo que la situación siguió igual por otros seis meses, hasta el domingo trágico en que José Arcadio Buendía le ganó una pelea de gallos a Prudencio Aguilar. Furioso, exaltado por la sangre de su animal, el perdedor se apartó de José Arcadio Buendía para que toda la gallera pudiera oír lo que iba a decirle.

—Te felicito —gritó—. A ver si por fin ese gallo le hace el favor a tu mujer.

José Arcadio Buendía, sereno, recogió su gallo. «Vuelvo en seguida», dijo a todos. Y luego, a Prudencio Aguilar:

—Y tú, anda a tu casa y ármate, porque te voy a matar.

Diez minutos después volvió con la lanza cebada de su abuelo. En la puerta de la gallera, donde se había concentrado medio pueblo, Prudencio Aguilar lo esperaba. No tuvo tiempo de defenderse. La lanza de José Arcadio Buendía, arrojada con la fuerza de un toro y con la misma dirección certera con que el primer Aureliano Buendía exterminó a los tigres de la región, le atravesó la garganta. Esa noche, mientras se velaba el cadáver en la gallera, José Arcadio Buendía entró en el dormitorio cuando su mujer se estaba poniendo el pantalón de castidad. Blandiendo la lanza frente a ella, le ordenó: «Quítate eso.» Úrsula no puso en duda la decisión de su marido. «Tú serás responsable de lo que pase», murmuró. José Arcadio Buendía clavó la lanza en el piso de tierra.

—Si has de parir iguanas, criaremos iguanas —dijo—. Pero no habrá más muertos en este pueblo por culpa tuya.

Era una buena noche de junio, fresca y con luna, y estuvieron despiertos y retozando en la cama hasta el amanecer, indiferentes al viento que pasaba por el dormitorio, cargado con el llanto de los parientes de Prudencio Aguilar.

El asunto fue clasificado como un duelo de honor, pero a ambos les quedó un malestar en la conciencia. Una noche en que no podía dormir, Úrsula salió a tomar agua en el patio y vio a Prudencio Aguilar junto a la tinaja. Estaba lívido, con una expresión muy triste, tratando de cegar con un tapón de esparto el hueco de su garganta. No le produjo miedo, sino lástima. Volvió al cuarto a contarle a su esposo lo que había visto, pero él no le hizo caso. «Los muertos no salen», dijo. «Lo que pasa es que no podemos con el peso de la conciencia.» Dos noches después, Úrsula volvió a ver a Prudencio Aguilar en el baño, lavándose con el tapón de esparto la sangre cristalizada del cuello. Otra noche lo vio paseándose bajo la lluvia. José Arcadio Buendía, fastidiado por las alucinaciones de su mujer, salió al patio armado con la lanza. Allí estaba el muerto con su expresión triste.

—Vete al carajo —le gritó José Arcadio Buendía—. Cuantas veces regreses volveré a matarte.

Prudencio Aguilar no se fue ni José Arcadio Buendía se atrevió a arrojar la lanza. Desde entonces no pudo dormir bien. Lo atormentaba la inmensa desolación con que el muerto lo había mirado desde la lluvia, la honda nostalgia con que añoraba a los vivos, la ansiedad con que registraba la casa buscando el agua para mojar su tapón de esparto. «Debe estar sufriendo mucho», le decía a Úrsula. «Se ve que está muy solo.» Ella estaba tan conmovida que la próxima vez que vio al muerto destapando las ollas de la hornilla comprendió lo que buscaba, y desde entonces le puso tazones de agua por toda la casa. Una noche en que lo encontró lavándose las heridas en su propio cuarto, José Arcadio Buendía no pudo resistir más.

—Está bien, Prudencio —le dijo—. Nos iremos de este pueblo, lo más lejos que podamos, y no regresaremos jamás. Ahora vete tranquilo.

Fue así como emprendieron la travesía de la sierra. Varios amigos de José Arcadio Buendía, jóvenes como él, embullados con la aventura, desmantelaron sus casas y cargaron con sus mujeres y sus hijos hacia la tierra que nadie les había prometido. Antes de partir, José Arcadio Buendía enterró la lanza en el patio y degolló uno tras otro sus magníficos gallos de pelea, confiando en que en esa forma le daba un poco de paz a Prudencio Aguilar. Lo único que se llevó Úrsula fue un baúl con sus ropas de recién casada, unos pocos útiles domésticos y el cofrecito con las piezas de oro que heredó de su padre. No se trazaron un itinerario definido. Solamente procuraban viajar en sentido contrario al camino de Riohacha para no dejar ningún rastro ni encontrar gente conocida. Fue un viaje absurdo. A los catorce meses, con el estómago estragado por la carne de mico y el caldo de culebras, Úrsula dio a luz un hijo con todas sus partes humanas. Había hecho la mitad del camino en una hamaca colgada de un palo que dos hombres llevaban en hombros, porque la hinchazón le desfiguró las piernas, y las varices se le reventaban como burbujas. Aunque daba lástima verlos con los vientres templados y los ojos lánguidos, los niños resistieron el viaje mejor que sus padres, y la mayor parte del tiempo les resultó divertido. Una mañana, después de casi dos años de travesía, fueron los primeros mortales que vieron la vertiente occidental de la sierra. Desde la cumbre nublada contemplaron la inmensa llanura acuática de la ciénaga grande, explayada hasta el otro lado del mundo. Pero nunca encontraron el mar. Una noche, después de varios meses de andar perdidos por entre los pantanos, lejos ya de los últimos indígenas que encontraron en el camino, acamparon a la orilla de un río pedregoso cuyas aguas parecían un torrente de vidrio helado. Años después, durante la segunda guerra civil, el coronel Aureliano Buendía trató de hacer aquella misma ruta para tomarse a Riohacha por sorpresa, y a los seis días de viaje comprendió que era una locura. Sin embargo, la noche en que acamparon junto al río, las huestes de su padre tenían un aspecto de náufragos sin escapatoria, pero su número había aumentado durante la travesía y todos estaban dispuestos (y lo consiguieron) a morirse de viejos. José Arcadio Buendía soñó esa noche que en aquel lugar se levantaba una ciudad ruidosa con casas de paredes de espejo. Preguntó qué ciudad era aquella, y le contestaron con un nombre que nunca había oído, que no tenía significado alguno, pero que tuvo en el sueño una resonancia sobrenatural: Macondo. Al día siguiente convenció a sus hombres de que nunca encontrarían el mar. Les ordenó derribar los árboles para hacer un claro junto al río, en el lugar más fresco de la orilla, y allí fundaron la aldea.

José Arcadio Buendía no logró descifrar el sueño de las casas con paredes de espejo hasta el día en que conoció el hielo. Entonces creyó entender su profundo significado. Pensó que en un futuro próximo podrían fabricarse bloques de hielo en gran escala, a partir de un material tan cotidiano como el agua, y construir con ellos las nuevas casas de la aldea. Macondo dejaría de ser un lugar ardiente, cuyas bisagras y aldabas se torcían de calor, para convertirse en una ciudad invernal. Si no perseveró en sus tentativas de construir una fábrica de hielo, fue porque entonces

36

estaba positivamente entusiasmado con la educación de sus hijos, en especial la de Aureliano, que había revelado desde el primer momento una rara intuición alquímica. El laboratorio había sido desempolvado. Revisando las notas de Melquíades, ahora serenamente, sin la exaltación de la novedad, en prolongadas y pacientes sesiones trataron de separar el oro de Úrsula del cascote adherido al fondo del caldero. El joven José Arcadio participó apenas en el proceso. Mientras su padre sólo tenía cuerpo y alma para el atanor, el voluntarioso primogénito, que siempre fue demasiado grande para su edad, se convirtió en un adolescente monumental. Cambió de voz. El bozo se le pobló de un vello incipiente. Una noche Úrsula entró en el cuarto cuando él se quitaba la ropa para dormir, y experimentó un confuso sentimiento de vergüenza y piedad: era el primer hombre que veía desnudo, después de su esposo, y estaba tan bien equipado para la vida, que le pareció anormal. Úrsula, encinta por tercera vez, vivió de nuevo sus terrores de recién casada.

Por aquel tiempo iba a la casa una mujer alegre, deslenguada, provocativa, que ayudaba en los oficios domésticos y sabía leer el porvenir en la baraja. Úrsula le habló de su hijo. Pensaba que su desproporción era algo tan desnaturalizado como la cola de cerdo del primo. La mujer soltó una risa expansiva que repercutió en toda la casa como un reguero de vidrio. «Al contrario», dijo. «Será feliz.» Para confirmar su pronóstico llevó los naipes a la casa pocos días después, y se encerró con José Arcadio en un depósito de granos contiguo a la cocina. Colocó las barajas con mucha calma en un viejo mesón de carpintería, hablando de cualquier cosa, mientras el muchacho esperaba cerca de ella más aburrido que intrigado. De pronto extendió la mano y lo tocó. «Qué bárbaro», dijo, sinceramente asustada, y fue todo lo que pudo decir. José Arcadio sintió que los huesos se le llenaban de espuma, que tenía un miedo lánguido y unos terribles deseos de llorar. La mujer no le hizo ninguna insinuación. Pero José Arcadio la siguió buscando toda la noche en el olor de humo que ella tenía en las axilas y que se le quedó metido debajo del pellejo. Quería estar con ella en todo momento, quería que ella fuera su madre, que nunca salieran del granero y que le dijera qué bárbaro, y que lo volviera a tocar y a decirle qué bárbaro. Un día no pudo soportar más y fue a buscarla a su casa. Hizo una visita formal, incomprensible, sentado en la sala sin pronunciar una palabra. En ese momento no la deseó. La encontraba distinta, enteramente ajena a la imagen que inspiraba su olor, como si fuera otra. Tomó el café y abandonó la casa deprimido. Esa noche, en el espanto de la vigilia, la volvió a desear con una ansiedad brutal, pero entonces no la quería como era en el granero, sino como había sido aquella tarde.

Días después, de un modo intempestivo, la mujer lo llamó a su casa, donde estaba sola con su madre, y lo hizo entrar en el dormitorio con el pretexto de enseñarle un truco de barajas. Entonces lo tocó con tanta libertad que él sufrió una desilusión después del estremecimiento inicial, y experimentó más miedo que placer. Ella le pidió que esa noche fuera a buscarla. Él estuvo de acuerdo, por salir del paso, sabiendo que no sería capaz de ir. Pero esa noche, en la cama ardiente, comprendió que tenía que ir a buscarla aunque no fuera capaz. Se vistió a tientas, oyendo en la oscuridad la reposada respiración de su hermano, la tos seca de su padre en el cuarto vecino, el asma de las gallinas en el patio, el zumbido de los mosquitos, el bombo de su corazón y el desmesurado bullicio del mundo que no había advertido hasta entonces, y salió a la calle dormida. Deseaba de todo corazón que la puerta estuviera atrancada, y no simplemente ajustada, como ella le había prometido. Pero estaba abierta. La empujó con la punta de los dedos y los goznes soltaron un quejido lúgubre y articulado que tuvo una resonancia helada en sus entrañas. Desde el instante en que entró, de medio lado y tratando de no hacer ruido, sintió el olor. Todavía estaba en la salita donde los tres hermanos de la mujer colgaban las hamacas en posiciones que él ignoraba y que no podía determinar en las tinieblas, así que le faltaba atravesarla a tientas, empujar la puerta del dormitorio y orientarse allí de tal modo que no fuera a equivocarse de cama. Lo consiguió. Tropezó con los hicos de las hamacas, que estaban más bajas de lo que él había supuesto, y un hombre que roncaba hasta entonces se revolvió en el sueño y dijo con una especie de desilusión: «Era miércoles.» Cuando empujó la puerta del dormitorio, no pudo impedir que raspara el desnivel del piso. De pronto, en la oscuridad absoluta, comprendió con una irremediable nostalgia que estaba completamente desorientado. En la estrecha habitación dormían la madre, otra hija con el marido y dos niños, y la mujer que tal vez no lo esperaba. Habría podido guiarse por el olor si el olor no hubiera estado en toda la casa, tan engañoso y al mismo tiempo tan definido como había estado siempre en su pellejo. Permaneció inmóvil un largo rato, preguntándose asombrado cómo había hecho para llegar a ese abismo de desamparo, cuando una mano con todos los dedos extendidos, que tanteaba en las tinieblas, le tropezó la cara. No se sorprendió, porque sin saberlo lo había estado esperando. Entonces se confió a aquella mano, y en un terrible estado de agotamiento se dejó llevar hasta un lugar sin formas donde le quitaron la ropa y lo zarandearon como un costal de papas y lo voltearon al derecho y al revés, en una oscuridad insondable en la que le sobraban los brazos, donde ya no olía más a mujer, sino a amoníaco, y donde trataba de acordarse del rostro de ella y se encontraba con el rostro de Úrsula, confusamente consciente de que estaba haciendo algo que desde hacía mucho tiempo deseaba que se pudiera hacer, pero que nunca se había imaginado que en realidad se pudiera hacer, sin saber cómo lo estaba haciendo porque no sabía dónde estaban los pies y dónde la cabeza, ni los pies de quién ni la cabeza de quién, y sintiendo que no podía resistir más el rumor glacial de sus riñones y el aire de sus tripas, y el miedo, y el ansia atolondrada de huir y al mismo tiempo de quedarse para siempre en aquel silencio exasperado y aquella soledad espantosa.

Se llamaba Pilar Ternera. Había formado parte del éxodo que culminó con la fundación de Macondo, arrastrada por su familia para separarla del hombre que la violó a los catorce años y siguió amándola hasta los veintidós, pero que nunca se decidió a hacer pública la situación porque era un hombre ajeno. Le prometió seguirla hasta el fin del mundo, pero más tarde, cuando arreglara sus asuntos, y ella se había cansado de esperarlo identificándolo siempre con los hombres altos y bajos, rubios y morenos, que las barajas le prometían por los caminos de la tierra y los caminos del mar, para dentro de tres días, tres meses o tres años. Había perdido en la espera la fuerza de los muslos, la dureza de los senos, el hábito de la ternura, pero conservaba intacta la locura del corazón. Trastornado por aquel juguete prodigioso, José Arcadio buscó su rastro todas las noches a través del laberinto del cuarto. En cierta ocasión encontró la puerta atrancada, y tocó varias veces, sabiendo que si había tenido el arresto de tocar la primera vez tenía que tocar hasta la última, y al cabo de una espera interminable ella le abrió la puerta. Durante el día, derrumbándose de sueño, gozaba en secreto con los recuerdos de la noche anterior. Pero cuando ella entraba en la casa, alegre, indiferente, dicharachera, él no tenía que hacer ningún esfuerzo para disimular su tensión, porque aquella mujer cuya risa explosiva espantaba a las palomas, no tenía nada que ver con el poder invisible que le enseñaba a respirar hacia dentro y a controlar los golpes del corazón, y le había permitido entender por qué los hombres le tienen miedo a la muerte. Estaba tan ensimismado que ni siquiera comprendió la alegría de todos cuando su padre y su hermano alborotaron la casa con la noticia de que habían logrado vulnerar el cascote metálico y separar el oro de Úrsula.

En efecto, tras complicadas y perseverantes jornadas, lo habían conseguido. Úrsula estaba feliz, y hasta dio gracias a Dios por la invención de la alquimia, mientras la gente de la aldea se apretujaba en el laboratorio, y les servían dulce de guayaba con galletitas para celebrar el prodigio, y José Arcadio Buendía les dejaba ver el crisol con el oro rescatado, como si acabara de inventarlo. De tanto mostrarlo, terminó frente a su hijo mayor, que en los últimos tiempos apenas se asomaba por el laboratorio. Puso frente a sus ojos el mazacote seco y amarillento, y le preguntó: «¿Qué te parece?» José Arcadio, sinceramente, contestó:

—Mierda de perro.

Su padre le dio con el revés de la mano un violento golpe en la boca que le hizo saltar la sangre y las lágrimas. Esa noche Pilar Ternera le puso compresas de árnica en la hinchazón, adivinando el frasco y los algodones en la oscuridad, y le hizo todo lo que quiso sin que él se molestara, para amarlo sin lastimarlo. Lograron tal estado de intimidad que un momento después, sin darse cuenta, estaban hablando en murmullos.

—Quiero estar solo contigo —decía él—. Un día de estos le cuento todo a todo el mundo y se acaban los escondrijos.

Ella no trató de apaciguarlo.

—Sería muy bueno —dijo—. Si estamos solos, dejamos la lámpara encendida para vernos bien, y yo puedo gritar todo lo que quiera sin que nadie tenga que meterse y tú me dices en la oreja todas las porquerías que se te ocurran.

Esta conversación, el rencor mordiente que sentía contra su padre, y la inminente posibilidad del amor desaforado le inspiraron una serena valentía. De un modo espontáneo, sin ninguna preparación, le contó todo a su hermano.

Al principio, el pequeño Aureliano sólo comprendía el riesgo, la inmensa posibilidad de peligro que implicaban las aventuras de su hermano, pero no lograba concebir la fascinación del objetivo. Poco a poco se fue contaminando de ansiedad. Se hacía contar las minuciosas peripecias, se identificaba con el sufrimiento y el gozo del hermano, se sentía asustado y feliz. Lo esperaba despierto hasta el amanecer, en la cama solitaria que parecía tener una estera de brasas, y seguían hablando sin sueño hasta la hora de levantarse, de modo que muy pronto padecieron ambos la misma somnolencia, sintieron el mismo desprecio por la alquimia y la sabiduría de su padre, y se refugiaron en la soledad. «Estos niños andan como zurumbáticos», decía Úrsula. «Deben tener lombrices.» Les preparó una repugnante pócima de paico machacado, que ambos bebieron con imprevisto estoicismo, y se sentaron al mismo tiempo en sus bacinillas once veces en un solo día, y expulsaron unos parásitos rosados que mostraron a todos con gran júbilo, porque les permitieron desorientar a Úrsula en cuanto al origen de sus distraimientos y languideces. Aureliano no sólo podía entonces entender, sino que podía vivir como cosa propia las experiencias de su hermano, porque en una ocasión en que éste explicaba con muchos pormenores el mecanismo del amor, lo interrumpió para preguntarle: «¿Qué se siente?» José Arcadio le dio una respuesta inmediata:

—Es como un temblor de tierra.

Un jueves de enero, a las dos de la madrugada, nació Amaranta. Antes de que nadie entrara en el cuarto, Úrsula la examinó minuciosamente. Era liviana y acuosa como una lagartija, pero todas sus partes eran humanas. Aureliano no se dio cuenta de la novedad sino cuando sintió la casa llena de gente. Protegido por la confusión salió en busca de su hermano, que no estaba en la cama desde las once, y fue una decisión tan impulsiva que ni siquiera tuvo tiempo de preguntarse cómo haría para sacarlo del dormitorio de Pilar Ternera. Estuvo rondando la casa varias horas, silbando claves privadas, hasta que la proximidad del alba lo obligó a regresar. En el cuarto de su madre, jugando con la hermanita recién nacida y con una cara que se le caía de inocencia, encontró a José Arcadio.

Úrsula había cumplido apenas su reposo de cuarenta días, cuando volvieron los gitanos. Eran los mismos saltimbanquis y malabaristas que llevaron el hielo. A diferencia de la tribu de Melquíades, habían demostrado en poco tiempo que no eran heraldos del progreso, sino mercachifles de diversiones. Inclusive cuando llevaron el hielo, no lo anunciaron en función de su utilidad en la vida de los hombres, sino como una simple curiosidad de circo. Esta vez, entre muchos otros juegos de artificio, llevaban una estera voladora. Pero no la ofrecieron como un aporte fundamental al desarrollo del transporte, sino como un objeto de recreo. La gente, desde luego, desenterró sus últimos pedacitos de oro para disfrutar de un vuelo fugaz sobre las casas de la aldea. Amparados por la deliciosa impunidad del desorden colectivo, José Arcadio y Pilar vivieron horas de desahogo. Fueron dos novios dichosos entre la muchedumbre, y hasta llegaron a sospechar que el amor podía ser un sentimiento más reposado y profundo que la felicidad desaforada pero momentánea de sus noches secretas. Pilar, sin embargo, rompió el encanto. Estimulada por el entusiasmo con que José Arcadio disfrutaba de su compañía, equivocó la forma y la ocasión, y de un solo golpe le echó el mundo encima. «Ahora sí eres un hombre», le dijo. Y como él no entendió lo que ella quería decirle, se lo explicó letra por letra:

—Vas a tener un hijo.

José Arcadio no se atrevió a salir de su casa en varios días. Le bastaba con escuchar la risotada trepidante de Pilar en la cocina para correr a refugiarse en el laboratorio, donde los artefactos de alquimia habían revivido con la bendición de Úrsula. José Arcadio Buendía recibió con alborozo al hijo extraviado y lo inició en la búsqueda de la piedra filosofal, que había por fin emprendido. Una tarde se entusiasmaron los muchachos con la estera voladora que pasó veloz al nivel de la ventana del laboratorio llevando al gitano conductor y a varios niños de la aldea que hacían alegres saludos con la mano, y José Arcadio Buendía ni siquiera la miró. «Déjenlos que sueñen», dijo. «Nosotros volaremos mejor que ellos con recursos más científicos que ese miserable sobrecamas.» A pesar de su fingido interés, José Arcadio no entendió nunca los poderes del *huevo filosófico*, que simplemente le parecía un frasco mal hecho. No lograba escapar de su preocupación. Perdió el apetito y el sueño, sucumbió al mal humor, igual que su padre ante el fracaso de alguna de sus empresas, y fue tal su trastorno que el propio José Arcadio Buendía lo relevó de los deberes en el laboratorio creyendo que había tomado la alquimia demasiado a pecho. Aureliano, por supuesto, comprendió que la aflicción del hermano no tenía origen en la búsqueda de la piedra filosofal, pero no consiguió arrancarle una confidencia. Había perdido su antigua espontaneidad. De cómplice y comunicativo se hizo hermético y hostil. Ansioso de soledad, mordido por un virulento rencor contra el mundo, una noche abandonó la cama como de costumbre, pero no fue a casa de Pilar Ternera, sino a confundirse con el tumulto de la feria. Después de deambular por entre toda suerte de máquinas de artificio, sin interesarse por ninguna, se fijó en algo que no estaba en juego: una gitana muy joven, casi una niña, agobiada de abalorios, la mujer más bella que José Arcadio había visto en su vida. Estaba entre la multitud que presenciaba el triste espectáculo del hombre que se convirtió en víbora por desobedecer a sus padres.

José Arcadio no puso atención. Mientras se desarrollaba el triste interrogatorio del hombre-víbora, se había abierto paso por entre la multitud hasta la primera fila en que se encontraba la gitana, y se había detenido detrás de ella. Se apretó contra sus espaldas. La muchacha trató de separarse, pero José Arcadio se apretó con más fuerza contra sus espaldas. Entonces ella lo sintió. Se quedó inmóvil contra él, temblando de sorpresa y pavor, sin poder creer en la evidencia, y por último volvió la cabeza y lo miró con una sonrisa trémula. En ese instante dos gitanos metieron al hombre-víbora en su jaula y la llevaron al interior de la tienda. El gitano que dirigía el espectáculo anunció:

—Y ahora, señoras y señores, vamos a mostrar la prueba terrible de la mujer que tendrá que ser decapitada todas las noches a esta hora durante ciento cincuenta años, como castigo por haber visto lo que no debía.

José Arcadio y la muchacha no presenciaron la decapitación. Fueron a la carpa de ella, donde se besaron con una ansiedad desesperada mientras se iban quitando la ropa. La gitana se deshizo de sus corpiños superpuestos, de sus numerosos pollerines de encaje almidonado, de su inútil corset alambrado, de su carga de abalorios, y quedó prácticamente convertida en nada. Era una ranita lánguida, de senos incipientes y piernas tan delgadas que no le ganaban en diámetro a los brazos de José Arcadio, pero tenía una decisión y un calor que compensaban su fragilidad. Sin embargo, José Arcadio no podía responderle porque estaban en una especie de carpa pública, por donde los gitanos pasaban con sus cosas de circo y arreglaban sus asuntos, y hasta se demoraban junto a la cama a echar una partida de dados. La lámpara colgada en la vara central iluminaba todo el ámbito. En una pausa de las caricias, José Arcadio se estiró desnudo en la cama, sin saber qué hacer, mientras la muchacha trataba de alentarlo. Una gitana de carnes espléndidas entró poco después acompañada de un hombre que no hacía parte de la farándula, pero que tampoco era de la aldea, y ambos empezaron a desvestirse frente a la cama. Sin proponérselo, la mujer miró a José Arcadio y examinó con una especie de fervor patético su magnífico animal en reposo.

—Muchacho —exclamó—, que Dios te la conserve.

La compañera de José Arcadio les pidió que los dejaran tranquilos, y la pareja se acostó en el suelo, muy cerca de la cama. La pasión de los otros despertó la fiebre de José Arcadio. Al primer contacto, los huesos de la muchacha parecieron desarticularse con un crujido desordenado como el de un fichero de dominó, y su piel se deshizo en un sudor pálido y sus ojos se llenaron de lágrimas y todo su cuerpo exhaló un lamento lúgubre y un vago olor de lodo. Pero soportó el impacto con una firmeza de carácter y una valentía admirables. José Arcadio se sintió entonces levantado en vilo hacia un estado de inspiración seráfica, donde su corazón se desbarató en un manantial de obscenidades tiernas que le entraban a la muchacha por los oídos y le salían por la boca traducidas a su idioma. Era jueves. La noche del sábado José Arcadio se amarró un trapo rojo en la cabeza y se fue con los gitanos.

Cuando Úrsula descubrió su ausencia, lo buscó por toda la aldea. En el desmantelado campamento de los gitanos no había más que un reguero de desperdicios entre las cenizas todavía humeantes de los fogones apagados. Alguien que andaba por ahí buscando abalorios entre la basura le dijo a Úrsula que la noche anterior había visto a su hijo en el tumulto de la farándula, empujando una carretilla con la jaula del hombre-víbora. «¡Se metió de gitano!», le gritó ella a su marido, quien no había dado la menor señal de alarma ante la desaparición.

—Ojalá fuera cierto —dijo José Arcadio Buendía, machacando en el mortero la materia mil veces machacada y recalentada y vuelta a machacar—. Así aprenderá a ser hombre.

Úrsula preguntó por dónde se habían ido los gitanos. Siguió preguntando en el camino que le indicaron, y creyendo que todavía tenía tiempo de alcanzarlos, siguió alejándose de la aldea, hasta que tuvo conciencia de estar tan lejos que ya no pensó en regresar. José Arcadio Buendía no descubrió la falta de su mujer sino a las ocho de la noche, cuando dejó la materia recalentándose en una cama de estiércol, y fue a ver qué le pasaba a la pequeña Amaranta que estaba ronca de llorar. En pocas horas reunió un grupo de hombres bien equipados, puso a Amaranta en manos de una mujer que se ofreció para amamantarla, y se perdió por senderos invisibles en pos de Úrsula. Aureliano los acompañó. Unos pescadores indígenas, cuya lengua desconocían, les indicaron por señas al amanecer que no habían visto pasar a nadie. Al cabo de tres días de búsqueda inútil, regresaron a la aldea.

Durante varias semanas, José Arcadio Buendía se dejó vencer por la consternación. Se ocupaba como una madre de la pequeña Amaranta. La bañaba y cambiaba de ropa, la llevaba a ser amamantada cuatro veces al día y hasta le cantaba en la noche las canciones que Úrsula nunca supo cantar. En cierta ocasión Pilar Ternera se ofreció para hacer los oficios de la casa mientras regresaba Úrsula. Aureliano, cuya misteriosa intuición se había sensibilizado en la desdicha, experimentó un fulgor de clarividencia al verla entrar. Entonces supo que de algún modo inexplicable ella tenía la culpa de la fuga de su hermano y la consiguiente desaparición de su madre, y la acosó de tal modo, con una callada e implacable hostilidad, que la mujer no volvió a la casa.

El tiempo puso las cosas en su puesto. José Arcadio Buendía y su hijo no supieron en qué momento estaban otra vez en el laboratorio sacudiendo el polvo, prendiendo fuego al atanor, entregados una vez más a la paciente manipulación de la materia dormida desde hacía varios meses en su cama de estiércol. Hasta Amaranta, acostada en una canastilla de mimbre, observaba con curiosidad la absorbente labor de su padre y su hermano en el cuarto enrarecido por los vapores del mercurio. En cierta ocasión, meses después de la partida de Úrsula, empezaron a suceder cosas extrañas. Un frasco vacío que durante mucho tiempo estuvo olvidado en un armario se hizo tan pesado que fue imposible moverlo. Una cazuela de agua colocada en la mesa de trabajo hirvió sin fuego durante media hora hasta evaporarse por completo. José Arcadio Buendía y su hijo observaban aquellos fenómenos con asustado alborozo, sin lograr explicárselos, pero interpretándolos como anuncios de la materia. Un día la canastilla de Amaranta empezó a moverse con un impulso propio y dio una vuelta completa en el cuarto, ante la consternación de Aureliano, que se apresuró a detenerla. Pero su padre no se alteró. Puso la canastilla en su puesto y la amarro a la pata de una mesa, convencido de que el acontecimiento esperado era inminente. Fue en esa ocasión cuando Aureliano le oyó decir:

—Si no temes a Dios, témele a los metales.

De pronto, casi cinco meses después de su desaparición, volvió Úrsula. Llegó exaltada, rejuvenecida, con ropas nuevas de un estilo desconocido en la aldea. José Arcadio Buendía apenas si pudo resistir el impacto. «¡Era esto!», gritaba. «Yo sabía que iba a ocurrir.» Y lo creía de veras, porque en sus prolongados encierros, mientras manipulaba la materia, rogaba en el fondo de su corazón que el prodigio esperado no fuera el hallazgo de la piedra filosofal, ni la liberación del soplo que hace vivir los metales, ni la facultad de convertir en oro las bisagras y cerraduras de la casa, sino lo que ahora había ocurrido: el regreso de Úrsula. Pero ella no compartía su alborozo. Le dio un beso convencional, como si no hubiera estado ausente más de una hora, y le dijo:

—Asómate a la puerta.

José Arcadio Buendía tardó mucho tiempo para restablecerse de la perplejidad cuando salió a la calle y vio la muchedumbre. No eran gitanos. Eran hombres y mujeres como ellos, de cabellos lacios y piel parda, que hablaban su misma lengua y se lamentaban de los mismos dolores. Traían mulas cargadas de cosas de comer, carretas de bueyes con muebles y utensilios domésticos, puros y simples accesorios terrestres puestos en venta sin aspavientos por los mercachifles de la realidad cotidiana. Venían del otro lado de la ciénaga, a sólo dos días de viaje, donde había pueblos que recibían el correo todos los meses y conocían las máquinas del bienestar. Úrsula no había alcanzado a los gitanos, pero encontró la ruta que su marido no pudo descubrir en su frustrada búsqueda de los grandes inventos.

El hijo de Pilar Ternera fue llevado a casa de sus abuelos a las dos semanas de nacido. Úrsula lo admitió de mala gana, vencida una vez más por la terquedad de su marido que no pudo tolerar la idea de que un retoño de su sangre quedara navegando a la deriva, pero impuso la condición de que se ocultara al niño su verdadera identidad. Aunque recibió el nombre de José Arcadio, terminaron por llamarlo simplemente Arcadio para evitar confusiones. Había por aquella época tanta actividad en el pueblo y tantos trajines en la casa, que el cuidado de los niños quedó relegado a un nivel secundario. Se los encomendaron a Visitación, una india guajira que llegó al pueblo con un hermano, huyendo de una peste de insomnio que flagelaba a su tribu desde hacía varios años. Ambos eran tan dóciles y serviciales que Úrsula se hizo cargo de ellos para que la ayudaran en los oficios domésticos. Fue así como Arcadio y Amaranta hablaron la lengua guajira antes que el castellano, y aprendieron a tomar caldo de lagartijas y a comer huevos de arañas sin que Úrsula se diera cuenta, porque andaba demasiado ocupada en un prometedor negocio de animalitos de caramelo. Macondo estaba transformado. Las gentes que llegaron con Úrsula divulgaron la buena calidad de su suelo y su posición privilegiada con respecto a la ciénaga, de modo que la escueta aldea de otro tiempo se convirtió muy pronto en un pueblo activo, con tiendas y talleres de artesanía, y una ruta de comercio permanente por donde llegaron los primeros árabes de pantuflas y argollas en las orejas, cambiando collares de vidrio por guacamayas. José Arcadio Buendía no tuvo un instante de reposo. Fascinado por una realidad inmediata que entonces le resultó más fantástica que el vasto universo de su imaginación, perdió todo interés por el laboratorio de alquimia, puso a descansar la materia extenuada por largos meses de manipulación, y volvió a ser el hombre emprendedor de los primeros tiempos que decidía el trazado de las calles y la posición de las nuevas casas, de manera que nadie disfrutara de privilegios que no tuvieran todos. Adquirió tanta autoridad entre los recién llegados que no se echaron cimientos ni se pararon cercas sin consultárselo, y se determinó que fuera él quien dirigiera la repartición de la tierra. Cuando volvieron los gitanos saltimbanquis, ahora con su feria ambulante transformada en un gigantesco establecimiento de juegos de suerte y azar, fueron recibidos con alborozo porque se pensó que José Arcadio regresaba con ellos. Pero José Arcadio no volvió, ni llevaron al hombrevíbora que según pensaba Úrsula era el único que podría darles razón de su hijo, así que no se les permitió a los gitanos instalarse en el pueblo ni volver a pisarlo en el futuro, porque se los consideró como mensajeros de la concupiscencia y la perversión. José Arcadio Buendía, sin embargo, fue explícito en el sentido de que la antigua tribu de Melquíades, que tanto contribuyó al engrandecimiento de la aldea con su milenaria sabiduría y sus fabulosos inventos, encontraría siempre las puertas abiertas. Pero la tribu de Melquíades, según contaron los trotamundos, había sido borrada de la faz de la tierra por haber sobrepasado los límites del conocimiento humano.

Emancipado al menos por el momento de las torturas de la fantasía, José Arcadio Buendía impuso en poco tiempo un estado de orden y trabajo, dentro del cual sólo se permitió una licencia: la liberación de los pájaros que desde la época de la fundación alegraban el tiempo con sus flautas, y la instalación en su lugar de relojes musicales en todas las casas. Eran unos preciosos relojes de madera labrada que los árabes cambiaban por guacamayas, y que José Arcadio Buendía sincronizó con tanta precisión, que cada media hora el pueblo se alegraba con los acordes progresivos de una misma pieza, hasta alcanzar la culminación de un mediodía exacto y unánime con el valse completo. Fue también José Arcadio Buendía quien decidió por esos años que en las calles del pueblo se sembraran almendros en vez de acacias, y quien descubrió sin revelarlos nunca los métodos para hacerlos eternos. Muchos años después, cuando Macondo fue un campamento de casas de madera y techos de zinc, todavía perduraban en las calles más antiguas los almendros rotos y polvorientos, aunque nadie sabía entonces quién los había sembrado. Mientras su padre ponía en orden el pueblo y su madre consolidaba el patrimonio doméstico con su maravillosa industria de gallitos y peces azucarados que dos veces al día salían de la casa ensartados en palos de balso, Aureliano vivía horas interminables en el laboratorio abandonado, aprendiendo por pura investigación el arte de la platería. Se había estirado tanto, que en poco tiempo dejó de servirle la ropa abandonada por su hermano y empezó a usar la de su padre, pero fue necesario que Visitación les cosiera alforzas a las camisas y sisas a los pantalones, porque Aureliano no había sacado la corpulencia de los otros. La adolescencia le había quitado la dulzura de la voz y lo había vuelto silencioso y definitivamente solitario, pero en cambio le había restituido la expresión intensa que tuvo en los ojos al nacer. Estaba tan concentrado en sus experimentos de platería que apenas si abandonaba el laboratorio para comer. Preocupado por su ensimismamiento, José Arcadio Buendía le dio llaves de la casa y un poco de dinero, pensando que tal vez le hiciera falta una mujer. Pero Aureliano gastó el dinero en ácido muriático para preparar agua regia y embelleció las llaves con un baño de oro. Sus exageraciones eran apenas comparables a las de Arcadio y Amaranta, que ya habían empezado a mudar los dientes y todavía andaban agarrados todo el día a las mantas de los indios, tercos en su decisión de no hablar el castellano, sino la lengua guajira. «No tienes de qué quejarte» le decía Úrsula a su marido. «Los hijos heredan las locuras de sus padres.» Y mientras se lamentaba de su mala suerte, convencida de que las extravagancias de sus hijos eran algo tan espantoso como una cola de cerdo, Aureliano fijó en ella una mirada que la envolvió en un ámbito de incertidumbre.

—Alguien va a venir —le dijo.

Úrsula, como siempre que él expresaba un pronóstico, trató de desalentarlo con su lógica casera. Era normal que alguien llegara. Decenas de forasteros pasaban a diario por Macondo sin suscitar inquietudes ni anticipar anuncios secretos. Sin embargo, por encima de toda lógica, Aureliano estaba seguro de su presagio.

—No sé quién será —insistió—, pero el que sea ya viene en camino.

El domingo, en efecto, llegó Rebeca. No tenía más de once años. Había hecho el penoso viaje desde Manaure con unos traficantes de pieles que recibieron el encargo de entregarla junto con una carta en la casa de José Arcadio Buendía, pero que no pudieron explicar con precisión quién era la persona que les había pedido el favor. Todo su equipaje estaba compuesto por el baulito de la ropa, un pequeño mecedor de madera con florecitas de colores pintadas a mano y un talego de lona que hacía un permanente ruido de cloc cloc cloc, donde llevaba los huesos de sus padres. La carta dirigida a José Arcadio Buendía estaba escrita en términos muy cariñosos por alguien que lo seguía queriendo mucho a pesar del tiempo y la distancia y que se sentía obligado por un elemental sentido humanitario a hacer la caridad de mandarle esa pobre huerfanita desamparada, que era prima de Úrsula en segundo grado y por consiguiente parienta también de José Arcadio Buendía, aunque en grado más lejano, porque era hija de ese inolvidable amigo que fue Nicanor Ulloa y su muy digna esposa Rebeca Montiel, a quienes Dios tuviera en su santo reino, cuyos restos adjuntaba a la presente para que les dieran cristiana sepultura. Tanto los nombres mencionados como la firma de la carta eran perfectamente legibles, pero ni José Arcadio Buendía ni Úrsula recordaban haber tenido parientes con esos nombres ni conocían a nadie que se llamara como el remitente y mucho menos en la remota población de

Manaure. A través de la niña fue imposible obtener ninguna información complementaria. Desde el momento en que llegó se sentó a chuparse el dedo en el mecedor y a observar a todos con sus grandes ojos espantados, sin que diera señal alguna de entender lo que le preguntaban. Llevaba un traje de diagonal teñido de negro, gastado por el uso, y unos desconchados botines de charol. Tenía el cabello sostenido detrás de las orejas con moños de cintas negras. Usaba un escapulario con las imágenes borradas por el sudor y en la muñeca derecha un colmillo de animal carnívoro montado en un soporte de cobre como amuleto contra el mal de ojo. Su piel verde, su vientre redondo y tenso como un tambor, revelaban una mala salud y un hambre más viejas que ella misma, pero cuando le dieron de comer se quedó con el plato en las piernas sin probarlo. Se llegó inclusive a creer que era sordomuda, hasta que los indios le preguntaron en su lengua si quería un poco de agua y ella movió los ojos como si los hubiera reconocido y dijo que sí con la cabeza.

Se quedaron con ella porque no había más remedio. Decidieron llamarla Rebeca, que de acuerdo con la carta era el nombre de su madre, porque Aureliano tuvo la paciencia de leer frente a ella todo el santoral y no logró que reaccionara con ningún nombre. Como en aquel tiempo no había cementerio en Macondo, pues hasta entonces no había muerto nadie, conservaron el talego con los huesos en espera de que hubiera un lugar digno para sepultarlos, y durante mucho tiempo estorbaron por todas partes y se les encontraba donde menos se suponía, siempre con su cloqueante cacareo de gallina clueca. Pasó mucho tiempo antes de que Rebeca se incorporara a la vida familiar. Se sentaba en el mecedorcito a chuparse el dedo en el rincón más apartado de la casa. Nada le llamaba la atención, salvo la música de los relojes, que cada media hora buscaba con ojos asustados, como si esperara encontrarla en algún lugar del aire. No lograron que comiera en varios días. Nadie entendía cómo no se había muerto de hambre, hasta que los indígenas, que se daban cuenta de todo porque recorrían la casa sin cesar con sus pies sigilosos, descubrieron que a Rebeca sólo le gustaba comer la tierra húmeda del patio y las tortas de cal que arrancaba de las paredes con las uñas. Era evidente que sus padres, o quienquiera que la hubiese criado, la habían reprendido por ese hábito, pues lo practicaba a escondidas y con conciencia de culpa, procurando trasponer las raciones para comerlas cuando nadie la viera. Desde entonces la sometieron a una vigilancia implacable. Echaban hiel de vaca en el patio y untaban ají picante en las paredes, creyendo derrotar con esos métodos su vicio pernicioso, pero ella dio tales muestras de astucia e ingenio para procurarse la tierra, que Úrsula se vio forzada a emplear recursos más drásticos. Ponía jugo de naranja con ruibarbo en una cazuela que dejaba al sereno toda la noche, y le daba la pócima al día siguiente en ayunas. Aunque nadie le había dicho que aquél era el remedio específico para el vicio de comer tierra, pensaba que cualquier sustancia amarga en el estómago vacío tenía que hacer reaccionar al hígado. Rebeca era tan rebelde y tan fuerte a pesar de su raquitismo, que tenían que barbearla como a un becerro para que tragara la medicina, y apenas si podían reprimir sus pataletas y soportar los enrevesados jeroglíficos que ella alternaba con mordiscos y escupitajos, y que según decían los escandalizados indígenas eran las obscenidades más gruesas que se podían concebir en su idioma. Cuando Úrsula lo supo, complementó el tratamiento con correazos. No se estableció nunca si lo que surtió efecto fue el ruibarbo o las tollinas, o las dos cosas combinadas, pero la verdad es que en pocas semanas Rebeca empezó a dar muestras de restablecimiento. Participó en los juegos de Arcadio y Amaranta, que la recibieron como una hermana mayor, y comió con apetito sirviéndose bien de los cubiertos. Pronto se reveló que hablaba el castellano con tanta fluidez como la lengua de los indios, que tenía una habilidad notable para los oficios manuales y que cantaba el valse de los relojes con una letra muy graciosa que ella misma había inventado. No tardaron en considerarla como un miembro más de la familia. Era con Úrsula más afectuosa que nunca lo fueron sus propios hijos, y llamaba hermanitos a Amaranta y a Arcadio, y tío a Aureliano y abuelito a José Arcadio Buendía. De modo que terminó por merecer tanto como los otros el nombre de Rebeca Buendía, el único que tuvo siempre y que llevó con dignidad hasta la muerte.

Una noche, por la época en que Rebeca se curó del vicio de comer tierra y fue llevada a dormir en el cuarto de los otros niños, la india que dormía con ellos despertó por casualidad y oyó un extraño ruido intermitente en el rincón. Se incorporó alarmada, creyendo que había entrado un animal en el cuarto, y entonces vio a Rebeca en el mecedor, chupándose el dedo y con los ojos alumbrados como los de un gato en la oscuridad. Pasmada de terror, atribulada por la fatalidad de su destino, Visitación reconoció en esos ojos los síntomas de la enfermedad cuya amenaza los había obligado, a ella y a su hermano, a desterrarse para siempre de un reino milenario en el cual eran príncipes. Era la peste del insomnio.

Cataure, el indio, no amaneció en la casa. Su hermana se quedó, porque su corazón fatalista le indicaba que la dolencia letal había de perseguirla de todos modos hasta el último rincón de la tierra. Nadie entendió en la casa la alarma de Visitación. «Si no volvemos a dormir, mejor», decía José Arcadio Buendía, de buen humor. «Así nos rendirá más la vida.» Pero la india les explicó que lo más temible de la enfermedad del insomnio no era la imposibilidad de dormir, pues el cuerpo no sentía cansancio alguno, sino su inexorable evolución hacia una manifestación más crítica: el olvido. Quería decir que cuando el enfermo se acostumbraba a su estado de vigilia, empezaban a borrarse de su memoria los recuerdos de la infancia, luego el nombre y la noción de las cosas, y por último la identidad de las personas y aun la conciencia del propio ser, hasta hundirse en una especie de idiotez sin pasado. José Arcadio Buendía, muerto de risa, consideró que se trataba de una de tantas dolencias inventadas por la superstición de los indígenas. Pero Úrsula, por si acaso, tomó la precaución de separar a Rebeca de los otros niños.

Al cabo de varias semanas, cuando el terror de Visitación parecía aplacado, José Arcadio Buendía se encontró una noche dando vueltas en la cama sin poder dormir. Úrsula, que también había despertado, le preguntó qué le pasaba, y él le contestó: «Estoy pensando otra vez en Prudencio Aguilar.» No durmieron un minuto, pero al día siguiente se sentían tan descansados que se olvidaron de la mala noche. Aureliano comentó asombrado a la hora del almuerzo que se sentía muy bien a pesar de que había pasado toda la noche en el laboratorio dorando un prendedor que pensaba regalarle a Úrsula el día de su cumpleaños. No se alarmaron hasta el tercer día, cuando a la hora de acostarse se sintieron sin sueño, y cayeron en la cuenta de que llevaban más de cincuenta horas sin dormir.

—Los niños también están despiertos —dijo la india con su convicción fatalista—. Una vez que entra en la casa, nadie escapa a la peste.

Habían contraído, en efecto, la enfermedad del insomnio. Úrsula, que había aprendido de su madre el valor medicinal de las plantas, preparó e hizo beber a todos un brebaje de acónito, pero no consiguieron dormir, sino que estuvieron todo el día soñando despiertos. En ese estado de alucinada lucidez no sólo veían las imágenes de sus propios sueños, sino que los unos veían las imágenes soñadas por los otros. Era como si la casa se hubiera llenado de visitantes. Sentada en su mecedor en un rincón de la cocina, Rebeca soñó que un hombre muy parecido a ella, vestido de lino blanco y con el cuello de la camisa cerrado por un botón de oro, le llevaba un ramo de rosas. Lo acompañaba una mujer de manos delicadas que separó una rosa y se la puso a la niña en el pelo. Úrsula comprendió que el hombre y la mujer eran los padres de Rebeca, pero aunque hizo un grande esfuerzo por reconocerlos, confirmó su certidumbre de que nunca los había visto. Mientras tanto, por un descuido que José Arcadio Buendía no se perdonó jamás, los animalitos de caramelo fabricados en la casa seguían siendo vendidos en el pueblo. Niños y adultos chupaban encantados los deliciosos gallitos verdes del insomnio, los exquisitos peces rosados del insomnio y los tiernos caballitos amarillos del insomnio, de modo que el alba del lunes sorprendió despierto a todo el pueblo. Al principio nadie se alarmó. Al contrario, se alegraron de no dormir, porque entonces había tanto que hacer en Macondo que el tiempo apenas alcanzaba. Trabajaron tanto, que pronto no tuvieron nada más que hacer, y se encontraron a las tres de la madrugada con los brazos cruzados, contando el número de notas que tenía el valse de los relojes. Los que querían dormir, no por cansancio sino por nostalgia de los sueños, recurrieron a toda clase de métodos agotadores. Se reunían a conversar sin tregua, a repetirse durante horas y horas los mismos chistes, a complicar hasta los límites de la exasperación el cuento del gallo capón, que era un juego infinito en que el narrador preguntaba si querían que les contara el cuento del gallo capón, y cuando contestaban que sí, el narrador decía que no les había pedido que dijeran que sí, sino que si querían que les contara el cuento del gallo capón, y cuando contestaban que no, el narrador decía que no les había pedido que dijeran que no, sino que si querían que les contara el cuento del gallo capón, y cuando se quedaban callados el narrador decía que no les había pedido que se quedaran callados, sino que si querían que les contara el cuento del gallo capón, y nadie podía irse, porque el narrador decía que no les había pedido que se fueran, sino que si querían que les contara el cuento del gallo capón, y así sucesivamente, en un círculo vicioso que se prolongaba por noches enteras.

Cuando José Arcadio Buendía se dio cuenta de que la peste había invadido el pueblo, reunió a los jefes de familia para explicarles lo que sabía sobre la enfermedad del insomnio, y se acordaron medidas para impedir que el flagelo se propagara a otras poblaciones de la ciénaga. Fue así como se quitaron a los chivos las campanitas que los árabes cambiaban por guacamayas, y se pusieron a la entrada del pueblo a disposición de quienes desatendían los consejos y súplicas de los centinelas e insistían en visitar la población. Todos los forasteros que por aquel tiempo recorrían las calles de Macondo tenían que hacer sonar su campanita para que los enfermos supieran que estaba sano. No se les permitía comer ni beber nada durante su estancia, pues no había duda de que la enfermedad sólo se transmitía por la boca, y todas las cosas de comer y de beber estaban contaminadas de insomnio. En esa forma se mantuvo la peste circunscrita al perímetro de la población. Tan eficaz fue la cuarentena, que llegó el día en que la situación de emergencia se tuvo por cosa natural, y se organizó la vida de tal modo que el trabajo recobró su ritmo y nadie volvió a preocuparse por la inútil costumbre de dormir.

Fue Aureliano quien concibió la fórmula que había de defenderlos durante varios meses de las evasiones de la memoria. La descubrió por casualidad. Insomne experto, por haber sido uno de los primeros, había aprendido a la perfección el arte de la platería. Un día estaba buscando el pequeño yunque que utilizaba para laminar los metales, y no recordó su nombre. Su padre se lo dijo: «tas». Aureliano escribió el nombre en un papel que pegó con goma en la base del yunquecito: *tas*. Así estuvo seguro de no olvidarlo en el futuro. No se le ocurrió que fuera aquella la primera manifestación del olvido, porque el objeto tenía un nombre difícil de recordar. Pero pocos días después descubrió que tenía dificultades para recordar casi todas las cosas del laboratorio. Entonces las marcó con el nombre respectivo, de modo que le bastaba con leer la inscripción para identificarlas. Cuando su padre le comunicó su alarma por haber olvidado hasta los hechos más impresionantes de su niñez, Aureliano le explicó su método, y José Arcadio Buendía lo puso en práctica en toda la casa y más tarde lo impuso a todo el pueblo. Con un hisopo entintado marcó cada cosa con su nombre: *mesa, silla, reloj, puerta, pared, cama, cacerola*. Fue al corral y marcó los animales y las plantas: *vaca, chivo, puerco, gallina, yuca, malanga, guineo*. Poco a poco, estudiando las infinitas posibilidades del olvido, se dio cuenta de que podía llegar un día en que se reconocieran las cosas por sus inscripciones, pero no se recordara su utilidad. Entonces fue más explícito. El letrero que colgó en la cerviz de la vaca era una muestra ejemplar de la forma en que los habitantes de Macondo estaban dispuestos a luchar contra el olvido: *Esta es la vaca, hay que ordeñarla todas las mañanas para que produzca leche y a la leche hay que hervirla para mezclarla con el café y hacer café con leche*. Así continuaron viviendo en una realidad escurridiza, momentáneamente capturada por las palabras, pero que había de fugarse sin remedio cuando olvidaran los valores de la letra escrita.

En la entrada del camino de la ciénaga se había puesto un anuncio que decía *Macondo* y otro más grande en la calle central que decía *Dios existe*. En todas las casas se habían escrito claves para memorizar los objetos y los sentimientos. Pero el sistema exigía tanta vigilancia y tanta fortaleza moral, que muchos sucumbieron al hechizo de una realidad imaginaria, inventada por ellos mismos, que les resultaba menos práctica pero más reconfortante. Pilar Ternera fue quien más contribuyó a popularizar esa mistificación, cuando concibió el artificio de leer el pasado en las barajas como antes había leído el futuro. Mediante ese recurso, los insomnes empezaron a vivir en un mundo construido por las alternativas inciertas de los naipes, donde el padre se recordaba apenas como el hombre moreno que había llegado a principios de abril y la madre se recordaba apenas como la mujer trigueña que usaba un anillo de oro en la mano izquierda, y donde una fecha de nacimiento quedaba reducida al último martes en que cantó la alondra en el laurel. Derrotado por aquellas prácticas de consolación, José Arcadio Buendía decidió entonces construir la máquina de la memoria que una vez había deseado para acordarse de los maravillosos inventos de los gitanos. El artefacto se fundaba en la posibilidad de repasar todas las mañanas, y desde el principio hasta el fin, la totalidad de los conocimientos adquiridos en la vida. Lo imaginaba como un diccionario giratorio que un individuo situado en el eje pudiera operar mediante una manivela, de modo que en pocas horas pasaran frente a sus ojos las nociones más necesarias para vivir. Había logrado escribir cerca de catorce mil fichas, cuando apareció por el camino de la ciénaga un anciano estrafalario con la campanita triste de los durmientes, cargando una maleta ventruda amarrada con cuerdas y un carrito cubierto de trapos negros. Fue directamente a la casa de José Arcadio Buendía.

Visitación no lo conoció al abrirle la puerta, y pensó que llevaba el propósito de vender algo, ignorante de que nada podía venderse en un pueblo que se hundía sin remedio en el tremedal del olvido. Era un hombre decrépito. Aunque su voz estaba también cuarteada por la incertidumbre y sus manos parecían dudar de la existencia de las cosas, era evidente que venía del mundo donde todavía los hombres podían dormir y recordar. José Arcadio Buendía lo encontró sentado en la sala, abanicándose con un remendado sombrero negro, mientras leía con atención compasiva los letreros pegados en las paredes. Lo saludó con amplias muestras de afecto, temiendo haberlo conocido en otro tiempo y ahora no recordarlo. Pero el visitante advirtió su falsedad. Se sintió olvidado, no con el olvido remediable del corazón, sino con otro olvido más cruel e irrevocable que él conocía muy bien, porque era el olvido de la muerte. Entonces comprendió. Abrió la maleta atiborrada de objetos indescifrables, y de entre ellos sacó un maletín con muchos frascos. Le dio a beber a José Arcadio Buendía una sustancia de color apacible, y la luz se hizo en su memoria. Los ojos se le humedecieron de llanto, antes de verse a sí mismo en una sala absurda donde los objetos estaban marcados, y antes de avergonzarse de las solemnes tonterías escritas en las paredes, y aun antes de reconocer al recién llegado en un deslumbrante resplandor de alegría. Era Melquíades.

Mientras Macondo celebraba la reconquista de los recuerdos, José Arcadio Buendía y Melquíades le sacudieron el polvo a su vieja amistad. El gitano iba dispuesto a quedarse en el pueblo. Había estado en la muerte, en efecto, pero había regresado porque no pudo soportar la soledad. Repudiado por su tribu, desprovisto de toda facultad sobrenatural como castigo por su fidelidad a la vida, decidió refugiarse en aquel rincón del mundo todavía no descubierto por la muerte, dedicado a la explotación de un laboratorio de daguerrotipia. José Arcadio Buendía no había oído hablar nunca de ese invento. Pero cuando se vio a sí mismo y a toda su familia plasmados en una edad eterna sobre una lámina de metal tornasol, se quedó mudo de estupor. De esa época databa el oxidado daguerrotipo en el que apareció José Arcadio Buendía con el pelo erizado y ceniciento, el acartonado cuello de la camisa prendido con un botón de cobre y una expresión de solemnidad asombrada, y que Úrsula describía muerta de risa como «un general asustado». En verdad, José Arcadio Buendía estaba asustado la diáfana mañana de diciembre en que le hicieron el daguerrotipo, porque pensaba que la gente se iba gastando poco a poco a medida que su imagen pasaba a las placas metálicas. Por una curiosa inversión de la costumbre, fue Úrsula quien le sacó aquella idea de la cabeza, como fue también ella quien olvidó sus antiguos resquemores y decidió que Melquíades se quedara viviendo en la casa, aunque nunca permitió que le hicieran un daguerrotipo porque (según sus propias palabras textuales) no quería quedar para burla de sus nietos. Aquella mañana vistió a los niños con sus ropas mejores, les empolvó la cara y les dio una cucharada de jarabe de tuétano a cada uno para que pudieran permanecer absolutamente inmóviles durante casi dos minutos frente a la aparatosa cámara de Melquíades. En el daguerrotipo familiar, el único que existió jamás, Aureliano apareció vestido de terciopelo negro, entre Amaranta y Rebeca. Tenía la misma languidez y la misma mirada clarividente que había de tener años más tarde frente al pelotón de fusilamiento Pero aún no había sentido la premonición de su destino. Era un orfebre experto, estimado en toda la ciénaga por el preciosismo de su trabajo. En el taller que compartía con el disparatado laboratorio de Melquíades, apenas si se le oía respirar. Parecía refugiado en otro tiempo, mientras su padre y el gitano interpretaban a gritos las predicciones de Nostradamus, entre un estrépito de frascos y cubetas, y el desastre de los ácidos derramados y el bromuro de plata perdido por los codazos y traspiés que daban a cada instante. Aquella consagración al trabajo, el buen juicio con que administraba sus intereses, le habían permitido a Aureliano ganar en poco tiempo más dinero que Úrsula con su deliciosa fauna de caramelo, pero todo el mundo se extrañaba de que fuera ya un hombre hecho y derecho y no se le hubiera conocido mujer. En realidad no la había tenido.

Meses después volvió Francisco el Hombre, un anciano trotamundos de casi 200 años que pasaba con frecuencia por Macondo divulgando las canciones compuestas por él mismo. En ellas, Francisco el Hombre relataba con detalles minuciosos las noticias ocurridas en los pueblos de su itinerario, desde Manaure hasta los confines de la ciénaga, de modo que si alguien tenía un recado que mandar o un acontecimiento que divulgar, le pagaba dos centavos para que lo incluyera en su repertorio. Fue así como se enteró Úrsula de la muerte de su madre, por pura casualidad, una noche que escuchaba las canciones con la esperanza de que dijeran algo de su hijo José Arcadio. Francisco el Hombre, así llamado porque derrotó al diablo en un duelo de improvisación de cantos, y cuyo verdadero nombre no conoció nadie, desapareció de Macondo durante la peste del insomnio y una noche reapareció sin ningún anuncio en la tienda de Catarino. Todo el pueblo fue a escucharlo para saber qué había pasado en el mundo. En esa ocasión llegaron con él una mujer tan gorda que cuatro indios tenían que llevarla cargada en un mecedor, y una mulata adolescente de aspecto desamparado que la protegía del sol con un paraguas. Aureliano fue esa noche a la tienda de Catarino. Encontró a Francisco el Hombre, como un camaleón monolítico, sentado en medio de un círculo de curiosos. Cantaba las noticias con su vieja voz descordada, acompañándose con el mismo acordeón arcaico que le regaló Sir Walter Raleigh en la Guayana, mientras llevaba el compás con sus grandes pies caminadores agrietados por el salitre. Frente a una puerta del fondo por donde entraban y salían algunos hombres, estaba sentada y se abanicaba en silencio la matrona del mecedor. Catarino, con una rosa de fieltro en la oreja, vendía a la concurrencia tazones de guarapo fermentado, y aprovechaba la ocasión para acercarse a los hombres y ponerles la mano donde no debía. Hacia la medianoche el calor era insoportable. Aureliano escuchó las noticias hasta el final sin encontrar ninguna que le interesara a su familia. Se disponía a regresar a casa cuando la matrona le hizo una señal con la mano.

—Entra tú también —le dijo—. Sólo cuesta veinte centavos.

Aureliano echó una moneda en la alcancía que la matrona tenía en las piernas y entró en el cuarto sin saber para qué. La mulata adolescente, con sus teticas de perra, estaba desnuda en la cama. Antes de Aureliano, esa noche, sesenta y tres hombres habían pasado por el cuarto. De tanto ser usado, y amasado en sudores y suspiros, el aire de la habitación empezaba a convertirse en lodo. La muchacha quitó la sábana empapada y le pidió a Aureliano que la tuviera de un lado. Pesaba como un lienzo. La exprimieron, torciéndola por los extremos, hasta que recobró su peso natural. Voltearon la estera, y el sudor salía del otro lado. Aureliano ansiaba que aquella operación no terminara nunca. Conocía la mecánica teórica del amor, pero no podía tenerse en pie a causa del desaliento de sus rodillas, y aunque tenía la piel erizada y ardiente no podía resistir a la urgencia de expulsar el peso de las tripas. Cuando la muchacha acabó de arreglar la cama y le ordenó que se desvistiera, él le hizo una explicación atolondrada: «Me hicieron entrar. Me dijeron que echara veinte centavos en la alcancía y que no me demorara.» La muchacha comprendió su ofuscación. «Si echas otros veinte centavos a la salida, puedes demorarte un poco más», dijo suavemente. Aureliano se desvistió, atormentado por el pudor, sin poder quitarse la idea de que su desnudez no resistía la comparación con su hermano. A pesar de los esfuerzos de la muchacha, él se sintió cada vez más indiferente, y terriblemente solo. «Echaré otros veinte centavos», dijo con voz desolada. La muchacha se lo agradeció en silencio. Tenía la espalda en carne viva. Tenía el pellejo pegado a las costillas y la respiración alterada por un agotamiento insondable. Dos años antes, muy lejos de allí, se había quedado dormida sin apagar la vela y había despertado cercada por el fuego. La casa donde vivía con la abuela que la había criado quedó reducida a cenizas. Desde entonces la abuela la llevaba de pueblo en pueblo, acostándola por veinte centavos, para pagarse el valor de la casa incendiada. Según los cálculos de la muchacha, todavía le faltaban unos diez años de setenta hombres por noche, porque tenía que pagar además los gastos de viaje y alimentación de ambas y el sueldo de los indios que cargaban el mecedor. Cuando la matrona tocó la puerta por segunda vez, Aureliano salió del cuarto sin haber hecho nada, aturdido por el deseo de llorar. Esa noche no pudo dormir pensando en la muchacha, con una mezcla de deseo y conmiseración. Sentía una necesidad irresistible de amarla y protegerla. Al amanecer, extenuado por el insomnio y la fiebre, tomó la serena decisión de casarse con ella para liberarla del despotismo de la abuela y disfrutar todas las noches de la satisfacción que ella le daba a setenta hombres. Pero a las diez de la mañana, cuando llegó a la tienda de Catarino, la muchacha se había ido del pueblo.

El tiempo aplacó su propósito atolondrado, pero agravó su sentimiento de frustración. Se refugió en el trabajo. Se resignó a ser un hombre sin mujer toda la vida para ocultar la vergüenza de su inutilidad. Mientras tanto, Melquíades terminó de plasmar en sus placas todo lo que era plasmable en Macondo, y abandonó el laboratorio de daguerrotipia a los delirios de José Arcadio Buendía, quien había resuelto utilizarlo para obtener la prueba científica de la existencia de Dios. Mediante un complicado proceso de exposiciones superpuestas tomadas en distintos lugares de la casa, estaba seguro de hacer tarde o temprano el daguerrotipo de Dios, si existía, o poner término de una vez por todas a la suposición de su existencia. Melquíades profundizó en las interpretaciones de Nostradamus. Estaba hasta muy tarde, asfixiándose dentro de su descolorido chaleco de terciopelo, garrapateando papeles con sus minúsculas manos de gorrión, cuyas sortijas habían perdido la lumbre de otra época. Una noche creyó encontrar una predicción sobre el futuro de Macondo. Sería una ciudad luminosa, con grandes casas de vidrio, donde no quedaba ningún rastro de la estirpe de los Buendía. «Es una equivocación», tronó José Arcadio Buendía. «No serán casas de vidrio sino de hielo, como yo lo soñé, y siempre habrá un Buendía, por los siglos de los siglos.» En aquella casa extravagante, Úrsula pugnaba por preservar el sentido común, habiendo ensanchado el negocio de animalitos de caramelo con un horno que producía toda la noche canastos y canastos de pan y una prodigiosa variedad de pudines, merengues y bizcochuelos, que se esfumaban en pocas horas por los vericuetos de la ciénaga. Había llegado a una edad en que tenía derecho a descansar, pero era, sin embargo, cada vez mas activa. Tan ocupada estaba en sus prósperas empresas, que una tarde miró por distracción hacia el patio, mientras la india la ayudaba a endulzar la masa, y vio dos adolescentes desconocidas y hermosas bordando en bastidor a la luz del crepúsculo. Eran Rebeca y Amaranta. Apenas se habían quitado el luto de la abuela, que guardaron con inflexible rigor durante tres años, y la ropa de color parecía haberles dado un nuevo lugar en el mundo. Rebeca, al contrario de lo que pudo esperarse, era la más bella. Tenía un cutis diáfano, unos ojos grandes y reposados y unas manos mágicas que parecían elaborar con hilos invisibles la trama del bordado. Amaranta, la menor, era un poco sin gracia, pero tenía la distinción natural, el estiramiento interior de la abuela muerta. Junto a ellas, aunque ya revelaba el impulso físico de su padre, Arcadio parecía un niño. Se había dedicado a aprender el arte de la platería con Aureliano, quien además le había enseñado a leer y escribir. Úrsula se dio cuenta de pronto que la casa se había llenado de gente, que sus hijos estaban a punto de casarse y tener hijos, y que se verían obligados a dispersarse por falta de espacio. Entonces sacó el dinero acumulado en largos años de dura labor, adquirió compromisos con sus clientes, y emprendió la ampliación de la casa. Dispuso que se construyera una sala formal para las visitas, otra más cómoda y fresca para el uso diario, un comedor para una mesa de doce puestos donde se sentara la familia con todos sus invitados; nueve dormitorios con ventanas hacia el patio y un largo corredor protegido del resplandor del mediodía por un jardín de rosas, con un pasamanos para poner macetas de helechos y tiestos de begonias. Dispuso ensanchar la cocina para construir dos hornos, destruir el viejo granero donde Pilar Ternera le leyó el porvenir a José Arcadio, y construir otro dos veces más grande para que nunca faltaran los alimentos en la casa. Dispuso construir en el patio, a la sombra del castaño, un baño para las mujeres y otro para los hombres, y al fondo una caballeriza grande, un gallinero alambrado, un establo de ordeña y una pajarera abierta a los cuatro vientos para que se instalaran a su gusto los pájaros sin rumbo. Seguida por docenas de albañiles y carpinteros, como si hubiera contraído la fiebre alucinante de su esposo, Úrsula ordenaba la posición de la luz y la conducta del calor, y repartía el espacio sin el menor sentido de sus límites. La primitiva construcción de los fundadores se llenó de herramientas y materiales, de obreros agobiados por el sudor, que le pedían a todo el mundo el favor de no estorbar, sin pensar que eran ellos quie-

73

nes estorbaban, exasperados por el talego de huesos humanos que los perseguía por todas partes con su sordo cascabeleo. En aquella incomodidad, respirando cal viva y melaza de alquitrán, nadie entendió muy bien cómo fue surgiendo de las entrañas de la tierra no sólo la casa más grande que habría nunca en el pueblo, sino la más hospitalaria y fresca que hubo jamás en el ámbito de la ciénaga. José Arcadio Buendía, tratando de sorprender a la Divina Providencia en medio del cataclismo, fue quien menos lo entendió. La nueva casa estaba casi terminada cuando Úrsula lo sacó de su mundo quimérico para informarle que había orden de pintar la fachada de azul, y no de blanco como ellos querían. Le mostró la disposición oficial escrita en un papel. José Arcadio Buendía, sin comprender lo que decía su esposa, descifró la firma.

—¿Quién es este tipo? —preguntó.

—El corregidor —dijo Úrsula desconsolada—. Dicen que es una autoridad que mandó el gobierno.

Don Apolinar Moscote, el corregidor, había llegado a Macondo sin hacer ruido. Se bajó en el Hotel de Jacob —instalado por uno de los primeros árabes que llegaron haciendo cambalache de chucherías por guacamayas— y al día siguiente alquiló un cuartito con puerta hacia la calle, a dos cuadras de la casa de los Buendía. Puso una mesa y una silla que le compró a Jacob, clavó en la pared un escudo de la república que había traído consigo, y pintó en la puerta el letrero: *Corregidor*. Su primera disposición fue ordenar que todas las casas se pintaran de azul para celebrar el aniversario de la independencia nacional. José Arcadio Buendía, con la copia de la orden en la mano, lo encontró durmiendo la siesta en una hamaca que había colgado en el escueto despacho. «¿Usted escribió este papel?», le preguntó. Don Apolinar Moscote, un hombre maduro, tímido, de complexión sanguínea, contestó que sí. «¿Con qué derecho?», volvió a preguntar José Arcadio Buendía. Don Apolinar Moscote buscó un papel en la gaveta de la mesa y se lo mostró: «He sido nombrado corregidor de este pueblo.» José Arcadio Buendía ni siquiera miró el nombramiento.

—En este pueblo no mandamos con papeles —dijo sin perder la calma—. Y para que lo sepa de una vez, no necesitamos ningún corregidor porque aquí no hay nada que corregir.

Ante la impavidez de don Apolinar Moscote, siempre sin levantar la voz, hizo un pormenorizado recuento de cómo habían fundado la aldea, de cómo se habían repartido la tierra, abierto los caminos e introducido las mejoras que les había ido exigiendo la necesidad, sin haber molestado a gobierno alguno y sin que nadie los molestara. «Somos tan pacíficos que ni siquiera nos hemos muerto de muerte natural», dijo. «Ya ve que todavía no tenemos cementerio.» No se dolió de que el gobierno no los hubiera ayudado. Al contrario, se alegraba de que hasta entonces los hubiera dejado crecer en paz, y esperaba que así los siguiera dejando, porque ellos no habían fundado un pueblo para que el primer advenedizo les fuera a decir lo que debían hacer. Don Apolinar Moscote se había puesto un saco de dril, blanco como sus pantalones, sin perder en ningún momento la pureza de sus ademanes.

—De modo que si usted se quiere quedar aquí, como otro ciudadano común y corriente, sea muy bienvenido —concluyó José Arcadio Buendía—. Pero si viene a implantar el desorden obligando a la gente que pinte su casa de azul, puede agarrar sus corotos y largarse por donde vino. Porque mi casa ha de ser blanca como una paloma.

Don Apolinar Moscote se puso pálido. Dio un paso atrás y apretó las mandíbulas para decir con una cierta aflicción:

—Quiero advertirle que estoy armado.

José Arcadio Buendía no supo en qué momento se le subió a las manos la fuerza juvenil con que derribaba un caballo. Agarró a don Apolinar Moscote por la solapa y lo levantó a la altura de sus ojos.

—Esto lo hago —le dijo— porque prefiero cargarlo vivo y no tener que seguir cargándolo muerto por el resto de mi vida.

Así lo llevó por la mitad de la calle, suspendido por las solapas, hasta que lo puso sobre sus dos pies en el camino de la ciénaga. Una semana después estaba de regreso con seis soldados descalzos y harapientos, armados con escopetas, y una carreta de bueyes donde viajaban su mujer y sus siete hijas. Más tarde llegaron otras dos carretas con los muebles, los baúles y los utensilios domésticos. Instaló la familia en el Hotel de Jacob, mientras conseguía una casa, y volvió a abrir el despacho protegido por los soldados. Los fundadores de Macondo, resueltos a expulsar a los invasores, fueron con sus hijos mayores a ponerse a disposición de José Arcadio Buendía. Pero él se opuso, según explicó, porque don Apolinar Moscote había vuelto con su mujer y sus hijas, y no era cosa de hombres abochornar a otros delante de su familia. Así que decidió arreglar la situación por las buenas.

Aureliano lo acompañó. Ya para entonces había empezado a cultivar el bigote negro de puntas engomadas, y tenía la voz un poco estentórea que había de caracterizarlo en la guerra. Desarmados, sin hacer caso de la guardia, entraron al despacho del corregidor. Don Apolinar Moscote no perdió la serenidad. Les presentó a dos de sus hijas que se encontraban allí por casualidad: Amparo, de dieciséis años, morena como su madre, y Remedios, de apenas nueve años, una preciosa niña con piel de lirio y ojos verdes. Eran graciosas y bien educadas. Tan pronto como ellos entraron, antes de ser presentadas, les acercaron sillas para que se sentaran. Pero ambos permanecieron de pie.

—Muy bien, amigo —dijo José Arcadio Buendía—, usted se queda aquí, pero no porque tenga en la puerta esos bandoleros de trabuco, sino por consideración a su señora esposa y a sus hijas.

Don Apolinar Moscote se desconcertó, pero José Arcadio Buendía no le dio tiempo de replicar. «Sólo le ponemos dos condiciones», agregó. «La primera: que cada quién pinta su casa del color que le dé la gana. La segunda: que los soldados se van en seguida. Nosotros le garantizamos el orden.» El corregidor levantó la mano derecha con todos los dedos extendidos.

—¿Palabra de honor?

—Palabra de enemigo —dijo José Arcadio Buendía. Y añadió en un tono amargo—: Porque una cosa le quiero decir: usted y yo seguimos siendo enemigos.

Esa misma tarde se fueron los soldados. Pocos días después José Arcadio Buendía le consiguió una casa a la familia del corregidor. Todo el mundo quedó en paz, menos Aureliano. La imagen de Remedios, la hija menor del corregidor, que por su edad hubiera podido ser hija suya, le quedó doliendo en alguna parte del cuerpo. Era una sensación física que casi le molestaba para caminar, como una piedrecita en el zapato.

La casa nueva, blanca como una paloma, fue estrenada con un baile. Úrsula había concebido aquella idea desde la tarde en que vio a Rebeca y Amaranta convertidas en adolescentes, y casi puede decirse que el principal motivo de la construcción fue el deseo de procurar a las muchachas un lugar digno donde recibir las visitas. Para que nada restara esplendor a ese propósito, trabajó como un galeote mientras se ejecutaban las reformas, de modo que antes de que estuvieran terminadas había encargado costosos menesteres para la decoración y el servicio, y el invento maravilloso que había de suscitar el asombro del pueblo y el júbilo de la juventud: la pianola. La llevaron a pedazos, empacada en varios cajones que fueron descargados junto con los muebles vieneses, la cristalería de Bohemia, la vajilla de la Compañía de las Indias, los manteles de Holanda y una rica variedad de lámparas y palmatorias, y floreros, paramentos y tapices. La casa importadora envió por su cuenta un experto italiano, Pietro Crespi, para que armara y afinara la pianola, instruyera a los compradores en su manejo y los enseñara a bailar la música de moda impresa en seis rollos de papel.

Pietro Crespi era joven y rubio, el hombre más hermoso y mejor educado que se había visto en Macondo, tan escrupuloso en el vestir que a pesar del calor sofocante trabajaba con la almilla brocada y el grueso saco de paño oscuro. Empapado en sudor, guardando una distancia reverente con los dueños de la casa, estuvo varias semanas encerrado en la sala, con una consagración similar a la de Aureliano en su taller de orfebre. Una mañana, sin abrir la puerta, sin convocar a ningún testigo del milagro, colocó el primer rollo en la pianola, y el martilleo atormentador y el estrépito constante de los listones de madera cesaron en un silencio de asombro, ante el orden y la limpieza de la música. Todos se precipitaron a la sala. José Arcadio Buendía pareció fulminado no por la belleza de la melodía, sino por el tecleo autónomo de la pianola, e instaló en la sala la cámara de Melquíades con la esperanza de obtener el daguerrotipo del ejecutante invisible. Ese día el italiano almorzó con ellos. Rebeca y Amaranta, sirviendo la mesa, se intimidaron con la fluidez con que manejaba los cubiertos aquel hombre angélico de manos pálidas y sin anillos. En la sala de estar, contigua a la sala de visita, Pietro Crespi las enseñó a bailar. Les indicaba los pasos sin tocarlas, marcando el compás con un metrónomo, bajo la amable vigilancia de Úrsula, que no abandonó la sala un solo instante mientras sus hijas recibían las lecciones. Pietro Crespi llevaba en esos días unos pantalones especiales, muy flexibles y ajustados, y unas zapatillas de baile. «No tienes por qué preocuparte tanto», le decía José Arcadio Buendía a su mujer. «Este hombre es marica.» Pero ella no desistió de la vigilancia mientras no terminó el aprendizaje y el italiano se marchó de Macondo. Entonces empezó la organización de la fiesta. Úrsula hizo una lista severa de los invitados, en la cual los únicos escogidos fueron los descendientes de los fundadores, salvo la familia de Pilar Ternera, que ya había tenido otros dos hijos de padres desconocidos. Era en realidad una selección de clase, sólo que determinada por sentimientos de amistad, pues los favorecidos no sólo eran los más antiguos allegados a la casa de José Arcadio Buendía desde antes de emprender el éxodo que culminó con la fundación de Macondo, sino que sus hijos y nietos eran los compañeros habituales de Aureliano y Arcadio desde la infancia, y sus hijas eran las únicas que visitaban la casa para bordar con Rebeca y Amaranta. Don Apolinar Moscote, el gobernante benévolo cuya actuación se reducía a sostener con sus escasos recursos a dos policías armados con bolillos de palo, era una autoridad ornamental. Para sobrellevar los gastos domésticos, sus hijas abrieron un taller de costura, donde lo mismo hacían flores de fieltro que bocadillos de guayaba y esquelas de amor por encargo. Pero a pesar de ser recatadas y serviciales, las más bellas del pueblo y las más diestras en los bailes nuevos, no consiguieron que se las tomara en cuenta para la fiesta.

Mientras Úrsula y las muchachas desempacaban muebles, pulían las vajillas y colgaban cuadros de doncellas en barcas cargadas de rosas, infundiendo un soplo de vida nueva a los espacios pelados que construyeron los albañiles, José Arcadio Buendía renunció a la persecución de la imagen de Dios, convencido de su inexistencia, y destripó la pianola para descifrar su magia secreta. Dos días antes de la fiesta, empantanado en un reguero de clavijas y martinetes sobrantes, chapuceando entre un enredijo de cuerdas que desenrollaba por un extremo y se volvían a enrollar por el otro, consiguió malcomponer el instrumento. Nunca hubo tantos sobresaltos y correndillas como en aquellos días, pero las nuevas lámparas de alquitrán se encendieron en la fecha y a la hora previstas. La casa se abrió, todavía olorosa a resinas y a cal húmeda, y los hijos y nietos de los fundadores conocieron el corredor de los helechos y las begonias, los aposentos silenciosos, el jardín saturado por la fragancia de las rosas, y se reunieron en la sala de visita frente al invento desconocido que había sido cubierto con una sábana blanca. Quienes conocían el pianoforte, popular en otras poblaciones de la ciénaga, se sintieron un poco descorazonados, pero más amarga fue la desilusión de Úrsula cuando colocó el primer rollo para que Amaranta y Rebeca abrieran el baile, y el mecanismo no funcionó. Melquíades, ya casi ciego, desmigajándose de decrepitud, recurrió a las artes de su antiquísima sabiduría para tratar de componerlo. Al fin José Arcadio Buendía logró mover por equivocación un dispositivo atascado, y la música salió primero a borbotones, y luego en un manantial de notas enrevesadas. Golpeando contra las cuerdas puestas sin orden ni concierto y templadas con temeridad, los martinetes se desquiciaron. Pero los porfiados descendientes de los veintiún intrépidos que desentrañaron la sierra buscando el mar por el occidente, eludieron los escollos del trastrueque melódico, y el baile se prolongó hasta el amanecer.

Pietro Crespi volvió a componer la pianola. Rebeca y Amaranta lo ayudaron a ordenar las cuerdas y lo secundaron en sus risas por lo enrevesado de los valses. Era en extremo afectuoso, y de índole tan honrada, que Úrsula renunció a la vigilancia. La víspera de su viaje se improvisó con la pianola restaurada un baile para despedirlo, y él hizo con Rebeca una demostración virtuosa de las danzas modernas. Arcadio y Amaranta los igualaron en gracia y destreza. Pero la exhibición fue interrumpida porque Pilar Ternera, que estaba en la puerta con los curiosos, se peleó a mordiscos y tirones de pelo con una mujer que se atrevió a comentar que el joven Arcadio tenía nalgas de mujer. Hacia la medianoche, Pietro Crespi se despidió con un discursito sentimental y prometió volver muy pronto. Rebeca lo acompañó hasta la puerta, y luego de haber cerrado la casa y apagado las lámparas, se fue a su cuarto a llorar. Fue un llanto inconsolable que se prolongó por varios días, y cuya causa no conoció ni siquiera Amaranta. No era extraño su hermetismo. Aunque parecía expansiva y cordial, tenía un carácter solitario y un corazón impenetrable. Era una adolescente espléndida, de huesos largos y firmes, pero se empecinaba en seguir usando el mecedorcito de madera con que llegó a la casa, muchas veces reforzado y ya desprovisto de brazos. Nadie había descubierto que aún a esa edad conservaba el hábito de chuparse el dedo. Por eso no perdía ocasión de encerrarse en el baño, y había adquirido la costumbre de dormir con la cara vuelta contra la pared. En las tardes de lluvia, bordando con un grupo de amigas en el corredor de las begonias, perdía el hilo de la conversación y una lágrima de nostalgia le salaba el paladar cuando veía las vetas de tierra húmeda y los montículos de barro construidos por las lombrices en el jardín. Esos gustos secretos, derrotados en otro tiempo por las naranjas con ruibarbo, estallaron en un anhelo irreprimible cuando empezó a llorar. Volvió a comer tierra. La primera vez lo hizo casi por curiosidad, segura de que el mal sabor sería el mejor remedio contra la tentación. Y en efecto no pudo soportar la tierra en la boca. Pero insistió, vencida por el ansia creciente, y poco a poco fue rescatando el apetito ancestral, el gusto de los minerales primarios, la satisfacción sin resquicios del alimento original. Se echaba puñados de tierra en los bolsillos, y los comía a granitos sin ser vista, con un confuso sentimiento de dicha y de rabia, mientras adiestraba a sus amigas en las puntadas más difíciles y conversaba de otros hombres que no merecían el sacrificio de que se comiera por ellos la cal de las paredes. Los puñados de tierra hacían menos remoto y más cierto al único hombre que merecía aquella degradación, como si el suelo que él pisaba con sus finas botas de charol en otro lugar del mundo le transmitiera a ella el peso y la temperatura de su sangre en un sabor mineral que dejaba un rescoldo áspero en la boca y un sedimento de paz en el corazón. Una tarde, sin ningún motivo, Amparo Moscote pidió permiso para conocer la casa. Amaranta y Rebeca, desconcertadas por la visita imprevista, la atendieron con un formalismo duro. Le mostraron la mansión reformada, le hicieron oír los rollos de la pianola y le ofrecieron naranjada con galletitas. Amparo dio una lección de dignidad, de encanto personal, de buenas maneras, que impresionó a Úrsula en los breves instantes en que asistió a la visita. Al cabo de dos horas, cuando la conversación empezaba a languidecer, Amparo aprovechó un descuido de Amaranta y le entregó una carta a Rebeca. Ella alcanzó a ver el nombre de la muy distinguida señorita doña Rebeca Buendía, escrito con la misma letra metódica, la misma tinta verde y la misma disposición preciosista de las palabras con que estaban escritas las instrucciones de manejo de la pianola, y dobló la carta con la punta de los dedos y se la escondió en el corpiño mirando a Amparo Moscote con una expresión de gratitud sin término ni condiciones y una callada promesa de complicidad hasta la muerte.

La repentina amistad de Amparo Moscote y Rebeca Buendía despertó las esperanzas de Aureliano. El recuerdo de la pequeña Remedios no había dejado de torturarlo, pero no encontraba la ocasión de verla. Cuando paseaba por el pueblo con sus amigos más próximos, Magnífico Visbal y Gerineldo Márquez —hijos de los fundadores de iguales nombres—, la buscaba con mirada ansiosa en el taller de costura y sólo veía a las hermanas mayores. La presencia de Amparo Moscote en la casa fue como una premonición. «Tiene que venir con ella», se decía Aureliano en voz baja. «Tiene que venir.» Tantas veces se lo repitió, y con tanta convicción, que una tarde en que armaba en el taller un pescadito de oro, tuvo la certidumbre de que ella había respondido a su llamado. Poco después, en efecto, oyó la vocecita infantil, y al levantar la vista con el corazón helado de pavor, vio a la niña en la puerta con vestido de organdí rosado y botitas blancas.

—Ahí no entres, Remedios —dijo Amparo Moscote en el corredor—. Están trabajando.

Pero Aureliano no le dio tiempo de atender. Levantó el pescadito dorado prendido de una cadenita que le salía por la boca, y le dijo:

—Entra.

Remedios se aproximó e hizo sobre el pescadito algunas preguntas, que Aureliano no pudo contes-

84

tar porque se lo impedía un asma repentina. Quería quedarse para siempre junto a ese cutis de lirio, junto a esos ojos de esmeralda, muy cerca de esa voz que a cada pregunta le decía señor con el mismo respeto con que se lo decía a su padre. Melquíades estaba en el rincón, sentado al escritorio, garabateando signos indescifrables. Aureliano lo odió. No pudo hacer nada, salvo decirle a Remedios que le iba a regalar el pescadito, y la niña se asustó tanto con el ofrecimiento que abandonó a toda prisa el taller. Aquella tarde perdió Aureliano la recóndita paciencia con que había esperado la ocasión de verla. Descuidó el trabajo. La llamó muchas veces, en desesperados esfuerzos de concentración, pero Remedios no respondió. La buscó en el taller de sus hermanas, en los visillos de su casa, en la oficina de su padre, pero solamente la encontró en la imagen que saturaba su propia y terrible soledad. Pasaba horas enteras con Rebeca en la sala de visita escuchando los valses de la pianola. Ella los escuchaba porque era la música con que Pietro Crespi la había enseñado a bailar. Aureliano los escuchaba simplemente porque todo, hasta la música, le recordaba a Remedios.

La casa se llenó de amor. Aureliano lo expresó en versos que no tenían principio ni fin. Los escribía en los ásperos pergaminos que le regalaba Melquíades, en las paredes del baño, en la piel de sus brazos, y en todos aparecía Remedios transfigurada: Remedios en el aire soporífero de las dos de la tarde, Remedios en la callada respiración de las rosas, Remedios en la clepsidra secreta de las polillas, Remedios en el vapor del pan al amanecer, Remedios en todas partes y Remedios para siempre. Rebeca esperaba el amor a las cuatro de la tarde bordando junto a la ventana. Sabía que la mula del correo no llegaba sino cada quince días, pero ella la esperaba siempre, convencida de que iba a llegar un día cualquiera por equivocación. Sucedió todo lo contrario: una vez la mula no llegó en la fecha prevista. Loca de desesperación, Rebeca se levantó a medianoche y comió puñados de tierra en el jardín, con una avidez suicida, llorando de dolor y de furia, masticando lombrices tiernas y astillándose las muelas con huesos de caracoles. Vomitó hasta el amanecer. Se hundió en un estado de postración febril, perdió la conciencia, y su corazón se abrió en un delirio sin pudor. Úrsula, escandalizada, forzó la cerradura del baúl, y encontró en el fondo, atadas con cintas color de rosa, las dieciséis cartas perfumadas y los esqueletos de hojas y pétalos conservados en libros antiguos y las mariposas disecadas que al tocarlas se convirtieron en polvo.

Aureliano fue el único capaz de comprender tanta desolación. Esa tarde, mientras Úrsula trataba de rescatar a Rebeca del manglar del delirio, él fue con Magnífico Visbal y Gerineldo Márquez a la tienda de Catarino. El establecimiento había sido ensanchado con una galería de cuartos de madera donde vivían mujeres solas olorosas a flores muertas. Un conjunto de acordeón y tambores ejecutaba las canciones de Francisco el Hombre, que desde hacía varios años había desaparecido de Macondo. Los tres amigos bebieron guarapo fermentado. Magnífico y Gerineldo, contemporáneos de Aureliano, pero más diestros en las cosas del mundo, bebían metódicamente con las mujeres sentadas en las piernas. Una de ellas, marchita y con la dentadura orificada, le hizo a Aureliano una caricia estremecedora. Él la rechazó. Había descubierto que mientras más bebía más se acordaba de Remedios, pero soportaba mejor la tortura de su recuerdo. No supo en qué momento empezó a flotar. Vio a sus amigos y a las mujeres navegando en una reverberación radiante, sin peso ni volumen, diciendo palabras que no salían de sus labios y haciendo señales misteriosas que no correspondían a sus gestos. Catarino le puso una mano en la espalda y le dijo: «Van a ser las once.» Aureliano volvió la cabeza, vio el enorme rostro desfigurado con una flor de fieltro en la oreja, y entonces perdió la memoria, como en los tiempos del olvido, y la volvió a recobrar en una madrugada ajena y en un cuarto que le era completamente extraño, donde estaba Pilar Ternera en combinación, descalza, desgreñada, alumbrándolo con una lámpara y pasmada de incredulidad.

—¡Aureliano!

Aureliano se afirmó en los pies y levantó la cabeza. Ignoraba cómo había llegado hasta allí, pero sabía cuál era el propósito, porque lo llevaba escondido desde la infancia en un estanco inviolable del corazón.

—Vengo a dormir con usted —dijo.

Tenía la ropa embadurnada de fango y de vómito. Pilar Ternera, que entonces vivía solamente con sus dos hijos menores, no le hizo ninguna pregunta. Lo llevó a la cama. Le limpió la cara con un estropajo húmedo, le quitó la ropa, y luego se desnudó por completo y bajó el mosquitero para que no la vieran sus hijos si despertaban. Se había cansado de esperar al hombre que se quedó, a los hombres que se fueron, a los incontables hombres que erraron el camino de su casa confundidos por la incertidumbre de las barajas. En la espera se le había agrietado la piel,

87

se le habían vaciado los senos, se le había apagado el rescoldo del corazón. Buscó a Aureliano en la oscuridad, le puso la mano en el vientre y lo besó en el cuello con una ternura maternal. «Mi pobre niñito», murmuró. Aureliano se estremeció. Con una destreza reposada, sin el menor tropiezo, dejó atrás los acantilados del dolor y encontró a Remedios convertida en un pantano sin horizontes, olorosa a animal crudo y a ropa recién planchada. Cuando salió a flote estaba llorando. Primero fueron unos sollozos involuntarios y entrecortados. Después se vació en un manantial desatado, sintiendo que algo tumefacto y doloroso se había reventado en su interior. Ella esperó, rascándole la cabeza con la yema de los dedos, hasta que su cuerpo se desocupó de la materia oscura que no lo dejaba vivir. Entonces Pilar Ternera le preguntó: «¿Quién es?» Y Aureliano se lo dijo. Ella soltó la risa que en otro tiempo espantaba a las palomas y que ahora ni siquiera despertaba a los niños. «Tendrás que acabar de criarla», se burló. Pero debajo de la burla encontró Aureliano un remanso de comprensión. Cuando abandonó el cuarto, dejando allí no sólo la incertidumbre de su virilidad sino también el peso amargo que durante tantos meses soportó en el corazón, Pilar Ternera le había hecho una promesa espontánea.

—Voy a hablar con la niña —le dijo—, y vas a ver que te la sirvo en bandeja.

Cumplió. Pero en un mal momento, porque la casa había perdido la paz de otros días. Al descubrir la pasión de Rebeca, que no fue posible mantener en secreto a causa de sus gritos, Amaranta sufrió un acceso de calenturas. También ella padecía la espina de un amor solitario. Encerrada en el baño se desahogaba del tormento de una pasión sin esperanzas escribiendo cartas febriles que se conformaba con esconder en el fondo del baúl. Úrsula apenas si se dio abasto para atender a las dos enfermas. No consiguió en prolongados e insidiosos interrogatorios averiguar las causas de la postración de Amaranta. Por último, en otro instante de inspiración, forzó la cerradura del baúl y encontró las cartas atadas con cintas de color de rosa, hinchadas de azucenas frescas y todavía húmedas de lágrimas, dirigidas y nunca enviadas a Pietro Crespi. Llorando de furia maldijo la hora en que se le ocurrió comprar la pianola, prohibió las clases de bordado y decretó una especie de luto sin muerto que había de prolongarse hasta que las hijas desistieran de sus esperanzas Fue inútil la intervención de José Arcadio Buendía, que había rectificado su primera impresión sobre Pietro Crespi, y admiraba su habilidad para el manejo de las máquinas musicales. De modo que cuando Pilar Ternera le dijo a Aureliano que Remedios estaba decidida a casarse, él comprendió que la noticia acabaría de atribular a sus padres. Pero le hizo frente a la situación. Convocados a la sala de visita para una entrevista formal, José Arcadio Buendía y Úrsula escucharon impávidos la declaración de su hijo. Al conocer el nombre de la novia, sin embargo, José Arcadio Buendía enrojeció de indignación. «El amor es una peste», tronó. «Habiendo tantas muchachas bonitas y decentes, lo único que se te ocurre es casarte con la hija del enemigo.» Pero Úrsula estuvo de acuerdo con la elección. Confesó su afecto hacia las siete hermanas Moscote, por su hermosura, su laboriosidad, su recato y su buena educación, y celebró el acierto de su hijo. Vencido por el entusiasmo de su mujer, José Arcadio

Buendía puso entonces una condición: Rebeca, que era la correspondida, se casaría con Pietro Crespi. Úrsula llevaría a Amaranta en un viaje a la capital de la provincia, cuando tuviera tiempo, para que el contacto con gente distinta la aliviara de su desilusión. Rebeca recobró la salud tan pronto como se enteró del acuerdo, y escribió a su novio una carta jubilosa que sometió a la aprobación de sus padres y puso al correo sin servirse de intermediarios. Amaranta fingió aceptar la decisión y poco a poco se restableció de las calenturas, pero se prometió a sí misma que Rebeca se casaría solamente pasando por encima de su cadáver.

El sábado siguiente, José Arcadio Buendía se puso el traje de paño oscuro, el cuello de celuloide y las botas de gamuza que había estrenado la noche de la fiesta, y fue a pedir la mano de Remedios Moscote. El corregidor y su esposa lo recibieron al mismo tiempo complacidos y conturbados, porque ignoraban el propósito de la visita imprevista, y luego creyeron que él había confundido el nombre de la pretendida. Para disipar el error, la madre despertó a Remedios y la llevó en brazos a la sala, todavía atarantada de sueño. Le preguntaron si en verdad estaba decidida a casarse, y ella contestó lloriqueando que solamente quería que la dejaran dormir. José Arcadio Buendía, comprendiendo el desconcierto de los Moscote, fue a aclarar las cosas con Aureliano. Cuando regresó, los esposos Moscote se habían vestido con ropa formal, habían cambiado la posición de los muebles y puesto flores nuevas en los floreros, y lo esperaban en compañía de sus hijas mayores. Agobiado por la ingratitud de la ocasión y por la molestia del cuello duro, José Arcadio Buendía confirmó que, en efecto, Remedios era la elegida. «Esto no tiene sentido», dijo consternado don Apolinar Moscote. «Tenemos seis hijas más, todas solteras y en edad de merecer, que estarían encantadas de ser esposas dignísimas de caballeros serios y trabajadores como su hijo, y Aurelito pone sus ojos precisamente en la única que todavía se orina en la cama.» Su esposa, una mujer bien conservada, de párpados y ademanes afligidos, le reprochó su incorrección. Cuando terminaron de tomar el batido de frutas, habían aceptado complacidos la decisión de Aureliano. Sólo que la señora de Moscote suplicaba el favor de hablar a solas con Úrsula. Intrigada, protestando de que la enredaran en asuntos de hombres, pero en realidad intimidada por la emoción, Úrsula fue a visitarla al día siguiente. Media hora después regresó con la noticia de que Remedios era impúber. Aureliano no lo consideró como un tropiezo grave. Había esperado tanto, que podía esperar cuanto fuera necesario, hasta que la novia estuviera en edad de concebir.

La armonía recobrada sólo fue interrumpida por la muerte de Melquíades. Aunque era un acontecimiento previsible, no lo fueron las circunstancias. Pocos meses después de su regreso se había operado en él un proceso de envejecimiento tan apresurado y crítico, que pronto se le tuvo por uno de esos bisabuelos inútiles que deambulan como sombras por los dormitorios, arrastrando los pies, recordando mejores tiempos en voz alta, y de quienes nadie se ocupa ni se acuerda en realidad hasta el día en que amanecen muertos en la cama. Al principio, José Arcadio Buendía lo secundaba en sus tareas, entusiasmado con la novedad de la daguerrotipia y las predicciones de Nostradamus. Pero poco a poco lo fue abandonando a su soledad, porque cada vez se les hacía más difícil la comunicación. Estaba perdiendo la vista y el oído, parecía confundir a los interlocutores con personas que conoció en épocas remotas de la humanidad, y contestaba a las preguntas con un intrincado batiburrillo de idiomas. Caminaba tanteando el aire, aunque se movía por entre las cosas con una fluidez inexplicable, como si estuviera dotado de un instinto de orientación fundado en presentimientos inmediatos. Un día olvidó ponerse la dentadura postiza, que dejaba de noche en un vaso de agua junto a la cama, y no se la volvió a poner. Cuando Úrsula dispuso la ampliación de la casa, le hizo construir un cuarto especial contiguo al taller de Aureliano, lejos de los ruidos y el trajín domésticos, con una ventana inundada de luz y un estante donde ella misma ordenó los libros casi deshechos por el polvo y las polillas, los quebradizos papeles apretados de signos indescifrables y el vaso con la dentadura postiza donde habían prendido unas plantitas acuáticas de minúsculas flores amarillas. El nuevo lugar pareció agradar a Melquíades, porque no volvió a vérsele ni siquiera en el comedor. Sólo iba al taller de Aureliano, donde pasaba horas y horas garabateando su literatura enigmática en los pergaminos que llevó consigo y que parecían fabricados en una materia árida que se resquebrajaba como hojaldres. Allí tomaba los alimentos que Visitación le llevaba dos veces al día, aunque en los últimos tiempos perdió el apetito y sólo se alimentaba de legumbres. Pronto adquirió el aspecto de desamparo propio de los vegetarianos. La piel se le cubrió de un musgo tierno, semejante al que prosperaba en el chaleco anacrónico que no se quitó jamás, y su respiración exhaló un tufo de animal dormido. Aureliano terminó por olvidarse de él, absorto en la redacción de sus versos, pero en cierta ocasión creyó entender algo de lo que decía en sus bordoneantes monólogos, y le prestó atención. En realidad, lo único que pudo aislar en las parrafadas pedregosas fue el insistente martilleo de la palabra equinoccio equinoccio equinoccio, y el nombre de Alexander Von Humboldt. Arcadio se aproximó un poco más a él cuando empezó a ayudar a Aureliano en la platería. Melquíades correspondió a aquel esfuerzo de comunicación soltando a veces frases en castellano que tenían muy poco que ver con la realidad. Una tarde, sin embargo, pareció iluminado por una emoción repentina. Años después, frente al pelotón de fusilamiento, Arcadio había de acordarse del temblor con que Melquíades le hizo escuchar varias páginas de su escritura impenetrable, que por supuesto no entendió, pero que al ser leídas en voz alta parecían encíclicas cantadas. Luego sonrió por primera vez en mucho tiempo y dijo en castellano: «Cuando me muera, quemen mercurio durante tres días en mi cuarto.» Arcadio se lo contó a José Arcadio Buendía, y éste trató de obtener una información más explícita, pero sólo consiguió una respuesta: «He alcanzado la inmortalidad.» Cuando la respiración de Melquíades empezó a oler, Arcadio lo llevó a bañarse al río los jueves en la mañana. Pareció mejorar. Se desnudaba y se metía en el agua junto con los muchachos, y su misterioso sentido de orientación le permitía eludir los sitios profundos y peligrosos. «Somos del agua», dijo en cierta ocasión. Así pasó mucho tiempo sin que nadie lo viera en la casa, salvo la noche en que hizo un conmovedor esfuerzo por componer la pianola, y cuando iba al río con Arcadio llevando bajo el brazo la totuma y la bola de jabón de corozo envueltas en una toalla. Un jueves, antes de que lo llamaran para ir al río, Aureliano le oyó decir: «He muerto de fiebre en los médanos de Singapur.» Ese día se metió en el agua por un mal camino y no lo encontraron hasta la mañana siguiente, varios kilómetros más abajo, varado en un recodo luminoso y con un gallinazo solitario parado en el vientre. Contra las escandalizadas protestas de Úrsula, que lo lloró con más dolor que a su propio padre, José Arcadio Buendía se opuso a que lo enterraran. «Es inmortal —dijo— y él mismo reveló la fórmula de la resurrección.» Revivió el olvidado atanor y puso a hervir un caldero de mercurio junto al cadáver que poco a poco se iba llenando de burbujas azules. Don Apolinar Moscote se atrevió a recordarle que un ahogado insepulto era un peligro para la salud pública. «Nada de eso, puesto que está vivo», fue la réplica de José Arcadio Buendía, que completó las setenta y dos horas de sahumerios mercuriales cuando ya el cadáver empezaba a reventarse en una floración lívida, cuyos silbidos tenues impregnaron la casa de un vapor pestilente. Sólo entonces permitió que lo enterraran, pero no de cualquier modo, sino con los honores reservados al más grande benefactor de Macondo. Fue el primer entierro y el más concurrido que se vio en el pueblo, superado apenas un siglo después por el carnaval funerario de la Mamá Grande. Lo sepultaron en una tumba erigida en el centro del terreno que destinaron para el cementerio, con una lápida donde quedó escrito lo único que se supo de él: MELQUÍADES. Le hicieron sus nueve noches de velorio. En el tumulto que se reunía en el patio a tomar café, contar chistes y jugar barajas,

Amaranta encontró una ocasión de confesarle su amor a Pietro Crespi, que pocas semanas antes había formalizado su compromiso con Rebeca y estaba instalando un almacén de instrumentos músicos y juguetes de cuerda, en el mismo sector donde vegetaban los árabes que en otro tiempo cambiaban baratijas por guacamayas, y que la gente conocía como la Calle de los Turcos. El italiano, cuya cabeza cubierta de rizos charolados suscitaba en las mujeres una irreprimible necesidad de suspirar, trató a Amaranta como una chiquilla caprichosa a quien no valía la pena tomar demasiado en cuenta.

—Tengo un hermano menor —le dijo—. Va a venir a ayudarme en la tienda.

Amaranta se sintió humillada y le dijo a Pietro Crespi, con un rencor virulento, que estaba dispuesta a impedir la boda de su hermana aunque tuviera que atravesar en la puerta su propio cadáver. Se impresionó tanto el italiano con el dramatismo de la amenaza, que no resistió la tentación de comentarla con Rebeca. Fue así como el viaje de Amaranta, siempre aplazado por las ocupaciones de Úrsula, se arregló en menos de una semana. Amaranta no opuso resistencia, pero cuando le dio a Rebeca el beso de despedida, le susurró al oído:

—No te hagas ilusiones. Aunque me lleven al fin del mundo encontraré la manera de impedir que te cases, así tenga que matarte.

Con la ausencia de Úrsula, con la presencia invisible de Melquíades que continuaba su deambular sigiloso por los cuartos, la casa pareció enorme y vacía. Rebeca había quedado a cargo del orden doméstico, mientras la india se ocupaba de la panadería. Al anochecer, cuando llegaba Pietro Crespi precedido de un fresco hálito de espliego y llevando siempre un juguete de regalo, su novia le recibía la visita en la sala principal con puertas y ventanas abiertas para estar a salvo de toda suspicacia. Era una precaución innecesaria, porque el italiano había demostrado ser tan respetuoso que ni siquiera tocaba la mano de la mujer que sería su esposa antes de un año. Aquellas visitas fueron llenando la casa de juguetes prodigiosos. Las bailarinas de cuerda, las cajas de música, los monos acróbatas, los caballos trotadores, los payasos tamborileros, la rica y asombrosa fauna mecánica que llevaba Pietro Crespi, disiparon la aflicción de José Arcadio Buendía por la muerte de Melquíades, y lo transportaron de nuevo a sus antiguos tiempos de alquimista. Vivía entonces en un paraíso de animales destripados, de mecanismos deshechos, tratando de perfeccionarlos con un sistema de movimiento continuo fundado en los principios del péndulo. Aureliano, por su parte, había descuidado el taller para enseñar a leer y escribir a la pequeña Remedios. Al principio, la niña prefería sus muñecas al hombre que llegaba todas las tardes, y que era el culpable de que la separaran de sus juegos para bañarla y vestirla y sentarla en la sala a recibir la visita. Pero la paciencia y la devoción de Aureliano terminaron por seducirla, hasta el punto de que pasaba muchas horas con él estudiando el sentido de las letras y dibujando en un cuaderno con lápices de colores casitas con vacas en los corrales y soles redondos con rayos amarillos que se ocultaban detrás de las lomas.

Sólo Rebeca era infeliz con la amenaza de Amaranta. Conocía el carácter de su hermana, la altivez de su espíritu, y la asustaba la virulencia de su rencor. Pasaba horas enteras chupándose el dedo en el baño, aferrándose a un agotador esfuerzo de voluntad para no comer tierra. En busca de un alivio a la zozobra llamó a Pilar Ternera para que le leyera el porvenir. Después de un sartal de imprecisiones convencionales, Pilar Ternera pronosticó:

—No serás feliz mientras tus padres permanezcan insepultos.

Rebeca se estremeció. Como en el recuerdo de un sueño se vio a sí misma entrando a la casa, muy niña, con el baúl y el mecedorcito de madera y un talego cuyo contenido no conoció jamás. Se acordó de un caballero calvo, vestido de lino y con el cuello de la camisa cerrado con un botón de oro, que nada tenía que ver con el rey de copas. Se acordó de una mujer muy joven y muy bella, de manos tibias y perfumadas, que nada tenían en común con las manos reumáticas de la sota de oros, y que le ponía flores en el cabello para sacarla a pasear en la tarde por un pueblo de calles verdes.

—No entiendo —dijo.

Pilar Ternera pareció desconcertada:

—Yo tampoco, pero eso es lo que dicen las cartas.

Rebeca quedó tan preocupada con el enigma, que se lo contó a José Arcadio Buendía y éste la reprendió por dar crédito a pronósticos de barajas, pero se dio a la silenciosa tarea de registrar armarios y baúles, remover muebles y voltear camas y entablados, buscando el talego de huesos. Recordaba no haberlo visto desde los tiempos de la reconstrucción. Llamó en secreto a los albañiles y uno de ellos reveló que había emparedado el talego en algún dormitorio porque le estorbaba para trabajar. Después de varios días de auscultaciones, con la oreja pegada a las paredes, percibieron el cloc cloc profundo. Perforaron el muro y allí estaban los huesos en el talego intacto. Ese mismo día lo sepultaron en una tumba sin lápida, improvisada junto a la de Melquíades, y José Arcadio Buendía regresó a la casa liberado de una carga que por un momento pesó tanto en su conciencia como el recuerdo de Prudencio Aguilar. Al pasar por la cocina le dio un beso en la frente a Rebeca.

—Quítate las malas ideas de la cabeza —le dijo—. Serás feliz.

La amistad de Rebeca abrió a Pilar Ternera las puertas de la casa, cerradas por Úrsula desde el nacimiento de Arcadio. Llegaba a cualquier hora del día, como un tropel de cabras, y descargaba su energía febril en los oficios más pesados. A veces entraba al taller y ayudaba a Arcadio a sensibilizar las láminas del daguerrotipo con una eficacia y una ternura que terminaron por confundirlo. Lo aturdía esa mujer. La resolana de su piel, su olor a humo, el desorden de su risa en el cuarto oscuro perturbaban su atención y lo hacían tropezar con las cosas.

En cierta ocasión Aureliano estaba allí, trabajando en orfebrería, y Pilar Ternera se apoyó en la mesa para admirar su paciente laboriosidad. De pronto ocurrió. Aureliano comprobó que Arcadio estaba en el cuarto oscuro, antes de levantar la vista y encontrarse con los ojos de Pilar Ternera, cuyo pensamiento era perfectamente visible, como expuesto a la luz del mediodía.

—Bueno —dijo Aureliano—. Dígame qué es.

Pilar Ternera se mordió los labios con una sonrisa triste.

—Que eres bueno para la guerra —dijo—. Donde pones el ojo pones el plomo.

Aureliano descansó con la comprobación del

presagio. Volvió a concentrarse en su trabajo, como si nada hubiera pasado, y su voz adquirió una reposada firmeza.

—Lo reconozco —dijo—. Llevará mi nombre.

José Arcadio Buendía consiguió por fin lo que buscaba: conectó a una bailarina de cuerda el mecanismo del reloj, y el juguete bailó sin interrupción al compás de su propia música durante tres días. Aquel hallazgo lo excitó mucho más que cualquiera de sus empresas descabelladas. No volvió a comer. No volvió a dormir. Sin la vigilancia y los cuidados de Úrsula se dejó arrastrar por su imaginación hacia un estado de delirio perpetuo del cual no se volvería a recuperar. Pasaba las noches dando vueltas en el cuarto, pensando en voz alta, buscando la manera de aplicar los principios del péndulo a las carretas de bueyes, a las rejas del arado, a todo lo que fuera útil puesto en movimiento. Lo fatigó tanto la fiebre del insomnio, que una madrugada no pudo reconocer al anciano de cabeza blanca y ademanes inciertos que entró en su dormitorio. Era Prudencio Aguilar. Cuando por fin lo identificó, asombrado de que también envejecieran los muertos, José Arcadio Buendía se sintió sacudido por la nostalgia. «Prudencio —exclamó—, ¡cómo has venido a parar tan lejos!» Después de muchos años de muerte, era tan intensa la añoranza de los vivos, tan apremiante la necesidad de compañía, tan aterradora la proximidad de la otra muerte que existía dentro de la muerte, que Prudencio Aguilar había terminado por querer al peor de sus enemigos. Tenía mucho tiempo de estar buscándolo. Les preguntaba por él a los muertos de Riohacha, a los muertos que llegaban del Valle de Upar, a los que llegaban de la ciénaga, y nadie le daba razón, porque Macondo fue un pueblo desconocido para los muertos hasta que llegó Melquíades y lo señaló con un puntito negro en los abigarrados mapas de la muerte. José Arcadio Buendía conversó con Prudencio Aguilar hasta el amanecer. Pocas horas después, estragado por la vigilia, entró al taller de Aureliano y le preguntó: «¿Qué día es hoy?» Aureliano le contestó que era martes. «Eso mismo pensaba yo», dijo José Arcadio Buendía. «Pero de pronto me he dado cuenta de que sigue siendo lunes como ayer. Mira el cielo, mira las paredes, mira las begonias. También hoy es lunes.» Acostumbrado a sus manías, Aureliano no le hizo caso. Al día siguiente, miércoles, José Arcadio Buendía volvió al taller. «Esto es un desastre —dijo—. Mira el aire, oye el zumbido del sol, igual que ayer y antier. También hoy es lunes.» Esa noche, Pietro Crespi lo encontró en el corredor, llorando con el llantito sin gracia de los viejos, llorando por Prudencio Aguilar, por Melquíades, por los padres de Rebeca, por su papá y su mamá, por todos los que podía recordar y que entonces estaban solos en la muerte. Le regaló un oso de cuerda que caminaba en dos patas por un alambre, pero no consiguió distraerlo de su obsesión. Le preguntó qué había pasado con el proyecto que le expuso días antes, sobre la posibilidad de construir una máquina de péndulo que le sirviera al hombre para volar, y él contestó que era imposible porque el péndulo podía levantar cualquier cosa en el aire pero no podía levantarse a sí mismo. El jueves volvió a aparecer en el taller con un doloroso aspecto de tierra arrasada. «¡La máquina del tiempo se ha descompuesto —casi sollozó— y Úrsula y Amaranta tan lejos!» Aureliano lo reprendió como a un niño y él adoptó un aire sumiso. Pasó seis horas examinando las cosas, tratando de encontrar una diferencia con el aspecto que tuvieron el día anterior, pendiente de descubrir en ellas algún cambio que revelara el transcurso del tiempo. Estuvo toda la noche en la cama con los ojos abiertos, llamando a Prudencio Aguilar, a Melquíades, a todos los muertos, para que fueran a compartir su desazón. Pero nadie acudió. El viernes, antes de que se levantara nadie, volvió a vigilar la apariencia de la naturaleza, hasta que no tuvo la menor duda de que seguía siendo lunes. Entonces agarró la tranca de una puerta y con la violencia salvaje de su fuerza descomunal destrozó hasta convertirlos en polvo los aparatos de alquimia, el gabinete de daguerrotipia, el taller de orfebrería, gritando como un endemoniado en un idioma altisonante y fluido pero completamente incomprensible. Se disponía a terminar con el resto de la casa cuando Aureliano pidió ayuda a los vecinos. Se necesitaron diez hombres para tumbarlo, catorce para amarrarlo, veinte para arrastrarlo hasta el castaño del patio, donde lo dejaron atado, ladrando en lengua extraña y echando espumarajos verdes por la boca. Cuando llegaron Úrsula y Amaranta todavía estaba atado de pies y manos al tronco del castaño, empapado de lluvia y en un estado de inocencia total. Le hablaron, y él las miró sin reconocerlas y les dijo algo incomprensible. Úrsula le soltó las muñecas y los tobillos, ulcerados por la presión de las sogas, y lo dejó amarrado solamente por la cintura. Más tarde le construyeron un cobertizo de palma para protegerlo del sol y la lluvia.

Aureliano Buendía y Remedios Moscote se casaron
un domingo de marzo ante el altar que el padre Nicanor Reyna hizo construir en la sala de visitas. Fue la
culminación de cuatro semanas de sobresaltos en casa
de los Moscote, pues la pequeña Remedios llegó a
la pubertad antes de superar los hábitos de la infancia. A pesar de que la madre la había aleccionado
sobre los cambios de la adolescencia, una tarde de febrero irrumpió dando gritos de alarma en la sala donde sus hermanas conversaban con Aureliano, y les
mostró el calzón embadurnado de una pasta achoco-
latada. Se fijó un mes para la boda. Apenas si hubo
tiempo de enseñarla a lavarse, a vestirse sola, a comprender los asuntos elementales de un hogar. La pusieron a orinar en ladrillos calientes para corregirle el
hábito de mojar la cama. Costó trabajo convencerla
de la inviolabilidad del secreto conyugal, porque Remedios estaba tan aturdida y al mismo tiempo tan ma-
ravillada con la revelación, que quería comentar con
todo el mundo los pormenores de la noche de bodas.
Fue un esfuerzo agotador, pero en la fecha prevista
para la ceremonia la niña era tan diestra en las cosas
del mundo como cualquiera de sus hermanas. Don

Apolinar Moscote la llevó del brazo por la calle adornada con flores y guirnaldas, entre el estampido de los cohetes y la música de varias bandas, y ella saludaba con la mano y daba las gracias con una sonrisa a quienes le deseaban buena suerte desde las ventanas. Aureliano, vestido de paño negro, con los mismos botines de charol con ganchos metálicos que había de llevar pocos años después frente al pelotón de fusilamiento, tenía una palidez intensa y una bola dura en la garganta cuando recibió a su novia en la puerta de la casa y la llevó al altar. Ella se comportó con tanta naturalidad, con tanta discreción, que no perdió la compostura ni siquiera cuando Aureliano dejó caer el anillo al tratar de ponérselo. En medio del murmullo y el principio de confusión de los convidados, ella mantuvo en alto el brazo con el mitón de encaje y permaneció con el anular dispuesto, hasta que su novio logró parar el anillo con el botín para que no siguiera rodando hasta la puerta, y regresó ruborizado al altar. Su madre y sus hermanas sufrieron tanto con el temor de que la niña hiciera una incorrección durante la ceremonia, que al final fueron ellas quienes cometieron la impertinencia de cargarla para darle un beso. Desde aquel día se reveló el sentido de responsabilidad, la gracia natural, el reposado dominio que siempre había de tener Remedios ante las circunstancias adversas. Fue ella quien de su propia iniciativa puso aparte la mejor porción que cortó del pastel de bodas y se la llevó en un plato con un tenedor a José Arcadio Buendía. Amarrado al tronco del castaño, encogido en un banquito de madera bajo el cobertizo de palmas, el enorme anciano descolorido por el sol y la lluvia hizo una vaga sonrisa de gratitud y se comió el pastel con los dedos masticando un salmo ininteligible. La única persona infeliz en aquella celebración estrepitosa que se prolongó hasta el amanecer del lunes fue Rebeca Buendía. Era su fiesta frustrada. Por acuerdo de Úrsula, su matrimonio debía celebrarse en la misma fecha, pero Pietro Crespi recibió el viernes una carta con el anuncio de la muerte inminente de su madre. La boda se aplazó. Pietro Crespi se fue para la capital de la provincia una hora después de recibir la carta, y en el camino se cruzó con su madre que llegó puntual la noche del sábado y cantó en la boda de Aureliano el aria triste que había preparado para la boda de su hijo. Pietro Crespi regresó a la medianoche del domingo a barrer las cenizas de la fiesta, después de haber reventado cinco caballos en el camino tratando de estar en tiempo para su boda. Nunca se averiguó quién escribió la carta. Atormentada por Úrsula, Amaranta lloró de indignación y juró su inocencia frente al altar que los carpinteros no habían acabado de desarmar.

El padre Nicanor Reyna —a quien don Apolinar Moscote había llevado de la ciénaga para que oficiara la boda— era un anciano endurecido por la ingratitud de su ministerio. Tenía la piel triste, casi en los puros huesos, y el vientre pronunciado y redondo y una expresión de ángel viejo que era más de inocencia que de bondad. Llevaba el propósito de regresar a su parroquia después de la boda, pero se espantó con la aridez de los habitantes de Macondo, que prosperaban en el escándalo, sujetos a la ley natural, sin bautizar a los hijos ni santificar las fiestas. Pensando que a ninguna tierra le hacía tanta falta la simiente de Dios, decidió quedarse una semana más para cristianizar a circuncisos y gentiles, legalizar concubinarios y sacramentar moribundos. Pero nadie le prestó atención. Le contestaban que durante muchos años habían estado sin cura, arreglando los negocios del alma directamente con Dios, y habían perdido la malicia del pecado mortal. Cansado de predicar en el desierto, el padre Nicanor se dispuso a emprender la construcción de un templo, el más grande del mundo, con santos de tamaño natural y vidrios de colores en las paredes, para que fuera gente desde Roma a honrar a Dios en el centro de la impiedad. Andaba por todas partes pidiendo limosnas con un platillo de cobre. Le daban mucho, pero él quería más, porque el templo debía tener una campana cuyo clamor sacara a flote a los ahogados. Suplicó tanto, que perdió la voz. Sus huesos empezaron a llenarse de ruidos. Un sábado, no habiendo recogido ni siquiera el valor de las puertas, se dejó confundir por la desesperación. Improvisó un altar en la plaza y el domingo recorrió el pueblo con una campanita, como en los tiempos del insomnio, convocando a la misa campal. Muchos fueron por curiosidad. Otros por nostalgia. Otros para que Dios no fuera a tomar como agravio personal el desprecio a su intermediario. Así que a las ocho de la mañana estaba medio pueblo en la plaza, donde el padre Nicanor cantó los evangelios con voz lacerada por la súplica. Al final, cuando los asistentes empezaron a desbandarse, levantó los brazos en señal de atención.

—Un momento —dijo—. Ahora vamos a presenciar una prueba irrebatible del infinito poder de Dios.

El muchacho que había ayudado a misa le llevó una taza de chocolate espeso y humeante que él se tomó sin respirar. Luego se limpió los labios con un pañuelo que sacó de la manga, extendió los brazos y cerró los ojos. Entonces el padre Nicanor se elevó doce centímetros sobre el nivel del suelo. Fue un recurso convincente. Anduvo varios días por entre las casas, repitiendo la prueba de la levitación mediante el estímulo del chocolate, mientras el monaguillo recogía tanto dinero en un talego, que en menos de un mes emprendió la construcción del templo. Nadie puso en duda el origen divino de la demostración, salvo José Arcadio Buendía, que observó sin inmutarse el tropel de gente que una mañana se reunió en torno al castaño para asistir una vez más a la revelación. Apenas se estiró un poco en el banquillo y se encogió de hombros cuando el padre Nicanor empezó a levantarse del suelo junto con la silla en que estaba sentado.

—*Hoc est simplicisimum* —dijo José Arcadio Buendía—: *homo iste statum quartum materiae invenit.*

El padre Nicanor levantó la mano y las cuatro patas de la silla se posaron en tierra al mismo tiempo.

—*Nego* —dijo—. *Factum hoc existentiam Dei probat sine dubio.*

Fue así como se supo que era latín la endiablada jerga de José Arcadio Buendía. El padre Nicanor aprovechó la circunstancia de ser la única persona que había podido comunicarse con él, para tratar de infundir la fe en su cerebro trastornado. Todas las tardes se sentaba junto al castaño, predicando en latín, pero José Arcadio Buendía se empecinó en no admitir vericuetos retóricos ni transmutaciones de chocolate, y exigió como única prueba el daguerrotipo de Dios. El padre Nicanor le llevó entonces medallas y estampitas y hasta una reproducción del paño de la Verónica, pero José Arcadio Buendía los rechazó por ser objetos artesanales sin fundamento científico. Era tan terco, que el padre Nicanor renunció a sus propósitos de evangelización y siguió visitándolo por sentimientos humanitarios. Pero entonces fue José Arcadio Buendía quien tomó la iniciativa y trató de quebrantar la fe del cura con martingalas racionalistas. En cierta ocasión en que el padre Nicanor llevó al castaño un tablero y una caja de fichas para invitarlo a jugar a las damas, José Arcadio Buendía no aceptó, según dijo, porque nunca pudo entender el sentido de una contienda entre dos adversarios que estaban de acuerdo en los principios. El padre Nicanor, que jamás había visto de ese modo el juego de damas, no pudo volverlo a jugar. Cada vez más asombrado de la lucidez de José Arcadio Buendía, le preguntó cómo era posible que lo tuvieran amarrado de un árbol.

—*Hoc est simplicisimum* —contestó él—: porque estoy loco.

Desde entonces, preocupado por su propia fe, el cura no volvió a visitarlo, y se dedicó por completo a apresurar la construcción del templo. Rebeca sintió renacer la esperanza. Su porvenir estaba condicionado a la terminación de la obra, desde un domingo en que el padre Nicanor almorzaba en la casa y toda la familia sentada a la mesa habló de la solemnidad y el esplendor que tendrían los actos religiosos cuando se construyera el templo. «La más afortunada será Rebeca», dijo Amaranta. Y como Rebeca no entendió lo que ella quería decirle, se lo explicó con una sonrisa inocente:

—Te va a tocar inaugurar la iglesia con tu boda.

Rebeca trató de anticiparse a cualquier comentario. Al paso que llevaba la construcción, el templo no estaría terminado antes de diez años. El padre Nicanor no estuvo de acuerdo: la creciente generosidad de los fieles permitía hacer cálculos más optimistas. Ante la sorda indignación de Rebeca, que no pudo terminar el almuerzo, Úrsula celebró la idea de Amaranta y contribuyó con un aporte considerable para que se apresuraran los trabajos. El padre Nicanor consideró que con otro auxilio como ese el templo estaría listo en tres años. A partir de entonces Rebeca no volvió a dirigirle la palabra a Amaranta, convencida de que su iniciativa no había tenido la inocencia que ella supo aparentar. «Era lo menos grave que podía hacer», le replicó Amaranta en la virulenta discusión que tuvieron aquella noche. «Así no tendré que matarte en los próximos tres años.» Rebeca aceptó el reto.

Cuando Pietro Crespi se enteró del nuevo aplazamiento, sufrió una crisis de desilusión, pero Rebeca le dio una prueba definitiva de lealtad. «Nos fugaremos cuando tú lo dispongas», le dijo. Pietro Crespi, sin embargo, no era hombre de aventuras. Carecía del carácter impulsivo de su novia, y consideraba el respeto a la palabra empeñada como un capital que no se podía dilapidar. Entonces Rebeca recurrió a métodos más audaces. Un viento misterioso apagaba las lámparas de la sala de visita y Úrsula sorprendía a los novios besándose en la oscuridad. Pietro Crespi le daba explicaciones atolondradas sobre la mala calidad de las modernas lámparas de alquitrán y hasta ayudaba a instalar en la sala sistemas de iluminación más seguros. Pero otra vez fallaba el combustible o se atascaban las mechas, y Úrsula encontraba a Rebeca sentada en las rodillas del novio. Terminó por no aceptar ninguna explicación. Depositó en la india la responsabilidad de la panadería y se sentó en un mecedor a vigilar la visita de los novios, dispuesta a no dejarse derrotar por maniobras que ya eran viejas en su juventud. «Pobre mamá», decía Rebeca con burlona indignación, viendo bostezar a Úrsula en el sopor de las visitas. «Cuando se muera saldrá penando en ese mecedor.» Al cabo de tres meses de amores vigilados, aburrido con la lentitud de la construcción que pasaba a inspeccionar todos los días, Pietro Crespi resolvió darle al padre Nicanor el dinero que le hacía falta para terminar el templo. Amaranta no se impacientó. Mientras conversaba con las amigas que todas las tardes iban a bordar o tejer en el corredor, trataba de concebir nuevas triquiñuelas. Un error de cálculo echó a perder la que consideró más eficaz: quitar las bolitas de naftalina que Rebeca había puesto a su vestido de novia antes de guardarlo en la cómoda del dormitorio. Lo hizo cuando faltaban menos de dos meses para la terminación del templo. Pero Rebeca estaba tan impaciente ante la proximidad de la boda, que quiso preparar el vestido con más anticipación de la que había previsto Amaranta. Al abrir la cómoda y desenvolver primero los papeles y luego el lienzo protector, encontró el raso del vestido y el punto del velo y hasta la corona de azahares pulverizados por las polillas. Aunque estaba segura de haber puesto en el envoltorio dos puñados de bolitas de naftalina, el desastre parecía tan accidental que no se atrevió a culpar a Amaranta. Faltaba menos de un mes para la boda, pero Amparo Moscote se comprometió a coser un nuevo vestido en una semana. Amaranta se sintió desfallecer el mediodía lluvioso en que Amparo entró a la casa envuelta en una espumarada de punto para hacerle a Rebeca la última prueba del vestido.

Perdió la voz y un hilo de sudor helado descendió por el cauce de su espina dorsal. Durante largos meses había temblado de pavor esperando aquella hora, porque si no concebía el obstáculo definitivo para la boda de Rebeca, estaba segura de que en el último instante, cuando hubieran fallado todos los recursos de su imaginación, tendría valor para envenenarla. Esa tarde, mientras Rebeca se ahogaba de calor dentro de la coraza de raso que Amparo Moscote iba armando en su cuerpo con un millar de alfileres y una paciencia infinita, Amaranta equivocó varias veces los puntos del crochet y se pinchó el dedo con la aguja, pero decidió con espantosa frialdad que la fecha sería el último viernes antes de la boda, y el modo sería un chorro de láudano en el café.

Un obstáculo mayor, tan insalvable como imprevisto, obligó a un nuevo e indefinido aplazamiento. Una semana antes de la fecha fijada para la boda, la pequeña Remedios despertó a medianoche empapada en un caldo caliente que explotó en sus entrañas con una especie de eructo desgarrador, y murió tres días después envenenada por su propia sangre con un par de gemelos atravesados en el vientre. Amaranta sufrió una crisis de conciencia. Había suplicado a Dios con tanto fervor que algo pavoroso ocurriera para no tener que envenenar a Rebeca, que se sintió culpable por la muerte de Remedios. No era ese el obstáculo por el que tanto había suplicado. Remedios había llevado a la casa un soplo de alegría. Se había instalado con su esposo en una alcoba cercana al taller, que decoró con las muñecas y juguetes de su infancia reciente, y su alegre vitalidad desbordaba las cuatro paredes de la alcoba y pasaba como un ventarrón de buena salud por el corredor de las begonias.

Cantaba desde el amanecer. Fue ella la única persona que se atrevió a mediar en las disputas de Rebeca y Amaranta. Se echó encima la dispendiosa tarea de atender a José Arcadio Buendía. Le llevaba los alimentos, lo asistía en sus necesidades cotidianas, lo lavaba con jabón y estropajo, le mantenía limpios de piojos y liendres los cabellos y la barba, conservaba en buen estado el cobertizo de palma y lo reforzaba con lonas impermeables en tiempos de tormenta. En sus últimos meses había logrado comunicarse con él en frases de latín rudimentario. Cuando nació el hijo de Aureliano y Pilar Ternera y fue llevado a la casa y bautizado en ceremonia íntima con el nombre de Aureliano José, Remedios decidió que fuera considerado como su hijo mayor. Su instinto maternal sorprendió a Úrsula. Aureliano, por su parte, encontró en ella la justificación que le hacía falta para vivir. Trabajaba todo el día en el taller y Remedios le llevaba a media mañana un tazón de café sin azúcar. Ambos visitaban todas las noches a los Moscote. Aureliano jugaba con el suegro interminables partidos de dominó, mientras Remedios conversaba con sus hermanas o trataba con su madre asuntos de gente mayor. El vínculo con los Buendía consolidó en el pueblo la autoridad de don Apolinar Moscote. En frecuentes viajes a la capital de la provincia consiguió que el gobierno construyera una escuela para que la atendiera Arcadio, que había heredado el entusiasmo didáctico del abuelo. Logró por medio de la persuasión que la mayoría de las casas fueran pintadas de azul para la fiesta de la independencia nacional. A instancias del padre Nicanor dispuso el traslado de la tienda de Catarino a una calle apartada, y clausuró varios lugares de escándalo que prosperaban en el

III

centro de la población. Una vez regresó con seis policías armados de fusiles a quienes encomendó el mantenimiento del orden, sin que nadie se acordara del compromiso original de no tener gente armada en el pueblo. Aureliano se complacía de la eficacia de su suegro. «Te vas a poner tan gordo como él», le decían sus amigos. Pero el sedentarismo, que acentuó sus pómulos y concentró el fulgor de sus ojos, no aumentó su peso ni alteró la parsimonia de su carácter, y por el contrario endureció en sus labios la línea recta de la meditación solitaria y la decisión implacable. Tan hondo era el cariño que él y su esposa habían logrado despertar en la familia de ambos, que cuando Remedios anunció que iba a tener un hijo, hasta Rebeca y Amaranta hicieron una tregua para tejer en lana azul, por si nacía varón, y en lana rosada, por si nacía mujer. Fue ella la última persona en que pensó Arcadio, pocos años después, frente al pelotón de fusilamiento.

Úrsula dispuso un duelo de puertas y ventanas cerradas, sin entrada ni salida para nadie como no fuera para asuntos indispensables; prohibió hablar en voz alta durante un año, y puso el daguerrotipo de Remedios en el lugar en que se veló el cadáver, con una cinta negra terciada y una lámpara de aceite encendida para siempre. Las generaciones futuras, que nunca dejaron extinguir la lámpara, habían de desconcertarse ante aquella niña de faldas rizadas, botitas blancas y lazo de organdí en la cabeza, que no lograban hacer coincidir con la imagen académica de una bisabuela. Amaranta se hizo cargo de Aureliano José. Lo adoptó como un hijo que había de compartir su soledad, y aliviarla del láudano involuntario que echaron sus súplicas desatinadas en el café de

Remedios. Pietro Crespi entraba en puntillas al anochecer, con una cinta negra en el sombrero, y hacía una visita silenciosa a una Rebeca que parecía desangrarse dentro del vestido negro con mangas hasta los puños. Habría sido tan irreverente la sola idea de pensar en una nueva fecha para la boda, que el noviazgo se convirtió en una relación eterna, un amor de cansancio que nadie volvió a cuidar, como si los enamorados que en otros días descomponían las lámparas para besarse hubieran sido abandonados al albedrío de la muerte. Perdido el rumbo, completamente desmoralizada, Rebeca volvió a comer tierra.

De pronto —cuando el duelo llevaba tanto tiempo que ya se habían reanudado las sesiones de punto de cruz— alguien empujó la puerta de la calle a las dos de la tarde, en el silencio mortal del calor, y los horcones se estremecieron con tal fuerza en los cimientos, que Amaranta y sus amigas bordando en el corredor, Rebeca chupándose el dedo en el dormitorio, Úrsula en la cocina, Aureliano en el taller y hasta José Arcadio Buendía bajo el castaño solitario, tuvieron la impresión de que un temblor de tierra estaba desquiciando la casa. Llegaba un hombre descomunal. Sus espaldas cuadradas apenas si cabían por las puertas. Tenía una medallita de la Virgen de los Remedios colgada en el cuello de bisonte, los brazos y el pecho completamente bordados de tatuajes crípticos, y en la muñeca derecha la apretada esclava de cobre de los *niños-en-cruz*. Tenía el cuero curtido por la sal de la intemperie, el pelo corto y rapado como las crines de un mulo, las mandíbulas férreas y la mirada triste. Tenía un cinturón dos veces más grueso que la cincha de un caballo, botas con polainas y espuelas y con los tacones herrados, y su presencia daba la impresión trepidatoria de un sacudimiento sísmico. Atravesó la sala de visitas y la sala de estar, llevando en la mano unas alforjas medio desbaratadas, y apareció como un trueno en el corredor de las begonias, donde Amaranta y sus amigas estaban paralizadas con las agujas en el aire. «Buenas», les dijo él con la voz cansada, y tiró las alforjas en la mesa de labor y pasó de largo hacia el fondo de la casa. «Buenas», le dijo a la asustada Rebeca que lo vio pasar por la puerta de su dormitorio. «Buenas», le dijo a Aureliano, que estaba con los cinco sentidos alerta en el mesón de orfebrería. No se entretuvo con nadie. Fue directamente a la cocina, y allí se paró por primera vez en el término de un viaje que había empezado al otro lado del mundo. «Buenas», dijo. Úrsula se quedó una fracción de segundo con la boca abierta, lo miró a los ojos, lanzó un grito y saltó a su cuello gritando y llorando de alegría. Era José Arcadio. Regresaba tan pobre como se fue, hasta el extremo de que Úrsula tuvo que darle dos pesos para pagar el alquiler del caballo. Hablaba el español cruzado con jerga de marineros. Le preguntaron dónde había estado, y contestó: «Por ahí.» Colgó la hamaca en el cuarto que le asignaron y durmió tres días. Cuando despertó, y después de tomarse dieciséis huevos crudos, salió directamente hacia la tienda de Catarino, donde su corpulencia monumental provocó un pánico de curiosidad entre las mujeres. Ordenó música y aguardiente para todos por su cuenta. Hizo apuestas de pulso con cinco hombres al mismo tiempo. «Es imposible», decían, al convencerse de que no lograban moverle el brazo. «Tiene niños-en-cruz.» Catarino, que no creía en artificios de fuerza, apostó doce pesos a que no movía el mostrador. José

Arcadio lo arrancó de su sitio, lo levantó en vilo sobre la cabeza y lo puso en la calle. Se necesitaron once hombres para meterlo. En el calor de la fiesta exhibió sobre el mostrador su masculinidad inverosímil, enteramente tatuada con una maraña azul y roja de letreros en varios idiomas. A las mujeres que lo asediaron con su codicia les preguntó quién pagaba más. La que tenía más ofreció veinte pesos. Entonces él propuso rifarse entre todas a diez pesos el número. Era un precio desorbitado, porque la mujer más solicitada ganaba ocho pesos en una noche, pero todas aceptaron. Escribieron sus nombres en catorce papeletas que metieron en un sombrero, y cada mujer sacó una. Cuando sólo faltaban por sacar dos papeletas, se estableció a quiénes correspondían.

—Cinco pesos más cada una —propuso José Arcadio— y me reparto entre ambas.

De eso vivía. Le había dado sesenta y cinco veces la vuelta al mundo, enrolado en una tripulación de marineros apátridas. Las mujeres que se acostaron con él aquella noche en la tienda de Catarino lo llevaron desnudo a la sala de baile para que vieran que no tenía un milímetro del cuerpo sin tatuar, por el frente y por la espalda, y desde el cuello hasta los dedos de los pies. No lograba incorporarse a la familia. Dormía todo el día y pasaba la noche en el barrio de tolerancia haciendo suertes de fuerza. En las escasas ocasiones en que Úrsula logró sentarlo a la mesa, dio muestras de una simpatía radiante, sobre todo cuando contaba sus aventuras en países remotos. Había naufragado y permanecido dos semanas a la deriva en el mar del Japón, alimentándose con el cuerpo de un compañero que sucumbió a la insolación, cuya carne salada y vuelta a salar y cocinada al sol tenía un sabor granuloso y dulce. En un mediodía radiante del Golfo de Bengala su barco había vencido un dragón de mar en cuyo vientre encontraron el casco, las hebillas y las armas de un cruzado. Había visto en el Caribe el fantasma de la nave corsaria de Víctor Hugues, con el velamen desgarrado por los vientos de la muerte, la arboladura carcomida por las cucarachas de mar, y equivocado para siempre el rumbo de la Guadalupe. Úrsula lloraba en la mesa como si estuviera leyendo las cartas que nunca llegaron, en las cuales relataba José Arcadio sus hazañas y desventuras. «Y tanta casa aquí, hijo mío», sollozaba. «¡Y tanta comida tirada a los puercos!» Pero en el fondo no podía concebir que el muchacho que se llevaron los gitanos fuera el mismo atarván que se comía medio lechón en el almuerzo y cuyas ventosidades marchitaban las flores. Algo similar le ocurría al resto de la familia. Amaranta no podía disimular la repugnancia que le producían en la mesa sus eructos bestiales. Arcadio, que nunca conoció el secreto de su filiación, apenas si contestaba a las preguntas que él le hacía con el propósito evidente de conquistar sus afectos. Aureliano trató de revivir los tiempos en que dormían en el mismo cuarto, procuró restaurar la complicidad de la infancia, pero José Arcadio los había olvidado porque la vida del mar le saturó la memoria con demasiadas cosas que recordar. Sólo Rebeca sucumbió al primer impacto. La tarde en que lo vio pasar frente a su dormitorio pensó que Pietro Crespi era un currutaco de alfeñique junto a aquel protomacho cuya respiración volcánica se percibía en toda la casa. Buscaba su proximidad con cualquier pretexto. En cierta ocasión, José Arcadio le miró el cuerpo con una atención descarada, y le dijo: «Eres muy mujer, hermanita.» Rebeca perdió el dominio de sí misma. Volvió a comer tierra y cal de las paredes con la avidez de otros días, y se chupó el dedo con tanta ansiedad que se le formó un callo en el pulgar. Vomitó un líquido verde con sanguijuelas muertas. Pasó noches en vela tiritando de fiebre, luchando contra el delirio, esperando, hasta que la casa trepidaba con el regreso de José Arcadio al amanecer. Una tarde, cuando todos dormían la siesta, no resistió más y fue a su dormitorio. Lo encontró en calzoncillos, despierto, tendido en la hamaca que había colgado de los horcones con cables de amarrar barcos. La impresionó tanto su enorme desnudez tarabiscoteada que sintió el impulso de retroceder. «Perdone», se excusó. «No sabía que estaba aquí.» Pero apagó la voz para no despertar a nadie. «Ven acá», dijo él. Rebeca obedeció. Se detuvo junto a la hamaca, sudando hielo, sintiendo que se le formaban nudos en las tripas, mientras José Arcadio le acariciaba los tobillos con la yema de los dedos, y luego las pantorrillas y luego los muslos, murmurando: «Ay, hermanita; ay, hermanita.» Ella tuvo que hacer un esfuerzo sobrenatural para no morirse cuando una potencia ciclónica asombrosamente regulada la levantó por la cintura y la despojó de su intimidad con tres zarpazos, y la descuartizó como a un pajarito. Alcanzó a dar gracias a Dios por haber nacido, antes de perder la conciencia en el placer inconcebible de aquel dolor insoportable, chapaleando en el pantano humeante de la hamaca que absorbió como un papel secante la explosión de su sangre.

Tres días después se casaron en la misa de cinco. José Arcadio había ido el día anterior a la tienda de Pietro Crespi. Lo había encontrado dictando una lección de cítara y no lo llevó aparte para hablarle. «Me caso con Rebeca», le dijo. Pietro Crespi se puso pálido, le entregó la cítara a uno de los discípulos, y dio la clase por terminada. Cuando quedaron solos en el salón atiborrado de instrumentos músicos y juguetes de cuerda, Pietro Crespi dijo:

—Es su hermana.

—No me importa —replicó José Arcadio.

Pietro Crespi se enjugó la frente con el pañuelo impregnado de espliego.

—Es contra natura —explicó— y, además, la ley lo prohíbe.

José Arcadio se impacientó no tanto con la argumentación como con la palidez de Pietro Crespi.

—Me cago dos veces en natura —dijo—. Y se lo vengo a decir para que no se tome la molestia de ir a preguntarle nada a Rebeca.

Pero su comportamiento brutal se quebrantó al ver que a Pietro Crespi se le humedecían los ojos.

—Ahora —le dijo en otro tono—, que si lo que le gusta es la familia, ahí le queda Amaranta.

El padre Nicanor reveló en el sermón del domingo que José Arcadio y Rebeca no eran hermanos. Úrsula no perdonó nunca lo que consideró como una inconcebible falta de respeto, y cuando regresaron de la iglesia prohibió a los recién casados que volvieran a pisar la casa. Para ella era como si hubieran muerto. Así que alquilaron una casita frente al cementerio y se instalaron en ella sin más muebles que la hamaca de José Arcadio. La noche de bodas, a Rebeca le mordió el pie un alacrán que se había metido en su pantufla. Se le adormeció la lengua, pero eso no impidió que pasaran una luna de miel escandalosa. Los vecinos se asustaban con los gritos que despertaban a todo el barrio hasta ocho veces en una noche, y hasta tres veces en la siesta, y rogaban que una pasión tan desaforada no fuera a perturbar la paz de los muertos.

Aureliano fue el único que se preocupó por ellos. Les compró algunos muebles y les proporcionó dinero, hasta que José Arcadio recuperó el sentido de la realidad y empezó a trabajar las tierras de nadie que colindaban con el patio de la casa. Amaranta, en cambio, no logró superar jamás su rencor contra Rebeca, aunque la vida le ofreció una satisfacción con que no había soñado: por iniciativa de Úrsula, que no sabía cómo reparar la vergüenza, Pietro Crespi siguió almorzando los martes en la casa, sobrepuesto al fracaso con una serena dignidad. Conservó la cinta negra en el sombrero como una muestra de aprecio por la familia, y se complacía en demostrar su afecto a Úrsula llevándole regalos exóticos: sardinas portuguesas, mermelada de rosas turcas y, en cierta ocasión, un primoroso mantón de Manila. Amaranta lo atendía con una cariñosa diligencia. Adivinaba sus gustos, le arrancaba los hilos descosidos en los puños de la camisa, y bordó una docena de pañuelos con sus iniciales para el día de su cumpleaños. Los martes, después del almuerzo, mientras ella bordaba en el corredor, él le hacía una alegre compañía. Para Pietro Crespi, aquella mujer que siempre consideró y trató como una niña, fue una revelación. Aunque su tipo carecía de gracia, tenía una rara sensibilidad para apreciar las cosas del mundo, y una ternura secreta. Un martes, cuando nadie dudaba de que tarde o temprano tenía que ocurrir, Pietro Crespi le pidió que se casara con él. Ella no interrumpió su labor. Esperó a que pasara el caliente rubor de sus orejas e imprimió a su voz un sereno énfasis de madurez.

—Por supuesto, Crespi —dijo—, pero cuando uno se conozca mejor. Nunca es bueno precipitar las cosas.

Úrsula se ofuscó. A pesar del aprecio que le tenía a Pietro Crespi, no lograba establecer si su decisión era buena o mala desde el punto de vista moral, después del prolongado y ruidoso noviazgo con Rebeca. Pero terminó por aceptarlo como un hecho sin calificación, porque nadie compartió sus dudas. Aureliano, que era el hombre de la casa, la confundió más con su enigmática y terminante opinión:

—Estas no son horas de andar pensando en matrimonios.

Aquella opinión que Úrsula sólo comprendió algunos meses después era la única sincera que podía expresar Aureliano en ese momento, no sólo con respecto al matrimonio, sino a cualquier asunto que no fuera la guerra. Él mismo, frente al pelotón de fusilamiento, no había de entender muy bien cómo se fue encadenando la serie de sutiles pero irrevocables casualidades que lo llevaron hasta ese punto. La muerte de Remedios no le produjo la conmoción que temía. Fue más bien un sordo sentimiento de rabia que paulatinamente se disolvió en una frustración solitaria y pasiva, semejante a la que experimentó en los tiempos en que estaba resignado a vivir sin mujer. Volvió a hundirse en el trabajo, pero conservó la costumbre de jugar dominó con su suegro. En una casa amordazada por el luto, las conversaciones nocturnas consolidaron la amistad de los dos hombres. «Vuelve a casarte, Aurelito», le decía el suegro. «Tengo seis hijas para escoger.» En cierta ocasión, en vísperas de las elecciones, don Apolinar Moscote regresó de uno de sus frecuentes viajes, preocupado por la situación política del país. Los liberales estaban decididos a lanzarse a la guerra. Como Aureliano tenía en esa época nociones muy confusas sobre las diferencias entre conservadores y liberales, su suegro le daba lecciones esquemáticas. Los liberales, le decía, eran masones; gente de mala índole, partidaria de ahorcar a los curas, de implantar el matrimonio civil y el divorcio, de reconocer iguales derechos a los hijos naturales que a los legítimos, y de despedazar al país en un sistema federal que despojara de poderes a la autoridad suprema. Los conservadores, en cambio, que habían recibido el poder directamente de Dios, propugnaban por la estabilidad del orden público y la moral familiar; eran los defensores de la fe de Cristo, del principio de autoridad, y no estaban dispuestos a permitir que el país fuera descuartizado en entidades autónomas. Por sentimientos humanitarios, Aureliano simpatizaba con la actitud liberal respecto de los derechos de los hijos naturales, pero de todos modos no entendía cómo se llegaba al extremo de hacer una guerra por cosas que no podían tocarse con las manos. Le pareció una exageración que su suegro se hiciera enviar para las elecciones seis soldados armados con fusiles, al mando de un sargento, en un pueblo sin pasiones políticas. No sólo llegaron, sino que fueron de casa en casa decomisando armas de cacería, machetes y hasta cuchillos de cocina, antes de repartir entre los hombres mayores de veintiún años las papeletas azules con los nombres de los candidatos conservadores, y las papeletas rojas con los nombres de los candidatos liberales. La víspera de las elecciones el propio don Apolinar Moscote leyó un bando que prohibía desde la medianoche del sábado, y por cuarenta y ocho horas, la venta de bebidas alcohólicas y la reunión de más de tres personas que no fueran de la misma familia. Las elecciones transcurrieron sin incidentes. Desde las ocho de la mañana del domingo se instaló en la plaza la urna de madera custodiada por los seis soldados. Se votó con entera libertad, como pudo comprobarlo el propio Aureliano, que estuvo casi todo el día con su suegro vigilando que nadie votara más de una vez. A las cuatro de la tarde, un repique de redoblante en la plaza anunció el término de la jornada, y don Apolinar Moscote selló la urna con una etiqueta cruzada con su firma. Esa noche, mientras jugaba dominó con Aureliano, le ordenó al sargento romper la etiqueta para contar los votos. Había casi tantas papeletas rojas como azules, pero el sargento sólo dejó diez rojas y completó la diferencia con azules. Luego volvieron a sellar la urna con una etiqueta nueva y al día siguiente a primera hora se la llevaron para la capital de la provincia. «Los liberales irán a la guerra», dijo Aureliano. Don Apolinar no desatendió sus fichas de dominó. «Si lo dices por los cambios de papeletas, no irán», dijo. «Se dejan algunas rojas para que no haya reclamos.» Aureliano comprendió las desventajas de la oposición. «Si yo fuera liberal —dijo— iría a la guerra por esto de las papeletas.» Su suegro lo miró por encima del marco de los anteojos.

—Ay, Aurelito —dijo—, si tú fueras liberal, aunque fueras mi yerno, no hubieras visto el cambio de las papeletas.

Lo que en realidad causó indignación en el pueblo no fue el resultado de las elecciones, sino el hecho de que los soldados no hubieran devuelto las armas. Un grupo de mujeres habló con Aureliano para que consiguiera con su suegro la restitución de los cuchillos de cocina. Don Apolinar Moscote le explicó, en estricta reserva, que los soldados se habían llevado las armas decomisadas como prueba de que los liberales se estaban preparando para la guerra. Lo alarmó el cinismo de la declaración. No hizo ningún comentario, pero cierta noche en que Gerineldo Márquez y Magnífico Visbal hablaban con otros amigos del incidente de los cuchillos, le preguntaron si era liberal o conservador. Aureliano no vaciló:

—Si hay que ser algo, sería liberal —dijo—, porque los conservadores son unos tramposos.

Al día siguiente, a instancias de sus amigos, fue a visitar al doctor Alirio Noguera para que le tratara un supuesto dolor en el hígado. Ni siquiera sabía cuál era el sentido de la patraña. El doctor Alirio Noguera había llegado a Macondo pocos años antes con un botiquín de globulitos sin sabor y una divisa médica que no convenció a nadie: *Un clavo saca otro clavo.* En realidad era un farsante. Detrás de su inocente fachada de médico sin prestigio se escondía un terrorista que tapaba con unas cáligas de media pierna las cicatrices que dejaron en sus tobillos cinco años de cepo. Capturado en la primera aventura federalista, logró escapar a Curazao disfrazado con el traje que más detestaba en este mundo: una sotana. Al cabo de un prolongado destierro, embullado por las exaltadas noticias que llevaban a Curazao los exiliados de todo el Caribe, se embarcó en una goleta de contrabandistas y apareció en Riohacha con los frasquitos de glóbulos que no eran más que de azúcar refinada, y un diploma de la Universidad de Leipzig falsificado por él mismo. Lloró de desencanto. El fervor federalista, que los exiliados definían como un polvorín a punto de estallar, se había disuelto en una vaga ilusión electoral. Amargado por el fracaso, ansioso de un lugar seguro donde esperar la vejez, el falso homeópata se refugió en Macondo. En el estrecho cuartito atiborrado de frascos vacíos que alquiló a un lado de la plaza, vivió varios años de los enfermos sin esperanzas que después de haber probado todo se consolaban con glóbulos de azúcar. Sus instintos de agitador permanecieron en reposo mientras don Apolinar Moscote fue una autoridad decorativa. El tiempo se le iba en recordar y en luchar contra el asma. La proximidad de las elecciones fue el hilo que le permitió encontrar de nuevo la madeja de la subversión. Estableció contacto con la gente joven del pueblo, que carecía de formación política, y se empeñó en una sigilosa campaña de instigación. Las numerosas papeletas rojas que aparecieron en la urna, y que fueron atribuidas por don Apolinar Moscote a la novelería propia de la juventud, eran parte de su plan: obligó a sus discípulos a votar para convencerlos de que las elecciones eran una farsa. «Lo único eficaz —decía— es la violencia.» La mayoría de los amigos de Aureliano andaban entusiasmados con la idea de liquidar el orden conservador, pero nadie se había atrevido a incluirlo en los planes, no sólo por sus vínculos con el corregidor, sino por su carácter solitario y evasivo. Se sabía, además, que había votado azul por indicación del suegro. Así que fue una simple casualidad que revelara sus sentimientos políticos, y fue un puro golpe de curiosidad el que lo metió en la ventolera de visitar al médico para tratarse un dolor que no tenía. En el cuchitril oloroso a telaraña alcanforada se encontró con una especie de iguana polvorienta cuyos pulmones silbaban al respirar. Antes de hacerle ninguna pregunta el doctor lo llevó a la ventana y le examinó por dentro el párpado inferior. «No es ahí», dijo Aureliano, según le habían indicado. Se hundió el hígado con la punta de los dedos, y agregó: «Es aquí donde tengo el dolor que no me deja dormir.» Entonces el doctor Noguera cerró la ventana con el pretexto de que había mucho sol, y le explicó en términos simples por qué era un deber patriótico asesinar a los conservadores. Durante varios días llevó Aureliano un frasquito en el bolsillo de la camisa. Lo sacaba cada dos horas, ponía tres globulitos en la palma de la mano y se los echaba de golpe en la boca para disolverlos lentamente en la lengua. Don Apolinar Moscote se burló de su fe en la homeopatía, pero quienes estaban en el complot reconocieron en él a uno más de los suyos. Casi todos los hijos de los fundadores estaban implicados, aunque ninguno sabía concretamente en qué consistía la acción que ellos mismos tramaban. Sin embargo, el día en que el médico le reveló el secreto a Aureliano, éste le sacó el cuerpo a la conspiración. Aunque entonces estaba convencido de la urgencia de liquidar al régimen conservador, el plan lo horrorizó. El doctor Noguera era un místico del atentado personal. Su sistema se reducía a coordinar una serie de acciones individuales que en un golpe maestro de alcance nacional liquidara a los funcionarios del régimen con sus respectivas familias, sobre todo a los niños, para exterminar el conservatismo en la semilla. Don Apolinar Moscote, su esposa y sus seis hijas, por supuesto, estaban en la lista.

—Usted no es liberal ni es nada —le dijo Aureliano sin alterarse—. Usted no es más que un matarife.

—En ese caso —replicó el doctor con igual calma— devuélveme el frasquito. Ya no te hace falta.

Sólo seis meses después supo Aureliano que el doctor lo había desahuciado como hombre de acción, por ser un sentimental sin porvenir, con un carácter pasivo y una definida vocación solitaria. Trataron de cercarlo temiendo que denunciara la conspiración. Aureliano los tranquilizó: no diría una palabra, pero la noche en que fueran a asesinar a la familia Moscote lo encontrarían a él defendiendo la puerta. Demostró una decisión tan convincente, que el plan se aplazó para una fecha indefinida. Fue por esos días que Úrsula consultó su opinión sobre el matrimonio de Pietro Crespi y Amaranta, y él contestó que los tiempos no estaban para pensar en eso. Desde hacía una semana llevaba bajo la camisa una pistola arcaica. Vigilaba a sus amigos. Iba por las tardes a tomar el café con José Arcadio y Rebeca, que empezaban a ordenar su casa, y desde las siete jugaba dominó con el suegro. A la hora del almuerzo conversaba con Arcadio, que era ya un adolescente monumental, y lo encontraba cada vez más exaltado con la inminencia de la guerra. En la escuela, donde Arcadio tenía alumnos mayores que él revueltos con niños que apenas empezaban a hablar, había prendido la fiebre liberal. Se hablaba de fusilar al padre Nicanor, de convertir el templo en escuela, de implantar el amor libre. Aureliano procuró atemperar sus ímpetus. Le recomendó discreción y prudencia. Sordo a su razonamiento sereno, a su sentido de la realidad, Arcadio le reprochó en público su debilidad de carácter. Aureliano esperó. Por fin, a principios de diciembre, Úrsula irrumpió trastornada en el taller.

—¡Estalló la guerra!

En efecto, había estallado desde hacía tres meses. La ley marcial imperaba en todo el país. El único que lo supo a tiempo fue don Apolinar Moscote, pero no le dio la noticia ni a su mujer, mientras llegaba el pelotón del ejército que había de ocupar el pueblo por sorpresa. Entraron sin ruido antes del amanecer, con dos piezas de artillería ligera tiradas por mulas, y establecieron el cuartel en la escuela. Se impuso el toque de queda a las seis de la tarde. Se hizo una requisa más drástica que la anterior, casa por casa, y esta vez se llevaron hasta las herramientas de labranza. Sacaron a rastras al doctor Noguera, lo amarraron a un árbol de la plaza y lo fusilaron sin fórmula de juicio. El padre Nicanor trató de impresionar a las autoridades militares con el milagro de la levitación, y un soldado lo descalabró de un culatazo. La exaltación liberal se apagó en un terror silencioso. Aureliano, pálido, hermético, siguió jugando dominó con su suegro. Comprendió que a pesar de su título actual de jefe civil y militar de la plaza, don Apolinar Moscote era otra vez una autoridad decorativa. Las decisiones las tomaba un capitán del ejército que todas las mañanas recaudaba una manlieva extraordinaria para la defensa del orden público. Cuatro soldados al mando suyo arrebataron a su familia una mujer que había sido mordida por un perro rabioso y la mataron a culatazos en plena calle. Un domingo, dos semanas después de la ocupación, Aureliano entró en la casa de Gerineldo Márquez y con su parsimonia habitual pidió un tazón de café sin azúcar. Cuando los dos quedaron solos en la cocina, Aureliano imprimió a su voz una autoridad que nunca se le había conocido. «Prepara los muchachos», dijo. «Nos vamos a la guerra.» Gerineldo Márquez no lo creyó.

—¿Con qué armas? —preguntó.

—Con las de ellos —contestó Aureliano.

El martes a medianoche, en una operación descabellada, veintiún hombres menores de treinta años al mando de Aureliano Buendía, armados con cuchillos de mesa y hierros afilados, tomaron por sorpresa la guarnición, se apoderaron de las armas y fusilaron en el patio al capitán y los cuatro soldados que habían asesinado a la mujer.

Esa misma noche, mientras se escuchaban las descargas del pelotón de fusilamiento, Arcadio fue nombrado jefe civil y militar de la plaza. Los rebeldes casados apenas tuvieron tiempo de despedirse de sus esposas, a quienes abandonaron a sus propios recursos. Se fueron al amanecer, aclamados por la población liberada del terror, para unirse a las fuerzas del general revolucionario Victorio Medina, que según las últimas noticias andaba por el rumbo de Manaure. Antes de irse, Aureliano sacó a don Apolinar Moscote de un armario. «Usted se queda tranquilo, suegro», le dijo. «El nuevo gobierno garantiza, bajo palabra de honor, su seguridad personal y la de su familia.» Don Apolinar Moscote tuvo dificultades para identificar aquel conspirador de botas altas y fusil terciado a la espalda con quien había jugado dominó hasta las nueve de la noche.

—Esto es un disparate, Aurelito —exclamó.

—Ningún disparate —dijo Aureliano—. Es la guerra. Y no me vuelva a decir Aurelito, que ya soy el coronel Aureliano Buendía.

El coronel Aureliano Buendía promovió treinta y dos levantamientos armados y los perdió todos. Tuvo diecisiete hijos varones de diecisiete mujeres distintas, que fueron exterminados uno tras otro en una sola noche, antes de que el mayor cumpliera treinta y cinco años. Escapó a catorce atentados, a setenta y tres emboscadas y a un pelotón de fusilamiento. Sobrevivió a una carga de estricnina en el café que habría bastado para matar a un caballo. Rechazó la Orden del Mérito que le otorgó el presidente de la república. Llegó a ser comandante general de las fuerzas revolucionarias, con jurisdicción y mando de una frontera a la otra, y el hombre más temido por el gobierno, pero nunca permitió que le tomaran una fotografía. Declinó la pensión vitalicia que le ofrecieron después de la guerra y vivió hasta la vejez de los pescaditos de oro que fabricaba en su taller de Macondo. Aunque peleó siempre al frente de sus hombres, la única herida que recibió se la produjo él mismo después de firmar la capitulación de Neerlandia que puso término a casi veinte años de guerras civiles. Se disparó un tiro de pistola en el pecho y el proyectil le salió por la espalda sin lastimar ningún centro vital. Lo único que quedó de todo eso fue una calle con su nombre en Macondo. Sin embargo, según declaró pocos años antes de morir de viejo, ni siquiera eso esperaba la madrugada en que se fue con sus veintiún hombres a reunirse con las fuerzas del general Victorio Medina.

—Ahí te dejamos a Macondo —fue todo cuanto le dijo a Arcadio antes de irse—. Te lo dejamos bien, procura que lo encontremos mejor.

Arcadio le dio una interpretación muy personal a la recomendación. Se inventó un uniforme con galones y charreteras de mariscal, inspirado en las láminas de un libro de Melquíades, y se colgó al cinto el sable con borlas doradas del capitán fusilado. Emplazó las dos piezas de artillería a la entrada del pueblo, uniformó a sus antiguos alumnos, exacerbados por sus proclamas incendiarias, y los dejó vagar armados por las calles para dar a los forasteros una impresión de invulnerabilidad. Fue un truco de doble filo, porque el gobierno no se atrevió a atacar la plaza durante diez meses, pero cuando lo hizo descargó contra ella una fuerza tan desproporcionada que liquidó la resistencia en media hora. Desde el primer día de su mandato Arcadio reveló su afición por los bandos. Leyó hasta cuatro diarios para ordenar y disponer cuanto le pasaba por la cabeza. Implantó el servicio militar obligatorio desde los dieciocho años, declaró de utilidad pública los animales que transitaban por las calles después de las seis de la tarde e impuso a los hombres mayores de edad la obligación de usar un brazal rojo. Recluyó al padre Nicanor en la casa cural, bajo amenaza de fusilamiento, y le prohibió decir misa y tocar las campanas como no fuera para celebrar las victorias liberales. Para que nadie pusiera en duda la severidad de sus propósitos, mandó que un pelotón de fusilamiento se entrenara en la plaza pública disparando contra un espantapájaros. Al principio nadie lo tomó en serio. Eran, a fin de cuentas, los muchachos de la escuela jugando a gente mayor. Pero una noche, al entrar Arcadio en la tienda de Catarino, el trompetista de la banda lo saludó con un toque de fanfarria que provocó las risas de la clientela, y Arcadio lo hizo fusilar por irrespeto a la autoridad. A quienes protestaron los puso a pan y agua con los tobillos en un cepo que instaló en un cuarto de la escuela. «¡Eres un asesino!», le gritaba Úrsula cada vez que se enteraba de alguna nueva arbitrariedad. «Cuando Aureliano lo sepa te va a fusilar a ti y yo seré la primera en alegrarme.» Pero todo fue inútil. Arcadio siguió apretando los torniquetes de un rigor innecesario, hasta convertirse en el más cruel de los gobernantes que hubo nunca en Macondo. «Ahora sufran la diferencia», dijo don Apolinar Moscote en cierta ocasión. «Esto es el paraíso liberal.» Arcadio lo supo. Al frente de una patrulla asaltó la casa, destrozó los muebles, vapuleó a las hijas y se llevó a rastras a don Apolinar Moscote. Cuando Úrsula irrumpió en el patio del cuartel, después de haber atravesado el pueblo clamando de vergüenza y blandiendo de rabia un rebenque alquitranado, el propio Arcadio se disponía a dar la orden de fuego al pelotón de fusilamiento.

—¡Atrévete, bastardo! —gritó Úrsula.

Antes de que Arcadio tuviera tiempo de reaccionar, le descargó el primer vergajazo. «Atrévete, asesino», gritaba. «Y mátame también a mí, hijo de mala madre. Así no tendré ojos para llorar la vergüenza de haber criado un fenómeno.» Azotándolo sin misericordia, lo persiguió hasta el fondo del patio, donde Arcadio se enrolló como un caracol. Don Apolinar Moscote estaba inconsciente, amarrado en el poste donde antes tenían el espantapájaros despedazado por los tiros de entrenamiento. Los muchachos del pelotón se dispersaron, temerosos de que Úrsula terminara desahogándose con ellos. Pero ni siquiera los miró. Dejó a Arcadio con el uniforme arrastrado, bramando de dolor y rabia, y desató a don Apolinar Moscote para llevarlo a su casa. Antes de abandonar el cuartel, soltó a los presos del cepo.

A partir de entonces fue ella quien mandó en el pueblo. Restableció la misa dominical, suspendió el uso de los brazales rojos y descalificó los bandos atrabiliarios. Pero a despecho de su fortaleza, siguió llorando la desdicha de su destino. Se sintió tan sola, que buscó la inútil compañía del marido olvidado bajo el castaño. «Mira en lo que hemos quedado», le decía, mientras las lluvias de junio amenazaban con derribar el cobertizo de palma. «Mira la casa vacía, nuestros hijos desperdigados por el mundo, y nosotros dos solos otra vez como al principio.» José Arcadio Buendía, hundido en un abismo de inconsciencia, era sordo a sus lamentos. Al comienzo de su locura anunciaba con latinajos apremiantes sus urgencias cotidianas. En fugaces escampadas de lucidez, cuando Amaranta le llevaba la comida, él le comunicaba sus pesares más molestos y se prestaba con docilidad a sus ventosas y sinapismos. Pero en la época en que Úrsula fue a lamentarse a su lado había perdido todo contacto con la realidad. Ella lo bañaba por partes sentado en el banquito, mientras le daba noticias de la familia. «Aureliano se ha ido a la guerra, hace ya más de cuatro meses, y no hemos vuelto a saber de él», le decía, restregándole la espalda con un estropajo enjabonado. «José Arcadio volvió, hecho un hombrazo más alto que tú y todo bordado en punto de cruz, pero sólo vino a traer la vergüenza a nuestra casa.» Creyó observar, sin embargo, que su marido entristecía con las malas noticias. Entonces optó por mentirle. «No me creas lo que te digo», decía, mientras echaba cenizas sobre sus excrementos para recogerlos con la pala. «Dios quiso que José Arcadio y Rebeca se casaran, y ahora son muy felices.» Llegó a ser tan sincera en el engaño que ella misma acabó consolándose con sus propias mentiras. «Arcadio ya es un hombre serio —decía—, y muy valiente, y muy buen mozo con su uniforme y su sable.» Era como hablarle a un muerto, porque José Arcadio Buendía estaba ya fuera del alcance de toda preocupación. Pero ella insistió. Lo veía tan manso, tan indiferente a todo, que decidió soltarlo. Él ni siquiera se movió del banquito. Siguió expuesto al sol y a la lluvia, como si las sogas fueran innecesarias, porque un dominio superior a cualquier atadura visible lo mantenía amarrado al tronco del castaño. Hacia el mes de agosto, cuando el invierno empezaba a eternizarse, Úrsula pudo por fin darle una noticia que parecía verdad.

—Fíjate que nos sigue atosigando la buena suerte —le dijo—. Amaranta y el italiano de la pianola se van a casar.

Amaranta y Pietro Crespi, en efecto, habían profundizado en la amistad, amparados por la confianza de Úrsula, que esta vez no creyó necesario vigilar las visitas. Era un noviazgo crepuscular. El italiano llegaba al atardecer, con una gardenia en el ojal, y le traducía a Amaranta sonetos de Petrarca. Permanecían en el corredor sofocado por el orégano y las rosas, él leyendo y ella tejiendo encaje de bolillo, indiferentes a los sobresaltos y las malas noticias de la guerra, hasta que los mosquitos los obligaban a refugiarse en la sala. La sensibilidad de Amaranta, su discreta pero envolvente ternura, habían ido urdiendo en torno al novio una telaraña invisible que él tenía que apartar materialmente con sus dedos pálidos y sin anillos para abandonar la casa a las ocho. Habían hecho un precioso álbum con las tarjetas postales que Pietro Crespi recibía de Italia. Eran imágenes de enamorados en parques solitarios, con viñetas de corazones flechados y cintas doradas sostenidas por palomas. «Yo conozco este parque en Florencia», decía Pietro Crespi repasando las postales. «Uno extiende la mano y los pájaros bajan a comer.» A veces, ante una acuarela de Venecia, la nostalgia transformaba en tibios aromas de flores el olor de fango y mariscos podridos de los canales. Amaranta suspiraba, reía, soñaba con una segunda patria de hombres y mujeres hermosos que hablaban una lengua de niños, con ciudades antiguas de cuya pasada grandeza sólo quedaban los gatos entre los escombros. Después de atravesar el océano en su búsqueda, después de haberlo confundido con la pasión en los manoseos vehementes de Rebeca, Pietro Crespi había encontrado el amor. La dicha trajo consigo la prosperidad. Su almacén ocupaba entonces casi una cuadra, y era un invernadero de fantasía, con reproducciones del campanario de Florencia que daban la hora con un concierto de carillones, y cajas musicales de Sorrento, y polveras de China que cantaban al destaparlas tonadas de cinco notas, y todos los instrumentos músicos que se podían imaginar y todos los artificios de cuerda que se podían concebir. Bruno Crespi, su hermano menor, estaba al frente del almacén, porque él no se daba abasto para atender la escuela de música. Gracias a él, la Calle de los Turcos, con su deslumbrante exposición de chucherías, se transformó en un remanso melódico para olvidar las arbitrariedades de Arcadio y la pesadilla remota de la guerra. Cuando Úrsula dispuso la reanudación de la misa dominical, Pietro Crespi le regaló al templo un armonio alemán, organizó un coro infantil y preparó un repertorio gregoriano que puso una nota espléndida en el ritual taciturno del padre Nicanor. Nadie ponía en duda que haría de Amaranta una esposa feliz. Sin apresurar los sentimientos, dejándose arrastrar por la fluidez natural del corazón, llegaron a un punto en que sólo hacía falta fijar la fecha de la boda. No encontrarían obstáculos. Úrsula se acusaba íntimamente de haber torcido con aplazamientos reiterados el destino de Rebeca, y no estaba dispuesta a acumular remordimientos. El rigor del luto por la muerte de Remedios había sido relegado a un lugar secundario por la mortificación de la guerra, la ausencia de Aureliano, la brutalidad de Arcadio y la expulsión de José Arcadio y Rebeca. Ante la inminencia de la boda, el propio Pietro Crespi había insinuado que Aureliano José, en quien fomentó un cariño casi paternal, fuera considerado como su hijo mayor. Todo hacía pensar que Amaranta se orientaba hacia una felicidad sin tropiezos. Pero al contrario de Rebeca, ella no revelaba la menor ansiedad. Con la misma paciencia con que abigarraba manteles y tejía primores de pasamanería y bordaba pavorreales en punto de cruz, esperó a que Pietro Crespi no soportara más las urgencias del corazón. Su hora llegó con las lluvias aciagas de octubre. Pietro Crespi le quitó del regazo la canastilla de bordar y le apretó la mano entre las suyas. «No soporto más esta espera», le dijo. «Nos casamos el mes entrante.» Amaranta no tembló al contacto de sus manos de hielo. Retiró la suya, como un animalito escurridizo, y volvió a su labor.

—No seas ingenuo, Crespi —sonrió—, ni muerta me casaré contigo.

Pietro Crespi perdió el dominio de sí mismo. Lloró sin pudor, casi rompiéndose los dedos de desesperación, pero no logró quebrantarla. «No pierdas el tiempo», fue todo cuanto dijo Amaranta. «Si en verdad me quieres tanto, no vuelvas a pisar esta casa.» Úrsula creyó enloquecer de vergüenza. Pietro Crespi agotó los recursos de la súplica. Llegó a increíbles extremos de humillación. Lloró toda una tarde en el regazo de Úrsula, que hubiera vendido el alma por consolarlo. En noches de lluvia se le vio merodear por la casa con un paraguas de seda, tratando de sorprender una luz en el dormitorio de Amaranta. Nunca estuvo mejor vestido que en esa época. Su augusta cabeza de emperador atormentado adquirió un extraño aire de grandeza. Importunó a las amigas de Amaranta, las que iban a bordar en el corredor, para que trataran de persuadirla. Descuidó los negocios. Pasaba el día en la trastienda, escribiendo esquelas desatinadas, que hacía llegar a Amaranta con membranas de pétalos y mariposas disecadas, y que ella devolvía sin abrir. Se encerraba horas y horas a tocar la cítara. Una noche cantó. Macondo despertó en una especie de estupor, angelizado por una cítara que no merecía ser de este mundo y una voz como no podía concebirse que hubiera otra en la tierra con tanto amor. Pietro Crespi vio entonces la luz en todas las ventanas del pueblo, menos en la de Amaranta. El dos de noviembre, día de todos los muertos, su hermano abrió el almacén y encontró todas las lámparas encendidas y todas las cajas musicales destapadas y todos los relojes trabados en una hora interminable, y en medio de aquel concierto disparatado encontró a Pietro Crespi en el escritorio de la trastienda, con las muñecas cortadas a navaja y las dos manos metidas en una palangana de benjuí.

Úrsula dispuso que se le velara en la casa. El padre Nicanor se oponía a los oficios religiosos y a la sepultura en tierra sagrada. Úrsula se le enfrentó. «De algún modo que ni usted ni yo podemos entender, ese hombre era un santo», dijo. «Así que lo voy a enterrar, contra su voluntad, junto a la tumba de Melquíades.» Lo hizo, con el respaldo de todo el pueblo, en funerales magníficos. Amaranta no abandonó el dormitorio. Oyó desde su cama el llanto de Úrsula, los pasos y murmullos de la multitud que invadió la casa, los aullidos de las plañideras, y luego un hondo silencio oloroso a flores pisoteadas. Durante mucho tiempo siguió sintiendo el hálito de lavanda de Pietro Crespi al atardecer, pero tuvo fuerzas para no sucumbir al delirio. Úrsula la abandonó. Ni siquiera levantó los ojos para apiadarse de ella, la tarde en que Amaranta entró en la cocina y puso la mano en las brasas del fogón, hasta que le dolió tanto que no sintió más dolor, sino la pestilencia de su propia carne chamuscada. Fue una cura de burro para el remordimiento. Durante varios días anduvo por la casa con la mano metida en un tazón con claras de huevo, y cuando sanaron las quemaduras pareció como si las claras de huevo hubieran cicatrizado también las úlceras de su corazón. La única huella externa que le dejó la tragedia fue la venda de gasa negra que se puso en la mano quemada, y que había de llevar hasta la muerte.

Arcadio dio una rara muestra de generosidad, al proclamar mediante un bando el duelo oficial por la muerte de Pietro Crespi. Úrsula lo intérpretó como el regreso del cordero extraviado. Pero se equivocó. Había perdido a Arcadio, no desde que vistió el uniforme militar, sino desde siempre. Creía haberlo criado como a un hijo, como crió a Rebeca, sin privilegios ni discriminaciones. Sin embargo, Arcadio era un niño solitario y asustado durante la peste del insomnio, en medio de la fiebre utilitaria de Úrsula, de los delirios de José Arcadio Buendía, del hermetismo de Aureliano, de la rivalidad mortal entre Amaranta y Rebeca. Aureliano le enseñó a leer y escribir, pensando en otra cosa, como lo hubiera hecho un extraño. Le regalaba su ropa, para que Visitación la redujera, cuando ya estaba de tirar. Arcadio sufría con sus zapatos demasiado grandes, con sus pantalones remendados, con sus nalgas de mujer. Nunca logró comunicarse con nadie mejor que lo hizo con Visitación y Cataure en su lengua. Melquíades fue el único que en realidad se ocupó de él, que le hacía escuchar sus textos incomprensibles y le daba instrucciones sobre el arte de la daguerrotipia. Nadie se imaginaba cuánto lloró su muerte en secreto, y con qué desesperación trató de revivirlo en el estudio inútil de sus papeles. La escuela, donde se le ponía atención y se le respetaba, y luego el poder, con sus bandos terminantes y su uniforme de gloria, lo liberaron del peso de una antigua amargura. Una noche, en la tienda de Catarino, alguien se atrevió a decirle: «No mereces el apellido que llevas.» Al contrario de lo que todos esperaban, Arcadio no lo hizo fusilar.

—A mucha honra —dijo—, no soy un Buendía.

Quienes conocían el secreto de su filiación, pensaron por aquella réplica que también él estaba al corriente, pero en realidad no lo estuvo nunca. Pilar Ternera, su madre, que le había hecho hervir la sangre en el cuarto de daguerrotipia, fue para él una obsesión tan irresistible como lo fue primero para José Arcadio y luego para Aureliano. A pesar de que había perdido sus encantos y el esplendor de su risa, él la buscaba y la encontraba en el rastro de su olor de humo. Poco antes de la guerra, un mediodía en que ella fue más tarde que de costumbre a buscar a su hijo menor a la escuela, Arcadio la estaba esperando en el cuarto donde solía hacer la siesta, y donde después instaló el cepo. Mientras el niño jugaba en el patio, él esperó en la hamaca, temblando de ansiedad, sabiendo que Pilar Ternera tenía que pasar por ahí. Llegó. Arcadio la agarró por la muñeca y trató de meterla en la hamaca. «No puedo, no puedo», dijo Pilar Ternera horrorizada. «No te imaginas cómo quisiera complacerte, pero Dios es testigo que no puedo.» Arcadio la agarró por la cintura con su tremenda fuerza hereditaria, y sintió que el mundo se borraba al contacto de su piel. «No te hagas la santa», decía. «Al fin, todo el mundo sabe que eres una puta.» Pilar se sobrepuso al asco que le inspiraba su miserable destino.

—Los niños se van a dar cuenta —murmuró—. Es mejor que esta noche dejes la puerta sin tranca.

Arcadio la esperó aquella noche tiritando de fiebre en la hamaca. Esperó sin dormir, oyendo los grillos alborotados de la madrugada sin término y el horario implacable de los alcaravanes, cada vez más convencido de que lo habían engañado. De pronto, cuando la ansiedad se había descompuesto en rabia, la puerta se abrió. Pocos meses después, frente al pelotón de fusilamiento, Arcadio había de revivir los pasos perdidos en el salón de clases, los tropiezos contra los escaños, y por último la densidad de un cuerpo en las tinieblas del cuarto y los latidos del aire bombeado por un corazón que no era el suyo. Extendió la mano y encontró otra mano con dos sortijas en un mismo dedo, que estaba a punto de naufragar en la oscuridad. Sintió la nervadura de sus venas, el pulso de su infortunio, y sintió la palma húmeda con la línea de la vida tronchada en la base del pulgar por el zarpazo de la muerte. Entonces comprendió que no era esa la mujer que esperaba, porque no olía a humo sino a brillantina de florecitas, y tenía los senos inflados y ciegos con pezones de hombre, y el sexo pétreo y redondo como una nuez, y la ternura caótica de la inexperiencia exaltada. Era virgen y tenía el nombre inverosímil de Santa Sofía de la Piedad. Pilar Ternera le había pagado cincuenta pesos, la mitad de sus ahorros de toda la vida, para que hiciera lo que estaba haciendo. Arcadio la había visto muchas veces, atendiendo la tiendecita de víveres de sus padres, y nunca se había fijado en ella, porque tenía la rara virtud de no existir por completo sino en el momento oportuno. Pero desde aquel día se enroscó como un gato al calor de su axila. Ella iba a la escuela a la hora de la siesta, con el consentimiento de sus padres, a quienes Pilar Ternera había pagado la otra mitad de sus ahorros. Más tarde, cuando las tropas del gobierno los desalojaron del local, se amaban entre las latas de manteca y los sacos de maíz de la trastienda. Por la época en que Arcadio fue nombrado jefe civil y militar, tuvieron una hija.

Los únicos parientes que se enteraron fueron José Arcadio y Rebeca, con quienes Arcadio mantenía entonces relaciones íntimas, fundadas no tanto en el parentesco como en la complicidad. José Arcadio había doblegado la cerviz al yugo matrimonial. El carácter firme de Rebeca, la voracidad de su vientre, su tenaz ambición, absorbieron la descomunal energía del marido, que de holgazán y mujeriego se convirtió en un enorme animal de trabajo. Tenían una casa limpia y ordenada. Rebeca la abría de par en par al amanecer, y el viento de las tumbas entraba por las ventanas y salía por las puertas del patio, y dejaba las paredes blanqueadas y los muebles curtidos por el salitre de los muertos. El hambre de tierra, el cloc cloc de los huesos de sus padres, la impaciencia de su sangre frente a la pasividad de Pietro Crespi estaban relegados al desván de la memoria. Todo el día bordaba junto a la ventana, ajena a la zozobra de la guerra, hasta que los potes de cerámica empezaban a vibrar en el aparador y ella se levantaba a calentar la comida, mucho antes de que aparecieran los escuálidos perros rastreadores y luego el coloso de polainas y espuelas y con escopeta de dos cañones, que a veces llevaba un venado al hombro y casi siempre un sartal de conejos o de patos silvestres. Una tarde, al principio de su gobierno, Arcadio fue a visitarlos de un modo intempestivo. No lo veían desde que abandonaron la casa, pero se mostró tan cariñoso y familiar que lo invitaron a compartir el guisado.

Sólo cuando tomaban el café reveló Arcadio el motivo de su visita: había recibido una denuncia contra José Arcadio. Se decía que empezó arando su patio y había seguido derecho por las tierras contiguas, derribando cercas y arrasando ranchos con sus bueyes, hasta apoderarse por la fuerza de los mejores predios del contorno. A los campesinos que no había despojado, porque no le interesaban sus tierras, les impuso una contribución que cobraba cada sábado con los perros de presa y la escopeta de dos cañones. No lo negó. Fundaba su derecho en que las tierras usurpadas habían sido distribuidas por José Arcadio Buendía en los tiempos de la fundación, y creía posible demostrar que su padre estaba loco desde entonces, puesto que dispuso de un patrimonio que en realidad pertenecía a la familia. Era un alegato innecesario, porque Arcadio no había ido a hacer justicia. Ofreció simplemente crear una oficina de registro de la propiedad para que José Arcadio legalizara los títulos de la tierra usurpada, con la condición de que delegara en el gobierno local el derecho de cobrar las contribuciones. Se pusieron de acuerdo. Años después, cuando el coronel Aureliano Buendía examinó los títulos de propiedad, encontró que estaban registradas a nombre de su hermano todas las tierras que se divisaban desde la colina de su patio hasta el horizonte, inclusive el cementerio, y que en los once meses de su mandato Arcadio había cargado no sólo con el dinero de las contribuciones, sino también con el que cobraba al pueblo por el derecho de enterrar a los muertos en predios de José Arcadio.

Úrsula tardó varios meses en saber lo que ya era del dominio público, porque la gente se lo ocultaba para no aumentarle el sufrimiento. Empezó por sospecharlo. «Arcadio está construyendo una casa», le confió con fingido orgullo a su marido, mientras trataba de meterle en la boca una cucharada de jarabe de totumo. Sin embargo, suspiró involuntariamente: «No sé por qué todo esto me huele mal.» Más tarde, cuando se enteró de que Arcadio no sólo había terminado la casa sino que había encargado un mobiliario vienés, confirmó la sospecha de que estaba disponiendo de los fondos públicos. «Eres la vergüenza de nuestro apellido», le gritó un domingo después de misa, cuando lo vio en la casa nueva jugando barajas con sus oficiales. Arcadio no le prestó atención. Sólo entonces supo Úrsula que tenía una hija de seis meses, y que Santa Sofía de la Piedad, con quien vivía sin casarse, estaba otra vez encinta. Resolvió escribirle al coronel Aureliano Buendía, en cualquier lugar en que se encontrara, para ponerlo al corriente de la situación. Pero los acontecimientos que se precipitaron por aquellos días no sólo impidieron sus propósitos, sino que la hicieron arrepentirse de haberlos concebido. La guerra, que hasta entonces no había sido más que una palabra para designar una circunstancia vaga y remota, se concretó en una realidad dramática. A fines de febrero llegó a Macondo una anciana de aspecto ceniciento, montada en un burro cargado de escobas. Parecía tan inofensiva, que las patrullas de vigilancia la dejaron pasar sin preguntas, como uno más de los vendedores que a menudo llegaban de los pueblos de la ciénaga. Fue directamente al cuartel. Arcadio la recibió en el local donde antes estuvo el salón de clases, y que entonces estaba transformado en una especie de campamento de retaguardia, con hamacas enrolladas y colgadas en las argollas y petates amontonados en los rincones, y fusiles y carabinas y hasta escopetas de cacería dispersos por el suelo. La anciana se cuadró en un saludo militar antes de identificarse:

—Soy el coronel Gregorio Stevenson.

Llevaba malas noticias. Los últimos focos de resistencia liberal, según dijo, estaban siendo exterminados. El coronel Aureliano Buendía, a quien había dejado batiéndose en retirada por los lados de Riohacha, le encomendó la misión de hablar con Arcadio. Debía entregar la plaza sin resistencia, poniendo como condición que se respetaran bajo palabra de honor la vida y las propiedades de los liberales. Arcadio examinó con una mirada de conmiseración a aquel extraño mensajero que habría podido confundirse con una abuela fugitiva.

—Usted, por supuesto, trae algún papel escrito —dijo.

—Por supuesto —contestó el emisario—, no lo traigo. Es fácil comprender que en las actuales circunstancias no se lleve encima nada comprometedor.

Mientras hablaba, se sacó del corpiño y puso en la mesa un pescadito de oro. «Creo que con esto será suficiente», dijo. Arcadio comprobó que en efecto era uno de los pescaditos hechos por el coronel Aureliano Buendía. Pero alguien podía haberlo comprado antes de la guerra, o haberlo robado, y no tenía por tanto ningún mérito de salvoconducto. El mensajero llegó hasta el extremo de violar un secreto de guerra para acreditar su identidad. Reveló que iba en misión a Curazao, donde esperaba reclutar exiliados de todo el Caribe y adquirir armas y pertrechos suficientes para intentar un desembarco a fin de año. Confiando en ese plan, el coronel Aureliano Buendía no era partidario de que en aquel momento se hicieran sacrificios inútiles. Pero Arcadio fue inflexible. Hizo encarcelar al mensajero, mientras comprobaba su identidad, y resolvió defender la plaza hasta la muerte.

No tuvo que esperar mucho tiempo. Las noticias del fracaso liberal fueron cada vez más concretas. A fines de marzo, en una madrugada de lluvias prematuras, la calma tensa de las semanas anteriores se resolvió abruptamente con un desesperado toque de corneta, seguido de un cañonazo que desbarató la torre del templo. En realidad, la voluntad de resistencia de Arcadio era una locura. No disponía de más de cincuenta hombres mal armados, con una dotación máxima de veinte cartuchos cada uno. Pero entre ellos, sus antiguos alumnos, excitados con proclamas altisonantes, estaban decididos a sacrificar el pellejo por una causa perdida. En medio del tropel de botas, de órdenes contradictorias, de cañonazos que hacían temblar la tierra, de disparos atolondrados y de toques de corneta sin sentido, el supuesto coronel Stevenson consiguió hablar con Arcadio. «Evíteme la indignidad de morir en el cepo con estos trapos de mujer», le dijo. «Si he de morir, que sea peleando.» Logró convencerlo. Arcadio ordenó que le entregaran un arma con veinte cartuchos y lo dejaron con cinco hombres defendiendo el cuartel mientras él iba con su estado mayor a ponerse al frente de la resistencia. No alcanzó a llegar al camino de la ciénaga. Las barricadas habían sido despedazadas y los defensores se batían al descubierto en las calles, primero hasta donde les alcanzaba la dotación de los fusiles, y luego con pistolas contra fusiles y por último cuerpo a cuerpo. Ante la inminencia de la derrota, algunas mujeres se echaron a la calle armadas de palos y cuchillos de cocina. En aquella confusión, Arcadio encontró a Amaranta que andaba buscándolo como una loca, en camisa de dormir, con dos viejas pistolas de José Arcadio Buendía. Le dio su fusil a un oficial que había sido desarmado en la refriega, y se evadió con Amaranta por una calle adyacente para llevarla a casa. Úrsula estaba en la puerta, esperando, indiferente a las descargas que habían abierto una tronera en la fachada de la casa vecina. La lluvia cedía, pero las calles estaban resbaladizas y blandas como jabón derretido, y había que adivinar las distancias en la oscuridad. Arcadio dejó a Amaranta con Úrsula y trató de enfrentarse a dos soldados que soltaron una andanada ciega desde la esquina. Las viejas pistolas guardadas muchos años en un ropero no funcionaron. Protegiendo a Arcadio con su cuerpo, Úrsula intentó arrastrarlo hasta la casa.

—Ven, por Dios —le gritaba—. ¡Ya basta de locuras!

Los soldados los apuntaron.

—¡Suelte a ese hombre, señora —gritó uno de ellos—, o no respondemos!

Arcadio empujó a Úrsula hacia la casa y se entregó. Poco después terminaron los disparos y empezaron a repicar las campanas. La resistencia había sido aniquilada en menos de media hora. Ni uno solo de los hombres de Arcadio sobrevivió al asalto, pero antes de morir se llevaron por delante a trescientos soldados. El último baluarte fue el cuartel. Antes de ser atacado, el supuesto coronel Gregorio Stevenson puso en libertad a los presos y ordenó a sus hombres que salieran a batirse en la calle. La extraordinaria movilidad y la puntería certera con que disparó sus veinte cartuchos por las diferentes ventanas dieron la impresión de que el cuartel estaba bien resguardado, y los atacantes lo despedazaron a cañonazos. El capitán que dirigió la operación se asombró de encontrar los escombros desiertos, y un solo hombre en calzoncillos, muerto, con el fusil sin carga, todavía agarrado por un brazo que había sido arrancado de cuajo. Tenía una frondosa cabellera de mujer enrollada en la nuca con una peineta, y en el cuello un escapulario con un pescadito de oro. Al voltearlo con la puntera de la bota para alumbrarle la cara, el capitán se quedó perplejo. «Mierda», exclamó. Otros oficiales se acercaron.

—Miren dónde vino a aparecer este hombre —les dijo el capitán—. Es Gregorio Stevenson.

Al amanecer, después de un consejo de guerra sumario, Arcadio fue fusilado contra el muro del cementerio. En las dos últimas horas de su vida no logró entender por qué había desaparecido el miedo que lo atormentó desde la infancia. Impasible, sin preocuparse siquiera por demostrar su reciente valor, escuchó los interminables cargos de la acusación. Pensaba en Úrsula, que a esa hora debía estar bajo el castaño tomando el café con José Arcadio Buendía. Pensaba en su hija de ocho meses, que aún no tenía nombre, y en el que iba a nacer en agosto. Pensaba en Santa Sofía de la Piedad, a quien la noche anterior dejó salando un venado para el almuerzo del sábado, y añoró su cabello chorreado sobre los hombros y sus pestañas que parecían artificiales. Pensaba en su gente sin sentimentalismos, en un severo ajuste de cuentas con la vida, empezando a comprender cuánto quería en realidad a las personas que más había odiado. El presidente del consejo de guerra inició su discurso final, antes de que Arcadio cayera en la cuenta de que habían transcurrido dos horas. «Aunque los cargos comprobados no tuvieran sobrados méritos —decía el presidente—, la temeridad irresponsable y criminal con que el acusado empujó a sus subordinados a una muerte inútil, bastaría para merecerle la pena capital.» En la escuela desportillada donde experimentó por primera vez la seguridad del poder, a pocos metros del cuarto donde conoció la incertidumbre del amor, Arcadio encontró ridículo el formalismo de la muerte. En realidad no le importaba la muerte sino la vida, y por eso la sensación que experimentó cuando pronunciaron la sentencia no fue una sensación de miedo sino de nostalgia. No habló mientras no le preguntaron cuál era su última voluntad.

—Díganle a mi mujer —contestó con voz bien timbrada— que le ponga a la niña el nombre de Úrsula. —Hizo una pausa y confirmó—: Úrsula, como la abuela. Y díganle también que si el que va a nacer nace varón, que le ponga José Arcadio, pero no por el tío, sino por el abuelo.

Antes de que lo llevaran al paredón, el padre Nicanor trató de asistirlo. «No tengo nada de qué arrepentirme», dijo Arcadio, y se puso a las órdenes del pelotón después de tomarse una taza de café negro. El jefe del pelotón, especialista en ejecuciones sumarias, tenía un nombre que era mucho más que una casualidad: capitán Roque Carnicero. Camino del cementerio, bajo la llovizna persistente, Arcadio observó que en el horizonte despuntaba un miércoles radiante. La nostalgia se desvanecía con la niebla y dejaba en su lugar una inmensa curiosidad. Sólo cuando le ordenaron ponerse de espaldas al muro, Arcadio vio a Rebeca con el pelo mojado y un vestido de flores rosadas, abriendo la casa de par en par. Hizo un esfuerzo para que lo reconociera. En efecto, Rebeca miró casualmente hacia el muro y se quedó paralizada de estupor, y apenas pudo reaccionar para hacerle a Arcadio una señal de adiós con la mano. Arcadio le contestó en la misma forma. En ese instante lo apuntaron las bocas ahumadas de los fusiles, y oyó letra por letra las encíclicas cantadas de Melquíades, y sintió los pasos perdidos de Santa Sofía de la Piedad, virgen, en el salón de clases, y experimentó en la nariz la misma dureza de hielo que le había llamado la atención en las fosas nasales del cadáver de Remedios. «¡Ah, carajo! —alcanzó a pensar—, se me olvidó decir que si nacía mujer le pusieran Remedios.» Entonces, acumulado en un zarpazo desgarrador, volvió a sentir todo el terror que le atormentó en la vida. El capitán dio la orden de fuego. Arcadio apenas tuvo tiempo de sacar el pecho y levantar la cabeza, sin comprender de dónde fluía el líquido ardiente que le quemaba los muslos.

—¡Cabrones! —gritó—. ¡Viva el partido liberal!

would make

En mayo terminó la guerra. Dos semanas antes de que el gobierno hiciera el anuncio oficial, en una proclama altisonante que prometía un despiadado castigo para los promotores de la rebelión, el coronel Aureliano Buendía cayó prisionero cuando estaba a punto de alcanzar la frontera occidental disfrazado de hechicero indígena. De los veintiún hombres que lo siguieron a la guerra, catorce murieron en combate, seis estaban heridos, y sólo uno lo acompañaba en el momento de la derrota final: el coronel Gerineldo Márquez. La noticia de la captura fue dada en Macondo con un bando extraordinario. «Está vivo», le informó Úrsula a su marido. «Roguemos a Dios para que sus enemigos tengan clemencia.» Después de tres días de llanto, una tarde en que batía un dulce de leche en la cocina, oyó claramente la voz de su hijo muy cerca del oído. «Era Aureliano», gritó, corriendo hacia el castaño para darle la noticia al esposo. «No sé cómo ha sido el milagro, pero está vivo y vamos a verlo muy pronto.» Lo dio por hecho. Hizo lavar los pisos de la casa y cambiar la posición de los muebles. Unas semanas después, un rumor sin origen que no sería respaldado por el bando, confirmó dramáticamente el presagio. El coronel Aureliano Buendía había sido condenado a muerte, y la sentencia sería ejecutada en Macondo, para escarmiento de la población.

Un lunes, a las diez y veinte de la mañana, Amaranta estaba vistiendo a Aureliano José, cuando percibió un tropel remoto y un toque de corneta, un segundo antes de que Úrsula irrumpiera en el cuarto con un grito: «Ya lo traen.» La tropa pugnaba por someter a culatazos a la muchedumbre desbordada. Úrsula y Amaranta corrieron hasta la esquina, abriéndose paso a empellones, y entonces lo vieron. Parecía un pordiosero. Tenía la ropa desgarrada, el cabello y la barba enmarañados, y estaba descalzo. Caminaba sin sentir el polvo abrasante, con las manos amarradas a la espalda con una soga que sostenía en la cabeza de su montura un oficial de a caballo. Junto a él, también astroso y derrotado, llevaban al coronel Gerineldo Márquez. No estaban tristes. Parecían más bien turbados por la muchedumbre que gritaba a la tropa toda clase de improperios.

—¡Hijo mío! —gritó Úrsula en medio de la algazara, y le dio un manotazo al soldado que trató de detenerla. El caballo del oficial se encabritó. Entonces el coronel Aureliano Buendía se detuvo, trémulo, esquivó los brazos de su madre y fijó en sus ojos una mirada dura.

—Váyase a casa, mamá —dijo—. Pida permiso a las autoridades y venga a verme a la cárcel.

Miró a Amaranta, que permanecía indecisa a dos pasos detrás de Úrsula, y le sonrió al preguntarle: «¿Qué te pasó en la mano?» Amaranta levantó la mano con la venda negra. «Una quemadura», dijo, y apartó a Úrsula para que no la atropellaran los caballos. La tropa disparó. Una guardia especial rodeó a los prisioneros y los llevó al trote al cuartel.

Al atardecer, Úrsula visitó en la cárcel al coronel Aureliano Buendía. Había tratado de conseguir el permiso a través de don Apolinar Moscote, pero éste había perdido toda autoridad frente a la omnipotencia de los militares. El padre Nicanor estaba postrado por una calentura hepática. Los padres del coronel Gerineldo Márquez, que no estaba condenado a muerte, habían tratado de verlo y fueron rechazados a culatazos. Ante la imposibilidad de conseguir intermediarios, convencida de que su hijo sería fusilado al amanecer, Úrsula hizo un envoltorio con las cosas que quería llevarle y fue sola al cuartel.

—Soy la madre del coronel Aureliano Buendía —se anunció.

Los centinelas le cerraron el paso. «De todos modos voy a entrar», les advirtió Úrsula. «De manera que si tienen orden de disparar, empiecen de una vez.» Apartó a uno de un empellón y entró a la antigua sala de clases, donde un grupo de soldados desnudos engrasaba sus armas. Un oficial en uniforme de campaña, sonrosado, con lentes de cristales muy gruesos y ademanes ceremoniosos, hizo a los centinelas una señal para que se retiraran.

—Soy la madre del coronel Aureliano Buendía —repitió Úrsula.

—Usted querrá decir —corrigió el oficial con una sonrisa amable— que es la señora madre del *señor* Aureliano Buendía.

Úrsula reconoció en su modo de hablar rebuscado la cadencia lánguida de la gente del páramo, los cachacos.

—Como usted diga, señor —admitió—, siempre que me permita verlo.

Había órdenes superiores de no permitir visitas a los condenados a muerte, pero el oficial asumió la responsabilidad de concederle una entrevista de quince minutos. Úrsula le mostró lo que llevaba en el envoltorio: una muda de ropa limpia, los botines que se puso su hijo para la boda y el dulce de leche que guardaba para él desde el día en que presintió su regreso. Encontró al coronel Aureliano Buendía en el cuarto del cepo, tendido en un catre y con los brazos abiertos, porque tenía las axilas empedradas de golondrinos. Le habían permitido afeitarse. El bigote denso de puntas retorcidas acentuaba la angulosidad de sus pómulos. A Úrsula le pareció que estaba más pálido que cuando se fue, un poco más alto y más solitario que nunca. Estaba enterado de los pormenores de la casa: el suicidio de Pietro Crespi, las arbitrariedades y el fusilamiento de Arcadio, la impavidez de José Arcadio Buendía bajo el castaño. Sabía que Amaranta había consagrado su viudez de virgen a la crianza de Aureliano José, y que éste empezaba a dar muestras de muy buen juicio y leía y escribía al mismo tiempo que aprendía a hablar. Desde el momento en que entró al cuarto, Úrsula se sintió cohibida por la madurez de su hijo, por su aura de dominio, por el resplandor de autoridad que irradiaba su piel. Se sorprendió que estuviera tan bien informado «Ya sabe usted que soy adivino», bromeó él. Y agregó en serio: «Esta mañana, cuando me trajeron, tuve la impresión de que ya había pasado por todo esto.» En verdad, mientras la muchedumbre tronaba a su paso, él estaba concentrado en sus pensamientos, asombrado de la forma en que había envejecido el pueblo en un año. Los almendros tenían las hojas rotas. Las casas pintadas de azul, pintadas luego de rojo y luego vueltas a pintar de azul, habían terminado por adquirir una coloración indefinible.

—¿Qué esperabas? —suspiró Úrsula—. El tiempo pasa.

—Así es —admitió Aureliano—, pero no tanto.

De este modo la visita tanto tiempo esperada, para la que ambos habían preparado las preguntas e inclusive previsto las respuestas, fue otra vez la conversación cotidiana de siempre. Cuando el centinela anunció el término de la entrevista, Aureliano sacó de debajo de la estera del catre un rollo de papeles sudados. Eran sus versos. Los inspirados por Remedios, que había llevado consigo cuando se fue, y los escritos después, en las azarosas pausas de la guerra. «Prométame que no los va a leer nadie», dijo. «Esta misma noche encienda el horno con ellos.» Úrsula lo prometió y se incorporó para darle un beso de despedida.

—Te traje un revólver —murmuró.

El coronel Aureliano Buendía comprobó que el centinela no estaba a la vista. «No me sirve de nada», replicó en voz baja. «Pero démelo, no sea que la registren a la salida.» Úrsula sacó el revólver del corpiño y él lo puso debajo de la estera del catre. «Y ahora no se despida», concluyó con un énfasis calmado. «No suplique a nadie ni se rebaje ante nadie. Hágase el cargo que me fusilaron hace mucho tiempo.» Úrsula se mordió los labios para no llorar.

—Ponte piedras calientes en los golondrinos —dijo.

Dio media vuelta y salió del cuarto. El coronel Aureliano Buendía permaneció de pie, pensativo, hasta que se cerró la puerta. Entonces volvió a acostarse con los brazos abiertos. Desde el principio de la adolescencia, cuando empezó a ser consciente de sus presagios, pensó que la muerte había de anunciarse con una señal definida, inequívoca, irrevocable, pero le faltaban pocas horas para morir, y la señal no llegaba. En cierta ocasión una mujer muy bella entró a su campamento de Tucurinca y pidió a los centinelas que le permitieran verlo. La dejaron pasar, porque conocían el fanatismo de algunas madres que enviaban a sus hijas al dormitorio de los guerreros más notables, según ellas mismas decían, para mejorar la raza. El coronel Aureliano Buendía estaba aquella noche terminando el poema del hombre que se había extraviado en la lluvia, cuando la muchacha entró al cuarto. Él le dio la espalda para poner la hoja en la gaveta con llave donde guardaba sus versos. Y entonces lo sintió. Agarró la pistola en la gaveta sin volver la cara.

—No dispare, por favor —dijo.

Cuando se volvió con la pistola montada, la muchacha había bajado la suya y no sabía qué hacer. Así había logrado eludir cuatro de once emboscadas. En cambio, alguien que nunca fue capturado entró una noche al cuartel revolucionario de Manaure y asesinó a puñaladas a su íntimo amigo, el coronel Magnífico Visbal, a quien había cedido el catre para que sudara una calentura. A pocos metros, durmiendo en una hamaca en el mismo cuarto, él no se dio cuenta de nada. Eran inútiles sus esfuerzos por sistematizar los presagios. Se presentaban de pronto, en una ráfaga de lucidez sobrenatural, como una convicción absoluta y momentánea, pero inasible. En ocasiones eran tan naturales, que no los identificaba como presagios sino cuando se cumplían. Otras veces eran terminantes y no se cumplían. Con frecuencia no eran más que golpes vulgares de superstición. Pero cuando lo condenaron a muerte y le pidieron expresar su última voluntad, no tuvo la menor dificultad para identificar el presagio que le inspiró la respuesta:

—Pido que la sentencia se cumpla en Macondo —dijo.

El presidente del tribunal se disgustó.

—No sea vivo, Buendía —le dijo—. Es una estratagema para ganar tiempo.

—Si no la cumplen, allá ustedes —dijo el coronel—, pero esa es mi última voluntad.

Desde entonces lo habían abandonado los presagios. El día en que Úrsula lo visitó en la cárcel, después de mucho pensar, llegó a la conclusión de que quizá la muerte no se anunciaría aquella vez, porque no dependía del azar sino de la voluntad de sus verdugos. Pasó la noche en vela atormentado por el dolor de los golondrinos. Poco antes del alba oyó pasos en el corredor. «Ya vienen», se dijo, y pensó sin motivo en José Arcadio Buendía, que en aquel momento estaba pensando en él, bajo la madrugada lúgubre del castaño. No sintió miedo, ni nostalgia, sino una rabia intestinal ante la idea de que aquella muerte artificiosa no le permitiría conocer el final de tantas cosas que dejaba sin terminar. La puerta se abrió y entró el centinela con un tazón de café. Al día siguiente a la misma hora todavía estaba como entonces, rabiando con el dolor de las axilas, y ocurrió exactamente lo mismo. El jueves compartió el dulce de leche con los centinelas y se puso la ropa limpia, que le quedaba estrecha, y los botines de charol. Todavía el viernes no lo habían fusilado.

En realidad, no se atrevían a ejecutar la sentencia. La rebeldía del pueblo hizo pensar a los militares que el fusilamiento del coronel Aureliano Buendía tendría graves consecuencias políticas no sólo en Macondo sino en todo el ámbito de la ciénaga, así que consultaron a las autoridades de la capital provincial. La noche del sábado, mientras esperaban la respuesta, el capitán Roque Carnicero fue con otros oficiales a la tienda de Catarino. Sólo una mujer, casi presionada con amenazas, se atrevió a llevarlo al cuarto. «No se quieren acostar con un hombre que saben que se va a morir», le confesó ella. «Nadie sabe cómo será, pero todo el mundo anda diciendo que el oficial que fusile al coronel Aureliano Buendía, y todos los soldados del pelotón, uno por uno, serán asesinados sin remedio, tarde o temprano, así se escondan en el fin del mundo.» El capitán Roque Carnicero lo comentó con los otros oficiales, y éstos lo comentaron con sus superiores. El domingo, aunque nadie lo había revelado con franqueza, aunque ningún acto militar había turbado la calma tensa de aquellos días, todo el pueblo sabía que los oficiales estaban dispuestos a eludir con toda clase de pretextos la responsabilidad de la ejecución. En el correo del lunes llegó la orden oficial: la ejecución debía cumplirse en el término de veinticuatro horas. Esa noche los oficiales metieron en una gorra siete papeletas con sus nombres, y el inclemente destino del capitán Roque Carnicero lo señaló con la papeleta premiada. «La mala suerte no tiene resquicios», dijo él con profunda amargura. «Nací hijo de puta y muero hijo de puta.» A las cinco de la mañana eligió el pelotón por sorteo, lo formó en el patio, y despertó al condenado con una frase premonitoria:

—Vamos, Buendía —le dijo—. Nos llegó la hora.

—Así que era esto —replicó el coronel—. Estaba soñando que se me habían reventado los golondrinos.

Rebeca Buendía se levantaba a las tres de la madrugada desde que supo que Aureliano sería fusilado. Se quedaba en el dormitorio a oscuras, vigilando por la ventana entreabierta el muro del cementerio, mientras la cama en que estaba sentada se estremecía con los ronquidos de José Arcadio. Esperó toda la semana con la misma obstinación recóndita con que en otra época esperaba las cartas de Pietro Crespi. «No lo fusilarán aquí», le decía José Arcadio. «Lo fusilarán a medianoche en el cuartel para que nadie sepa quién formó el pelotón, y lo enterrarán allá mismo.» Rebeca siguió esperando. «Son tan brutos que lo fusilarán aquí», decía. Tan segura estaba, que había previsto la forma en que abriría la puerta para decirle adiós con la mano. «No lo van a traer por la calle —insistía José Arcadio—, con sólo seis soldados asustados, sabiendo que la gente está dispuesta a todo.» Indiferente a la lógica de su marido, Rebeca continuaba en la ventana.

—Ya verás que son así de brutos —decía.

El martes a las cinco de la mañana José Arcadio había tomado el café y soltado los perros, cuando Rebeca cerró la ventana y se agarró de la cabecera de la cama para no caer. «Ahí lo traen», suspiró. «Qué hermoso está.» José Arcadio se asomó a la ventana, y lo vio, trémulo en la claridad del alba, con unos pantalones que habían sido suyos en la juventud. Estaba ya de espaldas al muro y tenía las manos apoyadas en la cintura porque los nudos ardientes de las axilas le impedían bajar los brazos. «Tanto joderse uno», murmuraba el coronel Aureliano Buendía. «Tanto joderse para que lo maten a uno seis *maricas* sin poder hacer nada.» Lo repetía con tanta rabia, que casi parecía fervor, y el capitán Roque Carnicero se conmovió porque creyó que estaba rezando. Cuando el pelotón lo apuntó, la rabia se había materializado en una sustancia viscosa y amarga que le adormeció la lengua y lo obligó a cerrar los ojos. Entonces desapareció el resplandor de aluminio del amanecer, y volvió a verse a sí mismo, muy niño, con pantalones cortos y un lazo en el cuello, y vio a su padre en una tarde espléndida conduciéndolo al interior de la carpa, y vio el hielo. Cuando oyó el grito, creyó que era la orden final al pelotón. Abrió los ojos con una curiosidad de escalofrío, esperando encontrarse con la trayectoria incandescente de los proyectiles, pero sólo encontró al capitán Roque Carnicero con los brazos en alto, y a José Arcadio atravesando la calle con su escopeta pavorosa lista para disparar.

—No haga fuego —le dijo el capitán a José Arcadio—. Usted viene mandado por la Divina Providencia

Allí empezó otra guerra. El capitán Roque Carnicero y sus seis hombres se fueron con el coronel Aureliano Buendía a liberar al general revolucionario Victorio Medina, condenado a muerte en Riohacha. Pensaron ganar tiempo atravesando la sierra por el camino que siguió José Arcadio Buendía para fundar a Macondo, pero antes de una semana se convencieron de que era una empresa imposible. De modo que tuvieron que hacer la peligrosa ruta de las estribaciones, sin más municiones que las del pelotón de fusilamiento. Acampaban cerca de los pueblos, y uno de ellos, con un pescadito de oro en la mano, entraba disfrazado a pleno día y hacía contacto con los liberales en reposo, que a la mañana siguiente salían a cazar y no regresaban nunca. Cuando avistaron a Riohacha desde un recodo de la sierra, el general Victorio Medina había sido fusilado. Los hombres del coronel Aureliano Buendía lo proclamaron jefe de las fuerzas revolucionarias del litoral del Caribe, con el grado de general. Él asumió el cargo, pero rechazó el ascenso, y se puso a sí mismo la condición de no aceptarlo mientras no derribaran el régimen conservador. Al cabo de tres meses habían logrado armar a más de mil hombres, pero fueron exterminados. Los sobrevivientes alcanzaron la frontera oriental. La próxima vez que se supo de ellos habían desembarcado en el Cabo de la Vela, procedentes del archipiélago de las Antillas, y un parte del gobierno, divulgado por telégrafo y publicado en bandos jubilosos por todo el país, anunció la muerte del coronel Aureliano Buendía. Pero dos días después, un telegrama múltiple, que casi le dio alcance al anterior, anunciaba otra rebelión en los llanos del sur. Así empezó la leyenda de la ubicuidad del coronel Aureliano Buendía. Informaciones simultáneas y contradictorias lo declaraban victorioso en Villanueva, derrotado en Guacamayal, devorado por los indios Motilones, muerto en una aldea de la ciénaga y otra vez sublevado en Urumita. Los dirigentes liberales, que en aquel momento estaban negociando una participación en el parlamento, lo señalaron como un aventurero sin representación de partido. El gobierno nacional lo asimiló a la categoría de <u>bandolero</u> y puso a su cabeza un precio de cinco mil pesos. Al cabo de dieciséis derrotas, el coronel Aureliano Buendía salió de la Guajira con dos mil indígenas bien armados, y la guarnición sorprendida durante el sueño abandonó Riohacha. Allí estableció su cuartel general, y proclamó la guerra total contra el régimen. La primera notificación que recibió del gobierno fue la amenaza de fusilar al coronel Gerineldo Márquez en el término de cuarenta y ocho horas, si no se replegaba con sus fuerzas hasta la frontera oriental. El coronel Roque Carnicero, que entonces era jefe de su estado mayor, le entregó el telegrama con un gesto de consternación, pero él lo leyó con imprevisible alegría.

—¡Qué bueno! —exclamó—. Ya tenemos telégrafo en Macondo.

Su respuesta fue terminante. En tres meses esperaba establecer su cuartel general en Macondo. Si entonces no encontraba vivo al coronel Gerineldo Márquez, fusilaría sin fórmula de juicio a toda la oficialidad que tuviera prisionera en ese momento, empezando por los generales, e impartiría órdenes a sus subordinados para que procedieran en igual forma hasta el término de la guerra. Tres meses después, cuando entró victorioso a Macondo, el primer abrazo que recibió en el camino de la ciénaga fue el del coronel Gerineldo Márquez.

La casa estaba llena de niños. Úrsula había recogido a Santa Sofía de la Piedad, con la hija mayor y un par de gemelos que nacieron cinco meses después del fusilamiento de Arcadio. Contra la última voluntad del fusilado, bautizó a la niña con el nombre de Remedios. «Estoy segura que eso fue lo que Arcadio quiso decir», alegó. «No le pondremos Úrsula, porque se sufre mucho con ese nombre.» A los gemelos les puso José Arcadio Segundo y Aureliano Segundo. Amaranta se hizo cargo de todos. Colocó asientitos de madera en la sala, y estableció un parvulario con otros niños de familias vecinas. Cuando regresó el coronel Aureliano Buendía, entre estampidos de cohetes y repiques de campanas, un coro infantil le dio la bienvenida en la casa. Aureliano José, largo como su abuelo, vestido de oficial revolucionario, le rindió honores militares.

No todas las noticias eran buenas. Un año después de la fuga del coronel Aureliano Buendía, José Arcadio y Rebeca se fueron a vivir en la casa construida por Arcadio. Nadie se enteró de su intervención para impedir el fusilamiento. En la casa nueva, situada en el mejor rincón de la plaza, a la sombra de un almendro privilegiado con tres nidos de petirrojos, con una puerta grande para las visitas y cuatro ventanas para la luz, establecieron un hogar hospitalario. Las antiguas amigas de Rebeca, entre ellas cuatro hermanas Moscote que continuaban solteras, reanudaron las sesiones de bordado interrumpidas años antes en el corredor de las begonias. José Arcadio siguió disfrutando de las tierras usurpadas, cuyos títulos fueron reconocidos por el gobierno conservador. Todas las tardes se le veía regresar a caballo, con sus perros montunos y su escopeta de dos cañones, y un sartal de conejos colgados en la montura. Una tarde de setiembre, ante la amenaza de una tormenta, regresó a casa más temprano que de costumbre. Saludó a Rebeca en el comedor, amarró los perros en el patio, colgó los conejos en la cocina para salarlos más tarde y fue al dormitorio a cambiarse de ropa. Rebeca declaró después que cuando su marido entró al dormitorio ella se encerró en el baño y no se dio cuenta de nada. Era una versión difícil de creer, pero no había otra más verosímil, y nadie pudo concebir un motivo para que Rebeca asesinara al hombre que la había hecho feliz. Ese fue tal vez el único misterio que nunca se esclareció en Macondo. Tan pronto como José Arcadio cerró la puerta del dormitorio, el estampido de un pistoletazo retumbó en la casa. Un hilo de sangre salió por debajo de la puerta, atravesó la sala, salió a la calle, siguió en un curso directo por los andenes desparejos, descendió escalinatas y subió pretiles, pasó de largo por la Calle de los Turcos, dobló una esquina a la derecha y otra a la izquierda, volteó en ángulo recto frente a la casa de los Buendía, pasó por debajo de la puerta cerrada, atravesó la sala de visitas pegado a las paredes para no manchar los tapices, siguió por la otra sala, eludió en una curva amplia la mesa del comedor, avanzó por el corredor de las begonias y pasó sin ser visto por debajo de la silla de Amaranta que daba una lección de aritmética a Aureliano José, y se metió por el granero y apareció en la cocina donde Úrsula se disponía a partir treinta y seis huevos para el pan.

—¡Ave María Purísima! —gritó Úrsula.

Siguió el hilo de sangre en sentido contrario, y en busca de su origen atravesó el granero, pasó por el corredor de las begonias donde Aureliano José cantaba que tres y tres son seis y seis y tres son nueve, y atravesó el comedor y las salas y siguió en línea recta por la calle, y dobló luego a la derecha y después a la izquierda hasta la Calle de los Turcos, sin recordar que todavía llevaba puestos el delantal de hornear y las babuchas caseras, y salió a la plaza y se metió por la puerta de una casa donde no había estado nunca, y empujó la puerta del dormitorio y casi se ahogó con el olor a pólvora quemada, y encontró a José Arcadio tirado boca abajo en el suelo sobre las polainas que se acababa de quitar, y vio el cabo original del hilo de sangre que ya había dejado de fluir de su oído derecho. No encontraron ninguna herida en su cuerpo ni pudieron localizar el arma. Tampoco fue posible quitar el penetrante olor a pólvora del cadáver. Primero lo lavaron tres veces con jabón y estropajo, después lo frotaron con sal y vinagre, luego con ceniza y limón, y por último lo metieron en un tonel de lejía y lo dejaron reposar seis horas. Tanto lo restregaron que los arabescos del tatuaje empezaban a decolorarse. Cuando concibieron el recurso desesperado de sazonarlo con pimienta y comino y hojas de laurel y hervirlo un día entero a fuego lento, ya había empezado a descomponerse y tuvieron que enterrarlo a las volandas. Lo encerraron herméticamente en un ataúd especial de dos metros y treinta centímetros de largo y un metro y diez centímetros de ancho, reforzado por dentro con planchas de hierro y atornillado con pernos de acero, y aun así se percibía el olor en las calles por donde pasó el entierro. El padre Nicanor, con el hígado hinchado y tenso como un tambor, le echó la bendición desde la cama. Aunque en los meses siguientes reforzaron la tumba con muros superpuestos y echaron entre ellos ceniza apelmazada, aserrín y cal viva, el cementerio siguió oliendo a pólvora hasta muchos años después, cuando los ingenieros de la compañía bananera recubrieron la sepultura con una coraza de hormigón. Tan pronto como sacaron el cadáver, Rebeca cerró las puertas de su casa y se enterró en vida, cubierta con una gruesa costra de desdén que ninguna tentación terrenal consiguió romper. Salió a la calle en una ocasión, ya muy vieja, con unos zapatos color de plata antigua y un sombrero de flores minúsculas, por la época en que pasó por el pueblo el Judío

Errante y provocó un calor tan intenso que los pájaros rompían las alambreras de las ventanas para morir en los dormitorios. La última vez que alguien la vio con vida fue cuando mató de un tiro certero a un ladrón que trató de forzar la puerta de su casa. Salvo Argénida, su criada y confidente, nadie volvió a tener contacto con ella desde entonces. En un tiempo se supo que escribía cartas al obispo, a quien consideraba como su primo hermano, pero nunca se dijo que hubiera recibido respuesta. El pueblo la olvidó.

A pesar de su regreso triunfal, el coronel Aureliano Buendía no se entusiasmaba con las apariencias. Las tropas del gobierno abandonaban las plazas sin resistencia, y eso suscitaba en la población liberal una ilusión de victoria que no convenía defraudar, pero los revolucionarios conocían la verdad, y más que nadie el coronel Aureliano Buendía. Aunque en ese momento mantenía más de cinco mil hombres bajo su mando y dominaba dos estados del litoral, tenía conciencia de estar acorralado contra el mar, y metido en una situación política tan confusa que cuando ordenó restaurar la torre de la iglesia desbaratada por un cañonazo del ejército, el padre Nicanor comentó en su lecho de enfermo: «Esto es un disparate: los defensores de la fe de Cristo destruyen el templo y los masones lo mandan componer.» Buscando una tronera de escape pasaba horas y horas en la oficina telegráfica, conferenciando con los jefes de otras plazas, y cada vez salía con la impresión más definida de que la guerra estaba estancada. Cuando se recibían noticias de nuevos triunfos liberales se proclamaban con bandos de júbilo, pero él medía en los mapas su verdadero alcance, y comprendía que sus huestes estaban penetrando en la selva, defen diéndose de la malaria y los mosquitos, avanzando en sentido contrario al de la realidad. «Estamos perdiendo el tiempo», se quejaba ante sus oficiales. «Estaremos perdiendo el tiempo mientras los cabrones del partido estén mendigando un asiento en el congreso.» En noches de vigilia, tendido bocarriba en la hamaca que colgaba en el mismo cuarto en que estuvo condenado a muerte, evocaba la imagen de los abogados vestidos de negro que abandonaban el palacio presidencial en el hielo de la madrugada con el cuello de los abrigos levantado hasta las orejas, frotándose las manos, cuchicheando, refugiándose en los cafetines lúgubres del amanecer, para especular sobre lo que quiso decir el presidente cuando dijo que sí, o lo que quiso decir cuando dijo que no, y para suponer inclusive lo que el presidente estaba pensando cuando dijo una cosa enteramente distinta, mientras él espantaba mosquitos a treinta y cinco grados de temperatura, sintiendo aproximarse el alba temible en que tendría que dar a sus hombres la orden de tirarse al mar.

Una noche de incertidumbre en que Pilar Ternera cantaba en el patio con la tropa, él pidió que le leyera el porvenir en las barajas. «Cuídate la boca», fue todo lo que sacó en claro Pilar Ternera después de extender y recoger los naipes tres veces. «No sé lo que quiere decir, pero la señal es muy clara: cuídate la boca.» Dos días después alguien le dio a un ordenanza un tazón de café sin azúcar, y el ordenanza se lo pasó a otro, y éste a otro, hasta que llegó de mano en mano al despacho del coronel Aureliano Buendía. No había pedido café, pero ya que estaba ahí, el coronel se lo tomó. Tenía una carga de nuez vómica suficiente para matar un caballo. Cuando lo llevaron a su casa estaba tieso y arqueado y tenía la lengua partida entre los dientes. Úrsula se lo disputó a la muerte. Después de limpiarle el estómago con vomitivos, lo envolvió en frazadas calientes y le dio claras de huevos durante dos días, hasta que el cuerpo estragado recobró la temperatura normal. Al cuarto día estaba fuera de peligro. Contra su voluntad, presionado por Úrsula y los oficiales, permaneció en la cama una semana más. Sólo entonces supo que no habían quemado sus versos. «No me quise precipitar», le explicó Úrsula. «Aquella noche, cuando iba a prender el horno, me dije que era mejor esperar que trajeran el cadáver.» En la neblina de la convalecencia, rodeado de las polvorientas muñecas de Remedios, el coronel Aureliano Buendía evocó en la lectura de sus versos los instantes decisivos de su existencia. Volvió a escribir. Durante muchas horas, al margen de los sobresaltos de una guerra sin futuro, resolvió en versos rimados sus experiencias a la orilla de la muerte. Entonces sus pensamientos se hicieron tan claros, que pudo examinarlos al derecho y al revés. Una noche le preguntó al coronel Gerineldo Márquez:

—Dime una cosa, compadre: ¿por qué estás peleando?

—Por qué ha de ser, compadre —contestó el coronel Gerineldo Márquez—: por el gran partido liberal.

—Dichoso tú que lo sabes —contestó él—. Yo, por mi parte, apenas ahora me doy cuenta que estoy peleando por orgullo.

—Eso es malo —dijo el coronel Gerineldo Márquez.

Al coronel Aureliano Buendía le divirtió su alarma. «Naturalmente», dijo. «Pero en todo caso, es mejor eso que no saber por qué se pelea.» Lo miró a los ojos, y agregó sonriendo:

—O que pelear como tú por algo que no significa nada para nadie.

Su orgullo le había impedido hacer contactos con los grupos armados del interior del país, mientras los dirigentes del partido no rectificaran en público su declaración de que era un bandolero. Sabía, sin embargo, que tan pronto como pusiera de lado esos escrúpulos rompería el círculo vicioso de la guerra. La convalecencia le permitió reflexionar. Entonces consiguió que Úrsula le diera el resto de la herencia enterrada y sus cuantiosos ahorros; nombró al coronel Gerineldo Márquez jefe civil y militar de Macondo, y se fue a establecer contacto con los grupos rebeldes del interior.

El coronel Gerineldo Márquez no sólo era el hombre de más confianza del coronel Aureliano Buendía, sino que Úrsula lo recibía como un miembro de la familia. Frágil, tímido, de una buena educación natural, estaba sin embargo mejor constituido para la guerra que para el gobierno. Sus asesores políticos lo enredaban con facilidad en laberintos teóricos. Pero consiguió imponer en Macondo el ambiente de paz rural con que soñaba el coronel Aureliano Buendía para morirse de viejo fabricando pescaditos de oro. Aunque vivía en casa de sus padres, almorzaba donde Úrsula dos o tres veces por semana. Inició a Aureliano José en el manejo de las armas de fuego, le dio una instrucción militar prematura y durante varios meses lo llevó a vivir al cuartel, con el consentimiento de Úrsula, para que se fuera haciendo hombre. Muchos años antes, siendo casi un niño, Gerineldo Márquez había declarado su amor a Amaranta. Ella estaba entonces tan ilusionada con su pasión solitaria por Pietro Crespi, que se rió de él. Gerineldo Márquez esperó. En cierta ocasión le envió a Amaranta un papelito desde la cárcel, pidiéndole el favor de bordar una docena de pañuelos de batista con las iniciales de su padre. Le mandó el dinero. Al cabo de una semana, Amaranta le llevó a la cárcel la docena de pañuelos bordados, junto con el dinero, y se quedaron varias horas hablando del pasado. «Cuando salga de aquí me casaré contigo», le dijo Gerineldo Márquez al despedirse. Amaranta se rió, pero siguió pensando en él mientras enseñaba a leer a los niños, y deseó revivir para él su pasión juvenil por Pietro Crespi. Los sábados, día de visita a los presos, pasaba por casa de los padres de Gerineldo Márquez y los acompañaba a la cárcel. Uno de esos sábados, Úrsula se sorprendió al verla en la cocina, esperando a que salieran los bizcochos del horno para escoger los mejores y envolverlos en una servilleta que había bordado para la ocasión.

—Cásate con él —le dijo—. Difícilmente encontrarás otro hombre como ese.

Amaranta fingió una reacción de disgusto.

—No necesito andar cazando hombres —replicó—. Le llevo estos bizcochos a Gerineldo porque me da lástima que tarde o temprano lo van a fusilar.

Lo dijo sin pensarlo, pero fue por esa época que el gobierno hizo pública la amenaza de fusilar al coronel Gerineldo Márquez si las fuerzas rebeldes no entregaban a Riohacha. Las visitas se suspendieron. Amaranta se encerró a llorar, agobiada por un sentimiento de culpa semejante al que la atormentó cuando murió Remedios, como si otra vez hubieran sido sus palabras irreflexivas las responsables de una muerte. Su madre la consoló. Le aseguró que el coronel Aureliano Buendía haría algo por impedir el fusilamiento, y prometió que ella misma se encargaría de atraer a Gerineldo Márquez, cuando terminara la guerra. Cumplió la promesa antes del término previsto. Cuando Gerineldo Márquez volvió a la casa investido de su nueva dignidad de jefe civil y militar, lo recibió como a un hijo, concibió exquisitos halagos para retenerlo, y rogó con todo el ánimo de su corazón que recordara su propósito de casarse con Amaranta. Sus súplicas parecían certeras. Los días en que iba a almorzar a la casa, el coronel Gerineldo Márquez se quedaba la tarde en el corredor de las begonias jugando damas chinas con Amaranta. Úrsula les llevaba café con leche y bizcochos y se hacía cargo de los niños para que no los molestaran. Amaranta, en realidad, se esforzaba por encender en su corazón las cenizas olvidadas de su pasión juvenil. Con una ansiedad que llegó a ser intolerable esperó los días de almuerzo, las tardes de damas chinas, y el tiempo se le iba volando en compañía de aquel guerrero de nombre nostálgico cuyos dedos temblaban imperceptiblemente al mover las fichas. Pero el día en que el coronel Gerineldo Márquez le reiteró su voluntad de casarse, ella lo rechazó.

—No me casaré con nadie —le dijo—, pero menos contigo. Quieres tanto a Aureliano que te vas a casar conmigo porque no puedes casarte con él.

El coronel Gerineldo Márquez era un hombre paciente. «Volveré a insistir», dijo. «Tarde o temprano te convenceré.» Siguió visitando la casa. Encerrada en el dormitorio, mordiendo un llanto secreto, Amaranta se metía los dedos en los oídos para no escuchar la voz del pretendiente que le contaba a Úrsula las últimas noticias de la guerra, y a pesar de que se moría por verlo, tuvo fuerzas para no salir a su encuentro.

El coronel Aureliano Buendía disponía entonces de tiempo para enviar cada dos semanas un informe pormenorizado a Macondo. Pero sólo una vez, casi ocho meses después de haberse ido, le escribió a Úrsula. Un emisario especial llevó a la casa un sobre lacrado, dentro del cual había un papel escrito con la caligrafía preciosista del coronel: *Cuiden mucho a papá porque se va a morir*. Úrsula se alarmó. «Si Aureliano lo dice, Aureliano lo sabe», dijo. Y pidió ayuda para llevar a José Arcadio Buendía a su dormitorio. No sólo era tan pesado como siempre, sino que en su prolongada estancia bajo el castaño había desarrollado la facultad de aumentar de peso voluntariamente, hasta el punto de que siete hombres no pudieron con él y tuvieron que llevarlo a rastras a la cama. Un tufo de hongos tiernos, de flor de palo, de antigua y reconcentrada intemperie impregnó el aire del dormitorio cuando empezó a respirarlo el viejo colosal macerado por el sol y la lluvia. Al día siguiente no amaneció en la cama. Después de buscarlo por todos los cuartos, Úrsula lo encontró otra vez bajo el castaño. Entonces lo amarraron a la cama. A pesar de su fuerza intacta, José Arcadio Buendía no estaba en condiciones de luchar. Todo le daba lo mismo. Si volvió al castaño no fue por su voluntad sino por una costumbre del cuerpo. Úrsula lo atendía, le daba de comer, le llevaba noticias de Aureliano. Pero en realidad, la única persona con quien él podía tener contacto desde hacía mucho tiempo, era Prudencio Aguilar. Ya casi pulverizado por la profunda decrepitud de la muerte, Prudencio Aguilar iba dos veces al día a conversar con él. Hablaban de gallos. Se pro-

metían establecer un criadero de animales magníficos, no tanto por disfrutar de unas victorias que entonces no les harían falta, sino por tener algo con qué
distraerse en los tediosos domingos de la muerte. Era
Prudencio Aguilar quien lo limpiaba, le daba de comer y le llevaba noticias espléndidas de un desconocido que se llamaba Aureliano y que era coronel en
la guerra. Cuando estaba solo, José Arcadio Buendía
se consolaba con el sueño de los cuartos infinitos.
Soñaba que se levantaba de la cama, abría la puerta y
pasaba a otro cuarto igual, con la misma cama de cabecera de hierro forjado, el mismo sillón de mimbre
y el mismo cuadrito de la Virgen de los Remedios en
la pared del fondo. De ese cuarto pasaba a otro exactamente igual, cuya puerta abría para pasar a otro
exactamente igual, y luego a otro exactamente igual,
hasta el infinito. Le gustaba irse de cuarto en cuarto,
como en una galería de espejos paralelos, hasta que
Prudencio Aguilar le tocaba el hombro. Entonces
regresaba de cuarto en cuarto, despertando hacia
atrás, recorriendo el camino inverso, y encontraba a
Prudencio Aguilar, en el cuarto de la realidad. Pero
una noche, dos semanas después de que lo llevaron a
la cama, Prudencio Aguilar le tocó el hombro en un
cuarto intermedio, y él se quedó allí para siempre,
creyendo que era el cuarto real. A la mañana siguiente Úrsula le llevaba el desayuno cuando vio acercarse
a un hombre por el corredor. Era pequeño y macizo,
con un traje de paño negro y un sombrero también
negro, enorme, hundido hasta los ojos taciturnos.
«Dios mío», pensó Úrsula. «Hubiera jurado que era
Melquíades.» Era Cataure, el hermano de Visitación,
que había abandonado la casa huyendo de la peste
del insomnio, y de quien nunca se volvió a tener no-

ticia. Visitación le preguntó por qué había vuelto, y él le contestó en su lengua solemne:

—He venido al sepelio del rey.

Entonces entraron al cuarto de José Arcadio Buendía, lo sacudieron con todas sus fuerzas, le gritaron al oído, le pusieron un espejo frente a las fosas nasales, pero no pudieron despertarlo. Poco después, cuando el carpintero le tomaba las medidas para el ataúd, vieron a través de la ventana que estaba cayendo una llovizna de minúsculas flores amarillas. Cayeron toda la noche sobre el pueblo en una tormenta silenciosa, y cubrieron los techos y atascaron las puertas, y sofocaron a los animales que durmieron a la intemperie. Tantas flores cayeron del cielo, que las calles amanecieron tapizadas de una colcha compacta, y tuvieron que despejarlas con palas y rastrillos para que pudiera pasar el entierro.

Sentada en el mecedor de mimbre, con la labor interrumpida en el regazo, Amaranta contemplaba a Aureliano José con el mentón embadurnado de espuma, afilando la navaja barbera en la penca para afeitarse por primera vez. Se sangró las espinillas, se cortó el labio superior tratando de modelarse un bigote de pelusas rubias, y después de todo quedó igual que antes, pero el laborioso proceso le dejó a Amaranta la impresión de que en aquel instante había empezado a envejecer.

—Estás idéntico a Aureliano cuando tenía tu edad —dijo—. Ya eres un hombre.

Lo era desde hacía mucho tiempo, desde el día ya lejano en que Amaranta creyó que aún era un niño y siguió desnudándose en el baño delante de él, como lo había hecho siempre, como se acostumbró a hacerlo desde que Pilar Ternera se lo entregó para que acabara de criarlo. La primera vez que él la vio, lo único que le llamó la atención fue la profunda depresión entre los senos. Era entonces tan inocente que preguntó qué le había pasado, y Amaranta fingió excavarse el pecho con la punta de los dedos y contestó: «Me sacaron tajadas y tajadas y tajadas.» Tiempo después, cuando ella se restableció del suicidio de Pietro Crespi y volvió a bañarse con Aureliano José, éste ya no se fijó en la depresión, sino que experimentó un estremecimiento desconocido ante la visión de los senos espléndidos de pezones morados. Siguió examinándola, descubriendo palmo a palmo el milagro de su intimidad, y sintió que su piel se erizaba en la contemplación, como se erizaba la piel de ella al contacto del agua. Desde muy niño tenía la costumbre de abandonar la hamaca para amanecer en la cama de Amaranta, cuyo contacto tenía la virtud de disipar el miedo a la oscuridad. Pero desde el día en que tuvo conciencia de su desnudez, no era el miedo a la oscuridad lo que lo impulsaba a meterse en su mosquitero, sino el anhelo de sentir la respiración tibia de Amaranta al amanecer. Una madrugada, por la época en que ella rechazó al coronel Gerineldo Márquez, Aureliano José despertó con la sensación de que le faltaba el aire. Sintió los dedos de Amaranta como unos gusanitos calientes y ansiosos que buscaban su vientre. Fingiendo dormir cambió de posición para eliminar toda dificultad, y entonces sintió la mano sin la venda negra buceando como un molusco ciego entre las algas de su ansiedad. Aunque aparentaron ignorar lo que ambos sabían, y lo que cada uno sabía que el otro sabía, desde aquella noche quedaron mancornados por una complicidad inviolable. Aureliano José no podía conciliar el sueño mientras no escuchaba el valse de las doce en el reloj de la sala, y la madura doncella cuya piel empezaba a entristecer no tenía un instante de sosiego mientras no sentía deslizarse en el mosquitero aquel sonámbulo que ella había criado, sin pensar que sería un paliativo para su soledad. Entonces no sólo durmieron juntos, desnudos, intercambiando caricias agotadoras, sino que se perseguían por los rincones de la casa y se encerraban en los dormitorios a cualquier hora, en un permanente estado de exaltación sin alivio. Estuvieron a punto de ser sorprendidos por Úrsula, una tarde en que entró al granero cuando ellos empezaban a besarse. «¿Quieres mucho a tu tía?», le preguntó ella de un modo inocente a Aureliano José. Él contestó que sí. «Haces bien», concluyó Úrsula, y acabó de medir la harina para el pan y regresó a la cocina. Aquel episodio sacó a Amaranta del delirio. Se dio cuenta de que había llegado demasiado lejos, de que ya no estaba jugando a los besitos con un niño, sino chapaleando en una pasión otoñal, peligrosa y sin porvenir, y la cortó de un tajo. Aureliano José, que entonces terminaba su adiestramiento militar, acabó por admitir la realidad y se fue a dormir al cuartel. Los sábados iba con los soldados a la tienda de Catarino. Se consolaba de su abrupta soledad, de su adolescencia prematura, con mujeres olorosas a flores muertas que él idealizaba en las tinieblas y las convertía en Amaranta mediante ansiosos esfuerzos de imaginación.

Poco después empezaron a recibirse noticias contradictorias de la guerra. Mientras el propio gobierno admitía los progresos de la rebelión, los oficiales de Macondo tenían informes confidenciales de la inminencia de una paz negociada. A principios de abril, un emisario especial se identificó ante el coronel Gerineldo Márquez. Le confirmó que, en efecto, los dirigentes del partido habían establecido contactos con jefes rebeldes del interior, y estaban en vísperas de concertar el armisticio a cambio de tres ministerios para los liberales, una representación minoritaria en el parlamento y la amnistía general para los rebeldes que depusieran las armas. El emisario llevaba una orden altamente confidencial del coronel Aureliano Buendía, que estaba en desacuerdo con los términos del armisticio. El coronel Gerineldo Márquez debía seleccionar a cinco de sus mejores hombres y prepararse para abandonar con ellos el país. La orden se cumplió dentro de la más estricta reserva. Una semana antes de que se anunciara el acuerdo, y en medio de una tormenta de rumores contradictorios, el coronel Aureliano Buendía y diez oficiales de confianza, entre ellos el coronel Roque Carnicero, llegaron sigilosamente a Macondo después de la medianoche, dispersaron la guarnición, enterraron las armas y destruyeron los archivos. Al amanecer habían abandonado el pueblo con el coronel Gerineldo Márquez y sus cinco oficiales. Fue una operación tan rápida y confidencial, que Úrsula no se enteró de ella sino a última hora, cuando alguien dio unos golpecitos en la ventana de su dormitorio y murmuró: «Si quiere ver al coronel Aureliano Buendía, asómese ahora mismo a la puerta.» Úrsula saltó de la cama y salió a la puerta en ropa de dormir, y apenas alcanzó a percibir el galope de la caballada que abandonaba el pueblo en medio de una muda polvareda. Sólo al día siguiente se enteró de que Aureliano José se había ido con su padre.

Diez días después de que un comunicado conjunto del gobierno y la oposición anunció el término de la guerra, se tuvieron noticias del primer levantamiento armado del coronel Aureliano Buendía en la frontera occidental. Sus fuerzas escasas y mal armadas fueron dispersadas en menos de una semana. Pero en el curso de ese año, mientras liberales y conservadores trataban de que el país creyera en la reconciliación, intentó otros siete alzamientos. Una noche cañoneó a Riohacha desde una goleta, y la guarnición sacó de sus camas y fusiló en represalia a los catorce liberales más conocidos de la población. Ocupó por más de quince días una aduana fronteriza, y desde allí dirigió a la nación un llamado a la guerra general. Otra de sus expediciones se perdió tres meses en la selva, en una disparatada tentativa de atravesar más de mil quinientos kilómetros de territorios vírgenes para proclamar la guerra en los suburbios de la capital. En cierta ocasión estuvo a menos de veinte kilómetros de Macondo, y fue obligado por las patrullas del gobierno a internarse en las montañas muy cerca de la región encantada donde su padre encontró muchos años antes el fósil de un galeón español.

Por esa época murió Visitación. Se dio el gusto de morirse de muerte natural, después de haber renunciado a un trono por temor al insomnio, y su última voluntad fue que desenterraran de debajo de su cama el sueldo ahorrado en más de veinte años, y se lo mandaran al coronel Aureliano Buendía para que siguiera la guerra. Pero Úrsula no se tomó el trabajo de sacar ese dinero, porque en aquellos días se rumoreaba que el coronel Aureliano Buendía había sido muerto en un desembarco cerca de la capital provincial. El anuncio oficial —el cuarto en menos de dos años— fue tenido por cierto durante casi seis meses, pues nada volvió a saberse de él. De pronto, cuando ya Úrsula y Amaranta habían superpuesto un nuevo luto a los anteriores, llegó una noticia insólita. El coronel Aureliano Buendía estaba vivo, pero aparentemente había desistido de hostigar al gobierno de su país, y se había sumado al federalismo triunfante en otras repúblicas del Caribe. Aparecía con nombres distintos cada vez más lejos de su tierra. Después había de saberse que la idea que entonces lo animaba era la unificación de las fuerzas federalistas de la América Central, para barrer con los regímenes conservadores desde Alaska hasta la Patagonia. La primera noticia directa que Úrsula recibió de él, varios años después de haberse ido, fue una carta arrugada y borrosa que le llegó de mano en mano desde Santiago de Cuba.

—Lo hemos perdido para siempre —exclamó Úrsula al leerla—. Por ese camino pasará la Navidad en el fin del mundo.

La persona a quien se lo dijo, que fue la primera a quien mostró la carta, era el general conservador José Raquel Moncada, alcalde de Macondo desde que terminó la guerra. «Este Aureliano —comentó el general Moncada—, lástima que no sea conservador.» Lo admiraba de veras. Como muchos civiles conservadores, José Raquel Moncada había hecho la guerra en defensa de su partido y había alcanzado el título de general en el campo de batalla, aunque carecía de vocación militar. Al contrario, también como muchos de sus copartidarios, era antimilitarista. Consideraba a la gente de armas como holgazanes sin principios, intrigantes y ambiciosos, expertos en enfrentar a los civiles para medrar en el desorden. Inteligente, simpático, sanguíneo, hombre de buen comer y fanático de las peleas de gallos, había sido en cierto momento el adversario más temible del coronel Aureliano Buendía. Logró imponer su autoridad sobre los militares de carrera en un amplio sector del litoral. Cierta vez en que se vio forzado por conveniencias estratégicas a abandonar una plaza a las fuerzas del coronel Aureliano Buendía, le dejó a éste dos cartas. En una de ellas, muy extensa, lo invitaba a una campaña conjunta para humanizar la guerra. La otra carta era para su esposa, que vivía en territorio liberal, y la dejó con la súplica de hacerla llegar a su destino. Desde entonces, aun en los períodos más encarnizados de la guerra, los dos comandantes concertaron treguas para intercambiar prisioneros. Eran pausas con un cierto ambiente festivo que el general Moncada aprovechaba para enseñar a jugar ajedrez al coronel Aureliano Buendía. Se hicieron grandes amigos. Llegaron inclusive a pensar en la posibilidad de coordinar a los elementos populares de ambos partidos para liquidar la influencia de los militares y los políticos profesionales, e instaurar un régimen humanitario que aprovechara lo mejor de cada doctrina. Cuando terminó la guerra, mientras el coronel Aureliano Buendía se escabullía por los desfiladeros de la subversión permanente, el general Moncada fue nombrado corregidor de Macondo. Vistió su traje civil, sustituyó a los militares por agentes de la policía desarmados, hizo respetar las leyes de amnistía y auxilió a algunas familias de liberales muertos en campaña. Consiguió que Macondo fuera erigido en municipio y fue por tanto su primer alcalde, y creó un ambiente de confianza que hizo pensar en la guerra como en una absurda pesadilla del pasado. El padre Nicanor, consumido por las fiebres hepáticas, fue reemplazado por el padre Coronel, a quien llamaban *El Cachorro*, veterano de la primera guerra federalista. Bruno Crespi, casado con Amparo Moscote, y cuya tienda de juguetes e instrumentos musicales no se cansaba de prosperar, construyó un teatro, que las compañías españolas incluyeron en sus itinerarios. Era un vasto salón al aire libre, con escaños de madera, un telón de terciopelo con máscaras griegas, y tres taquillas en forma de cabezas de león por cuyas bocas abiertas se vendían los boletos. Fue también por esa época que se restauró el edificio de la escuela. Se hizo cargo de ella don Melchor Escalona, un maestro viejo mandado de la ciénaga, que hacía caminar de rodillas en el patio de caliche a los alumnos desaplicados y les hacía comer ají picante a los lenguaraces, con la complacencia de los padres. Aureliano Segundo y José Arcadio Segundo, los voluntariosos gemelos de Santa Sofía de la Piedad, fueron los primeros que se sentaron en el salón de clases con sus pizarras y sus gises y sus jarritos de aluminio marcados con sus nombres. Remedios, heredera de la belleza pura de su madre, empezaba a ser conocida como Remedios, la bella. A pesar del tiempo, de los lutos superpuestos y las aflicciones acumuladas, Úrsula se resistía a envejecer. Ayudada por Santa Sofía de la Piedad había dado un nuevo impulso a su industria de repostería, y no sólo recuperó en pocos años la fortuna que su hijo se gastó en la guerra, sino que volvió a atiborrar de oro puro los calabazos enterrados en el dormitorio. «Mientras Dios me dé vida —solía decir— no faltará la plata en esta casa de locos.» Así estaban las cosas cuando Aureliano José desertó de las tropas federalistas de Nicaragua, se enroló en la tripulación de un buque alemán, y apareció en la cocina de la casa, macizo como un caballo, prieto y peludo como un indio, y con la secreta determinación de casarse con Amaranta.

Cuando Amaranta lo vio entrar, sin que él hubiera dicho nada, supo de inmediato por qué había vuelto. En la mesa no se atrevían a mirarse a la cara. Pero dos semanas después del regreso, estando Úrsula presente, él fijó sus ojos en los de ella y le dijo: «Siempre pensaba mucho en ti.» Amaranta le huía. Se prevenía contra los encuentros casuales. Procuraba no separarse de Remedios, la bella. Le indignó el rubor que doró sus mejillas el día en que el sobrino le preguntó hasta cuándo pensaba llevar la venda negra en la mano, porque interpretó la pregunta como una alusión a su virginidad. Cuando él llegó, ella pasó la aldaba en su dormitorio, pero durante tantas noches percibió sus ronquidos pacíficos en el cuarto contiguo, que descuidó esa precaución. Una madrugada, casi dos meses después del regreso, lo sintió entrar en el dormitorio. Entonces, en vez de huir, en vez de gritar como lo había previsto, se dejó saturar por una suave sensación de descanso. Lo sintió deslizarse en el mosquitero, como lo había hecho cuando era niño, como lo había hecho desde siempre y no pudo reprimir el sudor helado y el crotaloteo de los dientes cuando se dio cuenta de que él estaba completamente desnudo. «Vete», murmuró, ahogándose de curiosidad. «Vete o me pongo a gritar.» Pero Aureliano José sabía entonces lo que tenía que hacer, porque ya no era un niño asustado por la oscuridad sino un animal de campamento. Desde aquella noche se reiniciaron las sordas batallas sin consecuencias que se prolongaban hasta el amanecer. «Soy tu tía», murmuraba Amaranta, agotada. «Es casi como si fuera tu madre, no sólo por la edad, sino porque lo único que me faltó fue darte de mamar.» Aureliano escapaba al alba y regresaba a la madrugada siguiente, cada vez más excitado por la comprobación de que ella no pasaba la aldaba. No había dejado de desearla un solo instante. La encontraba en los oscuros dormitorios de los pueblos vencidos, sobre todo en los más abyectos, y la materializaba en el tufo de la sangre seca en las vendas de los heridos, en el pavor instantáneo del peligro de muerte, a toda hora y en todas partes. Había huido de ella tratando de aniquilar su recuerdo no sólo con la distancia, sino con un encarnizamiento aturdido que sus compañeros de armas calificaban de temeridad, pero mientras más revolcaba su imagen en el muladar de la guerra, más la guerra se parecía a Amaranta. Así padeció el exilio, buscando la manera de matarla con su propia muerte, hasta que le oyó contar a alguien el viejo cuento del hombre que se casó con una tía que además era su prima, y cuyo hijo terminó siendo abuelo de sí mismo.

—¿Es que uno se puede casar con una tía? —preguntó él, asombrado.

—No sólo se puede —le contestó un soldado— sino que estamos haciendo esta guerra contra los curas para que uno se pueda casar con su propia madre.

Quince días después desertó. Encontró a Amaranta más ajada que en el recuerdo, más melancólica y pudibunda, y ya doblando en realidad el último cabo de la madurez, pero más febril que nunca en las tinieblas del dormitorio y más desafiante que nunca en la agresividad de su resistencia: «Eres un bruto», le decía Amaranta, acosada por sus perros de presa. «No es cierto que se le pueda hacer esto a una pobre tía, como no sea con dispensa especial del Papa.» Aureliano José prometía ir a Roma, prometía recorrer Europa de rodillas, y besar las sandalias del Sumo Pontífice sólo para que ella bajara sus puentes levadizos.

—No es sólo eso —rebatía Amaranta—. Es que nacen los hijos con cola de puerco.

Aureliano José era sordo a todo argumento.

—Aunque nazcan armadillos —suplicaba.

Una madrugada, vencido por el dolor insoportable de la virilidad reprimida, fue a la tienda de Catarino. Encontró una mujer de senos fláccidos, cariñosa y barata, que le apaciguó el vientre por algún tiempo. Trató de aplicarle a Amaranta el tratamiento del desprecio. La veía en el corredor, cosiendo en una máquina de manivela que había aprendido a manejar con habilidad admirable, y ni siquiera le dirigía la palabra. Amaranta se sintió liberada de un lastre, y ella misma no comprendió por qué volvió a pensar entonces en el coronel Gerineldo Márquez, por qué evocaba con tanta nostalgia las tardes de damas chinas, y por qué llegó inclusive a desearlo como hombre de dormitorio. Aureliano José no se imaginaba cuánto terreno había perdido, la noche en que no pudo resistir más la farsa de la indiferencia, y volvió al cuarto de Amaranta. Ella lo rechazó con una determinación inflexible, inequívoca, y echó para siempre la aldaba del dormitorio.

Pocos meses después del regreso de Aureliano José, se presentó en la casa una mujer exuberante, perfumada de jazmines, con un niño de unos cinco años. Afirmó que era hijo del coronel Aureliano Buendía y lo llevaba para que Úrsula lo bautizara. Nadie puso en duda el origen de aquel niño sin nombre: era igual al coronel por los tiempos en que lo llevaron a conocer el hielo. La mujer contó que había nacido con los ojos abiertos mirando a la gente con criterio de persona mayor, y que le asustaba su manera de fijar la mirada en las cosas sin parpadear. «Es idéntico», dijo Úrsula. «Lo único que falta es que haga rodar las sillas con sólo mirarlas.» Lo bautiza-

ron con el nombre de Aureliano, y con el ap̶
su madre, porque la ley no le permitía llevar e̶
do del padre mientras éste no lo reconociera. ̶
neral Moncada sirvió de padrino. Aunque Amar̶
insistió en que se lo dejaran para acabar de criarlo, la
madre se opuso.

Úrsula ignoraba entonces la costumbre de mandar doncellas a los dormitorios de los guerreros,
como se les soltaban gallinas a los gallos finos, pero
en el curso de ese año se enteró: nueve hijos más del
coronel Aureliano Buendía fueron llevados a la casa
para ser bautizados. El mayor, un extraño moreno
de ojos verdes que nada tenía que ver con la familia
paterna, había pasado de los diez años. Llevaron niños de todas las edades, de todos los colores, pero
todos varones, y todos con un aire de soledad que no
permitía poner en duda el parentesco. Sólo dos se
distinguieron del montón. Uno, demasiado grande
para su edad, que hizo añicos los floreros y varias
piezas de la vajilla, porque sus manos parecían tener
la propiedad de despedazar todo lo que tocaban. El
otro era un rubio con los mismos ojos garzos de su
madre, a quien habían dejado el cabello largo y con
bucles, como a una mujer. Entró a la casa con mucha
familiaridad, como si hubiera sido criado en ella, y
fue directamente a un arcón del dormitorio de Úrsula, y exigió: «Quiero la bailarina de cuerda.» Úrsula
se asustó. Abrió el arcón, rebuscó entre los anticuados y polvorientos objetos de los tiempos de Melquíades y encontró envuelta en un par de medias la
bailarina de cuerda que alguna vez llevó Pietro Crespi a la casa, y de la cual nadie había vuelto a acordarse. En menos de dos años bautizaron con el nombre
de Aureliano, y con el apellido de la madre, a todos

os hijos que diseminó el coronel a lo largo y a lo ancho de sus territorios de guerra: diecisiete. Al principio Úrsula les llenaba los bolsillos de dinero y Amaranta intentaba quedarse con ellos. Pero terminaron por limitarse a hacerles un regalo y a servirles de madrinas. «Cumplimos con bautizarlos», decía Úrsula, anotando en una libreta el nombre y la dirección de las madres y el lugar y fecha de nacimiento de los niños. «Aureliano ha de llevar bien sus cuentas, así que será él quien tome las determinaciones cuando regrese.» En el curso de un almuerzo, comentando con el general Moncada aquella desconcertante proliferación, expresó el deseo de que el coronel Aureliano Buendía volviera alguna vez para reunir a todos sus hijos en la casa.

—No se preocupe, comadre —dijo enigmáticamente el general Moncada—. Vendrá más pronto de lo que usted se imagina.

Lo que el general Moncada sabía, y que no quiso revelar en el almuerzo, era que el coronel Aureliano Buendía estaba ya en camino para ponerse al frente de la rebelión más prolongada, radical y sangrienta de cuantas se habían intentado hasta entonces.

La situación volvió a ser tan tensa como en los meses que precedieron a la primera guerra. Las riñas de gallos, animadas por el propio alcalde, fueron suspendidas. El capitán Aquiles Ricardo, comandante de la guarnición, asumió en la práctica el poder municipal. Los liberales lo señalaron como un provocador. «Algo tremendo va a ocurrir», le decía Úrsula a Aureliano José. «No salgas a la calle después de las seis de la tarde.» Eran súplicas inútiles. Aureliano José, al igual que Arcadio en otra época, había dejado de pertenecerle. Era como si el regreso a la casa, la posibilidad de existir sin molestarse por las urgencias cotidianas, hubieran despertado en él la vocación concupiscente y desidiosa de su tío José Arcadio. Su pasión por Amaranta se extinguió sin dejar cicatrices. Andaba un poco al garete, jugando billar, sobrellevando su soledad con mujeres ocasionales, saqueando los resquicios donde Úrsula olvidaba el dinero traspuesto. Terminó por no volver a la casa sino para cambiarse de ropa. «Todos son iguales», se lamentaba Úrsula. «Al principio se crían muy bien, son obedientes y formales y parecen incapaces de matar una mosca, y apenas les sale la barba se tiran a la perdición.» Al contrario de Arcadio, que nunca conoció su verdadero origen, él se enteró de que era hijo de Pilar Ternera, quien le había colgado una hamaca para que hiciera la siesta en su casa. Eran, más que madre e hijo, cómplices en la soledad. Pilar Ternera había perdido el rastro de toda esperanza. Su risa había adquirido tonalidades de órgano, sus senos habían sucumbido al tedio de las caricias eventuales, su vientre y sus muslos habían sido víctimas de su irrevocable destino de mujer repartida, pero su corazón envejecía sin amargura. Gorda, lenguaraz, con ínfulas de matrona en desgracia, renunció a la ilusión estéril de las barajas y encontró un remanso de consolación en los amores ajenos. En la casa donde Aureliano José dormía la siesta, las muchachas del vecindario recibían a sus amantes casuales. «Me prestas el cuarto, Pilar», le decían simplemente, cuando ya estaban dentro. «Por supuesto», decía Pilar. Y si alguien estaba presente, le explicaba:

—Soy feliz sabiendo que la gente es feliz en la cama.

Nunca cobraba el servicio. Nunca negaba el favor, como no se lo negó a los incontables hombres que la buscaron hasta en el crepúsculo de su madurez, sin proporcionarle dinero ni amor, y sólo algunas veces placer. Sus cinco hijas, herederas de una semilla ardiente, se perdieron por los vericuetos de la vida desde la adolescencia. De los dos varones que alcanzó a criar, uno murió peleando en las huestes del coronel Aureliano Buendía y otro fue herido y capturado a los catorce años, cuando intentaba robarse un huacal de gallinas en un pueblo de la ciénaga. En cierto modo, Aureliano José fue el hombre alto y moreno que durante medio siglo le anunció el rey de copas, y que como todos los enviados de las barajas llegó a su corazón cuando ya estaba marcado por el signo de la muerte. Ella lo vio en los naipes.

—No salgas esta noche —le dijo—. Quédate a dormir aquí, que Carmelita Montiel se ha cansado de rogarme que la meta en tu cuarto.

Aureliano José no captó el profundo sentido de súplica que tenía aquella oferta.

—Dile que me espere a la medianoche —dijo.

Se fue al teatro donde una compañía española anunciaba *El puñal del Zorro*, que en realidad era la obra de Zorrilla con el nombre cambiado por orden del capitán Aquiles Ricardo, porque los liberales les llamaban *godos* a los conservadores. Sólo en el momento de entregar el boleto en la puerta, Aureliano José se dio cuenta de que el capitán Aquiles Ricardo, con dos soldados armados de fusiles, estaba cateando a la concurrencia. «Cuidado, capitán», le advirtió Aureliano José. «Todavía no ha nacido el hombre que me ponga las manos encima.» El capitán intentó catearlo por la fuerza, y Aureliano José, que andaba desarmado, se echó a correr. Los soldados desobede-

cieron la orden de disparar. «Es un Buendía», ex
có uno de ellos. Ciego de furia, el capitán le arreba
entonces el fusil, se abrió en el centro de la calle, y
apuntó.

—¡Cabrones! —alcanzó a gritar—. Ojalá fuera el
coronel Aureliano Buendía.

Carmelita Montiel, una virgen de veinte años,
acababa de bañarse con agua de azahares y estaba regando hojas de romero en la cama de Pilar Ternera,
cuando sonó el disparo. Aureliano José estaba destinado a conocer con ella la felicidad que le negó Amaranta, a tener siete hijos y a morirse de viejo en sus
brazos, pero la bala de fusil que le entró por la espalda y le despedazó el pecho estaba dirigida por una
mala interpretación de las barajas. El capitán Aquiles
Ricardo, que era en realidad quien estaba destinado a
morir esa noche, murió en efecto cuatro horas antes
que Aureliano José. Apenas sonó el disparo fue de-
rribado por dos balazos simultáneos, cuyo origen no
se estableció nunca, y un grito multitudinario estremeció la noche.

—¡Viva el partido liberal! ¡Viva el coronel Aureliano Buendía!

A las doce, cuando Aureliano José acabó de
desangrarse y Carmelita Montiel encontró en blanco
los naipes de su porvenir, más de cuatrocientos hombres habían desfilado frente al teatro y habían descargado sus revólveres contra el cadáver abandonado
del capitán Aquiles Ricardo. Se necesitó una patrulla
para poner en una carretilla el cuerpo apelmazado de
plomo, que se desbarataba como un pan ensopado.

Contrariado por las impertinencias del ejército
regular, el general José Raquel Moncada movilizó
sus influencias políticas, volvió a vestir el uniforme y

fatura civil y militar de Macondo. No es-
mbargo, que su actitud conciliatoria pu-
r lo inevitable. Las noticias de setiembre
adictorias. Mientras el gobierno anun-
ntenía el control en todo el país, los liberales recibían informes secretos de levantamientos
armados en el interior. El régimen no admitió el estado de guerra mientras no se proclamó en un bando
que se le había seguido consejo de guerra en ausencia
al coronel Aureliano Buendía, y había sido condenado a muerte. Se ordenaba cumplir la sentencia a la
primera guarnición que lo capturara. «Esto quiere
decir que ha vuelto», se alegró Úrsula ante el general
Moncada. Pero él mismo lo ignoraba.

En realidad, el coronel Aureliano Buendía estaba
en el país desde hacía más de un mes. Precedido de
rumores contradictorios, supuesto al mismo tiempo
en los lugares más apartados, el propio general Moncada no creyó en su regreso sino cuando se anunció
oficialmente que se había apoderado de dos estados
del litoral. «La felicito, comadre», le dijo a Úrsula,
mostrándole el telegrama. «Muy pronto lo tendrá
aquí.» Úrsula se preocupó entonces por primera vez.
«¿Y usted qué hará, compadre?», preguntó. El general Moncada se había hecho esa pregunta muchas
veces.

—Lo mismo que él, comadre —contestó—:
cumplir con mi deber.

El primero de octubre, al amanecer, el coronel
Aureliano Buendía con mil hombres bien armados
atacó a Macondo y la guarnición recibió la orden de
resistir hasta el final. A mediodía, mientras el general
Moncada almorzaba con Úrsula, un cañonazo rebelde que retumbó en todo el pueblo pulverizó la facha-

da de la tesorería municipal. «Están tan bien armados como nosotros —suspiró el general Moncada—, pero además pelean con más ganas.» A las dos de la tarde, mientras la tierra temblaba con los cañonazos de ambos lados, se despidió de Úrsula con la certidumbre de que estaba librando una batalla perdida.

—Ruego a Dios que esta noche no tenga a Aureliano en la casa —dijo—. Si es así, dele un abrazo de mi parte, porque yo no espero verlo más nunca.

Esa noche fue capturado cuando trataba de fugarse de Macondo, después de escribirle una extensa carta al coronel Aureliano Buendía, en la cual le recordaba los propósitos comunes de humanizar la guerra, y le deseaba una victoria definitiva contra la corrupción de los militares y las ambiciones de los políticos de ambos partidos. Al día siguiente el coronel Aureliano Buendía almorzó con él en casa de Úrsula, donde fue recluido hasta que un consejo de guerra revolucionario decidiera su destino. Fue una reunión familiar. Pero mientras los adversarios olvidaban la guerra para evocar recuerdos del pasado, Úrsula tuvo la sombría impresión de que su hijo era un intruso. La había tenido desde que lo vio entrar protegido por un ruidoso aparato militar que volteó los dormitorios al derecho y al revés hasta convencerse de que no había ningún riesgo. El coronel Aureliano Buendía no sólo lo aceptó, sino que impartió órdenes de una severidad terminante, y no permitió que nadie se le acercara a menos de tres metros, ni siquiera Úrsula, mientras los miembros de su escolta no terminaron de establecer las guardias alrededor de la casa. Vestía un uniforme de dril ordinario, sin insignias de ninguna clase, y unas botas altas con espuelas embadurnadas de barro y sangre seca. Llevaba al cinto una escuadra con la funda desabrochada, y la mano siempre apoyada en la culata revelaba la misma tensión vigilante y resuelta de la mirada. Su cabeza, ahora con entradas profundas, parecía horneada a fuego lento. Su rostro cuarteado por la sal del Caribe había adquirido una dureza metálica. Estaba preservado contra la vejez inminente por una vitalidad que tenía algo que ver con la frialdad de las entrañas. Era más alto que cuando se fue, más pálido y óseo, y manifestaba los primeros síntomas de resistencia a la nostalgia. «Dios mío», se dijo Úrsula, alarmada. «Ahora parece un hombre capaz de todo.» Lo era. El rebozo azteca que le llevó a Amaranta, las evocaciones que hizo en el almuerzo, las divertidas anécdotas que contó eran simples rescoldos de su humor de otra época. No bien se cumplió la orden de enterrar a los muertos en la fosa común, asignó al coronel Roque Carnicero la misión de apresurar los juicios de guerra, y él se empeñó en la agotadora tarea de imponer las reformas radicales que no dejaran piedra sobre piedra en la revenida estructura del régimen conservador. «Tenemos que anticiparnos a los políticos del partido», decía a sus asesores. «Cuando abran los ojos a la realidad se encontrarán con los hechos consumados.» Fue entonces cuando decidió revisar los títulos de propiedad de la tierra, hasta cien años atrás, y descubrió las tropelías legalizadas de su hermano José Arcadio. Anuló los registros de una plumada. En un último gesto de cortesía, desatendió sus asuntos por una hora y visitó a Rebeca para ponerla al corriente de su determinación.

En la penumbra de la casa, la viuda solitaria que en un tiempo fue la confidente de sus amores reprimidos, y cuya obstinación le salvó la vida, era un espectro del pasado. Cerrada de negro hasta los puños, con el corazón convertido en cenizas, apenas si tenía noticias de la guerra. El coronel Aureliano Buendía tuvo la impresión de que la fosforescencia de sus huesos traspasaba la piel, y que ella se movía a través de una atmósfera de fuegos fatuos, en un aire estancado donde aún se percibía un recóndito olor a pólvora. Empezó por aconsejarle que moderara el rigor de su luto, que ventilara la casa, que le perdonara al mundo la muerte de José Arcadio. Pero ya Rebeca estaba a salvo de toda vanidad. Después de buscarla inútilmente en el sabor de la tierra, en las cartas perfumadas de Pietro Crespi, en la cama tempestuosa de su marido, había encontrado la paz en aquella casa donde los recuerdos se materializaron por la fuerza de la evocación implacable, y se paseaban como seres humanos por los cuartos clausurados. Estirada en su mecedor de mimbre, mirando al coronel Aureliano Buendía como si fuera él quien pareciera un espectro del pasado, Rebeca ni siquiera se conmovió con la noticia de que las tierras usurpadas por José Arcadio serían restituidas a sus dueños legítimos.

—Se hará lo que tú dispongas, Aureliano —suspiró—. Siempre creí, y lo confirmo ahora, que eres un descastado.

La revisión de los títulos de propiedad se consumó al mismo tiempo que los juicios sumarios, presididos por el coronel Gerineldo Márquez, y que concluyeron con el fusilamiento de toda la oficialidad del ejército regular prisionera de los revolucionarios. El último consejo de guerra fue el del general José Raquel Moncada. Úrsula intervino. «Es el mejor gobernante que hemos tenido en Macondo», le dijo al coronel Aureliano Buendía. «Ni siquiera tengo nada que decirte de su buen corazón, del afecto que nos tiene, porque tú lo conoces mejor que nadie.» El coronel Aureliano Buendía fijó en ella una mirada de reprobación:

—No puedo arrogarme la facultad de administrar justicia —replicó—. Si usted tiene algo que decir, dígalo ante el consejo de guerra.

Úrsula no sólo lo hizo, sino que llevó a declarar a todas las madres de los oficiales revolucionarios que vivían en Macondo. Una por una, las viejas fundadoras del pueblo, varias de las cuales habían participado en la temeraria travesía de la sierra, exaltaron las virtudes del general Moncada. Úrsula fue la última en el desfile. Su dignidad luctuosa, el peso de su nombre, la convincente vehemencia de su declaración hicieron vacilar por un momento el equilibrio de la justicia. «Ustedes han tomado muy en serio este juego espantoso, y han hecho bien, porque están cumpliendo con su deber», dijo a los miembros del tribunal. «Pero no olviden que mientras Dios nos dé vida, nosotras seguiremos siendo madres, y por muy revolucionarios que sean tenemos derecho de bajarles los pantalones y darles una cueriza a la primera falta de respeto.» El jurado se retiró a deliberar cuando todavía resonaban estas palabras en el ámbito de la escuela convertida en cuartel. A la medianoche, el general José Raquel Moncada fue sentenciado a muerte. El coronel Aureliano Buendía, a pesar de las violentas recriminaciones de Úrsula, se negó a conmutarle la pena. Poco antes del amanecer, visitó al sentenciado en el cuarto del cepo.

—Recuerda, compadre —le dijo—, que no te fusilo yo. Te fusila la revolución.

El general Moncada ni siquiera se levantó del catre al verlo entrar.

—Vete a la mierda, compadre —replicó.

Hasta ese momento, desde su regreso, el coronel Aureliano Buendía no se había concedido la oportunidad de verlo con el corazón. Se asombró de cuánto había envejecido, del temblor de sus manos, de la conformidad un poco rutinaria con que esperaba la muerte, y entonces experimentó un hondo desprecio por sí mismo que confundió con un principio de misericordia.

—Sabes mejor que yo —dijo— que todo consejo de guerra es una farsa, y que en verdad tienes que pagar los crímenes de otros, porque esta vez vamos a ganar la guerra a cualquier precio. Tú, en mi lugar, ¿no hubieras hecho lo mismo?

El general Moncada se incorporó para limpiar los gruesos anteojos de carey con el faldón de la camisa. «Probablemente», dijo. «Pero lo que me preocupa no es que me fusiles, porque al fin y al cabo, para la gente como nosotros esto es la muerte natural.» Puso los lentes en la cama y se quitó el reloj de leontina. «Lo que me preocupa —agregó— es que de tanto odiar a los militares, de tanto combatirlos, de tanto pensar en ellos, has terminado por ser igual a ellos. Y no hay un ideal en la vida que merezca tanta abyección.» Se quitó el anillo matrimonial y la medalla de la Virgen de los Remedios y los puso junto con los lentes y el reloj.

—A este paso —concluyó— no sólo serás el dictador más despótico y sanguinario de nuestra historia, sino que fusilarás a mi comadre Úrsula tratando de apaciguar tu conciencia.

El coronel Aureliano Buendía permaneció impasible. El general Moncada le entregó entonces los lentes, la medalla, el reloj y el anillo, y cambió de tono.

—Pero no te hice venir para regañarte —dijo—. Quería suplicarte el favor de mandarle estas cosas a mi mujer.

El coronel Aureliano Buendía se las guardó en los bolsillos.

—¿Sigue en Manaure?

—Sigue en Manaure —confirmó el general Moncada—, en la misma casa detrás de la iglesia donde mandaste aquella carta.

—Lo haré con mucho gusto, José Raquel —dijo el coronel Aureliano Buendía.

Cuando salió al aire azul de neblina, el rostro se le humedeció como en otro amanecer del pasado, y sólo entonces comprendió por qué había dispuesto que la sentencia se cumpliera en el patio, y no en el muro del cementerio. El pelotón, formado frente a la puerta, le rindió honores de jefe de estado.

—Ya pueden traerlo —ordenó.

El coronel Gerineldo Márquez fue el primero que percibió el vacío de la guerra. En su condición de jefe civil y militar de Macondo sostenía dos veces por semana conversaciones telegráficas con el coronel Aureliano Buendía. Al principio, aquellas entrevistas determinaban el curso de una guerra de carne y hueso cuyos contornos perfectamente definidos permitían establecer en cualquier momento el punto exacto en que se encontraba, y prever sus rumbos futuros. Aunque nunca se dejaba arrastrar al terreno de las confidencias, ni siquiera por sus amigos más próximos, el coronel Aureliano Buendía conservaba entonces el tono familiar que permitía identificarlo al otro extremo de la línea. Muchas veces prolongó las conversaciones más allá del término previsto y las dejó derivar hacia comentarios de carácter doméstico. Poco a poco, sin embargo, y a medida que la guerra se iba intensificando y extendiendo, su imagen se fue borrando en un universo de irrealidad. Los puntos y rayas de su voz eran cada vez más remotos e inciertos, y se unían y combinaban para formar palabras que paulatinamente fueron perdiendo todo sentido. El coronel Gerineldo Márquez se limitaba entonces a escuchar, abrumado por la impresión de estar en contacto telegráfico con un desconocido de otro mundo.

—Comprendido, Aureliano —concluía en el manipulador—. ¡Viva el partido liberal!

Terminó por perder todo contacto con la guerra. Lo que en otro tiempo fue una actividad real, una pasión irresistible de su juventud, se convirtió para él en una referencia remota: un vacío. Su único refugio era el costurero de Amaranta. La visitaba todas las tardes. Le gustaba contemplar sus manos mientras rizaba espumas de olán en la máquina de manivela que hacía girar Remedios, la bella. Pasaban muchas horas sin hablar, conformes con la compañía recíproca, pero mientras Amaranta se complacía íntimamente en mantener vivo el fuego de su devoción, él ignoraba cuáles eran los secretos designios de aquel corazón indescifrable. Cuando se conoció la noticia de su regreso, Amaranta se había ahogado de ansiedad. Pero cuando lo vio entrar en la casa confundido con la ruidosa escolta del coronel Aureliano Buendía, y lo vio maltratado por el rigor del destierro, envejecido por la edad y el olvido, sucio de sudor y polvo, oloroso a rebaño, feo, con el brazo izquierdo en cabestrillo, se sintió desfallecer de desilusión. «Dios mío —pensó—: no era éste el que esperaba.» Al día siguiente, sin embargo, él volvió a la casa afeitado y limpio, con el bigote perfumado de agua de alhucema y sin el cabestrillo ensangrentado. Le llevaba un breviario de pastas nacaradas.

—Qué raros son los hombres —dijo ella, porque no encontró otra cosa que decir—. Se pasan la vida peleando contra los curas y regalan libros de oraciones.

Desde entonces, aun en los días más crít[...]
guerra, la visitó todas las tardes. Muchas vec[...]
do no estaba presente Remedios, la bella, era [...]
le daba vueltas a la rueda de la máquina de [...]
Amaranta se sentía turbada por la perseverai[...]a, la
lealtad, la sumisión de aquel hombre investido de
tanta autoridad, que sin embargo se despojaba de sus
armas en la sala para entrar indefenso al costurero.
Pero durante cuatro años él le reiteró su amor, y ella
encontró siempre la manera de rechazarlo sin herir-
lo, porque aunque no conseguía quererlo ya no podía vivir sin él. Remedios, la bella, que parecía indiferente a todo, y de quien se pensaba que era retrasada
mental, no fue insensible a tanta devoción, e intervino en favor del coronel Gerineldo Márquez. Amaranta descubrió de pronto que aquella niña que había criado, que apenas despuntaba a la adolescencia,
era ya la criatura más bella que se había visto en Macondo. Sintió renacer en su corazón el rencor que en
otro tiempo experimentó contra Rebeca, y rogándo-
le a Dios que no la arrastrara hasta el extremo de
desearle la muerte, la desterró del costurero. Fue por
esa época que el coronel Gerineldo Márquez empezó a sentir el hastío de la guerra. Apeló a sus reservas
de persuasión, a su inmensa y reprimida ternura, dispuesto a renunciar por Amaranta a una gloria que le
había costado el sacrificio de sus mejores años. Pero
no logró convencerla. Una tarde de agosto, agobiada
por el peso insoportable de su propia obstinación,
Amaranta se encerró en el dormitorio a llorar su soledad hasta la muerte, después de darle la respuesta
definitiva a su pretendiente tenaz.

—Olvidémonos para siempre —le dijo—, ya somos demasiado viejos para estas cosas.

El coronel Gerineldo Márquez acudió aquella tarde a un llamado telegráfico del coronel Aureliano Buendía. Fue una conversación rutinaria que no había de abrir ninguna brecha en la guerra estancada. Al terminar, el coronel Gerineldo Márquez contempló las calles desoladas, el agua cristalizada en los almendros, y se encontró perdido en la soledad.

—Aureliano —dijo tristemente en el manipulador—, está lloviendo en Macondo.

Hubo un largo silencio en la línea. De pronto, los aparatos saltaron con los signos despiadados del coronel Aureliano Buendía.

—No seas pendejo, Gerineldo —dijeron los signos—. Es natural que esté lloviendo en agosto.

Tenían tanto tiempo de no verse, que el coronel Gerineldo Márquez se desconcertó con la agresividad de aquella reacción. Sin embargo, dos meses después, cuando el coronel Aureliano Buendía volvió a Macondo, el desconcierto se transformó en estupor. Hasta Úrsula se sorprendió de cuánto había cambiado. Llegó sin ruido, sin escolta, envuelto en una manta a pesar del calor, y con tres amantes que instaló en una misma casa, donde pasaba la mayor parte del tiempo tendido en una hamaca. Apenas si leía los despachos telegráficos que informaban de operaciones rutinarias. En cierta ocasión el coronel Gerineldo Márquez le pidió instrucciones para la evacuación de una localidad fronteriza que amenazaba con convertirse en un conflicto internacional.

—No me molestes por pequeñeces —le ordenó él—. Consúltalo con la Divina Providencia.

Era tal vez el momento más crítico de la guerra. Los terratenientes liberales, que al principio apoyaban la revolución, habían suscrito alianzas secretas con los terratenientes conservadores para impedir la revisión de los títulos de propiedad. Los políticos que capitalizaban la guerra desde el exilio habían repudiado públicamente las determinaciones drásticas del coronel Aureliano Buendía, pero hasta esa desautorización parecía tenerlo sin cuidado. No había vuelto a leer sus versos, que ocupaban más de cinco tomos, y que permanecían olvidados en el fondo del baúl. De noche, o a la hora de la siesta, llamaba a la hamaca a una de sus mujeres y obtenía de ella una satisfacción rudimentaria, y luego dormía con un sueño de piedra que no era perturbado por el más ligero indicio de preocupación. Sólo él sabía entonces que su aturdido corazón estaba condenado para siempre a la incertidumbre. Al principio, embriagado por la gloria del regreso, por las victorias inverosímiles, se había asomado al abismo de la grandeza. Se complacía en mantener a la diestra al duque de Marlborough, su gran maestro en las artes de la guerra, cuyo atuendo de pieles y uñas de tigre suscitaba el respeto de los adultos y el asombro de los niños. Fue entonces cuando decidió que ningún ser humano, ni siquiera Úrsula, se le aproximara a menos de tres metros. En el centro del círculo de tiza que sus edecanes trazaban dondequiera que él llegara, y en el cual sólo él podía entrar, decidía con órdenes breves e inapelables el destino del mundo. La primera vez que estuvo en Manaure después del fusilamiento del general Moncada se apresuró a cumplir la última voluntad de su víctima, y la viuda recibió los lentes, la medalla, el reloj y el anillo, pero no le permitió pasar de la puerta.

—No entre, coronel —le dijo—. Usted mandará en su guerra, pero yo mando en mi casa.

201

El coronel Aureliano Buendía no dio ninguna
muestra de rencor, pero su espíritu sólo encontró el
sosiego cuando su guardia personal saqueó y redujo
a cenizas la casa de la viuda. «Cuídate el corazón,
Aureliano», le decía entonces el coronel Gerineldo
Márquez. «Te estás pudriendo vivo.» Por esa época
convocó una segunda asamblea de los principales comandantes rebeldes. Encontró de todo: idealistas,
ambiciosos, aventureros, resentidos sociales y hasta
delincuentes comunes. Había, inclusive, un antiguo
funcionario conservador refugiado en la revuelta
para escapar a un juicio por malversación de fondos.
Muchos no sabían ni siquiera por qué peleaban. En
medio de aquella muchedumbre abigarrada, cuyas
diferencias de criterio estuvieron a punto de provocar una explosión interna, se destacaba una autoridad
tenebrosa: el general Teófilo Vargas. Era un indio puro, montaraz, analfabeto, dotado de una malicia taciturna y una vocación mesiánica que suscitaba en sus
hombres un fanatismo demente. El coronel Aureliano Buendía promovió la reunión con el propósito de
unificar el mando rebelde contra las maniobras de
los políticos. El general Teófilo Vargas se adelantó a
sus intenciones: en pocas horas desbarató la coali-
ción de los comandantes mejor calificados y se apo-
deró del mando central. «Es una fiera de cuidado»,
les dijo el coronel Aureliano Buendía a sus oficiales.
«Para nosotros, ese hombre es más peligroso que el
Ministro de la Guerra.» Entonces un capitán muy
joven que siempre se había distinguido por su timidez levantó un índice cauteloso.

—Es muy simple, coronel —propuso—: hay que
matarlo.

El coronel Aureliano Buendía no se alarmó por

la frialdad de la proposición, sino por la forma en que se anticipó una fracción de segundo a su propio pensamiento.

—No esperen que yo dé esa orden —dijo.

No la dio, en efecto. Pero quince días después el general Teófilo Vargas fue despedazado a machetazos en una emboscada, y el coronel Aureliano Buendía asumió el mando central. La misma noche en que su autoridad fue reconocida por todos los comandos rebeldes, despertó sobresaltado, pidiendo a gritos una manta. Un frío interior que le rayaba los huesos y lo mortificaba inclusive a pleno sol le impidió dormir bien varios meses, hasta que se le convirtió en una costumbre. La embriaguez del poder empezó a descomponerse en ráfagas de desazón. Buscando un remedio contra el frío, hizo fusilar al joven oficial que propuso el asesinato del general Teófilo Vargas. Sus órdenes se cumplían antes de ser impartidas, aun antes de que él las concibiera, y siempre llegaban mucho más lejos de donde él se hubiera atrevido a hacerlas llegar. Extraviado en la soledad de su inmenso poder, empezó a perder el rumbo. Le molestaba la gente que lo aclamaba en los pueblos vencidos, y que le parecía la misma que aclamaba al enemigo. Por todas partes encontraba adolescentes que lo miraban con sus propios ojos, que hablaban con su propia voz, que lo saludaban con la misma desconfianza con que él los saludaba a ellos, y que decían ser sus hijos. Se sintió disperso, repetido, y más solitario que nunca. Tuvo la convicción de que sus propios oficiales le mentían. Se peleó con el duque de Marlborough. «El mejor amigo —solía decir entonces— es el que acaba de morir.» Se cansó de la incertidumbre, el círculo vicioso de aquella guerra eterna que siempre lo encontraba a él en el mismo lugar, sólo que cada vez más viejo, más acabado, más sin saber por qué, ni cómo, ni hasta cuándo. Siempre había alguien fuera del círculo de tiza. Alguien a quien le hacía falta dinero, que tenía un hijo con tos ferina o que quería irse a dormir para siempre porque ya no podía soportar en la boca el sabor a mierda de la guerra y que, sin embargo, se cuadraba con sus últimas reservas de energía para informar: «Todo normal, mi coronel.» Y la normalidad era precisamente lo más espantoso de aquella guerra infinita: que no pasaba nada. Solo, abandonado por los presagios, huyendo del frío que había de acompañarlo hasta la muerte, buscó un último refugio en Macondo, al calor de sus recuerdos más antiguos. Era tan grave su desidia que cuando le anunciaron la llegada de una comisión de su partido autorizada para discutir la encrucijada de la guerra, él se dio vuelta en la hamaca sin despertar por completo.

—Llévenlos donde las putas —dijo.

Eran seis abogados de levita y chistera que soportaban con un duro estoicismo el bravo sol de noviembre. Úrsula los hospedó en la casa. Se pasaban la mayor parte del día encerrados en el dormitorio en conciliábulos herméticos, y al anochecer pedían una escolta y un conjunto de acordeones y tomaban por su cuenta la tienda de Catarino. «No los molesten», ordenaba el coronel Aureliano Buendía. «Al fin y al cabo, yo sé lo que quieren.» A principios de diciembre, la entrevista largamente esperada, que muchos habían previsto como una discusión interminable, se resolvió en menos de una hora.

En la calurosa sala de visitas, junto al espectro de la pianola amortajada con una sábana blanca, el coronel Aureliano Buendía no se sentó esta vez dentro del círculo de tiza que trazaron sus edecanes. Ocupó una silla entre sus asesores políticos, y envuelto en la manta de lana escuchó en silencio las breves propuestas de los emisarios. Pedían, en primer término, renunciar a la revisión de los títulos de propiedad de la tierra para recuperar el apoyo de los terratenientes liberales. Pedían, en segundo término, renunciar a la lucha contra la influencia clerical para obtener el respaldo del pueblo católico. Pedían, por último, renunciar a las aspiraciones de igualdad de derechos entre los hijos naturales y los legítimos para preservar la integridad de los hogares.

—Quiere decir —sonrió el coronel Aureliano Buendía cuando terminó la lectura— que sólo estamos luchando por el poder.

—Son reformas tácticas —replicó uno de los delegados—. Por ahora, lo esencial es ensanchar la base popular de la guerra. Después veremos.

Uno de los asesores políticos del coronel Aureliano Buendía se apresuró a intervenir.

—Es un contrasentido —dijo—. Si estas reformas son buenas, quiere decir que es bueno el régimen conservador. Si con ellas lograremos ensanchar la base popular de la guerra, como dicen ustedes, quiere decir que el régimen tiene una amplia base popular. Quiere decir, en síntesis, que durante casi veinte años hemos estado luchando contra los sentimientos de la nación.

Iba a seguir, pero el coronel Aureliano Buendía lo interrumpió con una señal. «No pierda el tiempo, doctor», dijo. «Lo importante es que desde este momento sólo luchamos por el poder.» Sin dejar de sonreír, tomó los pliegos que le entregaron los delegados y se dispuso a firmar.

—Puesto que es así —concluyó—, no tenemos ningún inconveniente en aceptar.

Sus hombres se miraron consternados.

—Me perdona, coronel —dijo suavemente el coronel Gerineldo Márquez—, pero esto es una traición.

El coronel Aureliano Buendía detuvo en el aire la pluma entintada, y descargó sobre él todo el peso de su autoridad.

—Entréegueme sus armas —ordenó.

El coronel Gerineldo Márquez se levantó y puso las armas en la mesa.

—Preséntese en el cuartel —le ordenó el coronel Aureliano Buendía—. Queda usted a disposición de los tribunales revolucionarios.

Luego firmó la declaración y entregó los pliegos a los emisarios, diciéndoles:

—Señores, ahí tienen sus papeles. Que les aprovechen.

Dos días después, el coronel Gerineldo Márquez, acusado de alta traición, fue condenado a muerte. Derrumbado en su hamaca, el coronel Aureliano Buendía fue insensible a las súplicas de clemencia. La víspera de la ejecución, desobedeciendo la orden de no molestarlo, Úrsula lo visitó en el dormitorio. Cerrada de negro, investida de una rara solemnidad, permaneció de pie los tres minutos de la entrevista. «Sé que fusilarás a Gerineldo —dijo serenamente—, y no puedo hacer nada por impedirlo. Pero una cosa te advierto: tan pronto como vea el cadáver, te lo juro por los huesos de mi padre y mi madre, por la memoria de José Arcadio Buendía, te lo juro ante Dios, que te he de sacar de donde te metas y te mataré con mis propias manos.» Antes de abandonar el cuarto, sin esperar ninguna réplica, concluyó:

—Es lo mismo que habría hecho si hubieras nacido con cola de puerco.

Aquella noche interminable, mientras el coronel Gerineldo Márquez evocaba sus tardes muertas en el costurero de Amaranta, el coronel Aureliano Buendía rasguñó durante muchas horas, tratando de romperla, la dura cáscara de su soledad. Sus únicos instantes felices, desde la tarde remota en que su padre lo llevó a conocer el hielo, habían transcurrido en el taller de platería, donde se le iba el tiempo armando pescaditos de oro. Había tenido que promover treinta y dos guerras, y había tenido que violar todos sus pactos con la muerte y revolcarse como un cerdo en el muladar de la gloria, para descubrir con casi cuarenta años de retraso los privilegios de la simplicidad.

Al amanecer, estragado por la tormentosa vigilia, apareció en el cuarto del cepo una hora antes de la ejecución. «Terminó la farsa, compadre», le dijo al coronel Gerineldo Márquez. «Vámonos de aquí, antes de que acaben de fusilarte los mosquitos.» El coronel Gerineldo Márquez no pudo reprimir el desprecio que le inspiraba aquella actitud.

—No, Aureliano —replicó—. Vale más estar muerto que verte convertido en un chafarote.

—No me verás —dijo el coronel Aureliano Buendía—. Ponte los zapatos y ayúdame a terminar con esta guerra de mierda.

Al decirlo, no imaginaba que era más fácil empezar una guerra que terminarla. Necesitó casi un año de rigor sanguinario para forzar al gobierno a proponer condiciones de paz favorables a los rebeldes, y otro año para persuadir a sus partidarios de la conveniencia de aceptarlas. Llegó a inconcebibles extremos de crueldad para sofocar las rebeliones de sus propios oficiales, que se resistían a feriar la victoria, y terminó apoyándose en fuerzas enemigas para acabar de someterlos.

Nunca fue mejor guerrero que entonces. La certidumbre de que por fin peleaba por su propia liberación, y no por ideales abstractos, por consignas que los políticos podían voltear al derecho y al revés según las circunstancias, le infundió un entusiasmo enardecido. El coronel Gerineldo Márquez, que luchó por el fracaso con tanta convicción y tanta lealtad como antes había luchado por el triunfo, le reprochaba su temeridad inútil. «No te preocupes», sonreía él. «Morirse es mucho más difícil de lo que uno cree.» En su caso era verdad. La seguridad de que su día estaba señalado lo invistió de una inmunidad misteriosa, una inmortalidad a término fijo que lo hizo invulnerable a los riesgos de la guerra, y le permitió finalmente conquistar una derrota que era mucho más difícil, mucho más sangrienta y costosa que la victoria.

En casi veinte años de guerra, el coronel Aureliano Buendía había estado muchas veces en la casa, pero el estado de urgencia en que llegaba siempre, el aparato militar que lo acompañaba a todas partes, el aura de leyenda que doraba su presencia y a la cual no fue insensible ni la propia Úrsula, terminaron por convertirlo en un extraño. La última vez que estuvo en Macondo, y tomó una casa para sus tres concubinas, no se le vio en la suya sino dos o tres veces, cuando tuvo tiempo de aceptar invitaciones a comer. Remedios, la bella, y los gemelos, nacidos en plena guerra, apenas si lo conocían. Amaranta no lograba conciliar la imagen del hermano que pasó la adolescencia fabricando pescaditos de oro, con la del guerrero mítico que había interpuesto entre él y el resto de la humanidad una distancia de tres metros. Pero cuando se conoció la proximidad del armisticio y se pensó que él regresaba otra vez convertido en un ser humano, rescatado por fin para el corazón de los suyos, los afectos familiares aletargados por tanto tiempo renacieron con más fuerza que nunca.

—Al fin —dijo Úrsula— tendremos otra vez un hombre en la casa.

Amaranta fue la primera en sospechar que lo habían perdido para siempre. Una semana antes del armisticio, cuando él entró en la casa sin escolta, precedido por dos ordenanzas descalzos que depositaron en el corredor los aperos de la mula y el baúl de los versos, único saldo de su antiguo equipaje imperial, ella lo vio pasar frente al costurero y lo llamó. El coronel Aureliano Buendía pareció tener dificultad para reconocerla.

—Soy Amaranta —dijo ella de buen humor, feliz de su regreso, y le mostró la mano con la venda negra—. Mira.

El coronel Aureliano Buendía le hizo la misma sonrisa de la primera vez en que la vio con la venda, la remota mañana en que volvió a Macondo sentenciado a muerte.

—¡Qué horror —dijo—, cómo se pasa el tiempo!

El ejército regular tuvo que proteger la casa. Llegó vejado, escupido, acusado de haber recrudecido la guerra sólo para venderla más cara. Temblaba de fiebre y de frío y tenía otra vez las axilas empedradas de golondrinos. Seis meses antes, cuando oyó hablar del armisticio, Úrsula había abierto y barrido la alcoba nupcial, y había quemado mirra en los rincones, pensando que él regresaría dispuesto a envejecer despacio entre las enmohecidas muñecas de Remedios. Pero en realidad, en los dos últimos años él le había pagado sus cuotas finales a la vida, inclusive la del envejecimiento. Al pasar frente al taller de platería, que Úrsula había preparado con especial diligencia, ni siquiera advirtió que las llaves estaban puestas en el candado. No percibió los minúsculos y desgarradores destrozos que el tiempo había hecho en la casa, y que después de una ausencia tan prolongada habrían parecido un desastre a cualquier hombre que conservara vivos sus recuerdos. No le dolieron las peladuras de cal en las paredes, ni los sucios algodones de telaraña en los rincones, ni el polvo de las begonias, ni las nervaduras del comején en las vigas, ni el musgo de los quicios, ni ninguna de las trampas insidiosas que le tendía la nostalgia. Se sentó en el corredor, envuelto en la manta y sin quitarse las botas, como esperando apenas que escampara, y permaneció toda la tarde viendo llover sobre las begonias. Úrsula comprendió entonces que no lo tendría en la casa por mucho tiempo. «Si no es la guerra —pensó— sólo puede ser la muerte.» Fue una suposición tan nítida, tan convincente, que la identificó como un presagio.

Esa noche, en la cena, el supuesto Aureliano Segundo desmigajó el pan con la mano derecha y tomó la sopa con la izquierda. Su hermano gemelo, el supuesto José Arcadio Segundo, desmigajó el pan con la mano izquierda y tomó la sopa con la derecha. Era tan precisa la coordinación de sus movimientos que no parecían dos hermanos sentados el uno frente al otro, sino un artificio de espejos. El espectáculo que los gemelos habían concebido desde que tuvieron conciencia de ser iguales fue repetido en honor del recién llegado. Pero el coronel Aureliano Buendía no lo advirtió. Parecía tan ajeno a todo que ni siquiera se fijó en Remedios, la bella, que pasó desnuda hacia el dormitorio. Úrsula fue la única que se atrevió a perturbar su abstracción.

—Si has de irte otra vez —le dijo a mitad de la cena—, por lo menos trata de recordar cómo éramos esta noche.

Entonces el coronel Aureliano Buendía se dio cuenta, sin asombro, que Úrsula era el único ser humano que había logrado desentrañar su miseria, y por primera vez en muchos años se atrevió a mirarla a la cara. Tenía la piel cuarteada, los dientes carcomidos, el cabello marchito y sin color, y la mirada atónita. La comparó con el recuerdo más antiguo que tenía de ella, la tarde en que él tuvo el presagio de que una olla de caldo hirviendo iba a caerse de la mesa, y la encontró despedazada. En un instante descubrió los arañazos, los verdugones, las mataduras, las úlceras y cicatrices que había dejado en ella más de medio siglo de vida cotidiana, y comprobó que esos estragos no suscitaban en él ni siquiera un sentimiento de piedad. Hizo entonces un último esfuerzo para buscar en su corazón el sitio donde se le habían podrido los afectos, y no pudo encontrarlo. En otra época, al menos experimentaba un confuso sentimiento de vergüenza cuando sorprendía en su propia piel el olor de Úrsula, y en más de una ocasión sintió sus pensamientos interferidos por el pensamiento de ella. Pero todo eso había sido arrasado por la guerra. La propia Remedios, su esposa, era en aquel momento la imagen borrosa de alguien que pudo haber sido su hija. Las incontables mujeres que conoció en el desierto del amor, y que dispersaron su simiente en todo el litoral, no habían dejado rastro alguno en sus sentimientos. La mayoría de ellas entraba en el cuarto en la oscuridad y se iba antes del alba, y al día siguiente eran apenas un poco de tedio en la memoria corporal. El único afecto que prevalecía contra el tiempo y la guerra fue el que sintió por su hermano José Arcadio, cuando ambos eran niños, y no estaba fundado en el amor, sino en la complicidad.

—Perdone —se excusó ante la petición de Úrsula—. Es que esta guerra ha acabado con todo.

En los días siguientes se ocupó de destruir todo rastro de su paso por el mundo. Simplificó el taller de platería hasta sólo dejar los objetos impersonales, regaló sus ropas a los ordenanzas y enterró sus armas en el patio con el mismo sentido de penitencia con que su padre enterró la lanza que dio muerte a Prudencio Aguilar. Sólo conservó una pistola, y con una sola bala. Úrsula no intervino. La única vez que lo disuadió fue cuando él estaba a punto de destruir el daguerrotipo de Remedios que se conservaba en la sala, alumbrado por una lámpara eterna. «Ese retrato dejó de pertenecerte hace mucho tiempo», le dijo. «Es una reliquia de familia.» La víspera del armisticio, cuando ya no quedaba en la casa un solo objeto que permitiera recordarlo, llevó a la panadería el baúl con los versos en el momento en que Santa Sofía de la Piedad se preparaba para encender el horno.

—Préndalo con esto —le dijo él, entregándole el primer rollo de papeles amarillentos—. Arde mejor, porque son cosas muy viejas.

Santa Sofía de la Piedad, la silenciosa, la condescendiente, la que nunca contrarió ni a sus propios hijos, tuvo la impresión de que aquel era un acto prohibido.

—Son papeles importantes —dijo.

—Nada de eso —dijo el coronel—. Son cosas que se escriben para uno mismo.

—Entonces —dijo ella— quémelos usted mismo, coronel.

No sólo lo hizo, sino que despedazó el baúl con una hachuela y echó las astillas al fuego. Horas antes, Pilar Ternera había estado a visitarlo. Después de tantos años de no verla, el coronel Aureliano Buendía se asombró de cuánto había envejecido y engordado, y de cuánto había perdido el esplendor de su risa, pero se asombró también de la profundidad que había logrado en la lectura de las barajas. «Cuídate la boca», le dijo ella, y él se preguntó si la otra vez que se lo dijo, en el apogeo de la gloria, no había sido una visión sorprendentemente anticipada de su destino. Poco después, cuando su médico personal acabó de extirparle los golondrinos, él le preguntó sin demostrar un interés particular cuál era el sitio exacto del corazón. El médico lo auscultó y le pintó luego un círculo en el pecho con un algodón sucio de yodo.

El martes del armisticio amaneció tibio y lluvioso. El coronel Aureliano Buendía apareció en la cocina antes de las cinco y tomó su habitual café sin azúcar. «Un día como este viniste al mundo», le dijo Úrsula. «Todos se asustaron con tus ojos abiertos.» Él no le puso atención, porque estaba pendiente de los aprestos de tropa, los toques de corneta y las voces de mando que estropeaban el alba. Aunque después de tantos años de guerra debían parecerle familiares, esta vez experimentó el mismo desaliento en las rodillas, y el mismo cabrilleo de la piel que había experimentado en su juventud en presencia de una mujer desnuda. Pensó confusamente, al fin capturado en una trampa de la nostalgia, que tal vez si se hubiera casado con ella hubiera sido un hombre sin guerra y sin gloria, un artesano sin nombre, un animal feliz. Ese estremecimiento tardío, que no figuraba en sus previsiones, le amargó el desayuno. A las siete de la mañana, cuando el coronel Gerineldo Márquez fue a buscarlo en compañía de un grupo de oficiales rebeldes, lo encontró más taciturno que nunca, más pensativo y solitario. Úrsula trató de echarle sobre los hombros una manta nueva. «Qué va a pensar el gobierno», le dijo. «Se imaginarán que te has rendido porque ya no tenías ni con qué comprar una manta.» Pero él no la aceptó. Ya en la puerta, viendo que seguía la lluvia, se dejó poner un viejo sombrero de fieltro de José Arcadio Buendía.

—Aureliano —le dijo entonces Úrsula—, prométeme que si te encuentras por ahí con la mala hora, pensarás en tu madre.

Él le hizo una sonrisa distante, levantó la mano con todos los dedos extendidos, y sin decir una palabra abandonó la casa y se enfrentó a los gritos, vituperios y blasfemias que habían de perseguirlo hasta la salida del pueblo. Úrsula pasó la tranca en la puerta decidida a no quitarla en el resto de su vida. «Nos pudriremos aquí dentro», pensó. «Nos volveremos ceniza en esta casa sin hombres, pero no le daremos a este pueblo miserable el gusto de vernos llorar.» Estuvo toda la mañana buscando un recuerdo de su hijo en los más secretos rincones, y no pudo encontrarlo.

El acto se celebró a veinte kilómetros de Macondo, a la sombra de una ceiba gigantesca en torno a la cual había de fundarse más tarde el pueblo de Neerlandia. Los delegados del gobierno y los partidos, y la comisión rebelde que entregó las armas, fueron servidos por un bullicioso grupo de novicias de hábitos blancos, que parecían un revuelo de palomas asustadas por la lluvia. El coronel Aureliano Buendía llegó en una mula embarrada. Estaba sin afeitar, más atormentado por el dolor de los golondrinos que por el inmenso fracaso de sus sueños, pues había llegado al término de toda esperanza, más allá de la gloria y de la nostalgia de la gloria. De acuerdo con lo dispuesto por él mismo, no hubo música, ni cohetes, ni campanas de júbilo, ni vítores, ni ninguna otra manifestación que pudiera alterar el carácter luctuoso del armisticio. Un fotógrafo ambulante, que tomó el único retrato suyo que hubiera podido conservarse, fue obligado a destruir las placas sin revelarlas.

El acto duró apenas el tiempo indispensable para que se estamparan las firmas. En torno de la rústica mesa colocada en el centro de una remendada carpa de circo, donde se sentaron los delegados, estaban los últimos oficiales que permanecieron fieles al coronel Aureliano Buendía. Antes de tomar las firmas, el delegado personal del presidente de la república trató de leer en voz alta el acta de la rendición, pero el coronel Aureliano Buendía se opuso. «No perdamos el tiempo en formalismos», dijo, y se dispuso a firmar los pliegos sin leerlos. Uno de sus oficiales rompió entonces el silencio soporífero de la carpa.

—Coronel —dijo—, háganos el favor de no ser el primero en firmar.

El coronel Aureliano Buendía accedió. Cuando el documento dio la vuelta completa a la mesa, en medio de un silencio tan nítido que habrían podido descifrarse las firmas por el garrapateo de la pluma en el papel, el primer lugar estaba todavía en blanco. El coronel Aureliano Buendía se dispuso a ocuparlo.

—Coronel —dijo entonces otro de sus oficiales—, todavía tiene tiempo de quedar bien.

Sin inmutarse, el coronel Aureliano Buendía firmó la primera copia. No había acabado de firmar la última cuando apareció en la puerta de la carpa un coronel rebelde llevando del cabestro una mula cargada con dos baúles. A pesar de su extremada juventud, tenía un aspecto árido y una expresión paciente. Era el tesorero de la revolución en la circunscripción de Macondo. Había hecho un penoso viaje de seis días, arrastrando la mula muerta de hambre, para llegar a tiempo al armisticio. Con una parsimonia exasperante descargó los baúles, los abrió, y fue poniendo en la mesa, uno por uno, setenta y dos ladrillos de oro. Nadie recordaba la existencia de aquella fortuna. En el desorden del último año, cuando el mando central saltó en pedazos y la revolución degeneró en una sangrienta rivalidad de caudillos, era imposible determinar ninguna responsabilidad. El oro de la rebelión, fundido en bloques que luego fueron recubiertos de barro cocido, quedó fuera de todo control. El coronel Aureliano Buendía hizo incluir los setenta y dos ladrillos de oro en el inventario de la rendición, y clausuró el acto sin permitir discursos. El escuálido adolescente permaneció frente a él, mirándolo a los ojos con sus serenos ojos color de almíbar.

—¿Algo más? —le preguntó el coronel Aureliano Buendía.

El joven coronel apretó los dientes.

—El recibo —dijo.

El coronel Aureliano Buendía se lo extendió de su puño y letra. Luego tomó un vaso de limonada y un pedazo de bizcocho que repartieron las novicias, y se retiró a una tienda de campaña que le habían preparado por si quería descansar. Allí se quitó la camisa, se sentó en el borde del catre, y a las tres y cuarto de la tarde se disparó un tiro de pistola en el círculo de yodo que su médico personal le había pintado en el pecho. A esa hora, en Macondo, Úrsula destapó la olla de la leche en el fogón, extrañada de que se demorara tanto para hervir, y la encontró llena de gusanos.

—¡Han matado a Aureliano! —exclamó.

Miró hacia el patio, obedeciendo a una costumbre de su soledad, y entonces vio a José Arcadio Buendía empapado, triste de lluvia y mucho más viejo que cuando murió. «Lo han matado a traición —precisó Úrsula— y nadie le hizo la caridad de cerrarle los ojos.» Al anochecer vio a través de las lágrimas los raudos y luminosos discos anaranjados que cruzaron el cielo como una exhalación, y pensó que eran una señal de la muerte. Estaba todavía bajo el castaño, sollozando en las rodillas de su esposo, cuando llevaron al coronel Aureliano Buendía envuelto en la manta acartonada de sangre seca y con los ojos abiertos de rabia.

Estaba fuera de peligro. El proyectil siguió una trayectoria tan limpia que el médico le metió por el pecho y le sacó por la espalda un cordón empapado de yodo. «Esta es mi obra maestra», le dijo satisfecho. «Era el único punto por donde podía pasar una bala sin lastimar ningún centro vital.» El coronel Aureliano Buendía se vio rodeado de novicias misericordiosas que entonaban salmos desesperados por el eterno descanso de su alma, y entonces se arrepintió de no haberse dado el tiro en el paladar como lo tenía previsto, sólo por burlar el pronóstico de Pilar Ternera.

—Si todavía me quedara autoridad —le dijo al doctor—, lo haría fusilar sin fórmula de juicio. No por salvarme la vida, sino por hacerme quedar en ridículo.

El fracaso de la muerte le devolvió en pocas horas el prestigio perdido. Los mismos que inventaron la patraña de que había vendido la guerra por un aposento cuyas paredes estaban construidas con ladrillos de oro, definieron la tentativa de suicidio como un acto de honor, y lo proclamaron mártir. Luego, cuando rechazó la Orden del Mérito que le otorgó el presidente de la república, hasta sus más encarnizados rivales desfilaron por su cuarto pidiéndole que desconociera los términos del armisticio y promoviera una nueva guerra. La casa se llenó de regalos de desagravio. Tardíamente impresionado por el respaldo masivo de sus antiguos compañeros de armas, el coronel Aureliano Buendía no descartó la posibilidad de complacerlos. Al contrario, en cierto momento pareció tan entusiasmado con la idea de una nueva guerra que el coronel Gerineldo Márquez pensó que sólo esperaba un pretexto para proclamarla. El pretexto se le ofreció, efectivamente, cuando el presidente de la república se negó a asignar las pensiones de guerra a los antiguos combatientes, liberales o conservadores, mientras cada expediente no fuera revisado por una comisión especial, y la ley de asignaciones aprobada por el congreso. «Esto es un atropello», tronó el coronel Aureliano Buendía. «Se morirán de viejos esperando el correo.» Abandonó por primera vez el mecedor que Úrsula compró para la convalecencia, y dando vueltas en la alcoba dictó un mensaje terminante para el presidente de la república. En ese telegrama, que nunca fue publicado, denunciaba la primera violación del tratado de Neerlandia y amenazaba con proclamar la guerra a muerte si la asignación de las pensiones no era resuelta en el término de quince días. Era tan justa su actitud, que permitía esperar, inclusive, la adhesión de los antiguos combatientes conservadores. Pero la única respuesta del gobierno fue el refuerzo de la guardia militar que se había puesto en la puerta de la casa, con el pretexto de protegerla, y la prohibición de toda clase de visitas. Medidas similares se adoptaron en todo el país con otros caudillos de cuidado. Fue una operación tan oportuna, drástica y eficaz, que dos meses después del armisticio, cuando el coronel Aureliano Buendía fue dado de alta, sus instigadores más decididos estaban muertos o expatriados, o habían sido asimilados para siempre por la administración pública.

El coronel Aureliano Buendía abandonó el cuarto en diciembre, y le bastó con echar una mirada al corredor para no volver a pensar en la guerra. Con una vitalidad que parecía imposible a sus años, Úrsula había vuelto a rejuvenecer la casa. «Ahora van a ver quién soy yo», dijo cuando supo que su hijo viviría. «No habrá una casa mejor, ni más abierta a todo el mundo, que esta casa de locos.» La hizo lavar y pintar, cambió los muebles, restauró el jardín y sembró flores nuevas, y abrió puertas y ventanas para que entrara hasta los dormitorios la deslumbrante claridad del verano. Decretó el término de los numerosos lutos superpuestos, y ella misma cambió los viejos trajes rigurosos por ropas juveniles. La música de la pianola volvió a alegrar la casa. Al oírla, Amaranta se acordó de Pietro Crespi, de su gardenia crepuscular y su olor de lavanda, y en el fondo de su marchito corazón floreció un rencor limpio, purificado por el tiempo. Una tarde en que trataba de poner orden en la sala, Úrsula pidió ayuda a los soldados que custodiaban la casa. El joven comandante de la guardia les concedió el permiso. Poco a poco, Úrsula les fue asignando nuevas tareas. Los invitaba a comer, les regalaba ropas y zapatos y les enseñaba a leer y escribir. Cuando el gobierno suspendió la vigilancia, uno de ellos se quedó viviendo en la casa, y estuvo a su servicio por muchos años. El día de Año Nuevo, enloquecido por los desaires de Remedios, la bella, el joven comandante de la guardia amaneció muerto de amor junto a su ventana.

Años después, en su lecho de agonía, Aureliano Segundo había de recordar la lluviosa tarde de junio en que entró en el dormitorio a conocer a su primer hijo. Aunque era lánguido y llorón, sin ningún rasgo de un Buendía, no tuvo que pensar dos veces para ponerle nombre.

—Se llamará José Arcadio —dijo.

Fernanda del Carpio, la hermosa mujer con quien se había casado el año anterior, estuvo de acuerdo. En cambio Úrsula no pudo ocultar un vago sentimiento de zozobra. En la larga historia de la familia, la tenaz repetición de los nombres le había permitido sacar conclusiones que le parecían terminantes. Mientras los Aurelianos eran retraídos, pero de mentalidad lúcida, los José Arcadio eran impulsivos y emprendedores, pero estaban marcados por un signo trágico. Los únicos casos de clasificación imposible eran los de José Arcadio Segundo y Aureliano Segundo. Fueron tan parecidos y traviesos durante la infancia que ni la propia Santa Sofía de la Piedad podía distinguirlos. El día del bautismo, Amaranta les puso esclavas con sus respectivos nombres y los vistió con ropas de colores distintos marcadas con las iniciales de cada uno, pero cuando empezaron a asistir a la escuela optaron por cambiarse la ropa y las esclavas y por llamarse ellos mismos con los nombres cruzados. El maestro Melchor Escalona, acostumbrado a conocer a José Arcadio Segundo por la camisa verde, perdió los estribos cuando descubrió que éste tenía la esclava de Aureliano Segundo, y que el otro decía llamarse, sin embargo, Aureliano Segundo a pesar de que tenía la camisa blanca y la esclava marcada con el nombre de José Arcadio Segundo. Desde entonces no se sabía con certeza quién era quién. Aun cuando crecieron y la vida los hizo diferentes, Úrsula seguía preguntándose si ellos mismos no habrían cometido un error en algún momento de su intrincado juego de confusiones, y habían quedado cambiados para siempre. Hasta el principio de la adolescencia fueron dos mecanismos sincrónicos. Despertaban al mismo tiempo, sentían deseos de ir al baño a la misma hora, sufrían los mismos trastornos de salud y hasta soñaban las mismas cosas. En la casa, donde se creía que coordinaban sus actos por el simple deseo de confundir, nadie se dio cuenta de la realidad hasta un día en que Santa Sofía de la Piedad le dio a uno un vaso de limonada, y más tardó en probarlo que el otro en decir que le faltaba azúcar. Santa Sofía de la Piedad, que en efecto había olvidado ponerle azúcar a la limonada, se lo contó a Úrsula. «Así son todos», dijo ella, sin sorpresa. «Locos de nacimiento.» El tiempo acabó de desordenar las cosas. El que en los juegos de confusión se quedó con el nombre de Aureliano Segundo se volvió monumental como el abuelo, y el que se quedó con el nombre de José Arcadio Segundo se volvió óseo como el coronel, y lo único que conservaron en común fue el aire solitario de la familia. Tal vez fue ese entrecruzamiento de estaturas, nombres y caracteres lo que le hizo sospechar a Úrsula que estaban barajados desde la infancia.

La diferencia decisiva se reveló en plena guerra cuando José Arcadio Segundo le pidió al coronel Gerineldo Márquez que lo llevara a ver los fusilamientos. Contra el parecer de Úrsula, sus deseos fueron satisfechos. Aureliano Segundo, en cambio, se estremeció ante la sola idea de presenciar una ejecución. Prefería la casa. A los doce años le preguntó a Úrsula qué había en el cuarto clausurado. «Papeles», le contestó ella. «Son los libros de Melquíades y las cosas raras que escribía en sus últimos años.» La respuesta, en vez de tranquilizarlo, aumentó su curiosidad. Insistió tanto, prometió con tanto ahínco no maltratar las cosas, que Úrsula le dio las llaves. Nadie había vuelto a entrar al cuarto desde que sacaron el cadáver de Melquíades y pusieron en la puerta el candado cuyas piezas se soldaron con la herrumbre. Pero cuando Aureliano Segundo abrió las ventanas entró una luz familiar que parecía acostumbrada a iluminar el cuarto todos los días y no había el menor rastro de polvo o telaraña, sino que todo estaba barrido y limpio, mejor barrido y más limpio que el día del entierro, y la tinta no se había secado en el tintero ni el óxido había alterado el brillo de los metales, ni se había extinguido el rescoldo del atanor donde José Arcadio Buendía vaporizó el mercurio. En los anaqueles estaban los libros empastados en una materia acartonada y pálida como la piel humana curtida, y estaban los manuscritos intactos. A pesar del encierro de muchos años, el aire parecía más puro que en el resto de la casa. Todo era tan reciente, que varias semanas después, cuando Úrsula entró al cuarto con un cubo de agua y una escoba para lavar los pisos, no tuvo nada que hacer. Aureliano Segundo estaba abstraído en la lectura de un libro. Aunque carecía de pastas y el título no aparecía por ninguna parte, el niño gozaba con la historia de una mujer que se sentaba a la mesa y sólo comía granos de arroz que prendía con alfileres, y con la historia del pescador que le pidió prestado a su vecino un plomo para su red y el pescado con que lo recompensó más tarde tenía un diamante en el estómago, y con la lámpara que satisfacía los deseos y las alfombras que volaban. Asombrado, le preguntó a Úrsula si todo aquello era verdad, y ella le contestó que sí, que muchos años antes los gitanos llevaban a Macondo las lámparas maravillosas y las esteras voladoras.

—Lo que pasa —suspiró— es que el mundo se va acabando poco a poco y ya no vienen esas cosas.

Cuando terminó el libro, muchos de cuyos cuentos estaban inconclusos porque faltaban páginas, Aureliano Segundo se dio a la tarea de descifrar los manuscritos. Fue imposible. Las letras parecían ropa puesta a secar en un alambre, y se asemejaban más a la escritura musical que a la literaria. Un mediodía ardiente, mientras escrutaba los manuscritos, sintió que no estaba solo en el cuarto. Contra la reverberación de la ventana, sentado con las manos en las rodillas, estaba Melquíades. No tenía más de cuarenta años. Llevaba el mismo chaleco anacrónico y el sombrero de alas de cuervo, y por sus sienes pálidas chorreaba la grasa del cabello derretida por el calor, como lo vieron Aureliano y José Arcadio cuando eran niños. Aureliano Segundo lo reconoció de inmediato, porque aquel recuerdo hereditario se había transmitido de generación en generación, y había llegado a él desde la memoria de su abuelo.

—Salud —dijo Aureliano Segundo.

—Salud, joven —dijo Melquíades.

Desde entonces, durante varios años, se vieron casi todas las tardes. Melquíades le hablaba del mundo, trataba de infundirle su vieja sabiduría, pero se negó a traducir los manuscritos. «Nadie debe conocer su sentido mientras no hayan cumplido cien años», explicó. Aureliano Segundo guardó para siempre el secreto de aquellas entrevistas. En una ocasión sintió que su mundo privado se derrumbaba, porque Úrsula entró en el momento en que Melquíades estaba en el cuarto. Pero ella no lo vio.

—¿Con quién hablas? —le preguntó.

—Con nadie —dijo Aureliano Segundo.

—Así era tu bisabuelo —dijo Úrsula—. También él hablaba solo.

José Arcadio Segundo, mientras tanto, había satisfecho la ilusión de ver un fusilamiento. Por el resto de su vida recordaría el fogonazo lívido de los seis disparos simultáneos y el eco del estampido que se despedazó por los montes, y la sonrisa triste y los ojos perplejos del fusilado, que permaneció erguido mientras la camisa se le empapaba de sangre, y que seguía sonriendo aun cuando lo desataron del poste y lo metieron en un cajón lleno de cal. «Está vivo», pensó él. «Lo van a enterrar vivo.» Se impresionó tanto, que desde entonces detestó las prácticas militares y la guerra, no por las ejecuciones sino por la espantosa costumbre de enterrar vivos a los fusilados. Nadie supo entonces en qué momento empezó a tocar las campanas en la torre, y a ayudarle a misa al padre Antonio Isabel, sucesor de *El Cachorro*, y a cuidar gallos de pelea en el patio de la casa cural. Cuando el coronel Gerineldo Márquez se enteró, lo reprendió duramente por estar aprendiendo oficios repudiados por los liberales. «La cuestión —contestó él— es que a mí me parece que he salido conservador.» Lo creía como si fuera una determinación de la fatalidad. El coronel Gerineldo Márquez, escandalizado, se lo contó a Úrsula.

—Mejor —aprobó ella—. Ojalá se meta de cura, para que Dios entre por fin a esta casa.

Muy pronto se supo que el padre Antonio Isabel lo estaba preparando para la primera comunión. Le enseñaba el catecismo mientras le afeitaba el pescuezo a los gallos. Le explicaba con ejemplos simples, mientras ponían en sus nidos a las gallinas cluecas, cómo se le ocurrió a Dios en el segundo día de la creación que los pollos se formaran dentro del huevo. Desde entonces manifestaba el párroco los primeros síntomas del delirio senil que lo llevó a decir, años más tarde, que probablemente el diablo había ganado la rebelión contra Dios, y que era aquél quien estaba sentado en el trono celeste, sin revelar su verdadera identidad para atrapar a los incautos. Fogueado por la intrepidez de su preceptor, José Arcadio Segundo llegó en pocos meses a ser tan ducho en martingalas teológicas para confundir al demonio, como diestro en las trampas de la gallera. Amaranta le hizo un traje de lino con cuello y corbata, le compró un par de zapatos blancos y grabó su nombre con letras doradas en el lazo del cirio. Dos noches antes de la primera comunión, el padre Antonio Isabel se encerró con él en la sacristía para confesarlo, con la ayuda de un diccionario de pecados. Fue una lista tan larga, que el anciano párroco, acostumbrado a acostarse a las seis, se quedó dormido en el sillón antes de terminar. El interrogatorio fue para José

Arcadio Segundo una revelación. No le sorprendió que el padre le preguntara si había hecho cosas malas con mujer, y contestó honradamente que no, pero se desconcertó con la pregunta de si las había hecho con animales. El primer viernes de mayo comulgó torturado por la curiosidad. Más tarde le hizo la pregunta a Petronio, el enfermo sacristán que vivía en la torre y que según decían se alimentaba de murciélagos, y Petronio le contestó: «Es que hay cristianos corrompidos que hacen sus cosas con las burras.» José Arcadio Segundo siguió demostrando tanta curiosidad, pidió tantas explicaciones, que Petronio perdió la paciencia.

—Yo voy los martes en la noche —confesó—. Si prometes no decírselo a nadie, el otro martes te llevo.

El martes siguiente, en efecto, Petronio bajó de la torre con un banquito de madera que nadie supo hasta entonces para qué servía, y llevó a José Arcadio Segundo a una huerta cercana. El muchacho se aficionó tanto a aquellas incursiones nocturnas, que pasó mucho tiempo antes de que se le viera en la tienda de Catarino. Se hizo hombre de gallos. «Te llevas esos animales a otra parte», le ordenó Úrsula la primera vez que lo vio entrar con sus finos animales de pelea. «Ya los gallos han traído demasiadas amarguras a esta casa para que ahora vengas tú a traernos otras.» José Arcadio Segundo se los llevó sin discusión, pero siguió criándolos donde Pilar Ternera, su abuela, que puso a su disposición cuanto le hacía falta, a cambio de tenerlo en la casa. Pronto demostró en la gallera la sabiduría que le infundió el padre Antonio Isabel, y dispuso de suficiente dinero no sólo para enriquecer sus crías, sino para procurarse satisfacciones de hombre. Úrsula lo comparaba en aquel tiempo con su hermano y no podía entender cómo los dos gemelos que parecieron una sola persona en la infancia habían terminado por ser tan distintos. La perplejidad no le duró mucho tiempo, porque muy pronto empezó Aureliano Segundo a dar muestras de holgazanería y disipación. Mientras estuvo encerrado en el cuarto de Melquíades fue un hombre ensimismado, como lo fue el coronel Aureliano Buendía en su juventud. Pero poco antes del tratado de Neerlandia una casualidad lo sacó de su ensimismamiento y lo enfrentó a la realidad del mundo. Una mujer joven, que andaba vendiendo números para la rifa de un acordeón, lo saludó con mucha familiaridad. Aureliano Segundo no se sorprendió porque ocurría con frecuencia que lo confundieran con su hermano. Pero no aclaró el equívoco, ni siquiera cuando la muchacha trató de ablandarle el corazón con lloriqueos, y terminó por llevarlo a su cuarto. Le tomó tanto cariño desde aquel primer encuentro, que hizo trampas en la rifa para que él se ganara el acordeón. Al cabo de dos semanas, Aureliano Segundo se dio cuenta de que la mujer se había estado acostando alternativamente con él y con su hermano, creyendo que eran el mismo hombre, y en vez de aclarar la situación se las arregló para prolongarla. No volvió al cuarto de Melquíades. Pasaba las tardes en el patio, aprendiendo a tocar de oídas el acordeón, contra las protestas de Úrsula, que en aquel tiempo había prohibido la música en la casa a causa de los lutos, y que además menospreciaba el acordeón como un instrumento propio de los vagabundos herederos de Francisco el Hombre. Sin embargo, Aureliano Segundo llegó a ser un virtuoso del acordeón y siguió siéndolo después de que se casó y tuvo hijos y fue uno de los hombres más respetados de Macondo.

Durante casi dos meses compartió la mujer con su hermano. Lo vigilaba, le descomponía los planes, y cuando estaba seguro de que José Arcadio Segundo no visitaría esa noche la amante común, se iba a dormir con ella. Una mañana descubrió que estaba enfermo. Dos días después encontró a su hermano aferrado a una viga del baño, empapado en sudor y llorando a lágrima viva, y entonces comprendió. Su hermano le confesó que la mujer lo había repudiado por llevarle lo que ella llamaba una enfermedad de la mala vida. Le contó también cómo trataba de curarlo Pilar Ternera. Aureliano Segundo se sometió a escondidas a los ardientes lavados de permanganato y las aguas diuréticas, y ambos se curaron por separado después de tres meses de sufrimientos secretos. José Arcadio Segundo no volvió a ver a la mujer. Aureliano Segundo obtuvo su perdón y se quedó con ella hasta la muerte.

Se llamaba Petra Cotes. Había llegado a Macondo en plena guerra, con un marido ocasional que vivía de las rifas, y cuando el hombre murió, ella siguió con el negocio. Era una mulata limpia y joven, con unos ojos amarillos y almendrados que le daban a su rostro la ferocidad de una pantera, pero tenía un corazón generoso y una magnífica vocación para el amor. Cuando Úrsula se dio cuenta de que José Arcadio Segundo era gallero y Aureliano Segundo tocaba el acordeón en las fiestas ruidosas de su concubina, creyó enloquecer de confusión. Era como si en ambos se hubieran concentrado los defectos de la familia y ninguna de sus virtudes. Entonces decidió que nadie volviera a llamarse Aureliano y José Arcadio. Sin embargo, cuando Aureliano Segundo tuvo su primer hijo, no se atrevió a contrariarlo.

lineage

—De acuerdo —dijo Úrsula—, pero con una condición: yo me encargo de criarlo.

Aunque ya era centenaria y estaba a punto de quedarse ciega por las cataratas, conservaba intactos el dinamismo físico, la integridad del carácter y el equilibrio mental. Nadie mejor que ella para formar al hombre virtuoso que había de restaurar el prestigio de la familia, un hombre que nunca hubiera oído hablar de la guerra, los gallos de pelea, las mujeres de mala vida y las empresas delirantes, cuatro calamidades que, según pensaba Úrsula, habían determinado la decadencia de su estirpe. «Este será cura», prometió solemnemente. «Y si Dios me da vida, ha de llegar a ser Papa.» Todos rieron al oírla, no sólo en el dormitorio, sino en toda la casa, donde estaban reunidos los bulliciosos amigotes de Aureliano Segundo. La guerra, relegada al desván de los malos recuerdos, fue momentáneamente evocada con los taponazos del champaña.

→ *loft* *attic*

—A la salud del Papa —brindó Aureliano Segundo.

Los invitados brindaron a coro. Luego el dueño de casa tocó el acordeón, se reventaron cohetes y se ordenaron tambores de júbilo para el pueblo. En la madrugada, los invitados ensopados en champaña sacrificaron seis vacas y las pusieron en la calle a disposición de la muchedumbre. Nadie se escandalizó. Desde que Aureliano Segundo se hizo cargo de la casa, aquellas festividades eran cosa corriente, aunque no existiera un motivo tan justo como el nacimiento de un Papa. En pocos años, sin esfuerzos, a puros golpes de suerte, había acumulado una de las más grandes fortunas de la ciénaga, gracias a la proliferación sobrenatural de sus animales. Sus yeguas parían trillizos, las gallinas ponían dos veces por día, y los cerdos engordaban con tal desenfreno, que nadie podía explicarse tan desordenada fecundidad, como no fuera por artes de magia. «Economiza ahora», le decía Úrsula a su atolondrado bisnieto. «Esta suerte no te va a durar toda la vida.» Pero Aureliano Segundo no le ponía atención. Mientras más destapaba champaña para ensopar a sus amigos, más alocadamente parían sus animales, y más se convencía él de que su buena estrella no era cosa de su conducta sino influencia de Petra Cotes, su concubina, cuyo amor tenía la virtud de exasperar a la naturaleza. Tan persuadido estaba de que era ese el origen de su fortuna, que nunca tuvo a Petra Cotes lejos de sus crías, y aun cuando se casó y tuvo hijos siguió viviendo con ella con el consentimiento de Fernanda. Sólido, monumental como sus abuelos, pero con un gozo vital y una simpatía irresistible que ellos no tuvieron, Aureliano Segundo apenas si tenía tiempo de vigilar sus ganados. Le bastaba con llevar a Petra Cotes a sus criaderos, y pasearla a caballo por sus tierras, para que todo animal marcado con su hierro sucumbiera a la peste irremediable de la proliferación.

Como todas las cosas buenas que les ocurrieron en su larga vida, aquella fortuna desmandada tuvo origen en la casualidad. Hasta el final de las guerras, Petra Cotes seguía sosteniéndose con el producto de sus rifas, y Aureliano Segundo se las arreglaba para saquear de vez en cuando las alcancías de Úrsula. Formaban una pareja frívola, sin más preocupaciones que la de acostarse todas las noches, aun en las fechas prohibidas, y retozar en la cama hasta el amanecer. «Esa mujer ha sido tu perdición», le gritaba Úrsula al bisnieto cuando lo veía entrar a la casa como un sonámbulo. «Te tiene tan embobado, que un día de estos te veré retorciéndote de cólicos, con un sapo metido en la barriga.» José Arcadio Segundo, que demoró mucho tiempo para descubrir la suplantación, no lograba entender la pasión de su hermano. Recordaba a Petra Cotes como una mujer convencional, más bien perezosa en la cama, y completamente desprovista de recursos para el amor. Sordo al clamor de Úrsula y a las burlas de su hermano, Aureliano Segundo sólo pensaba entonces en encontrar un oficio que le permitiera sostener una casa para Petra Cotes, y morirse con ella, sobre ella y debajo de ella, en una noche de desafuero febril. Cuando el coronel Aureliano Buendía volvió a abrir el taller, seducido al fin por los encantos pacíficos de la vejez, Aureliano Segundo pensó que sería un buen negocio dedicarse a la fabricación de pescaditos de oro. Pasó muchas horas en el cuartito caluroso viendo cómo las duras láminas de metal, trabajadas por el coronel con la paciencia inconcebible del desengaño, se iban convirtiendo poco a poco en escamas doradas. El oficio le pareció tan laborioso, y era tan persistente y apremiante el recuerdo de Petra Cotes, que al cabo de tres semanas desapareció del taller. Fue en esa época que le dio a Petra Cotes por rifar conejos. Se reproducían y se volvían adultos con tanta rapidez, que apenas daban tiempo para vender los números de la rifa. Al principio, Aureliano Segundo no advirtió las alarmantes proporciones de la proliferación. Pero una noche, cuando ya nadie en el pueblo quería oír hablar de las rifas de conejos, sintió un estruendo en la pared del patio. «No te asustes», dijo Petra Cotes. «Son los conejos.» No pudieron dormir más, atormentados por el tráfago de los animales. Al

232

amanecer, Aureliano Segundo abrió la puerta y vio el patio empedrado de conejos, azules en el resplandor del alba. Petra Cotes, muerta de risa, no resistió la tentación de hacerle una broma.

—Estos son los que nacieron anoche —dijo.

—¡Qué horror! —dijo él—. ¿Por qué no pruebas con vacas?

Pocos días después, tratando de desahogar su patio, Petra Cotes cambió los conejos por una vaca, que dos meses más tarde parió trillizos. Así empezaron las cosas. De la noche a la mañana, Aureliano Segundo se hizo dueño de tierras y ganados, y apenas si tenía tiempo de ensanchar las caballerizas y pocilgas desbordadas. Era una prosperidad de delirio que a él mismo le causaba risa, y no podía menos que asumir actitudes extravagantes para descargar su buen humor. «Apártense, vacas, que la vida es corta», gritaba. Úrsula se preguntaba en qué enredos se había metido, si no estaría robando, si no había terminado por volverse cuatrero, y cada vez que lo veía destapando champaña por el puro placer de echarse la espuma por la cabeza, le reprochaba a gritos el desperdicio. Lo molestó tanto, que un día en que Aureliano Segundo amaneció con el humor rebosado, apareció con un cajón de dinero, una lata de engrudo y una brocha, y cantando a voz en cuello las viejas canciones de Francisco el Hombre, empapeló la casa por dentro y por fuera, y de arriba abajo, con billetes de a peso. La antigua mansión pintada de blanco desde los tiempos en que llevaron la pianola, adquirió el aspecto equívoco de una mezquita. En medio del alboroto de la familia, del escándalo de Úrsula, del júbilo del pueblo que abarrotó la calle para presenciar la glorificación del despilfarro, Aureliano Segundo terminó por empapelar desde la fachada hasta la cocina, inclusive los baños y dormitorios, y arrojó los billetes sobrantes en el patio.

—Ahora —dijo finalmente— espero que nadie en esta casa me vuelva a hablar de plata.

Así fue. Úrsula hizo quitar los billetes adheridos a las grandes tortas de cal, y volvió a pintar la casa de blanco. «Dios mío», suplicaba. «Haznos tan pobres como éramos cuando fundamos este pueblo, no sea que en la otra vida nos vayas a cobrar esta dilapidación.» Sus súplicas fueron escuchadas en sentido contrario. En efecto, uno de los trabajadores que desprendía los billetes tropezó por descuido con un enorme San José de yeso que alguien había dejado en la casa en los últimos años de la guerra, y la imagen hueca se despedazó contra el suelo. Estaba atiborrada de monedas de oro Nadie recordaba quién había llevado aquel santo de tamaño natural. «Lo trajeron tres hombres», explicó Amaranta. «Me pidieron que lo guardáramos mientras pasaba la lluvia, y yo les dije que lo pusieran ahí, en el rincón, donde nadie fuera a tropezar con él, y ahí lo pusieron con mucho cuidado, y ahí ha estado desde entonces, porque nunca volvieron a buscarlo.» En los últimos tiempos, Úrsula le había puesto velas y se había postrado ante él, sin sospechar que en lugar de un santo estaba adorando casi doscientos kilogramos de oro. La tardía comprobación de su involuntario paganismo agravó su desconsuelo. Escupió el espectacular montón de monedas, lo metió en tres sacos de lona, y lo enterró en un lugar secreto, en espera de que tarde o temprano los tres desconocidos fueran a reclamarlo. Mucho después, en los años difíciles de su decrepitud, Úrsula solía intervenir en las conversaciones de los numerosos viajeros que entonces pasaban por la casa, y les preguntaba si durante la guerra no habían dejado allí un San José de yeso para que lo guardaran mientras pasaba la lluvia.

Estas cosas, que tanto consternaban a Úrsula, eran corrientes en aquel tiempo. Macondo naufragaba en una prosperidad de milagro. Las casas de barro y cañabrava de los fundadores habían sido reemplazadas por construcciones de ladrillo, con persianas de madera y pisos de cemento, que hacían más llevadero el calor sofocante de las dos de la tarde. De la antigua aldea de José Arcadio Buendía sólo quedaban entonces los almendros polvorientos, destinados a resistir a las circunstancias más arduas, y el río de aguas diáfanas cuyas piedras prehistóricas fueron pulverizadas por las enloquecidas almádenas de José Arcadio Segundo, cuando se empeñó en despejar el cauce para establecer un servicio de navegación. Fue un sueño delirante, comparable apenas a los de su bisabuelo, porque el lecho pedregoso y los numerosos tropiezos de la corriente impedían el tránsito desde Macondo hasta el mar. Pero José Arcadio Segundo, en un imprevisto arranque de temeridad, se empecinó en el proyecto. Hasta entonces no había dado ninguna muestra de imaginación. Salvo su precaria aventura con Petra Cotes, nunca se le había conocido mujer. Úrsula lo tenía como el ejemplar más apagado que había dado la familia en toda su historia, incapaz de destacarse ni siquiera como alborotador de galleras, cuando el coronel Aureliano Buendía le contó la historia del galeón español encallado a doce kilómetros del mar, cuyo costillar carbonizado vio él mismo durante la guerra. El relato, que a tanta gente durante tanto tiempo le pareció fantástico, fue una revelación para José Arcadio Segundo. Remató sus gallos al mejor postor, reclutó hombres y compró herramientas, y se empeñó en la descomunal empresa de romper piedras, excavar canales, despejar escollos y hasta emparejar cataratas. «Ya esto me lo sé de memoria», gritaba Úrsula. «Es como si el tiempo diera vueltas en redondo y hubiéramos vuelto al principio.» Cuando estimó que el río era navegable, José Arcadio Segundo hizo a su hermano una exposición pormenorizada de sus planes, y éste le dio el dinero que le hacía falta para su empresa. Desapareció por mucho tiempo. Se había dicho que su proyecto de comprar un barco no era más que una triquiñuela para alzarse con el dinero del hermano, cuando se divulgó la noticia de que una extraña nave se aproximaba al pueblo. Los habitantes de Macondo, que ya no recordaban las empresas colosales de José Arcadio Buendía, se precipitaron a la ribera y vieron con ojos pasmados de incredulidad la llegada del primer y último barco que atracó jamás en el pueblo. No era más que una balsa de troncos, arrastrada mediante gruesos cables por veinte hombres que caminaban por la ribera. En la proa, con un brillo de satisfacción en la mirada, José Arcadio Segundo dirigía la dispendiosa maniobra. Junto con él llegaba un grupo de matronas espléndidas que se protegían del sol abrasante con vistosas sombrillas, y tenían en los hombros preciosos pañolones de seda, y ungüentos de colores en el rostro, y flores naturales en el cabello, y serpientes de oro en los brazos y diamantes en los dientes. La balsa de troncos fue el único vehículo que José Arcadio Segundo pudo remontar hasta Macondo, y sólo por una vez, pero nunca reconoció el fracaso de su empresa sino que proclamó su hazaña como una victoria de la voluntad. Rindió cuentas escrupulosas a su hermano, y muy pronto volvió a hundirse en la rutina de los gallos. Lo único que quedó de aquella desventurada iniciativa fue el soplo de renovación que llevaron las matronas de Francia, cuyas artes magníficas cambiaron los métodos tradicionales del amor, y cuyo sentido del bienestar social arrasó con la anticuada tienda de Catarino y transformó la calle en un bazar de farolitos japoneses y organillos nostálgicos. Fueron ellas las promotoras del carnaval sangriento que durante tres días hundió a Macondo en el delirio, y cuya única consecuencia perdurable fue haberle dado a Aureliano Segundo la oportunidad de conocer a Fernanda del Carpio.

Remedios, la bella, fue proclamada reina. Úrsula, que se estremecía ante la belleza inquietante de la bisnieta, no pudo impedir la elección. Hasta entonces había conseguido que no saliera a la calle, como no fuera para ir a misa con Amaranta, pero la obligaba a cubrirse la cara con una mantilla negra. Los hombres menos piadosos, los que se disfrazaban de curas para decir misas sacrílegas en la tienda de Catarino, asistían a la iglesia con el único propósito de ver aunque fuera un instante el rostro de Remedios, la bella, de cuya hermosura legendaria se hablaba con un fervor sobrecogido en todo el ámbito de la ciénaga. Pasó mucho tiempo antes de que lo consiguieran, y más les hubiera valido que la ocasión no llegara nunca, porque la mayoría de ellos no pudo recuperar jamás la placidez del sueño. El hombre que lo hizo posible, un forastero, perdió para siempre la serenidad, se enredó en los tremedales de la abyección y la miseria, y años después fue despedazado por un tren nocturno cuando se quedó dormido sobre los rieles. Desde el momento en que se le vio en la iglesia, con un vestido de pana verde y un chaleco bordado, nadie puso en duda que iba desde muy lejos, tal vez de una remota ciudad del exterior, atraído por la fascinación mágica de Remedios, la bella. Era tan hermoso, tan gallardo y reposado, de una prestancia tan bien llevada, que Pietro Crespi junto a él habría parecido un sietemesino, y muchas mujeres murmuraron entre sonrisas de despecho que era él quien verdaderamente merecía la mantilla. No alternó con nadie en Macondo. Aparecía al amanecer del domingo, como un príncipe de cuento, en un caballo con estribos de plata y gualdrapas de terciopelo, y abandonaba el pueblo después de la misa.

Era tal el poder de su presencia, que desde la primera vez que se le vio en la iglesia todo el mundo dio por sentado que entre él y Remedios, la bella, se había establecido un duelo callado y tenso, un pacto secreto, un desafío irrevocable cuya culminación no podía ser solamente el amor sino también la muerte. El sexto domingo, el caballero apareció con una rosa amarilla en la mano. Oyó la misa de pie, como lo hacía siempre, y al final se interpuso al paso de Remedios, la bella, y le ofreció la rosa solitaria. Ella la recibió con un gesto natural, como si hubiera estado preparada para aquel homenaje, y entonces se descubrió el rostro por un instante y dio las gracias con una sonrisa. Fue todo cuanto hizo. Pero no sólo para el caballero, sino para todos los hombres que tuvieron el desdichado privilegio de vivirlo, aquel fue un instante eterno.

El caballero instalaba desde entonces la banda de música junto a la ventana de Remedios, la bella, y a veces hasta el amanecer. Aureliano Segundo fue el único que sintió por él una compasión cordial, y trató de quebrantar su perseverancia. «No pierda más el tiempo», le dijo una noche. «Las mujeres de esta casa son peores que las mulas.» Le ofreció su amistad, lo invitó a bañarse en champaña, trató de hacerle entender que las hembras de su familia tenían entrañas de pedernal, pero no consiguió vulnerar su obstinación. Exasperado por las interminables noches de música, el coronel Aureliano Buendía lo amenazó con curarle la aflicción a pistoletazos. Nada lo hizo desistir, salvo su propio y lamentable estado de desmoralización. De apuesto e impecable se hizo vil y harapiento. Se rumoreaba que había abandonado poder y fortuna en su lejana nación, aunque en verdad no se conoció nunca su origen. Se volvió hombre de pleitos, pendenciero de cantina, y amaneció revolcado en sus propias excrecencias en la tienda de Catarino. Lo más triste de su drama era que Remedios, la bella, no se fijó en él ni siquiera cuando se presentaba a la iglesia vestido de príncipe. Recibió la rosa amarilla sin la menor malicia, más bien divertida por la extravagancia del gesto, y se levantó la mantilla para verle mejor la cara y no para mostrarle la suya.

En realidad, Remedios, la bella, no era un ser de este mundo. Hasta muy avanzada la pubertad, Santa Sofía de la Piedad tuvo que bañarla y ponerle la ropa, y aun cuando pudo valerse por sí misma había que vigilarla para que no pintara animalitos en las paredes con una varita embadurnada de su propia caca. Llegó a los veinte años sin aprender a leer y escribir, sin servirse de los cubiertos en la mesa, paseándose desnuda por la casa, porque su naturaleza se resistía a cualquier clase de convencionalismos. Cuando el joven comandante de la guardia le declaró su amor, lo rechazó sencillamente porque la asombró su frivolidad. «Fíjate qué simple es», le dijo a Amaranta. «Dice que se está muriendo por mí, como si yo fuera un cólico miserere.» Cuando en efecto lo encontraron muerto junto a su ventana, Remedios, la bella, confirmó su impresión inicial.

—Ya ven —comentó—. Era completamente simple.

Parecía como si una lucidez penetrante le permitiera ver la realidad de las cosas más allá de cualquier formalismo. Ese era al menos el punto de vista del coronel Aureliano Buendía, para quien Remedios, la bella, no era en modo alguno retrasada mental, como se creía, sino todo lo contrario. «Es como si viniera de regreso de veinte años de guerra», solía decir. Úrsula, por su parte, le agradecía a Dios que hubiera premiado a la familia con una criatura de una pureza excepcional, pero al mismo tiempo la conturbaba su hermosura, porque le parecía una virtud contradictoria, una trampa diabólica en el centro de la candidez. Fue por eso que decidió apartarla del mundo, preservarla de toda tentación terrenal, sin saber que Remedios, la bella, ya desde el vientre de su madre, estaba a salvo de cualquier contagio. Nunca le pasó por la cabeza la idea de que la eligieran reina de la belleza en el pandemónium de un carnaval. Pero Aureliano Segundo, embullado con la ventolera de disfrazarse de tigre, llevó al padre Antonio Isabel a la casa para que convenciera a Úrsula de que el carnaval no era una fiesta pagana, como ella decía, sino una tradición católica. Finalmente convencida, aunque a regañadientes, dio el consentimiento para la coronación.

La noticia de que Remedios Buendía iba a ser la

soberana del festival rebasó en pocas horas los límites de la ciénaga, llegó hasta lejanos territorios donde se ignoraba el inmenso prestigio de su belleza, y suscitó la inquietud de quienes todavía consideraban su apellido como un símbolo de la subversión. Era una inquietud infundada. Si alguien resultaba inofensivo en aquel tiempo, era el envejecido y desencantado coronel Aureliano Buendía, que poco a poco había ido perdiendo todo contacto con la realidad de la nación. Encerrado en su taller, su única relación con el resto del mundo era el comercio de pescaditos de oro. Uno de los antiguos soldados que vigilaron su casa en los primeros días de la paz iba a venderlos a las poblaciones de la ciénaga, y regresaba cargado de monedas y de noticias. Que el gobierno conservador, decía, con el apoyo de los liberales, estaba reformando el calendario para que cada presidente estuviera cien años en el poder. Que por fin se había firmado el concordato con la Santa Sede, y que había venido desde Roma un cardenal con una corona de diamantes y en un trono de oro macizo, y que los ministros liberales se habían hecho retratar de rodillas en el acto de besarle el anillo. Que la corista principal de una compañía española, de paso por la capital, había sido secuestrada en su camerino por un grupo de enmascarados, y el domingo siguiente había bailado desnuda en la casa de verano del presidente de la república. «No me hables de política», le decía el coronel. «Nuestro asunto es vender pescaditos.» El rumor público de que no quería saber nada de la situación del país porque se estaba enriqueciendo con su taller provocó las risas de Úrsula cuando llegó a sus oídos. Con su terrible sentido práctico, ella no podía entender el negocio del coronel, que cambiaba los pescaditos por monedas de oro, y luego convertía las monedas de oro en pescaditos, y así sucesivamente, de modo que tenía que trabajar cada vez más a medida que más vendía, para satisfacer un círculo vicioso exasperante. En verdad, lo que le interesaba a él no era el negocio sino el trabajo. Le hacía falta tanta concentración para engarzar escamas, incrustar minúsculos rubíes en los ojos, laminar agallas y montar timones, que no le quedaba un solo vacío para llenarlo con la desilusión de la guerra. Tan absorbente era la atención que le exigía el preciosismo de su artesanía, que en poco tiempo envejeció más que en todos los años de guerra, y la posición le torció la espina dorsal y la milimetría le desgastó la vista, pero la concentración implacable lo premió con la paz del espíritu. La última vez que se le vio atender algún asunto relacionado con la guerra fue cuando un grupo de veteranos de ambos partidos solicitó su apoyo para la aprobación de las pensiones vitalicias, siempre prometidas y siempre en el punto de partida. «Olvídense de eso», les dijo él. «Ya ven que yo rechacé mi pensión para quitarme la tortura de estarla esperando hasta la muerte.» Al principio, el coronel Gerineldo Márquez lo visitaba al atardecer, y ambos se sentaban en la puerta de la calle a evocar el pasado. Pero Amaranta no pudo soportar los recuerdos que le suscitaba aquel hombre cansado cuya calvicie lo precipitaba al abismo de una ancianidad prematura, y lo atormentó con desaires injustos, hasta que no volvió sino en ocasiones especiales, y desapareció finalmente anulado por la parálisis. Taciturno, silencioso, insensible al nuevo soplo de vitalidad que estremecía la casa, el coronel Aureliano Buendía apenas si comprendió que el secreto de una buena vejez no es otra cosa que un pacto honrado con la soledad. Se levantaba a las cinco después de un sueño superficial, tomaba en la cocina su eterno tazón de café amargo, se encerraba todo el día en el taller, y a las cuatro de la tarde pasaba por el corredor arrastrando un taburete, sin fijarse siquiera en el incendio de los rosales, ni en el brillo de la hora, ni en la impavidez de Amaranta, cuya melancolía hacía un ruido de marmita perfectamente perceptible al atardecer, y se sentaba en la puerta de la calle hasta que se lo permitían los mosquitos. Alguien se atrevió alguna vez a perturbar su soledad.

—¿Cómo está, coronel? —le dijo al pasar.

—Aquí —contestó él—. Esperando que pase mi entierro.

De modo que la inquietud causada por la reaparición pública de su apellido, a propósito del reinado de Remedios, la bella, carecía de fundamento real. Muchos, sin embargo, no lo creyeron así. Inocente de la tragedia que lo amenazaba, el pueblo se desbordó en la plaza pública, en una bulliciosa explosión de alegría. El carnaval había alcanzado su más alto nivel de locura, Aureliano Segundo había satisfecho por fin su sueño de disfrazarse de tigre y andaba feliz entre la muchedumbre desaforada, ronco de tanto roncar, cuando apareció por el camino de la ciénaga una comparsa multitudinaria llevando en andas doradas a la mujer más fascinante que hubiera podido concebir la imaginación. Por un momento, los pacíficos habitantes de Macondo se quitaron las máscaras para ver mejor la deslumbrante criatura con corona de esmeraldas y capa de armiño, que parecía investida de una autoridad legítima, y no simplemente de una soberanía de lentejuelas y papel crespón. No faltó

243

quien tuviera la suficiente clarividencia para sospechar que se trataba de una provocación. Pero Aureliano Segundo se sobrepuso de inmediato a la perplejidad, declaró huéspedes de honor a los recién llegados, y sentó salomónicamente a Remedios, la bella, y a la reina intrusa en el mismo pedestal. Hasta la medianoche, los forasteros disfrazados de beduinos participaron del delirio y hasta lo enriquecieron con una pirotecnia suntuosa y unas virtudes acrobáticas que hicieron pensar en las artes de los gitanos. De pronto, en el paroxismo de la fiesta, alguien rompió el delicado equilibrio.

—¡Viva el partido liberal! —gritó—. ¡Viva el coronel Aureliano Buendía!

Las descargas de fusilería ahogaron el esplendor de los fuegos artificiales, y los gritos de terror anularon la música, y el júbilo fue aniquilado por el pánico. Muchos años después seguiría afirmándose que la guardia real de la soberana intrusa era un escuadrón del ejército regular que debajo de sus ricas chilabas escondía fusiles de reglamento. El gobierno rechazó el cargo en un bando extraordinario y prometió una investigación terminante del episodio sangriento. Pero la verdad no se esclareció nunca, y prevaleció para siempre la versión de que la guardia real, sin provocación de ninguna índole, tomó posiciones de combate a una seña de su comandante y disparó sin piedad contra la muchedumbre. Cuando se restableció la calma, no quedaba en el pueblo uno solo de los falsos beduinos, y quedaron tendidos en la plaza, entre muertos y heridos, nueve payasos, cuatro colombinas, diecisiete reyes de baraja, un diablo, tres músicos, dos Pares de Francia y tres emperatrices japonesas. En la confusión del pánico, José Arcadio

Segundo logró poner a salvo a Remedios, la bella, y Aureliano Segundo llevó en brazos a la casa a la soberana intrusa, con el traje desgarrado y la capa de armiño embarrada de sangre. Se llamaba Fernanda del Carpio. La habían seleccionado como la más hermosa entre las cinco mil mujeres más hermosas del país, y la habían llevado a Macondo con la promesa de nombrarla reina de Madagascar. Úrsula se ocupó de ella como si fuera una hija. El pueblo, en lugar de poner en duda su inocencia, se compadeció de su candidez. Seis meses después de la masacre, cuando se restablecieron los heridos y se marchitaron las últimas flores en la fosa común, Aureliano Segundo fue a buscarla a la distante ciudad donde vivía con su padre, y se casó con ella en Macondo, en una fragorosa parranda de veinte días.

El matrimonio estuvo a punto de acabarse a los dos meses porque Aureliano Segundo, tratando de desagraviar a Petra Cotes, le hizo tomar un retrato vestida de reina de Madagascar. Cuando Fernanda lo supo volvió a hacer sus baúles de recién casada y se marchó de Macondo sin despedirse. Aureliano Segundo la alcanzó en el camino de la ciénaga. Al cabo de muchas súplicas y propósitos de enmienda logró llevarla de regreso a la casa, y abandonó a la concubina.

Petra Cotes, consciente de su fuerza, no dio muestras de preocupación. Ella lo había hecho hombre. Siendo todavía un niño lo sacó del cuarto de Melquíades, con la cabeza llena de ideas fantásticas y sin ningún contacto con la realidad, y le dio un lugar en el mundo. La naturaleza lo había hecho reservado y esquivo, con tendencias a la meditación solitaria, y ella le había moldeado el carácter opuesto, vital, expansivo, desabrochado, y le había infundido el júbilo de vivir y el placer de la parranda y el despilfarro, hasta convertirlo, por dentro y por fuera, en el hombre con que había soñado para ella desde la adolescencia. Se había casado, pues, como tarde o temprano se casan los hijos. Él no se atrevió a anticiparle la noticia. Asumió una actitud tan infantil frente a la situación que fingía falsos rencores y resentimientos imaginarios, buscando el modo de que fuera Petra Cotes quien provocara la ruptura. Un día en que Aureliano Segundo le hizo un reproche injusto, ella eludió la trampa y puso las cosas en su puesto.

—Lo que pasa —dijo— es que te quieres casar con la reina.

Aureliano Segundo, avergonzado, fingió un colapso de cólera, se declaró incomprendido y ultrajado, y no volvió a visitarla. Petra Cotes, sin perder un solo instante su magnífico dominio de fiera en reposo, oyó la música y los cohetes de la boda, el alocado bullicio de la parranda pública, como si todo eso no fuera más que una nueva travesura de Aureliano Segundo. A quienes se compadecieron de su suerte, los tranquilizó con una sonrisa. «No se preocupen», les dijo. «A mí las reinas me hacen los mandados.» A una vecina que le llevó velas compuestas para que alumbrara con ellas el retrato del amante perdido, le dijo con una seguridad enigmática:

—La única vela que lo hará venir está siempre encendida.

Tal como ella lo había previsto, Aureliano Segundo volvió a su casa tan pronto como pasó la luna de miel. Llevó a sus amigotes de siempre, un fotógrafo ambulante y el traje y la capa de armiño sucia de sangre que Fernanda había usado en el carnaval. Al calor de la parranda que se prendió esa tarde, hizo vestir de reina a Petra Cotes, la coronó soberana absoluta y vitalicia de Madagascar, y repartió copias del retrato entre sus amigos. Ella no sólo se prestó al juego, sino que se compadeció íntimamente de él, pensando que debía estar muy asustado cuando concibió aquel extravagante recurso de reconciliación. A las siete de la noche, todavía vestida de reina, lo recibió en la cama. Tenía apenas dos meses de casado, pero ella se dio cuenta en seguida de que las cosas no andaban bien en el lecho nupcial, y experimentó el delicioso placer de la venganza consumada. Dos días después, sin embargo, cuando él no se atrevió a volver, sino que mandó un intermediario para que arreglara los términos de la separación, ella comprendió que iba a necesitar más paciencia de la prevista, porque él parecía dispuesto a sacrificarse por las apariencias. Tampoco entonces se alteró. Volvió a facilitar las cosas con una sumisión que confirmó la creencia generalizada de que era una pobre mujer, y el único recuerdo que conservó de Aureliano Segundo fue un par de botines de charol que, según él mismo había dicho, eran los que quería llevar puestos en el ataúd. Los guardó envueltos en trapos en el fondo de un baúl, y se preparó para apacentar una espera sin desesperación.

—Tarde o temprano tiene que venir —se dijo—, aunque sólo sea a ponerse estos botines.

No tuvo que esperar tanto como suponía. En realidad, Aureliano Segundo comprendió desde la noche de bodas que volvería a casa de Petra Cotes mucho antes de que tuviera necesidad de ponerse los botines de charol: Fernanda era una mujer perdida para el mundo. Había nacido y crecido a mil kilómetros del mar, en una ciudad lúgubre por cuyas callejuelas de piedra traqueteaban todavía, en noches de espantos, las carrozas de los virreyes. Treinta y dos campanarios tocaban a muerto a las seis de la tarde. En la casa señorial embaldosada de losas sepulcrales, jamás se conoció el sol. El aire había muerto en los

248

cipreses del patio, en las pálidas colgaduras de los dormitorios, en las arcadas rezumantes del jardín de los nardos. Fernanda no tuvo hasta la pubertad otra noticia del mundo que los melancólicos ejercicios de piano ejecutados en alguna casa vecina por alguien que durante años y años se permitió el albedrío de no hacer la siesta. En el cuarto de su madre enferma, verde y amarilla bajo la polvorienta luz de los vitrales, escuchaba las escalas metódicas, tenaces, descorazonadas, y pensaba que esa música estaba en el mundo, mientras ella se consumía tejiendo coronas de palmas fúnebres. Su madre, sudando la calentura de las cinco, le hablaba del esplendor del pasado. Siendo muy niña, una noche de luna, Fernanda vio una hermosa mujer vestida de blanco que atravesó el jardín hacia el oratorio. Lo que más le inquietó de aquella visión fugaz fue que la sintió exactamente igual a ella, como si se hubiera visto a sí misma con veinte años de anticipación. «Es tu bisabuela, la reina», le dijo su madre en las treguas de la tos. «Se murió de un mal aire que le dio al cortar una vara de nardos.» Muchos años después, cuando empezó a sentirse igual a su bisabuela, Fernanda puso en duda la visión de la infancia, pero la madre le reprochó su incredulidad.

—Somos inmensamente ricos y poderosos —le dijo—. Un día serás reina.

Ella lo creyó, aunque sólo ocupaban la larga mesa con manteles de lino y servicios de plata, para tomar una taza de chocolate con agua y un pan de dulce. Hasta el día de la boda soñó con un reinado de leyenda, a pesar de que su padre, don Fernando, tuvo que hipotecar la casa para comprarle el ajuar. No era ingenuidad ni delirio de grandeza. Así la educaron. Desde que tuvo uso de razón recordaba haber hecho sus necesidades en una bacinilla de oro con el escudo de armas de la familia. Salió de la casa por primera vez a los doce años, en un coche de caballos que sólo tuvo que recorrer dos cuadras para llevarla al convento. Sus compañeras de clases se sorprendieron de que la tuvieran apartada, en una silla de espaldar muy alto, y de que ni siquiera se mezclara con ellas durante el recreo. «Ella es distinta», explicaban las monjas. «Va a ser reina.» Sus compañeras lo creyeron, porque ya entonces era la doncella más hermosa, distinguida y discreta que habían visto jamás. Al cabo de ocho años, habiendo aprendido a versificar en latín, a tocar el clavicordio, a conversar de cetrería con los caballeros y de apologética con los arzobispos, a dilucidar asuntos de estado con los gobernantes extranjeros y asuntos de Dios con el Papa, volvió a casa de sus padres a tejer palmas fúnebres. La encontró saqueada. Quedaban apenas los muebles indispensables, los candelabros y el servicio de plata, porque los útiles domésticos habían sido vendidos, uno a uno, para sufragar los gastos de su educación. Su madre había sucumbido a la calentura de las cinco. Su padre, don Fernando, vestido de negro, con un cuello laminado y una leontina de oro atravesada en el pecho, le daba los lunes una moneda de plata para los gastos domésticos, y se llevaba las coronas fúnebres terminadas la semana anterior. Pasaba la mayor parte del día encerrado en el despacho, y en las pocas ocasiones en que salía a la calle regresaba antes de las seis, para acompañarla a rezar el rosario. Nunca llevó amistad íntima con nadie. Nunca oyó hablar de las guerras que desangraron el país. Nunca dejó de oír los ejercicios de piano a las tres de la tarde. Empezaba inclusive a perder la ilusión de ser reina, cuando sonaron dos aldabonazos perentorios en el portón, y le abrió a un militar apuesto, de ademanes ceremoniosos, que tenía una cicatriz en la mejilla y una medalla de oro en el pecho. Se encerró con su padre en el despacho. Dos horas después, su padre fue a buscarla al costurero. «Prepare sus cosas», le dijo. «Tiene que hacer un largo viaje.» Fue así como la llevaron a Macondo. En un solo día, con un zarpazo brutal, la vida le echó encima todo el peso de una realidad que durante años le habían escamoteado sus padres. De regreso a casa se encerró en el cuarto a llorar, indiferente a las súplicas y explicaciones de don Fernando, tratando de borrar la quemadura de aquella burla inaudita. Se había prometido no abandonar el dormitorio hasta la muerte, cuando Aureliano Segundo llegó a buscarla. Fue un golpe de suerte inconcebible, porque en el aturdimiento de la indignación, en la furia de la vergüenza, ella le había mentido para que nunca conociera su verdadera identidad. Las únicas pistas reales de que disponía Aureliano Segundo cuando salió a buscarla eran su inconfundible dicción del páramo y su oficio de tejedora de palmas fúnebres. La buscó sin piedad. Con la temeridad atroz con que José Arcadio Buendía atravesó la sierra para fundar a Macondo, con el orgullo ciego con que el coronel Aureliano Buendía promovió sus guerras inútiles, con la tenacidad insensata con que Úrsula aseguró la supervivencia de la estirpe, así buscó Aureliano Segundo a Fernanda, sin un solo instante de desaliento. Cuando preguntó dónde vendían palmas fúnebres, lo llevaron de casa en casa para que escogiera las mejores. Cuando preguntó dónde estaba la mujer más bella que se había dado sobre la tierra, todas las madres le llevaron a sus hijas. Se extravió por desfiladeros de niebla, por tiempos reservados al olvido, por laberintos de desilusión. Atravesó un páramo amarillo donde el eco repetía los pensamientos y la ansiedad provocaba espejismos premonitorios. Al cabo de semanas estériles, llegó a una ciudad desconocida donde todas las campanas tocaban a muerto. Aunque nunca los había visto, ni nadie se los había descrito, reconoció de inmediato los muros carcomidos por la cal de los huesos, los decrépitos balcones de maderas destripadas por los hongos, y clavado en el portón y casi borrado por la lluvia el cartoncito más triste del mundo: *Se venden palmas fúnebres.* Desde entonces hasta la mañana helada en que Fernanda abandonó la casa al cuidado de la Madre Superiora apenas si hubo tiempo para que las monjas cosieran el ajuar, y metieran en seis baúles los candelabros, el servicio de plata y la bacinilla de oro, y los incontables e inservibles destrozos de una catástrofe familiar que había tardado dos siglos en consumarse. Don Fernando declinó la invitación de acompañarlos. Prometió ir más tarde, cuando acabara de liquidar sus compromisos, y desde el momento en que le echó la bendición a su hija volvió a encerrarse en el despacho, a escribirle las esquelas con viñetas luctuosas y el escudo de armas de la familia que habían de ser el primer contacto humano que Fernanda y su padre tuvieran en toda la vida. Para ella, esa fue la fecha real de su nacimiento. Para Aureliano Segundo fue casi al mismo tiempo el principio y el fin de la felicidad.

Fernanda llevaba un precioso calendario con llavecitas doradas en el que su director espiritual había marcado con tinta morada las fechas de abstinencia venérea. Descontando la Semana Santa, los domingos, las fiestas de guardar, los primeros viernes, los retiros, los sacrificios y los impedimentos cíclicos, su anuario útil quedaba reducido a 42 días desperdigados en una maraña de cruces moradas. Aureliano Segundo, convencido de que el tiempo echaría por tierra aquella alambrada hostil, prolongó la fiesta de la boda más allá del término previsto. Agotada de tanto mandar al basurero botellas vacías de brandy y champaña para que no congestionaran la casa, y al mismo tiempo intrigada de que los recién casados durmieran a horas distintas y en habitaciones separadas mientras continuaban los cohetes y la música y los sacrificios de reses, Úrsula recordó su propia experiencia y se preguntó si Fernanda no tendría también un cinturón de castidad que tarde o temprano provocara las burlas del pueblo y diera origen a una tragedia. Pero Fernanda le confesó que simplemente estaba dejando pasar dos semanas antes de permitir el primer contacto con su esposo. Transcurrido el término, en efecto, abrió la puerta de su dormitorio con la resignación al sacrificio con que lo hubiera hecho una víctima expiatoria, y Aureliano Segundo vio a la mujer más bella de la tierra, con sus gloriosos ojos de animal asustado y los largos cabellos color de cobre extendidos en la almohada. Tan fascinado estaba con la visión que tardó un instante en darse cuenta de que Fernanda se había puesto un camisón blanco, largo hasta los tobillos y con mangas hasta los puños, y con un ojal grande y redondo primorosamente ribeteado a la altura del vientre. Aureliano Segundo no pudo reprimir una explosión de risa.

—Esto es lo más obsceno que he visto en mi

vida —gritó, con una carcajada que resonó en toda la casa—. Me casé con una hermanita de la caridad.

Un mes después, no habiendo conseguido que la esposa se quitara el camisón, se fue a hacer el retrato de Petra Cotes vestida de reina. Más tarde, cuando logró que Fernanda regresara a casa, ella cedió a sus apremios en la fiebre de la reconciliación, pero no supo proporcionarle el reposo con que él soñaba cuando fue a buscarla a la ciudad de los treinta y dos campanarios. Aureliano Segundo sólo encontró en ella un hondo sentimiento de desolación. Una noche, poco antes de que naciera el primer hijo, Fernanda se dio cuenta de que su marido había vuelto en secreto al lecho de Petra Cotes.

—Así es —admitió él. Y explicó en un tono de postrada resignación—: Tuve que hacerlo, para que siguieran pariendo los animales.

Le hizo falta un poco de tiempo para convencerla de tan peregrino expediente, pero cuando por fin lo consiguió, mediante pruebas que parecieron irrefutables, la única promesa que le impuso Fernanda fue que no se dejara sorprender por la muerte en la cama de su concubina. Así continuaron viviendo los tres, sin estorbarse, Aureliano Segundo puntual y cariñoso con ambas, Petra Cotes pavoneándose de la reconciliación, y Fernanda fingiendo que ignoraba la verdad.

El pacto no logró, sin embargo, que Fernanda se incorporara a la familia. En vano insistió Úrsula para que tirara la golilla de lana con que se levantaba cuando había hecho el amor, y que provocaba los cuchicheos de los vecinos. No logró convencerla de que utilizara el baño, o el beque nocturno, y de que le vendiera la bacinilla de oro al coronel Aureliano Buendía para que la convirtiera en pescaditos. Amaranta se

254

sintió tan incómoda con su dicción viciosa, y con su hábito de usar un eufemismo para designar cada cosa, que siempre hablaba delante de ella en jerigonza.

—*Esfetafa* —decía— *esfe defe lasfa quefe lesfe ti-fiefenenfe asfacofo afa sufu profopifiafa mifierfedafa.*

Un día, irritada con la burla, Fernanda quiso saber qué era lo que decía Amaranta, y ella no usó eufemismos para contestarle.

—Digo —dijo— que tú eres de las que confunden el culo con las témporas.

Desde aquel día no volvieron a dirigirse la palabra. Cuando las obligaban las circunstancias, se mandaban recados, o se decían las cosas indirectamente. A pesar de la visible hostilidad de la familia, Fernanda no renunció a la voluntad de imponer los hábitos de sus mayores. Terminó con la costumbre de comer en la cocina, y cuando cada quien tenía hambre, e impuso la obligación de hacerlo a horas exactas en la mesa grande del comedor arreglada con manteles de lino, y con los candelabros y el servicio de plata. La solemnidad de un acto que Úrsula había considerado siempre como el más sencillo de la vida cotidiana creó un ambiente de estiramiento contra el cual se rebeló primero que nadie el callado José Arcadio Segundo. Pero la costumbre se impuso, así como la de rezar el rosario antes de la cena, y llamó tanto la atención de los vecinos, que muy pronto circuló el rumor de que los Buendía no se sentaban a la mesa como los otros mortales, sino que habían convertido el acto de comer en una misa mayor. Hasta las supersticiones de Úrsula, surgidas más bien de la inspiración momentánea que de la tradición, entraron en conflicto con las que Fernanda heredó de sus padres, y que estaban perfectamente definidas y catalogadas para cada ocasión. Mientras Úrsula disfrutó del dominio pleno de sus facultades, subsistieron algunos de los antiguos hábitos y la vida de la familia conservó una cierta influencia de sus corazonadas, pero cuando perdió la vista y el peso de los años la relegó a un rincón, el círculo de rigidez iniciado por Fernanda desde el momento en que llegó terminó por cerrarse completamente, y nadie más que ella determinó el destino de la familia. El negocio de repostería y animalitos de caramelo, que Santa Sofía de la Piedad mantenía por voluntad de Úrsula, era considerado por Fernanda como una actividad indigna, y no tardó en liquidarlo. Las puertas de la casa, abiertas de par en par desde el amanecer hasta la hora de acostarse, fueron cerradas durante la siesta, con el pretexto de que el sol recalentaba los dormitorios, y finalmente se cerraron para siempre. El ramo de sábila y el pan que estaban colgados en el dintel desde los tiempos de la fundación fueron reemplazados por un nicho del Corazón de Jesús. El coronel Aureliano Buendía alcanzó a darse cuenta de aquellos cambios y previó sus consecuencias. «Nos estamos volviendo gente fina», protestaba. «A este paso, terminaremos peleando otra vez contra el régimen conservador, pero ahora para poner un rey en su lugar.» Fernanda, con muy buen tacto, se cuidó de no tropezar con él. Le molestaba íntimamente su espíritu independiente, su resistencia a toda forma de rigidez social. La exasperaban sus tazones de café a las cinco, el desorden de su taller, su manta deshilachada y su costumbre de sentarse en la puerta de la calle al atardecer. Pero tuvo que permitir esa pieza suelta del mecanismo familiar, porque tenía la certidumbre de que el viejo coronel era un animal apaciguado por los años y la desilusión, que en un arranque de rebeldía senil podría desarraigar los cimientos de la casa. Cuando su esposo decidió ponerle al primer hijo el nombre del bisabuelo, ella no se atrevió a oponerse, porque sólo tenía un año de haber llegado. Pero cuando nació la primera hija expresó sin reservas su determinación de que se llamara Renata, como su madre. Úrsula había resuelto que se llamara Remedios. Al cabo de una tensa controversia, en la que Aureliano Segundo actuó como mediador divertido, la bautizaron con el nombre de Renata Remedios, pero Fernanda la siguió llamando Renata a secas, mientras la familia de su marido y todo el pueblo siguieron llamándola Meme, diminutivo de Remedios.

Al principio, Fernanda no hablaba de su familia, pero con el tiempo empezó a idealizar a su padre. Hablaba de él en la mesa como un ser excepcional que había renunciado a toda forma de vanidad, y se estaba convirtiendo en santo. Aureliano Segundo, asombrado de la intempestiva magnificación del suegro, no resistía a la tentación de hacer pequeñas burlas a espaldas de su esposa. El resto de la familia siguió el ejemplo. La propia Úrsula, que era en extremo celosa de la armonía familiar y que sufría en secreto con las fricciones domésticas, se permitió decir alguna vez que el pequeño tataranieto tenía asegurado su porvenir pontifical, porque era «nieto de santo e hijo de reina y de cuatrero». A pesar de aquella sonriente conspiración, los niños se acostumbraron a pensar en el abuelo como en un ser legendario, que les transcribía versos piadosos en las cartas y les mandaba en cada Navidad un cajón de regalos que apenas si cabía por la puerta de la calle. Eran, en realidad, los últimos desperdicios del patrimonio señorial. Con ellos se construyó en el dormitorio de los niños un altar con santos de tamaño natural, cuyos ojos de vidrio les imprimían una inquietante apariencia de vida y cuyas ropas de paño artísticamente bordadas eran mejores que las usadas jamás por ningún habitante de Macondo. Poco a poco, el esplendor funerario de la antigua y helada mansión se fue trasladando a la luminosa casa de los Buendía. «Ya nos han mandado todo el cementerio familiar», comentó Aureliano Segundo en cierta ocasión. «Sólo faltan los sauces y las losas sepulcrales.» Aunque en los cajones no llegó nunca nada que sirviera a los niños para jugar, éstos pasaban el año esperando a diciembre, porque al fin y al cabo los anticuados y siempre imprevisibles regalos constituían una novedad en la casa. En la décima Navidad, cuando ya el pequeño José Arcadio se preparaba para viajar al seminario, llegó con más anticipación que en los años anteriores el enorme cajón del abuelo, muy bien clavado e impermeabilizado con brea, y dirigido con el habitual letrero de caracteres góticos a la muy distinguida señora doña Fernanda del Carpio de Buendía. Mientras ella leía la carta en el dormitorio, los niños se apresuraron a abrir la caja. Ayudados como de costumbre por Aureliano Segundo, rasparon los sellos de brea, desclavaron la tapa, sacaron el aserrín protector, y encontraron dentro un largo cofre de plomo cerrado con pernos de cobre. Aureliano Segundo quitó los ocho pernos, ante la impaciencia de los niños, y apenas tuvo tiempo de lanzar un grito y hacerlos a un lado, cuando levantó la plataforma de plomo y vio a don Fernando vestido de negro y con un crucifijo en el pecho, con la piel reventada en eructos pestilentes y cocinándose a fuego lento en un espumoso y borboritante caldo de perlas vivas.

Poco después del nacimiento de la niña, se anunció el inesperado jubileo del coronel Aureliano Buendía, ordenado por el gobierno para celebrar un nuevo aniversario del tratado de Neerlandia. Fue una determinación tan inconsecuente con la política oficial, que el coronel se pronunció violentamente contra ella y rechazó el homenaje. «Es la primera vez que oigo la palabra jubileo», decía. «Pero cualquier cosa que quiera decir, no puede ser sino una burla.» El estrecho taller de orfebrería se llenó de emisarios. Volvieron, mucho más viejos y mucho más solemnes, los abogados de trajes oscuros que en otro tiempo revolotearon como cuervos en torno al coronel. Cuando éste los vio aparecer, como en otro tiempo llegaban a empantanar la guerra, no pudo soportar el cinismo de sus panegíricos. Les ordenó que lo dejaran en paz, insistió que él no era un prócer de la nación como ellos decían, sino un artesano sin recuerdos, cuyo único sueño era morirse de cansancio en el olvido y la miseria de sus pescaditos de oro. Lo que más le indignó fue la noticia de que el propio presidente de la república pensaba asistir a los actos de Macondo para imponerle la Orden del Mérito. El coronel Aureliano Buendía le mandó a decir, palabra por palabra, que esperaba con verdadera ansiedad aquella tardía pero merecida ocasión de darle un tiro, no para cobrarle las arbitrariedades y anacronismos de su régimen, sino por faltarle al respeto a un viejo que no le hacía mal a nadie. Fue tal la vehemencia con que pronunció la amenaza, que el presidente de la república canceló el viaje a última hora y le mandó la condecoración con un representante personal. El coronel Gerineldo Márquez, asediado por presiones de toda índole, abandonó su lecho de paralítico para persuadir a su antiguo compañero de armas. Cuando éste vio aparecer el mecedor cargado por cuatro hombres y vio sentado en él, entre grandes almohadas, al amigo que compartió sus victorias e infortunios desde la juventud, no dudó un solo instante de que hacía aquel esfuerzo para expresarle su solidaridad. Pero cuando conoció el verdadero propósito de su visita, lo hizo sacar del taller.

—Demasiado tarde me convenzo —le dijo— que te habría hecho un gran favor si te hubiera dejado fusilar.

De modo que el jubileo se llevó a cabo sin asistencia de ninguno de los miembros de la familia. Fue una casualidad que coincidiera con la semana del carnaval, pero nadie logró quitarle al coronel Aureliano Buendía la empecinada idea de que también aquella coincidencia había sido prevista por el gobierno para recalcar la crueldad de la burla. Desde el taller solitario oyó las músicas marciales, la artillería de aparato, las campanas del Te Deum, y algunas frases de los discursos pronunciados frente a la casa cuando bautizaron la calle con su nombre. Los ojos se le humedecieron de indignación, de rabiosa impotencia, y por primera vez desde la derrota se dolió de no tener los arrestos de la juventud para promover una guerra sangrienta que borrara hasta el último vestigio del régimen conservador. No se habían extinguido los ecos del homenaje, cuando Úrsula llamó a la puerta del taller.

—No me molesten —dijo él—. Estoy ocupado.

—Abre —insistió Úrsula con voz cotidiana—. Esto no tiene nada que ver con la fiesta.

Entonces el coronel Aureliano Buendía quitó la tranca, y vio en la puerta diecisiete hombres de los más variados aspectos, de todos los tipos y colores, pero todos con un aire solitario que habría bastado para identificarlos en cualquier lugar de la tierra. Eran sus hijos. Sin ponerse de acuerdo, sin conocerse entre sí, habían llegado desde los más apartados rincones del litoral cautivados por el ruido del jubileo. Todos llevaban con orgullo el nombre de Aureliano, y el apellido de su madre. Durante los tres días que permanecieron en la casa, para satisfacción de Úrsula y escándalo de Fernanda, ocasionaron trastornos de guerra. Amaranta buscó entre antiguos papeles la libreta de cuentas donde Úrsula había apuntado los nombres y las fechas de nacimiento y bautismo de todos, y agregó frente al espacio correspondiente a cada uno el domicilio actual. Aquella lista habría permitido hacer una recapitulación de veinte años de guerra. Habrían podido reconstruirse con ella los itinerarios nocturnos del coronel, desde la madrugada en que salió de Macondo al frente de veintiún hombres hacia una rebelión quimérica, hasta que regresó por última vez envuelto en la manta acartonada de sangre. Aureliano Segundo no desperdició la ocasión de festejar a los primos con una estruendosa parranda de champaña y acordeón, que se interpretó como un atrasado ajuste de cuentas con el carnaval malogrado por el jubileo. Hicieron añicos media vajilla, destrozaron los rosales persiguiendo un toro para mantearlo, mataron las gallinas a tiros, obligaron a bailar a Amaranta los valses tristes de Pietro Crespi, consiguieron que Remedios, la bella, se pusiera unos pantalones de hombre para subirse a la cucaña, y soltaron en el comedor un cerdo embadurnado de sebo que revolcó a Fernanda, pero nadie lamentó los percances, porque la casa se estremeció con un terremoto de buena salud. El coronel Aureliano Buendía, que al principio los recibió con desconfianza y hasta puso en duda la filiación de algunos, se divirtió con sus locuras, y antes de que se fueran le regaló a cada uno un pescadito de oro. Hasta el esquivo José Arcadio Segundo les ofreció una tarde de gallos, que estuvo a punto de terminar en tragedia, porque varios de los Aurelianos eran tan duchos en componendas de galleras que descubrieron al primer golpe de vista las triquiñuelas del padre Antonio Isabel. Aureliano Segundo, que vio las ilimitadas perspectivas de parranda que ofrecía aquella desaforada parentela, decidió que todos se quedaran a trabajar con él. El único que aceptó fue Aureliano Triste, un mulato grande con los ímpetus y el espíritu explorador del abuelo, que ya había probado fortuna en medio mundo, y le daba lo mismo quedarse en cualquier parte. Los otros, aunque todavía estaban solteros, consideraban resuelto su destino. Todos eran artesanos hábiles, hombres de su casa, gente de paz. El miércoles de ceniza, antes de que volvieran a dispersarse en el litoral, Amaranta consiguió que se pusieran ropas dominicales y la acompañaran a la iglesia. Más divertidos que piadosos, se dejaron conducir hasta el comulgatorio, donde el padre Antonio Isabel les puso en la frente la cruz de ceniza. De regreso a casa, cuando el menor quiso limpiarse la frente, descubrió que la mancha era indeleble, y que lo eran también las de sus hermanos. Probaron con agua y jabón, con tierra y estropajo, y por último con piedra pómez y lejía, y no consiguieron borrarse la cruz. En cambio, Amaranta y los demás que fueron a misa se la quitaron sin dificultad. «Así van mejor», los despidió Úrsula. «De ahora en adelante nadie podrá confundirlos.» Se fueron en tropel, precedidos por la banda de músicos y reventando cohetes, y dejaron en el pueblo la impresión de que la estirpe de los Buendía tenía semillas para muchos siglos. Aureliano Triste, con su cruz de ceniza en la frente, instaló en las afueras del pueblo la fábrica de hielo con que soñó José Arcadio Buendía en sus delirios de inventor.

Meses después de su llegada, cuando ya era conocido y apreciado, Aureliano Triste andaba buscando una casa para llevar a su madre y a una hermana soltera (que no era hija del coronel) y se interesó por el caserón decrépito que parecía abandonado en una esquina de la plaza. Preguntó quién era el dueño. Alguien le dijo que era una casa de nadie, donde en otro tiempo vivió una viuda solitaria que se alimentaba de tierra y cal de las paredes, y que en sus últimos años sólo se la vio dos veces en la calle con un sombrero de minúsculas flores artificiales y unos zapatos color de plata antigua, cuando atravesó la plaza hasta la oficina de correos para mandarle cartas al obispo. Le dijeron que su única compañera fue una sirvienta desalmada que mataba perros y gatos y cuanto animal penetraba a la casa, y echaba los cadáveres en mitad de la calle para fregar al pueblo con la hedentina de la putrefacción. Había pasado tanto tiempo desde que el sol momificó el pellejo vacío del último animal, que todo el mundo daba por sentado que la dueña de la casa y la sirvienta habían muerto mucho antes de que terminaran las guerras, y que si todavía la casa estaba en pie era porque no habían tenido en años recientes un invierno riguroso o un viento demoledor. Los goznes desmigajados por el óxido, las puertas apenas sostenidas por cúmulos de telaraña, las ventanas soldadas por la humedad y el piso roto por la hierba y las flores silvestres, en cuyas grietas anidaban los lagartos y toda clase de sabandijas, parecían confirmar la versión de que allí no había estado un ser humano por lo menos en medio siglo. Al impulsivo Aureliano Triste no le hacían falta tantas pruebas para proceder. Empujó con el hombro la puerta principal, y la carcomida armazón de madera se derrumbó sin estrépito, en un callado cataclismo de polvo y tierra de nidos de comején. Aureliano Triste permaneció en el umbral, esperando que se desvaneciera la niebla, y entonces vio en el centro de la sala a la escuálida mujer vestida todavía con ropas del siglo anterior, con unas pocas hebras amarillas en el cráneo pelado, y con unos ojos grandes, aun hermosos, en los cuales se habían apagado las últimas estrellas de la esperanza, y el pellejo del rostro agrietado por la aridez de la soledad. Estremecido por la visión de otro mundo, Aureliano Triste apenas se dio cuenta de que la mujer lo estaba apuntando con una anticuada pistola de militar.

—Perdone —murmuró.

Ella permaneció inmóvil en el centro de la sala atiborrada de cachivaches, examinando palmo a palmo al gigante de espaldas cuadradas con un tatuaje de ceniza en la frente, y a través de la neblina del polvo lo vio en la neblina de otro tiempo, con una escopeta de dos cañones terciada a la espalda y un sartal de conejos en la mano.

—¡Por el amor de Dios —exclamó en voz baja—, no es justo que ahora me vengan con este recuerdo!

—Quiero alquilar la casa —dijo Aureliano Triste.

La mujer levantó entonces la pistola, apuntando con pulso firme la cruz de ceniza, y montó el gatillo con una determinación inapelable.

—Váyase —ordenó.

Aquella noche, durante la cena, Aureliano Triste le contó el episodio a la familia, y Úrsula lloró de consternación. «Dios santo», exclamó apretándose la cabeza con las manos. «¡Todavía está viva!» El tiempo, las guerras, los incontables desastres cotidianos la habían hecho olvidarse de Rebeca. La única que no había perdido un solo instante la conciencia de que estaba viva, pudriéndose en su sopa de larvas, era la implacable y envejecida Amaranta. Pensaba en ella al amanecer, cuando el hielo del corazón la despertaba en la cama solitaria, y pensaba en ella cuando se jabonaba los senos marchitos y el vientre macilento, y cuando se ponía los blancos pollerines y corpiños de olán de la vejez, y cuando se cambiaba en la mano la venda negra de la terrible expiación. Siempre, a toda hora, dormida y despierta, en los instantes más sublimes y en los más abyectos, Amaranta pensaba en Rebeca, porque la soledad le había seleccionado los recuerdos, y había incinerado los entorpecedores montones de basura nostálgica que la vida había acumulado en su corazón, y había purificado, magnificado y eternizado los otros, los más amargos. Por ella sabía Remedios, la bella, de la existencia de Rebeca. Cada vez que pasaban por la casa decrépita le contaba un incidente ingrato, una fábula de oprobio, tratando en esa forma de que su extenuante rencor fuera compartido por la sobrina, y por consiguiente prolongado más allá de la muerte, pero no consiguió sus propósitos porque Remedios era inmune a toda clase de sentimientos apasionados, y mucho más a los ajenos. Úrsula, en cambio, que había sufrido un proceso contrario al de Amaranta, evocó a Rebeca con un recuerdo limpio de impurezas, pues la imagen de la criatura de lástima que llevaron a la casa con el talego de huesos de sus padres prevaleció sobre la ofensa que la hizo indigna de continuar vinculada al tronco familiar. Aureliano Segundo resolvió que había que llevarla a la casa y protegerla, pero su buen propósito fue frustrado por la inquebrantable intransigencia de Rebeca, que había necesitado muchos años de sufrimiento y miseria para conquistar los privilegios de la soledad, y no estaba dispuesta a renunciar a ellos a cambio de una vejez perturbada por los falsos encantos de la misericordia.

En febrero, cuando volvieron los dieciséis hijos del coronel Aureliano Buendía, todavía marcados con la cruz de ceniza, Aureliano Triste les habló de Rebeca en el fragor de la parranda, y en medio día restauraron la apariencia de la casa, cambiaron puertas y ventanas, pintaron la fachada de colores alegres, apuntalaron las paredes y vaciaron cemento nuevo en el piso, pero no obtuvieron autorización para continuar las reformas en el interior. Rebeca ni siquiera se asomó a la puerta. Dejó que terminaran la atolondrada restauración, y luego hizo un cálculo de los costos y les mandó con Argénida, la vieja sirvienta que seguía acompañándola, un puñado de monedas retiradas de la circulación desde la última guerra, y que Rebeca seguía creyendo útiles. Fue entonces cuando se supo hasta qué punto inconcebible había llegado su desvinculación con el mundo, y se comprendió que sería imposible rescatarla de su empecinado encierro mientras le quedara un aliento de vida.

En la segunda visita que hicieron a Macondo los hijos del coronel Aureliano Buendía, otro de ellos, Aureliano Centeno, se quedó trabajando con Aureliano Triste. Era uno de los primeros que habían lle-

gado a la casa para el bautismo, y Úrsula y Amaranta
lo recordaban muy bien porque había destrozado en
pocas horas cuanto objeto quebradizo pasó por sus
manos. El tiempo había moderado su primitivo impulso de crecimiento, y era un hombre de estatura
mediana marcado con cicatrices de viruela, pero su
asombroso poder de destrucción manual continuaba
intacto. Tantos platos rompió, inclusive sin tocarlos,
que Fernanda optó por comprarle un servicio de peltre antes de que liquidara las últimas piezas de su
costosa vajilla, y aun los resistentes platos metálicos
estaban al poco tiempo desconchados y torcidos.
Pero a cambio de aquel poder irremediable, exasperante inclusive para él mismo, tenía una cordialidad
que suscitaba la confianza inmediata, y una estupen-
da capacidad de trabajo. En poco tiempo incrementó
de tal modo la producción de hielo, que rebasó el
mercado local, y Aureliano Triste tuvo que pensar
en la posibilidad de extender el negocio a otras poblaciones de la ciénaga. Fue entonces cuando concibió el paso decisivo no sólo para la modernización
de su industria, sino para vincular la población con el
resto del mundo.

—Hay que traer el ferrocarril —dijo.

Fue la primera vez que se oyó esa palabra en Macondo. Ante el dibujo que trazó Aureliano Triste en
la mesa, y que era un descendiente directo de los
esquemas con que José Arcadio Buendía ilustró el
proyecto de la guerra solar, Úrsula confirmó su impresión de que el tiempo estaba dando vueltas en redondo. Pero al contrario de su abuelo, Aureliano
Triste no perdía el sueño ni el apetito, ni atormentaba a nadie con crisis de mal humor, sino que concebía los proyectos más desatinados como posibilida-

des inmediatas, elaboraba cálculos racionales sobre costos y plazos, y los llevaba a término sin intermedios de exasperación. Aureliano Segundo, que si algo tenía del bisabuelo y algo le faltaba del coronel Aureliano Buendía era una absoluta impermeabilidad para el escarmiento, soltó el dinero para llevar el ferrocarril con la misma frivolidad con que lo soltó para la absurda compañía de navegación del hermano. Aureliano Triste consultó el calendario y se fue el miércoles siguiente para estar de vuelta cuando pasaran las lluvias. No se tuvieron más noticias. Aureliano Centeno, desbordado por las abundancias de la fábrica, había empezado ya a experimentar la elaboración de hielo con base de jugos de frutas en lugar de agua, y sin saberlo ni proponérselo concibió los fundamentos esenciales de la invención de los helados, pensando en esa forma diversificar la producción de una empresa que suponía suya, porque el hermano no daba señales de regreso después de que pasaron las lluvias y transcurrió todo un verano sin noticias. A principios del otro invierno, sin embargo, una mujer que lavaba ropa en el río a la hora de más calor, atravesó la calle central lanzando alaridos en un alarmante estado de conmoción.

—Ahí viene —alcanzó a explicar— un asunto espantoso como una cocina arrastrando un pueblo.

En ese momento la población fue estremecida por un silbato de resonancias pavorosas y una descomunal respiración acezante. Las semanas precedentes se había visto a las cuadrillas que tendieron durmientes y rieles, y nadie les prestó atención porque pensaron que era un nuevo artificio de los gitanos que volvían con su centenario y desprestigiado dale que dale de pitos y sonajas pregonando las excelencias de quién iba a saber qué pendejo menjunje de jarapellinosos genios jerosolimitanos. Pero cuando se restablecieron del desconcierto de los silbatazos y resoplidos, todos los habitantes se echaron a la calle y vieron a Aureliano Triste saludando con la mano desde la locomotora, y vieron hechizados el tren adornado de flores que por primera vez llegaba con ocho meses de retraso. El inocente tren amarillo que tantas incertidumbres y evidencias, y tantos halagos y desventuras, y tantos cambios, calamidades y nostalgias había de llevar a Macondo.

Deslumbrada por tantas y tan maravillosas invenciones, la gente de Macondo no sabía por dónde empezar a asombrarse. Se trasnochaban contemplando las pálidas bombillas eléctricas alimentadas por la planta que llevó Aureliano Triste en el segundo viaje del tren, y a cuyo obsesionante tumtum costó tiempo y trabajo acostumbrarse. Se indignaron con las imágenes vivas que el próspero comerciante don Bruno Crespi proyectaba en el teatro con taquillas de bocas de león, porque un personaje muerto y sepultado en una película, y por cuya desgracia se derramaron lágrimas de aflicción, reapareció vivo y convertido en árabe en la película siguiente. El público, que pagaba dos centavos para compartir las vicisitudes de los personajes, no pudo soportar aquella burla inaudita y rompió la silletería. El alcalde, a instancias de don Bruno Crespi, explicó mediante un bando que el cine era una máquina de ilusión que no merecía los desbordamientos pasionales del público. Ante la desalentadora explicación, muchos estimaron que habían sido víctimas de un nuevo y aparatoso asunto de gitanos, de modo que optaron por no volver al cine, considerando que ya tenían bastante con sus propias penas para llorar por fingidas desventuras de seres imaginarios. Algo semejante ocurrió con los gramófonos de cilindros que llevaron las alegres matronas de Francia en sustitución de los anticuados organillos, y que tan hondamente afectaron por un tiempo los intereses de la banda de músicos. Al principio, la curiosidad multiplicó la clientela de la calle prohibida, y hasta se supo de señoras respetables que se disfrazaron de villanos para observar de cerca la novedad del gramófono, pero tanto y de tan cerca lo observaron, que muy pronto llegaron a la conclusión de que no era un molino de sortilegio, como todos pensaban y como las matronas decían, sino un truco mecánico que no podía compararse con algo tan conmovedor, tan humano y tan lleno de verdad cotidiana como una banda de músicos. Fue una desilusión tan grave, que cuando los gramófonos se popularizaron hasta el punto de que hubo uno en cada casa, todavía no se les tuvo como objetos para entretenimiento de adultos, sino como una cosa buena para que la destriparan los niños. En cambio, cuando alguien del pueblo tuvo oportunidad de comprobar la cruda realidad del teléfono instalado en la estación del ferrocarril, que a causa de la manivela se consideraba como una versión rudimentaria del gramófono, hasta los más incrédulos se desconcertaron. Era como si Dios hubiera resuelto poner a prueba toda capacidad de asombro, y mantuviera a los habitantes de Macondo en un permanente vaivén entre el alborozo y el desencanto, la duda y la revelación, hasta el extremo de que ya nadie podía saber a ciencia cierta dónde estaban los límites de la realidad. Era un intrincado frangollo de verdades y espejismos, que convulsionó de impaciencia al espectro de José Arcadio Buendía bajo el castaño y lo obligó a caminar por toda la casa aun a pleno día. Desde que el ferrocarril fue inaugurado oficialmente y empezó a llegar con regularidad los miércoles a las once, y se construyó la primitiva estación de madera con un escritorio, el teléfono y una ventanilla para vender los pasajes, se vieron por las calles de Macondo hombres y mujeres que fingían actitudes comunes y corrientes, pero que en realidad parecían gente de circo. En un pueblo escaldado por el escarmiento de los gitanos no había un buen porvenir para aquellos equilibristas del comercio ambulante que con igual desparpajo ofrecían una olla pitadora que un régimen de vida para la salvación del alma al séptimo día; pero entre los que se dejaban convencer por cansancio y los incautos de siempre, obtenían estupendos beneficios. Entre esas criaturas de farándula, con pantalones de montar y polainas, sombrero de corcho, espejuelos con armaduras de acero, ojos de topacio y pellejo de gallo fino, uno de tantos miércoles llegó a Macondo y almorzó en la casa el rechoncho y sonriente Mr. Herbert.

Nadie lo distinguió en la mesa mientras no se comió el primer racimo de bananos. Aureliano Segundo lo había encontrado por casualidad, protestando en español trabajoso porque no había un cuarto libre en el Hotel de Jacob, y como lo hacía con frecuencia con muchos forasteros se lo llevó a la casa. Tenía un negocio de globos cautivos, que había llevado por medio mundo con excelentes ganancias, pero no había conseguido elevar a nadie en Macondo porque consideraban ese invento como un retroceso, después de haber visto y probado las esteras voladoras de los gitanos. Se iba, pues, en el próximo tren. Cuando llevaron a la mesa el atigrado racimo de banano que solían colgar en el comedor durante el almuerzo, arrancó la primera fruta sin mucho entusiasmo. Pero siguió comiendo mientras hablaba, saboreando, masticando, más bien con distracción de sabio que con deleite de buen comedor, y al terminar el primer racimo suplicó que le llevaran otro. Entonces sacó de la caja de herramientas que siempre llevaba consigo un pequeño estuche de aparatos ópticos. Con la incrédula atención de un comprador de diamantes examinó meticulosamente un banano seccionando sus partes con un estilete especial, pesándolas en un granatario de farmacéutico y calculando su cnvergadura con un calibrador de armero. Luego sacó de la caja una serie de instrumentos con los cuales midió la temperatura, el grado de humedad de la atmósfera y la intensidad de la luz. Fue una ceremonia tan intrigante, que nadie comió tranquilo esperando que Mr. Herbert emitiera por fin un juicio revelador, pero no dijo nada que permitiera vislumbrar sus intenciones. ⟶ *illuminate*?

En los días siguientes se le vio con una malla y una canastilla cazando mariposas en los alrededores del pueblo. El miércoles llegó un grupo de ingenieros, agrónomos, hidrólogos, topógrafos y agrimensores que durante varias semanas exploraron los mismos lugares donde Mr. Herbert cazaba mariposas. Más tarde llegó el señor Jack Brown en un vagón suplementario que engancharon en la cola del tren amarillo, y que era todo laminado de plata, con poltronas de terciopelo episcopal y techo de vidrios azules. En el vagón especial llegaron también, revoloteando en torno al señor Brown, los solemnes abogados vestidos de negro que en otra época siguieron por todas partes al coronel Aureliano Buendía, y esto hizo pensar a la gente que los agrónomos, hidrólogos, topógrafos y agrimensores, así como Mr.

Herbert con sus globos cautivos y sus mariposas de colores, y el señor Brown con su mausoleo rodante y sus feroces perros alemanes, tenían algo que ver con la guerra. No hubo, sin embargo, mucho tiempo para pensarlo, porque los suspicaces habitantes de Macondo apenas empezaban a preguntarse qué cuernos era lo que estaba pasando, cuando ya el pueblo se había transformado en un campamento de casas de madera con techos de zinc, poblado por forasteros que llegaban de medio mundo en el tren, no sólo en los asientos y plataformas sino hasta en el techo de los vagones. Los gringos, que después llevaron sus mujeres lánguidas con trajes de muselina y grandes sombreros de gasa, hicieron un pueblo aparte al otro lado de la línea del tren, con calles bordeadas de palmeras, casas con ventanas de redes metálicas, mesitas blancas en las terrazas y ventiladores de aspas colgados en el cielorraso, y extensos prados azules con pavorreales y codornices. El sector estaba cercado por una malla metálica, como un gigantesco gallinero electrificado que en los frescos meses del verano amanecía negro de golondrinas achicharradas. Nadie sabía aún qué era lo que buscaban, o si en verdad no eran más que filántropos, y ya habían ocasionado un trastorno colosal, mucho más perturbador que el de los antiguos gitanos, pero menos transitorio y comprensible. Dotados de recursos que en otra época estuvieron reservados a la Divina Providencia, modificaron el régimen de lluvias, apresuraron el ciclo de las cosechas, y quitaron el río de donde estuvo siempre y lo pusieron con sus piedras blancas y sus corrientes heladas en el otro extremo de la población, detrás del cementerio. Fue en esa ocasión cuando construyeron una fortaleza de hormigón sobre la descolorida tumba de José Arcadio, para que el olor a pólvora del cadáver no contaminara las aguas. Para los forasteros que llegaban sin amor, convirtieron la calle de las cariñosas matronas de Francia en un pueblo más extenso que el otro, y un miércoles de gloria llevaron un tren cargado de putas inverosímiles, hembras babilónicas adiestradas en recursos inmemoriales, y provistas de toda clase de ungüentos y dispositivos para estimular a los inermes, despabilar a los tímidos, saciar a los voraces, exaltar a los modestos, escarmentar a los múltiples y corregir a los solitarios. La Calle de los Turcos, enriquecida con luminosos almacenes de ultramarinos que desplazaron los viejos bazares de colorines, bordoneaba la noche del sábado con las muchedumbres de aventureros que se atropellaban entre las mesas de suerte y azar, los mostradores de tiro al blanco, el callejón donde se adivinaba el porvenir y se interpretaban los sueños, y las mesas de fritangas y bebidas, que amanecían el domingo desparramadas por el suelo, entre cuerpos que a veces eran de borrachos felices y casi siempre de curiosos abatidos por los disparos, trompadas, navajinas y botellazos de la pelotera. Fue una invasión tan tumultuosa e intempestiva, que en los primeros tiempos fue imposible caminar por la calle con el estorbo de los muebles y los baúles, y el trajín de carpintería de quienes paraban sus casas en cualquier terreno pelado sin permiso de nadie, y el escándalo de las parejas que colgaban sus hamacas entre los almendros y hacían el amor bajo los toldos, a pleno día y a la vista de todo el mundo. El único rincón de serenidad fue establecido por los pacíficos negros antillanos que construyeron una calle marginal, con casas de madera sobre pilotes, en cuyos pórticos se sentaban al atardecer cantando himnos melancólicos en su farragoso papiamento. Tantos cambios ocurrieron en tan poco tiempo, que ocho meses después de la visita de Mr. Herbert los antiguos habitantes de Macondo se levantaban temprano a conocer su propio pueblo.

—Miren la vaina que nos hemos buscado —solía decir entonces el coronel Aureliano Buendía—, no más por invitar un gringo a comer guineo.

Aureliano Segundo, en cambio, no cabía de contento con la avalancha de forasteros. La casa se llenó de pronto de huéspedes desconocidos, de invencibles parranderos mundiales, y fue preciso agregar dormitorios en el patio, ensanchar el comedor y cambiar la antigua mesa por una de dieciséis puestos, con nuevas vajillas y servicios, y aun así hubo que establecer turnos para almorzar. Fernanda tuvo que atragantarse sus escrúpulos y atender como a reyes a invitados de la más perversa condición, que embarraban con sus botas el corredor, se orinaban en el jardín, extendían sus petates en cualquier parte para hacer la siesta, y hablaban sin fijarse en susceptibilidades de damas ni remilgos de caballeros. Amaranta se escandalizó de tal modo con la invasión de la plebe, que volvió a comer en la cocina como en los viejos tiempos. El coronel Aureliano Buendía, persuadido de que la mayoría de quienes entraban a saludarlo en el taller no lo hacían por simpatía o estimación, sino por la curiosidad de conocer una reliquia histórica, un fósil de museo, optó por encerrarse con tranca y no se le volvió a ver sino en muy escasas ocasiones sentado en la puerta de la calle. Úrsula, en cambio, aun en los tiempos en que ya arrastraba los pies y caminaba tanteando en las paredes, experimentaba un alborozo pueril cuando se aproximaba la llegada del tren. «Hay que hacer carne y pescado», ordenaba a las cuatro cocineras, que se afanaban por estar a tiempo bajo la imperturbable dirección de Santa Sofía de la Piedad. «Hay que hacer de todo —insistía— porque nunca se sabe qué quieren comer los forasteros.» El tren llegaba a la hora de más calor. Al almuerzo, la casa trepidaba con un alboroto de mercado, y los sudorosos comensales, que ni siquiera sabían quiénes eran sus anfitriones, irrumpían en tropel para ocupar los mejores puestos en la mesa, mientras las cocineras tropezaban entre sí con las enormes ollas de sopa, los calderos de carnes, las bangañas de legumbres, las bateas de arroz, y repartían con cucharones inagotables los toneles de limonada. Era tal el desorden, que Fernanda se exasperaba con la idea de que muchos comían dos veces, y en más de una ocasión quiso desahogarse en improperios de verdulera porque algún comensal confundido le pedía la cuenta. Había pasado más de un año desde la visita de Mr. Herbert, y lo único que se sabía era que los gringos pensaban sembrar banano en la región encantada que José Arcadio Buendía y sus hombres habían atravesado buscando la ruta de los grandes inventos. Otros dos hijos del coronel Aureliano Buendía, con su cruz de ceniza en la frente, llegaron arrastrados por aquel eructo volcánico, y justificaron su determinación con una frase que tal vez explicaba las razones de todos.

—Nosotros venimos —dijeron— porque todo el mundo viene.

Remedios, la bella, fue la única que permaneció inmune a la peste del banano. Se estancó en una adolescencia magnífica, cada vez más impermeable a los formalismos, más indiferente a la malicia y la suspi-

277

cacia, feliz en un mundo propio de realidades simples. No entendía por qué las mujeres se complicaban la vida con corpiños y pollerines, de modo que se cosió un balandrán de cañamazo que sencillamente se metía por la cabeza y resolvía sin más trámites el problema del vestir, sin quitarle la impresión de estar desnuda, que según ella entendía las cosas era la única forma decente de estar en casa. La molestaron tanto para que se cortara el cabello de lluvia que ya le daba a las pantorrillas, y para que se hiciera moños con peinetas y trenzas con lazos colorados, que simplemente se rapó la cabeza y les hizo pelucas a los santos. Lo asombroso de su instinto simplificador era que mientras más se desembarazaba de la moda buscando la comodidad, y mientras más pasaba por encima de los convencionalismos en obediencia a la espontaneidad, más perturbadora resultaba su belleza increíble y más provocador su comportamiento con los hombres. Cuando los hijos del coronel Aureliano Buendía estuvieron por primera vez en Macondo, Úrsula recordó que llevaban en las venas la misma sangre de la bisnieta, y se estremeció con un espanto olvidado. «Abre bien los ojos», la previno. «Con cualquiera de ellos, los hijos te saldrán con cola de puerco.» Ella hizo tan poco caso de la advertencia, que se vistió de hombre y se revolcó en arena para subirse en la cucaña, y estuvo a punto de ocasionar una tragedia entre los diecisiete primos trastornados por el insoportable espectáculo. Era por eso que ninguno de ellos dormía en la casa cuando visitaban el pueblo, y los cuatro que se habían quedado vivían por disposición de Úrsula en cuartos de alquiler. Sin embargo, Remedios, la bella, se habría muerto de risa si hubiera conocido aquella precaución.

Hasta el último instante en que estuvo en la tierra ignoró que su irreparable destino de hembra perturbadora era un desastre cotidiano. Cada vez que aparecía en el comedor, contrariando las órdenes de Úrsula, ocasionaba un pánico de exasperación entre los forasteros. Era demasiado evidente que estaba desnuda por completo bajo el burdo camisón, y nadie podía entender que su cráneo pelado y perfecto no era un desafío, y que no era una criminal provocación el descaro con que se descubría los muslos para quitarse el calor, y el gusto con que se chupaba los dedos después de comer con las manos. Lo que ningún miembro de la familia supo nunca fue que los forasteros no tardaron en darse cuenta de que Remedios, la bella, soltaba un hálito de perturbación, una ráfaga de tormento, que seguía siendo perceptible varias horas después de que ella había pasado. Hombres expertos en trastornos de amor, probados en el mundo entero, afirmaban no haber padecido jamás una ansiedad semejante a la que producía el olor natural de Remedios, la bella. En el corredor de las begonias, en la sala de visitas, en cualquier lugar de la casa, podía señalarse el lugar exacto en que estuvo y el tiempo transcurrido desde que dejó de estar. Era un rastro definido, inconfundible, que nadie de la casa podía distinguir porque estaba incorporado desde hacía mucho tiempo a los olores cotidianos, pero que los forasteros identificaban de inmediato. Por eso eran ellos los únicos que entendían que el joven comandante de la guardia se hubiera muerto de amor, y que un caballero venido de otras tierras se hubiera echado a la desesperación. Inconsciente del ámbito inquietante en que se movía, del insoportable estado de íntima calamidad que provocaba a su paso,

Remedios, la bella, trataba a los hombres sin la menor malicia y acababa de trastornarlos con sus inocentes complacencias. Cuando Úrsula logró imponer la orden de que comiera con Amaranta en la cocina para que no la vieran los forasteros, ella se sintió más cómoda porque al fin y al cabo quedaba a salvo de toda disciplina. En realidad, le daba lo mismo comer en cualquier parte, y no a horas fijas sino de acuerdo con las alternativas de su apetito. A veces se levantaba a almorzar a las tres de la madrugada, dormía todo el día, y pasaba varios meses con los horarios trastocados, hasta que algún incidente casual volvía a ponerla en orden. Cuando las cosas andaban mejor, se levantaba a las once de la mañana, y se encerraba hasta dos horas completamente desnuda en el baño, matando alacranes mientras se despejaba del denso y prolongado sueño. Luego se echaba agua de la alberca con una totuma. Era un acto tan prolongado, tan meticuloso, tan rico en situaciones ceremoniales, que quien no la conociera bien habría podido pensar que estaba entregada a una merecida adoración de su propio cuerpo. Para ella, sin embargo, aquel rito solitario carecía de toda sensualidad, y era simplemente una manera de perder el tiempo mientras le daba hambre. Un día, cuando empezaba a bañarse, un forastero levantó una teja del techo y se quedó sin aliento ante el tremendo espectáculo de su desnudez. Ella vio los ojos desolados a través de las tejas rotas y no tuvo una reacción de vergüenza, sino de alarma.

—Cuidado —exclamó—. Se va a caer.

—Nada más quiero verla —murmuró el forastero.

—Ah, bueno —dijo ella—. Pero tenga cuidado, que esas tejas están podridas.

El rostro del forastero tenía una dolorosa expresión de estupor, y parecía batallar sordamente contra sus impulsos primarios para no disipar el espejismo. Remedios, la bella, pensó que estaba sufriendo con el temor de que se rompieran las tejas, y se bañó más de prisa que de costumbre para que el hombre no siguiera en peligro. Mientras se echaba agua de la alberca, le dijo que era un problema que el techo estuviera en ese estado, pues ella creía que la cama de hojas podridas por la lluvia era lo que llenaba el baño de alacranes. El forastero confundió aquella cháchara con una forma de disimular la complacencia, de modo que cuando ella empezó a jabonarse cedió a la tentación de dar un paso adelante.

—Déjeme jabonarla —murmuró.

—Le agradezco la buena intención —dijo ella—, pero me basto con mis dos manos.

—Aunque sea la espalda —suplicó el forastero.

—Sería una ociosidad —dijo ella—. Nunca se ha visto que la gente se jabone la espalda.

Después, mientras se secaba, el forastero le suplicó con los ojos llenos de lágrimas que se casara con él. Ella le contestó sinceramente que nunca se casaría con un hombre tan simple que perdía casi una hora, y hasta se quedaba sin almorzar, sólo por ver bañarse a una mujer. Al final, cuando se puso el balandrán, el hombre no pudo soportar la comprobación de que en efecto no se ponía nada debajo, como todo el mundo sospechaba, y se sintió marcado para siempre con el hierro ardiente de aquel secreto. Entonces quitó dos tejas más para descolgarse en el interior del baño.

—Está muy alto —lo previno ella, asustada—. ¡Se va a matar!

Las tejas podridas se despedazaron en un estrépito de desastre, y el hombre apenas alcanzó a lanzar un grito de terror, y se rompió el cráneo y murió sin agonía en el piso de cemento. Los forasteros que oyeron el estropicio en el comedor, y se apresuraron a llevarse el cadáver, percibieron en su piel el sofocante olor de Remedios, la bella. Estaba tan compenetrado con el cuerpo, que las grietas del cráneo no manaban sangre sino un aceite ambarino impregnado de aquel perfume secreto, y entonces comprendieron que el olor de Remedios, la bella, seguía torturando a los hombres más allá de la muerte, hasta el polvo de sus huesos. Sin embargo, no relacionaron aquel accidente de horror con los otros dos hombres que habían muerto por Remedios, la bella. Faltaba todavía una víctima para que los forasteros, y muchos de los antiguos habitantes de Macondo, dieran crédito a la leyenda de que Remedios Buendía no exhalaba un aliento de amor, sino un flujo mortal. La ocasión de comprobarlo se presentó meses después, una tarde en que Remedios, la bella, fue con un grupo de amigas a conocer las nuevas plantaciones. Para la gente de Macondo era una distracción reciente recorrer las húmedas e interminables avenidas bordeadas de bananos, donde el silencio parecía llevado de otra parte, todavía sin usar, y era por eso tan torpe para transmitir la voz. A veces no se entendía muy bien lo dicho a medio metro de distancia, y sin embargo resultaba perfectamente comprensible al otro extremo de la plantación. Para las muchachas de Macondo aquel juego novedoso era motivo de risas y sobresaltos, de sustos y burlas, y por las noches se hablaba del paseo como de una experiencia de sueño. Era tal el prestigio de aquel silencio, que Úrsula no tuvo corazón para privar de la diversión a Remedios, la bella, y le permitió ir una tarde, siempre que se pusiera un sombrero y un traje adecuado. Desde que el grupo de amigas entró en la plantación, el aire se impregnó de una fragancia mortal. Los hombres que trabajaban en las zanjas se sintieron poseídos por una rara fascinación, amenazados por un peligro invisible, y muchos sucumbieron a los terribles deseos de llorar. Remedios, la bella, y sus espantadas amigas lograron refugiarse en una casa próxima cuando estaban a punto de ser asaltadas por un tropel de machos feroces. Poco después fueron rescatadas por los cuatro Aurelianos, cuyas cruces de ceniza infundían un respeto sagrado, como si fueran una marca de casta, un sello de invulnerabilidad. Remedios, la bella, no le contó a nadie que uno de los hombres, aprovechando el tumulto, le alcanzó a agredir el vientre con una mano que más bien parecía una garra de águila aferrándose al borde de un precipicio. Ella se enfrentó al agresor en una especie de deslumbramiento instantáneo, y vio los ojos desconsolados que quedaron impresos en su corazón como una brasa de lástima. Esa noche, el hombre se jactó de su audacia y presumió de su suerte en la Calle de los Turcos, minutos antes de que la patada de un caballo le destrozara el pecho, y una muchedumbre de forasteros lo viera agonizar en mitad de la calle, ahogándose en vómitos de sangre.

La suposición de que Remedios, la bella, poseía poderes de muerte estaba entonces sustentada por cuatro hechos irrebatibles. Aunque algunos hombres ligeros de palabra se complacían en decir que bien valía sacrificar la vida por una noche de amor con tan conturbadora mujer, la verdad fue que ninguno hizo esfuerzos por conseguirlo. Tal vez, no sólo para rendirla sino también para conjurar sus peligros, habría bastado con un sentimiento tan primitivo y simple como el amor, pero eso fue lo único que no se le ocurrió a nadie. Úrsula no volvió a ocuparse de ella. En otra época, cuando todavía no renunciaba al propósito de salvarla para el mundo, procuró que se interesara por los asuntos elementales de la casa. «Los hombres piden más de lo que tú crees», le decía enigmáticamente. «Hay mucho que cocinar, mucho que barrer, mucho que sufrir por pequeñeces, además de lo que crees.» En el fondo se engañaba a sí misma tratando de adiestrarla para la felicidad doméstica, porque estaba convencida de que una vez satisfecha la pasión, no había un hombre sobre la tierra capaz de soportar así fuera por un día una negligencia que estaba más allá de toda comprensión. El nacimiento del último José Arcadio, y su inquebrantable voluntad de educarlo para Papa, terminaron por hacerla desistir de sus preocupaciones por la bisnieta. La abandonó a su suerte, confiando que tarde o temprano ocurriera un milagro, y que en este mundo donde había de todo hubiera también un hombre con suficiente cachaza para cargar con ella. Ya desde mucho antes, Amaranta había renunciado a toda tentativa de convertirla en una mujer útil. Desde las tardes olvidadas del costurero, cuando la sobrina apenas se interesaba por darle vuelta a la manivela de la máquina de coser, llegó a la conclusión simple de que era boba. «Vamos a tener que rifarte», le decía, perpleja ante su impermeabilidad a la palabra de los hombres. Más tarde, cuando Úrsula se empeñó en que Remedios, la bella, asistiera a misa con la cara cubierta con una mantilla, Amaranta pensó que aquel recurso misterioso resultaría tan provocador, que muy pronto habría un hombre lo bastante intrigado como para buscar con paciencia el punto débil de su corazón. Pero cuando vio la forma insensata en que despreció a un pretendiente que por muchos motivos era más apetecible que un príncipe, renunció a toda esperanza. Fernanda no hizo siquiera la tentativa de comprenderla. Cuando vio a Remedios, la bella, vestida de reina en el carnaval sangriento, pensó que era una criatura extraordinaria. Pero cuando la vio comiendo con las manos, incapaz de dar una respuesta que no fuera un prodigio de simplicidad, lo único que lamentó fue que los bobos de familia tuvieran una vida tan larga. A pesar de que el coronel Aureliano Buendía seguía creyendo y repitiendo que Remedios, la bella, era en realidad el ser más lúcido que había conocido jamás, y que lo demostraba a cada momento con su asombrosa habilidad para burlarse de todos, la abandonaron a la buena de Dios. Remedios, la bella, se quedó vagando por el desierto de la soledad, sin cruces a cuestas, madurándose en sus sueños sin pesadillas, en sus baños interminables, en sus comidas sin horarios, en sus hondos y prolongados silencios sin recuerdos, hasta una tarde de marzo en que Fernanda quiso doblar en el jardín sus sábanas de bramante, y pidió ayuda a las mujeres de la casa. Apenas habían empezado, cuando Amaranta advirtió que Remedios, la bella, estaba transparentada por una palidez intensa.

—¿Te sientes mal? —le preguntó.

Remedios, la bella, que tenía agarrada la sábana por otro extremo, hizo una sonrisa de lástima.

—Al contrario —dijo—, nunca me he sentido mejor.

Acabó de decirlo, cuando Fernanda sintió que un delicado viento de luz le arrancó las sábanas de las manos y las desplegó en toda su amplitud. Amaranta sintió un temblor misterioso en los encajes de sus pollerines y trató de agarrarse de la sábana para no caer, en el instante en que Remedios, la bella, empezaba a elevarse. Úrsula, ya casi ciega, fue la única que tuvo serenidad para identificar la naturaleza de aquel viento irreparable, y dejó las sábanas a merced de la luz, viendo a Remedios, la bella, que le decía adiós con la mano, entre el deslumbrante aleteo de las sábanas que subían con ella, que abandonaban con ella el aire de los escarabajos y las dalias, y pasaban con ella a través del aire donde terminaban las cuatro de la tarde, y se perdieron con ella para siempre en los altos aires donde no podían alcanzarla ni los más altos pájaros de la memoria.

Los forasteros, por supuesto, pensaron que Remedios, la bella, había sucumbido por fin a su irrevocable destino de abeja reina, y que su familia trataba de salvar la honra con la patraña de la levitación. Fernanda, mordida por la envidia, terminó por aceptar el prodigio, y durante mucho tiempo siguió rogando a Dios que le devolviera las sábanas. La mayoría creyó en el milagro, y hasta se encendieron velas y se rezaron novenarios. Tal vez no se hubiera vuelto a hablar de otra cosa en mucho tiempo, si el bárbaro exterminio de los Aurelianos no hubiera sustituido el asombro por el espanto. Aunque nunca lo identificó como un presagio, el coronel Aureliano Buendía había previsto en cierto modo el trágico final de sus hijos. Cuando Aureliano Serrador y Aureliano Arcaya, los dos que llegaron en el tumulto, manifestaron la voluntad de quedarse en Macondo, su padre trató de disuadirlos. No entendía qué iban a hacer en un pueblo que de la noche a la mañana se había convertido en un lugar de peligro. Pero Aureliano Centeno y Aureliano Triste, apoyados por Aureliano Segundo, les dieron trabajo en sus empresas. El coronel Aureliano Buendía tenía motivos todavía muy confusos para no patrocinar aquella determinación. Desde que vio al señor Brown en el primer automóvil que llegó a Macondo —un convertible anaranjado con una corneta que espantaba a los perros con sus ladridos—, el viejo guerrero se indignó con los serviles aspavientos de la gente, y se dio cuenta de que algo había cambiado en la índole de los hombres desde los tiempos en que abandonaban mujeres e hijos y se echaban una escopeta al hombro para irse a la guerra. Las autoridades locales, después del armisticio de Neerlandia, eran alcaldes sin iniciativa, jueces decorativos, escogidos entre los pacíficos y cansados conservadores de Macondo. «Este es un régimen de pobres diablos», comentaba el coronel Aureliano Buendía cuando veía pasar a los policías descalzos armados de bolillos de palo. «Hicimos tantas guerras, y todo para que no nos pintaran la casa de azul.» Cuando llegó la compañía bananera, sin embargo, los funcionarios locales fueron sustituidos por forasteros autoritarios, que el señor Brown se llevó a vivir en el gallinero electrificado, para que gozaran, según explicó, de la dignidad que correspondía a su investidura, y no padecieran el calor y los mosquitos y las incontables incomodidades y privaciones del pueblo. Los antiguos policías fueron reemplazados por sicarios de machetes. Encerrado en el taller, el coronel Aureliano Buendía pensaba en estos cambios, y por primera vez en sus callados años de soledad lo atormentó la definida certidumbre de que había sido un error no proseguir la guerra hasta sus últimas consecuencias. Por esos días, un hermano del olvidado coronel Magnífico Visbal llevó su nieto de siete años a tomar un refresco en los carritos de la plaza, y porque el niño tropezó por accidente con un cabo de la policía y le derramó el refresco en el uniforme, el bárbaro lo hizo picadillo a machetazos y decapitó de un tajo al abuelo que trató de impedirlo. Todo el pueblo vio pasar al decapitado cuando un grupo de hombres lo llevaba a su casa, y la cabeza arrastrada que una mujer llevaba cogida por el pelo, y el talego ensangrentado donde habían metido los pedazos del niño.

Para el coronel Aureliano Buendía fue el límite de la expiación. Se encontró de pronto padeciendo la misma indignación que sintió en la juventud, frente al cadáver de la mujer que fue muerta a palos porque la mordió un perro con mal de rabia. Miró a los grupos de curiosos que estaban frente a la casa y con su antigua voz estentórea, restaurada por un hondo desprecio contra sí mismo, les echó encima la carga de odio que ya no podía soportar en el corazón.

—¡Un día de estos —gritó— voy a armar a mis muchachos para que acaben con estos gringos de mierda!

En el curso de esa semana, por distintos lugares del litoral, sus diecisiete hijos fueron cazados como conejos por criminales invisibles que apuntaron al centro de sus cruces de ceniza. Aureliano Triste salía de la casa de su madre, a las siete de la noche, cuando un disparo de fusil surgido de la oscuridad le perforó la frente. Aureliano Centeno fue encontrado en la hamaca que solía colgar en la fábrica, con un punzón de picar hielo clavado hasta la empuñadura entre las cejas. Aureliano Serrador había dejado a su novia en casa de sus padres después de llevarla al cine, y regresaba por la iluminada Calle de los Turcos cuando alguien que nunca fue identificado entre la muchedumbre disparó un tiro de revólver que lo derribó dentro de un caldero de manteca hirviendo. Pocos minutos después, alguien llamó a la puerta del cuarto donde Aureliano Arcaya estaba encerrado con una mujer, y le gritó: «Apúrate, que están matando a tus hermanos.» La mujer que estaba con él contó después que Aureliano Arcaya saltó de la cama y abrió la puerta, y fue esperado con una descarga de máuser que le desbarató el cráneo. Aquella noche de muerte, mientras la casa se preparaba para velar los cuatro cadáveres, Fernanda recorrió el pueblo como una loca buscando a Aureliano Segundo, a quien Petra Cotes encerró en un ropero creyendo que la consigna de exterminio incluía a todo el que llevara el nombre del coronel. No le dejó salir hasta el cuarto día, cuando los telegramas recibidos de distintos lugares del litoral permitieron comprender que la saña del enemigo invisible estaba dirigida solamente contra los hermanos marcados con cruces de ceniza. Amaranta buscó la libreta de cuentas donde había anotado los datos de los sobrinos, y a medida que llegaban los telegramas iba tachando nombres, hasta que sólo quedó el del mayor. Lo recordaban muy bien por el contraste de su piel oscura con los grandes ojos verdes. Se llamaba Aureliano Amador, era carpintero, y vivía en un pueblo perdido en las estribaciones de la sierra. Después de esperar dos semanas el telegrama de su muerte, Aureliano Segundo le mandó un emisario para prevenirlo, pensando que ignoraba la amenaza que pesaba sobre él. El emisario regresó con la noticia de que Aureliano Amador estaba a salvo. La noche del exterminio habían ido a buscarlo dos hombres a su casa, y habían descargado sus revólveres contra él, pero no le habían acertado a la cruz de ceniza. Aureliano Amador logró saltar la cerca del patio, y se perdió en los laberintos de la sierra que conocía palmo a palmo gracias a la amistad de los indios con quienes comerciaba en maderas. No había vuelto a saberse de él.

Fueron días negros para el coronel Aureliano Buendía. El presidente de la república le dirigió un telegrama de pésame, en el que prometía una investigación exhaustiva, y rendía homenaje a los muertos. Por orden suya, el alcalde se presentó al entierro con cuatro coronas fúnebres que pretendió colocar sobre los ataúdes, pero el coronel lo puso en la calle. Después del entierro, redactó y llevó personalmente un telegrama violento para el presidente de la república, que el telegrafista se negó a tramitar. Entonces lo enriqueció con términos de singular agresividad, lo metió en un sobre y lo puso al correo. Como le había ocurrido con la muerte de su esposa, como tantas veces le ocurrió durante la guerra con la muerte de sus mejores amigos, no experimentaba un sentimiento de pesar, sino una rabia ciega y sin dirección, una extenuante impotencia. Llegó hasta denunciar la complicidad del padre Antonio Isabel, por haber marcado a sus hijos con ceniza indeleble para que fueran identificados por sus enemigos. El decrépito sacerdote que ya no hilvanaba muy bien las ideas y empezaba a espantar a los feligreses con las disparatadas interpretaciones que intentaba en el púlpito, apareció una tarde en la casa con el tazón donde preparaba las cenizas del miércoles, y trató de ungir con ellas a toda la familia para demostrar que se quitaban con agua. Pero el espanto de la desgracia había calado tan hondo, que ni la misma Fernanda se prestó al experimento, y nunca más se vio un Buendía arrodillado en el comulgatorio el miércoles de ceniza.

El coronel Aureliano Buendía no logró recobrar la serenidad en mucho tiempo. Abandonó la fabricación de pescaditos, comía a duras penas, y andaba como un sonámbulo por toda la casa, arrastrando la manta y masticando una cólera sorda. Al cabo de tres meses tenía el pelo ceniciento, el antiguo bigote de puntas engomadas chorreando sobre los labios sin color, pero en cambio sus ojos eran otra vez las dos brasas que asustaron a quienes lo vieron nacer y que en otro tiempo hacían rodar las sillas con sólo mirarlas. En la furia de su tormento trataba inútilmente de provocar los presagios que guiaron su juventud por senderos de peligro hasta el desolado yermo de la gloria. Estaba perdido, extraviado en una casa ajena donde ya nada ni nadie le suscitaba el menor vestigio de afecto. Una vez abrió el cuarto de Melquíades, buscando los rastros de un pasado anterior a la guerra, y sólo encontró los escombros, la basura, los montones de porquería acumulados por tantos años de abandono. En las pastas de los libros que nadie había vuelto a leer, en los viejos pergaminos macerados por la humedad había prosperado una flora lívida, y en el aire que había sido el más puro y luminoso de la casa flotaba un insoportable olor de recuerdos podridos. Una mañana encontró a Úrsula llorando bajo el castaño, en las rodillas de su esposo muerto. El coronel Aureliano Buendía era el único habitante de la casa que no seguía viendo al potente anciano agobiado por medio siglo de intemperie. «Saluda a tu padre», le dijo Úrsula. Él se detuvo un instante frente al castaño, y una vez más comprobó que tampoco aquel espacio vacío le suscitaba ningún afecto.

—¿Qué dice? —preguntó.

—Está muy triste —contestó Úrsula— porque cree que te vas a morir.

—Dígale —sonrió el coronel— que uno no se muere cuando debe, sino cuando puede.

El presagio del padre muerto removió el último rescoldo de soberbia que le quedaba en el corazón, pero él lo confundió con un repentino soplo de fuerza. Fue por eso que asedió a Úrsula para que le revelara en qué lugar del patio estaban enterradas las monedas de oro que encontraron dentro del San José de yeso. «Nunca lo sabrás», le dijo ella, con una firmeza inspirada en un viejo escarmiento. «Un día —agregó— ha de aparecer el dueño de esa fortuna, y sólo él podrá desenterrarla.» Nadie sabía por qué un hombre que siempre fue tan desprendido había empezado a codiciar el dinero con semejante ansiedad, y no las modestas cantidades que le habrían bastado para resolver una emergencia, sino una fortuna de magnitudes desatinadas cuya sola mención dejó sumido en un mar de asombro a Aureliano Segundo. Los viejos copartidarios a quienes acudió en demanda de ayuda se escondieron para no recibirlo. Fue por esa época que se le oyó decir: «La única diferencia actual entre liberales y conservadores es que los liberales van a misa de cinco y los conservadores van a misa de ocho.» Sin embargo, insistió con tanto ahínco, suplicó de tal modo, quebrantó a tal punto sus principios de dignidad, que con un poco de aquí y otro poco de allá, deslizándose por todas partes con una diligencia sigilosa y una perseverancia despiadada, consiguió reunir en ocho meses más dinero del que Úrsula tenía enterrado. Entonces visitó al enfermo coronel Gerineldo Márquez para que lo ayudara a promover la guerra total.

En un cierto momento, el coronel Gerineldo Márquez era en verdad el único que habría podido mover, aun desde su mecedor de paralítico, los enmohecidos hilos de la rebelión. Después del armisticio de Neerlandia, mientras el coronel Aureliano Buendía se refugiaba en el exilio de sus pescaditos de oro, él se mantuvo en contacto con los oficiales rebeldes que le fueron fieles hasta la derrota. Hizo con ellos la guerra triste de la humillación cotidiana, de las súplicas y los memoriales, del vuelva mañana, del ya casi, del estamos estudiando su caso con la debida atención; la guerra perdida sin remedio contra los muy atentos y seguros servidores que debían asignar y no asignaron nunca las pensiones vitalicias. La otra guerra, la sangrienta de veinte años, no les causó tantos estragos como la guerra corrosiva del eterno aplazamiento. El propio coronel Gerineldo Márquez, que escapó a tres atentados, sobrevivió a cinco heridas y salió ileso de incontables batallas, sucumbió al asedio atroz de la espera y se hundió en la derrota miserable de la vejez pensando en Amaranta entre los rombos de luz de una casa prestada. Los últimos veteranos de quienes se tuvo noticia aparecieron retratados en un periódico, con la cara levantada de indignidad, junto a un anónimo presidente de la república que les regaló unos botones con su efigie para que los usaran en la solapa, y les restituyó una bandera sucia de sangre y de pólvora para que la pusieran sobre sus ataúdes. Los otros, los más dignos, todavía esperaban una carta en la penumbra de la caridad pública, muriéndose de hambre, sobreviviendo de rabia, pudriéndose de viejos en la exquisita mierda de la gloria. De modo que cuando el coronel Aureliano Buendía lo invitó a promover una conflagración mortal que arrasara con todo vestigio de un régimen de corrupción y de escándalo sostenido por el invasor extranjero, el coronel Gerineldo Márquez no pudo reprimir un estremecimiento de compasión.

—Ay, Aureliano —suspiró—, ya sabía que estabas viejo, pero ahora me doy cuenta que estás mucho más viejo de lo que pareces.

En el aturdimiento de los últimos años, Úrsula había dispuesto de muy escasas treguas para atender a la formación papal de José Arcadio, cuando éste tuvo que ser preparado a las volandas para irse al seminario. Meme, su hermana, repartida entre la rigidez de Fernanda y las amarguras de Amaranta, llegó casi al mismo tiempo a la edad prevista para mandarla al colegio de las monjas donde harían de ella una virtuosa del clavicordio. Úrsula se sentía atormentada por graves dudas acerca de la eficacia de los métodos con que había templado el espíritu del lánguido aprendiz de Sumo Pontífice, pero no le echaba la culpa a su trastabillante vejez ni a los nubarrones que apenas le permitían vislumbrar el contorno de las cosas, sino a algo que ella misma no lograba definir pero que concebía confusamente como un progresivo desgaste del tiempo. «Los años de ahora ya no vienen como los de antes», solía decir, sintiendo que la realidad cotidiana se le escapaba de las manos. Antes, pensaba, los niños tardaban mucho para crecer. No había sino que recordar todo el tiempo que se necesitó para que José Arcadio, el mayor, se fuera con los gitanos, y todo lo que ocurrió antes de que volviera pintado como una culebra y hablando como un astrónomo, y las cosas que ocurrieron en la casa antes de que Amaranta y Arcadio olvidaran la lengua de los indios y aprendieran el castellano. Había que ver las de sol y sereno que soportó el pobre José Arcadio Buendía bajo el castaño, y todo lo que hubo que llorar su muerte antes de que llevaran moribundo a un coronel Aureliano Buendía que después de tanta guerra y después de tanto sufrir por él, aún no cumplía cincuenta años. En otra época, después de pasar todo el día haciendo animalitos de caramelo, todavía le sobraba tiempo para ocuparse de los niños, para verles en el blanco del ojo que estaban necesitando una pócima de aceite de ricino. En cambio ahora, cuando no tenía nada que hacer y andaba con José Arcadio acaballado en la cadera desde el amanecer hasta la noche, la mala clase del tiempo le había obligado a dejar las cosas a medias. La verdad era que Úrsula se resistía a envejecer aun cuando ya había perdido la cuenta de su edad, y estorbaba por todos lados, y trataba de meterse en todo, y fastidiaba a los forasteros con la preguntadera de si no habían dejado en la casa, por los tiempos de la guerra, un San José de yeso para que lo guardaran mientras pasaba la lluvia. Nadie supo a ciencia cierta cuándo empezó a perder la vista. Todavía en sus últimos años, cuando ya no podía levantarse de la cama, parecía simplemente que estaba vencida por la decrepitud, pero nadie descubrió que estuviera ciega. Ella lo había notado desde antes del nacimiento de José Arcadio. Al principio creyó que se trataba de una debilidad transitoria, y tomaba a escondidas jarabe de tuétano y se echaba miel de abeja en los ojos, pero muy pronto se fue convenciendo de que se hundía sin remedio en las tinieblas, hasta el punto de que nunca tuvo una noción muy clara del invento de la luz eléctrica, porque cuando instalaron los primeros focos sólo alcanzó a percibir el resplandor. No se lo dijo a nadie, pues habría sido un reconocimiento público de su inutilidad. Se empeñó en un callado aprendizaje de las distancias de las cosas, y de las voces de la gente, para seguir viendo con la memoria cuando ya no se lo permitieran las sombras de las cataratas. Más tarde había de descubrir el auxilio imprevisto de los olores, que se definieron en las tinieblas con una fuerza mucho más convincente que los volúmenes y el color, y la salvaron definitivamente de la vergüenza de una renuncia. En la oscuridad del cuarto podía ensartar la aguja y tejer un ojal, y sabía cuándo estaba la leche a punto de hervir. Conoció con tanta seguridad el lugar en que se encontraba cada cosa, que ella misma se olvidaba a veces de que estaba ciega. En cierta ocasión, Fernanda alborotó la casa porque había perdido su anillo matrimonial, y Úrsula lo encontró en una repisa del dormitorio de los niños. Sencillamente, mientras los otros andaban descuidadamente por todos lados, ella los vigilaba con sus cuatro sentidos para que nunca la tomaran por sorpresa, y al cabo de algún tiempo descubrió que cada miembro de la familia repetía todos los días, sin darse cuenta, los mismos recorridos, los mismos actos, y que casi repetía las mismas palabras a la misma hora. Sólo cuando se salían de esa meticulosa rutina corrían el riesgo de perder algo. De modo que cuando oyó a Fernanda consternada porque había perdido el anillo, Úrsula recordó que lo único distinto que había hecho aquel día era asolear las esteras de los niños porque Meme había descubierto una chinche la noche anterior. Como los niños asistieron a la limpieza, Úrsula pensó que Fernanda había puesto el anillo en el único lugar en que ellos no podían alcanzarlo: la repisa. Fernanda, en cambio, lo buscó únicamente en los trayectos de su itinerario cotidiano, sin saber que la búsqueda de las cosas perdidas está entorpecida por los hábitos rutinarios, y es por eso que cuesta tanto trabajo encontrarlas.

La crianza de José Arcadio ayudó a Úrsula en la tarea agotadora de mantenerse al corriente de los mínimos cambios de la casa. Cuando se daba cuenta de que Amaranta estaba vistiendo a los santos del dormitorio, fingía que le enseñaba al niño las diferencias de los colores.

—Vamos a ver —le decía—, cuéntame de qué color está vestido San Rafael Arcángel.

En esa forma, el niño le daba la información que le negaban sus ojos, y mucho antes de que él se fuera al seminario ya podía Úrsula distinguir por la textura los distintos colores de la ropa de los santos. A veces ocurrían accidentes imprevistos. Una tarde estaba Amaranta bordando en el corredor de las begonias, y Úrsula tropezó con ella.

—Por el amor de Dios —protestó Amaranta—, fíjese por dónde camina.

—Eres tú —dijo Úrsula—, la que estás sentada donde no debe ser.

Para ella era cierto. Pero aquel día empezó a darse cuenta de algo que nadie había descubierto, y era que en el transcurso del año el sol iba cambiando imperceptiblemente de posición, y quienes se sentaban en el corredor tenían que ir cambiando de lugar poco a poco y sin advertirlo. A partir de entonces, Úrsula no tenía sino que recordar la fecha para conocer el lugar exacto en que estaba sentada Amaranta. Aunque el temblor de las manos era cada vez más perceptible y no podía con el peso de los pies, nunca se vio su menudita figura en tantos lugares al mismo tiempo. Era casi tan diligente como cuando llevaba encima todo el peso de la casa. Sin embargo, en la impenetrable soledad de la decrepitud dispuso de tal clarividencia para examinar hasta los más insignificantes acontecimientos de la familia, que por primera vez vio con claridad las verdades que sus ocupaciones de otro tiempo le habían impedido ver. Por la época en que preparaban a José Arcadio para el seminario, ya había hecho una recapitulación infinitesimal de la vida de la casa desde la fundación de Macondo, y había cambiado por completo la opinión que siempre tuvo de sus descendientes. Se dio cuenta de que el coronel Aureliano Buendía no le había perdido el cariño a la familia a causa del endurecimiento de la guerra, como ella creía antes, sino que nunca había querido a nadie, ni siquiera a su esposa Remedios o a las incontables mujeres de una noche que pasaron por su vida, y mucho menos a sus hijos. Vislumbró que no había hecho tantas guerras por idealismo, como todo el mundo creía, ni había renunciado por cansancio a la victoria inminente, como todo el mundo creía, sino que había ganado y perdido por el mismo motivo, por pura y pecaminosa soberbia. Llegó a la conclusión de que aquel hijo por quien ella habría dado la vida era simplemente un hombre incapacitado para el amor. Una noche, cuando lo tenía en el vientre, lo oyó llorar. Fue un lamento tan definido, que José Arcadio Buendía despertó a su lado y se alegró con la idea de que el niño iba a ser ventrílocuo. Otras personas pronosticaron que sería adivino. Ella, en cambio, se estremeció con la certidumbre de que aquel bramido profundo era un primer indicio de la temible cola de cerdo, y rogó a Dios que le dejara morir la criatura en el vientre. Pero la lucidez de la decrepitud le permitió ver, y así lo repitió muchas veces, que el llanto de los niños en el vientre de la madre no es un anuncio de ventriloquía ni de facultad adivinatoria, sino una señal inequívoca de incapacidad para el amor. Aquella desvalorización de la imagen del hijo le suscitó de un golpe toda la compasión que le estaba debiendo. Amaranta, en cambio, cuya dureza de corazón la espantaba, cuya concentrada amargura la amargaba, se le esclareció en el último examen como la mujer más tierna que había existido jamás, y comprendió con una lastimosa clarividencia que las injustas torturas a que había sometido a Pietro Crespi no eran dictadas por una voluntad de venganza, como todo el mundo creía, ni el lento martirio con que frustró la vida del coronel Gerineldo Márquez había sido determinado por la mala hiel de su amargura, como todo el mundo creía, sino que ambas acciones habían sido una lucha a muerte entre un amor sin medidas y una cobardía invencible, y había triunfado finalmente el miedo irracional que Amaranta le tuvo siempre a su propio y atormentado corazón. Fue por esa época que Úrsula empezó a nombrar a Rebeca, a evocarla con un viejo cariño exaltado por el arrepentimiento tardío y la admiración repentina, habiendo comprendido que solamente ella, Rebeca, la que nunca se alimentó de su leche sino de la tierra, de la tierra y la cal de las paredes, la que no llevó en las venas sangre de sus venas sino la sangre desconocida de los desconocidos cuyos huesos seguían cloqueando en la tumba, Rebeca, la del corazón impaciente, la del vientre desaforado, era la única que tuvo la valentía sin frenos que Úrsula había deseado para su estirpe.

—Rebeca —decía, tanteando las paredes—, ¡qué injustos hemos sido contigo!

En la casa, sencillamente, creían que desvariaba, sobre todo desde que le dio por andar con el brazo derecho levantado, como el arcángel Gabriel. Fernanda se dio cuenta, sin embargo, de que había un sol de clarividencia en las sombras de ese desvarío, pues Úrsula podía decir sin titubeos cuánto dinero se había gastado en la casa durante el último año. Amaranta tuvo una idea semejante cierto día en que su madre meneaba en la cocina una olla de sopa, y dijo de pronto, sin saber que la estaban oyendo, que el molino de maíz que le compraron a los primeros gitanos, y que había desaparecido desde antes de que José Arcadio le diera sesenta y cinco veces la vuelta al mundo, estaba todavía en casa de Pilar Ternera. También casi centenaria, pero entera y ágil a pesar de la inconcebible gordura que espantaba a los niños como en otro tiempo su risa espantaba a las palomas, Pilar Ternera no se sorprendió del acierto de Úrsula, porque su propia experiencia empezaba a indicarle que una vejez alerta puede ser más atinada que las averiguaciones de barajas.

Sin embargo, cuando Úrsula se dio cuenta de que no le había alcanzado el tiempo para consolidar la vocación de José Arcadio, se dejó aturdir por la consternación. Empezó a cometer errores, tratando de ver con los ojos las cosas que la intuición le permitía ver con mayor claridad. Una mañana le echó al niño en la cabeza el contenido de un tintero creyendo que era agua de florida. Ocasionó tantos tropiezos con la terquedad de intervenir en todo, que se sintió trastornada por ráfagas de mal humor, y trataba de quitarse las tinieblas que por fin la estaban enredando como un camisón de telaraña. Fue entonces cuando se le ocurrió que su torpeza no era la primera victoria de la decrepitud y la oscuridad, sino una falla del tiempo. Pensaba que antes, cuando Dios no hacía con los meses y los años las mismas trampas que hacían los turcos al medir una yarda de percal, las cosas eran diferentes. Ahora no sólo crecían los niños más de prisa, sino que hasta los sentimientos evolucionaban de otro modo. No bien Remedios, la bella, había subido al cielo en cuerpo y alma, y ya la desconsiderada Fernanda andaba refunfuñando en los rincones porque se había llevado las sábanas. No bien se habían enfriado los cuerpos de los Aurelianos en sus tumbas, y ya Aureliano Segundo tenía otra vez la casa prendida, llena de borrachos que tocaban el acordeón y se ensopaban en champaña, como si no hubieran muerto cristianos sino perros, y como si aquella casa de locos que tantos dolores de cabeza y tantos animalitos de caramelo había costado, estuviera predestinada a convertirse en un basurero de perdición. Recordando estas cosas mientras alistaban el baúl de José Arcadio, Úrsula se preguntaba si no era preferible acostarse de una vez en la sepultura y que le echaran la tierra encima, y le preguntaba a Dios, sin miedo, si de verdad creía que la gente estaba hecha de fierro para soportar tantas penas y mortificaciones; y preguntando y preguntando iba atizando su propia ofuscación, y sentía unos irreprimibles deseos de soltarse a despotricar como un forastero, y de permitirse por fin un instante de rebeldía, el instante tantas veces anhelado y tantas veces aplazado de meterse la resignación por el fundamento y cagarse de una vez en todo, y sacarse del corazón los infinitos montones de malas palabras que había tenido que atragantarse en todo un siglo de conformidad.

—¡Carajo! —gritó.

Amaranta, que empezaba a meter la ropa en el baúl, creyó que la había picado un alacrán.

—¿Dónde está? —preguntó alarmada.

—¿Qué?

—¡El animal! —aclaró Amaranta.

Úrsula se puso un dedo en el corazón.

—Aquí —dijo.

Un jueves a las dos de la tarde, José Arcadio se fue al seminario. Úrsula había de evocarlo siempre como lo imaginó al despedirlo, lánguido y serio y sin derramar una lágrima, como ella le había enseñado, ahogándose de calor dentro del vestido de pana verde con botones de cobre y un lazo almidonado en el cuello. Dejó el comedor impregnado de la penetrante fragancia de agua de florida que ella le echaba en la cabeza para poder seguir su rastro en la casa. Mientras duró el almuerzo de despedida, la familia disimuló el nerviosismo con expresiones de júbilo, y celebró con exagerado entusiasmo las ocurrencias del padre Antonio Isabel. Pero cuando se llevaron el baúl forrado de terciopelo con esquinas de plata, fue como si hubieran sacado de la casa un ataúd. El único que se negó a participar en la despedida fue el coronel Aureliano Buendía.

—Esta era la última vaina que nos faltaba —refunfuñó—: ¡un Papa!

Tres meses después, Aureliano Segundo y Fernanda llevaron a Meme al colegio, y regresaron con un clavicordio que ocupó el lugar de la pianola. Fue por esa época que Amaranta empezó a tejer su propia mortaja. La fiebre del banano se había apaciguado. Los antiguos habitantes de Macondo se encontraban arrinconados por los advenedizos, trabajosamente asidos a sus precarios recursos de antaño, pero reconfortados en todo caso por la impresión de haber sobrevivido a un naufragio. En la casa siguieron recibiendo invitados a almorzar, y en realidad no se restableció la antigua rutina mientras no se fue, años después, la compañía bananera. Sin embargo, hubo cambios radicales en el tradicional sentido de hospitalidad, porque entonces era Fernanda quien imponía sus leyes. Con Úrsula relegada a las tinieblas, y con Amaranta abstraída en la labor del sudario, la antigua aprendiza de reina tuvo libertad para seleccionar a los comensales e imponerles las rígidas normas que le inculcaran sus padres. Su severidad hizo de la casa un reducto de costumbres revenidas, en un pueblo convulsionado por la vulgaridad con que los forasteros despilfarraban sus fáciles fortunas. Para ella, sin más vueltas, la gente de bien era la que no tenía nada que ver con la compañía bananera. Hasta José Arcadio Segundo, su cuñado, fue víctima de su celo discriminatorio, porque en el embullamiento de la primera hora volvió a rematar sus estupendos gallos de pelea y se empleó de capataz en la compañía bananera.

—Que no vuelva a pisar este hogar —dijo Fernanda—, mientras tenga la sarna de los forasteros.

Fue tal la estrechez impuesta en la casa, que Aureliano Segundo se sintió definitivamente más cómodo donde Petra Cotes. Primero, con el pretexto de aliviarle la carga a la esposa, trasladó las parrandas. Luego, con el pretexto de que los animales estaban perdiendo fecundidad, trasladó los establos y caballerizas. Por último, con el pretexto de que en casa de la concubina hacía menos calor, trasladó la pequeña oficina donde atendía sus negocios. Cuando Fernanda se dio cuenta de que era una viuda a quien todavía no se le había muerto el marido, ya era demasiado tarde para que las cosas volvieran a su estado anterior. Aureliano Segundo apenas si comía en la casa, y las únicas apariencias que seguía guardando, como las de dormir con la esposa, no bastaban para convencer a nadie. Una noche, por descuido, lo sorprendió la mañana en la cama de Petra Cotes. Fernanda, al contrario de lo que él esperaba, no le hizo el menor reproche ni soltó el más leve suspiro de resentimiento, pero ese mismo día le mandó a casa de la concubina sus dos baúles de ropa. Los mandó a pleno sol y con instrucciones de llevarlos por la mitad de la calle, para que todo el mundo los viera, creyendo que el marido descarriado no podría soportar la vergüenza y volvería al redil con la cabeza humillada. Pero aquel gesto heroico fue apenas una prueba más de lo mal que conocía Fernanda no sólo el carácter de su marido sino la índole de una comunidad que nada tenía que ver con la de sus padres, porque todo el que vio pasar los baúles se dijo que al fin y al cabo esa era la culminación natural de una historia cuyas intimidades no ignoraba nadie, y Aureliano Segundo celebró la libertad regalada con una parranda de tres días. Para mayor desventaja de la esposa, mientras ella empezaba a hacer una mala madurez con sus sombrías vestiduras talares, sus medallones anacrónicos y su orgullo fuera de lugar, la concubina parecía reventar en una segunda juventud, embutida en vistosos trajes de seda natural y con los ojos atigrados por la candela de la reivindicación. Aureliano

Segundo volvió a entregarse a ella con la fogosidad de la adolescencia, como antes, cuando Petra Cotes no lo quería por ser él sino porque lo confundía con su hermano gemelo, y acostándose con ambos al mismo tiempo pensaba que Dios le había deparado la fortuna de tener un hombre que hacía el amor como si fueran dos. Era tan apremiante la pasión restaurada, que en más de una ocasión se miraron a los ojos cuando se disponían a comer, y sin decirse nada taparon los platos y se fueron a morirse de hambre y de amor en el dormitorio. Inspirado en las cosas que había visto en sus furtivas visitas a las matronas francesas, Aureliano Segundo le compró a Petra Cotes una cama con baldaquín arzobispal, y puso cortinas de terciopelo en las ventanas y cubrió el cielorraso y las paredes del dormitorio con grandes espejos de cristal de roca. Se le vio entonces más parrandero y botarate que nunca. En el tren, que llegaba todos los días a las once, recibía cajas y más cajas de champaña y de brandy. Al regreso de la estación arrastraba a la cumbiamba improvisada a cuanto ser humano encontraba a su paso, nativo o forastero, conocido o por conocer, sin distinciones de ninguna clase. Hasta el escurridizo señor Brown, que sólo alternaba en lengua extraña, se dejó seducir por las tentadoras señas que le hacía Aureliano Segundo, y varias veces se emborrachó a muerte en casa de Petra Cotes y hasta hizo que los feroces perros alemanes que lo acompañaban a todas partes bailaran canciones texanas que él mismo masticaba de cualquier modo al compás del acordeón.

—Apártense vacas —gritaba Aureliano Segundo en el paroxismo de la fiesta—. Apártense que la vida es corta.

Nunca tuvo mejor semblante, ni lo quisieron más, ni fue más desaforado el paritorio de sus animales. Se sacrificaban tantas reses, tantos cerdos y gallinas en las interminables parrandas, que la tierra del patio se volvió negra y lodosa de tanta sangre. Aquello era un eterno tiradero de huesos y tripas, un muladar de sobras, y había que estar quemando recámaras de dinamita a todas horas para que los gallinazos no les sacaran los ojos a los invitados. Aureliano Segundo se volvió gordo, violáceo, atortugado, a consecuencia de un apetito apenas comparable al de José Arcadio cuando regresó de la vuelta al mundo. El prestigio de su desmandada voracidad, de su inmensa capacidad de despilfarro, de su hospitalidad sin precedente, rebasó los límites de la ciénaga y atrajo a los glotones mejor calificados del litoral. De todas partes llegaban tragaldabas fabulosos para tomar parte en los irracionales torneos de capacidad y resistencia que se organizaban en casa de Petra Cotes. Aureliano Segundo fue el comedor invicto, hasta el sábado de infortunio en que apareció Camila Sagastume, una hembra totémica conocida en el país entero con el buen nombre de La Elefanta. El duelo se prolongó hasta el amanecer del martes. En las primeras veinticuatro horas, habiendo despachado una ternera con yuca, ñame y plátanos asados, y además una caja y media de champaña, Aureliano Segundo tenía la seguridad de la victoria. Se veía más entusiasta, más vital que la imperturbable adversaria, poseedora de un estilo evidentemente más profesional, pero por lo mismo menos emocionante para el abigarrado público que desbordó la casa. Mientras Aureliano Segundo comía a dentelladas, desbocado por la ansiedad del triunfo, La Elefanta seccionaba la carne con las artes de un cirujano, y la comía sin prisa y hasta con un cierto placer. Era gigantesca y maciza, pero contra la corpulencia colosal prevalecía la ternura de la femineidad, y tenía un rostro tan hermoso, unas manos tan finas y bien cuidadas y un encanto personal tan irresistible, que cuando Aureliano Segundo la vio entrar a la casa comentó en voz baja que hubiera preferido no hacer el torneo en la mesa sino en la cama. Más tarde, cuando la vio consumir el cuadril de la ternera sin violar una sola regla de la mejor urbanidad, comentó seriamente que aquel delicado, fascinante e insaciable proboscidio era en cierto modo la mujer ideal. No estaba equivocado. La fama de quebrantahuesos que precedió a La Elefanta carecía de fundamento. No era trituradora de bueyes, ni mujer barbada en un circo griego, como se decía, sino directora de una academia de canto. Había aprendido a comer siendo ya una respetable madre de familia, buscando un método para que sus hijos se alimentaran mejor y no mediante estímulos artificiales del apetito sino mediante la absoluta tranquilidad del espíritu. Su teoría, demostrada en la práctica, se fundaba en el principio de que una persona que tuviera perfectamente arreglados todos los asuntos de su conciencia, podía comer sin tregua hasta que la venciera el cansancio. De modo que fue por razones morales, y no por interés deportivo, que desatendió la academia y el hogar para competir con un hombre cuya fama de gran comedor sin principios le había dado la vuelta al país. Desde la primera vez que lo vio, se dio cuenta de que a Aureliano Segundo no lo perdería el estómago sino el carácter. Al término de la primera noche, mientras La Elefanta continuaba impávida, Aureliano Segundo se estaba agotando de tanto hablar y reír. Durmieron cuatro horas. Al despertar, se bebió cada uno el jugo de cincuenta naranjas, ocho litros de café y treinta huevos crudos. Al segundo amanecer, después de muchas horas sin dormir y habiendo despachado dos cerdos, un racimo de plátanos y cuatro cajas de champaña, La Elefanta sospechó que Aureliano Segundo, sin saberlo, había descubierto el mismo método que ella, pero por el camino absurdo de la irresponsabilidad total. Era, pues, más peligroso de lo que ella pensaba. Sin embargo, cuando Petra Cotes llevó a la mesa dos pavos asados, Aureliano Segundo estaba a un paso de la congestión.

—Si no puede, no coma más —dijo La Elefanta—. Quedamos empatados.

Lo dijo de corazón, comprendiendo que tampoco ella podía comer un bocado más por el remordimiento de estar propiciando la muerte del adversario. Pero Aureliano Segundo lo interpretó como un nuevo desafío, y se atragantó de pavo hasta más allá de su increíble capacidad. Perdió el conocimiento. Cayó de bruces en el plato de huesos, echando espumarajos de perro por la boca, y ahogándose en ronquidos de agonía. Sintió, en medio de las tinieblas, que lo arrojaban desde lo más alto de una torre hacia un precipicio sin fondo, y en un último fogonazo de lucidez se dio cuenta de que al término de aquella inacabable caída lo estaba esperando la muerte.

—Llévenme con Fernanda —alcanzó a decir.

Los amigos que lo dejaron en la casa creyeron que le había cumplido a la esposa la promesa de no morir en la cama de la concubina. Petra Cotes había embetunado los botines de charol que él quería tener puestos en el ataúd, y ya andaba buscando a alguien

que los llevara, cuando fueron a decirle que Aureliano Segundo estaba fuera de peligro. Se restableció,
en efecto, en menos de una semana, y quince días
después estaba celebrando con una parranda sin precedentes el acontecimiento de la supervivencia. Siguió viviendo en casa de Petra Cotes, pero visitaba a
Fernanda todos los días y a veces se quedaba a comer
en familia, como si el destino hubiera invertido la situación, y lo hubiera dejado de esposo de la concubina y de amante de la esposa.

Fue un descanso para Fernanda. En los tedios del
abandono, sus únicas distracciones eran los ejercicios de clavicordio a la hora de la siesta, y las cartas
de sus hijos. En las detalladas esquelas que les mandaba cada quince días, no había una sola línea de verdad. Les ocultaba sus penas. Les escamoteaba la tristeza de una casa que a pesar de la luz sobre las
begonias, a pesar de la sofocación de las dos de la tarde, a pesar de las frecuentes ráfagas de fiesta que llegaban de la calle, era cada vez más parecida a la mansión colonial de sus padres. Fernanda vagaba sola
entre tres fantasmas vivos y el fantasma muerto de
José Arcadio Buendía, que a veces iba a sentarse con
una atención inquisitiva en la penumbra de la sala,
mientras ella tocaba el clavicordio. El coronel Aureliano Buendía era una sombra. Desde la última vez
que salió a la calle a proponerle una guerra sin porvenir al coronel Gerineldo Márquez, apenas si abandonaba el taller para orinar bajo el castaño. No recibía
más visitas que las del peluquero cada tres semanas.
Se alimentaba de cualquier cosa que le llevaba Úrsula
una vez al día, y aunque seguía fabricando pescaditos
de oro con la misma pasión de antes, dejó de venderlos cuando se enteró de que la gente no los compraba

como joyas sino como reliquias históricas. Había hecho en el patio una hoguera con las muñecas de Remedios, que decoraban su dormitorio desde el día de su matrimonio. La vigilante Úrsula se dio cuenta de lo que estaba haciendo su hijo, pero no pudo impedirlo.

—Tienes un corazón de piedra —le dijo.

—Esto no es asunto del corazón —dijo él—. El cuarto se está llenando de polillas.

Amaranta tejía su mortaja. Fernanda no entendía por qué le escribía cartas ocasionales a Meme, y hasta le mandaba regalos, y en cambio ni siquiera quería hablar de José Arcadio. «Se morirán sin saber por qué», contestó Amaranta cuando ella le hizo la pregunta a través de Úrsula, y aquella respuesta sembró en su corazón un enigma que nunca pudo esclarecer. Alta, espadada, altiva, siempre vestida con abundantes pollerines de espuma y con un aire de distinción que resistía a los años y a los malos recuerdos, Amaranta parecía llevar en la frente la cruz de ceniza de la virginidad. En realidad la llevaba en la mano, en la venda negra que no se quitaba ni para dormir, y que ella misma lavaba y planchaba. La vida se le iba en bordar el sudario. Se hubiera dicho que bordaba durante el día y desbordaba en la noche, y no con la esperanza de derrotar en esa forma la soledad, sino todo lo contrario, para sustentarla.

La mayor preocupación que tenía Fernanda en sus años de abandono era que Meme fuera a pasar las primeras vacaciones y no encontrara a Aureliano Segundo en la casa. La congestión puso término a aquel temor. Cuando Meme volvió, sus padres se habían puesto de acuerdo no sólo para que la niña creyera que Aureliano Segundo seguía siendo un esposo do-

mesticado, sino también para que no notara la tristeza de la casa. Todos los años, durante dos meses, Aureliano Segundo representaba su papel de marido
ejemplar, y promovía fiestas con helados y galletitas,
que la alegre y vivaz estudiante amenizaba con el clavicordio. Era evidente desde entonces que había heredado muy poco del carácter de la madre. Parecía
más bien una segunda versión de Amaranta, cuando
ésta no conocía la amargura y andaba alborotando la
casa con sus pasos de baile, a los doce, a los catorce
años, antes de que la pasión secreta por Pietro Crespi
torciera definitivamente el rumbo de su corazón.
Pero al contrario de Amaranta, al contrario de todos,
Meme no revelaba todavía el sino solitario de la familia, y parecía enteramente conforme con el mundo, aun cuando se encerraba en la sala a las dos de la
tarde a practicar el clavicordio con una disciplina inflexible. Era evidente que le gustaba la casa, que pasaba todo el año soñando con el alboroto de adolescentes que provocaba su llegada, y que no andaba
muy lejos de la vocación festiva y los desafueros hos-
pitalarios de su padre. El primer signo de esa herencia calamitosa se reveló en las terceras vacaciones,
cuando Meme apareció en la casa con cuatro monjas
y sesenta y ocho compañeras de clase, a quienes invitó a pasar una semana en familia, por propia iniciativa y sin ningún anuncio.

—¡Qué desgracia! —se lamentó Fernanda—.
¡Esta criatura es tan bárbara como su padre!

Fue preciso pedir camas y hamacas a los vecinos,
establecer nueve turnos en la mesa, fijar horarios
para el baño y conseguir cuarenta taburetes prestados para que las niñas de uniformes azules y botines
de hombre no anduvieran todo el día revoloteando

de un lado a otro. La invitación fue un fracaso, porque las ruidosas colegialas apenas acababan de desayunar cuando ya tenían que empezar los turnos para el almuerzo, y luego para la cena, y en toda la semana sólo pudieron hacer un paseo a las plantaciones. Al anochecer, las monjas estaban agotadas, incapacitadas para moverse, para impartir una orden más, y todavía el tropel de adolescentes incansables estaba en el patio cantando desabridos himnos escolares. Un día estuvieron a punto de atropellar a Úrsula, que se empeñaba cn ser útil precisamente donde más estorbaba. Otro día, las monjas armaron un alboroto porque el coronel Aureliano Buendía orinó bajo el castaño sin preocuparse de que las colegialas estuvieran en el patio. Amaranta estuvo a punto dc sembrar el pánico, porque una de las monjas entró a la cocina cuando ella estaba salando la sopa, y lo único que se le ocurrió fue preguntar qué eran aquellos puñados de polvo blanco.

—Arsénico —dijo Amaranta.

La noche de su llegada, las estudiantes se embrollaron de tal modo tratando de ir al excusado antes de acostarse, que a la una de la madrugada todavía estaban entrando las últimas. Fernanda compró entonces setenta y dos bacinillas, pero sólo consiguió convertir en un problema matinal el problema nocturno, porque desde el amanecer había frente al excusado una larga fila de muchachas, cada una con su bacinilla en la mano, esperando turno para lavarla. Aunque algunas sufrieron calenturas y a varias se les infectaron las picaduras de los mosquitos, la mayoría demostró una resistencia inquebrantable frente a las dificultades más penosas, y aun a la hora de más calor correteaban en el jardín. Cuando por fin se fueron, las flores estaban destrozadas, los muebles partidos y las paredes cubiertas de dibujos y letreros, pero Fernanda les perdonó los estragos en el alivio de la partida. Devolvió las camas y taburetes prestados y guardó las setenta y dos bacinillas en el cuarto de Melquíades. La clausurada habitación, en torno a la cual giró en otro tiempo la vida espiritual de la casa, fue conocida desde entonces como *el cuarto de las bacinillas*. Para el coronel Aureliano Buendía, ese era el nombre más apropiado, porque mientras el resto de la familia seguía asombrándose de que la pieza de Melquíades fuera inmune al polvo y la destrucción, él la veía convertida en un muladar. De todos modos, no parecía importarle quién tenía la razón, y si se enteró del destino del cuarto fue porque Fernanda estuvo pasando y perturbando su trabajo una tarde entera para guardar las bacinillas.

Por esos días reapareció José Arcadio Segundo en la casa. Pasaba de largo por el corredor, sin saludar a nadie, y se encerraba en el taller a conversar con el coronel. A pesar de que no podía verlo, Úrsula analizaba el taconeo de sus botas de capataz, y se sorprendía de la distancia insalvable que lo separaba de la familia, inclusive del hermano gemelo con quien jugaba en la infancia ingeniosos juegos de confusión, y con el cual no tenía ya ningún rasgo común. Era lineal, solemne, y tenía un estar pensativo, y una tristeza de sarraceno, y un resplandor lúgubre en el rostro color de otoño. Era el que más se parecía a su madre, Santa Sofía de la Piedad. Úrsula se reprochaba la tendencia a olvidarse de él al hablar de la familia, pero cuando lo sintió de nuevo en la casa, y advirtió que el coronel lo admitía en el taller durante las horas de trabajo, volvió a examinar sus viejos recuerdos, y confirmó la creencia de que en algún momento de la infancia se había cambiado con su hermano gemelo, porque era él y no el otro quien debía llamarse Aureliano. Nadie conocía los pormenores de su vida. En un tiempo se supo que no tenía una residencia fija, que criaba gallos en casa de Pilar Ternera, y que a veces se quedaba a dormir allí, pero que casi siempre pasaba la noche en los cuartos de las matronas francesas. Andaba al garete, sin afectos, sin ambiciones, como una estrella errante en el sistema planetario de Úrsula.

En realidad, José Arcadio Segundo no era miembro de la familia, ni lo sería jamás de otra, desde la madrugada distante en que el coronel Gerineldo Márquez lo llevó al cuartel, no para que viera un fusilamiento, sino para que no olvidara en el resto de su vida la sonrisa triste y un poco burlona del fusilado. Aquel no era sólo su recuerdo más antiguo, sino el único de su niñez. El otro, el de un anciano con un chaleco anacrónico y un sombrero de alas de cuervo que contaba maravillas frente a una ventana deslumbrante, no lograba situarlo en ninguna época. Era un recuerdo incierto, enteramente desprovisto de enseñanzas o nostalgia, al contrario del recuerdo del fusilado, que en realidad había definido el rumbo de su vida, y regresaba a su memoria cada vez más nítido a medida que envejecía, como si el transcurso del tiempo lo hubiera ido aproximando. Úrsula trató de aprovechar a José Arcadio Segundo para que el coronel Aureliano Buendía abandonara su encierro. «Convéncelo de que vaya al cine», le decía. «Aunque no le gusten las películas tendrá por lo menos una ocasión de respirar aire puro.» Pero no tardó en darse cuenta de que él era tan insensible a sus súplicas como hubiera podido serlo el coronel, y que estaban acorazados por la misma impermeabilidad a los afectos. Aunque nunca supo, ni lo supo nadie, de qué hablaban en los prolongados encierros del taller, entendió que fueran ellos los únicos miembros de la familia que parecían vinculados por las afinidades.

La verdad es que ni José Arcadio Segundo hubiera podido sacar al coronel de su encierro. La invasión escolar había rebasado los límites de su paciencia. Con el pretexto de que el dormitorio nupcial estaba a merced de las polillas a pesar de la destrucción de las apetitosas muñecas de Remedios, colgó una hamaca en el taller, y entonces lo abandonó solamente para ir al patio a hacer sus necesidades. Úrsula no conseguía hilvanar con él una conversación trivial. Sabía que no miraba los platos de comida, sino que los ponía en un extremo del mesón mientras terminaba el pescadito, y no le importaba si la sopa se llenaba de nata y se enfriaba la carne. Se endureció cada vez más desde que el coronel Gerineldo Márquez se negó a secundarlo en una guerra senil. Se encerró con tranca dentro de sí mismo, y la familia terminó por pensar en él como si hubiera muerto. No se le volvió a ver una reacción humana, hasta un once de octubre en que salió a la puerta de la calle para ver el desfile de un circo. Aquella había sido para el coronel Aureliano Buendía una jornada igual a todas las de sus últimos años. A las cinco de la madrugada lo despertó el alboroto de los sapos y los grillos en el exterior del muro. La llovizna persistía desde el sábado, y él no hubiera tenido necesidad de oír su minucioso cuchicheo en las hojas del jardín, porque de todos modos lo hubiera sentido en el frío de los huesos. Estaba, como siempre, arropado con la manta de lana, y con los largos calzoncillos de algodón crudo que seguía usando por comodidad, aunque a causa de su polvoriento anacronismo él mismo los llamaba «calzoncillos de godo». Se puso los pantalones estrechos, pero no se cerró las presillas ni se puso en el cuello de la camisa el botón de oro que usaba siempre, porque tenía el propósito de darse un baño. Luego se puso la manta en la cabeza, como un capirote, se peinó con los dedos el bigote chorreado, y fue a orinar en el patio. Faltaba tanto para que saliera el sol que José Arcadio Buendía dormitaba todavía bajo el cobertizo de palmas podridas por la llovizna. Él no lo vio, como no lo había visto nunca, ni oyó la frase incomprensible que le dirigió el espectro de su padre cuando despertó sobresaltado por el chorro de orín caliente que le salpicaba los zapatos. Dejó el baño para más tarde, no por el frío y la humedad, sino por la niebla opresiva de octubre. De regreso al taller percibió el olor de pabilo de los fogones que estaba encendiendo Santa Sofía de la Piedad, y esperó en la cocina a que hirviera el café para llevarse su tazón sin azúcar. Santa Sofía de la Piedad le preguntó, como todas las mañanas, en qué día de la semana estaban, y él contestó que era martes, once de octubre. Viendo a la impávida mujer dorada por el resplandor del fuego, que ni en ese ni en ningún otro instante de su vida parecía existir por completo, recordó de pronto que un once de octubre, en plena guerra, lo despertó la certidumbre brutal de que la mujer con quien había dormido estaba muerta. Lo estaba, en realidad, y no olvidaba la fecha porque también ella le había preguntado una hora antes en qué día estaban. A pesar de la evocación, tampoco esta vez tuvo conciencia de hasta qué punto lo habían abandonado los presagios, y mientras hervía el café siguió pensando por pura curiosidad, pero sin el más insignificante riesgo de nostalgia, en la mujer cuyo nombre no conoció nunca, y cuyo rostro no vio con vida porque había llegado hasta su hamaca tropezando en la oscuridad. Sin embargo, en el vacío de tantas mujeres como llegaron a su vida en igual forma, no recordó que fue ella la que en el delirio del primer encuentro estaba a punto de naufragar en sus propias lágrimas, y apenas una hora antes de morir había jurado amarlo hasta la muerte. No volvió a pensar en ella, ni en ninguna otra, después de que entró al taller con la taza humeante, y encendió la luz para contar los pescaditos de oro que guardaba en un tarro de lata. Había diecisiete. Desde que decidió no venderlos, seguía fabricando dos pescaditos al día, y cuando completaba veinticinco volvía a fundirlos en el crisol para empezar a hacerlos de nuevo. Trabajó toda la mañana, absorto, sin pensar en nada, sin darse cuenta de que a las diez arreció la lluvia y alguien pasó frente al taller gritando que cerraran las puertas para que no se inundara la casa, y sin darse cuenta ni siquiera de sí mismo hasta que Úrsula entró con el almuerzo y apagó la luz.

—¡Qué lluvia! —dijo Úrsula.

—Octubre —dijo él.

Al decirlo, no levantó la vista del primer pescadito del día, porque estaba engastando los rubíes de los ojos. Sólo cuando lo terminó y lo puso con los otros en el tarro, empezó a tomar la sopa. Luego se comió, muy despacio, el pedazo de carne guisada con cebolla, el arroz blanco y las tajadas de plátano fritas, todo junto en el mismo plato. Su apetito no se alteraba ni en las mejores ni en las más duras circunstancias. Al término del almuerzo experimentó la zozobra de la ociosidad. Por una especie de superstición científica, nunca trabajaba, ni leía, ni se bañaba, ni hacía el amor antes de que transcurrieran dos horas de digestión, y era una creencia tan arraigada que varias veces retrasó operaciones de guerra para no someter la tropa a los riesgos de una congestión. De modo que se acostó en la hamaca, sacándose la cera de los oídos con un cortaplumas, y a los pocos minutos se quedó dormido. Soñó que entraba en una casa vacía, de paredes blancas, y que lo inquietaba la pesadumbre de ser el primer ser humano que entraba en ella. En el sueño recordó que había soñado lo mismo la noche anterior y en muchas noches de los últimos años, y supo que la imagen se habría borrado de su memoria al despertar, porque aquel sueño recurrente tenía la virtud de no ser recordado sino dentro del mismo sueño. Un momento después, en efecto, cuando el peluquero llamó a la puerta del taller, el coronel Aureliano Buendía despertó con la impresión de que involuntariamente se había quedado dormido por breves segundos, y que no había tenido tiempo de soñar nada.

—Hoy no —le dijo al peluquero—. Nos vemos el viernes.

Tenía una barba de tres días, moteada de pelusas blancas, pero no creía necesario afeitarse si el viernes se iba a cortar el pelo y podía hacerlo todo al mismo tiempo. El sudor pegajoso de la siesta indeseable revivió en sus axilas las cicatrices de los golondrinos. Había escampado, pero aún no salía el sol. El coronel Aureliano Buendía emitió un eructo sonoro que le devolvió al paladar la acidez de la sopa, y que fue como una orden del organismo para que se echara la manta en los hombros y fuera al excusado. Allí permaneció más del tiempo necesario, acuclillado sobre la densa fermentación que subía del cajón de madera, hasta que la costumbre le indicó que era hora de reanudar el trabajo. Durante el tiempo que duró la espera volvió a recordar que era martes, y que José Arcadio Segundo no había estado en el taller porque era día de pago en las fincas de la compañía bananera. Ese recuerdo, como todos los de los últimos años, lo llevó sin que viniera a cuento a pensar en la guerra. Recordó que el coronel Gerineldo Márquez le había prometido alguna vez conseguirle un caballo con una estrella blanca en la frente, y que nunca se había vuelto a hablar de eso. Luego derivó hacia episodios dispersos, pero los evocó sin calificarlos, porque a fuerza de no poder pensar en otra cosa había aprendido a pensar en frío, para que los recuerdos ineludibles no le lastimaran ningún sentimiento. De regreso al taller, viendo que el aire empezaba a secar, decidió que era un buen momento para bañarse, pero Amaranta se le había anticipado. Así que empezó el segundo pescadito del día. Estaba engarzando la cola cuando el sol salió con tanta fuerza que la claridad crujió como un balandro. El aire lavado por la llovizna de tres días se llenó de hormigas voladoras. Entonces cayó en la cuenta de que tenía deseos de orinar, y los estaba aplazando hasta que acabara de armar el pescadito. Iba para el patio, a las cuatro y diez, cuando oyó los cobres lejanos, los retumbos del bombo y el júbilo de los niños, y por primera vez desde su juventud pisó conscientemente una trampa de la nostalgia, y revivió la prodigiosa tarde de gitanos en que su padre lo llevó a conocer el hielo. Santa Sofía de la Piedad abandonó lo que estaba haciendo en la cocina y corrió hacia la puerta.

—Es el circo —gritó.

En vez de ir al castaño, el coronel Aureliano Buendía fue también a la puerta de la calle y se mezcló con los curiosos que contemplaban el desfile. Vio una mujer vestida de oro en el cogote de un elefante. Vio un dromedario triste. Vio un oso vestido de holandesa que marcaba el compás de la música con un cucharón y una cacerola. Vio los payasos haciendo maromas en la cola del desfile, y le vio otra vez la cara a su soledad miserable cuando todo acabó de pasar, y no quedó sino el luminoso espacio en la calle, y el aire lleno de hormigas voladoras, y unos cuantos curiosos asomados al precipicio de la incertidumbre. Entonces fue al castaño, pensando en el circo, y mientras orinaba trató de seguir pensando en el circo, pero ya no encontró el recuerdo. Metió la cabeza entre los hombros, como un pollito, y se quedó inmóvil con la frente apoyada en el tronco del castaño. La familia no se enteró hasta el día siguiente, a las once de la mañana, cuando Santa Sofía de la Piedad fue a tirar la basura en el traspatio y le llamó la atención que estuvieran bajando los gallinazos.

Las últimas vacaciones de Meme coincidieron con el luto por la muerte del coronel Aureliano Buendía. En la casa cerrada no había lugar para fiestas. Se hablaba en susurros, se comía en silencio, se rezaba el rosario tres veces al día, y hasta los ejercicios de clavicordio en el calor de la siesta tenían una resonancia fúnebre. A pesar de su secreta hostilidad contra el coronel, fue Fernanda quien impuso el rigor de aquel duelo, impresionada por la solemnidad con que el gobierno exaltó la memoria del enemigo muerto. Aureliano Segundo volvió como de costumbre a dormir en la casa mientras pasaban las vacaciones de su hija, y algo debió hacer Fernanda para recuperar sus privilegios de esposa legítima, porque el año siguiente encontró Meme una hermanita recién nacida, a quien bautizaron, contra la voluntad de la madre, con el nombre de Amaranta Úrsula.

Meme había terminado sus estudios. El diploma que la acreditaba como concertista de clavicordio fue ratificado por el virtuosismo con que ejecutó temas populares del siglo XVII en la fiesta organizada para celebrar la culminación de sus estudios y con la cual se puso término al duelo. Los invitados admiraron, más que su arte, su rara dualidad. Su carácter frívolo y hasta un poco infantil no parecía adecuado para ninguna actividad seria, pero cuando se sentaba al clavicordio se transformaba en una muchacha diferente, cuya madurez imprevista le daba un aire de adulto. Así fue siempre. En verdad no tenía una vocación definida, pero había logrado las más altas calificaciones mediante una disciplina inflexible, para no contrariar a su madre. Habrían podido imponerle el aprendizaje de cualquier otro oficio y los resultados hubieran sido los mismos. Desde muy niña le molestaba el rigor de Fernanda, su costumbre de decidir por los demás, y habría sido capaz de un sacrificio mucho más duro que las lecciones de clavicordio, sólo por no tropezar con su intransigencia. En el acto de clausura, tuvo la impresión de que el pergamino con letras góticas y mayúsculas historiadas la liberaba de un compromiso que había aceptado no tanto por obediencia como por comodidad, y creyó que a partir de entonces ni la porfiada Fernanda volvería a preocuparse por un instrumento que hasta las monjas consideraban como un fósil de museo. En los primeros años creyó que sus cálculos eran errados, porque después de haber dormido a media ciudad no sólo en la sala de visitas, sino en cuantas veladas benéficas, sesiones escolares y conmemoraciones patrióticas se celebraban en Macondo, su madre siguió invitando a todo recién llegado que suponía capaz de apreciar las virtudes de la hija. Sólo después de la muerte de Amaranta, cuando la familia volvió a encerrarse por un tiempo en el luto, pudo Meme clausurar el clavicordio y olvidar la llave en cualquier ropero, sin que Fernanda se molestara en averiguar en qué momento ni por culpa de quién se había extraviado. Meme resistió las exhibiciones con el mismo estoicismo con que se consagró al aprendizaje. Era el precio de su libertad. Fernanda estaba tan complacida con su docilidad y tan orgullosa de la admiración que despertaba su arte, que nunca se opuso a que tuviera la casa llena de amigas, y pasara la tarde en las plantaciones y fuera al cine con Aureliano Segundo o con señoras de confianza, siempre que la película hubiera sido autorizada en el púlpito por el padre Antonio Isabel. En aquellos ratos de esparcimiento se revelaban los verdaderos gustos de Meme. Su felicidad estaba en el otro extremo de la disciplina, en las fiestas ruidosas, en los comadreos de enamorados, en los prolongados encierros con sus amigas, donde aprendían a fumar y conversaban de asuntos de hombres, y donde una vez se les pasó la mano con tres botellas de ron de caña y terminaron desnudas midiéndose y comparando las partes de sus cuerpos. Meme no olvidaría jamás la noche en que entró en la casa masticando rizomas de regaliz, y sin que advirtieran su trastorno se sentó a la mesa en que Fernanda y Amaranta cenaban sin dirigirse la palabra. Había pasado dos horas tremendas en el dormitorio de una amiga, llorando de risa y de miedo, y en el otro lado de la crisis había encontrado el raro sentimiento de valentía que le hizo falta para fugarse del colegio y decirle a su madre con esas o con otras palabras que bien podía ponerse una lavativa de clavicordio. Sentada en la cabecera de la mesa, tomando un caldo de pollo que le caía en el estómago como un elixir de resurrección, Meme vio entonces a Fernanda y Amaranta envueltas en el halo acusador de la realidad. Tuvo que hacer un grande esfuerzo para no echarles en cara sus remilgos, su pobreza de espíritu, sus delirios de grandeza. Desde las segundas vacaciones se había enterado de que su padre sólo vivía en la casa por guardar las apariencias, y conociendo a Fernanda como la conocía y habiéndoselas arreglado más tarde para conocer a Petra Cotes, le concedió la razón a su padre. También ella hubiera preferido ser la hija de la concubina. En el embotamiento del alcohol, Meme pensaba con deleite en el escándalo que se habría suscitado si en aquel momento hubiera expresado sus pensamientos, y fue tan intensa la íntima satisfacción de la picardía, que Fernanda la advirtió.

—¿Qué te pasa? —preguntó.

—Nada —contestó Meme—. Que apenas ahora descubro cuánto las quiero.

Amaranta se asustó con la evidente carga de odio que llevaba la declaración. Pero Fernanda se sintió tan conmovida que creyó volverse loca cuando Meme despertó a medianoche con la cabeza cuarteada por el dolor, y ahogándose en vómitos de hiel. Le dio un frasco de aceite de castor, le puso cataplasmas en el vientre y bolsas de hielo en la cabeza, y la obligó a cumplir la dieta y el encierro de cinco días ordenados por el nuevo y extravagante médico francés que, después de examinarla más de dos horas, llegó a la conclusión nebulosa de que tenía un trastorno propio de mujer. Abandonada por la valentía, en un miserable estado de desmoralización, a Meme no le quedó otro recurso que aguantar. Úrsula, ya completamente ciega, pero todavía activa y lúcida, fue la única que intuyó el diagnóstico exacto. «Para mí —pensó—, estas son las mismas cosas que les dan a los borrachos.» Pero no sólo rechazó la idea, sino que se reprochó la ligereza de pensamiento. Aureliano Segundo sintió un retortijón de conciencia cuando vio el estado de postración de Meme, y se prometió ocuparse más de ella en el futuro. Fue así como nació la relación de alegre camaradería entre el padre y la hija, que lo liberó a él por un tiempo de la amarga soledad de las parrandas, y la liberó a ella de la tutela de Fernanda sin tener que provocar la crisis doméstica que ya parecía inevitable. Aureliano Segundo aplazaba entonces cualquier compromiso para estar con Meme, por llevarla al cine o al circo, y le dedicaba la mayor parte de su ocio. En los últimos tiempos, el estorbo de la obesidad absurda que ya no le permitía amarrarse los cordones de los zapatos, y la satisfacción abusiva de toda clase de apetitos, habían empezado a agriarle el carácter. El descubrimiento de la hija le restituyó la antigua jovialidad, y el gusto de estar con ella lo iba apartando poco a poco de la disipación. Meme despuntaba en una edad frutal. No era bella, como nunca lo fue Amaranta, pero en cambio era simpática, descomplicada, y tenía la virtud de caer bien desde el primer momento. Tenía un espíritu moderno que lastimaba la anticuada sobriedad y el mal disimulado corazón cicatero de Fernanda, y que en cambio Aureliano Segundo se complacía en patrocinar. Fue él quien resolvió sacarla del dormitorio que ocupaba desde niña, y donde los pávidos ojos de los santos seguían alimentando sus terrores de adolescente, y le amuebló un cuarto con una cama tronal, un tocador amplio y cortinas de terciopelo, sin caer en la cuenta de que estaba haciendo una segunda versión del aposento de Petra Cotes. Era tan pródigo con Meme que ni siquiera sabía cuánto dinero le proporcionaba, porque ella misma se lo sacaba de los bolsillos, y la mantenía al tanto de cuanta novedad embellecedora llegaba a los comisariatos de la compañía bananera. El cuarto de Meme se llenó de almohadillas de piedra pómez para pulirse las uñas, rizadores de cabellos, brilladores de dientes, colirios para languidecer la mirada, y tantos y tan novedosos cosméticos y artefactos de belleza que cada vez que Fernanda entraba en el dormitorio se escandalizaba con la idea de que el tocador de la hija debía ser igual al de las matronas francesas. Sin embargo, Fernanda andaba en esa época con el tiempo dividido entre la pequeña Amaranta Úrsula, que era caprichosa y enfermiza, y una emocionante correspondencia con los médicos invisibles. De modo que cuando advirtió la complicidad del padre con la hija, la única promesa que le arrancó a Aureliano Segundo fue que nunca llevaría a Meme a casa de Petra Cotes. Era una advertencia sin sentido, porque la concubina estaba tan molesta con la camaradería de su amante con la hija que no quería saber nada de ella. La atormentaba un temor desconocido, como si el instinto le indicara que Meme, con sólo desearlo, podría conseguir lo que no pudo conseguir Fernanda: privarla de un amor que ya consideraba asegurado hasta la muerte. Por primera vez tuvo que soportar Aureliano Segundo las caras duras y las virulentas cantaletas de la concubina, y hasta temió que sus traídos y llevados baúles hicieran el camino de regreso a la casa de la esposa. Esto no ocurrió. Nadie conocía mejor a un hombre que Petra Cotes a su amante, y sabía que los baúles se quedarían donde los mandaran, porque si algo detestaba Aureliano Segundo era complicarse la vida con rectificaciones y mudanzas. De modo que los baúles se quedaron donde estaban, y Petra Cotes se empeñó en reconquistar al marido afilando las únicas armas con que no podía disputárselo la hija. Fue también un esfuerzo innecesario, porque Meme no tuvo nunca el propósito de intervenir en los asuntos de su padre, y seguramente si lo hubiera hecho habría sido en favor de la concubina. No le sobraba tiempo para molestar a nadie. Ella misma barría el dormitorio y arreglaba la cama, como le enseñaron las monjas. En la mañana se ocupaba de su ropa, bordando en el corredor o cosiendo en la vieja máquina de manivela de Amaranta. Mientras los otros hacían la siesta, practicaba dos horas el clavicordio, sabiendo que el sacrificio diario mantendría calmada a Fernanda. Por el mismo motivo seguía ofreciendo conciertos en bazares eclesiásticos y veladas escolares, aunque las solicitudes eran cada vez menos frecuentes. Al atardecer se arreglaba, se ponía sus trajes sencillos y sus duros borceguíes, y si no tenía algo que hacer con su padre iba a casas de amigas, donde permanecía hasta la hora de la cena. Era excepcional que Aureliano Segundo no fuera a buscarla entonces para llevarla al cine.

Entre las amigas de Meme había tres jóvenes norteamericanas que rompieron el cerco del gallinero electrificado y establecieron amistad con muchachas de Macondo. Una de ellas era Patricia Brown. Agradecido con la hospitalidad de Aureliano Segundo, el señor Brown le abrió a Meme las puertas de su casa y la invitó a los bailes de los sábados, que eran los únicos en que los gringos alternaban con los nativos. Cuando Fernanda lo supo, se olvidó por un momento de Amaranta Úrsula y los médicos invisibles, y armó todo un melodrama. «Imagínate —le dijo a Meme— lo que va a pensar el coronel en su tumba.» Estaba buscando, por supuesto, el apoyo de Úrsula. Pero la anciana ciega, al contrario de lo que todos esperaban, consideró que no había nada reprochable en que Meme asistiera a los bailes y cultivara amistad con las norteamericanas de su edad, siempre que conservara su firmeza de criterio y no se dejara convertir a la religión protestante. Meme captó muy bien el pensamiento de la tatarabuela, y al día siguiente de los bailes se levantaba más temprano que de costumbre para ir a misa. La oposición de Fernanda resistió hasta el día en que Meme la desarmó con la noticia de que los norteamericanos querían oírla tocar el clavicordio. El instrumento fue sacado una vez más de la casa y llevado a la del señor Brown, donde en efecto la joven concertista recibió los aplausos más sinceros y las felicitaciones más entusiastas. Desde entonces no sólo la invitaron a los bailes, sino también a los baños dominicales en la piscina, y a almorzar una vez por semana. Meme aprendió a nadar como una profesional, a jugar al tenis y a comer jamón de Virginia con rebanadas de piña. Entre bailes, piscina y tenis, se encontró de pronto desenredándose en inglés. Aureliano Segundo se entusiasmó tanto con los progresos de la hija que le compró a un vendedor viajero una enciclopedia inglesa en seis volúmenes y con numerosas láminas de colores, que Meme leía en sus horas libres. La lectura ocupó la atención que antes destinaba a los comadreos de enamorados o a los encierros experimentales con sus amigas, no porque se lo hubiera impuesto como disciplina, sino porque ya había perdido todo interés en comentar misterios que eran del dominio público. Recordaba la borrachera como una aventura infantil, y le parecía tan divertida que se la contó a Aureliano Segundo, y a éste le pareció más divertida que a ella. «Si tu madre lo supiera», le dijo, ahogándose de risa, como le decía siempre que ella le hacía una confidencia. Él le había hecho prometer que con la misma confianza lo pondría al corriente de su primer noviazgo, y Meme le había contado que simpatizaba con un pelirrojo norteamericano que fue a pasar vacaciones con sus padres. «Qué barbaridad», rió Aureliano Segundo. «Si tu madre lo supiera.» Pero Meme le contó también que el muchacho había regresado a su país y no había vuelto a dar señales de vida. Su madurez de criterio afianzó la paz doméstica. Aureliano Segundo dedicaba entonces más horas a Petra Cotes, y aunque ya el cuerpo y el alma no le daban para parrandas como las de antes, no perdía ocasión de promoverlas y de desenfundar el acordeón, que ya tenía algunas teclas amarradas con cordones de zapatos. En la casa, Amaranta bordaba su interminable mortaja, y Úrsula se dejaba arrastrar por la decrepitud hacia el fondo de las tinieblas, donde lo único que seguía siendo visible era el espectro de José Arcadio Buendía bajo el castaño. Fernanda consolidó su autoridad. Las cartas mensuales a su hijo José Arcadio no llevaban entonces una línea de mentira, y solamente le ocultaba su correspondencia con los médicos invisibles, que le habían diagnosticado un tumor benigno en el intestino grueso y estaban preparándola para practicarle una intervención telepática.

Se hubiera dicho que en la cansada mansión de los Buendía había paz y felicidad rutinaria para mucho tiempo si la intempestiva muerte de Amaranta no hubiera promovido un nuevo escándalo. Fue un acontecimiento inesperado. Aunque estaba vieja y apartada de todos, todavía se notaba firme y recta, y con la salud de piedra que tuvo siempre. Nadie conoció su pensamiento desde la tarde en que rechazó definitivamente al coronel Gerineldo Márquez y se encerró a llorar. Cuando salió, había agotado todas sus lágrimas. No se le vio llorar con la subida al cielo de Remedios, la bella, ni con el exterminio de los

Aurelianos, ni con la muerte del coronel Aureliano Buendía, que era la persona que más quiso en este mundo, aunque sólo pudo demostrárselo cuando encontraron su cadáver bajo el castaño. Ella ayudó a levantar el cuerpo. Lo vistió con sus arreos de guerrero, lo afeitó, lo peinó y le engomó el bigote mejor que él mismo no lo hacía en sus años de gloria. Nadie pensó que hubiera amor en aquel acto, porque estaban acostumbrados a la familiaridad de Amaranta con los ritos de la muerte. Fernanda se escandalizaba de que no entendiera las relaciones del catolicismo con la vida, sino únicamente sus relaciones con la muerte, como si no fuera una religión, sino un prospecto de convencionalismos funerarios. Amaranta estaba demasiado enredada en el berenjenal de sus recuerdos para entender aquellas sutilezas apologéticas. Había llegado a la vejez con todas sus nostalgias vivas. Cuando escuchaba los valses de Pietro Crespi sentía los mismos deseos de llorar que tuvo en la adolescencia, como si el tiempo y los escarmientos no sirvieran de nada. Los rollos de música que ella misma había echado a la basura, con el pretexto de que se estaban pudriendo con la humedad, seguían girando y golpeando martinetes en su memoria. Había tratado de hundirlos en la pasión pantanosa que se permitió con su sobrino Aureliano José, y había tratado de refugiarse en la protección serena y viril del coronel Gerineldo Márquez, pero no había conseguido derrotarlos ni con el acto más desesperado de su vejez, cuando bañaba al pequeño José Arcadio tres años antes de que lo mandaran al seminario, y lo acariciaba no como podía hacerlo una abuela con un nieto, sino como lo hubiera hecho una mujer con un hombre, como se contaba que lo hacían las matronas francesas, y como ella quiso hacerlo con Pietro Crespi, a los doce, los catorce años, cuando lo vio con sus pantalones de baile y la varita mágica con que llevaba el compás del metrónomo. A veces le dolía haber dejado a su paso aquel reguero de miseria, y a veces le daba tanta rabia que se pinchaba los dedos con las agujas, pero más le dolía y más rabia le daba y más la amargaba el fragante y agusanado guayabal de amor que iba arrastrando hacia la muerte. Como el coronel Aureliano Buendía pensaba en la guerra, sin poder evitarlo, Amaranta pensaba en Rebeca. Pero mientras su hermano había conseguido esterilizar los recuerdos, ella sólo había conseguido escaldarlos. Lo único que le rogó a Dios durante muchos años fue que no le mandara el castigo de morir antes que Rebeca. Cada vez que pasaba por su casa y advertía los progresos de la destrucción se complacía con la idea de que Dios la estaba oyendo. Una tarde, cuando cosía en el corredor, la asaltó la certidumbre de que ella estaría sentada en ese lugar, en esa misma posición y bajo esa misma luz, cuando le llevaran la noticia de la muerte de Rebeca. Se sentó a esperarla, como quien espera una carta, y era cierto que en una época arrancaba botones para volver a pegarlos, de modo que la ociosidad no hiciera más larga y angustiosa la espera. Nadie se dio cuenta en la casa de que Amaranta tejió entonces una preciosa mortaja para Rebeca. Más tarde, cuando Aureliano Triste contó que la había visto convertida en una imagen de aparición, con la piel cuarteada y unas pocas hebras amarillentas en el cráneo, Amaranta no se sorprendió, porque el espectro descrito era igual al que ella imaginaba desde hacía mucho tiempo. Había decidido restaurar el cadáver de Rebeca, disimular con parafina los estragos del

el opuesto con cabal

rostro y hacerle una peluca con el cabello de los santos. Fabricaría un cadáver hermoso, con la mortaja de lino y un ataúd forrado de peluche con vueltas de púrpura, y lo pondría a disposición de los gusanos en unos funerales espléndidos. Elaboró el plan con tanto odio que la estremeció la idea de que lo habría hecho de igual modo si hubiera sido con amor, pero no se dejó aturdir por la confusión, sino que siguió perfeccionando los detalles tan minuciosamente que llegó a ser, más que una especialista, una virtuosa en los ritos de la muerte. Lo único que no tuvo en cuenta en su plan tremendista fue que, a pesar de sus súplicas a Dios, ella podía morirse primero que Rebeca. Así ocurrió, en efecto. Pero en el instante final Amaranta no se sintió frustrada, sino por el contrario liberada de toda amargura, porque la muerte le deparó el privilegio de anunciarse con varios años de anticipación. La vio un mediodía ardiente, cosiendo con ella en el corredor, poco después de que Meme se fue al colegio. La reconoció en el acto, y no había nada pavoroso en la muerte, porque era una mujer vestida de azul con el cabello largo, de aspecto un poco anticuado, y con un cierto parecido a Pilar Ternera en la época en que las ayudaba en los oficios de cocina. Varias veces Fernanda estuvo presente y no la vio, a pesar de que era tan real, tan humana, que en alguna ocasión le pidió a Amaranta el favor de que le ensartara una aguja. La muerte no le dijo cuándo se iba a morir ni si su hora estaba señalada antes que la de Rebeca, sino que le ordenó empezar a tejer su propia mortaja el próximo seis de abril. La autorizó para que la hiciera tan complicada y primorosa como ella quisiera, pero tan honradamente como hizo la de Rebeca, y le advirtió que había de morir sin dolor, ni miedo, ni amargura, al anochecer del día en que la terminara. Tratando de perder la mayor cantidad posible de tiempo, Amaranta encargó las hilazas de lino bayal y ella misma fabricó el lienzo. Lo hizo con tanto cuidado que solamente esa labor le llevó cuatro años. Luego inició el bordado. A medida que se aproximaba el término ineludible, iba comprendiendo que sólo un milagro le permitiría prolongar el trabajo más allá de la muerte de Rebeca, pero la misma concentración le proporcionó la calma que le hacía falta para aceptar la idea de una frustración. Fue entonces cuando entendió el círculo vicioso de los pescaditos de oro del coronel Aureliano Buendía. El mundo se redujo a la superficie de su piel, y el interior quedó a salvo de toda amargura. Le dolió no haber tenido aquella revelación muchos años antes, cuando aún fuera posible purificar los recuerdos y reconstruir el universo bajo una luz nueva, y evocar sin estremecerse el olor de espliego de Pietro Crespi al atardecer, y rescatar a Rebeca de su salsa de miseria, no por odio ni por amor, sino por la comprensión sin medidas de la soledad. El odio que advirtió una noche en las palabras de Meme no la conmovió porque la afectara, sino porque se sintió repetida en otra adolescencia que parecía tan limpia como debió parecer la suya y que, sin embargo, estaba ya viciada por el rencor. Pero entonces era tan honda la conformidad con su destino que ni siquiera la inquietó la certidumbre de que estaban cerradas todas las posibilidades de rectificación. Su único objetivo fue terminar la mortaja. En vez de retardarla con preciosismos inútiles, como lo hizo al principio, apresuró la labor. Una semana antes calculó que daría la última puntada en la noche del cuatro de febrero, y sin reve-

334

larle el motivo le sugirió a Meme que anticipara un concierto de clavicordio que tenía previsto para el día siguiente, pero ella no le hizo caso. Amaranta buscó entonces la manera de retrasarse cuarenta y ocho horas, y hasta pensó que la muerte la estaba complaciendo, porque en la noche del cuatro de febrero una tempestad descompuso la planta eléctrica. Pero al día siguiente, a las ocho de la mañana, dio la última puntada en la labor más primorosa que mujer alguna había terminado jamás, y anunció sin el menor dramatismo que moriría al atardecer. No sólo previno a la familia, sino a toda la población, porque Amaranta se había hecho a la idea de que se podía reparar una vida de mezquindad con un último favor al mundo, y pensó que ninguno era mejor que llevarles cartas a los muertos.

La noticia de que Amaranta Buendía zarpaba al crepúsculo llevando el correo de la muerte se divulgó en Macondo antes del mediodía, y a las tres de la tarde había en la sala un cajón lleno de cartas. Quienes no quisieron escribir le dieron a Amaranta recados verbales que ella anotó en una libreta con el nombre y la fecha de muerte del destinatario. «No se preocupe», tranquilizaba a los remitentes. «Lo primero que haré al llegar será preguntar por él, y le daré su recado.» Parecía una farsa. Amaranta no revelaba trastorno alguno, ni el más leve signo de dolor, y hasta se notaba un poco rejuvenecida por el deber cumplido. Estaba tan derecha y esbelta como siempre. De no haber sido por los pómulos endurecidos y la falta de algunos dientes habría parecido mucho menos vieja de lo que era en realidad. Ella misma dispuso que se metieran las cartas en una caja embreada, e indicó la manera como debía colocarse en la tumba para preservarla mejor de la humedad. En la mañana había llamado a un carpintero que le tomó las medidas para el ataúd, de pie, en la sala, como si fueran para un vestido. Se le despertó tal dinamismo en las últimas horas que Fernanda creyó que se estaba burlando de todos. Úrsula, con la experiencia de que los Buendía se morían sin enfermedad, no puso en duda que Amaranta había tenido el presagio de la muerte, pero en todo caso la atormentó el temor de que en el trajín de las cartas y la ansiedad de que llegaran pronto, los ofuscados remitentes la fueran a enterrar viva. Así que se empeñó en despejar la casa, disputándose a gritos con los intrusos, y a las cuatro de la tarde lo había conseguido. A esa hora, Amaranta acababa de repartir sus cosas entre los pobres, y sólo había dejado sobre el severo ataúd de tablas sin pulir la muda de ropa y las sencillas babuchas de pana que había de llevar en la muerte. No pasó por alto esa precaución, al recordar que cuando murió el coronel Aureliano Buendía hubo que comprarle un par de zapatos nuevos, porque ya sólo le quedaban las pantuflas que usaba en el taller. Poco antes de las cinco, Aureliano Segundo fue a buscar a Meme para el concierto, y se sorprendió de que la casa estuviera preparada para el funeral. Si alguien parecía vivo a esa hora era la serena Amaranta, a quien el tiempo le había alcanzado hasta para rebanarse los callos. Aureliano Segundo y Meme se despidieron de ella con adioses de burla, y le prometieron que el sábado siguiente harían la parranda de la resurrección. Atraído por las voces públicas de que Amaranta Buendía estaba recibiendo cartas para los muertos, el padre Antonio Isabel llegó a las cinco con el viático, y tuvo que esperar más de quince minutos a que la moribunda saliera del baño. Cuando la vio aparecer con un camisón de madapolán y el cabello suelto en la espalda, el decrépito párroco creyó que era una burla, y despachó al monaguillo. Pensó, sin embargo, aprovechar la ocasión para confesar a Amaranta después de casi veinte años de reticencia. Amaranta replicó, sencillamente, que no necesitaba asistencia espiritual de ninguna clase porque tenía la conciencia limpia. Fernanda se escandalizó. Sin cuidarse de que no la oyeran, se preguntó en voz alta qué espantoso pecado habría cometido Amaranta cuando prefería una muerte sacrílega a la vergüenza de una confesión. Entonces Amaranta se acostó, y obligó a Úrsula a dar testimonio público de su virginidad.

—Que nadie se haga ilusiones —gritó, para que la oyera Fernanda—. Amaranta Buendía se va de este mundo como vino.

No se volvió a levantar. Recostada en almohadones, como si de veras estuviera enferma, tejió sus largas trenzas y se las enrolló sobre las orejas, como la muerte le había dicho que debía estar en el ataúd. Luego le pidió a Úrsula un espejo, y por primera vez en más de cuarenta años vio su rostro devastado por la edad y el martirio, y se sorprendió de cuánto se parecía a la imagen mental que tenía de sí misma. Úrsula comprendió por el silencio de la alcoba que había empezado a oscurecer.

—Despídete de Fernanda —le suplicó—. Un minuto de reconciliación tiene más mérito que toda una vida de amistad.

—Ya no vale la pena —replicó Amaranta.

Meme no pudo no pensar en ella cuando encendieron las luces del improvisado escenario y empezó la segunda parte del programa. A mitad de la pieza alguien le dio la noticia al oído, y el acto se suspendió. Cuando llegó a la casa, Aureliano Segundo tuvo que abrirse paso a empujones por entre la muchedumbre, para ver el cadáver de la anciana doncella, fea y de mal color, con la venda negra en la mano y envuelta en la mortaja primorosa. Estaba expuesto en la sala junto al cajón del correo.

Úrsula no volvió a levantarse después de las nueve noches de Amaranta. <u>Santa Sofía de la Piedad</u> se hizo cargo de ella. Le llevaba al dormitorio la comida, y el agua de bija para que se lavara, y la mantenía al corriente de cuanto pasaba en Macondo. Aureliano Segundo la visitaba con frecuencia, y llevaba ropas que ella ponía cerca de la cama, junto con las cosas más indispensables para el vivir diario, de modo que en poco tiempo se había construido un mundo al alcance de la mano. Logró despertar un gran afecto en la pequeña Amaranta Úrsula, que era idéntica a ella, y a quien enseñó a leer. Su lucidez, la habilidad para bastarse a sí misma, hacían pensar que estaba naturalmente vencida por el peso de los cien años, pero aunque era evidente que andaba mal de la vista nadie sospechó que estaba completamente ciega. Disponía entonces de tanto tiempo y de tanto silencio interior para vigilar la vida de la casa, que fue ella la primera en darse cuenta de la callada tribulación de Meme.

—Ven acá —le dijo—. Ahora que estamos solas, confiésale a esta pobre vieja lo que te pasa.

Meme eludió la conversación con una risa entrecortada. Úrsula no insistió, pero acabó de confirmar sus sospechas cuando Meme no volvió a visitarla. Sabía que se arreglaba más temprano que de costumbre, que no tenía un instante de sosiego mientras esperaba la hora de salir a la calle, que pasaba noches enteras dando vueltas en la cama en el dormitorio contiguo, y que la atormentaba el revoloteo de una mariposa. En cierta ocasión le oyó decir que iba a verse con Aureliano Segundo, y Úrsula se sorprendió de que Fernanda fuera tan corta de imaginación que no sospechó nada cuando su marido fue a la casa a preguntar por la hija. Era demasiado evidente que Meme andaba en asuntos sigilosos, en compromisos urgentes, en ansiedades reprimidas, desde mucho antes de la noche en que Fernanda alborotó la casa porque la encontró besándose con un hombre en el cine.

La propia Meme andaba entonces tan ensimismada que acusó a Úrsula de haberla denunciado. En realidad se denunció a sí misma. Desde hacía tiempo dejaba a su paso un reguero de pistas que habrían despertado al más dormido, y si Fernanda tardó tanto en descubrirlas fue porque también ella estaba obnubilada por sus relaciones secretas con los médicos invisibles. Aun así terminó por advertir los hondos silencios, los sobresaltos intempestivos, las alternativas del humor y las contradicciones de la hija. Se empeñó en una vigilancia disimulada pero implacable. La dejó ir con sus amigas de siempre, la ayudó a vestirse para las fiestas del sábado, y jamás le hizo una pregunta impertinente que pudiera alertarla. Tenía ya muchas pruebas de que Meme hacía cosas distintas de las que anunciaba, y todavía no dejó vislumbrar sus sospechas, en espera de la ocasión decisiva. Una noche, Meme le anunció que iba al cine con su padre. Poco después, Fernanda oyó los cohetes de la parranda y el inconfundible acordeón de Aureliano Segundo por el rumbo de Petra Cotes. Entonces se vistió, entró al cine, y en la penumbra de las lunetas reconoció a su hija. La aturdidora emoción del acierto le impidió ver al hombre con quien se estaba besando, pero alcanzó a percibir su voz trémula en medio de la rechifla y las risotadas ensordecedoras del público. «Lo siento, amor», le oyó decir, y sacó a Meme del salón sin decirle una palabra, y la sometió a la vergüenza de llevarla por la bulliciosa Calle de los Turcos, y la encerró con llave en el dormitorio.

Al día siguiente, a las seis de la tarde, Fernanda reconoció la voz del hombre que fue a visitarla. Era joven, cetrino, con unos ojos oscuros y melancólicos que no le habrían sorprendido tanto si hubiera conocido a los gitanos, y un aire de ensueño que a cualquier mujer de corazón menos rígido le habría bastado para entender los motivos de su hija. Vestía de lino muy usado, con zapatos defendidos desesperadamente con cortezas superpuestas de blanco de zinc, y llevaba en la mano un canotier comprado el último sábado. En su vida no estuvo ni estaría más asustado que en aquel momento, pero tenía una dignidad y un dominio que lo ponían a salvo de la humillación, y una prestancia legítima que sólo fracasaba en las manos percudidas y las uñas astilladas por el trabajo rudo. A Fernanda, sin embargo, le bastó el verlo una vez para intuir su condición de menestral. Se dio cuenta de que llevaba puesta su única muda de los domingos, y que debajo de la camisa tenía la piel carcomida por la sarna de la compañía bananera. No le permitió hablar. No le permitió siquiera pasar de la puerta que un momento después tuvo que cerrar porque la casa estaba llena de mariposas amarillas.

—Lárguese —le dijo—. Nada tiene que venir a buscar entre la gente decente.

Se llamaba Mauricio Babilonia. Había nacido y crecido en Macondo, y era aprendiz de mecánico en los talleres de la compañía bananera. Meme lo había conocido por casualidad, una tarde en que fue con Patricia Brown a buscar el automóvil para dar un paseo por las plantaciones. Como el chofer estaba enfermo, lo encargaron a él de conducirlas, y Meme pudo al fin satisfacer su deseo de sentarse junto al volante para observar de cerca el sistema de manejo. Al contrario del chofer titular, Mauricio Babilonia le hizo una demostración práctica. Eso fue por la época en que Meme empezó a frecuentar la casa del señor Brown, y todavía se consideraba indigno de damas el conducir un automóvil. Así que se conformó con la información teórica y no volvió a ver a Mauricio Babilonia en varios meses. Más tarde había de recordar que durante el paseo le llamó la atención su belleza varonil, salvo la brutalidad de las manos, pero que después había comentado con Patricia Brown la molestia que le produjo su seguridad un poco altanera. El primer sábado en que fue al cine con su padre, volvió a ver a Mauricio Babilonia con su muda de lino, sentado a poca distancia de ellos, y advirtió que él se desinteresaba de la película por volverse a mirarla, no tanto por verla como para que ella notara que la estaba mirando. A Meme le molestó la vulgaridad de aquel sistema. Al final, Mauricio Babilonia se acercó a saludar a Aureliano Segundo, y sólo entonces se enteró Meme de que se conocían, porque él había trabajado en la primitiva planta eléctrica de Aureliano Triste, y trataba a su padre con una actitud de subalterno. Esa comprobación la alivió del disgusto que le causaba su altanería. No se habían visto a solas, ni se habían cruzado una palabra distinta del saludo, la noche en que soñó que él la salvaba de un naufragio y ella no experimentaba un sentimiento de gratitud sino de rabia. Era como haberle dado una oportunidad que él deseaba, siendo que Meme anhelaba lo contrario, no sólo con Mauricio Babilonia, sino con cualquier otro hombre que se interesara en ella. Por eso le indignó tanto que después del sueño, en vez de detestarlo, hubiera experimentado una urgencia irresistible de verlo. La ansiedad se hizo más intensa en el curso de la semana, y el sábado era tan apremiante que tuvo que hacer un grande esfuerzo para que Mauricio Babilonia no notara al saludarla en el cine que se le estaba saliendo el corazón por la boca. Ofuscada por una confusa sensación de placer y rabia, le tendió la mano por primera vez, y sólo entonces Mauricio Babilonia se permitió estrechársela. Meme alcanzó en una fracción de segundo a arrepentirse de su impulso, pero el arrepentimiento se transformó de inmediato en una satisfacción cruel, al comprobar que también la mano de él estaba sudorosa y helada. Esa noche comprendió que no tendría un instante de sosiego mientras no le demostrara a Mauricio Babilonia la vanidad de su aspiración, y pasó la semana revoloteando en torno de esa ansiedad. Recurrió a toda clase de artimañas inútiles para que Patricia Brown la llevara a buscar el automóvil. Por último, se valió del pelirrojo norteamericano que por esa época fue a pasar vacaciones en Macondo, y con el pretexto de conocer los nuevos modelos de automóviles se hizo llevar a los talleres. Desde el momento en que lo vio, Meme dejó de engañarse a sí misma, y comprendió que lo que pasaba en realidad era que no podía soportar los deseos de estar a solas con Mauricio Babilonia, y la indignó la certidumbre de que éste lo había comprendido al verla llegar.

—Vine a ver los nuevos modelos —dijo Meme.

—Es un buen pretexto —dijo él.

Meme se dio cuenta de que se estaba achicharrando en la lumbre de su altivez, y buscó desesperadamente una manera de humillarlo. Pero él no le dio tiempo «No se asuste», le dijo en voz baja. «No es la primera vez que una mujer se vuelve loca por un hombre.» Se sintió tan desamparada que abandonó el taller sin ver los nuevos modelos, y pasó la noche de extremo a extremo dando vueltas en la cama y llorando de indignación. El pelirrojo norteamericano, que en realidad empezaba a interesarle, le pareció una criatura en pañales. Fue entonces cuando cayó en la cuenta de las mariposas amarillas que precedían las apariciones de Mauricio Babilonia. Las había visto antes, sobre todo en el taller de mecánica, y había pensado que estaban fascinadas por el olor de la pintura. Alguna vez las había sentido revoloteando sobre su cabeza en la penumbra del cine. Pero cuando Mauricio Babilonia empezó a perseguirla, como un espectro que sólo ella identificaba en la multitud, comprendió que las mariposas amarillas tenían algo que ver con él. Mauricio Babilonia estaba siempre en el público de los conciertos, en el cine, en la misa mayor, y ella no necesitaba verlo para descubrirlo, porque se lo indicaban las mariposas. Una vez Aureliano Segundo se impacientó tanto con el sofocante aleteo, que ella sintió el impulso de confiarle su secreto, como se lo había prometido, pero el instinto le indicó que esta vez él no iba a reír como de costumbre: «Qué diría tu madre si lo supiera.» Una mañana, mientras podaban las rosas, Fernanda lanzó un grito de espanto e hizo quitar a Meme del lugar en que estaba, y que era el mismo del jardín donde subió a los cielos Remedios, la bella. Había tenido por un instante la impresión de que el milagro iba a repetirse en su hija, porque la había perturbado un repentino aleteo. Eran las mariposas. Meme las vio, como si hubieran nacido de pronto en la luz, y el corazón le dio un vuelco. En ese momento entraba Mauricio Babilonia con un paquete que, según dijo, era un regalo de Patricia Brown. Meme se atragantó el rubor, asimiló la tribulación, y hasta consiguió una sonrisa natural para pedirle el favor de que lo pusiera en el pasamanos porque tenía los dedos sucios de tierra. Lo único que notó Fernanda en el hombre que pocos meses después había de expulsar de la casa sin recordar que lo hubiera visto alguna vez fue la textura biliosa de su piel.

—Es un hombre muy raro —dijo Fernanda—. Se le ve en la cara que se va a morir.

Meme pensó que su madre había quedado impresionada por las mariposas. Cuando acabaron de podar el rosal, se lavó las manos y llevó el paquete al dormitorio para abrirlo. Era una especie de juguete chino, compuesto por cinco cajas concéntricas, y en la última una tarjeta laboriosamente dibujada por alguien que apenas sabía escribir: *Nos vemos el sábado en el cine*. Meme sintió el estupor tardío de que la caja hubiera estado tanto tiempo en el pasamanos al alcance de la curiosidad de Fernanda, y aunque la halagaba la audacia y el ingenio de Mauricio Babilonia, la conmovió su ingenuidad de esperar que ella le cumpliera la cita. Meme sabía desde entonces que Aureliano Segundo tenía un compromiso el sábado en la noche. Sin embargo, el fuego de la ansiedad la abrasó de tal modo en el curso de la semana, que el sábado convenció a su padre de que la dejara sola en el teatro y volviera por ella al terminar la función. Una mariposa nocturna revoloteó sobre su cabeza mientras las luces estuvieron encendidas. Y entonces ocurrió. Cuando las luces se apagaron, Mauricio Babilonia se sentó a su lado. Meme se sintió chapaleando en un tremedal de zozobra, del cual sólo podía rescatarla, como había ocurrido en el sueño, aquel hombre oloroso a aceite de motor que apenas distinguía en la penumbra.

—Si no hubiera venido —dijo él—, no me hubiera visto más nunca.

Meme sintió el peso de su mano en la rodilla, y supo que ambos llegaban en aquel instante al otro lado del desamparo.

—Lo que me choca de ti —sonrió— es que siempre dices precisamente lo que no se debe.

Se volvió loca por él. Perdió el sueño y el apetito, y se hundió tan profundamente en la soledad, que hasta su padre se le convirtió en un estorbo. Elaboró un intrincado enredo de compromisos falsos para desorientar a Fernanda, perdió de vista a sus amigas, saltó por encima de los convencionalismos para verse con Mauricio Babilonia a cualquier hora y en cualquier parte. Al principio le molestaba su rudeza. La primera vez que se vieron a solas, en los prados desiertos detrás del taller de mecánica, él la arrastró sin misericordia a un estado animal que la dejó extenuada. Tardó algún tiempo en darse cuenta de que también aquella era una forma de la ternura, y fue entonces cuando perdió el sosiego, y no vivía sino para él, trastornada por la ansiedad de hundirse en su entorpecedor aliento de aceite refregado con lejía.

Poco antes de la muerte de Amaranta tropezó de pronto con un espacio de lucidez dentro de la locura, y tembló ante la incertidumbre del porvenir. Entonces oyó hablar de una mujer que hacía pronósticos de barajas, y fue a visitarla en secreto. Era Pilar Ternera. Desde que ésta la vio entrar, conoció los recónditos motivos de Meme. «Siéntate», le dijo. «No necesito de barajas para averiguar el porvenir de un Buendía.» Meme ignoraba, y lo ignoró siempre, que aquella pitonisa centenaria era su bisabuela. Tampoco lo hubiera creído después del agresivo realismo con que ella le reveló que la ansiedad del enamoramiento no encontraba reposo sino en la cama. Era el mismo punto de vista de Mauricio Babilonia, pero Meme se resistía a darle crédito, pues en el fondo suponía que estaba inspirado en un mal criterio de menestral. Ella pensaba entonces que el amor de un modo derrotaba al amor de otro modo, porque estaba en la índole de los hombres repudiar el hambre una vez satisfecho el apetito. Pilar Ternera no sólo disipó el error, sino que le ofreció la vieja cama de lienzo donde ella concibió a Arcadio, el abuelo de Meme, y donde concibió después a Aureliano José. Le enseñó además cómo prevenir la concepción indeseable mediante la vaporización de cataplasmas de mostaza, y le dio recetas de bebedizos que en casos de percances hacían expulsar «hasta los remordimientos de conciencia». Aquella entrevista le infundió a Meme el mismo sentimiento de valentía que experimentó la tarde de la borrachera. La muerte de Amaranta, sin embargo, la obligó a aplazar la decisión. Mientras duraron las nueve noches, ella no se apartó un instante de Mauricio Babilonia, que andaba confundido con la muchedumbre que invadió la casa. Vinieron luego el luto prolongado y el encierro obligatorio, y se separaron por un tiempo. Fueron días de tanta agitación interior, de tanta ansiedad irreprimible y tantos anhelos reprimidos, que la primera tarde en que Meme logró salir fue directamente a la casa de Pilar Ternera. Se entregó a Mauricio Babilonia sin resistencia, sin pudor, sin formalismos, y con una vocación tan fluida y una intuición tan sabia, que un hombre más suspicaz que el suyo hubiera podido confundirlas con una acendrada experiencia. Se amaron dos veces por semana durante más de tres meses, protegidos por la complicidad inocente de Aureliano Segundo, que acreditaba sin malicia las coartadas de la hija, sólo por verla liberada de la rigidez de su madre.

La noche en que Fernanda los sorprendió en el cine, Aureliano Segundo se sintió agobiado por el peso de la conciencia, y visitó a Meme en el dormitorio donde la encerró Fernanda, confiando en que ella se desahogaría con él de las confidencias que le estaba debiendo. Pero Meme lo negó todo. Estaba tan segura de sí misma, tan aferrada a su soledad, que Aureliano Segundo tuvo la impresión de que ya no existía ningún vínculo entre ellos, que la camaradería y la complicidad no eran más que una ilusión del pasado. Pensó hablar con Mauricio Babilonia, creyendo que su autoridad de antiguo patrón lo haría desistir de sus propósitos, pero Petra Cotes lo convenció de que aquellos eran asuntos de mujeres, así que quedó flotando en un limbo de indecisión, y apenas sostenido por la esperanza de que el encierro terminara con las tribulaciones de la hija.

Meme no dio muestra alguna de aflicción. Al contrario, desde el dormitorio contiguo percibió

Úrsula el ritmo sosegado de su sueño, la serenidad de sus quehaceres, el orden de sus comidas y la buena salud de su digestión. Lo único que intrigó a Úrsula después de casi dos meses de castigo, fue que Meme no se bañara en la mañana, como lo hacían todos, sino a las siete de la noche. Alguna vez pensó prevenirla contra los alacranes, pero Meme era tan esquiva con ella por la convicción de que la había denunciado, que prefirió no perturbarla con impertinencias de tatarabuela. Las mariposas amarillas invadían la casa desde el atardecer. Todas las noches, al regresar del baño, Meme encontraba a Fernanda desesperada, matando mariposas con la bomba de insecticida. «Esto es una desgracia», decía. «Toda la vida me contaron que las mariposas nocturnas llaman la mala suerte.» Una noche, mientras Meme estaba en el baño, Fernanda entró en su dormitorio por casualidad, y había tantas mariposas que apenas se podía respirar. Agarró cualquier trapo para espantarlas, y el corazón se le heló de pavor al relacionar los baños nocturnos de su hija con las cataplasmas de mostaza que rodaron por el suelo. No esperó un momento oportuno, como lo hizo la primera vez. Al día siguiente invitó a almorzar al nuevo alcalde, que como ella había bajado de los páramos, y le pidió que estableciera una guardia nocturna en el traspatio, porque tenía la impresión de que se estaban robando las gallinas. Esa noche, la guardia derribó a Mauricio Babilonia cuando levantaba las tejas para entrar en el baño donde Meme lo esperaba, desnuda y temblando de amor entre los alacranes y las mariposas, como lo había hecho casi todas las noches de los últimos meses. Un proyectil incrustado en la columna vertebral lo redujo a cama por el resto de su vida. Murió de viejo en la soledad, sin un quejido, sin una protesta, sin una sola tentativa de infidencia, atormentado por los recuerdos y por las mariposas amarillas que no le concedieron un instante de paz, y públicamente repudiado como ladrón de gallinas.

Los acontecimientos que habían de darle el golpe mortal a Macondo empezaban a vislumbrarse cuando llevaron a la casa al hijo de Meme Buendía. La situación pública era entonces tan incierta, que nadie tenía el espíritu dispuesto para ocuparse de escándalos privados, de modo que Fernanda contó con un ambiente propicio para mantener al niño escondido como si no hubiera existido nunca. Tuvo que recibirlo, porque las circunstancias en que se lo llevaron no hacían posible el rechazo. Tuvo que soportarlo contra su voluntad por el resto de su vida, porque a la hora de la verdad le faltó valor para cumplir la íntima determinación de ahogarlo en la alberca del baño. Lo encerró en el antiguo taller del coronel Aureliano Buendía. A Santa Sofía de la Piedad logró convencerla de que lo había encontrado flotando en una canastilla. Úrsula había de morir sin conocer su origen. La pequeña Amaranta Úrsula, que entró una vez al taller cuando Fernanda estaba alimentando al niño, también creyó en la versión de la canastilla flotante. Aureliano Segundo, definitivamente distanciado de la esposa por la forma irracional en que ésta manejó la tragedia de Meme, no supo de la existencia del nieto sino tres años después de que lo llevaron a la casa, cuando el niño escapó al cautiverio por un descuido de Fernanda, y se asomó al corredor por una fracción de segundo, desnudo y con los pelos enmarañados y con un impresionante sexo de moco de pavo, como si no fuera una criatura humana sino la definición enciclopédica de un antropófago.

Fernanda no contaba con aquella trastada de su incorregible destino. El niño fue como el regreso de una vergüenza que ella creía haber desterrado para siempre de la casa. Apenas se habían llevado a Mauricio Babilonia con la espina dorsal fracturada, y ya había concebido Fernanda hasta el detalle más ínfimo de un plan destinado a eliminar todo vestigio del oprobio. Sin consultarlo con su marido, hizo al día siguiente su equipaje, metió en una maletita las tres mudas que su hija podía necesitar, y fue a buscarla al dormitorio media hora antes de la llegada del tren.

—Vamos, Renata —le dijo.

No le dio ninguna explicación. Meme, por su parte, no la esperaba ni la quería. No sólo ignoraba para dónde iban, sino que le habría dado igual si la hubieran llevado al matadero. No había vuelto a hablar, ni lo haría en el resto de su vida, desde que oyó el disparo en el traspatio y el simultáneo aullido de dolor de Mauricio Babilonia. Cuando su madre le ordenó salir del dormitorio, no se peinó ni se lavó la cara, y subió al tren como un sonámbulo sin advertir siquiera las mariposas amarillas que seguían acompañándola. Fernanda no supo nunca, ni se tomó el trabajo de averiguarlo, si su silencio pétreo era una determinación de su voluntad, o si se había quedado muda por el impacto de la tragedia. Meme apenas se dio cuenta del viaje a través de la antigua región encantada. No vio las umbrosas e interminables plantaciones de banano a ambos lados de las líneas. No vio las casas blancas de los gringos, ni sus jardines aridecidos por el polvo y el calor, ni las mujeres con pantalones cortos y camisas de rayas azules que jugaban barajas en los pórticos. No vio las carretas de bueyes cargadas de racimos en los caminos polvorientos. No vio las doncellas que saltaban como sábalos en los ríos transparentes para dejarles a los pasajeros del tren la amargura de sus senos espléndidos, ni las barracas abigarradas y miserables de los trabajadores donde revoloteaban las mariposas amarillas de Mauricio Babilonia, y en cuyos portales había niños verdes y escuálidos sentados en sus bacinillas, y mujeres embarazadas que gritaban improperios al paso del tren. Aquella visión fugaz, que para ella era una fiesta cuando regresaba del colegio, pasó por el corazón de Meme sin despabilarlo. No miró a través de la ventanilla ni siquiera cuando se acabó la humedad ardiente de las plantaciones, y el tren pasó por la llanura de amapolas donde estaba todavía el costillar carbonizado del galeón español, y salió luego al mismo aire diáfano y al mismo mar espumoso y sucio donde casi un siglo antes fracasaron las ilusiones de José Arcadio Buendía.

A las cinco de la tarde, cuando llegaron a la estación final de la ciénaga, descendió del tren porque Fernanda lo hizo. Subieron a un cochecito que parecía un murciélago enorme, tirado por un caballo asmático, y atravesaron la ciudad desolada, en cuyas calles interminables y cuarteadas por el salitre, resonaba un ejercicio de piano igual al que escuchó Fernanda en las siestas de su adolescencia. Se embarcaron en un buque fluvial, cuya rueda de madera hacía un ruido de conflagración, y cuyas láminas de hierro carcomidas por el óxido reverberaban como la boca de un horno. Meme se encerró en el camarote. Dos veces al día dejaba Fernanda un plato de comida junto a la cama, y dos veces al día se lo llevaba intacto, no porque Meme hubiera resuelto morirse de hambre, sino porque le repugnaba el solo olor de los alimentos y su estómago expulsaba hasta el agua. Ni ella misma sabía entonces que su fertilidad había burlado a los vapores de mostaza, así como Fernanda no lo supo hasta casi un año después, cuando le llevaron al niño. En el camarote sofocante, trastornada por la vibración de las paredes de hierro y por el tufo insoportable del cieno removido por la rueda del buque, Meme perdió la cuenta de los días. Había pasado mucho tiempo cuando vio la última mariposa amarilla destrozándose en las aspas del ventilador y admitió como una verdad irremediable que Mauricio Babilonia había muerto. Sin embargo, no se dejó vencer por la resignación. Seguía pensando en él durante la penosa travesía a lomo de mula por el páramo alucinante donde se perdió Aureliano Segundo cuando buscaba a la mujer más hermosa que se había dado sobre la tierra, y cuando remontaron la cordillera por caminos de indios y entraron a la ciudad lúgubre en cuyos vericuetos de piedra resonaban los bronces funerarios de treinta y dos iglesias. Esa noche durmieron en la abandonada mansión colonial, sobre los tablones que Fernanda puso en el suelo de un aposento invadido por la maleza, y arropadas con piltrafas de cortinas que arrancaron de las ventanas y que se desmigaban a cada vuelta del cuerpo. Meme supo dónde estaban porque en el espanto del insomnio vio pasar al caballero vestido de negro que en una distante víspera de Navidad llevaron a la casa dentro de un cofre de plomo. Al día siguiente, después de misa, Fernanda la condujo a un edificio sombrío que Meme reconoció de inmediato por las evocaciones que su madre solía hacer del convento donde la educaron para reina, y entonces comprendió que había llegado al término del viaje. Mientras Fernanda hablaba con alguien en el despacho contiguo, ella se quedó en un salón ajedrezado con grandes óleos de arzobispos coloniales, temblando de frío, porque llevaba todavía un traje de etamina con florecitas negras y los duros borceguíes hinchados por el hielo del páramo. Estaba de pie en el centro del salón, pensando en Mauricio Babilonia bajo el chorro amarillo de los vitrales, cuando salió del despacho una novicia muy bella que llevaba su maletita con las tres mudas de ropa. Al pasar junto a Meme le tendió la mano sin detenerse.

—Vamos, Renata —le dijo.

Meme le tomó la mano y se dejó llevar. La última vez que Fernanda la vio, tratando de igualar su paso con el de la novicia, acababa de cerrarse detrás de ella el rastrillo de hierro de la clausura. Todavía pensaba en Mauricio Babilonia, en su olor de aceite y su ámbito de mariposas, y seguiría pensando en él todos los días de su vida, hasta la remota madrugada de otoño en que muriera de vejez, con sus nombres cambiados y sin haber dicho nunca una palabra, en un tenebroso hospital de Cracovia.

Fernanda regresó a Macondo en un tren protegido por policías armados. Durante el viaje advirtió la tensión de los pasajeros, los aprestos militares en los pueblos de la línea y el aire enrarecido por la certidumbre de que algo grave iba a suceder, pero careció de información mientras no llegó a Macondo y le contaron que José Arcadio Segundo estaba incitando a la huelga a los trabajadores de la compañía bananera. «Esto es lo último que nos faltaba», se dijo Fernanda. «Un anarquista en la familia.» La huelga estalló dos semanas después y no tuvo las consecuencias dramáticas que se temían. Los obreros aspiraban a que no se les obligara a cortar y embarcar banano los domingos, y la petición pareció tan justa que hasta el padre Antonio Isabel intercedió en favor de ella porque la encontró de acuerdo con la ley de Dios. El triunfo de la acción, así como de otras que se promovieron en los meses siguientes, sacó del anonimato al descolorido José Arcadio Segundo, de quien solía decirse que sólo había servido para llenar el pueblo de putas francesas. Con la misma decisión impulsiva con que remató sus gallos de pelea para establecer una empresa de navegación desatinada, había renunciado al cargo de capataz de cuadrilla de la compañía bananera y tomó el partido de los trabajadores. Muy pronto se le señaló como agente de una conspiración internacional contra el orden público. Una noche, en el curso de una semana oscurecida por rumores sombríos, escapó de milagro a cuatro tiros de revólver que le hizo un desconocido cuando salía de una reunión secreta. Fue tan tensa la atmósfera de los meses siguientes, que hasta Úrsula la percibió en su rincón de tinieblas, y tuvo la impresión de estar viviendo de nuevo los tiempos azarosos en que su hijo Aureliano cargaba en el bolsillo los glóbulos homeopáticos de la subversión. Trató de hablar con José Arcadio Segundo para enterarlo de ese precedente, pero Aureliano Segundo le informó que desde la noche del atentado se ignoraba su paradero.

—Lo mismo que Aureliano —exclamó Úrsula—. Es como si el mundo estuviera dando vueltas.

Fernanda permaneció inmune a la incertidumbre de esos días. Carecía de contactos con el mundo exterior desde el violento altercado que tuvo con su marido por haber determinado la suerte de Meme sin su consentimiento. Aureliano Segundo estaba dispuesto a rescatar a su hija, con la policía si era necesario, pero Fernanda le hizo ver papeles en los que se demostraba que había ingresado a la clausura por propia voluntad. En efecto, Meme los había firmado cuando ya estaba del otro lado del rastrillo de hierro, y lo hizo con el mismo desdén con que se dejó conducir. En el fondo, Aureliano Segundo no creyó en la legitimidad de las pruebas, como no creyó nunca que Mauricio Babilonia se hubiera metido al patio para robar gallinas, pero ambos expedientes le sirvieron para tranquilizar la conciencia, y pudo entonces volver sin remordimientos a la sombra de Petra Cotes, donde reanudó las parrandas ruidosas y las comilonas desaforadas. Ajena a la inquietud del pueblo, sorda a los tremendos pronósticos de Úrsula, Fernanda le dio la última vuelta a las tuercas de su plan consumado. Le escribió una extensa carta a su hijo José Arcadio, que ya iba a recibir las órdenes menores, y en ella le comunicó que su hermana Renata había expirado en la paz del Señor a consecuencia del vómito negro. Luego puso a Amaranta Úrsula al cuidado de Santa Sofía de la Piedad, y se dedicó a organizar su correspondencia con los médicos invisibles, trastornada por el percance de Meme. Lo primero que hizo fue fijar fecha definitiva para la aplazada intervención telepática. Pero los médicos invisibles le contestaron que no era prudente mientras persistiera el estado de agitación social en Macondo. Ella estaba tan urgida y tan mal informada, que les explicó en otra carta que no había tal estado de agitación, y que todo era fruto de las locuras de un cuñado suyo, que andaba por esos días con la ventolera sindical, como padeció en otro tiempo las de la gallera y la navegación. Aún no estaban de acuerdo el caluroso miércoles en que llamó a la puerta de la casa una monja anciana que llevaba una canastilla colgada del brazo. Al abrirle, Santa Sofía de la Piedad pensó que era un regalo y trató de quitarle la canastilla cubierta con un primoroso tapete de encaje. Pero la monja lo impidió, porque tenía instrucciones de entregársela personalmente, y bajo la reserva más estricta, a doña Fernanda del Carpio de Buendía. Era el hijo de Meme. El antiguo director espiritual de Fernanda le explicaba en una carta que había nacido dos meses antes, y que se habían permitido bautizarlo con el nombre de Aureliano, como su abuelo, porque la madre no despegó los labios para expresar su voluntad. Fernanda se sublevó íntimamente contra aquella burla del destino, pero tuvo fuerzas para disimularlo delante de la monja.

—Diremos que lo encontramos flotando en la canastilla —sonrió.

—No se lo creerá nadie —dijo la monja.

—Si se lo creyeron a las Sagradas Escrituras —replicó Fernanda—, no veo por qué no han de creérmelo a mí.

La monja almorzó en casa, mientras pasaba el tren de regreso, y de acuerdo con la discreción que le habían exigido no volvió a mencionar al niño, pero Fernanda la señaló como un testigo indeseable de su vergüenza, y lamentó que se hubiera desechado la costumbre medieval de ahorcar al mensajero de malas noticias. Fue entonces cuando decidió ahogar a la criatura en la alberca tan pronto como se fuera la monja, pero el corazón no le dio para tanto y prefirió esperar con paciencia a que la infinita bondad de Dios la liberara del estorbo.

El nuevo Aureliano había cumplido un año cuando la tensión pública estalló sin ningún anuncio. José Arcadio Segundo y otros dirigentes sindicales que habían permanecido hasta entonces en la clandestinidad aparecieron intempestivamente un fin de semana y promovieron manifestaciones en los pueblos de la zona bananera. La policía se conformó con vigilar el orden. Pero en la noche del lunes los dirigentes fueron sacados de sus casas y mandados con grillos de cinco kilos en los pies a la cárcel de la capital provincial. Entre ellos se llevaron a José Arcadio Segundo y a Lorenzo Gavilán, un coronel de la revolución mexicana, exiliado en Macondo, que decía haber sido testigo del heroísmo de su compadre Artemio Cruz. Sin embargo, antes de tres meses estaban en libertad, porque el gobierno y la compañía bananera no pudieron ponerse de acuerdo sobre quién debía alimentarlos en la cárcel. La inconformidad de los trabajadores se fundaba esta vez en la insalubridad de las viviendas, el engaño de los servicios médicos y la iniquidad de las condiciones de trabajo. Afirmaban, además, que no se les pagaba con dinero efectivo, sino con vales que sólo servían para comprar jamón de Virginia en los comisariatos de la compañía. José Arcadio Segundo fue encarcelado porque reveló que el sistema de los vales era un recurso de la compañía para financiar sus barcos fruteros, que de no haber sido por la mercancía de los comisariatos hubieran tenido que regresar vacíos desde Nueva Orleans hasta los puertos de embarque del banano. Los otros cargos eran del dominio público. Los médicos de la compañía no examinaban a los enfermos, sino que los hacían pararse en fila india frente a los dispensarios, y una enfermera les ponía en la lengua una píldora del color del piedralipe, así tuvieran paludismo, blenorragia o estreñimiento. Era una terapéutica tan generalizada, que los niños se ponían en la fila varias veces, y en vez de tragarse las píldoras se las llevaban a sus casas para señalar con ellas los numeros cantados en el juego de lotería. Los obreros de la compañía estaban hacinados en tambos miserables. Los ingenieros, en vez de construir letrinas, llevaban a los campamentos, por Navidad, un excusado portátil para cada cincuenta personas, y hacían demostraciones públicas de cómo utilizarlos para que duraran más. Los decrépitos abogados vestidos de negro que en otro tiempo asediaron al coronel Aureliano Buendía, y que entonces eran apoderados de la compañía bananera, desvirtuaban estos cargos con arbitrios que parecían cosa de magia. Cuando los trabajadores redactaron un pliego de peticiones unánime, pasó mucho tiempo sin que pudieran notificar oficialmente a la compañía bananera. Tan pronto como conoció el acuerdo, el señor Brown enganchó en el tren su suntuoso vagón de vidrio, y desapareció de Macondo junto con los representantes más conocidos de su empresa. Sin embargo, varios obreros encontraron a uno de ellos el sábado siguiente en un burdel, y le hicieron firmar una copia del pliego de peticiones cuando estaba desnudo con la mujer que se prestó para llevarlo a la trampa. Los luctuosos abogados demostraron en el juzgado que aquel hombre no tenía nada que ver con la compañía, y para que nadie pusiera en duda sus argumentos lo hicieron encarcelar por usurpador. Más tarde, el señor Brown fue sorprendido viajando de incógnito en un vagón de tercera clase, y le hicieron firmar otra copia del pliego de peticiones. Al día siguiente compareció ante los jueces con el pelo pintado de negro y hablando un castellano sin tropiezos. Los abogados demostraron que no era el señor Jack Brown, superintendente de la compañía bananera y nacido en Prattville, Alabama, sino un inofensivo vendedor de plantas medicinales, nacido en Macondo y allí mismo bautizado con el nombre de Dagoberto Fonseca. Poco después, frente a una nueva tentativa de los trabajadores, los abogados exhibieron en lugares públicos el certificado de defunción del señor Brown, autenticado por cónsules y cancilleres, y en el cual se daba fe de que el pasado nueve de junio había sido atropellado en Chicago por un carro de bomberos. Cansados de aquel delirio hermenéutico, los trabajadores repudiaron a las autoridades de Macondo y subieron con sus quejas a los tribunales supremos. Fue allí donde los ilusionistas del derecho demostraron que las reclamaciones carecían de toda validez, simplemente porque la compañía bananera no tenía, ni había tenido nunca ni tendría jamás trabajadores a su servicio, sino que los reclutaba ocasionalmente y con carácter temporal. De modo que se desbarató la patraña del jamón de Virginia, las píldoras milagrosas y los excusados pascuales, y se estableció por fallo de tribunal y se proclamó en bandos solemnes la inexistencia de los trabajadores.

La huelga grande estalló. Los cultivos se quedaron a medias, la fruta se pasó en las cepas y los trenes de ciento veinte vagones se pararon en los ramales. Los obreros ociosos desbordaron los pueblos. La Calle de los Turcos reverberó en un sábado de muchos días, y en el salón de billares del Hotel de Jacob hubo que establecer turnos de veinticuatro horas. Allí estaba José Arcadio Segundo, el día en que se anunció que el ejército había sido encargado de restablecer el orden público. Aunque no era hombre de presagios, la noticia fue para él como un anuncio de la muerte, que había esperado desde la mañana distante en que el coronel Gerineldo Márquez le permitió ver un fusilamiento. Sin embargo, el mal augurio no alteró su solemnidad. Hizo la jugada que tenía prevista y no erró la carambola. Poco después, las descargas de redoblante, los ladridos del clarín, los gritos y el tropel de la gente le indicaron que no sólo la partida de billar sino la callada y solitaria partida que jugaba consigo mismo desde la madrugada de la ejecución, habían por fin terminado. Entonces se asomó a la calle, y los vio. Eran tres regimientos cuya marcha pautada por tambor de galeotes hacía trepidar la tierra. Su resuello de dragón multicéfalo impregnó de un vapor pestilente la claridad del mediodía. Eran pequeños, macizos, brutos. Sudaban con sudor de caballo, y tenían un olor de carnaza macerada por el sol, y la impavidez taciturna e impenetrable de los hombres del páramo. Aunque tardaron más de una hora en pasar, hubiera podido pensarse que eran unas pocas escuadras girando en redondo, porque todos eran idénticos, hijos de la misma madre, y todos soportaban con igual estolidez el peso de los morrales y las cantimploras, y la vergüenza de los fusiles con las bayonetas caladas, y el incordio de la obediencia ciega y el sentido del honor. Úrsula los oyó pasar desde su lecho de tinieblas y levantó la mano con los dedos en cruz. Santa Sofía de la Piedad existió por un instante, inclinada sobre el mantel bordado que acababa de planchar, y pensó en su hijo, José Arcadio Segundo, que vio pasar sin inmutarse los últimos soldados por la puerta del Hotel de Jacob.

La ley marcial facultaba al ejército para asumir funciones de árbitro de la controversia, pero no se hizo ninguna tentativa de conciliación. Tan pronto como se exhibieron en Macondo, los soldados pusieron a un lado los fusiles, cortaron y embarcaron el banano y movilizaron los trenes. Los trabajadores, que hasta entonces se habían conformado con esperar, se echaron al monte sin más armas que sus machetes de labor, y empezaron a sabotear el sabotaje. Incendiaron fincas y comisariatos, destruyeron los rieles para impedir el tránsito de los trenes que empezaban a abrirse paso con fuego de ametralladoras, y cortaron los alambres del telégrafo y el teléfono. Las acequias se tiñeron de sangre. El señor Brown, que estaba vivo en el gallinero electrificado, fue sacado de Macondo con su familia y las de otros compatriotas suyos, y conducidos a territorio seguro bajo la protección del ejército. La situación amenazaba con evolucionar hacia una guerra civil desigual y sangrienta, cuando las autoridades hicieron un llamado a los trabajadores para que se concentraran en Macondo. El llamado anunciaba que el Jefe Civil y Militar de la provincia llegaría el viernes siguiente, dispuesto a interceder en el conflicto.

José Arcadio Segundo estaba entre la muchedumbre que se concentró en la estación desde la mañana del viernes. Había participado en una reunión de los dirigentes sindicales y había sido comisionado junto con el coronel Gavilán para confundirse con la multitud y orientarla según las circunstancias. No se sentía bien, y amasaba una pasta salitrosa en el paladar, desde que advirtió que el ejército había emplazado nidos de ametralladoras alrededor de la plazoleta, y que la ciudad alambrada de la compañía bananera estaba protegida con piezas de artillería. Hacia las doce, esperando un tren que no llegaba, más de tres mil personas, entre trabajadores, mujeres y niños, habían desbordado el espacio descubierto frente a la estación y se apretujaban en las calles adyacentes que el ejército cerró con filas de ametralladoras. Aquello parecía entonces, más que una recepción, una feria jubilosa. Habían trasladado los puestos de fritangas y las tiendas de bebidas de la Calle de los Turcos, y la gente soportaba con muy buen ánimo el fastidio de la espera y el sol abrasante. Un poco antes de las tres corrió el rumor de que el tren oficial no llegaría hasta el día siguiente. La muchedumbre cansada exhaló un suspiro de desaliento. Un teniente del ejército se subió entonces en el techo de la estación, donde había cuatro nidos de ametralladoras enfiladas hacia la multitud, y se dio un toque de silencio. Al lado de José Arcadio Segundo estaba una mujer descalza, muy gorda, con dos niños de unos cuatro y siete años. Cargó al menor, y le pidió a José Arcadio Segundo, sin conocerlo, que levantara al otro para que oyera mejor lo que iban a decir. José Arcadio Segundo se acaballó al niño en la nuca. Muchos años después, ese niño había de seguir contando, sin que nadie se lo creyera, que había visto al teniente leyendo con una bocina de gramófono el Decreto Número 4 del Jefe Civil y Militar de la provincia. Estaba firmado por el general Carlos Cortes

Vargas, y por su secretario, el mayor Enrique García Isaza, y en tres artículos de ochenta palabras declaraba a los huelguistas *cuadrilla de malhechores* y facultaba al ejército para matarlos a bala.

Leído el decreto, en medio de una ensordecedora rechifla de protesta, un capitán sustituyó al teniente en el techo de la estación, y con la bocina de gramófono hizo señas de que quería hablar. La muchedumbre volvió a guardar silencio.

—Señoras y señores —dijo el capitán con una voz baja, lenta, un poco cansada—, tienen cinco minutos para retirarse.

La rechifla y los gritos redoblados ahogaron el toque de clarín que anunció el principio del plazo. Nadie se movió.

—Han pasado cinco minutos —dijo el capitán en el mismo tono—. Un minuto más y se hará fuego.

José Arcadio Segundo, sudando hielo, se bajó al niño de los hombros y se lo entregó a la mujer. «Estos cabrones son capaces de disparar», murmuró ella. José Arcadio Segundo no tuvo tiempo de hablar, porque al instante reconoció la voz ronca del coronel Gavilán haciéndoles eco con un grito a las palabras de la mujer. Embriagado por la tensión, por la maravillosa profundidad del silencio y, además, convencido de que nada haría mover a aquella muchedumbre pasmada por la fascinación de la muerte, José Arcadio Segundo se empinó por encima de las cabezas que tenía enfrente, y por primera vez en su vida levantó la voz.

—¡Cabrones! —gritó—. Les regalamos el minuto que falta.

Al final de su grito ocurrió algo que no le produjo espanto, sino una especie de alucinación. El capitán dio la orden de fuego y catorce nidos de ametralladoras le respondieron en el acto. Pero todo parecía una farsa. Era como si las ametralladoras hubieran estado cargadas con engañifas de pirotecnia, porque se escuchaba su anhelante tableteo, y se veían sus escupitajos incandescentes, pero no se percibía la más leve reacción, ni una voz, ni siquiera un suspiro, entre la muchedumbre compacta que parecía petrificada por una invulnerabilidad instantánea. De pronto, a un lado de la estación, un grito de muerte desgarró el encantamiento: «Aaaay, mi madre.» Una fuerza sísmica, un aliento volcánico, un rugido de cataclismo, estallaron en el centro de la muchedumbre con una descomunal potencia expansiva. José Arcadio Segundo apenas tuvo tiempo de levantar al niño, mientras la madre con el otro era absorbida por la muchedumbre centrifugada por el pánico.

Muchos años después, el niño había de contar todavía, a pesar de que los vecinos seguían creyéndolo un viejo chiflado, que José Arcadio Segundo lo levantó por encima de su cabeza, y se dejó arrastrar, casi en el aire, como flotando en el terror de la muchedumbre, hacia una calle adyacente. La posición privilegiada del niño le permitió ver que en ese momento la masa desbocada empezaba a llegar a la esquina y la fila de ametralladoras abrió fuego. Varias voces gritaron al mismo tiempo:

—¡Tírense al suelo! ¡Tírense al suelo!

Ya los de las primeras líneas lo habían hecho, barridos por las ráfagas de metralla. Los sobrevivientes, en vez de tirarse al suelo, trataron de volver a la plazoleta, y el pánico dio entonces un coletazo de dragón, y los mandó en una oleada compacta contra la otra oleada compacta que se movía en sentido contrario, despedida por el otro coletazo de dragón de la calle opuesta, donde también las ametralladoras disparaban sin tregua. Estaban acorralados, girando en un torbellino gigantesco que poco a poco se reducía a su epicentro porque sus bordes iban siendo sistemáticamente recortados en redondo, como pelando una cebolla, por las tijeras insaciables y metódicas de la metralla. El niño vio una mujer arrodillada, con los brazos en cruz, en un espacio limpio, misteriosamente vedado a la estampida. Allí lo puso José Arcadio Segundo, en el instante de derrumbarse con la cara bañada en sangre, antes de que el tropel colosal arrasara con el espacio vacío, con la mujer arrodillada, con la luz del alto cielo de sequía, y con el puto mundo donde Úrsula Iguarán había vendido tantos animalitos de caramelo.

Cuando José Arcadio Segundo despertó estaba bocarriba en las tinieblas. Se dio cuenta de que iba en un tren interminable y silencioso, y de que tenía el cabello apelmazado por la sangre seca y le dolían todos los huesos. Sintió un sueño insoportable. Dispuesto a dormir muchas horas, a salvo del terror y el horror, se acomodó del lado que menos le dolía, y sólo entonces descubrió que estaba acostado sobre los muertos. No había un espacio libre en el vagón, salvo el corredor central. Debían de haber pasado varias horas después de la masacre, porque los cadáveres tenían la misma temperatura del yeso en otoño, y su misma consistencia de espuma petrificada, y quienes los habían puesto en el vagón tuvieron tiempo de arrumarlos en el orden y el sentido en que se transportaban los racimos de banano. Tratando de fugarse de la pesadilla, José Arcadio Segundo se arrastró de un vagón a otro, en la dirección en que avanzaba el tren, y en los relámpagos que estallaban por entre los listones de madera al pasar por los pueblos dormidos veía los muertos hombres, los muertos mujeres, los muertos niños, que iban a ser arrojados al mar como el banano de rechazo. Solamente reconoció a una mujer que vendía refrescos en la plaza y al coronel Gavilán, que todavía llevaba enrollado en la mano el cinturón con la hebilla de plata moreliana con que trató de abrirse camino a través del pánico. Cuando llegó al primer vagón dio un salto en la oscuridad, y se quedó tendido en la zanja hasta que el tren acabó de pasar. Era el más largo que había visto nunca, con casi doscientos vagones de carga, y una locomotora en cada extremo y una tercera en el centro. No llevaba ninguna luz, ni siquiera las rojas y verdes lámparas de posición, y se deslizaba a una velocidad nocturna y sigilosa. Encima de los vagones se veían los bultos oscuros de los soldados con las ametralladoras emplazadas.

Después de medianoche se precipitó un aguacero torrencial. José Arcadio Segundo ignoraba dónde había saltado, pero sabía que caminando en sentido contrario al del tren llegaría a Macondo. Al cabo de más de tres horas de marcha, empapado hasta los huesos, con un dolor de cabeza terrible, divisó las primeras casas a la luz del amanecer. Atraído por el olor del café, entró en una cocina donde una mujer con un niño en brazos estaba inclinada sobre el fogón.

—Buenos —dijo exhausto—. Soy José Arcadio Segundo Buendía.

Pronunció el nombre completo, letra por letra, para convencerse de que estaba vivo. Hizo bien, porque la mujer había pensado que era una aparición al ver en la puerta la figura escuálida, sombría, con la cabeza y la ropa sucias de sangre, y tocada por la solemnidad de la muerte. Lo conocía. Llevó una manta para que se arropara mientras se secaba la ropa en el fogón, le calentó agua para que se lavara la herida, que era sólo un desgarramiento de la piel, y le dio un pañal limpio para que se vendara la cabeza. Luego le sirvió un pocillo de café, sin azúcar, como le habían dicho que lo tomaban los Buendía, y abrió la ropa cerca del fuego.

José Arcadio Segundo no habló mientras no terminó de tomar el café.

—Debían ser como tres mil —murmuró.

—¿Qué?

—Los muertos —aclaró él—. Debían ser todos los que estaban en la estación.

La mujer lo midió con una mirada de lástima. «Aquí no ha habido muertos», dijo. «Desde los tiempos de tu tío, el coronel, no ha pasado nada en Macondo.» En tres cocinas donde se detuvo José Arcadio Segundo antes de llegar a la casa le dijeron lo mismo: «No hubo muertos.» Pasó por la plazoleta de la estación, y vio las mesas de fritangas amontonadas una encima de otra, y tampoco allí encontró rastro alguno de la masacre. Las calles estaban desiertas bajo la lluvia tenaz y las casas cerradas, sin vestigios de vida interior. La única noticia humana era el primer toque para misa. Llamó en la puerta de la casa del coronel Gavilán. Una mujer encinta, a quien había visto muchas veces, le cerró la puerta en la cara. «Se fue», dijo asustada. «Volvió a su tierra.» La entrada principal del gallinero alambrado estaba custodiada, como siempre, por dos policías locales que parecían de piedra bajo la lluvia, con impermeables y cascos de hule. En su callecita marginal, los negros antillanos cantaban a coro los salmos del sábado. José Arcadio Segundo saltó la cerca del patio y entró en la casa por la cocina. Santa Sofía de la Piedad apenas levantó la voz. «Que no te vea Fernanda», dijo. «Hace un rato se estaba levantando.» Como si cumpliera un pacto implícito, llevó al hijo al *cuarto de las bacinillas*, le arregló el desvencijado catre de Melquíades, y a las dos de la tarde, mientras Fernanda hacía la siesta, le pasó por la ventana un plato de comida.

Aureliano Segundo había dormido en casa porque allí lo sorprendió la lluvia, y a las tres de la tarde todavía seguía esperando que escampara. Informado en secreto por Santa Sofía de la Piedad, a esa hora visitó a su hermano en el cuarto de Melquíades. Tampoco él creyó la versión de la masacre ni la pesadilla del tren cargado de muertos que viajaba hacia el mar. La noche anterior habían leído un bando nacional extraordinario, para informar que los obreros habían obedecido la orden de evacuar la estación, y se dirigían a sus casas en caravanas pacíficas. El bando informaba también que los dirigentes sindicales, con un elevado espíritu patriótico, habían reducido sus peticiones a dos puntos: reforma de los servicios médicos y construcción de letrinas en las viviendas. Se informó más tarde que cuando las autoridades militares obtuvieron el acuerdo de los trabajadores, se apresuraron a comunicárselo al señor Brown, y que éste no sólo había aceptado las nuevas condiciones, sino que ofreció pagar tres días de jolgorios públicos para celebrar el término del conflicto. Sólo que cuando los militares le preguntaron para qué fecha podía anunciarse la firma del acuerdo, él miró a través de la ventana el cielo rayado de relámpagos, e hizo un profundo gesto de incertidumbre.

—Será cuando escampe —dijo—. Mientras dure la lluvia, suspendemos toda clase de actividades.

No llovía desde hacía tres meses y era tiempo de sequía. Pero cuando el señor Brown anunció su decisión se precipitó en toda la zona bananera el aguacero torrencial que sorprendió a José Arcadio Segundo en el camino de Macondo. Una semana después seguía lloviendo. La versión oficial, mil veces repetida y machacada en todo el país por cuanto medio de divulgación encontró el gobierno a su alcance, terminó por imponerse: no hubo muertos, los trabajadores satisfechos habían vuelto con sus familias, y la compañía bananera suspendía actividades mientras pasaba la lluvia. La ley marcial continuaba, en previsión de que fuera necesario aplicar medidas de emergencia para la calamidad pública del aguacero interminable, pero la tropa estaba acuartelada. Durante el día los militares andaban por los torrentes de las calles, con los pantalones enrollados a media pierna, jugando a los naufragios con los niños. En la noche, después del toque de queda, derribaban puertas a culatazos, sacaban a los sospechosos de sus camas y se los llevaban a un viaje sin regreso. Era todavía la búsqueda y el exterminio de los malhechores, asesinos, incendiarios y revoltosos del Decreto Número Cuatro, pero los militares lo negaban a los propios parientes de sus víctimas, que desbordaban la oficina de los comandantes en busca de noticias. «Seguro que fue un sueño», insistían los oficiales. «En Macondo no ha pasado nada, ni está pasando ni pasará nunca. Este es un pueblo feliz.» Así consumaron el exterminio de los jefes sindicales.

El único sobreviviente fue José Arcadio Segundo. Una noche de febrero se oyeron en la puerta los golpes inconfundibles de las culatas. Aureliano Segundo, que seguía esperando que escampara para salir, les abrió a seis soldados al mando de un oficial. Empapados de lluvia, sin pronunciar una palabra, registraron la casa cuarto por cuarto, armario por armario, desde las salas hasta el granero. Úrsula despertó cuando encendieron la luz del aposento, y no exhaló un suspiro mientras duró la requisa, pero mantuvo los dedos en cruz, moviéndolos hacia donde los soldados se movían. Santa Sofía de la Piedad alcanzó a prevenir a José Arcadio Segundo que dormía en el cuarto de Melquíades, pero él comprendió que era demasiado tarde para intentar la fuga. De modo que Santa Sofía de la Piedad volvió a cerrar la puerta, y él se puso la camisa y los zapatos, y se sentó en el catre a esperar que llegaran. En ese momento estaban requisando el taller de orfebrería. El oficial había hecho abrir el candado, y con una rápida barrida de la linterna había visto el mesón de trabajo y la vidriera con los frascos de ácidos y los instrumentos que seguían en el mismo lugar en que los dejó su dueño, y pareció comprender que en aquel cuarto no vivía nadie. Sin embargo, le preguntó astutamente a Aureliano Segundo si era platero, y él le explicó que aquel había sido el taller del coronel Aureliano Buendía. «Ajá», hizo el oficial, y encendió la luz y ordenó una requisa tan minuciosa, que no se les escaparon los dieciocho pescaditos de oro que se habían quedado sin fundir y que estaban escondidos detrás de los frascos en el tarro de lata. El oficial los examinó uno por uno en el mesón de trabajo y entonces se humanizó por completo. «Quisiera llevarme uno, si usted me lo permite», dijo. «En un tiempo fueron una clave de subversión, pero ahora son una reliquia.» Era joven, casi un adolescente, sin ningún signo de timidez, y con una simpatía natural que no se le había notado hasta entonces. Aureliano Segundo le regaló el pescadito. El oficial se lo guardó en el bolsillo de la camisa, con un brillo infantil en los ojos, y echó los otros en el tarro para ponerlos donde estaban.

—Es un recuerdo invaluable —dijo—. El coronel Aureliano Buendía fue uno de nuestros más grandes hombres.

Sin embargo, el golpe de humanización no modificó su conducta profesional. Frente al cuarto de Melquíades, que estaba otra vez con candado, Santa Sofía de la Piedad acudió a una última esperanza. «Hace como un siglo que no vive nadie en ese aposento», dijo. El oficial lo hizo abrir, lo recorrió con el haz de la linterna, y Aureliano Segundo y Santa Sofía de la Piedad vieron los ojos árabes de José Arcadio Segundo en el momento en que pasó por su cara la ráfaga de luz, y comprendieron que aquel era el fin de una ansiedad y el principio de otra que sólo encontraría un alivio en la resignación. Pero el oficial siguió examinando la habitación con la linterna, y no dio ninguna señal de interés mientras no descubrió las setenta y dos bacinillas apelotonadas en los armarios. Entonces encendió la luz. José Arcadio Segundo estaba sentado en el borde del catre, listo para salir, más solemne y pensativo que nunca. Al fondo estaban los anaqueles con los libros descosidos, los rollos de pergaminos, y la mesa de trabajo limpia y ordenada, y todavía fresca la tinta en los tinteros. Había la misma pureza en el aire, la misma diafanidad, el mismo privilegio contra el polvo y la destrucción que conoció Aureliano Segundo en la infancia, y que sólo el coronel Aureliano Buendía no pudo percibir. Pero el oficial no se interesó sino en las bacinillas.

—¿Cuántas personas viven en esta casa? —preguntó.

—Cinco.

El oficial, evidentemente, no entendió. Detuvo la mirada en el espacio donde Aureliano Segundo y Santa Sofía de la Piedad seguían viendo a José Arcadio Segundo, y también éste se dio cuenta de que el militar lo estaba mirando sin verlo. Luego apagó la luz y ajustó la puerta. Cuando les habló a los soldados, entendió Aureliano Segundo que el joven militar había visto el cuarto con los mismos ojos con que lo vio el coronel Aureliano Buendía.

—Es verdad que nadie ha estado en ese cuarto por lo menos en un siglo —dijo el oficial a los soldados—. Ahí debe haber hasta culebras.

Al cerrarse la puerta, José Arcadio Segundo tuvo la certidumbre de que su guerra había terminado. Años antes, el coronel Aureliano Buendía le había hablado de la fascinación de la guerra y había tratado de demostrarla con ejemplos incontables sacados de su propia experiencia. Él le había creído. Pero la noche en que los militares lo miraron sin verlo, mientras pensaba en la tensión de los últimos meses, en la miseria de la cárcel, en el pánico de la estación y en el tren cargado de muertos, José Arcadio Segundo llegó a la conclusión de que el coronel Aureliano Buendía no fue más que un farsante o un imbécil. No entendía que hubiera necesitado tantas palabras para explicar lo que se sentía en la guerra, si con una sola bastaba: miedo. En el cuarto de Melquíades, en cambio, protegido por la luz sobrenatural, por el ruido de la lluvia, por la sensación de ser invisible, encontró el reposo que no tuvo un solo instante de su vida anterior, y el único miedo que persistía era el de que lo enterraran vivo. Se lo contó a Santa Sofía de la Piedad, que le llevaba las comidas diarias, y ella le prometió luchar por estar viva hasta más allá de sus fuerzas, para asegurarse de que lo enterraran muerto. A salvo de todo temor, José Arcadio Segundo se dedicó entonces a repasar muchas veces los pergaminos de Melquíades, y tanto más a gusto cuanto menos los entendía. Acostumbrado al ruido de la lluvia, que a los dos meses se convirtió en una forma nueva del silencio, lo único que perturbaba su soledad eran las entradas y salidas de Santa Sofía de la Piedad. Por eso le suplicó que le dejara la comida en el alféizar de la ventana, y le echara candado a la puerta. El resto de la familia lo olvidó, inclusive Fernanda, que no tuvo inconveniente en dejarlo allí, cuando supo que los militares lo habían visto sin conocerlo. A los seis meses de encierro, en vista de que los militares se habían ido de Macondo, Aureliano Segundo quitó el candado buscando alguien con quien conversar mientras pasaba la lluvia. Desde que abrió la puerta se sintió agredido por la pestilencia de las bacinillas que estaban puestas en el suelo, y todas muchas veces ocupadas. José Arcadio Segundo, devorado por la pelambre, indiferente al aire enrarecido por los vapores nauseabundos, seguía leyendo y releyendo los pergaminos ininteligibles. Estaba iluminado por un resplandor seráfico. Apenas levantó la vista cuando sintió abrirse la puerta, pero a su hermano le bastó aquella mirada para ver repetido en ella el destino irreparable del bisabuelo.

—Eran más de tres mil —fue todo cuanto dijo José Arcadio Segundo—. Ahora estoy seguro que eran todos los que estaban en la estación.

Llovió cuatro años, once meses y dos días. Hubo épocas de llovizna en que todo el mundo se puso sus ropas de pontifical y se compuso una cara de convaleciente para celebrar la escampada, pero pronto se acostumbraron a interpretar las pausas como anuncios de recrudecimiento. Se desempedraba el cielo en unas tempestades de estropicio, y el norte mandaba unos huracanes que desportillaron techos y derribaron paredes, y desenterraron de raíz las últimas cepas de las plantaciones. Como ocurrió durante la peste del insomnio, que Úrsula se dio a recordar por aquellos días, la propia calamidad iba inspirando defensas contra el tedio. Aureliano Segundo fue uno de los que más hicieron para no dejarse vencer por la ociosidad. Había ido a la casa por algún asunto casual la noche en que el señor Brown convocó la tormenta, y Fernanda trató de auxiliarlo con un paraguas medio desvarillado que encontró en un armario. «No hace falta», dijo él. «Me quedo aquí hasta que escampe.» No era, por supuesto, un compromiso ineludible, pero estuvo a punto de cumplirlo al pie de la letra. Como su ropa estaba en casa de Petra Cotes, se quitaba cada tres días la que llevaba puesta, y esperaba en calzoncillos mientras la lavaban. Para no aburrirse, se entregó a la tarea de componer los numerosos desperfectos de la casa. Ajustó bisagras, aceitó cerraduras, atornilló aldabas y niveló fallebas. Durante varios meses se le vio vagar con una caja de herramientas que debieron olvidar los gitanos en los tiempos de José Arcadio Buendía, y nadie supo si fue por la gimnasia involuntaria, por el tedio invernal o por la abstinencia obligada, que la panza se le fue desinflando poco a poco como un pellejo, y la cara de tortuga beatífica se le hizo menos sanguínea y menos protuberante la papada, hasta que todo él terminó por ser menos paquidérmico y pudo amarrarse otra vez los cordones de los zapatos. Viéndolo montar picaportes y desconectar relojes, Fernanda se preguntó si no estaría incurriendo también en el vicio de hacer para deshacer, como el coronel Aureliano Buendía con los pescaditos de oro, Amaranta con los botones y la mortaja, José Arcadio Segundo con los pergaminos y Úrsula con los recuerdos. Pero no era cierto. Lo malo era que la lluvia lo trastornaba todo, y las máquinas más áridas echaban flores por entre los engranajes si no se les aceitaba cada tres días, y se oxidaban los hilos de los brocados y le nacían algas de azafrán a la ropa mojada. La atmósfera era tan húmeda que los peces hubieran podido entrar por las puertas y salir por las ventanas, navegando en el aire de los aposentos. Una mañana despertó Úrsula sintiendo que se acababa en un soponcio de placidez, y ya había pedido que le llevaran al padre Antonio Isabel, aunque fuera en andas, cuando Santa Sofía de la Piedad descubrió que tenía la espalda adoquinada de sanguijuelas. Se las desprendieron una por una, achicharrándolas con tizones, antes de que terminaran de desangrarla. Fue necesario excavar canales para desaguar la casa, y desembarazarla de sapos y caracoles, de modo que pudieran secarse los pisos, quitar los ladrillos de las patas de las camas y caminar otra vez con zapatos. Entretenido con las múltiples minucias que reclamaban su atención, Aureliano Segundo no se dio cuenta de que se estaba volviendo viejo, hasta una tarde en que se encontró contemplando el atardecer prematuro desde un mecedor, y pensando en Petra Cotes sin estremecerse. No habría tenido ningún inconveniente en regresar al amor insípido de Fernanda, cuya belleza se había reposado con la madurez, pero la lluvia lo había puesto a salvo de toda emergencia pasional, y le había infundido la serenidad esponjosa de la inapetencia. Se divirtió pensando en las cosas que hubiera podido hacer en otro tiempo con aquella lluvia que ya iba para un año. Había sido uno de los primeros que llevaron láminas de zinc a Macondo, mucho antes de que la compañía bananera las pusiera de moda, sólo por techar con ellas el dormitorio de Petra Cotes y solazarse con la impresión de intimidad profunda que en aquella época le producía la crepitación de la lluvia. Pero hasta esos recuerdos locos de su juventud estrafalaria lo dejaban impávido, como si en la última parranda hubiera agotado sus cuotas de salacidad, y sólo le hubiera quedado el premio maravilloso de poder evocarlas sin amargura ni arrepentimientos. Hubiera podido pensarse que el diluvio le había dado la oportunidad de sentarse a reflexionar, y que el trajín de los alicates y las alcuzas le había despertado la añoranza tardía de tantos oficios útiles como hubiera podido hacer y no hizo en la vida, pero ni lo uno ni lo otro era cierto, porque la tentación de sedentarismo y domesticidad que lo andaba rondando no era fruto de la recapacitación ni el escarmiento. Le llegaba de mucho más lejos, desenterrada por el trinche de la lluvia, de los tiempos en que leía en el cuarto de Melquíades las prodigiosas fábulas de los tapices volantes y las ballenas que se alimentaban de barcos con tripulaciones. Fue por esos días que en un descuido de Fernanda apareció en el corredor el pequeño Aureliano, y su abuelo conoció el secreto de su identidad. Le cortó el pelo, lo vistió, le enseñó a perderle el miedo a la gente, y muy pronto se vio que era un legítimo Aureliano Buendía, con sus pómulos altos, su mirada de asombro y su aire solitario. Para Fernanda fue un descanso. Hacía tiempo que había medido la magnitud de su soberbia, pero no encontraba cómo remediarla, porque mientras más pensaba en las soluciones, menos racionales le parecían. De haber sabido que Aureliano Segundo iba a tomar las cosas como las tomó, con una buena complacencia de abuelo, no le habría dado tantas vueltas ni tantos plazos, sino que desde el año anterior se hubiera liberado de la mortificación. Para Amaranta Úrsula, que ya había mudado los dientes, el sobrino fue como un juguete escurridizo que la consoló del tedio de la lluvia. Aureliano Segundo se acordó entonces de la enciclopedia inglesa que nadie había vuelto a tocar en el antiguo dormitorio de Meme. Empezó por mostrarles las láminas a los niños, en especial las de animales, y más tarde los mapas y las fotografías de países remotos y personajes célebres. Como no sabía inglés, y como apenas podía distinguir las ciudades más conocidas y las personalidades más corrientes, se dio a inventar nombres y leyendas para satisfacer la curiosidad insaciable de los niños.

Fernanda creía de veras que su esposo estaba esperando a que escampara para volver con la concubina. En los primeros meses de la lluvia temió que él intentara deslizarse hasta su dormitorio, y que ella iba a pasar por la vergüenza de revelarle que estaba incapacitada para la reconciliación desde el nacimiento de Amaranta Úrsula. Esa era la causa de su ansiosa correspondencia con los médicos invisibles, interrumpida por los frecuentes desastres del correo. Durante los primeros meses, cuando se supo que los trenes se descarrilaban en la tormenta, una carta de los médicos invisibles le indicó que se estaban perdiendo las suyas. Más tarde, cuando se interrumpieron los contactos con sus corresponsales ignotos, había pensado seriamente en ponerse la máscara de tigre que usó su marido en el carnaval sangriento, para hacerse examinar con un nombre ficticio por los médicos de la compañía bananera. Pero una de las tantas personas que pasaban a menudo por la casa llevando las noticias ingratas del diluvio le había dicho que la compañía estaba desmantelando sus dispensarios para llevárselos a tierras de escampada. Entonces perdió la esperanza. Se resignó a aguardar que pasara la lluvia y se normalizara el correo y, mientras tanto, se aliviaba de sus dolencias secretas con recursos de inspiración, porque hubiera preferido morirse a ponerse en manos del único médico que quedaba en Macondo, el francés extravagante que se alimentaba con hierba para burros. Se había aproximado a Úrsula, confiando en que ella conociera algún paliativo para sus quebrantos. Pero la tortuosa costumbre de no llamar las cosas por su nombre la llevó a poner lo anterior en lo posterior, y a sustituir lo parido por lo expulsado, y a cambiar flujos por ardores para que todo fuera menos vergonzoso, de manera que Úrsula concluyó razonablemente que los trastornos no eran uterinos, sino intestinales, y le aconsejó que tomara en ayunas una papeleta de calomel. De no haber sido por ese padecimiento que nada hubiera tenido de pudendo para alguien que no estuviera también enfermo de pudibundez, y de no haber sido por la pérdida de las cartas, a Fernanda no le habría importado la lluvia, porque al fin de cuentas toda la vida había sido para ella como si estuviera lloviendo. No modificó los horarios ni perdonó los ritos. Cuando todavía estaba la mesa alzada sobre ladrillos y puestas las sillas sobre tablones para que los comensales no se mojaran los pies, ella seguía sirviendo con manteles de lino y vajillas chinas, y prendiendo los candelabros en la cena, porque consideraba que las calamidades no podían tomarse de pretexto para el relajamiento de las costumbres. Nadie había vuelto a asomarse a la calle. Si de Fernanda hubiera dependido no habrían vuelto a hacerlo jamás, no sólo desde que empezó a llover, sino desde mucho antes, puesto que ella consideraba que las puertas se habían inventado para cerrarlas, y que la curiosidad por lo que ocurría en la calle era cosa de rameras. Sin embargo, ella fue la primera en asomarse cuando avisaron que estaba pasando el entierro del coronel Gerineldo Márquez, aunque lo que vio entonces por la ventana entreabierta la dejó en tal estado de aflicción que durante mucho tiempo estuvo arrepintiéndose de su debilidad.

No habría podido concebirse un cortejo más desolado. Habían puesto el ataúd en una carreta de bueyes sobre la cual construyeron un cobertizo de hojas de banano, pero la presión de la lluvia era tan intensa y las calles estaban tan empantanadas que a cada paso se atollaban las ruedas y el cobertizo estaba a punto de desbaratarse. Los chorros de agua triste que caían sobre el ataúd iban ensopando la bandera que le habían puesto encima, y que era en realidad la bandera sucia de sangre y de pólvora, repudiada por los veteranos más dignos. Sobre el ataúd habían puesto también el sable con borlas de cobre y seda, el mismo que el coronel Gerineldo Márquez colgaba en la percha de la sala para entrar inerme al costurero de Amaranta. Detrás de la carreta, algunos descalzos y todos con los pantalones a media pierna, chapaleaban en el fango los últimos sobrevivientes de la capitulación de Neerlandia, llevando en una mano el bastón de carreto y en la otra una corona de flores de papel descoloridas por la lluvia. Aparecieron como una visión irreal en la calle que todavía llevaba el nombre del coronel Aureliano Buendía, y todos miraron la casa al pasar, y doblaron por la esquina de la plaza, donde tuvieron que pedir ayuda para sacar la carreta atascada. Úrsula se había hecho llevar a la puerta por Santa Sofía de la Piedad. Siguió con tanta atención las peripecias del entierro que nadie dudó de que lo estaba viendo, sobre todo porque su alzada mano de arcángel anunciador se movía con los cabeceos de la carreta.

—Adiós, Gerineldo, hijo mío —gritó—. Salúdame a mi gente y dile que nos vemos cuando escampe.

Aureliano Segundo la ayudó a volver a la cama, y con la misma informalidad con que la trataba siempre le preguntó el significado de su despedida.

—Es verdad —dijo ella—. Nada más estoy esperando que pase la lluvia para morirme.

El estado de las calles alarmó a Aureliano Segundo. Tardíamente preocupado por la suerte de sus animales, se echó encima un lienzo encerado y fue a casa de Petra Cotes. La encontró en el patio, con el agua a la cintura, tratando de desencallar el cadáver de un caballo. Aureliano Segundo la ayudó con una tranca, y el enorme cuerpo tumefacto dio una vuelta de campana y fue arrastrado por el torrente de barro líquido. Desde que empezó la lluvia, Petra Cotes no había hecho más que desembarazar su patio de animales muertos. En las primeras semanas le mandó recados a Aureliano Segundo para que tomara providencias urgentes, y él había contestado que no había prisa, que la situación no era alarmante, que ya se pensaría en algo cuando escampara. Le mandó a decir que los potreros se estaban inundando, que el ganado se fugaba hacia las tierras altas donde no había qué comer, y que estaban a merced del tigre y la peste. «No hay nada que hacer», le contestó Aureliano Segundo. «Ya nacerán otros cuando escampe.» Petra Cotes los había visto morir a racimadas, y apenas si se daba abasto para destazar a los que se quedaban atollados. Vio con una impotencia sorda cómo el diluvio fue exterminando sin misericordia una fortuna que en un tiempo se tuvo como la más grande y sólida de Macondo, y de la cual no quedaba sino la pestilencia. Cuando Aureliano Segundo decidió ir a ver lo que pasaba, sólo encontró el cadáver del caballo, y una mula escuálida entre los escombros de la caballeriza. Petra Cotes lo vio llegar sin sorpresa, sin alegría ni resentimiento, y apenas se permitió una sonrisa irónica.

—¡A buena hora! —dijo.

Estaba envejecida, en los puros huesos, y sus lanceolados ojos de animal carnívoro se habían vuelto tristes y mansos de tanto mirar la lluvia. Aureliano

Segundo se quedó más de tres meses en su casa, no porque entonces se sintiera mejor allí que en la de su familia, sino porque necesitó todo ese tiempo para tomar la decisión de echarse otra vez encima el pedazo de lienzo encerado. «No hay prisa», dijo, como había dicho en la otra casa. «Esperemos que escampe en las próximas horas.» En el curso de la primera semana se fue acostumbrando a los desgastes que habían hecho el tiempo y la lluvia en la salud de su concubina, y poco a poco fue viéndola como era antes, acordándose de sus desafueros jubilosos y de la fecundidad de delirio que su amor provocaba en los animales, y en parte por amor y en parte por interés, una noche de la segunda semana la despertó con caricias apremiantes. Petra Cotes no reaccionó. «Duerme tranquilo», murmuró. «Ya los tiempos no están para estas cosas.» Aureliano Segundo se vio a sí mismo en los espejos del techo, vio la espina dorsal de Petra Cotes como una hilera de carretes ensartados en un mazo de nervios marchitos, y comprendió que ella tenía razón, no por los tiempos, sino por ellos mismos, que ya no estaban para esas cosas.

Aureliano Segundo regresó a la casa con sus baúles, convencido de que no sólo Úrsula, sino todos los habitantes de Macondo, estaban esperando que escampara para morirse. Los había visto al pasar, sentados en las salas con la mirada absorta y los brazos cruzados, sintiendo transcurrir un tiempo entero, un tiempo sin desbravar, porque era inútil dividirlo en meses y años, y los días en horas, cuando no podía hacerse nada más que contemplar la lluvia. Los niños recibieron alborozados a Aureliano Segundo, quien volvió a tocar para ellos el acordeón asmático. Pero el concierto no les llamó tanto la atención como las sesiones enciclopédicas, de modo que otra vez volvieron a reunirse en el dormitorio de Meme, donde la imaginación de Aureliano Segundo convirtió el dirigible en un elefante volador que buscaba un sitio para dormir entre las nubes. En cierta ocasión encontró un hombre de a caballo que a pesar de su atuendo exótico conservaba un aire familiar, y después de mucho examinarlo llegó a la conclusión de que era un retrato del coronel Aureliano Buendía. Se lo mostró a Fernanda, y también ella admitió el parecido del jinete no sólo con el coronel, sino con todos los miembros de la familia, aunque en verdad era un guerrero tártaro. Así se le fue pasando el tiempo, entre el coloso de Rodas y los encantadores de serpientes, hasta que su esposa le anunció que no quedaban más de seis kilos de carne salada y un saco de arroz en el granero.

—¿Y ahora qué quieres que haga? —preguntó él.

—Yo no sé —contestó Fernanda—. Eso es asunto de hombres.

—Bueno —dijo Aureliano Segundo—, algo se hará cuando escampe.

Siguió más interesado en la enciclopedia que en el problema doméstico, aun cuando tuvo que conformarse con una piltrafa y un poco de arroz en el almuerzo. «Ahora es imposible hacer nada», decía. «No puede llover toda la vida.» Y mientras más largas le daba a las urgencias del granero, más intensa se iba haciendo la indignación de Fernanda, hasta que sus protestas eventuales, sus desahogos poco frecuentes, se desbordaron en un torrente incontenible, desatado, que empezó una mañana como el monótono bordón de una guitarra, y que a medida que avanzaba el día fue subiendo de tono, cada vez más rico, más espléndido. Aureliano Segundo no tuvo conciencia de la cantaleta hasta el día siguiente, después del desayuno, cuando se sintió aturdido por un abejorreo que era entonces más fluido y alto que el rumor de la lluvia, y era Fernanda que se paseaba por toda la casa doliéndose de que la hubieran educado como una reina para terminar de sirvienta en una casa de locos, con un marido holgazán, idólatra, libertino, que se acostaba bocarriba a esperar que le llovieran panes del cielo, mientras ella se destroncaba los riñones tratando de mantener a flote un hogar emparapetado con alfileres, donde había tanto que hacer, tanto que soportar y corregir desde que amanecía Dios hasta la hora de acostarse, que llegaba a la cama con los ojos llenos de polvo de vidrio y, sin embargo, nadie le había dicho nunca buenos días, Fernanda, qué tal noche pasaste, Fernanda, ni le habían preguntado aunque fuera por cortesía por qué estaba tan pálida ni por qué despertaba con esas ojeras de violeta, a pesar de que ella no esperaba, por supuesto, que aquello saliera del resto de una familia que al fin y al cabo la había tenido siempre como un estorbo, como el trapito de bajar la olla, como un monigote pintado en la pared, y que siempre andaban desbarrando contra ella por los rincones, llamándola santurrona, llamándola farisea, llamándola lagarta, y hasta Amaranta, que en paz descanse, había dicho de viva voz que ella era de las que confundían el recto con las témporas, bendito sea Dios, qué palabras, y ella había aguantado todo con resignación por las intenciones del Santo Padre, pero no había podido soportar más cuando el malvado de José Arcadio Segundo dijo que la perdición de la familia había sido abrirle las puertas a una cachaca, imagínese, una cachaca mandona, válgame Dios, una cachaca hija de la mala saliva, de la misma índole de los cachacos que mandó el gobierno a matar trabajadores, dígame usted, y se refería a nadie menos que a ella, la ahijada del Duque de Alba, una dama con tanta alcurnia que le revolvía el hígado a las esposas de los presidentes, una fijodalga de sangre como ella que tenía derecho a firmar con once apellidos peninsulares, y que era el único mortal en ese pueblo de bastardos que no se sentía emberenjenado frente a dieciséis cubiertos, para que luego el adúltero de su marido dijera muerto de risa que tantas cucharas y tenedores, y tantos cuchillos y cucharitas no era cosa de cristianos, sino de ciempiés, y la única que podía determinar a ojos cerrados cuándo se servía el vino blanco, y de qué lado y en qué copa, y cuándo se servía el vino rojo, y de qué lado y en qué copa, y no como la montuna de Amaranta, que en paz descanse, que creía que el vino blanco se servía de día y el vino rojo de noche, y la única en todo el litoral que podía vanagloriarse de no haber hecho del cuerpo sino en bacinillas de oro, para que luego el coronel Aureliano Buendía, que en paz descanse, tuviera el atrevimiento de preguntar con su mala bilis de masón de dónde había merecido ese privilegio, si era que ella no cagaba mierda, sino astromelias, imagínese, con esas palabras, y para que Renata, su propia hija, que por indiscreción había visto sus aguas mayores en el dormitorio, contestara que de verdad la bacinilla era de mucho oro y de mucha heráldica, pero que lo que tenía dentro era pura mierda, mierda física, y peor todavía que las otras porque era mierda de cachaca, imagínese, su propia hija, de modo que nunca se había hecho ilusiones con el resto de la familia, pero de todos modos tenía derecho a esperar un poco de más consideración de parte de su esposo, puesto que bien o mal era su cónyuge de sacramento, su autor, su legítimo perjudicador, que se echó encima por voluntad libre y soberana la grave responsabilidad de sacarla del solar paterno, donde nunca se privó ni se dolió de nada, donde tejía palmas fúnebres por gusto de entretenimiento, puesto que su padrino había mandado una carta con su firma y el sello de su anillo impreso en el lacre, sólo para decir que las manos de su ahijada no estaban hechas para menesteres de este mundo, como no fuera tocar el clavicordio y, sin embargo, el insensato de su marido la había sacado de su casa con todas las admoniciones y advertencias y la había llevado a aquella paila de infierno donde no se podía respirar de calor, y antes de que ella acabara de guardar sus dietas de Pentecostés ya se había ido con sus baúles trashumantes y su acordeón de perdulario a holgar en adulterio con una desdichada a quien bastaba con verle las nalgas, bueno, ya estaba dicho, a quien bastaba con verle menear las nalgas de potranca para adivinar que era una, que era una, todo lo contrario de ella, que era una dama en el palacio o en la pocilga, en la mesa o en la cama, una dama de nación, temerosa de Dios, obediente de sus leyes y sumisa a sus designios, y con quien no podía hacer, por supuesto, las maromas y vagabundinas que hacía con la otra, que por supuesto se prestaba a todo, como las matronas francesas, y peor aún, pensándolo bien, porque éstas al menos tenían la honradez de poner un foco colorado en la puerta, semejantes porquerías, imagínese, ni más faltaba, con la hija única y bienamada de doña Renata Argote y don Fernando del Carpio, y sobre todo de éste, por supuesto, un santo varón, un cristiano de los grandes, Caballero de la Orden del Santo Sepulcro, de esos que reciben directamente de Dios el privilegio de conservarse intactos en la tumba, con la piel tersa como raso de novia y los ojos vivos y diáfanos como las esmeraldas.

—Eso sí no es cierto —la interrumpió Aureliano Segundo—, cuando lo trajeron ya apestaba.

Había tenido la paciencia de escucharla un día entero, hasta sorprenderla en una falta. Fernanda no le hizo caso, pero bajó la voz. Esa noche, durante la cena, el exasperante zumbido de la cantaleta había derrotado al rumor de la lluvia. Aureliano Segundo comió muy poco, con la cabeza baja, y se retiró temprano al dormitorio. En el desayuno del día siguiente Fernanda estaba trémula, con aspecto de haber dormido mal, y parecía desahogada por completo de sus rencores. Sin embargo, cuando su marido preguntó si no sería posible comerse un huevo tibio, ella no contestó simplemente que desde la semana anterior se habían acabado los huevos, sino que elaboró una virulenta diatriba contra los hombres que se pasaban el tiempo adorándose el ombligo y luego tenían la cachaza de pedir hígados de alondra en la mesa. Aureliano Segundo llevó a los niños a ver la enciclopedia, como siempre, y Fernanda fingió poner orden en el dormitorio de Meme, sólo para que él la oyera murmurar que, por supuesto, se necesitaba tener la cara dura para decirles a los pobres inocentes que el coronel Aureliano Buendía estaba retratado en la enciclopedia. En la tarde, mientras los niños hacían la siesta, Aureliano Segundo se sentó en el corredor, y hasta allá lo persiguió Fernanda, provocándolo, atormentándolo, girando en torno de él con su implacable zumbido de moscardón, diciendo que, por supuesto, mientras ya no quedaban más que piedras para comer, su marido se sentaba como un sultán de Persia a contemplar la lluvia, porque no era más que eso, un mampolón, un mantenido, un bueno para nada, más flojo que el algodón de borla, acostumbrado a vivir de las mujeres, y convencido de que se había casado con la esposa de Jonás, que se quedó tan tranquila con el cuento de la ballena. Aureliano Segundo la oyó más de dos horas, impasible, como si fuera sordo. No la interrumpió hasta muy avanzada la tarde cuando no pudo soportar más la resonancia de bombo que le atormentaba la cabeza.

—Cállate ya, por favor —suplicó.

Fernanda, por el contrario, levantó el tono. «No tengo por qué callarme», dijo. «El que no quiera oírme que se vaya.» Entonces Aureliano Segundo perdió el dominio. Se incorporó sin prisa, como si sólo pensara estirar los huesos, y con una furia perfectamente regulada y metódica fue agarrando uno tras otro los tiestos de begonias, las macetas de helechos, los potes de orégano, y uno tras otro los fue despedazando contra el suelo. Fernanda se asustó, pues en realidad no había tenido hasta entonces una conciencia clara de la tremenda fuerza interior de la cantaleta, pero ya era tarde para cualquier tentativa de rectificación. Embriagado por el torrente incontenible del desahogo, Aureliano Segundo rompió el cristal de la vidriera, y una por una, sin apresurarse, fue sacando las piezas de la vajilla y las hizo polvo contra el piso. Sistemático, sereno, con la misma parsimonia con que había empapelado la casa de billetes, fue rompiendo luego contra las paredes la cristalería de Bohemia, los floreros pintados a mano, los cuadros de las doncellas en barcas cargadas de rosas, los espejos de marcos dorados, y todo cuanto era rompible desde la sala hasta el granero, y terminó con la tinaja de la cocina que se reventó en el centro del patio con una explosión profunda. Luego se lavó las manos, se echó encima el lienzo encerado, y antes de medianoche volvió con unos tiesos colgajos de carne salada, varios sacos de arroz y maíz con gorgojo, y unos desmirriados racimos de plátanos. Desde entonces no volvieron a faltar las cosas de comer.

Amaranta Úrsula y el pequeño Aureliano habían de recordar el diluvio como una época feliz. A pesar del rigor de Fernanda, chapaleaban en los pantanos del patio, cazaban lagartos para descuartizarlos y jugaban a envenenar la sopa echándole polvo de alas de mariposas en los descuidos de Santa Sofía de la Piedad. Úrsula era su juguete más entretenido. La tuvieron por una gran muñeca decrépita que llevaban y traían por los rincones, disfrazada con trapos de colores y la cara pintada con hollín y achiote, y una vez estuvieron a punto de destriparle los ojos como le hacían a los sapos con las tijeras de podar. Nada les causaba tanto alborozo como sus desvaríos. En efecto, algo debió ocurrir en su cerebro en el tercer año de la lluvia, porque poco a poco fue perdiendo el sentido de la realidad, y confundía el tiempo actual con épocas remotas de su vida, hasta el punto de que en una ocasión pasó tres días llorando sin consuelo por la muerte de Petronila Iguarán, su bisabuela, enterrada desde hacía más de un siglo. Se hundió en un estado de confusión tan disparatado, que creía que el pequeño Aureliano era su hijo el coronel por los tiempos en que lo llevaron a conocer el hielo, y que el José Arcadio que estaba entonces en el seminario era el primogénito que se fue con los gitanos. Tanto habló de la familia, que los niños aprendieron a organizarle visitas imaginarias con seres que no sólo habían muerto desde hacía mucho tiempo, sino que habían existido en épocas distintas. Sentada en la cama con el pelo cubierto de ceniza y la cara tapada con un pañuelo rojo, Úrsula era feliz en medio de la parentela irreal que los niños describían sin omisión de detalles, como si de verdad la hubieran conocido. Úrsula conversaba con sus antepasados sobre acontecimientos anteriores a su propia existencia, gozaba con las noticias que le daban y lloraba con ellos por muertos mucho más recientes que los mismos contertulios. Los niños no tardaron en advertir que en el curso de esas visitas fantasmales Úrsula planteaba siempre una pregunta destinada a establecer quién era el que había llevado a la casa durante la guerra un San José de yeso de tamaño natural para que lo guardaran mientras pasaba la lluvia. Fue así como Aureliano Segundo se acordó de la fortuna enterrada en algún lugar que sólo Úrsula conocía, pero fueron inútiles las preguntas y las maniobras astutas que se le ocurrieron, porque en los laberintos de su desvarío ella parecía conservar un margen de lucidez para defender aquel secreto, que sólo había de revelar a quien demostrara ser el verdadero dueño del oro sepultado. Era tan hábil y tan estricta, que cuando Aureliano Segundo instruyó a uno de sus compañeros de parranda para que se hiciera pasar por el propietario de la fortuna, ella lo enredó en un interrogatorio minucioso y sembrado de trampas sutiles.

Convencido de que Úrsula se llevaría el secreto a la tumba, Aureliano Segundo contrató una cuadrilla de excavadores con el pretexto de que construyeran canales de desagüe en el patio y en el traspatio, y él mismo sondeó el suelo con barretas de hierro y con toda clase de detectores de metales, sin encontrar nada que se pareciera al oro en tres meses de exploraciones exhaustivas. Más tarde recurrió a Pilar Ternera con la esperanza de que las barajas vieran más que los cavadores, pero ella empezó por explicarle que era inútil cualquier tentativa mientras no fuera Úrsula quien cortara el naipe. Confirmó en cambio la existencia del tesoro, con la precisión de que eran siete mil doscientas catorce monedas enterradas en tres sacos de lona con jaretas de alambre de cobre, dentro de un círculo con un radio de ciento veintidós metros, tomando como centro la cama de Úrsula, pero advirtió que no sería encontrado antes de que acabara de llover y los soles de tres junios consecutivos convirtieran en polvo los barrizales. La profusión y la meticulosa vaguedad de los datos le parecieron a Aureliano Segundo tan semejantes a las fábulas espiritistas, que insistió en su empresa a pesar de que estaban en agosto y habría sido necesario esperar por lo menos tres años para satisfacer las condiciones del pronóstico. Lo primero que le causó asombro, aunque al mismo tiempo aumentó su confusión, fue el comprobar que había exactamente ciento veintidós metros de la cama de Úrsula a la cerca del traspatio. Fernanda temió que estuviera tan loco como su hermano gemelo cuando lo vio haciendo las mediciones, y peor aun cuando ordenó a las cuadrillas de excavadores profundizar un metro más en las zanjas. Presa de un delirio exploratorio comparable apenas al del bisabuelo cuando buscaba la ruta de los inventos, Aureliano Segundo perdió las últimas bolsas de grasa que le quedaban, y la antigua semejanza con el hermano gemelo se fue otra vez acentuando, no sólo por el escurrimiento de la figura, sino por el aire distante y la actitud ensimismada. No volvió a ocuparse de los niños. Comía a cualquier hora, embarrado de pies a cabeza, y lo hacía en un rincón de la cocina, contestando apenas a las preguntas ocasionales de Santa Sofía de la Piedad. Viéndolo trabajar en aquella forma, como nunca sonó que pudiera hacerlo, Fernanda creyó que su temeridad era diligencia, y que su codicia era abnegación y que su tozudez era perseverancia, y le remordieron las entrañas por la virulencia con que había despotricado contra su desidia. Pero Aureliano Segundo no estaba entonces para reconciliaciones misericordiosas. Hundido hasta el cuello en una ciénaga de ramazones muertas y flores podridas, volteó al derecho y al revés el suelo del jardín después de haber terminado con el patio y el traspatio, y barrenó tan profundamente los cimientos de la galería oriental de la casa, que una noche despertaron aterrorizados por lo que parecía ser un cataclismo, tanto por las trepidaciones como por el pavoroso crujido subterráneo, y era que tres aposentos se estaban desbarrancando y se había abierto una grieta de escalofrío desde el corredor hasta el dormitorio de Fernanda. Aureliano Segundo no renunció por eso a la exploración. Aun cuando ya se habían extinguido las últimas esperanzas y lo único que parecía tener algún sentido eran las predicciones de las barajas, reforzó los cimientos mellados, resanó la grieta con argamasa y continuó excavando en el costado occidental. Allí estaba todavía la segunda semana del junio siguiente, cuando la lluvia empezó a apaciguarse y las nubes se fueron alzando, y se vio que de un momento a otro iba a escampar. Así fue. Un viernes a las dos de la tarde se alumbró el mundo con un sol bobo, bermejo y áspero como polvo de ladrillo, y casi tan fresco como el agua, y no volvió a llover en diez años.

Macondo estaba en ruinas. En los pantanos de las calles quedaban muebles despedazados, esqueletos de animales cubiertos de lirios colorados, últimos recuerdos de las hordas de advenedizos que se fugaron de Macondo tan atolondradamente como habían llegado. Las casas paradas con tanta urgencia durante la fiebre del banano habían sido abandonadas. La compañía bananera desmanteló sus instalaciones. De la antigua ciudad alambrada sólo quedaban los escombros. Las casas de madera, las frescas terrazas donde transcurrían las serenas tardes de naipes, parecían arrasadas por una anticipación del viento profético que años después había de borrar a Macondo de la faz de la tierra. El único rastro humano que dejó aquel soplo voraz fue un guante de Patricia Brown en el automóvil sofocado por las trinitarias. La región encantada que exploró José Arcadio Buendía en los tiempos de la fundación, y donde luego prosperaron las plantaciones de banano, era un tremedal de cepas putrefactas, en cuyo horizonte remoto se alcanzó a ver por varios años la espuma silenciosa del mar. Aureliano Segundo padeció una crisis de aflicción el primer domingo que vistió ropas secas y salió a reconocer el pueblo. Los sobrevivientes de la catástrofe, los mismos que ya vivían en Macondo antes de que fuera sacudido por el huracán de la compañía bananera, estaban sentados en mitad de la calle gozando de los primeros soles. Todavía conservaban en la piel el verde de alga y el olor de rincón que les imprimió la lluvia, pero en el fondo de sus corazones parecían satisfechos de haber recuperado el pueblo en que nacieron. La Calle de los Turcos era otra vez la de antes, la de los tiempos en que los árabes de pantuflas y argollas en las orejas que recorrían el mundo cambiando guacamayas por chucherías hallaron en Macondo un buen recodo para descansar de su milenaria condición de gente trashumante. Al otro lado de la lluvia, la mercancía de los bazares estaba cayéndose a pedazos, los géneros abiertos en la puerta estaban veteados de musgo, los mostradores socavados por el comején y las paredes carcomidas por la humedad, pero los árabes de la tercera generación estaban sentados en el mismo lugar y en la misma actitud de sus padres y sus abuelos, taciturnos, impávidos, invulnerables al tiempo y al desastre, tan vivos o tan muertos como estuvieron después de la peste del insomnio y de las treinta y dos guerras del coronel Aureliano Buendía. Era tan asombrosa su fortaleza de ánimo frente a los escombros de las mesas de juego, los puestos de fritangas, las casetas de tiro al blanco y el callejón donde se interpretaban los sueños y se adivinaba el porvenir, que Aureliano Segundo les preguntó con su informalidad habitual de qué recursos misteriosos se habían valido para no naufragar en la tormenta, cómo diablos habían hecho para no ahogarse, y uno tras otro, de puerta en puerta, le devolvieron una sonrisa ladina y una mirada de ensueño, y todos le dieron, sin ponerse de acuerdo, la misma respuesta:

—Nadando.

Petra Cotes era tal vez el único nativo que tenía corazón de árabe. Había visto los últimos destrozos de sus establos y caballerizas arrastrados por la tormenta, pero había logrado mantener la casa en pie. En el último año, le había mandado recados apremiantes a Aureliano Segundo, y éste le había contestado que ignoraba cuándo volvería a su casa, pero que en todo caso llevaría un cajón de monedas de oro para empedrar el dormitorio. Entonces ella había escarbado en su corazón, buscando la fuerza que le permitiera sobrevivir a la desgracia, y había encontrado una rabia reflexiva y justa, con la cual había jurado restaurar la fortuna despilfarrada por el amante y acabada de exterminar por el diluvio. Fue una decisión tan inquebrantable, que Aureliano Segundo volvió a su casa ocho meses después del último recado, y la encontró verde, desgreñada, con los párpados hundidos y la piel escarchada por la sarna, pero estaba escribiendo números en pedacitos de papel, para hacer una rifa. Aureliano Segundo se quedó atónito, y estaba tan escuálido y tan solemne, que Petra Cotes no creyó que quien había vuelto a buscarla fuera el amante de toda la vida, sino el hermano gemelo.

—Estás loca —dijo él—. A menos que pienses rifar los huesos.

Entonces ella le dijo que se asomara al dormitorio, y Aureliano Segundo vio la mula. Estaba con el pellejo pegado a los huesos, como la dueña, pero tan viva y resuelta como ella. Petra Cotes la había alimentado con su rabia, y cuando no tuvo más hierbas, ni maíz, ni raíces, la albergó en su propio dormitorio y le dio a comer las sábanas de percal, los tapices persas, los sobrecamas de peluche, las cortinas de terciopelo y el palio bordado con hilos de oro y borlones de seda de la cama episcopal.

Úrsula tuvo que hacer un grande esfuerzo para cumplir su promesa de morirse cuando escampara. Las ráfagas de lucidez, que eran tan escasas durante la lluvia, se hicieron más frecuentes a partir de agosto, cuando empezó a soplar el viento árido que sofocaba los rosales y petrificaba los pantanos, y que acabó por esparcir sobre Macondo el polvo abrasante que cubrió para siempre los oxidados techos de zinc y los almendros centenarios. Úrsula lloró de lástima al descubrir que por más de tres años había quedado para juguete de los niños. Se lavó la cara pintorreteada, se quitó de encima las tiras de colorines, las lagartijas y los sapos resecos y las camándulas y antiguos collares de árabes que le habían colgado por todo el cuerpo, y por primera vez desde la muerte de Amaranta abandonó la cama sin auxilio de nadie para incorporarse de nuevo a la vida familiar. El ánimo de su corazón invencible la orientaba en las tinieblas. Quienes repararon en sus trastabilleos y tropezaron con su brazo arcangélico siempre alzado a la altura de la cabeza pensaron que a duras penas podía con su cuerpo, pero todavía no creyeron que estaba ciega. Ella no necesitaba ver para darse cuenta de que los canteros de flores, cultivados con tanto esmero desde la primera reconstrucción, habían sido destruidos por la lluvia y arrasados por las excavaciones de Aureliano Segundo, y que las paredes y el cemento de los pisos estaban cuarteados, los muebles flojos y descoloridos, las puertas desquiciadas, y la familia amenazada por un espíritu de resignación y pesadumbre que no hubiera sido concebible en sus tiempos. Moviéndose a tientas por los dormitorios vacíos percibía el trueno continuo del comején taladrando las maderas, y el tijereteo de la polilla en los roperos, y el estrépito devastador de las enormes hormigas coloradas que habían prosperado en el diluvio y estaban socavando los cimientos de la casa. Un día abrió el baúl de los santos, y tuvo que pedir auxilio a Santa Sofía de la Piedad para quitarse de encima las cucarachas que saltaron del interior, y que ya habían pulverizado la ropa. «No es posible vivir en esta negligencia», decía. «A este paso terminaremos devorados por las bestias.» Desde entonces no tuvo un instante de reposo. Levantada desde antes del amanecer, recurría a quien estuviera disponible, inclusive a los niños. Puso al sol las escasas ropas que todavía estaban en condiciones de ser usadas, ahuyentó las cucarachas con sorpresivos asaltos de insecticida, raspó las venas del comején en puertas y ventanas y asfixió con cal viva a las hormigas en sus madrigueras. La fiebre de restauración acabó por llevarla a los cuartos olvidados. Hizo desembarazar de escombros y telarañas la habitación donde a José Arcadio Buendía se le secó la mollera buscando la piedra filosofal, puso en orden el taller de platería que había sido revuelto por los soldados, y por último pidió las llaves del cuarto de Melquíades para ver en qué estado se encontraba. Fiel a la voluntad de José Arcadio Segundo, que había prohibido toda intromisión mientras no hubiera un indicio real de que había muerto, Santa Sofía de la Piedad recurrió a toda clase de subterfugios para desorientar a Úrsula. Pero era tan inflexible su determinación de no abandonar a los insectos ni el más recóndito e inservible rincón de la casa, que desbarató cuanto obstáculo le atravesaron, y al cabo de tres días de insistencia consiguió que le abrieran el cuarto. Tuvo que agarrarse del quicio para que no la derribara la pestilencia, pero no le hicieron falta más de dos segundos para recordar que ahí estaban guardadas las setenta y dos bacinillas de las colegialas, y que en una de las primeras noches de lluvia una patrulla de soldados había registrado la casa buscando a José Arcadio Segundo y no había podido encontrarlo.

—¡Bendito sea Dios! —exclamó, como si lo hubiera visto todo—. Tanto tratar de inculcarte las buenas costumbres, para que terminaras viviendo como un puerco.

José Arcadio Segundo seguía releyendo los pergaminos. Lo único visible en la intrincada maraña de pelos eran los dientes rayados de lama verde y los ojos inmóviles. Al reconocer la voz de la bisabuela, movió la cabeza hacia la puerta, trato de sonreír, y sin saberlo repitió una antigua frase de Úrsula.

—Qué quería —murmuró—, el tiempo pasa.

—Así es —dijo Úrsula—, pero no tanto.

Al decirlo, tuvo conciencia de estar dando la misma réplica que recibió del coronel Aureliano Buendía en su celda de sentenciado, y una vez más se estremeció con la comprobación de que el tiempo no pasaba, como ella lo acababa de admitir, sino que daba vueltas en redondo. Pero tampoco entonces le dio una oportunidad a la resignación. Regañó a José Arcadio Segundo como si fuera un niño, y se empeñó en que se bañara y se afeitara y le prestara su fuerza para acabar de restaurar la casa. La simple idea de abandonar el cuarto que le había proporcionado la paz aterrorizó a José Arcadio Segundo. Gritó que no había poder humano capaz de hacerlo salir, porque no quería ver el tren de doscientos vagones cargados de muertos que cada atardecer partía de Macondo hacia el mar. «Son todos los que estaban en la estación», gritaba. «Tres mil cuatrocientos ocho.» Sólo entonces comprendió Úrsula que él estaba en un mundo de tinieblas más impenetrable que el suyo, tan infranqueable y solitario como el del bisabuelo. Lo dejó en el cuarto, pero consiguió que no volvieran a poner el candado, que hicieran la limpieza todos los días, que tiraran las bacinillas a la basura y sólo dejaran una, y que mantuvieran a José Arcadio Segundo tan limpio y presentable como estuvo el bisabuelo en su largo cautiverio bajo el castaño. Al principio, Fernanda interpretaba aquel ajetreo como un acceso de locura senil, y a duras penas reprimía la exasperación. Pero José Arcadio le anunció por esa época desde Roma que pensaba ir a Macondo antes de hacer los votos perpetuos, y la buena noticia le infundió tal entusiasmo, que de la noche a la mañana se encontró regando las flores cuatro veces al día para que su hijo no fuera a formarse una mala impresión de la casa. Fue ese mismo incentivo el que la indujo a apresurar su correspondencia con los médicos invisibles, y a reponer en el corredor las macetas de helechos y orégano, y los tiestos de begonias, mucho antes de que Úrsula se enterara de que habían sido destruidos por la furia exterminadora de Aureliano Segundo. Más tarde vendió el servicio de plata, y compró vajillas de cerámica, soperas y cucharones de peltre y cubiertos de alpaca, y empobreció con ellos las alacenas acostumbradas a la loza de la Compañía de Indias y la cristalería de Bohemia. Úrsula trataba de ir siempre más lejos. «Que abran puertas y ventanas», gritaba. «Que hagan carne y pescado, que compren las tortugas más grandes, que vengan los forasteros a tender sus petates en los rincones y a orinarse en los rosales, que se sienten a la mesa a comer cuantas veces quieran, y que eructen y despotriquen y lo embarren todo con sus botas, y que hagan con nosotros lo que les dé la gana, porque esa es la única manera de espantar la ruina.» Pero era una ilusión vana. Estaba ya demasiado vieja y viviendo de sobra para repetir el milagro de los animalitos de caramelo, y ninguno de sus descendientes había heredado su fortaleza. La casa continuó cerrada por orden de Fernanda.

Aureliano Segundo, que había vuelto a llevarse sus baúles a casa de Petra Cotes, disponía apenas de los medios para que la familia no se muriera de hambre. Con la rifa de la mula, Petra Cotes y él habían comprado otros animales, con los cuales consiguieron enderezar un rudimentario negocio de lotería. Aureliano Segundo andaba de casa en casa, ofreciendo los billetitos que él mismo pintaba con tintas de colores para hacerlos más atractivos y convincentes, y acaso no se daba cuenta de que muchos se los compraban por gratitud, y la mayoría por compasión. Sin embargo, aun los más piadosos compradores adquirían la oportunidad de ganarse un cerdo por veinte centavos o una novilla por treinta y dos, y se entusiasmaban tanto con la esperanza, que la noche del martes desbordaban el patio de Petra Cotes esperando el momento en que un niño escogido al azar sacara de la bolsa el número premiado. Aquello no tardó en convertirse en una feria semanal, pues desde el atardecer se instalaban en el patio mesas de fritangas y puestos de bebidas, y muchos de los favorecidos sacrificaban allí mismo el animal ganado con la condición de que otros pusieran la música y el aguardiente, de modo que sin haberlo deseado Aureliano Segundo se encontró de pronto tocando otra vez el acordeón y participando en modestos torneos de voracidad. Estas humildes réplicas de las parrandas de otros días sirvieron para que el propio Aureliano Segundo descubriera cuánto habían decaído sus ánimos y hasta qué punto se había secado su ingenio de cumbiambero magistral. Era un hombre cambiado. Los ciento veinte kilos que llegó a tener en la época en que lo desafió La Elefanta se habían reducido a setenta y ocho; la candorosa y abotagada cara de tortuga se le había vuelto de iguana, y siempre andaba cerca del aburrimiento y el cansancio. Para Petra Cotes, sin embargo, nunca fue mejor hombre que entonces, tal vez porque confundía con el amor la compasión que él le inspiraba, y el sentimiento de solidaridad que en ambos había despertado la miseria. La cama desmantelada dejó de ser lugar de desafueros y se convirtió en refugio de confidencias. Liberados de los espejos repetidores que habían rematado para comprar animales de rifa, y de los damascos y terciopelos concupiscentes que se había comido la mula, se quedaban despiertos hasta muy tarde con la inocencia de dos abuelos desvelados, aprovechando para sacar cuentas y trasponer centavos el tiempo que antes malgastaban en malgastarse. A veces los sorprendían los primeros gallos haciendo y deshaciendo montoncitos de monedas, quitando un poco de aquí para ponerlo allá, de modo que esto alcanzara para contentar a Fernanda, y aquello para los zapatos de Amaranta Úrsula, y esto otro para Santa Sofía de la Piedad que no estrenaba un traje desde los tiempos del ruido, y esto para mandar hacer el cajón si se moría Úrsula, y esto para el café que subía un centavo por libra cada tres meses, y esto para el azúcar que cada vez endulzaba menos, y esto para la leña que todavía estaba mojada por el diluvio, y esto otro para el papel y la tinta de colores de los billetes, y aquello que sobraba para ir amortizando el valor de la ternera de abril, dc la cual milagrosamente salvaron el cuero, porque le dio carbunco sintomático cuando estaban vendidos casi todos los números de la rifa. Eran tan puras aquellas misas de pobreza, que siempre destinaban la mejor parte para Fernanda, y no lo hicieron nunca por remordimiento ni por caridad, sino porque su bienestar les importaba más que el de ellos mismos. Lo que en verdad les ocurría, aunque ninguno de los dos se daba cuenta, era que ambos pensaban en Fernanda como en la hija que hubieran querido tener y no tuvieron, hasta el punto de que en cierta ocasión se resignaron a comer mazamorra por tres días para que ella pudiera comprar un mantel holandés. Sin embargo, por más que se mataban trabajando, por mucho dinero que escamotearan y muchas triquiñuelas que concibieran, los ángeles de la guarda se les dormían de cansancio mientras ellos ponían y quitaban monedas tratando de que siquiera les alcanzaran para vivir. En el insomnio que les dejaban las malas cuentas, se preguntaban qué había pasado en el mundo para que los animales no parieran con el mismo desconcierto de antes, por qué el dinero se desbarataba en las manos, y por qué la gente que hacía poco tiempo quemaba mazos de billetes en la cumbiamba consideraba que era un asalto en despoblado cobrar doce centavos por la rifa de seis gallinas. Aureliano Segundo pensaba sin decirlo que el mal no estaba en el mundo, sino en algún lugar recóndito del misterioso corazón de Petra Cotes, donde algo había ocurrido durante el diluvio que volvió estériles a los animales y escurridizo el dinero. Intrigado con ese enigma, escarbó tan profundamente en los sentimientos de ella, que buscando el interés encontró el amor, porque tratando de que ella lo quisiera terminó por quererla. Petra Cotes, por su parte, lo iba queriendo más a medida que sentía aumentar su cariño, y fue así como en la plenitud del otoño volvió a creer en la superstición juvenil de que la pobreza era una servidumbre del amor. Ambos evocaban entonces como un estorbo las parrandas desatinadas, la riqueza aparatosa y la fornicación sin frenos, y se lamentaban de cuánta vida les había costado encontrar el paraíso de la soledad compartida. Locamente enamorados al cabo de tantos años de complicidad estéril, gozaban con el milagro de quererse tanto en la mesa como en la cama, y llegaron a ser tan felices, que todavía cuando eran dos ancianos agotados seguían retozando como conejitos y peleándose como perros.

Las rifas no dieron nunca para más. Al principio, Aureliano Segundo ocupaba tres días de la semana encerrado en su antigua oficina de ganadero, dibujando billete por billete, pintando con un cierto primor una vaquita roja, un cochinito verde o un grupo de gallinitas azules, según fuera el animal rifado, y modelaba con una buena imitación de las letras de imprenta el nombre que le pareció bueno a Petra Cotes para bautizar el negocio: *Rifas de la Divina Providencia*. Pero con el tiempo se sintió tan cansado después de dibujar hasta dos mil billetes a la semana, que mandó a hacer los animales, el nombre y los números en sellos de caucho, y entonces el trabajo se redujo a humedecerlos en almohadillas de distintos colores. En sus últimos años se les ocurrió sustituir los números por adivinanzas, de modo que el premio se repartiera entre todos los que acertaran, pero el sistema resultó ser tan complicado y se prestaba a tantas suspicacias, que desistieron a la segunda tentativa.

Aureliano Segundo andaba tan ocupado tratando de consolidar el prestigio de sus rifas, que apenas le quedaba tiempo para ver a los niños. Fernanda puso a Amaranta Úrsula en una escuelita privada donde no se recibían más de seis alumnas, pero se negó a permitir que Aureliano asisticra a la escuela pública. Consideraba que ya había cedido demasiado al aceptar que abandonara el cuarto. Además, en las escuelas de esa época sólo se recibían hijos legítimos de matrimonios católicos, y en el certificado de nacimiento que habían prendido con una nodriza en la batita de Aureliano cuando lo mandaron a la casa estaba registrado como expósito. De modo que se quedó encerrado, a merced de la vigilancia caritativa de Santa Sofía de la Piedad y de las alternativas mentales de Úrsula, descubriendo el estrecho mundo de la casa según se lo explicaban las abuelas. Era fino, estirado, de una curiosidad que sacaba de quicio a los adultos, pero al contrario de la mirada inquisitiva y a veces clarividente que tuvo el coronel a su edad, la suya era parpadeante y un poco distraída. Mientras Amaranta Úrsula estaba en el parvulario, él cazaba lombrices y torturaba insectos en el jardín. Pero una vez en que Fernanda lo sorprendió metiendo alacranes en una caja para ponerlos en la estera de Úrsula, lo recluyó en el antiguo dormitorio de Meme, donde se distrajo de sus horas solitarias repasando las láminas de la enciclopedia. Allí lo encontró Úrsula una tarde en que andaba asperjando la casa con agua serenada y un ramo de ortigas, y a pesar de que había estado con él muchas veces, le preguntó quién era.

—Soy Aureliano Buendía —dijo él.

—Es verdad —replicó ella—. Ya es hora de que empieces a aprender la platería.

Lo volvió a confundir con su hijo, porque el viento cálido que sucedió al diluvio e infundió en el cerebro de Úrsula ráfagas eventuales de lucidez había acabado de pasar. No volvió a recobrar la razón. Cuando entraba al dormitorio, encontraba allí a Petronila Iguarán, con el estorboso miriñaque y el saquito de mostacilla que se ponía para las visitas de compromiso, y encontraba a Tranquilina María Miniata Alacoque Buendía, su abuela, abanicándose con una pluma de pavorreal en su mecedor de tullida, y a su bisabuelo Aureliano Arcadio Buendía con su falso dormán de las guardias virreinales, y a Aureliano Iguarán, su padre, que había inventado una oración para que se achicharraran y se cayeran los gusanos de las vacas, y a la timorata de su madre, y al primo con la cola de cerdo, y a José Arcadio Buendía y a sus hijos muertos, todos sentados en sillas que habían sido recostadas contra la pared como si no estuvieran en una visita, sino en un velorio. Ella hilvanaba una cháchara colorida, comentando asuntos de lugares apartados y tiempos sin coincidencia, de modo que cuando Amaranta Úrsula regresaba de la escuela y Aureliano se cansaba de la enciclopedia, la encontraban sentada en la cama, hablando sola, y perdida en un laberinto de muertos. «¡Fuego!», gritó una vez aterrorizada, y por un instante sembró el pánico en la casa, pero lo que estaba anunciando era el incendio de una caballeriza que había presenciado a los cuatro años. Llegó a revolver de tal modo el pasado con la actualidad, que en las dos o tres ráfagas de lucidez que tuvo antes de morir, nadie supo a ciencia cierta si hablaba de lo que sentía o de lo que recordaba. Poco a poco se fue reduciendo, fetizándose, momificándose en vida, hasta el punto de que en sus últimos meses era una ciruela pasa perdida dentro del camisón, y el brazo siempre alzado terminó por parecer la pata de una marimonda. Se quedaba inmóvil varios días, y Santa Sofía de la Piedad tenía que sacudirla para convencerse de que estaba viva, y se la sentaba en las piernas para alimentarla con cucharaditas de agua de azúcar. Parecía una anciana recién nacida. Amaranta Úrsula y Aureliano la llevaban y la traían por el dormitorio, la acostaban en el altar para ver que era apenas más grande que el Niño Dios, y una tarde la escondieron en un armario del granero donde hubieran podido comérsela las ratas. Un domingo de ramos entraron al dormitorio mientras Fernanda estaba en misa, y cargaron a Úrsula por la nuca y los tobillos.

—Pobre la tatarabuelita —dijo Amaranta Úrsula—, se nos murió de vieja.

Úrsula se sobresaltó.

—¡Estoy viva! —dijo.

—Ya ves —dijo Amaranta Úrsula, reprimiendo la risa—, ni siquiera respira.

—¡Estoy hablando! —gritó Úrsula.

—Ni siquiera habla —dijo Aureliano—. Se murió como un grillito.

Entonces Úrsula se rindió a la evidencia. «Dios mío», exclamó en voz baja. «De modo que esto es la muerte.» Inició una oración interminable, atropellada, profunda, que se prolongó por más de dos días, y que el martes había degenerado en un revoltijo de súplicas a Dios y de consejos prácticos para que las hormigas coloradas no tumbaran la casa, para que nunca dejaran apagar la lámpara frente al daguerrotipo de Remedios, y para que cuidaran de que ningún Buendía fuera a casarse con alguien de su misma sangre, porque nacían los hijos con cola de puerco. Aureliano Segundo trató de aprovechar el delirio para que le confesara dónde estaba el oro enterrado, pero otra vez fueron inútiles las súplicas. «Cuando aparezca el dueño —dijo Úrsula— Dios ha de iluminarlo para que lo encuentre.» Santa Sofía de la Piedad tuvo la certeza de que la encontraría muerta de un momento a otro, porque observaba por esos días un cierto aturdimiento de la naturaleza: que las rosas olían a quenopodio, que se le cayó una totuma de garbanzos y los granos quedaron en el suelo en un orden geométrico perfecto y en forma de estrella de mar, y que una noche vio pasar por el cielo una fila de luminosos discos anaranjados.

Amaneció muerta el jueves santo. La última vez que la habían ayudado a sacar la cuenta de su edad, por los tiempos de la compañía bananera, la había calculado entre los ciento quince y los ciento veintidós años. La enterraron en una cajita que era apenas más grande que la canastilla en que fue llevado Aureliano, y muy poca gente asistió al entierro, en parte porque no eran muchos quienes se acordaban de ella, y en parte porque ese mediodía hubo tanto calor que los pájaros desorientados se estrellaban como perdigones contra las paredes y rompían las mallas metálicas de las ventanas para morirse en los dormitorios.

Al principio se creyó que era una peste. Las amas de casa se agotaban de tanto barrer pájaros muertos, sobre todo a la hora de la siesta, y los hombres los echaban al río por carretadas. El domingo de resurrección, el centenario padre Antonio Isabel afirmó en el púlpito que la muerte de los pájaros obedecía a la mala influencia del Judío Errante, que él mismo había visto la noche anterior. Lo describió como un híbrido de macho cabrío cruzado con hembra hereje, una bestia infernal cuyo aliento calcinaba el aire y cuya visita determinaría la concepción de engendros por las recién casadas. No fueron muchos quienes prestaron atención a su plática apocalíptica, porque el pueblo estaba convencido de que el párroco desvariaba a causa de la edad. Pero una mujer despertó a todos al amanecer del miércoles, porque encontró unas huellas de bípedo de pezuña hendida. Eran tan ciertas e inconfundibles, que quienes fueron a verlas no pusieron en duda la existencia de una criatura espantosa semejante a la descrita por el párroco, y se asociaron para montar trampas en sus patios. Fue así como lograron la captura. Dos semanas después de la muerte de Úrsula, Petra Cotes y Aureliano Segundo despertaron sobresaltados por un llanto de becerro descomunal que les llegaba del vecindario. Cuando se levantaron, ya un grupo de hombres estaba desensartando al monstruo de las afiladas varas que habían parado en el fondo de una fosa cubierta con hojas secas, y había dejado de berrear. Pesaba como un buey, a pesar de que su estatura no era mayor que la de un adolescente, y de sus heridas manaba una sangre verde y untuosa. Tenía el cuerpo cubierto de una pelambre áspera, plagada de garrapatas menudas, y el pellejo petrificado por una costra de rémora, pero al contrario de la descripción del párroco, sus partes humanas eran más de ángel valetudinario que de hombre, porque las manos eran tersas y hábiles, los ojos grandes y crepusculares, y tenía en los omoplatos los muñones cicatrizados y callosos de unas alas potentes, que debieron ser desbastadas con hachas de labrador. Lo colgaron por los tobillos en un almendro de la plaza, para que nadie se quedara sin verlo, y cuando empezó a pudrirse lo incineraron en una hoguera, porque no se pudo determinar si su naturaleza bastarda era de animal para echar en el río o de cristiano para sepultar. Nunca se estableció si en realidad fue por él que se murieron los pájaros, pero las recién casadas no concibieron los engendros anunciados, ni disminuyó la intensidad del calor.

Rebeca murió a fines de ese año. Argénida, su criada de toda la vida, pidió ayuda a las autoridades para derribar la puerta del dormitorio donde su patrona estaba encerrada desde hacía tres días, y la encontraron en la cama solitaria, enroscada como un camarón, con la cabeza pelada por la tiña y el pulgar metido en la boca. Aureliano Segundo se hizo cargo del entierro, y trató de restaurar la casa para venderla, pero la destrucción estaba tan encarnizada en ella que las paredes se desconchaban acabadas de pintar, y no hubo argamasa bastante gruesa para impedir que la cizaña triturara los pisos y la hiedra pudriera los horcones.

Todo andaba así desde el diluvio. La desidia de la gente contrastaba con la voracidad del olvido, que poco a poco iba carcomiendo sin piedad los recuerdos, hasta el extremo de que por esos tiempos, en un nuevo aniversario del tratado de Neerlandia, llegaron a Macondo unos emisarios del presidente de la república para entregar por fin la condecoración varias veces rechazada por el coronel Aureliano Buendía, y perdieron toda una tarde buscando a alguien que les indicara dónde podían encontrar a alguno de sus descendientes. Aureliano Segundo estuvo tentado de recibirla, creyendo que era una medalla de oro macizo, pero Petra Cotes lo persuadió de la indignidad cuando ya los emisarios aprestaban bandos y discursos para la ceremonia. También por esa época volvieron los gitanos, los últimos herederos de la ciencia de Melquíades, y encontraron el pueblo tan acabado y a sus habitantes tan apartados del resto del mundo, que volvieron a meterse en las casas arrastrando fierros imantados como si de veras fueran el último descubrimiento de los sabios babilonios, y volvieron a concentrar los rayos solares con la lupa gigantesca, y no faltó quien se quedara con la boca abierta viendo caer peroles y rodar calderos, y quienes pagaran cincuenta centavos para asombrarse con una gitana que se quitaba y se ponía la dentadura postiza. Un desvencijado tren amarillo que no traía ni se llevaba a nadie, y que apenas se detenía en la estación desierta, era lo único que quedaba del tren multitudinario en el cual enganchaba el señor Brown su vagón con techo de vidrio y poltronas de obispo, y de los trenes fruteros de ciento veinte vagones que demoraban pasando toda una tarde. Los delegados curiales que habían ido a investigar el informe sobre la extraña mortandad de los pájaros y el sacrificio del Judío Errante encontraron al padre Antonio Isabel jugando con los niños a la gallina ciega, y creyendo que su informe era producto de una alucinación senil, se lo llevaron a un asilo. Poco después mandaron al padre Augusto Ángel, un cruzado de las nuevas hornadas, intransigente, audaz, temerario, que tocaba personalmente las campanas varias veces al día para que no se aletargaran los espíritus, y que andaba de casa en casa despertando a los dormilones para que fueran a misa, pero antes de un año estaba también vencido por la negligencia que se respiraba en el aire, por el polvo ardiente que todo lo envejecía y atascaba, y por el sopor que le causaban las albóndigas del almuerzo en el calor insoportable de la siesta.

A la muerte de Úrsula, la casa volvió a caer en un abandono del cual no la podría rescatar ni siquiera una voluntad tan resuelta y vigorosa como la de Amaranta Úrsula, que muchos años después, siendo una mujer sin prejuicios, alegre y moderna, con los pies bien asentados en el mundo, abrió puertas y ventanas. Para espantar la ruina, restauró el jardín, exterminó las hormigas coloradas que ya andaban a pleno día por el corredor, y trató inútilmente de despertar el olvidado espíritu de hospitalidad. La pasión claustral de Fernanda puso un dique infranqueable a los cien años torrenciales de Úrsula. No sólo se negó a abrir las puertas cuando pasó el viento árido, sino que hizo clausurar las ventanas con crucetas de madera, obedeciendo a la consigna paterna de enterrarse en vida. La dispendiosa correspondencia con los médicos invisibles terminó en un fracaso. Después de numerosos aplazamientos, se encerró en su dormitorio en la fecha y la hora acordadas cubierta solamente por una sábana blanca y con la cabeza hacia el norte, y a la una de la madrugada sintió que le taparon la cara con un pañuelo embebido en un líquido glacial. Cuando despertó, el sol brillaba en la ventana y ella tenía una costura bárbara en forma de arco que empezaba en la ingle y terminaba en el esternón. Pero antes de que cumpliera el reposo previsto recibió una carta desconcertada de los médicos invisibles, quienes decían haberla registrado durante seis horas sin encontrar nada que correspondiera a los síntomas tantas veces y tan escrupulosamente descritos por ella. En realidad, su hábito pernicioso de no llamar las cosas por su nombre había dado origen a una nueva confusión, pues lo único que encontraron los cirujanos telepáticos fue un descendimiento del útero que podía corregirse con el uso de un pesario. La desilusionada Fernanda trató de obtener una información más precisa, pero los corresponsales ignotos no volvieron a contestar sus cartas. Se sintió tan agobiada por el peso de una palabra desconocida, que decidió amordazar la vergüenza para preguntar qué era un pesario, y sólo entonces supo que el médico francés se había colgado de una viga tres meses antes, y había sido enterrado contra la voluntad del pueblo por un antiguo compañero de armas del coronel Aureliano Buendía. Entonces se confió a su hijo José Arcadio, y éste le mandó los pesarios desde Roma, con un folletito explicativo que ella echó al excusado después de aprendérselo de memoria, para que nadie fuera a conocer la naturaleza de sus quebrantos. Era una precaución inútil, porque las únicas personas que vivían en la casa apenas si la tomaban en cuenta. Santa Sofía de la Piedad vagaba en una vejez solitaria, cocinando lo poco que se comían, y casi por completo dedicada al cuidado de José Arcadio Segundo. Amaranta Úrsula, heredera de ciertos encantos de Remedios, la bella, ocupaba en hacer sus tareas escolares el tiempo que antes perdía en atormentar a Úrsula, y empezaba a manifestar un buen juicio y una consagración a los estudios que hicieron renacer en Aureliano Segundo la buena esperanza que le inspiraba Meme. Le había prometido mandarla a terminar sus estudios en Bruselas, de acuerdo con una costumbre establecida en los tiempos de la compañía bananera, y esa ilusión lo había llevado a tratar de revivir las tierras devastadas por el diluvio. Las pocas veces que entonces se le veía en la casa, era por Amaranta Úrsula, pues con el tiempo se había convertido en un extraño para Fernanda, y el pequeño Aureliano se iba volviendo esquivo y ensimismado a medida que se acercaba a la pubertad. Aureliano Segundo confiaba en que la vejez ablandara el corazón de Fernanda, para que el niño pudiera incorporarse a la vida de un pueblo donde seguramente nadie se hubiera tomado el trabajo de hacer especulaciones suspicaces sobre su origen. Pero el propio Aureliano parecía preferir el encierro y la soledad, y no revelaba la menor malicia por conocer el mundo que empezaba en la puerta de la calle. Cuando Úrsula hizo abrir el cuarto de Melquíades, él se dio a rondarlo, a curiosear por la puerta entornada, y nadie supo en qué momento terminó vinculado a José Arcadio Segundo por un afecto recíproco. Aureliano Segundo descubrió esa amistad mucho tiempo después de iniciada, cuando oyó al niño hablando de la matanza de la estación. Ocurrió un día en que alguien se lamentó en la mesa de la ruina en que se hundió el pueblo cuando lo abandonó la compañía bananera, y Aureliano lo contradijo con una madurez y una versación de persona mayor. Su punto de vista, contrario a la interpretación general, era que Macondo fue un lugar próspero y bien encaminado hasta que lo desordenó y lo corrompió y lo exprimió la compañía bananera, cuyos ingenieros provocaron el diluvio como un pretexto para eludir compromisos con los trabajadores. Hablando con tan buen criterio que a Fernanda le pareció una parodia sacrílega de Jesús entre los doctores, el niño describió con detalles precisos y convincentes cómo el ejército ametralló a más de tres mil trabajadores acorralados en la estación, y cómo cargaron los cadáveres en un tren de doscientos vagones y los arrojaron al mar. Convencida como la mayoría de la gente de la verdad oficial de que no había pasado nada, Fernanda se escandalizó con la idea de que el niño había heredado los instintos anarquistas del coronel Aureliano Buendía, y le ordenó callarse. Aureliano Segundo, en cambio, reconoció la versión de su hermano gemelo. En realidad, a pesar de que todo el mundo lo tenía por loco, José Arcadio Segundo era en aquel tiempo el habitante más lúcido de la casa. Enseñó al pequeño Aureliano a leer y a escribir, lo inició en el estudio de los pergaminos, y le inculcó una interpretación tan personal de lo que significó para Macondo la compañía bananera, que muchos años después, cuando Aureliano se incorporara al mundo, había de pensarse que contaba una versión alucinada, porque era radicalmente contraria a la falsa que los historiadores habían admitido, y consagrado en los textos escolares. En el cuartito apartado, adonde nunca llegó el viento árido, ni el polvo ni el calor, ambos recordaban la visión atávica de un anciano con sombrero de alas de cuervo que hablaba del mundo a espaldas de la ventana, muchos años antes de que ellos nacieran. Ambos descubrieron al mismo tiempo que allí siempre era marzo y siempre era lunes, y entonces comprendieron que José Arcadio Buendía no estaba tan loco como contaba la familia, sino que era el único que había dispuesto de bastante lucidez para vislumbrar la verdad de que también el tiempo sufría tropiezos y accidentes, y podía por tanto astillarse y dejar en un cuarto una fracción eternizada. José Arcadio Segundo había logrado además clasificar las letras crípticas de los pergaminos. Estaba seguro de que correspondían a un alfabeto de cuarenta y siete a cincuenta y tres caracteres, que separados parecían arañitas y garrapatas, y que en la primorosa caligrafía de Melquíades parecían piezas de ropa puestas a secar en un alambre. Aureliano recordaba haber visto una tabla semejante en la enciclopedia inglesa, así que la llevó al cuarto para compararla con la de José Arcadio Segundo. Eran iguales, en efecto.

Por la época en que se le ocurrió la lotería de adivinanzas, Aureliano Segundo despertaba con un nudo en la garganta, como si estuviera reprimiendo las ganas de llorar. Petra Cotes lo interpretó como uno de los tantos trastornos provocados por la mala situación, y todas las mañanas, durante más de un año, le tocaba el paladar con un hisopo de miel de abejas y le daba jarabe de rábano. Cuando el nudo de la garganta se le hizo tan opresivo que le costaba trabajo respirar, Aureliano Segundo visitó a Pilar Ternera por si ella conocía alguna hierba de alivio. La inquebrantable abuela, que había llegado a los cien años al frente de un burdelito clandestino, no confió en supersticiones terapéuticas, sino que consultó el asunto con las barajas. Vio el caballo de oros con la garganta herida por el acero de la sota de espadas, y dedujo que Fernanda estaba tratando de que el marido volviera a la casa mediante el desprestigiado sistema de hincar alfileres en su retrato, pero que le había provocado un tumor interno por un conocimiento torpe de sus malas artes. Como Aureliano Segundo no tenía más retratos que los de la boda, y las copias estaban completas en el álbum familiar, siguió buscando por toda la casa en los descuidos de la esposa, y por fin encontró en el fondo del ropero media docena de pesarios en sus cajitas originales. Creyendo que las rojas llantitas de caucho eran objetos de hechicería, se metió una en el bolsillo para que la viera Pilar Ternera. Ella no pudo determinar su naturaleza, pero le pareció tan sospechosa, que de todos modos se hizo llevar la media docena y la quemó en una hoguera que prendió en el patio. Para conjurar el supuesto maleficio de Fernanda, le indicó a Aureliano Segundo que mojara una gallina clueca y la enterrara viva bajo el castaño, y él lo hizo de tan buena fe, que cuando acabó de disimular con hojas secas la tierra removida, ya sentía que respiraba mejor. Por su parte, Fernanda interpretó la desaparición como una represalia de los médicos invisibles, y se cosió en la parte interior de la camisola una faltriquera de jareta, donde guardó los pesarios nuevos que le mandó su hijo.

Seis meses después del enterramiento de la gallina, Aureliano Segundo despertó a medianoche con un acceso de tos, y sintiendo que lo estrangulaban por dentro con tenazas de cangrejo. Fue entonces

cuando comprendió que por muchos pesarios mágicos que destruyera y muchas gallinas de conjuro que
remojara, la única y triste verdad era que se estaba
muriendo. No se lo dijo a nadie. Atormentado por el
temor de morirse sin mandar a Bruselas a Amaranta
Úrsula, trabajó como nunca lo había hecho, y en vez
de una hizo tres rifas semanales. Desde muy temprano se le veía recorrer el pueblo, aun en los barrios
más apartados y miserables, tratando de vender los
billetitos con una ansiedad que sólo era concebible
en un moribundo. «Aquí está la Divina Providencia», pregonaba. «No la dejen ir, que sólo llega una
vez cada cien años.» Hacía conmovedores esfuerzos
por parecer alegre, simpático, locuaz, pero bastaba
verle el sudor y la palidez para saber que no podía
con su alma. A veces se desviaba por predios baldíos,
donde nadie lo viera, y se sentaba un momento a descansar de las tenazas que lo despedazaban por dentro. Todavía a la medianoche estaba en el barrio de
tolerancia, tratando de consolar con prédicas de buena suerte a las mujeres solitarias que sollozaban junto a las victrolas. «Este número no sale hace cuatro
meses», les decía, mostrándoles los billetitos. «No lo
dejes ir, que la vida es más corta de lo que uno cree.»
Acabaron por perderle el respeto, por burlarse de él,
y en sus últimos meses ya no le decían don Aureliano, como lo habían hecho siempre, sino que lo llamaban en su propia cara don Divina Providencia. La
voz se le iba llenando de notas falsas, se le fue des-
templando y terminó por apagársele en un ronquido
de perro, pero todavía tuvo voluntad para no dejar
que decayera la expectativa por los premios en el patio de Petra Cotes. Sin embargo, a medida que se
quedaba sin voz y se daba cuenta de que en poco

tiempo ya no podría soportar el dolor, iba comprendiendo que no era con cerdos y chivos rifados como su hija llegaría a Bruselas, de modo que concibió la idea de hacer la fabulosa rifa de las tierras destruidas por el diluvio, que bien podían ser restauradas por quien dispusiera de capital. Fue una iniciativa tan espectacular, que el propio alcalde se prestó para anunciarla con un bando, y se formaron sociedades para comprar billetes a cien pesos cada uno, que se agotaron en menos de una semana. La noche de la rifa, los ganadores hicieron una fiesta aparatosa, comparable apenas a las de los buenos tiempos de la compañía bananera, y Aureliano Segundo tocó en el acordeón por última vez las canciones olvidadas de Francisco el Hombre, pero ya no pudo cantarlas.

Dos meses después, Amaranta Úrsula se fue a Bruselas. Aureliano Segundo le entregó no sólo el dinero de la rifa extraordinaria, sino el que había logrado economizar en los meses anteriores, y el muy escaso que obtuvo por la venta de la pianola, el clavicordio y otros corotos caídos en desgracia. Según sus cálculos, ese fondo le alcanzaba para los estudios, así que sólo quedaba pendiente el valor del pasaje de regreso. Fernanda se opuso al viaje hasta el último momento, escandalizada con la idea de que Bruselas estuviera tan cerca de la perdición de París, pero se tranquilizó con una carta que le dio el padre Ángel para una pensión de jóvenes católicas atendida por religiosas, donde Amaranta Úrsula prometió vivir hasta el término de sus estudios. Además, el párroco consiguió que viajara al cuidado de un grupo de franciscanas que iban para Toledo, donde esperaban encontrar gente de confianza para mandarla a Bélgica. Mientras se adelantaba la apresurada correspon-

dencia que hizo posible esta coordinación, Aureliano Segundo, ayudado por Petra Cotes, se ocupó del
equipaje de Amaranta Úrsula. La noche en que pre-
pararon uno de los baúles nupciales de Fernanda, las
cosas estaban tan bien dispuestas que la estudiante sabía de memoria cuáles eran los trajes y las babuchas de pana con que debía hacer la travesía del
Atlántico, y el abrigo de paño azul con botones de
cobre, y los zapatos de cordobán con que debía des-
embarcar. Sabía también cómo debía caminar para
no caer al agua cuando subiera a bordo por la plataforma, que en ningún momento debía separarse de
las monjas ni salir del camarote como no fuera para
comer, y que por ningún motivo debía contestar a las
preguntas que los desconocidos de cualquier sexo le
hicieran en alta mar. Llevaba un frasquito con gotas
para el mareo y un cuaderno escrito de su puño y letra por el padre Ángel, con seis oraciones para conjurar la tempestad. Fernanda le fabricó un cinturón
de lona para que guardara el dinero, y le indicó la
forma de usarlo ajustado al cuerpo, de modo que no
tuviera que quitárselo ni siquiera para dormir. Trató
de regalarle la bacinilla de oro lavada con lejía y de-
sinfectada con alcohol, pero Amaranta Úrsula la rechazó por miedo de que se burlaran de ella sus compañeras de colegio. Pocos meses después, a la hora de
la muerte, Aureliano Segundo había de recordarla
como la vio la última vez, tratando de bajar sin conseguirlo el cristal polvoriento del vagón de segunda
clase, para escuchar las últimas recomendaciones de
Fernanda. Llevaba un traje de seda rosada con un
ramito de pensamientos artificiales en el broche del
hombro izquierdo; los zapatos de cordobán con tra-
billa y tacón bajo, y las medias satinadas con ligas

elásticas en las pantorrillas. Tenía el cuerpo menudo, el cabello suelto y largo y los ojos vivaces que tuvo Úrsula a su edad, y la forma en que se despedía, sin llorar pero sin sonreír, revelaba la misma fortaleza de carácter. Caminando junto al vagón a medida que aceleraba, y llevando a Fernanda del brazo para que no fuera a tropezar, Aureliano Segundo apenas pudo corresponderle con un saludo de la mano, cuando la hija le mandó un beso con la punta de los dedos. Los esposos permanecieron inmóviles bajo el sol abrasante, mirando cómo el tren se iba confundiendo con el punto negro del horizonte, y tomados del brazo por primera vez desde el día de la boda.

El nueve de agosto, antes de que se recibiera la primera carta de Bruselas, José Arcadio Segundo conversaba con Aureliano en el cuarto de Melquíades, y sin que viniera a cuento dijo:

—Acuérdate siempre de que eran más de tres mil y que los echaron al mar.

Luego se fue de bruces sobre los pergaminos, y murió con los ojos abiertos. En ese mismo instante, en la cama de Fernanda, su hermano gemelo llegó al final del prolongado y terrible martirio de los cangrejos de hierro que le carcomieron la garganta. Una semana antes había vuelto a la casa, sin voz, sin aliento y casi en los puros huesos, con sus baúles trashumantes y su acordeón de perdulario, para cumplir la promesa de morir junto a la esposa. Petra Cotes lo ayudó a recoger sus ropas y lo despidió sin derramar una lágrima, pero olvidó darle los zapatos de charol que él quería llevar en el ataúd. De modo que cuando supo que había muerto, se vistió de negro, envolvió los botines en un periódico, y le pidió permiso a Fernanda para ver al cadáver. Fernanda no la dejó pasar de la puerta.

—Póngase en mi lugar —suplicó Petra Cotes—. Imagínese cuánto lo habré querido para soportar esta humillación.

—No hay humillación que no la merezca una concubina —replicó Fernanda—. Así que espere a que se muera otro de los tantos para ponerle esos botines.

En cumplimiento de su promesa, Santa Sofía de la Piedad degolló con un cuchillo de cocina el cadáver de José Arcadio Segundo para asegurarse de que no lo enterraran vivo. Los cuerpos fueron puestos en ataúdes iguales, y allí se vio que volvían a ser idénticos en la muerte, como lo fueron hasta la adolescencia. Los viejos compañeros de parranda de Aureliano Segundo pusieron sobre su caja una corona que tenía una cinta morada con un letrero: *Apártense vacas que la vida es corta.* Fernanda se indignó tanto con la irreverencia que mandó tirar la corona en la basura. En el tumulto de última hora, los borrachitos tristes que los sacaron de la casa confundieron los ataúdes y los enterraron en tumbas equivocadas.

Aureliano no abandonó en mucho tiempo el cuarto de Melquíades. Se aprendió de memoria las leyendas fantásticas del libro desencuadernado, la síntesis de los estudios de Hermann, el tullido; los apuntes sobre la ciencia demonológica, las claves de la piedra filosofal, las *Centurias* de Nostradamus y sus investigaciones sobre la peste, de modo que llegó a la adolescencia sin saber nada de su tiempo, pero con los conocimientos básicos del hombre medieval. A cualquier hora que entrara en el cuarto, Santa Sofía de la Piedad lo encontraba absorto en la lectura. Le llevaba al amanecer un tazón de café sin azúcar, y al mediodía un plato de arroz con tajadas de plátano fritas, que era lo único que se comía en la casa después de la muerte de Aureliano Segundo. Se preocupaba por cortarle el pelo, por sacarle las liendres, por adaptarle la ropa vieja que encontraba en baúles olvidados, y cuando empezó a despuntarle el bigote le llevó la navaja barbera y la totumita para la espuma del coronel Aureliano Buendía. Ninguno de los hijos de éste se le pareció tanto, ni siquiera Aureliano José, sobre todo por los pómulos pronunciados, y la línea resuelta y un poco despiadada de los labios. Como le ocurrió a Úrsula con Aureliano Segundo cuando éste estudiaba en el cuarto, Santa Sofía de la Piedad creía que Aureliano hablaba solo. En realidad, conversaba con Melquíades. Un mediodía ardiente, poco después de la muerte de los gemelos, vio contra la reverberación de la ventana al anciano lúgubre con el sombrero de alas de cuervo, como la materialización de un recuerdo que estaba en su memoria desde mucho antes de nacer. Aureliano había terminado de clasificar el alfabeto de los pergaminos. Así que cuando Melquíades le preguntó si había descubierto en qué lengua estaban escritos, él no vaciló para contestar.

—En sánscrito —dijo.

Melquíades le reveló que sus oportunidades de volver al cuarto estaban contadas. Pero se iba tranquilo a las praderas de la muerte definitiva, porque Aureliano tenía tiempo de aprender el sánscrito en los años que faltaban para que los pergaminos cumplieran un siglo y pudieran ser descifrados. Fue él quien le indicó que en el callejón que terminaba en el río, y donde en los tiempos de la compañía bananera se adivinaba el porvenir y se interpretaban los sueños, un sabio catalán tenía una tienda de libros donde había un *Sanskrit Primer* que sería devorado por las polillas seis años después si él no se apresuraba a comprarlo. Por primera vez en su larga vida Santa Sofía de la Piedad dejó traslucir un sentimiento, y era un sentimiento de estupor, cuando Aureliano le pidió que le llevara el libro que había de encontrar entre la *Jerusalén Libertada* y los poemas de Milton, en el extremo derecho del segundo renglón de los anaqueles. Como no sabía leer, se aprendió de memoria la parrafada, y consiguió el dinero con la venta de uno de los diecisiete pescaditos de oro que quedaban en el taller, y que sólo ella y Aureliano sabían dónde los habían puesto la noche en que los soldados registraron la casa.

Aureliano avanzaba en los estudios del sánscrito, mientras Melquíades iba haciéndose cada vez menos asiduo y más lejano, esfumándose en la claridad radiante del mediodía. La última vez que Aureliano lo sintió era apenas una presencia invisible que murmuraba: «He muerto de fiebre en los médanos de Singapur.» El cuarto se hizo entonces vulnerable al polvo, al calor, al comején, a las hormigas coloradas, a las polillas que habían de convertir en aserrín la sabiduría de los libros y los pergaminos.

En la casa no faltaba qué comer. Al día siguiente de la muerte de Aureliano Segundo, uno de los amigos que habían llevado la corona con la inscripción irreverente le ofreció pagarle a Fernanda un dinero que le había quedado debiendo a su esposo. A partir de entonces, un mandadero llevaba todos los miércoles un canasto con cosas de comer, que alcanzaban bien para una semana. Nadie supo nunca que aquellas vituallas las mandaba Petra Cotes, con la idea de que la caridad continuada era una forma de humillar a quien la había humillado. Sin embargo, el rencor se le disipó mucho más pronto de lo que ella misma esperaba, y entonces siguió mandando la comida por orgullo y finalmente por compasión. Varias veces, cuando le faltaron ánimos para vender billetitos y la gente perdió el interés por las rifas, se quedó ella sin comer para que comiera Fernanda, y no dejó de cumplir el compromiso mientras no vio pasar su entierro.

Para Santa Sofía de la Piedad, la reducción de los habitantes de la casa debía haber sido el descanso a

425

que tenía derecho después de más de medio siglo de trabajo. Nunca se le había oído un lamento a aquella mujer sigilosa, impenetrable, que sembró en la familia los gérmenes angélicos de Remedios, la bella, y la misteriosa solemnidad de José Arcadio Segundo; que consagró toda una vida de soledad y silencio a la crianza de unos niños que apenas si recordaban que eran sus hijos y sus nietos, y que se ocupó de Aureliano como si hubiera salido de sus entrañas, sin saber ella misma que era su bisabuela. Sólo en una casa como aquélla era concebible que hubiera dormido siempre en un petate que tendía en el piso del granero, entre el estrépito nocturno de las ratas, y sin haberle contado a nadie que una noche la despertó la pavorosa sensación de que alguien la estaba mirando en la oscuridad, y era que una víbora se deslizaba por su vientre. Ella sabía que si se lo hubiera contado a Úrsula la hubiera puesto a dormir en su propia cama, pero eran los tiempos en que nadie se daba cuenta de nada mientras no se gritara en el corredor, porque los afanes de la panadería, los sobresaltos de la guerra, el cuidado de los niños, no dejaban tiempo para pensar en la felicidad ajena. Petra Cotes, a quien nunca vio, era la única que se acordaba de ella. Estaba pendiente de que tuviera un buen par de zapatos para salir, de que nunca le faltara un traje, aun en los tiempos en que hacía milagros con el dinero de las rifas. Cuando Fernanda llegó a la casa tuvo motivos para creer que era una sirvienta eternizada, y aunque varias veces oyó decir que era la madre de su esposo, aquello le resultaba tan increíble que más tardaba en saberlo que en olvidarlo. Santa Sofía de la Piedad no pareció molestarse nunca por aquella condición subalterna. Al contrario, se tenía la impresión de que le gustaba andar por los rincones, sin una tregua, sin un quejido, manteniendo ordenada y limpia la inmensa casa donde vivió desde la adolescencia, y que particularmente en los tiempos de la compañía bananera parecía más un cuartel que un hogar. Pero cuando murió Úrsula, la diligencia inhumana de Santa Sofía de la Piedad, su tremenda capacidad de trabajo, empezaron a quebrantarse. No era solamente que estuviera vieja y agotada, sino que la casa se precipitó de la noche a la mañana en una crisis de senilidad. Un musgo tierno se trepó por las paredes. Cuando ya no hubo un lugar pelado en los patios, la maleza rompió por debajo el cemento del corredor, lo resquebrajó como un cristal, y salieron por las grietas las mismas florecitas amarillas que casi un siglo antes había encontrado Úrsula en el vaso donde estaba la dentadura postiza de Melquíades. Sin tiempo ni recursos para impedir los desafueros de la naturaleza, Santa Sofía de la Piedad se pasaba el día en los dormitorios, espantando los lagartos que volverían a meterse por la noche. Una mañana vio que las hormigas coloradas abandonaron los cimientos socavados, atravesaron el jardín, subieron por el pasamanos donde las begonias habían adquirido un color de tierra, y entraron hasta el fondo de la casa. Trató primero de matarlas con una escoba, luego con insecticida y por último con cal, pero al otro día estaban otra vez en el mismo lugar, pasando siempre, tenaces e invencibles. Fernanda, escribiendo cartas a sus hijos, no se daba cuenta de la arremetida incontenible de la destrucción. Santa Sofía de la Piedad siguió luchando sola, peleando con la maleza para que no entrara en la cocina, arrancando de las paredes los borlones de telaraña que se reproducían en pocas horas, raspando el comején. Pero cuando vio que también el cuarto de Melquíades estaba telarañado y polvoriento, así lo barriera y sacudiera tres veces al día, y que a pesar de su furia limpiadora estaba amenazado por los escombros y el aire de miseria que sólo el coronel Aureliano Buendía y el joven militar habían previsto, comprendió que estaba vencida. Entonces se puso el gastado traje dominical, unos viejos zapatos de Úrsula y un par de medias de algodón que le había regalado Amaranta Úrsula, e hizo un atadito con las dos o tres mudas que le quedaban.

—Me rindo —le dijo a Aureliano—. Esta es mucha casa para mis pobres huesos.

Aureliano le preguntó para dónde iba, y ella hizo un gesto de vaguedad, como si no tuviera la menor idea de su destino. Trató de precisar, sin embargo, que iba a pasar sus últimos años con una prima hermana que vivía en Riohacha. No era una explicación verosímil. Desde la muerte de sus padres, no había tenido contacto con nadie en el pueblo, ni recibió cartas ni recados, ni se le oyó hablar de pariente alguno. Aureliano le dio catorce pescaditos de oro, porque ella estaba dispuesta a irse con lo único que tenía: un peso y veinticinco centavos. Desde la ventana del cuarto, él la vio atravesar el patio con su atadito de ropa, arrastrando los pies y arqueada por los años, y la vio meter la mano por un hueco del portón para poner la aldaba después de haber salido. Jamás se volvió a saber de ella.

Cuando se enteró de la fuga, Fernanda despotricó un día entero, mientras revisaba baúles, cómodas y armarios, cosa por cosa, para convencerse de que Santa Sofía de la Piedad no se había alzado con nada. Se quemó los dedos tratando de prender un fogón por primera vez en la vida, y tuvo que pedirle a Aureliano el favor de enseñarle a preparar el café. Con el tiempo, fue él quien hizo los oficios de cocina. Al levantarse, Fernanda encontraba el desayuno servido, y sólo volvía a abandonar el dormitorio para coger la comida que Aureliano le dejaba tapada en rescoldo, y que ella llevaba a la mesa para comérsela en manteles de lino y entre candelabros, sentada en una cabecera solitaria al extremo de quince sillas vacías. Aun en esas circunstancias, Aureliano y Fernanda no compartieron la soledad, sino que siguieron viviendo cada uno en la suya, haciendo la limpieza del cuarto respectivo, mientras la telaraña iba nevando los rosales, tapizando las vigas, acolchonando las paredes. Fue por esa época que Fernanda tuvo la impresión de que la casa se estaba llenando de duendes. Era como si los objetos, sobre todo los de uso diario, hubieran desarrollado la facultad de cambiar de lugar por sus propios medios. A Fernanda se le iba el tiempo en buscar las tijeras que estaba segura de haber puesto en la cama y, después de revolverlo todo, las encontraba en una repisa de la cocina, donde creía no haber estado en cuatro días. De pronto no había un tenedor en la gaveta de los cubiertos, y encontraba seis en el altar y tres en el lavadero. Aquella caminadera de las cosas era más desesperante cuando se sentaba a escribir. El tintero que ponía a la derecha aparecía a la izquierda, la almohadilla del papel secante se le perdía, y la encontraba dos días después debajo de la almohada, y las páginas escritas a José Arcadio se le confundían con las de Amaranta Úrsula, y siempre andaba con la mortificación de haber metido las cartas en sobres cambiados, como en efecto le ocurrió varias veces. En cierta ocasión perdió la pluma. Quince días después se la devolvió el cartero, que la había encontrado en su bolsa y andaba buscando al dueño de casa en casa. Al principio, ella creyó que eran cosas de los médicos invisibles, como la desaparición de los pesarios, y hasta empezó a escribirles una carta para suplicarles que la dejaran en paz, pero había tenido que interrumpirla para hacer algo, y cuando volvió al cuarto no sólo no encontró la carta empezada, sino que se olvidó del propósito de escribirla. Por un tiempo pensó que era Aureliano. Se dio a vigilarlo, a poner objetos a su paso tratando de sorprenderlo en el momento en que los cambiara de lugar, pero muy pronto se convenció de que Aureliano no abandonaba el cuarto de Melquíades sino para ir a la cocina o al excusado, y que no era hombre de burlas. De modo que terminó por creer que eran travesuras de duendes, y optó por asegurar cada cosa en el sitio donde tenía que usarla. Amarró las tijeras con una larga pita en la cabecera de la cama. Amarró el plumero y la almohadilla del papel secante en la pata de la mesa, y pegó con goma el tintero en la tabla, a la derecha del lugar en que solía escribir. Los problemas no se resolvieron de un día para otro, pues a las pocas horas de costura ya la pita de las tijeras no alcanzaba para cortar, como si los duendes la fueran disminuyendo. Le ocurría lo mismo con la pita de la pluma, y hasta con su propio brazo, que al poco tiempo de estar escribiendo no alcanzaba el tintero. Ni Amaranta Úrsula, en Bruselas, ni José Arcadio, en Roma, se enteraron jamás de esos insignificantes infortunios. Fernanda les contaba que era feliz, y en realidad lo era, justamente porque se sentía liberada de todo compromiso, como si la vida la hubiera arrastrado otra vez hasta el mundo de sus padres, donde no se sufría con los problemas diarios porque estaban resueltos de antemano en la imaginación. Aquella correspondencia interminable le hizo perder el sentido del tiempo, sobre todo después de que se fue Santa Sofía de la Piedad. Se había acostumbrado a llevar la cuenta de los días, los meses y los años, tomando como puntos de referencia las fechas previstas para el retorno de los hijos. Pero cuando éstos modificaron los plazos una y otra vez, las fechas se le confundieron, los términos se le traspapelaron, y las jornadas se parecieron tanto las unas a las otras, que no se sentían transcurrir. En lugar de impacientarse, experimentaba una honda complacencia con la demora. No la inquietaba que muchos años después de anunciarle las vísperas de sus votos perpetuos, José Arcadio siguiera diciendo que esperaba terminar los estudios de alta teología para emprender los de diplomacia, porque ella comprendía que era muy alta y empedrada de obstáculos la escalera de caracol que conducía a la silla de San Pedro. En cambio, el espíritu se le exaltaba con noticias que para otros hubieran sido insignificantes, como aquella de que su hijo había visto al Papa. Experimentó un gozo similar cuando Amaranta Úrsula le mandó decir que sus estudios se prolongaban más del tiempo previsto, porque sus excelentes calificaciones le habían merecido privilegios que su padre no tomó en consideración al hacer las cuentas.

Habían transcurrido más de tres años desde que Santa Sofía de la Piedad le llevó la gramática, cuando Aureliano consiguió traducir el primer pliego. No fue una labor inútil, pero constituía apenas un primer paso en un camino cuya longitud era imposible prever, porque el texto en castellano no significa-ba nada: eran versos cifrados. Aureliano carecía de elementos para establecer las claves que le permitieran desentrañarlos, pero como Melquíades le había dicho que en la tienda del sabio catalán estaban los libros que le harían falta para llegar al fondo de los pergaminos, decidió hablar con Fernanda para que le permitiera ir a buscarlos. En el cuarto devorado por los escombros, cuya proliferación incontenible había terminado por derrotarlo, pensaba en la forma más adecuada de formular la solicitud, se anticipaba a las circunstancias, calculaba la ocasión más adecuada, pero cuando encontraba a Fernanda retirando la comida del rescoldo, que era la única oportunidad para hablarle, la solicitud laboriosamente premeditada se le atragantaba, y se le perdía la voz. Fue aquella la única vez en que la espió. Estaba pendiente de sus pasos en el dormitorio. La oía ir hasta la puerta para recibir las cartas de sus hijos y entregarle las suyas al cartero, y escuchaba hasta muy altas horas de la noche el trazo duro y apasionado de la pluma en el papel, antes de oír el ruido del interruptor y el murmullo de las oraciones en la oscuridad. Sólo entonces se dormía, confiando en que el día siguiente le daría la oportunidad esperada. Se ilusionó tanto con la idea de que el permiso no le sería negado que una mañana se cortó el cabello que ya le daba a los hombros, se afeitó la barba enmarañada, se puso unos pantalones estrechos y una camisa de cuello postizo que no sabía de quién había heredado, y esperó en la cocina a que Fernanda fuera a desayunar. No llegó la mujer de todos los días, la de la cabeza alzada y la andadura pétrea, sino una anciana de una hermosura sobrenatural, con una amarillenta capa de armiño, una corona de cartón dorado, y la conducta lánguida de quien ha llorado en secreto. En realidad, desde que lo encontró en los baúles de Aureliano Segundo, Fernanda se había puesto muchas veces el apolillado vestido de reina. Cualquiera que la hubiera visto frente al espejo, extasiada en sus propios ademanes monárquicos, habría podido pensar que estaba loca. Pero no lo estaba. Simplemente, había convertido los atuendos reales en una máquina de recordar. La primera vez que se los puso no pudo evitar que se le formara un nudo en el corazón y que los ojos se le llenaran de lágrimas, porque en aquel instante volvió a percibir el olor de betún de las botas del militar que fue a buscarla a su casa para hacerla reina, y el alma se le cristalizó con la nostalgia de los sueños perdidos. Se sintió tan vieja, tan acabada, tan distante de las mejores horas de su vida, que inclusive añoró las que recordaba como las peores, y sólo entonces descubrió cuánta falta hacían las ráfagas de orégano en el corredor, y el vapor de los rosales al atardecer, y hasta la naturaleza bestial de los advenedizos. Su corazón de ceniza apelmazada, que había resistido sin quebrantos a los golpes más certeros de la realidad cotidiana, se desmoronó a los primeros embates de la nostalgia. La necesidad de sentirse triste se le iba convirtiendo en un vicio a medida que la devastaban los años. Se humanizó en la soledad. Sin embargo, la mañana en que entró en la cocina y se encontró con una taza de café que le ofrecía un adolescente óseo y pálido, con un resplandor alucinado en los ojos, la desgarró el zarpazo del ridículo. No sólo le negó el permiso, sino que desde entonces cargó las llaves de la casa en la bolsa donde guardaba los pesarios sin usar. Era una precaución inútil, porque de haberlo querido Aureliano hubiera podido escapar y hasta volver a casa sin ser visto. Pero el prolongado cautiverio, la incertidumbre del mundo, el hábito de obedecer, habían resecado en su corazón las semillas de la rebeldía. De modo que volvió a su clausura, pasando y repasando los pergaminos, y oyendo hasta muy avanzada la noche los sollozos de Fernanda en el dormitorio. Una mañana fue como de costumbre a prender el fogón, y encontró en las cenizas apagadas la comida que había dejado para ella el día anterior. Entonces se asomó al dormitorio, y la vio tendida en la cama, tapada con la capa de armiño, más bella que nunca, y con la piel convertida en una cáscara de marfil. Cuatro meses después, cuando llegó José Arcadio, la encontró intacta.

Era imposible concebir un hombre más parecido a su madre. Llevaba un traje de tafetán luctuoso, una camisa de cuello redondo y duro, y una delgada cinta de seda con un lazo, en lugar de la corbata. Era lívido, lánguido, de mirada atónita y labios débiles. El cabello negro, lustrado y liso, partido en el centro del cráneo por una línea recta y exangüe, tenía la misma apariencia postiza del pelo de los santos. La sombra de la barba bien destroncada en el rostro de parafina parecía un asunto de la conciencia. Tenía las manos pálidas, con nervaduras verdes y dedos parasitarios, y un anillo de oro macizo con un ópalo girasol, redondo, en el índice izquierdo. Cuando le abrió la puerta de la calle, Aureliano no hubiera tenido la necesidad de suponer quién era para darse cuenta de que venía de muy lejos. La casa se impregnó a su paso de la fragancia de agua de florida que Úrsula le echaba en la cabeza cuando era niño, para poder encontrarlo en las tinieblas. De algún modo imposible de precisar, después de tantos años de ausencia José

Arcadio seguía siendo un niño otoñal, terriblemente triste y solitario. Fue directamente al dormitorio de su madre, donde Aureliano había vaporizado mercurio durante cuatro meses en el atanor del abuelo de su abuelo, para conservar el cuerpo según la fórmula de Melquíades. José Arcadio no hizo ninguna pregunta. Le dio un beso en la frente al cadáver, le sacó de debajo de la falda la faltriquera de jareta donde había tres pesarios todavía sin usar, y la llave del ropero. Hacía todo con ademanes directos y decididos, en contraste con su languidez. Sacó del ropero un cofrecito damasquinado con el escudo familiar, y encontró en el interior perfumado de sándalo la carta voluminosa en que Fernanda desahogó el corazón de las incontables verdades que le había ocultado. La leyó de pie, con avidez pero sin ansiedad, y en la tercera página se detuvo, y examinó a Aureliano con una mirada de segundo reconocimiento.

—Entonces —dijo con una voz que tenía algo de navaja de afeitar—, tú eres el bastardo.

—Soy Aureliano Buendía.

—Vete a tu cuarto —dijo José Arcadio.

Aureliano se fue, y no volvió a salir ni siquiera por curiosidad cuando oyó el rumor de los funerales solitarios. A veces, desde la cocina, veía a José Arcadio deambulando por la casa, ahogándose en su respiración anhelante, y seguía escuchando sus pasos por los dormitorios en ruinas después de la medianoche. No oyó su voz en muchos meses, no sólo porque José Arcadio no le dirigía la palabra, sino porque él no tenía deseos de que ocurriera, ni tiempo de pensar en nada distinto de los pergaminos. A la muerte de Fernanda, había sacado el penúltimo pescadito y había ido a la librería del sabio catalán, en busca de los libros que le hacían falta. No le interesó nada de lo que vio en el trayecto, acaso porque carecía de recuerdos para comparar, y las calles desiertas y las casas desoladas eran iguales a como las había imaginado en un tiempo en que hubiera dado el alma por conocerlas. Se había concedido a sí mismo el permiso que le negó Fernanda, y sólo por una vez, con un objetivo único y por el tiempo mínimo indispensable, así que recorrió sin pausa las once cuadras que separaban la casa del callejón donde antes se interpretaban los sueños, y entró acezando en el abigarrado y sombrío local donde apenas había espacio para moverse. Más que una librería, aquello parecía un basurero de libros usados, puestos en desorden en los estantes mellados por el comején, en los rincones amelazados de telaraña, y aun en los espacios que debieron destinarse a los pasadizos. En una larga mesa, también agobiada de mamotretos, el propietario escribía una prosa incansable, con una caligrafía morada, un poco delirante, y en hojas sueltas de cuaderno escolar. Tenía una hermosa cabellera plateada que se le adelantaba en la frente como el penacho de una cacatúa, y sus ojos azules, vivos y estrechos, revelaban la mansedumbre del hombre que ha leído todos los libros. Estaba en calzoncillos, empapado en sudor, y no desatendió la escritura para ver quién había llegado. Aureliano no tuvo dificultad para rescatar de entre aquel desorden de fábula los cinco libros que buscaba, pues estaban en el lugar exacto que le indicó Melquíades. Sin decir una palabra, se los entregó junto con el pescadito de oro al sabio catalán, y éste los examinó, y sus párpados se contrajeron como dos almejas. «Debes estar loco», dijo en su lengua, alzándose de hombros, y le devolvió a Aureliano los cinco libros y el pescadito.

—Llévatelos —dijo en castellano—. El último hombre que leyó esos libros debió ser Isaac el Ciego, así que piensa bien lo que haces.

José Arcadio restauró el dormitorio de Meme, mandó limpiar y remendar las cortinas de terciopelo y el damasco del baldaquín de la cama virreinal, y puso otra vez en servicio el baño abandonado, cuya alberca de cemento estaba renegrida por una nata fibrosa y áspera. A esos dos lugares se redujo su imperio de pacotilla, de gastados géneros exóticos, de perfumes falsos y pedrería barata. Lo único que pareció estorbarle en el resto de la casa fueron los santos del altar doméstico, que una tarde quemó hasta convertirlos en ceniza, en una hoguera que prendió en el patio. Dormía hasta después de las once. Iba al baño con una deshilachada túnica de dragones dorados y unas chinelas de borlas amarillas, y allí oficiaba un rito que por su parsimonia y duración recordaba al de Remedios, la bella. Antes de bañarse, aromaba la alberca con las sales que llevaba en tres pomos alabastrados. No se hacía abluciones con la totuma, sino que se zambullía en las aguas fragantes, y permanecía hasta dos horas flotando bocarriba, adormecido por la frescura y por el recuerdo de Amaranta. A los pocos días de haber llegado abandonó el vestido de tafetán, que además de ser demasiado caliente para el pueblo era el único que tenía, y lo cambió por unos pantalones ajustados, muy parecidos a los que usaba Pietro Crespi en las clases de baile, y una camisa de seda tejida con el gusano vivo, y con sus iniciales bordadas en el corazón. Dos veces por semana lavaba la muda completa en la alberca, y se quedaba con la túnica hasta que se secaba, pues no tenía nada más que ponerse. Nunca comía en la casa.

Salía a la calle cuando aflojaba el calor de la siesta, y no regresaba hasta muy entrada la noche. Entonces continuaba su deambular angustioso, respirando como un gato, y pensando en Amaranta. Ella, y la mirada espantosa de los santos en el fulgor de la lámpara nocturna, eran los dos recuerdos que conservaba de la casa. Muchas veces, en el alucinante agosto romano, había abierto los ojos en mitad del sueño, y había visto a Amaranta surgiendo de un estanque de mármol brocatel, con sus pollerines de encaje y su venda en la mano, idealizada por la ansiedad del exilio. Al contrario de Aureliano José, que trató de sofocar aquella imagen en el pantano sangriento de la guerra, él trataba de mantenerla viva en un cenagal de concupiscencia, mientras entretenía a su madre con la patraña sin término de la vocación pontificia. Ni a él ni a Fernanda se les ocurrió pensar nunca que su correspondencia era un intercambio de fantasías. José Arcadio, que abandonó el seminario tan pronto como llegó a Roma, siguió alimentando la leyenda de la teología y el derecho canónico, para no poner en peligro la herencia fabulosa de que le hablaban las cartas delirantes de su madre, y que había de rescatarlo de la miseria y la sordidez que compartía con dos amigos en una buhardilla del Trastevere. Cuando recibió la última carta de Fernanda, dictada por el presentimiento de la muerte inminente, metió en una maleta los últimos desperdicios de su falso esplendor, y atravesó el océano en una bodega donde los emigrantes se apelotonaban como reses de matadero, comiendo macarrones fríos y queso agusanado. Antes de leer el testamento de Fernanda, que no era más que una minuciosa y tardía recapitulación de infortunios, ya los muebles desvencijados y la maleza del corredor le habían indicado que estaba metido en una trampa de la cual no saldría jamás, para siempre exiliado de la luz de diamante y el aire inmemorial de la primavera romana. En los insomnios agotadores del asma, medía y volvía a medir la profundidad de su desventura, mientras repasaba la casa tenebrosa donde los aspavientos seniles de Úrsula le infundieron el miedo del mundo. Para estar segura de no perderlo en las tinieblas, ella le había asignado un rincón del dormitorio, el único donde podría estar a salvo de los muertos que deambulaban por la casa desde el atardecer. «Cualquier cosa mala que hagas —le decía Úrsula— me la dirán los santos.» Las noches pávidas de su infancia se redujeron a ese rincón, donde permanecía inmóvil hasta la hora de acostarse sudando de miedo en un taburete, bajo la mirada vigilante y glacial de los santos acusetas. Era una tortura inútil, porque ya para esa época él tenía terror de todo lo que lo rodeaba, y estaba preparado para asustarse de todo lo que encontrara en la vida: las mujeres de la calle, que echaban a perder la sangre; las mujeres de la casa, que parían hijos con cola de puerco; los gallos de pelea, que provocaban muertes de hombres y remordimientos de conciencia para el resto de la vida; las armas de fuego, que con sólo tocarlas condenaban a veinte años de guerra; las empresas desacertadas, que sólo conducían al desencanto y la locura, y todo, en fin, todo cuanto Dios había creado con su infinita bondad, y que el diablo había pervertido. Al despertar, molido por el torno de las pesadillas, la claridad de la ventana y las caricias de Amaranta en la alberca, y el deleite con que lo empolvaba entre las piernas con una bellota de seda, lo liberaban del terror. Hasta Úrsula era distinta bajo la luz radiante del jardín, porque allí no le hablaba de cosas de pavor, sino que le frotaba los dientes con polvo de carbón para que tuviera la sonrisa radiante de un Papa, y le cortaba y le pulía las uñas para que los peregrinos que llegaran a Roma de todo el ámbito de la tierra se asombraran de la pulcritud de las manos del Papa cuando les echara la bendición, y lo peinaba como un Papa, y lo ensopaba con agua de florida para que su cuerpo y sus ropas tuvieran la fragancia de un Papa. En el patio de Castelgandolfo él había visto al Papa en un balcón, pronunciando el mismo discurso en siete idiomas para una muchedumbre de peregrinos, y lo único que en efecto le había llamado la atención era la blancura de sus manos, que parecían maceradas en lejía, el resplandor deslumbrante de sus ropas de verano, y su recóndito hálito de agua de colonia.

Casi un año después del regreso a la casa, habiendo vendido para comer los candelabros de plata y la bacinilla heráldica que a la hora de la verdad sólo tuvo de oro las incrustaciones del escudo, la única distracción de José Arcadio era recoger niños en el pueblo para que jugaran en la casa. Aparecía con ellos a la hora de la siesta, y los hacía saltar la cuerda en el jardín, cantar en el corredor y hacer maromas en los muebles de la sala, mientras él iba por entre los grupos impartiendo lecciones de buen comportamiento. Para esa época había acabado con los pantalones estrechos y la camisa de seda, y usaba una muda ordinaria comprada en los almacenes de los árabes, pero seguía manteniendo su dignidad lánguida y sus ademanes papales. Los niños se tomaron la casa como lo hicieron en el pasado las compañeras de Meme. Hasta muy entrada la noche se les oía cotorrear y cantar y bailar zapateados, de modo que la casa parecía un internado sin disciplina. Aureliano no se preocupó de la invasión mientras no fueron a molestarlo en el cuarto de Melquíades. Una mañana, dos niños empujaron la puerta, y se espantaron ante la visión del hombre cochambroso y peludo que seguía descifrando los pergaminos en la mesa de trabajo. No se atrevieron a entrar, pero siguieron rondando la habitación. Se asomaban cuchicheando por las hendijas, arrojaban animales vivos por las claraboyas y en una ocasión clavetearon por fuera la puerta y la ventana, y Aureliano necesitó medio día para forzarlas. Divertidos por la impunidad de sus travesuras, cuatro niños entraron otra mañana en el cuarto, mientras Aureliano estaba en la cocina, dispuestos a destruir los pergaminos. Pero tan pronto como se apoderaron de los pliegos amarillentos, una fuerza angélica los levantó del suelo, y los mantuvo suspendidos en el aire, hasta que regresó Aureliano y les arrebató los pergaminos. Desde entonces no volvieron a molestarlo.

Los cuatro niños mayores, que usaban pantalones cortos a pesar de que ya se asomaban a la adolescencia, se ocupaban de la apariencia personal de José Arcadio. Llegaban más temprano que los otros, y dedicaban la mañana a afeitarlo, a darle masajes con toallas calientes, a cortarle y pulirle las uñas de las manos y los pies, a perfumarlo con agua de florida. En varias ocasiones se metieron en la alberca, para jabonarlo de pies a cabeza, mientras él flotaba bocarriba, pensando en Amaranta. Luego lo secaban, le empolvaban el cuerpo, y lo vestían. Uno de los niños, que tenía el cabello rubio y crespo, y los ojos de vidrios rosados como los conejos, solía dormir en la casa. Eran tan firmes los vínculos que lo unían a José Arcadio que lo acompañaba en sus insomnios de asmático, sin hablar, deambulando con él por la casa en tinieblas. Una noche vieron en la alcoba donde dormía Úrsula un resplandor amarillo a través del cemento cristalizado, como si un sol subterráneo hubiera convertido en vitral el piso del dormitorio. No tuvieron que encender el foco. Les bastó con levantar las placas quebradas del rincón donde siempre estuvo la cama de Úrsula, y donde el resplandor era más intenso, para encontrar la cripta secreta que Aureliano Segundo se cansó de buscar en el delirio de las excavaciones. Allí estaban los tres sacos de lona cerrados con alambre de cobre y, dentro de ellos, los siete mil doscientos catorce doblones de a cuatro, que seguían relumbrando como brasas en la oscuridad.

El hallazgo del tesoro fue como una deflagración. En vez de regresar a Roma con la intempestiva fortuna, que era el sueño madurado en la miseria, José Arcadio convirtió la casa en un paraíso decadente. Cambió por terciopelo nuevo las cortinas y el baldaquín del dormitorio, y les hizo poner baldosas al piso del baño y azulejos a las paredes. La alacena del comedor se llenó de frutas azucaradas, jamones y encurtidos, y el granero en desuso volvió a abrirse para almacenar vinos y licores que el propio José Arcadio retiraba en la estación del ferrocarril, en cajas marcadas con su nombre. Una noche, él y los cuatro niños mayores hicieron una fiesta que se prolongó hasta el amanecer. A las seis de la mañana salieron desnudos del dormitorio, vaciaron la alberca y la llenaron de champaña. Se zambulleron en bandada, nadando como pájaros que volaran en un cielo dorado de burbujas fragantes, mientras José Arcadio flotaba bocarriba, al margen de la fiesta, evocando a Amaranta con los ojos abiertos. Permaneció así, ensimismado, rumiando la amargura de sus placeres equívocos, hasta después de que los niños se cansaron y se fueron en tropel al dormitorio, donde arrancaron las cortinas de terciopelo para secarse, y cuartearon en el desorden la luna de cristal de roca, y desbarataron el baldaquín de la cama tratando de acostarse en tumulto. Cuando José Arcadio volvía del baño, los encontró durmiendo apelotonados, desnudos, en una alcoba de naufragio. Enardecido no tanto por los estragos como por el asco y la lástima que sentía contra sí mismo en el desolado vacío de la saturnal, se armó con unas disciplinas de perrero eclesiástico que guardaba en el fondo del baúl, junto con un cilicio y otros fierros de mortificación y penitencia, y expulsó a los niños de la casa, aullando como un loco, y azotándolos sin misericordia, como no lo hubiera hecho con una jauría de coyotes. Quedó demolido, con una crisis de asma que se prolongó por varios días, y que le dio el aspecto de un agonizante. A la tercera noche de tortura, vencido por la asfixia, fue al cuarto de Aureliano a pedirle el favor de que le comprara en una botica cercana unos polvos para inhalar. Fue así como hizo Aureliano su segunda salida a la calle. Sólo tuvo que recorrer dos cuadras para llegar hasta la estrecha botica de polvorientas vidrieras con pomos de loza marcados en latín donde una muchacha con la sigilosa belleza de una serpiente del Nilo le despachó el medicamento que José Arcadio le había escrito en un papel. La segunda visión del pueblo desierto, alumbrado apenas por las amarillentas bombillas de las calles, no despertó en Aureliano más curiosidad que la primera vez. José Arcadio había alcanzado a pensar que había huido, cuando lo vio aparecer de nuevo, un poco anhelante a causa de la prisa, arrastrando las piernas que el encierro y la falta de movilidad habían vuelto débiles y torpes. Era tan cierta su indiferencia por el mundo que pocos días después José Arcadio violó la promesa que había hecho a su madre, y lo dejó en libertad para salir cuando quisiera.

—No tengo nada que hacer en la calle —le contestó Aureliano.

Siguió encerrado, absorto en los pergaminos que poco a poco iba desentrañando, y cuyo sentido, sin embargo, no lograba interpretar. José Arcadio le llevaba al cuarto rebanadas de jamón, flores azucaradas que dejaban en la boca un regusto primaveral, y en dos ocasiones un vaso de buen vino. No se interesó en los pergaminos, que consideraba más bien como un entretenimiento esotérico, pero le llamó la atención la rara sabiduría y el inexplicable conocimiento del mundo que tenía aquel pariente desolado. Supo entonces que era capaz de comprender el inglés escrito, y que entre pergamino y pergamino había leído de la primera página a la última, como si fuera una novela, los seis tomos de la enciclopedia. A eso atribuyó al principio el que Aureliano pudiera hablar de Roma como si hubiera vivido allí muchos años, pero muy pronto se dio cuenta de que tenía conocimientos que no eran enciclopédicos, como los precios de las cosas. «Todo se sabe», fue la única respuesta que recibió de Aureliano, cuando le preguntó cómo había obtenido aquellas informaciones. Aureliano, por su parte, se sorprendió de que José Arcadio visto de cerca fuera tan distinto de la imagen que se había formado de él cuando lo veía deambular por la casa. Era capaz de reír, de permitirse de vez en cuando una nostalgia del pasado de la casa, y de preocuparse por el ambiente de miseria en que se encontraba el cuarto de Melquíades. Aquel acercamiento entre dos solitarios de la misma sangre estaba muy lejos de la amistad, pero les permitió a ambos sobrellevar mejor la insondable soledad que al mismo tiempo los separaba y los unía. José Arcadio pudo entonces acudir a Aureliano para desenredar ciertos problemas domésticos que lo exasperaban. Aureliano, a su vez, podía sentarse a leer en el corredor, recibir las cartas de Amaranta Úrsula que seguían llegando con la puntualidad de siempre, y usar el baño de donde lo había desterrado José Arcadio desde su llegada.

Una calurosa madrugada ambos despertaron alarmados por unos golpes apremiantes en la puerta de la calle. Era un anciano oscuro, con unos ojos grandes y verdes que le daban a su rostro una fosforescencia espectral, y con una cruz de ceniza en la frente. Las ropas en piltrafas, los zapatos rotos, la vieja mochila que llevaba en el hombro como único equipaje, le daban el aspecto de un pordiosero, pero su conducta tenía una dignidad que estaba en franca contradicción con su apariencia. Bastaba con verlo una vez, aun en la penumbra de la sala, para darse cuenta de que la fuerza secreta que le permitía vivir no era el instinto de conservación, sino la costumbre del miedo. Era Aureliano Amador, el único sobreviviente de los diecisiete hijos del coronel Aureliano Buendía, que iba buscando una tregua en su larga y azarosa existencia de fugitivo. Se identificó, suplicó que le dieran refugio en aquella casa que en sus noches de paria había evocado como el último reducto de seguridad que le quedaba en la vida. Pero José Arcadio y Aureliano no lo recordaban. Creyendo que era un vagabundo, lo echaron a la calle a empellones. Ambos vieron entonces desde la puerta el final de un drama que había empezado desde antes de que José Arcadio tuviera uso de razón. Dos agentes de la policía que habían perseguido a Aureliano Amador durante años, que lo habían rastreado como perros por medio mundo, surgieron de entre los almendros de la acera opuesta y le hicieron dos tiros de máuser que le penetraron limpiamente por la cruz de ceniza.

En realidad, desde que expulsó a los niños de la casa, José Arcadio esperaba noticias de un trasatlántico que saliera para Nápoles antes de Navidad. Se lo había dicho a Aureliano, e inclusive había hecho planes para dejarle montado un negocio que le permitiera vivir, porque la canastilla de víveres no volvió a llegar desde el entierro de Fernanda. Sin embargo, tampoco aquel sueño final había de cumplirse. Una mañana de setiembre, después de tomar el café con Aureliano en la cocina, José Arcadio estaba terminando su baño diario cuando irrumpieron por entre los portillos de las tejas los cuatro niños que había expulsado de la casa. Sin darle tiempo de defenderse, se metieron vestidos en la alberca, lo agarraron por el pelo y le mantuvieron la cabeza hundida, hasta que cesó en la superficie la borboritación de la agonía, y el silencioso y pálido cuerpo de delfín se deslizó hasta el fondo de las aguas fragantes. Después se llevaron los tres sacos de oro que sólo ellos y su víctima sabían dónde estaban escondidos. Fue una acción tan rápida, metódica y brutal, que pareció un asalto de militares. Aureliano, encerrado en su cuarto, no se dio cuenta de nada. Esa tarde, habiéndolo echado de menos en la cocina, buscó a José Arcadio por toda la casa, y lo encontró flotando en los espejos perfumados de la alberca, enorme y tumefacto, y todavía pensando en Amaranta. Sólo entonces comprendió cuánto había empezado a quererlo.

Amaranta Úrsula regresó con los primeros ángeles de diciembre, empujada por brisas de velero, llevando al esposo amarrado por el cuello con un cordel de seda. Apareció sin ningún anuncio, con un vestido color de marfil, un hilo de perlas que le daba casi a las rodillas, sortijas de esmeraldas y topacios, y el cabello redondo y liso rematado en las orejas con puntas de golondrinas. El hombre con quien se había casado seis meses antes era un flamenco maduro, esbelto, con aires de navegante. No tuvo sino que empujar la puerta de la sala para comprender que su ausencia había sido más prolongada y demoledora de lo que ella suponía.

—Dios mío —gritó, más alegre que alarmada—, ¡cómo se ve que no hay una mujer en esta casa!

El equipaje no cabía en el corredor. Además del antiguo baúl de Fernanda con que la mandaron al colegio, llevaba dos roperos verticales, cuatro maletas grandes, un talego para las sombrillas, ocho cajas de sombreros, una jaula gigantesca con medio centenar de canarios, y el velocípedo del marido, desarmado dentro de un estuche especial que permitía llevarlo como un violoncelo. Ni siquiera se permitió un día de descanso al cabo del largo viaje. Se puso un gastado overol de lienzo que había llevado el esposo con otras prendas de motorista, y emprendió una nueva restauración de la casa. Desbandó las hormigas coloradas que ya se habían apoderado del corredor, resucitó los rosales, arrancó la maleza de raíz, y volvió a sembrar helechos, oréganos y begonias en los tiestos del pasamanos. Se puso al frente de una cuadrilla de carpinteros, cerrajeros y albañiles que resanaron las grietas de los pisos, enquiciaron puertas y ventanas, renovaron los muebles y blanquearon las paredes por dentro y por fuera, de modo que tres meses después de su llegada se respiraba otra vez el aire de juventud y de fiesta que hubo en los tiempos de la pianola. Nunca se vio en la casa a nadie con mejor humor a toda hora y en cualquier circunstancia, ni a nadie más dispuesto a cantar y bailar, y a tirar en la basura las cosas y las costumbres revenidas. De un escobazo acabó con los recuerdos funerarios y los montones de cherembecos inútiles y aparatos de superstición que se apelotonaban en los rincones, y lo único que conservó, por gratitud a Úrsula, fue el daguerrotipo de Remedios en la sala. «Miren qué lujo», gritaba muerta de risa. «¡Una bisabuela de catorce años!» Cuando uno de los albañiles le contó que la casa estaba poblada de aparecidos, y que el único modo de espantarlos era buscando los tesoros que habían dejado enterrados, ella replicó entre carcajadas que no creía en supersticiones de hombres. Era tan espontánea, tan emancipada, con un espíritu tan moderno y libre, que Aureliano no supo qué hacer con el cuerpo cuando la vio llegar. «¡Qué bárbaro!», gritó ella, feliz, con los brazos abiertos. «¡Miren cómo ha crecido mi adorado antropófago!» Antes de que él tuviera tiempo de reaccionar, ya ella había puesto un disco en el gramófono portátil que llevó consigo, y estaba tratando de enseñarle los bailes de moda. Lo obligó a cambiarse los escuálidos pantalones que heredó del coronel Aureliano Buendía, le regaló camisas juveniles y zapatos de dos colores, y lo empujaba a la calle cuando pasaba mucho tiempo en el cuarto de Melquíades.

Activa, menuda, indomable, como Úrsula, y casi tan bella y provocativa como Remedios, la bella, estaba dotada de un raro instinto para anticiparse a la moda. Cuando recibía por correo los figurines más recientes, apenas le servían para comprobar que no se había equivocado en los modelos que inventaba, y que cosía en la rudimentaria máquina de manivela de Amaranta. Estaba suscrita a cuanta revista de modas, información artística y música popular se publicara en Europa, y apenas les echaba una ojeada para darse cuenta de que las cosas iban en el mundo como ella las imaginaba. No era comprensible que una mujer con aquel espíritu hubiera regresado a un pueblo muerto, deprimido por el polvo y el calor, y menos con un marido que tenía dinero de sobra para vivir bien en cualquier parte del mundo, y que la amaba tanto que se había sometido a ser llevado y traído por ella con el dogal de seda. Sin embargo, a medida que el tiempo pasaba era más evidente su intención de quedarse, pues no concebía planes que no fueran a largo plazo, ni tomaba determinaciones que no estuvieran orientadas a procurarse una vida cómoda y una vejez tranquila en Macondo. La jaula de canarios demostraba que esos propósitos no eran improvisados. Recordando que su madre le había contado en una carta el exterminio de los pájaros, había retrasado el viaje varios meses hasta encontrar un barco que hiciera escala en las islas Afortunadas, y allí seleccionó las veinticinco parejas de canarios más finos para repoblar el cielo de Macondo. Esa fue la más lamentable de sus numerosas iniciativas frustradas. A medida que los pájaros se reproducían, Amaranta Úrsula los iba soltando por parejas, y más tardaban en sentirse libres que en fugarse del pueblo. En vano procuró encariñarlos con la pajarera que construyó Úrsula en la primera restauración. En vano les falsificó nidos de esparto en los almendros, y regó alpiste en los techos y alborotó a los cautivos para que sus cantos disuadieran a los desertores, porque éstos se remontaban a la primera tentativa y daban una vuelta en el cielo, apenas el tiempo indispensable para encontrar el rumbo de regreso a las islas Afortunadas.

Un año después del retorno, aunque no hubiera conseguido entablar una amistad ni promover una fiesta, Amaranta Úrsula seguía creyendo que era posible rescatar aquella comunidad elegida por el infortunio. Gastón, su marido, se cuidaba de no contrariarla, aunque desde el mediodía mortal en que descendió del tren comprendió que la determinación de su mujer había sido provocada por un espejismo de la nostalgia. Seguro de que sería derrotada por la realidad, no se tomó siquiera el trabajo de armar el velocípedo, sino que se dio a perseguir los huevos más lúcidos entre las telarañas que desprendían los albañiles, y los abría con las uñas y se gastaba las horas contemplando con una lupa las arañitas minúsculas que salían del interior. Más tarde, creyendo que Amaranta Úrsula continuaba con las reformas por no dar su brazo a torcer, resolvió armar el aparatoso velocípedo cuya rueda anterior era mucho más grande que la posterior, y se dedicó a capturar y disecar cuanto insecto aborigen encontraba en los contornos, que remitía en frascos de mermelada a su antiguo profesor de historia natural de la universidad de Lieja, donde había hecho estudios avanzados en entomología, aunque su vocación dominante era la de aeronauta. Cuando andaba en el velocípedo usaba pantalones de acróbata, medias de gaitero y cachucha de detective, pero cuando andaba de a pie vestía de lino crudo, intachable, con zapatos blancos, corbatín de seda, sombrero canotier y una vara de mimbre en la mano. Tenía unas pupilas pálidas que acentuaban su aire de navegante, y un bigotito de pelos de ardilla. Aunque era por lo menos quince años mayor que su mujer, sus gustos juveniles, su vigilante determinación de hacerla feliz, y sus virtudes de buen amante, compensaban la diferencia. En realidad, quienes veían aquel cuarentón de hábitos cautelosos, con su sedal al cuello y su bicicleta de circo, no hubieran podido pensar que tenía con su joven esposa un pacto de amor desenfrenado, y que ambos cedían al apremio recíproco en los lugares menos adecuados y donde los sorprendiera la inspiración, como lo hicieron desde que empezaron a verse, y con una pasión que el transcurso del tiempo y las circunstancias cada vez más insólitas iban profundizando y enriqueciendo. Gastón no sólo era un amante feroz, de una sabiduría y una imaginación inagotables, sino que era tal vez el primer hombre en la historia de la especie que hizo un aterrizaje de emergencia y estuvo a punto de matarse con su novia sólo por hacer el amor en un campo de violetas.

Se habían conocido tres años antes de casarse, cuando el biplano deportivo en que él hacía piruetas sobre el colegio en que estudiaba Amaranta Úrsula intentó una maniobra intrépida para eludir el asta de la bandera, y la primitiva armazón de lona y papel de aluminio quedó colgada por la cola en los cables de la energía eléctrica. Desde entonces, sin hacer caso de su pierna entablillada, él iba los fines de semana a recoger a Amaranta Úrsula en la pensión de religiosas donde vivió siempre, cuyo reglamento no era tan severo como deseaba Fernanda, y la llevaba a su club deportivo. Empezaron a amarse a 500 metros de altura, en el aire dominical de las landas, y más se sentían compenetrados mientras más minúsculos iban haciéndose los seres de la tierra. Ella le hablaba de Macondo como del pueblo más luminoso y plácido del mundo, y de una casa enorme, perfumada de orégano, donde quería vivir hasta la vejez con un marido leal y dos hijos indómitos que se llamaran Rodrigo y Gonzalo, y en ningún caso Aureliano y José Arcadio, y una hija que se llamara Virginia, y en ningún caso Remedios. Había evocado con una tenacidad tan anhelante el pueblo idealizado por la nostalgia, que Gastón comprendió que ella no quisiera casarse si no la llevaba a vivir en Macondo. Él estuvo de acuerdo, como lo estuvo más tarde con el sedal, porque creyó que era un capricho transitorio que más valía defraudar a tiempo. Pero cuando transcurrieron dos años en Macondo y Amaranta Úrsula seguía tan contenta como el primer día, él comenzó a dar señales de alarma. Ya para entonces había disecado cuanto insecto era disecable en la región, hablaba el castellano como un nativo, y había descifrado todos los crucigramas de las revistas que recibían por correo. No tenía el pretexto del clima para apresurar el regreso, porque la naturaleza lo había dotado de un hígado colonial, que resistía sin quebrantos el bochorno de la siesta y el agua con gusarapos. Le gustaba tanto la comida criolla, que una vez se comió un sartal de ochenta y dos huevos de iguana. Amaranta Úrsula, en cambio, se hacía llevar en el tren pescados y mariscos en cajas de hielo, carnes en latas y frutas almibaradas, que era lo único que podía comer, y seguía vistiéndose a la moda europea y recibiendo figurines por correo, a pesar de que no tenía donde ir ni a quién visitar, y de que a esas alturas su marido carecía de humor para apreciar sus vestidos cortos, sus fieltros ladeados y sus collares de siete vueltas. Su secreto parecía consistir en que siempre encontraba el modo de estar ocupada, resolviendo problemas domésticos que ella misma creaba y haciendo mal ciertas cosas que corregía al día siguiente, con una diligencia perniciosa que habría hecho pensar a Fernanda en el vicio hereditario de hacer para deshacer. Su genio festivo continuaba entonces tan despierto, que cuando recibía discos nuevos invitaba a Gastón a quedarse en la sala hasta muy tarde para ensayar los bailes que sus compañeras de colegio le describían con dibujos, y terminaban generalmente haciendo el amor en los mecedores vieneses o en el suelo pelado. Lo único que le faltaba para ser completamente feliz era el nacimiento de los hijos, pero respetaba el pacto que había hecho con su marido de no tenerlos antes de cumplir cinco años de casados.

Buscando algo con que llenar sus horas muertas Gastón solía pasar la mañana en el cuarto de Melquíades, con el esquivo Aureliano. Se complacía en evocar con él los rincones más íntimos de su tierra, que Aureliano conocía como si hubiera estado en ella mucho tiempo. Cuando Gastón le preguntó cómo había hecho para obtener informaciones que no estaban en la enciclopedia, recibió la misma respuesta que José Arcadio: «Todo se sabe.» Además del sánscrito, Aureliano había aprendido el inglés y el francés, y algo del latín y del griego. Como entonces salía todas las tardes, y Amaranta Úrsula le había asignado una suma semanal para sus gastos personales, su cuarto parecía una sección de la librería del sabio catalán. Leía con avidez hasta muy altas horas de la noche, aunque por la forma en que se refería a sus lecturas, Gastón pensaba que no compraba los libros para informarse sino para verificar la exactitud de sus conocimientos, y que ninguno le interesaba más que los pergaminos, a los cuales dedicaba las mejores horas de la mañana. Tanto a Gastón como a su esposa les habría gustado incorporarlo a la vida familiar, pero Aureliano era hombre hermético, con una nube de misterio que el tiempo iba haciendo más densa. Era una condición tan infranqueable, que Gastón fracasó en sus esfuerzos por intimar con él, y tuvo que buscarse otro entretenimiento para llenar sus horas muertas. Fue por esa época que concibió la idea de establecer un servicio de correo aéreo.

No era un proyecto nuevo. En realidad lo tenía bastante avanzado cuando conoció a Amaranta Úrsula, sólo que no era para Macondo sino para el Congo Belga, donde su familia tenía inversiones en aceite de palma. El matrimonio, la decisión de pasar unos meses en Macondo para complacer a la esposa, lo habían obligado a aplazarlo. Pero cuando vio que Amaranta Úrsula estaba empeñada en organizar una junta de mejoras públicas y hasta se reía de él por insinuar la posibilidad del regreso, comprendió que las cosas iban para largo, y volvió a establecer contacto con sus olvidados socios de Bruselas, pensando que para ser pionero daba lo mismo el Caribe que el África. Mientras progresaban las gestiones, preparó un campo de aterrizaje en la antigua región encantada que entonces parecía una llanura de pedernal resquebrajado, y estudió la dirección de los vientos, la geografía del litoral y las rutas más adecuadas para la navegación aérea, sin saber que su diligencia, tan parecida a la de Mr. Herbert, estaba infundiendo en el pueblo la peligrosa sospecha de que su propósito no era planear itinerarios sino sembrar banano. Entusiasmado con una ocurrencia que después de todo podía justificar su establecimiento definitivo en Macondo, hizo varios viajes a la capital de la provincia, se entrevistó con las autoridades, y obtuvo licencias y suscribió contratos de exclusividad. Mientras tanto, mantenía con los socios de Bruselas una correspondencia parecida a la de Fernanda con los médicos invisibles, y acabó de convencerlos de que embarcaran el primer aeroplano al cuidado de un mecánico experto, que lo armara en el puerto más próximo y lo llevara volando a Macondo. Un año después de las primeras mediciones y cálculos meteorológicos, confiando en las promesas reiteradas de sus corresponsales, había adquirido la costumbre de pasearse por las calles, mirando el cielo, pendiente de los rumores de la brisa, en espera de que apareciera el aeroplano.

Aunque ella no lo había notado, el regreso de Amaranta Úrsula determinó un cambio radical en la vida de Aureliano. Después de la muerte de José Arcadio, se había vuelto un cliente asiduo de la librería del sabio catalán. Además, la libertad de que entonces disfrutaba, y el tiempo de que disponía, le despertaron una cierta curiosidad por el pueblo, que conoció sin asombro. Recorrió las calles polvorientas y solitarias, examinando con un interés más científico que humano el interior de las casas en ruinas, las redes metálicas de las ventanas rotas por el óxido y los pájaros moribundos, y los habitantes abatidos por los recuerdos. Trató de reconstruir con la imaginación el arrasado esplendor de la antigua ciudad de la compañía bananera, cuya piscina seca estaba llena hasta los bordes de podridos zapatos de hombre y zapatillas de mujer, y en cuyas casas desbaratadas por la cizaña encontró el esqueleto de un perro alemán todavía atado a una argolla con una cadena de acero, y un teléfono que repicaba, repicaba, repicaba, hasta que él lo descolgó, entendió lo que una mujer angustiada y remota preguntaba en inglés, y le contestó que sí, que la huelga había terminado, que los tres mil muertos habían sido echados al mar, que la compañía bananera se había ido, y que Macondo estaba por fin en paz desde hacía muchos años. Aquellas correrías lo llevaron al postrado barrio de tolerancia, donde en otros tiempos se quemaban mazos de billetes para animar la cumbiamba, y que entonces era un vericueto de calles más afligidas y miserables que las otras, con algunos focos rojos todavía encendidos, y con yermos salones de baile adornados con piltrafas de guirnaldas, donde las macilentas y gordas viudas de nadie, las bisabuelas francesas y las matriarcas babilónicas, continuaban esperando junto a las victrolas. Aureliano no encontró quien recordara a su familia, ni siquiera al coronel Aureliano Buendía, salvo el más antiguo de los negros antillanos, un anciano cuya cabeza algodonada le daba el aspecto de un negativo de fotografía, que seguía cantando en el pórtico de la casa los salmos lúgubres del atardecer. Aureliano conversaba con él en el enrevesado papiamento que aprendió en pocas semanas, y a veces compartía el caldo de cabezas de gallo que preparaba la bisnieta, una negra grande, de huesos sólidos, caderas de yegua y tetas de melones vivos, y una cabeza redonda, perfecta, acorazada por un duro capacete de pelos de alambre, que parecía el almófar de un guerrero medieval. Se llamaba Nigromanta. Por esa época, Aureliano vivía de vender cubiertos, palmatorias y otros chécheres de la casa. Cuando andaba sin un céntimo, que era lo más frecuente, conseguía que en las fondas del mercado le regalaran las cabezas de gallo que iban a tirar en la basura, y se las llevaba a Nigromanta para que le hiciera sus sopas aumentadas con verdolaga y perfumadas con hierbabuena. Al morir el bisabuelo, Aureliano dejó de frecuentar la casa, pero se encontraba a Nigromanta bajo los oscuros almendros de la plaza, cautivando con sus silbos de animal montuno a los escasos trasnochadores. Muchas veces la acompañó, hablando en papiamento de las sopas de cabezas de gallo y otras exquisiteces de la miseria, y hubiera seguido haciéndolo si ella no lo hubiera hecho caer en la cuenta de que su compañía le ahuyentaba la clientela. Aunque algunas veces sintió la tentación, y aunque a la propia Nigromanta le hubiera parecido una culminación natural de la nostalgia compartida, no se acostaba con ella. De modo que Aureliano seguía siendo virgen cuando Amaranta Úrsula regresó a Macondo y le dio un abrazo fraternal que lo dejó sin aliento. Cada vez que la veía, y peor aun cuando ella le enseñaba los bailes de moda, él sentía el mismo desamparo de esponjas en los huesos que turbó a su tatarabuelo cuando Pilar Ternera le puso pretextos de barajas en el granero. Tratando de sofocar el tormento, se sumergió más a fondo en los pergaminos y eludió los halagos inocentes de aquella tía que emponzoñaba sus noches con efluvios de tribulación, pero mientras más la evitaba, con más ansiedad esperaba su risa pedregosa, sus aullidos de gata feliz y sus canciones de gratitud, agonizando de amor a cualquier hora y en los lugares menos pensados de la casa. Una noche, a diez metros de su cama, en el mesón de platería, los esposos del vientre desquiciado desbarataron la vidriera y terminaron amándose en un charco de ácido muriático. Aureliano no sólo no pudo dormir un minuto, sino que pasó el día siguiente con calentura, sollozando de rabia. Se le hizo eterna la llegada de la primera noche en que esperó a Nigromanta a la sombra de los almendros, atravesado por las agujas de hielo de la incertidumbre, y apretando en el puño el peso con cincuenta centavos que le había pedido a Amaranta Úrsula, no tanto porque los necesitara, como para complicarla, envilecerla y prostituirla de algún modo con su aventura. Nigromanta lo llevó a su cuarto alumbrado con veladoras de superchería, a su cama de tijeras con el lienzo percudido de malos amores, y a su cuerpo de perra brava, empedernida, desalmada, que se preparó para despacharlo como si fuera un niño asustado, y se encontró de pronto con un hombre cuyo poder tremendo exigió a sus entrañas un movimiento de reacomodación sísmica.

Se hicieron amantes. Aureliano ocupaba la mañana en descifrar pergaminos, y a la hora de la siesta iba al dormitorio soporífero donde Nigromanta lo esperaba para enseñarlo a hacer primero como las

lombrices, luego como los caracoles y por último
como los cangrejos, hasta que tenía que abandonarlo
para acechar amores extraviados. Pasaron varias semanas antes de que Aureliano descubriera que ella
tenía alrededor de la cintura un cintillo que parecía
hecho con una cuerda de violoncelo, pero que era
duro como el acero y carecía de remate, porque había nacido y crecido con ella. Casi siempre, entre
amor y amor, comían desnudos en la cama, en el calor alucinante y bajo las estrellas diurnas que el óxido iba haciendo despuntar en el techo de zinc. Era la
primera vez que Nigromanta tenía un hombre fijo,
un machucante de planta, como ella misma decía
muerta de risa, y hasta empezaba a hacerse ilusiones
de corazón cuando Aureliano le confió su pasión reprimida por Amaranta Úrsula, que no había conseguido remediar con la sustitución, sino que le iba
torciendo cada vez más las entrañas a medida que la
experiencia ensanchaba el horizonte del amor. Entonces Nigromanta siguió recibiéndolo con el mismo calor de siempre, pero se hizo pagar los servicios
con tanto rigor, que cuando Aureliano no tenía dinero se los cargaba en la cuenta que no llevaba con números sino con rayitas que iba trazando con la uña
del pulgar detrás de la puerta. Al anochecer, mientras ella se quedaba barloventeando en las sombras
de la plaza, Aureliano pasaba por el corredor como
un extraño, saludando apenas a Amaranta Úrsula y a
Gastón que de ordinario cenaban a esa hora, y volvía
a encerrarse en el cuarto, sin poder leer ni escribir, ni
siquiera pensar, por la ansiedad que le provocaban
las risas, los cuchicheos, los retozos preliminares, y
luego las explosiones de felicidad agónica que col-
maban las noches de la casa. Esa era su vida dos años

antes de que Gastón empezara a esperar el aeroplano, y seguía siendo igual la tarde en que fue a la librería del sabio catalán y encontró a cuatro muchachos despotricadores, encarnizados en una discusión sobre los métodos de matar cucarachas en la Edad Media. El viejo librero, conociendo la afición de Aureliano por libros que sólo había leído Beda el Venerable, lo instó con una cierta malignidad paternal a que terciara en la controversia, y él ni siquiera tomó aliento para explicar que las cucarachas, el insecto alado más antiguo sobre la tierra, era ya la víctima favorita de los chancletazos en el Antiguo Testamento, pero que como especie era definitivamente refractaria a cualquier método de exterminio, desde las rebanadas de tomate con bórax hasta la harina con azúcar, pues sus mil seiscientas tres variedades habían resistido a la más remota, tenaz y despiadada persecución que el hombre había desatado desde sus orígenes contra ser viviente alguno, inclusive el propio hombre, hasta el extremo de que así como se atribuía al género humano un instinto de reproducción, debía atribuírsele otro más definido y apremiante, que era el instinto de matar cucarachas, y que si éstas habían logrado escapar a la ferocidad humana era porque se habían refugiado en las tinieblas, donde se hicieron invulnerables por el miedo congénito del hombre a la oscuridad, pero en cambio se volvieron susceptibles al esplendor del mediodía, de modo que ya en la Edad Media, en la actualidad y por los siglos de los siglos, el único método eficaz para matar cucarachas era el deslumbramiento solar.

Aquel fatalismo enciclopédico fue el principio de una gran amistad. Aureliano siguió reuniéndose todas las tardes con los cuatro discutidores, que se llamaban Álvaro, Germán, Alfonso y Gabriel, los primeros y últimos amigos que tuvo en la vida. Para un hombre como él, encastillado en la realidad escrita, aquellas sesiones tormentosas que empezaban en la librería a las seis de la tarde y terminaban en los burdeles al amanecer, fueron una revelación. No se le había ocurrido pensar hasta entonces que la literatura fuera el mejor juguete que se había inventado para burlarse de la gente, como lo demostró Álvaro en una noche de parranda. Había de transcurrir algún tiempo antes de que Aureliano se diera cuenta de que tanta arbitrariedad tenía origen en el ejemplo del sabio catalán, para quien la sabiduría no valía la pena si no era posible servirse de ella para inventar una manera nueva de preparar los garbanzos.

La tarde en que Aureliano sentó cátedra sobre las cucarachas, la discusión terminó en la casa de las muchachitas que se acostaban por hambre, un burdel de mentiras en los arrabales de Macondo. La propietaria era una mamasanta sonriente, atormentada por la manía de abrir y cerrar puertas. Su eterna sonrisa parecía provocada por la credulidad de los clientes, que admitían como algo cierto un establecimiento que no existía sino en la imaginación, porque allí hasta las cosas tangibles eran irreales: los muebles que se desarmaban al sentarse, la victrola destripada en cuyo interior había una gallina incubando, el jardín de flores de papel, los almanaques de años anteriores a la llegada de la compañía bananera, los cuadros con litografías recortadas de revistas que nunca se editaron. Hasta las putitas tímidas que acudían del vecindario cuando la propietaria les avisaba que habían llegado clientes, eran una pura invención. Aparecían sin saludar, con los trajecitos floreados de cuando tenían cinco años menos, y se los quitaban con la misma inocencia con que se los habían puesto, y en el paroxismo del amor exclamaban asombradas qué barbaridad, mira cómo se está cayendo ese techo, y tan pronto como recibían su peso con cincuenta centavos se lo gastaban en un pan y un pedazo de queso que les vendía la propietaria, más risueña que nunca, porque solamente ella sabía que tampoco esa comida era verdad. Aureliano, cuyo mundo de entonces empezaba en los pergaminos de Melquíades y terminaba en la cama de Nigromanta, encontró en el burdelito imaginario una cura de burro para la timidez. Al principio no lograba llegar a ninguna parte, en unos cuartos donde la dueña entraba en los mejores momentos del amor y hacía toda clase de comentarios sobre los encantos íntimos de los protagonistas. Pero con el tiempo llegó a familiarizarse tanto con aquellos percances del mundo que una noche más desquiciada que las otras se desnudó en la salita de recibo y recorrió la casa llevando en equilibrio una botella de cerveza sobre su masculinidad inconcebible. Fue él quien puso de moda las extravagancias que la propietaria celebraba con su sonrisa eterna, sin protestar, sin creer en ellas, lo mismo que cuando Germán trató de incendiar la casa para demostrar que no existía, que cuando Alfonso le torció el pescuezo al loro y lo echó en la olla donde empezaba a hervir el sancocho de gallina.

Aunque Aureliano se sentía vinculado a los cuatro amigos por un mismo cariño y una misma solidaridad, hasta el punto de que pensaba en ellos como si fueran uno solo, estaba más cerca de Gabriel que de los otros. El vínculo nació la noche en que él habló casualmente del coronel Aureliano Buendía, y Gabriel fue el único que no creyó que se estuviera burlando de alguien. Hasta la dueña, que no solía intervenir en las conversaciones, discutió con una rabiosa pasión de comadrona que el coronel Aureliano Buendía, de quien en efecto había oído hablar alguna vez, era un personaje inventado por el gobierno como un pretexto para matar liberales. Gabriel, en cambio, no ponía en duda la realidad del coronel Aureliano Buendía, porque había sido compañero de armas y amigo inseparable de su bisabuelo, el coronel Gerineldo Márquez. Aquellas veleidades de la memoria eran todavía más críticas cuando se hablaba de la matanza de los trabajadores. Cada vez que Aureliano tocaba el punto, no sólo la propietaria, sino algunas personas mayores que ella, repudiaban la patraña de los trabajadores acorralados en la estación, y del tren de doscientos vagones cargados de muertos, e inclusive se obstinaban en lo que después de todo había quedado establecido en expedientes judiciales y en los textos de la escuela primaria: que la compañía bananera no había existido nunca. De modo que Aureliano y Gabriel estaban vinculados por una especie de complicidad, fundada en hechos reales en los que nadie creía, y que habían afectado sus vidas hasta el punto de que ambos se encontraban a la deriva en la resaca de un mundo acabado, del cual sólo quedaba la nostalgia. Gabriel dormía donde lo sorprendiera la hora. Aureliano lo acomodó varias veces en el taller de platería, pero se pasaba las noches en vela, perturbado por el trasiego de los muertos que andaban hasta el amanecer por los dormitorios. Más tarde se lo encomendó a Nigromanta, quien lo llevaba a su cuartito multitudinario cuando estaba libre, y le anotaba las cuentas con rayitas verticales detrás de la puerta, en los pocos espacios disponibles que habían dejado las deudas de Aureliano.

A pesar de su vida desordenada, todo el grupo trataba de hacer algo perdurable, a instancias del sabio catalán. Era él, con su experiencia de antiguo profesor de letras clásicas y su depósito de libros raros, quien los había puesto en condiciones de pasar una noche entera buscando la trigesimoséptima situación dramática, en un pueblo donde ya nadie tenía interés ni posibilidades de ir más allá de la escuela primaria. Fascinado por el descubrimiento de la amistad, aturdido por los hechizos de un mundo que le había sido vedado por la mezquindad de Fernanda, Aureliano abandonó el escrutinio de los pergaminos, precisamente cuando empezaban a revelársele como predicciones en versos cifrados. Pero la comprobación posterior de que el tiempo alcanzaba para todo sin que fuera necesario renunciar a los burdeles, le dio ánimos para volver al cuarto de Melquíades, decidido a no flaquear en su empeño hasta descubrir las últimas claves. Eso fue por los días en que Gastón empezaba a esperar el aeroplano, y Amaranta Úrsula se encontraba tan sola, que una mañana apareció en el cuarto.

—Hola, antropófago —le dijo—. Otra vez en la cueva.

Era irresistible, con su vestido inventado, y uno de los largos collares de vértebras de sábalo, que ella misma fabricaba. Había desistido del sedal, convencida de la fidelidad del marido, y por primera vez desde el regreso parecía disponer de un rato de ocio. Aureliano no hubiera tenido necesidad de verla para saber que había llegado. Ella se acodó en la mesa de trabajo, tan cercana e inerme que Aureliano percibió el hondo rumor de sus huesos, y se interesó en los pergaminos. Tratando de sobreponerse a la turbación, él atrapó la voz que se le fugaba, la vida que se le iba, la memoria que se le convertía en un pólipo petrificado, y le habló del destino levítico del sánscrito, de la posibilidad científica de ver el futuro transparentado en el tiempo como se ve a contraluz lo escrito en el reverso de un papel, de la necesidad de cifrar las predicciones para que no se derrotaran a sí mismas, y de las *Centurias* de Nostradamus y de la destrucción de Cantabria anunciada por San Millán. De pronto, sin interrumpir la plática, movido por un impulso que dormía en él desde sus orígenes, Aureliano puso su mano sobre la de ella, creyendo que aquella decisión final ponía término a la zozobra. Sin embargo, ella le agarró el índice con la inocencia cariñosa con que lo hizo muchas veces en la infancia, y lo tuvo agarrado mientras él seguía contestando sus preguntas. Permanecieron así, vinculados por un índice de hielo que no transmitía nada en ningún sentido, hasta que ella despertó de su sueño momentáneo y se dio una palmada en la frente. «¡Las hormigas!», exclamó. Y entonces se olvidó de los manuscritos, llegó hasta la puerta con un paso de baile, y desde allí le mandó a Aureliano con la punta de los dedos el mismo beso con que se despidió de su padre la tarde en que la mandaron a Bruselas.

—Después me explicas —dijo—. Se me había olvidado que hoy es día de echar cal en los huecos de las hormigas.

Siguió yendo al cuarto ocasionalmente, cuando tenía algo que hacer por esos lados, y permanecía allí breves minutos, mientras su marido continuaba escrutando el cielo. Ilusionado con aquel cambio, Aureliano se quedaba entonces a comer en familia, como no lo hacía desde los primeros meses del regreso de Amaranta Úrsula. A Gastón le agradó. En las conversaciones de sobremesa, que solían prolongarse por más de una hora, se dolía de que sus socios lo estuvieran engañando. Le habían anunciado el embarque del aeroplano en un buque que no llegaba, y aunque sus agentes marítimos insistían en que no llegaría nunca porque no figuraba en las listas de los barcos del Caribe, sus socios se obstinaban en que el despacho era correcto, y hasta insinuaban la posibilidad de que Gastón les mintiera en sus cartas. La correspondencia alcanzó tal grado de suspicacia recíproca, que Gastón optó por no volver a escribir, y empezó a sugerir la posibilidad de un viaje rápido a Bruselas, para aclarar las cosas, y regresar con el aeroplano. Sin embargo, el proyecto se desvaneció tan pronto como Amaranta Úrsula reiteró su decisión de no moverse de Macondo aunque se quedara sin marido. En los primeros tiempos, Aureliano compartió la idea generalizada de que Gastón era un tonto en velocípedo, y eso le suscitó un vago sentimiento de piedad. Más tarde, cuando obtuvo en los burdeles una información más profunda sobre la naturaleza de los hombres, pensó que la mansedumbre de Gastón tenía origen en la pasión desmandada. Pero cuando lo conoció mejor, y se dio cuenta de que su verdadero carácter estaba en contradicción con su conducta sumisa, concibió la maliciosa sospecha de que hasta la espera del aeroplano era una farsa. Entonces pensó que Gastón no era tan tonto como lo aparentaba, sino al contrario, un hombre de una constancia, una habilidad y una paciencia infinitas, que se había propuesto vencer a la esposa por el cansancio de la eterna complacencia, del nunca decirle que no, del simular una conformidad sin límites, dejándola enredarse en su propia telaraña, hasta el día en que no pudiera soportar más el tedio de las ilusiones al alcance de la mano, y ella misma hiciera las maletas para volver a Europa. La antigua piedad de Aureliano se transformó en una animadversión virulenta. Le pareció tan perverso el sistema de Gastón, pero al mismo tiempo tan eficaz, que se atrevió a prevenir a Amaranta Úrsula. Sin embargo, ella se burló de su suspicacia, sin vislumbrar siquiera la desgarradora carga de amor, de incertidumbre y de celos que llevaba dentro. No se le había ocurrido pensar que suscitaba en Aureliano algo más que un afecto fraternal, hasta que se pinchó un dedo tratando de destapar una lata de melocotones, y él se precipitó a chuparle la sangre con una avidez y una devoción que le erizaron la piel.

—¡Aureliano! —rió ella, inquieta—. Eres demasiado malicioso para ser un buen murciélago.

Entonces Aureliano se desbordó. Dándole besitos huérfanos en el cuenco de la mano herida, abrió los pasadizos más recónditos de su corazón, y se sacó una tripa interminable y macerada, el terrible animal parasitario que había incubado en el martirio. Le contó cómo se levantaba a medianoche para llorar de desamparo y de rabia en la ropa íntima que ella dejaba secando en el baño. Le contó con cuánta ansiedad le pedía a Nigromanta que chillara como una gata, y sollozara en su oído gastón gastón gastón, y con cuánta astucia saqueaba sus frascos de perfume para encontrarlo en el cuello de las muchachitas que se acostaban por hambre. Espantada con la pasión de aquel desahogo, Amaranta Úrsula fue cerrando los dedos, contrayéndolos como un molusco, hasta que su mano herida, liberada de todo dolor y todo vestigio de misericordia, se convirtió en un nudo de esmeraldas y topacios, y huesos pétreos e insensibles.

—¡Bruto! —dijo, como si estuviera escupiendo—. Me voy a Bélgica en el primer barco que salga.

Álvaro había llegado una de esas tardes a la librería del sabio catalán, pregonando a voz en cuello su último hallazgo: un burdel zoológico. Se llamaba *El Niño de Oro*, y era un inmenso salón al aire libre, por donde se paseaban a voluntad no menos de doscientos alcaravanes que daban la hora con un cacareo ensordecedor. En los corrales de alambre que rodeaban la pista de baile, y entre grandes camelias amazónicas, había garzas de colores, caimanes cebados como cerdos, serpientes de doce cascabeles, y una tortuga de concha dorada que se zambullía en un minúsculo océano artificial. Había un perrazo blanco, manso y pederasta, que sin embargo prestaba servicios de padrote para que le dieran de comer. El aire tenía una densidad ingenua, como si lo acabaran de inventar, y las bellas mulatas que esperaban sin esperanza entre pétalos sangrientos y discos pasados de moda, conocían oficios de amor que el hombre había dejado olvidados en el paraíso terrenal. La primera noche en que el grupo visitó aquel invernadero de ilusiones, la espléndida y taciturna anciana que vigilaba el ingreso en un mecedor de bejuco, sintió que el tiempo regresaba a sus manantiales primarios, cuando entre los cinco que llegaban descubrió un hombre óseo, cetrino, de pómulos tártaros, marcado para siempre y desde el principio del mundo por la viruela de la soledad.

—¡Ay —suspiró—, Aureliano!

Estaba viendo otra vez al coronel Aureliano Buendía, como lo vio a la luz de una lámpara mucho antes de las guerras, mucho antes de la desolación de la gloria y el exilio del desencanto, la remota madrugada en que él fue a su dormitorio para impartir la primera orden de su vida: la orden de que le dieran amor. Era Pilar Ternera. Años antes, cuando cumplió los ciento cuarenta y cinco, había renunciado a la perniciosa costumbre de llevar las cuentas de su edad, y continuaba viviendo en el tiempo estático y marginal de los recuerdos, en un futuro perfectamente revelado y establecido, más allá de los futuros perturbados por las acechanzas y las suposiciones insidiosas de las barajas.

Desde aquella noche, Aureliano se había refugiado en la ternura y la comprensión compasiva de la tatarabuela ignorada. Sentada en el mecedor de bejuco, ella evocaba el pasado, reconstruía la grandeza y el infortunio de la familia y el arrasado esplendor de Macondo, mientras Álvaro asustaba a los caimanes con sus carcajadas de estrépito, y Alfonso inventaba la historia truculenta de los alcaravanes que les sacaron los ojos a picotazos a cuatro clientes que se portaron mal la semana anterior, y Gabriel estaba en el cuarto de la mulata pensativa que no cobraba el amor con dinero, sino con cartas para un novio contrabandista que estaba preso al otro lado del Orinoco, porque los guardias fronterizos lo habían purgado y lo habían sentado luego en una bacinilla que quedó llena de mierda con diamantes. Aquel burdel verdadero, con aquella dueña maternal, era el mundo con que Aureliano había soñado en su prolongado cautiverio. Se sentía tan bien, tan próximo al acompañamiento perfecto, que no pensó en otro refugio la tarde en que Amaranta Úrsula le desmigajó las ilusiones. Fue dispuesto a desahogarse con palabras, a que alguien le zafara los nudos que le oprimían el pecho, pero sólo consiguió soltarse en un llanto fluido y cálido y reparador, en el regazo de Pilar Ternera. Ella lo dejó terminar, rascándole la cabeza con la yema de los dedos, y sin que él le hubiera revelado que estaba llorando de amor, ella reconoció de inmediato el llanto más antiguo de la historia del hombre.

—Bueno, niñito —lo consoló—: ahora dime quién es.

Cuando Aureliano se lo dijo, Pilar Ternera emitió una risa profunda, la antigua risa expansiva que había terminado por parecer un cucurrucuteo de palomas. No había ningún misterio en el corazón de un Buendía que fuera impenetrable para ella, porque un siglo de naipes y de experiencias le había enseñado que la historia de la familia era un engranaje de repeticiones irreparables, una rueda giratoria que hubiera seguido dando vueltas hasta la eternidad, de no haber sido por el desgaste progresivo e irremediable del eje.

—No te preocupes —sonrió—. En cualquier lugar en que esté ahora, ella te está esperando.

Eran las cuatro y media de la tarde, cuando Amaranta Úrsula salió del baño. Aureliano la vio pasar frente a su cuarto, con una bata de pliegues tenues y una toalla enrollada en la cabeza como un turbante. La siguió casi en puntillas, tambaleándose de la borrachera, y entró al dormitorio nupcial en el momento en que ella se abrió la bata y se la volvió a cerrar espantada. Hizo una señal silenciosa hacia el cuarto contiguo, cuya puerta estaba entreabierta, y donde Aureliano sabía que Gastón empezaba a escribir una carta.

—Vete —dijo sin voz.

Aureliano sonrió, la levantó por la cintura con las dos manos, como una maceta de begonias, y la tiró bocarriba en la cama. De un tirón brutal, la despojó de la túnica de baño antes de que ella tuviera tiempo de impedirlo, y se asomó al abismo de una desnudez recién lavada que no tenía un matiz de la piel, ni una veta de vellos, ni un lunar recóndito que él no hubiera imaginado en las tinieblas de otros cuartos. Amaranta Úrsula se defendía sinceramente, con astucias de hembra sabia, comadrejeando el escurridizo y flexible y fragante cuerpo de comadreja, mientras trataba de destroncarle los riñones con las rodillas y le alacraneaba la cara con las uñas, pero sin que él ni ella emitieran un suspiro que no pudiera confundirse con la respiración de alguien que contemplara el parsimonioso crepúsculo de abril por la ventana abierta. Era una lucha feroz, una batalla a muerte, que sin embargo parecía desprovista de toda violencia, porque estaba hecha de agresiones distorsionadas y evasivas espectrales, lentas, cautelosas, solemnes, de modo que entre una y otra había tiempo para que volvieran a florecer las petunias y Gastón olvidara sus sueños de aeronauta en el cuarto vecino, como si fueran dos amantes enemigos tratando de reconciliarse en el fondo de un estanque diáfano. En el fragor del encarnizado y ceremonioso forcejeo, Amaranta Úrsula comprendió que la meticulosidad de su silencio era tan irracional, que habría podido despertar las sospechas del marido contiguo, mucho más que los estrépitos de guerra que trataban de evitar. Entonces empezó a reír con los labios apretados, sin renunciar a la lucha, pero defendiéndose con mordiscos falsos y descomadrejeando el cuerpo poco a poco, hasta que ambos tuvieron conciencia de ser al mismo tiempo adversarios y cómplices, y la brega degeneró en un retozo convencional y las agresiones se volvieron caricias. De pronto, casi jugando, como una travesura más, Amaranta Úrsula descuidó la defensa, y cuando trató de reaccionar, asustada de lo que ella misma había hecho posible, ya era demasiado tarde. Una conmoción descomunal la inmovilizó en su centro de gravedad, la sembró en su sitio, y su voluntad defensiva fue demolida por la ansiedad irresistible de descubrir qué eran los silbos anaranjados y los globos invisibles que la esperaban al otro lado de la muerte. Apenas tuvo tiempo de estirar la mano y buscar a ciegas la toalla, y meterse una mordaza entre los dientes, para que no se le salieran los chillidos de gata que ya le estaban desgarrando las entrañas.

Pilar Ternera murió en el mecedor de bejuco, una noche de fiesta, vigilando la entrada de su paraíso. De acuerdo con su última voluntad, la enterraron sin ataúd, sentada en el mecedor que ocho hombres bajaron con cabuyas en un hueco enorme, excavado en el centro de la pista de baile. Las mulatas vestidas de negro, pálidas de llanto, improvisaban oficios de tinieblas mientras se quitaban los aretes, los prendedores y las sortijas, y los iban echando en la fosa, antes de que la sellaran con una lápida sin nombre ni fechas y le pusieran encima un promontorio de camelias amazónicas. Después de envenenar a los animales, clausuraron puertas y ventanas con ladrillos y argamasa, y se dispersaron por el mundo con sus baúles de madera, tapizados por dentro con estampas de santos, cromos de revistas, y retratos de novios efímeros, remotos y fantásticos, que cagaban diamantes, o se comían a los caníbales, o eran coronados reyes de barajas en alta mar.

Era el final. En la tumba de Pilar Ternera, entre salmos y abalorios de putas, se pudrían los escombros del pasado, los pocos que quedaban después de que el sabio catalán remató la librería y regresó a la aldea mediterránea donde había nacido, derrotado por la nostalgia de una primavera tenaz. Nadie hubiera podido presentir su decisión. Había llegado a Macondo en el esplendor de la compañía bananera, huyendo de una de tantas guerras, y no se le había ocurrido nada más práctico que instalar aquella librería de incunables y ediciones originales en varios idiomas, que los clientes casuales hojeaban con recelo, como si fueran libros de muladar, mientras esperaban el turno para que les interpretaran los sueños en la casa de enfrente. Estuvo media vida en la calurosa trastienda, garrapateando su escritura preciosista en tinta violeta y en hojas que arrancaba de cuadernos escolares, sin que nadie supiera a ciencia cierta qué era lo que escribía. Cuando Aureliano lo conoció tenía dos cajones llenos de aquellas páginas abigarradas que de algún modo hacían pensar en los pergaminos de Melquíades, y desde entonces hasta cuando se fue había llenado un tercero, así que era razonable pensar que no había hecho nada más durante su permanencia en Macondo. Las únicas personas con quienes se relacionó fueron los cuatro amigos, a quienes les cambió por libros los trompos y las cometas, y los puso a leer a Séneca y a Ovidio cuando todavía estaban en la escuela primaria. Trataba a los clásicos con una familiaridad casera, como si todos hubieran sido en alguna época sus compañeros de cuarto, y sabía muchas cosas que simplemente no se debían saber, como que San Agustín usaba debajo del hábito un jubón de lana que no se quitó en catorce años, y que Arnaldo de Vilanova, el nigromante, se volvió impotente desde niño por una mordedura de alacrán. Su fervor por la palabra escrita era una urdimbre de respeto solemne e irreverencia comadrera. Ni sus propios manuscritos estaban a salvo de esa dualidad. Habiendo aprendido el catalán para traducirlos, Alfonso se metió un rollo de páginas en los bolsillos, que siempre tenía llenos de recortes de periódicos y manuales de oficios raros, y una noche los perdió en la casa de las muchachitas que se acostaban por hambre. Cuando el abuelo sabio se enteró, en vez de hacerle el escándalo temido comentó muerto de risa que aquel era el destino natural de la literatura. En cambio, no hubo poder humano capaz de persuadirlo de que no se llevara los tres cajones cuando regresó a su aldea natal, y se soltó en improperios cartagineses contra los inspectores del ferrocarril que trataban de mandarlos como carga, hasta que consiguió quedarse con ellos en el vagón de pasajeros. «El mundo habrá acabado de joderse —dijo entonces— el día en que los hombres viajen en primera clase y la literatura en el vagón de carga.» Eso fue lo último que se le oyó decir. Había pasado una semana negra con los preparativos finales del viaje, porque a medida que se aproximaba la hora se le iba descomponiendo el humor, y se le traspapelaban las intenciones, y las cosas que ponía en un lugar aparecían en otro, asediado por los mismos duendes que atormentaban a Fernanda.

—Collons —maldecía—. Me cago en el canon 27 del sínodo de Londres.

Germán y Aureliano se hicieron cargo de él. Lo auxiliaron como a un niño, le prendieron los pasajes y los documentos migratorios en los bolsillos con alfileres de nodriza, le hicieron una lista pormenorizada de lo que debía hacer desde que saliera de Macondo hasta que desembarcara en Barcelona, pero de todos modos echó a la basura sin darse cuenta un pantalón con la mitad de su dinero. La víspera del viaje, después de clavetear los cajones y meter la ropa en la misma maleta con que había llegado, frunció sus párpados de almejas, señaló con una especie de bendición procaz los montones de libros con los que había sobrellevado el exilio, y dijo a sus amigos:

—¡Ahí les dejo esa mierda!

Tres meses después se recibieron en un sobre grande veintinueve cartas y más de cincuenta retratos, que se le habían acumulado en los ocios de altamar. Aunque no ponía fechas, era evidente el orden en que había escrito las cartas. En las primeras contaba con su humor habitual las peripecias de la travesía, las ganas que le dieron de echar por la borda al sobrecargo que no le permitió meter los tres cajones en el camarote, la imbecilidad lúcida de una señora que se aterraba con el número 13, no por superstición sino porque le parecía un número que se había quedado sin terminar, y la apuesta que se ganó en la primera cena porque reconoció en el agua de a bordo el sabor a remolachas nocturnas de los manantiales de Lérida. Con el transcurso de los días, sin embargo, la realidad de a bordo le importaba cada vez menos, y hasta los acontecimientos más recientes y triviales le parecían dignos de añoranza, porque a medida que el barco se alejaba, la memoria se le iba volviendo triste. Aquel proceso de nostalgización progresiva era también evidente en los retratos. En los primeros parecía feliz, con su camisa de inválido y su mechón nevado, en el cabrilleante octubre del Caribe. En los últimos se le veía con un abrigo oscuro y una bufanda de seda, pálido de sí mismo y taciturnado por la ausencia, en la cubierta de un barco de pesadumbre que empezaba a sonambular por océanos otoñales. Germán y Aureliano le contestaban las cartas. Escribió tantas en los primeros meses, que se sentían entonces más cerca de él que cuando estaba en Macondo, y casi se aliviaban de la rabia de que se hubiera ido. Al principio mandaba a decir que todo seguía igual, que en la casa donde nació estaba todavía el caracol rosado, que los arenques secos tenían el mismo sabor en la yesca de pan, que las cascadas de la aldea continuaban perfumándose al atardecer. Eran otra vez las hojas de cuaderno rezurcidas con garrapatitas moradas, en las cuales dedicaba un párrafo especial a cada uno. Sin embargo, y aunque él mismo no parecía advertirlo, aquellas cartas de recuperación y estímulo se iban transformando poco a poco en pastorales de desengaño. En las noches de invierno, mientras hervía la sopa en la chimenea, añoraba el calor de su trastienda, el zumbido del sol en los almendros polvorientos, el pito del tren en el sopor de la siesta, lo mismo que añoraba en Macondo la sopa de invierno en la chimenea, los pregones del vendedor de café y las alondras fugaces de la primavera. Aturdido por dos nostalgias enfrentadas como dos espejos, perdió su maravilloso sentido de la irrealidad, hasta que terminó por recomendarles a todos que se fueran de Macondo, que olvidaran cuanto él les había enseñado del mundo y del corazón humano, que se cagaran en Horacio, y que en cualquier lugar en que estuvieran recordaran siempre que el pasado era mentira, que la memoria no tenía caminos de regreso, que toda primavera antigua era irrecuperable, y que el amor más desatinado y tenaz era de todos modos una verdad efímera.

Álvaro fue el primero que atendió el consejo de abandonar a Macondo. Lo vendió todo, hasta el tigre cautivo que se burlaba de los transeúntes en el patio de su casa, y compró un pasaje eterno en un tren que nunca acababa de viajar. En las tarjetas postales que mandaba desde las estaciones intermedias, describía a gritos las imágenes instantáneas que había visto por la ventanilla del vagón, y era como ir haciendo trizas y tirando al olvido el largo poema de la fugacidad: los negros quiméricos en los algodonales de la Luisiana, los caballos alados en la hierba azul de Kentucky, los amantes griegos en el crepúsculo infernal de Arizona, la muchacha de suéter rojo que pintaba acuarelas en los lagos de Michigan, y que le hizo con los pinceles un adiós que no era de despedida sino de esperanza, porque ignoraba que estaba viendo pasar un tren sin regreso. Luego se fueron Alfonso y Germán, un sábado, con la idea de regresar el lunes, y nunca se volvió a saber de ellos. Un año después de la partida del sabio catalán, el único que quedaba en Macondo era Gabriel, todavía al garete, a merced de la azarosa caridad de Nigromanta, y contestando los cuestionarios del concurso de una revista francesa, cuyo premio mayor era un viaje a París. Aureliano, que era quien recibía la suscripción, lo ayudaba a llenar los formularios, a veces en su casa, y casi siempre entre los pomos de loza y el aire de valeriana de la única botica que quedaba en Macondo, donde vivía Mercedes, la sigilosa novia de Gabriel. Era lo último que iba quedando de un pasado cuyo aniquilamiento no se consumaba, porque seguía aniquilándose indefinidamente, consumiéndose dentro de sí mismo, acabándose a cada minuto pero sin acabar de acabarse jamás. El pueblo había llegado a tales extremos de inactividad, que cuando Gabriel ganó el concurso y se fue a París con dos mudas de ropa, un par de zapatos y las obras completas de Rabelais, tuvo que hacer señas al maquinista para que el tren se detuviera a recogerlo. La antigua Calle de los Turcos era entonces un rincón de abandono, donde los últimos árabes se dejaban llevar hacia la muerte por la costumbre milenaria de sentarse en la puerta, aunque hacía muchos años que habían vendido la última yarda de diagonal, y en las vitrinas sombrías solamente quedaban los maniquíes decapitados. La ciudad de la compañía bananera, que tal vez Patricia Brown trataba de evocar para sus nietos en las noches de intolerancia y pepinos en vinagre de Prattville, Alabama, era una llanura de hierba silvestre. El cura anciano que había sustituido al padre Ángel, y cuyo nombre nadie se tomó el trabajo de averiguar, esperaba la piedad de Dios tendido a la bartola en una hamaca, atormentado por la artritis y el insomnio de la duda, mientras los lagartos y las ratas se disputaban la herencia del templo vecino. En aquel Macondo olvidado hasta por los pájaros, donde el polvo y el calor se habían hecho tan tenaces que costaba trabajo respirar, recluidos por la soledad y el amor y por la soledad del amor en una casa donde era casi imposible dormir por el estruendo de las hormigas coloradas, Aureliano y Amaranta Úrsula eran los únicos seres felices, y los más felices sobre la tierra.

Gastón había vuelto a Bruselas. Cansado de esperar el aeroplano, un día metió en una maletita las cosas indispensables y su archivo de correspondencia y se fue con el propósito de regresar por el aire, antes de que sus privilegios fueran cedidos a un grupo de aviadores alemanes que había presentado a las autoridades provinciales un proyecto más ambicioso que el suyo. Desde la tarde del primer amor, Aureliano y Amaranta Úrsula habían seguido aprovechando los escasos descuidos del esposo, amándose con ardores amordazados en encuentros azarosos y casi siempre interrumpidos por regresos imprevistos. Pero cuando se vieron solos en la casa sucumbieron en el delirio de los amores atrasados. Era una pasión insensata, desquiciante, que hacía temblar de pavor en su tumba los huesos de Fernanda, y los mantenía en un estado de exaltación perpetua. Los chillidos de Amaranta Úrsula, sus canciones agónicas, estallaban lo mismo a las dos de la tarde en la mesa del comedor, que a las dos de la madrugada en el granero. «Lo que más me duele —reía— es tanto tiempo que perdimos.» En el aturdimiento de la pasión, vio las hormigas devastando el jardín, saciando su hambre prehistórica en las maderas de la casa, y vio el torrente de lava viva apoderándose otra vez del corredor, pero solamente se preocupó de combatirlo cuando lo encontró en su dormitorio. Aureliano abandonó los pergaminos, no volvió a salir de la casa, y contestaba de cualquier modo las cartas del sabio catalán. Perdieron el sentido de la realidad, la noción del tiempo, el ritmo de los hábitos cotidianos. Volvieron a cerrar puertas y ventanas para no demorarse en trámites de desnudamientos, y andaban por la casa como siempre quiso estar Remedios, la bella, y se revolcaban en cueros en los barrizales del patio, y una tarde estuvieron a punto de ahogarse cuando se amaban en la alberca. En poco tiempo hicieron más estragos que las hormigas coloradas: destrozaron los muebles de la sala, rasgaron con sus locuras la hamaca que había resistido a los tristes amores de campamento del coronel Aureliano Buendía, y destriparon los colchones y los vaciaron en los pisos para sofocarse en tempestades de algodón. Aunque Aureliano era un amante tan feroz como su rival, era Amaranta Úrsula quien comandaba con su ingenio disparatado y su voracidad lírica aquel paraíso de desastres, como si hubiera concentrado en el amor la indómita energía que la tatarabuela consagró a la fabricación de animalitos de caramelo. Además, mientras ella cantaba de placer y se moría de risa de sus propias invenciones, Aureliano se iba haciendo más absorto y callado, porque su pasión era ensimismada y calcinante. Sin embargo, ambos llegaron a tales extremos de virtuosismo, que cuando se agotaban en la exaltación le sacaban mejor partido al cansancio. Se entregaron a la idolatría de sus cuerpos, al descubrir que los tedios del amor tenían posibilidades inexploradas, mucho más ricas que las del deseo. Mientras él amasaba con claras de huevo los senos eréctiles de Amaranta Úrsula, o suavizaba con manteca de coco sus muslos elásticos y su vientre aduraznado, ella jugaba a las muñecas con la portentosa criatura de Aureliano, y le pintaba ojos de payaso con carmín de labios y bigotes de turco con carboncillo de las cejas, y le ponía corbatines de organza y sombreritos de papel plateado. Una noche se embadurnaron de pies a cabeza con melocotones en almíbar, se lamieron como perros y se amaron como locos en el piso del corredor, y fueron despertados por un torrente de hormigas carniceras que se disponían a devorarlos vivos.

En las pausas del delirio, Amaranta Úrsula contestaba las cartas de Gastón. Lo sentía tan distante y ocupado, que su regreso le parecía imposible. En una de las primeras cartas él contó que en realidad sus socios habían mandado el aeroplano, pero que una agencia marítima de Bruselas lo había embarcado por error con destino a Tanganyka, donde se lo entregaron a la dispersa comunidad de los Makondos. Aquella confusión ocasionó tantos contratiempos que solamente la recuperación del aeroplano podía tardar dos años. Así que Amaranta Úrsula descartó la posibilidad de un regreso inoportuno. Aureliano, por su parte, no tenía más contacto con el mundo que las cartas del sabio catalán y las noticias que recibía de Gabriel a través de Mercedes, la boticaria silenciosa. Al principio eran contactos reales. Gabriel se había hecho reembolsar el pasaje de regreso para quedarse en París, vendiendo los periódicos atrasados y las botellas vacías que las camareras sacaban de un hotel lúgubre de la calle Dauphine. Aureliano podía imaginarlo entonces con un suéter de cuello alto que sólo se quitaba cuando las terrazas de Montparnasse se llenaban de enamorados primaverales, y durmiendo de día y escribiendo de noche para confundir el hambre, en el cuarto oloroso a espuma de coliflores hervidos donde había de morir Rocamadour. Sin embargo, sus noticias se fueron haciendo poco a poco tan inciertas, y tan esporádicas y melancólicas las cartas del sabio, que Aureliano se acostumbró a pensar en ellos como Amaranta Úrsula pensaba en su marido, y ambos quedaron flotando en un universo vacío, donde la única realidad cotidiana y eterna era el amor.

De pronto, como un estampido en aquel mundo de inconsciencia feliz, llegó la noticia del regreso de Gastón. Aureliano y Amaranta Úrsula abrieron los ojos, sondearon sus almas, se miraron a la cara con la mano en el corazón, y comprendieron que estaban tan identificados que preferían la muerte a la separación. Entonces ella le escribió al marido una carta de verdades contradictorias, en la que reiteraba su amor y sus ansias de volver a verlo, al mismo tiempo que admitía como un designio fatal la imposibilidad de vivir sin Aureliano. Al contrario de lo que ambos esperaban, Gastón les mandó una respuesta tranquila, casi paternal, con dos hojas enteras consagradas a prevenirlos contra las veleidades de la pasión, y un párrafo final con votos inequívocos por que fueran tan felices como él lo fue en su breve experiencia conyugal. Era una actitud tan imprevista, que Amaranta Úrsula se sintió humillada con la idea de haber proporcionado al marido el pretexto que él deseaba para abandonarla a su suerte. El rencor se le agravó seis meses después, cuando Gastón volvió a escribirle desde Leopoldville, donde por fin había recibido el aeroplano, sólo para pedir que le mandaran el velocípedo, que de todo lo que había dejado en Macondo era lo único que tenía para él un valor sentimental. Aureliano sobrellevó con paciencia el despecho de Amaranta Úrsula, se esforzó por demostrarle que podía ser tan buen marido en la bonanza como en la adversidad, y las urgencias cotidianas que los asediaban cuando se les acabaron los últimos dineros de Gastón crearon entre ellos un vínculo de solidaridad que no era tan deslumbrante y capitoso como la pasión, pero que les sirvió para amarse tanto y ser tan felices como en los tiempos alborotados de la salacidad. Cuando murió Pilar Ternera estaban esperando un hijo.

En el sopor del embarazo, Amaranta Úrsula trató de establecer una industria de collares de vértebras de pescados. Pero a excepción de Mercedes, que le compró una docena, no encontró a quién vendérselos. Aureliano tuvo conciencia por primera vez de que su don de lenguas, su sabiduría enciclopédica, su rara facultad de recordar sin conocerlos los pormenores de hechos y lugares remotos, eran tan inútiles como el cofre de pedrería legítima de su mujer, que entonces debía valer tanto como todo el dinero de que hubieran podido disponer, juntos, los últimos habitantes de Macondo. Sobrevivían de milagro. Aunque Amaranta Úrsula no perdía el buen humor, ni su ingenio para las travesuras eróticas, adquirió la costumbre de sentarse en el corredor después del almuerzo, en una especie de siesta insomne y pensativa. Aureliano la acompañaba. A veces permanecían en silencio hasta el anochecer, el uno frente a la otra, mirándose a los ojos, amándose en el sosiego con tanto amor como antes se amaron en el escándalo. La incertidumbre del futuro les hizo volver el corazón hacia el pasado. Se vieron a sí mismos en el paraíso perdido del diluvio, chapaleando en los pantanos del patio, matando lagartijas para colgárselas a Úrsula, jugando a enterrarla viva, y aquellas evocaciones les revelaron la verdad de que habían sido felices juntos desde que tenían memoria. Profundizando en el pasado, Amaranta Úrsula recordó la tarde en que entró al taller de platería y su madre le contó que el pequeño Aureliano no era hijo de nadie porque había sido encontrado flotando en una canastilla. Aunque la versión les pareció inverosímil, carecían de información para sustituirla por la verdadera. De lo único que estaban seguros, después de examinar todas las posibilidades, era de que Fernanda no fue la madre de Aureliano. Amaranta Úrsula se inclinó a creer que era hijo de Petra Cotes, de quien sólo recordaba fábulas de infamia, y aquella suposición les produjo en el alma una torcedura de horror.

Atormentado por la certidumbre de que era hermano de su mujer, Aureliano se dio una escapada a la casa cural para buscar en los archivos rezumantes y apolillados alguna pista cierta de su filiación. La partida de bautismo más antigua que encontró fue la de Amaranta Buendía, bautizada en la adolescencia por el padre Nicanor Reyna, por la época en que éste andaba tratando de probar la existencia de Dios mediante artificios de chocolate. Llegó a ilusionarse con la posibilidad de ser uno de los diecisiete Aurelianos, cuyas partidas de nacimiento rastreó a través de cuatro tomos, pero las fechas de bautismo eran demasiado remotas para su edad. Viéndolo extraviado en laberintos de sangre, trémulo de incertidumbre, el párroco artrítico que lo observaba desde la hamaca le preguntó compasivamente cuál era su nombre.

—Aureliano Buendía —dijo él.

—Entonces no te mates buscando —exclamó el párroco con una convicción terminante—. Hace muchos años hubo aquí una calle que se llamaba así, y por esos entonces la gente tenía la costumbre de ponerles a los hijos los nombres de las calles.

Aureliano tembló de rabia.

—¡Ah! —dijo—, entonces usted tampoco cree.

—¿En qué?

—Que el coronel Aureliano Buendía hizo treinta y dos guerras civiles y las perdió todas —contestó Aureliano—. Que el ejército acorraló y ametralló a tres mil trabajadores, y que se llevaron los cadáveres para echarlos al mar en un tren de doscientos vagones.

El párroco lo midió con una mirada de lástima.

—Ay, hijo —suspiró—. A mí me bastaría con estar seguro de que tú y yo existimos en este momento.

De modo que Aureliano y Amaranta Úrsula aceptaron la versión de la canastilla, no porque la creyeran, sino porque los ponía a salvo de sus terrores. A medida que avanzaba el embarazo se iban convirtiendo en un ser único, se integraban cada vez más en la soledad de una casa a la que sólo le hacía falta un último soplo para derrumbarse. Se habían reducido a un espacio esencial, desde el dormitorio de Fernanda, donde vislumbraron los encantos del amor sedentario, hasta el principio del corredor, donde Amaranta Úrsula se sentaba a tejer botitas y sombreritos de recién nacido, y Aureliano a contestar las cartas ocasionales del sabio catalán. El resto de la casa se rindió al asedio tenaz de la destrucción. El taller de platería, el cuarto de Melquíades, los reinos primitivos y silenciosos de Santa Sofía de la Piedad quedaron en el fondo de una selva doméstica que nadie hubiera tenido la temeridad de desentrañar. Cercados por la voracidad de la naturaleza, Aureliano y Amaranta Úrsula seguían cultivando el orégano y las begonias y defendían su mundo con demarcaciones de cal, construyendo las últimas trincheras de la guerra inmemorial entre el hombre y las hormigas. El cabello largo y descuidado, los moretones que le amanecían en la cara, la hinchazón de las piernas, la deformación del antiguo y amoroso cuerpo de comadreja, le habían cambiado a Amaranta Úrsula la apariencia juvenil de cuando llegó a la casa con la jaula de canarios desafortunados y el esposo cautivo pero no le alteraron la vivacidad del espíritu. «Mierda», solía reír. «¡Quién hubiera pensado que de veras íbamos a terminar viviendo como antropófagos!» El último hilo que los vinculaba con el mundo se rompió en el sexto mes de embarazo, cuando recibieron una carta que evidentemente no era del sabio catalán. Había sido franqueada en Barcelona, pero la cubierta estaba escrita con tinta azul convencional por una caligrafía administrativa, y tenía el aspecto inocente e impersonal de los recados enemigos. Aureliano se la arrebató de las manos a Amaranta Úrsula cuando se disponía a abrirla.

—Esta no —le dijo—. No quiero saber lo que dice.

Tal como él lo presentía, el sabio catalán no volvió a escribir. La carta ajena, que nadie leyó, quedó a merced de las polillas en la repisa donde Fernanda olvidó alguna vez su anillo matrimonial, y allí siguió consumiéndose en el fuego interior de su mala noticia, mientras los amantes solitarios navegaban contra la corriente de aquellos tiempos de postrimerías, tiempos impenitentes y aciagos, que se desgastaban en el empeño inútil de hacerlos derivar hacia el desierto del desencanto y el olvido. Conscientes de aquella amenaza, Aureliano y Amaranta Úrsula pasaron los últimos meses tomados de la mano, terminando con amores de lealtad el hijo empezado con desafueros de fornicación. De noche, abrazados en la cama, no los amedrentaban las explosiones sublunares de las hormigas, ni el fragor de las polillas, ni el silbido constante y nítido del crecimiento de la maleza en los cuartos vecinos. Muchas veces fueron despertados por el tráfago de los muertos. Oyeron a Úrsula peleando con las leyes de la creación para preservar la estirpe, y a José Arcadio Buendía buscando la verdad quimérica de los grandes inventos, y a Fernanda rezando, y al coronel Aureliano Buendía embruteciéndose con engaños de guerras y pescaditos de oro, y a Aureliano Segundo agonizando de soledad en el aturdimiento de las parrandas, y entonces aprendieron que las obsesiones dominantes prevalecen contra la muerte, y volvieron a ser felices con la certidumbre de que ellos seguirían amándose con sus naturalezas de aparecidos, mucho después de que otras especies de animales futuros les arrebataran a los insectos el paraíso de miseria que los insectos estaban acabando de arrebatarles a los hombres.

Un domingo, a las seis de la tarde, Amaranta Úrsula sintió los apremios del parto. La sonriente comadrona de las muchachitas que se acostaban por hambre la hizo subir en la mesa del comedor, se le acaballó en el vientre, y la maltrató con galopes cerriles hasta que sus gritos fueron acallados por los berridos de un varón formidable. A través de las lágrimas, Amaranta Úrsula vio que era un Buendía de los grandes, macizo y voluntarioso como los José Arcadios, con los ojos abiertos y clarividentes de los Aurelianos, y predispuesto para empezar la estirpe otra vez por el principio y purificarla de sus vicios perniciosos y su vocación solitaria, porque era el único en un siglo que había sido engendrado con amor.

—Es todo un antropófago —dijo—. Se llamará Rodrigo.

—No —la contradijo su marido—. Se llamará Aureliano y ganará treinta y dos guerras.

Después de cortarle el ombligo, la comadrona se puso a quitarle con un trapo el ungüento azul que le cubría el cuerpo, alumbrada por Aureliano con una lámpara. Sólo cuando lo voltearon boca abajo se dieron cuenta de que tenía algo más que el resto de los hombres, y se inclinaron para examinarlo. Era una cola de cerdo.

No se alarmaron. Aureliano y Amaranta Úrsula

no conocían el precedente familiar, ni recordaban las pavorosas admoniciones de Úrsula, y la comadrona acabó de tranquilizarlos con la suposición de que aquella cola inútil podía cortarse cuando el niño mudara los dientes. Luego no tuvieron ocasión de volver a pensar en eso, porque Amaranta Úrsula se desangraba en un manantial incontenible. Trataron de socorrerla con apósitos de telaraña y apelmazamientos de ceniza, pero era como querer cegar un surtidor con las manos. En las primeras horas, ella hacía esfuerzos por conservar el buen humor. Le tomaba la mano al asustado Aureliano, y le suplicaba que no se preocupara, que la gente como ella no estaba hecha para morirse contra la voluntad, y se reventaba de risa con los recursos truculentos de la comadrona. Pero a medida que a Aureliano lo abandonaban las esperanzas, ella se iba haciendo menos visible, como si la estuvieran borrando de la luz, hasta que se hundió en el sopor. Al amanecer del lunes llevaron una mujer que rezó junto a su cama oraciones de cauterio, infalibles en hombres y animales, pero la sangre apasionada de Amaranta Úrsula era insensible a todo artificio distinto del amor. En la tarde, después de veinticuatro horas de desesperación, supieron que estaba muerta porque el caudal se agotó sin auxilios, y se le afiló el perfil, y los verdugones de la cara se le desvanecieron en una aurora de alabastro, y volvió a sonreír.

Aureliano no comprendió hasta entonces cuánto quería a sus amigos, cuánta falta le hacían, y cuánto hubiera dado por estar con ellos en aquel momento. Puso al niño en la canastilla que su madre le había preparado, le tapó la cara al cadáver con una manta, y vagó sin rumbo por el pueblo desierto, buscando un desfiladero de regreso al pasado. Llamó a la puerta de la botica, donde no había estado en los últimos tiempos y lo que encontró fue un taller de carpintería. La anciana que le abrió la puerta con una lámpara en la mano se compadeció de su desvarío e insistió en que no, que allí no había habido nunca una botica, ni había conocido jamás una mujer de cuello esbelto y ojos adormecidos que se llamara Mercedes. Lloró con la frente apoyada en la puerta de la antigua librería del sabio catalán, consciente de que estaba pagando los llantos atrasados de una muerte que no quiso llorar a tiempo para no romper los hechizos del amor. Se rompió los puños contra los muros de argamasa de *El Niño de Oro*, clamando por Pilar Ternera, indiferente a los luminosos discos anaranjados que cruzaban por el cielo, y que tantas veces había contemplado con una fascinación pueril en noches de fiesta, desde el patio de los alcaravanes. En el último salón abierto del desmantelado barrio de tolerancia, un conjunto de acordeones tocaba los cantos de Rafael Escalona, el sobrino del obispo, heredero de los secretos de Francisco el Hombre. El cantinero, que tenía un brazo seco y como achicharrado por haberlo levantado contra su madre, invitó a Aureliano a tomarse una botella de aguardiente, y Aureliano lo invitó a otra. El cantinero le habló de la desgracia de su brazo. Aureliano le habló de la desgracia de su corazón, seco y como achicharrado por haberlo levantado contra su hermana. Terminaron llorando juntos y Aureliano sintió por un momento que el dolor había terminado. Pero cuando volvió a quedar solo en la última madrugada de Macondo, se abrió de brazos en la mitad de la plaza, dispuesto a despertar al mundo entero, y gritó con toda su alma:

—¡Los amigos son unos hijos de puta!

Nigromanta lo rescató de un charco de vómito y de lágrimas. Lo llevó a su cuarto, lo limpió, le hizo tomar una taza de caldo. Creyendo que eso lo consolaba, tachó con una raya de carbón los incontables amores que él seguía debiéndole, y evocó voluntariamente sus tristezas más solitarias para no dejarlo solo en el llanto. Al amanecer, después de un sueño torpe y breve, Aureliano recobró la conciencia de su dolor de cabeza. Abrió los ojos y se acordó del niño.

No lo encontró en la canastilla. Al primer impacto experimentó una deflagración de alegría, creyendo que Amaranta Úrsula había despertado de la muerte para ocuparse del niño. Pero el cadáver era un promontorio de piedras bajo la manta. Consciente de que al llegar había encontrado abierta la puerta del dormitorio, Aureliano atravesó el corredor saturado por los suspiros matinales del orégano, y se asomó al comedor, donde estaban todavía los escombros del parto: la olla grande, las sábanas ensangrentadas, los tiestos de ceniza, y el retorcido ombligo del niño en un pañal abierto sobre la mesa, junto a las tijeras y el sedal. La idea de que la comadrona había vuelto por el niño en el curso de la noche le proporcionó una pausa de sosiego para pensar. Se derrumbó en el mecedor, el mismo en que se sentó Rebeca en los tiempos originales de la casa para dictar lecciones de bordado, y en el que Amaranta jugaba damas chinas con el coronel Gerineldo Márquez, y en el que Amaranta Úrsula cosía la ropita del niño, y en aquel relámpago de lucidez tuvo conciencia de que era incapaz de resistir sobre su alma el peso abrumador de tanto pasado. Herido por las lanzas mortales de las nostalgias propias y ajenas, admiró la impavidez de la telaraña en los rosales muertos, la perseverancia de la cizaña, la paciencia del aire en el radiante amanecer de febrero. Y entonces vio al niño. Era un pellejo hinchado y reseco, que todas las hormigas del mundo iban arrastrando trabajosamente hacia sus madrigueras por el sendero de piedras del jardín. Aureliano no pudo moverse. No porque lo hubiera paralizado el estupor, sino porque en aquel instante prodigioso se le revelaron las claves definitivas de Melquíades, y vio el epígrafe de los pergaminos perfectamente ordenado en el tiempo y el espacio de los hombres: *El primero de la estirpe está amarrado en un árbol y al último se lo están comiendo las hormigas.*

Aureliano no había sido más lúcido en ningún acto de su vida que cuando olvidó sus muertos y el dolor de sus muertos, y volvió a clavar las puertas y las ventanas con las crucetas de Fernanda para no dejarse perturbar por ninguna tentación del mundo, porque entonces sabía que en los pergaminos de Melquíades estaba escrito su destino. Los encontró intactos entre las plantas prehistóricas y los charcos humeantes y los insectos luminosos que habían desterrado del cuarto todo vestigio del paso de los hombres por la tierra, y no tuvo serenidad para sacarlos a la luz, sino que allí mismo, de pie, sin la menor dificultad, como si hubieran estado escritos en castellano bajo el resplandor deslumbrante del mediodía, empezó a descifrarlos en voz alta. Era la historia de la familia, escrita por Melquíades hasta en sus detalles más triviales, con cien años de anticipación. La había redactado en sánscrito, que era su lengua materna, y había cifrado los versos pares con la clave privada del emperador Augusto, y los impares con claves militares lacedemonias. La protección final, que Aureliano empezaba a vislumbrar cuando se dejó confundir por el amor de Amaranta Úrsula, radicaba en que Melquíades no había ordenado los hechos en el tiempo convencional de los hombres, sino que concentró un siglo de episodios cotidianos, de modo que todos coexistieran en un instante. Fascinado por el hallazgo, Aureliano leyó en voz alta, sin saltos, las encíclicas cantadas que el propio Melquíades le hizo escuchar a Arcadio, y que eran en realidad las predicciones de su ejecución, y encontró anunciado el nacimiento de la mujer más bella del mundo que estaba subiendo al cielo en cuerpo y alma, y conoció el origen de dos gemelos póstumos que renunciaban a descifrar los pergaminos, no sólo por incapacidad e inconstancia, sino porque sus tentativas eran prematuras. En este punto, impaciente por conocer su propio origen, Aureliano dio un salto. Entonces empezó el viento, tibio, incipiente, lleno de voces del pasado, de murmullos de geranios antiguos, de suspiros de desengaños anteriores a las nostalgias más tenaces. No lo advirtió porque en aquel momento estaba descubriendo los primeros indicios de su ser, en un abuelo concupiscente que se dejaba arrastrar por la frivolidad a través de un páramo alucinado, en busca de una mujer hermosa a quien no haría feliz. Aureliano lo reconoció, persiguió los caminos ocultos de su descendencia, y encontró el instante de su propia concepción entre los alacranes y las mariposas amarillas de un baño crepuscular, donde un menestral saciaba su lujuria con una mujer que se le entregaba por rebeldía. Estaba tan absorto, que no sintió tampoco la segunda arremetida del viento, cuya potencia ciclónica arrancó de los quicios las puertas y las ventanas, descuajó el techo de la galería oriental y desarraigó los cimientos. Sólo entonces descubrió que Amaranta Úrsula no era su hermana, sino su tía, y que Francis Drake había asaltado a Riohacha solamente para que ellos pudieran buscarse por los laberintos más intrincados de la sangre, hasta engendrar el animal mitológico que había de poner término a la estirpe. Macondo era ya un pavoroso remolino de polvo y escombros centrifugado por la cólera del huracán bíblico, cuando Aureliano saltó once páginas para no perder el tiempo en hechos demasiado conocidos, y empezó a descifrar el instante que estaba viviendo, descifrándolo a medida que lo vivía, profetizándose a sí mismo en el acto de descifrar la última página de los pergaminos, como si se estuviera viendo en un espejo hablado. Entonces dio otro salto para anticiparse a las predicciones y averiguar la fecha y las circunstancias de su muerte. Sin embargo, antes de llegar al verso final ya había comprendido que no saldría jamás de ese cuarto, pues estaba previsto que la ciudad de los espejos (o los espejismos) sería arrasada por el viento y desterrada de la memoria de los hombres en el instante en que Aureliano Babilonia acabara de descifrar los pergaminos, y que todo lo escrito en ellos era irrepetible desde siempre y para siempre, porque las estirpes condenadas a cien años de soledad no tenían una segunda oportunidad sobre la tierra.

Si algún día no
te trajo.

no quiero estar un tin listening
no quiero esta rew unit → leyendas
                                of Spain

se han roke
no sé

que diablos hago amandote

Siento que tu me
cortas la respiración
Cada vez que te acercas
Solo un poco a mi

Maconda es un
aldea desconocida
y remota. Viven
allí unas docenas de
personas, quienes
se fueron de otra
ciudad porque
su fundador ~~José~~ José
Arcadia Buendia
y su esposa, Ursa
~~fueron it~~ tenían
vergüenza de que
eran casados aunque
eran parientes.
Vino una chica, quien
se ~~llama~~ nombran Rebecca
por falta de nombre,
quien trajo la peste
de insomnia al pueblo.
Sin saberlo, Ursula
transmitió la peste a
todo la población a
travez de sus dulces que
producía en casa.
Ahora nadie puede dormir